G000077401

About the author

Gillian de Vries grew up in rural Dorset, England, where her roots are still deeply attached. The family emigrated to Australia and, on leaving high school, she joined the Royal Australian Navy in which she spent twelve happy years, including three in America.

She returned to England several times over the years before she took the opportunity to spend four years studying writing and editing in Australia. Some time later, after working in a university, she returned to England. She has written a number of articles and short stories. She also edits a National Trust property's monthly newsletter, while an earlier, unpublished, novel is undergoing revision. *The Strathvern Secrets* is her first published novel.

The Strathvern Secrets

Gillian De Vries

The Strathvern Secrets

Vanguard Press

VANGUARD PAPERBACK

© Copyright 2018
Gillian De Vries

The right of Gillian De Vries to be identified as author of
this work has been asserted by her in accordance with the
Copyright, Designs and Patents Act 1988.

All Rights Reserved

No reproduction, copy or transmission of this publication
may be made without written permission.
No paragraph of this publication may be reproduced,
copied or transmitted save with the written permission of the
publisher, or in accordance with the provisions
of the Copyright Act 1956 (as amended).

Any person who commits any unauthorised act in relation to
this publication may be liable to criminal
prosecution and civil claims for damages.

A CIP catalogue record for this title is
available from the British Library.

ISBN 978 1 784653 30 9

Vanguard Press is an imprint of
Pegasus Elliot MacKenzie Publishers Ltd.
www.pegasuspublishers.com

First Published in 2018

Vanguard Press
Sheraton House Castle Park
Cambridge England

Printed & Bound in Great Britain

Chapter 1

There was nothing fragile about Ellie Madison as she strode the hill tracks towards the high crags and desolate places to reach Maw's Hearth. She was, though, concerned about Farley. She hadn't seen him for almost two weeks, which wasn't unusual, though they had an agreement that he'd call at least every second day. There had been no call. Alone in the Highlands or on the islands, trouble could be over the next hill or round the next bend. Another day and she'd call the police.

With him she had tramped almost every inch of her portion of the Scottish Highlands in all seasons, poking about in its caves and glens, discovering geological oddities and artefacts from the past. Some said she was obsessed with her love of the empty, cruel land, but they spoke such things without understanding or knowing either her or Farley. Her message was blunt to anyone who would consider desecrating it with so much as one croft filled to its rafters with tourist trinkets – tread lightly and leave no hint you've been.

To those with varying interests in the heritage, archaeological and geological preservation of the highlands, she was a guardian and warrior rolled into one. For others, who saw commercial goldmines vetoed at every turn, she was nothing more than a thirty-five-year-old woman who could paint quite well and wasn't averse to giving her opinions. However, Ellie knew it was Farley Orman's voice that had the most influence on hearts and minds, occasionally winning the support of opponents.

Eleven hikers and painters with various levels of physical fitness trailed behind her. According to her friends, she had the stamina of an ox despite her slim frame. She'd thought this group a rum lot when they first met her at Kilcomb's pub earlier that morning, she explaining the day's walk and their responsibilities. After cups of tea and coffee they had set off at nine o'clock with a damp, cold wind slapping gently at their faces. So much for summer 1998, she thought ruefully.

The group included two archaeologists from Argentina who proved to be the liveliest members of the group, their banter soon breaking through the stiffer attitude of several English folk. Of course, there was always one, in this case two, who were determined not to join in. Well, that was their choice. She was not going to fret about it.

Over the last forty minutes since a stop for hot drinks from thermos flasks and energy food to keep them going to lunch time, the climb had gradually increased. They crossed a soggy patch of moorland grass and, a short while later, Ellie came to a halt as did Kipp her Pyrenean Mountain Dog. She rarely went anywhere without him, his white frame perching next to her in the passenger seat of the Land Rover, beside her in the village and galloping across the wide acres they knew and loved.

Ellie, tucking strands of wavy chestnut hair back behind her ear, watched as the stragglers caught up. One of them, an Englishman called Byron Oakes, was taking a lot of photographs and jotting in a pocket-sized notebook.

"And what're you scribbling about, Byron?" she asked rather bluntly. Most of the others were admiring the view across the hills and a loch they'd passed.

"Descriptions of views, the weather, that kind of thing. Impossible to recall all the details of a place when you're back in the humdrum of life," he said with a little cocking of his right eyebrow. He smiled at her, his teeth straight and white in a tanned face. He was taller than her by six inches, broad shouldered and looked fit. Late thirties, she guessed, and wondered if he was an athlete.

"Only if you have a mind to. Now then, I'd better get this lot on the move." Nice looking man. She gave herself a mental shake. What was on the inside was more important – and outside and inside didn't always go together. She'd known that almost all her life. "Okay everyone, we're about to start the climb. Yell out if I'm going too fast. Don't forget I've been doing this for over fifteen years. Kipp will give you a nudge if you need it."

"What if you're going too slowly?" said one of the sturdy Argentine chaps, grinning.

"Then when I go to the Andes on one of your archaeological digs you can have pity on me!"

Laughter rippled across the boggy area as Ellie turned away and followed the narrow, sometimes vague path towards Maw's Hearth. Over the years she had taken hikers, painters, writers, historians, botanists and a host of others to numerous locations, but that part of her life hadn't begun until she'd been in Kilcomb for four years. Until then she'd mostly gone off on her own painting, sometimes accompanying the well-known photographer Farley Orman and his wife, Alice, on their treks, learning, observing, and becoming passionate about the Highlands. It had been her idea to start the hikes and painting treks; educate the uneducated, she'd told them. Alice had thought it a wonderful way for people to understand why protecting the region was so important, but Farley wanted no part of it. He hated the idea of being a tour guide and nothing they said had ever changed his mind. Poor Alice, she thought.

The three of them had forged several new tracks, imprinting them as unobtrusively upon the landscape as possible. Now she used the less defined tracks to take only more experienced hikers and those interested in remote places. Local authorities were insisting they stick to the regular paths more often. So, to keep them happy and for safety reasons, she and Farley, he more reluctantly, agreed. The last thing she wanted was someone suing them because they got lost or wandered off into a dangerous area. A path with unobtrusive markers at certain spots had saved them from the waspish tongues of the less observant on more than one occasion.

The group strode on through heather ablaze in purple and white mantles, across rocks sitting snugly on the tough heath and past clear, rippling streams. Patches of spongy moss and peat threatened to suck the soles off their boots. Late morning sunshine made intermittent appearances as clouds sailed north towards John O'Groats. All in all, a beautiful summer's day walk, Ellie thought, with little possibility of anything going disastrously awry. The next stop would be at the Knobbles, where they'd eat their packed lunches and gaze across hills and valleys towards the Isle of Skye, many miles in the distance. After that – the climb to Maw's Hearth.

Kipp bounded ahead, stopping and pushing his nose into the heather or under rocks as the scent took him. He barked at the ptarmigans that flapped off in fright, but he did not give chase and never went too far from Ellie or the last hiker.

There was no counting the number of times she had taken this route and it never failed to delight no matter the season: the smell of the heath and the twittering of birds under a warm sun in summer; pearly, autumn light so clear and translucent she wanted to stare at it forever; and in winter the first flutter of snow speckling the hills and landing on her hair and cheeks. Then there was spring with its unexpected first blooms popping up through thinning snow and birds beginning the building of new nests or sitting in patches of barely warm sunshine.

"You don't sound Scottish. Are you?" said Byron's voice unexpectedly behind her.

It clattered in on her thoughts. "No," she replied, resenting the intrusion. She had just glimpsed a hawk gliding over the crags.

"What brought you up here?"

"You're an inquisitive man, Byron Oakes. I don't discuss my life with strangers."

"Sorry, just being polite. Still, the winters must be hell."

"Not to me."

"So why did you come up here?" He was now walking beside her, matching her strides, breathing evenly. "Fresh air and freedom?"

"For goodness sake, man! It's none of your business." Ellie shot him an annoyed glance before increasing her pace and getting ahead.

Not exactly a good start, she castigated herself, but why did people think they had a right to pursue intimacy on these hikes, as if to 'know' something personal about her was a prize?

Unperturbed by the woman's hostility, Byron continued the hike to the Knobbles in the company of the Argentines and two middle-aged sisters from Portugal. They were entertaining and intelligent and he enjoyed the cross-cultural banter, but frequently his eyes looked ahead to the woman clad in an olive green weather-proof jacket, brown trousers and hiking boots. Clinging to her back like a limpet was a dark green pack. Her chestnut hair was cut to shoulder length, its wavy tendrils blowing wildly in gusts of wind. He sensed in her a spirited and determined nature and smiled to himself.

White clouds bustled in over the crags, drawing a thick curtain across the sun and deepening the shadows in hollows and pits. The carpet of heather seemed a richer shade of mauve, the white a greater contrast. It was breathtaking, but he still didn't fancy the winters up here. She could keep that.

Fifteen minutes from the Knobbles the path narrowed and ahead it wound steadily upwards. Ellie led them between boulders and over a stream before detouring across tussock grass around a small landslide.

"How much farther is it? I've got a stone in my boot."

The high-pitched voice of Moira, a woman from Norwich, seemed extraordinarily loud in the clear air and Ellie inwardly cringed.

"About ten minutes," she said, "but you can stop and tip the stone out. We won't leave you behind."

Much as I'd like to, Ellie thought, noticing Byron's amused expression. Whether at the woman's remark or her response she could not be sure.

Kipp was the first one to the top and barked his success. The response was mixed; most smiled and one or two hadn't seemed to notice, looking at the scenery instead. Moira glared.

"Stick to the path and go slowly," Ellie said loudly, standing to one side where the ground was flatter and broader.

The archaeologists went on first while Ellie waited for the last three, one of them the Norwich woman. If anyone was going to wander off the path it would be her. Byron ignored Ellie as he passed by, apparently engrossed in a conversation with a single – and attractive – London woman. She was welcome to his attentions. He asked too many questions.

"No one told me it was goin' to be this rough," Moira grumbled.

"This is the Highlands," Ellie said.

"Well, someone still should've told me this walk wasn't goin' to be easy."

"I explained clearly before we started out that there would be a few moderately difficult bits and it's in the walk information. Surely you checked the hike details before coming here."

The woman was looking at her foot. "And the stone's causin' me lots of pain. I'll have to get it out."

I rest my case, thought Ellie, and waited while the woman tipped out the stone.

Ellie loved the Knobbles. One section of the great expanse, oblong in shape, was sheltered by a long, jagged ridge of rock shelves and caves, while the ground was an uneven collection of small rocks.

"Don't just take in the views. If you look carefully you'll find carvings on the bigger stones towards the caves. No one seems to know who carved them, but they're worth looking at."

The hikers spread out, a few at one end of the ridge gazing silently over the master creation before them, the dark, still waters of lochs providing mirrors for the landscape. She could see Ben

Nevis, as well as lower hills, carpeted in heather and grass, and streams sparkling in shafts of sunlight. Other hikers walked slowly over the stones, heads bent looking for the carvings. Cameras and sketchpads came out as they always did, quickly followed by exclamations and chatter.

The Norwich woman hobbled over to her two friends, a married couple, and guessing by the down-turned mouth and frown she was telling them what a dreadful time she was having. No doubt the blister was the size of a saucer.

A cold wind whipped up as Ellie slid off her backpack. Above the ridge, two ospreys soared in the air stream and Ellie lifted the binoculars round her neck to her eyes. The sun popped out and for a moment she lost sight of the birds in the glare. They glided into view again, probably on an outing from whichever nearby loch they called home. She always thought of the ospreys as 'wanderers returned'. In the 1950s, after being absent from Scotland for forty years, they had begun returning entirely of their own volition and now, she'd heard, there were many pairs breeding.

"Beautiful," she said quietly, smiling. "Hatch lots of babies, you gorgeous pair."

Suddenly, the hair on the back of her neck stood up. A scream tore through the sharp air and Ellie whirled around, her heart thumping. Had someone ignored the warnings and gone too close to the edge? She saw, then, the young man from York with his arm around his wife's shoulders, a pretty woman whose hands covered her face. She was very distressed and Ellie walked over quickly, but not before Byron got there and began talking with the husband, Robert.

"What's going on?" Ellie asked, peeved Byron had arrived first.

"My wife's had a nasty shock. She was exploring along the base of the ridge and…" He glanced at her, then up at Ellie.

"And?"

"She found… she found a…"

Robert got no further as his wife, Natalie, broke from his embrace and walked away. He followed her. "Ask Byron," he said over his shoulder.

She didn't. Instead she looked intently at him and waited. His eyes, brown and bold, held hers, and then he said, "A man's body."

"A body? Is she sure?"

"Seems you like asking questions too. And the answer is yes, she's sure."

Ellie ignored the gibe. A few of the other hikers were drawing closer, curious. "I'd better go and have a look."

"I'll come with you."

"It's not your responsibility. I know the caves here."

"I'm sure you do, but I'm still coming. No matter how tough you think you are, staring at a rotting body isn't exactly fun."

She opened her mouth to object, but decided he was right. "No, I suppose not."

Paolo, one of the Argentines, joined them as they turned towards the ridge. "A problem?" he asked, dark brows drawn together in a frown.

"Not sure," she said quickly, glancing at Byron. "We're going to have a look. Can you keep an eye on everyone?"

"Of course," he said, nodding.

When they were out of his hearing Ellie asked Byron if Robert had said which cave.

"About halfway along he thought. His wife was too distraught to give precise details."

It wasn't many minutes before they found it. Tucked in a recess and sitting on the ground with its head slumped forwards, was the decomposing body of a man in hiking boots, jeans and a thick, dark blue anorak. There was a discoloured area on the anorak near the middle of his chest. Blood, Byron concluded, and stepped closer, leaning down. The knees of the jeans bore traces of green stains, grass perhaps, and there was a trace of blood above the right knee.

Straightening up he glanced at Ellie. She was staring at the body, her face ashen. Byron stepped closer to her.

"Are you all right?" he asked gently.

She blinked and turned her head slowly towards him as if the words reached her from a long way off and she had just heard them.

"It's Farley Orman," she said in a voice that had lost its strength.

Byron's heart missed a beat. "You know the man?"

"Yes. He lives… lived in Eigg."

"Isn't that an island off Mallaig?"

"There's a village up here, too. About six miles away."

"This is a lonely place to die."

"Not for a Highlander, not for Farley."

"Maybe. Does he have family?"

Ellie nodded. "Two sons and a daughter. His wife disappeared a few years ago."

He was surprised to see tears in her eyes and was about to ask how well she knew them, but changed his mind given her earlier response to his probing about her life.

"We should get everyone back down and report it to the police," he said, staring at the ugly bloodstains.

"Someone should stay with him."

"I don't think so. He's not going anywhere, Ellie, and there's nothing we can do to help him. It looks as if he's been dead a while. Hadn't anyone reported him missing?"

She gave a little snort. "You don't know Farley. He'd go up into the lonely places by himself for weeks on end taking the most extraordinary photographs."

Byron stared at her. "So this is *the* Farley Orman?" Stupid! Who else had a name like that?

"Yes." The expression on her face tightened as if warning him not to ask any more questions.

But he did. "So, where's his camera equipment?"

For a few moments she studied him intently then looked at the lifeless Farley. "I don't know. He never went anywhere without it."

Reluctantly, Byron, bringing up the rear, followed Paolo down from the Knobbles for the trek back to the village. Ellie had given him the telephone number of the local police and as soon as his mobile was in range, he phoned. At no stage did he speak to any of the hikers, including Paolo, about the situation. However, at the Knobbles, Moira had sidled up to Natalie, patted her hand, and found out the cause of the young woman's distress. In less than a minute the entire group knew. When Byron and Ellie joined them, they were bombarded with questions, but Ellie had told them there was nothing to worry about, that Paolo and Byron would return with them to the village.

Byron had tried to convince her that staying alone was unnecessary. She would not budge from her decision. Everything in him rebelled against leaving a woman alone up there. No matter how long she had lived in the Highlands this was madness.

By the time they reached a small car park half an hour later, the police were already there. There were two of them, a sergeant and his constable, both pulling on backpacks.

"Which one o' you is Byron Oakes?" asked the sergeant in a deep voice that seemed to come straight out of the hills themselves.

No lowlander this man. He was medium height, thicker of waist than he should be and his hair greying.

"I am," said Byron, walking towards him.

"I'm Sergeant Kennart and this is Constable Ashby. Are you fit enough to go back up the crag or d'you need to rest like most southerners?"

Byron studied the weathered face silently for a few moments. The man's expression gave little indication of the feelings behind the question.

"I'm fit enough," he said evenly.

"Right. You can tell me what happened on the way up. Who found the body?"

"The woman in the red jacket. Her name's Natalie Seabert."

The sergeant turned and walked towards the rest of the party who were standing several yards away. "I don't want any of you leaving the village until I say so. We'll be taking statements from everyone. Constable Ashby will go back wi' you to Kilcomb."

"You'll not be taking any statement from me," said the Norwich woman, her expression indignant. "I never saw a thing. It's this poor woman you need to talk to." She touched Natalie's arm.

"Madam, you'll do as I say. Constable, please get these people back to the village."

"You can't treat us like criminals!"

"Is that how you see yourself, madam?"

Her face turned bright pink and the little eyes glittered, but she did not answer. The sergeant returned to Byron.

"Let's go. Ellie will not like being up there alone wi' Farley's body."

"I volunteered to stay with her but she wouldn't have it."

"You're a stranger. You don't know Ellie," he said bluntly. "Now, what happened up there?"

Byron frowned. "Shouldn't you be talking with Natalie first?"

"I'll do the investigating in my own way, you just answer the question."

In the short time it took Byron to relate the events at the Knobbles, Jack Kennart's expression changed like the weather; cold and dark one moment, less hostile the next and eventually reaching a calmer harbour. Byron watched, fascinated.

"Aye, she'll be glad to see us," Jack said eventually without explaining. "You said there was no camera equipment."

"That's right. It seemed to worry Ellie."

"So it should. Farley Orman was more attached to his cameras than to any human being. Never went anywhere wi'out at least one camera."

"That's only natural when it was his livelihood."

"Natural? You think so?"

"Of course. Anyway, whatever I think, I didn't know the man, only his name and photos. I suppose he could've dropped whatever he was carrying."

"Possible, but unlikely. He knows this area better than anyone."

"Accidents can happen to the best, Sergeant Kennart."

The older man looked at him, scrutinising his features. "What do you do for a living, Mr Oakes?"

The question surprised Byron. "I'm an architect."

"And who d'you work for?"

"I have my own business, but I'm doing some work for Mayfair Hotels."

The momentary cocking of the bushy brown eyebrows made Byron smile, but not for long.

"So you're up here to spy out the land then." It was a statement not a question.

"Not exactly."

"Exactly what then, Mr Oakes?"

"I'm on holiday, nothing more nothing less."

"Don't think we're stupid because we live in the Highlands, laddie. We've been battling to keep the big hotels out of here. I'm guessing you haven't told Ellie. You'd have been down that crag quicker than you went up."

Byron did not like the turn in conversation. "They don't own me, Sergeant. I'm freelance. They contracted me to do some work for them."

"Then take some advice – don't trespass where you're not wanted."

***

The tears dried on Ellie's cheeks as she sat outside the cave in the warm sunshine. Hardened as she was to the tough realities of life in the Highlands, the sight of Farley's body had shocked her and filled her with pain that entwined itself round her heart. Anguish churned in the depths of her being. She could not understand what he was doing at the Knobbles or why his body was covered in blood and his camera equipment missing. A fortnight ago he'd told her he was going to Ben Hope, almost twenty miles north, to photograph an interesting cave and rock formations he had found in April when bad weather had prohibited extensive exploration. Why would he lie to her?

Unable to sit still any longer, Ellie stood up and walked across the rocks to the springy grass that carpeted a wide section near the caves on the western edge. There, with the sweet breath of summer riffling through her hair and caressing her cheeks, she gazed across bumpy green hills towards the Isle of Skye and wondered what the world would make of Farley's unexpected death. A shudder shook her body as she thought of journalists, television crews, photographers and countless nosy tourists trekking up the mountains despoiling and dishonouring the region as they came and went. Farley would not want that. *She* did not want that. Perhaps Jack Kennart could keep quiet concerning the exact location of Farley's death. He wouldn't want hundreds of people making a shrine out of the Knobbles. Still, even if he and Constable Ashby kept quiet, someone was eventually bound to talk – the Norfolk woman for one. She was probably telling the villagers even now.

Beside her, Kipp nudged her leg and she bent down and hugged him.

In Farley and Alice Orman, Ellie had found a committed and passionate team who had led many successful campaigns against further building development in the area. Now they were both gone – one was missing and the other dead. While there were numerous others who worked hard and faithfully for the cause, the Ormans had been a formidable duo. To her amazement, they had eventually included her. A couple of journalists from the local press had, more than once, labelled them the 'Three Iron Musketeers', a title that had found its way onto page three of *The Scottish Times* ahead of a three-column article on the loss of wild places to hotels and tourist venues. Ellie had protested, saying it was the Ormans who were the force and expertise behind the trio. Alice had a science degree, majoring in botany, and Farley was a gifted photographer and writer who spared neither pen nor tongue in getting his point to the 'ignorant masses and politicians'. She, born and raised in Plymouth, daughter of a Navy captain, simply loved the Highlands, immersed herself in her painting and did the best she could in supporting the Ormans and others.

Now there was one musketeer. What could she do without Farley? It had been hard enough when Alice disappeared, but being one musketeer held no appeal for her. It was Farley's fame as a photographer and the high regard in which he was held throughout Scotland that had given others greater success in their own fight. The battle depended on them now.

She glanced at her watch. Jack would be here soon and the questions and investigating begin. How deeply would they probe into Farley's life, into her life? Would she now, by acquaintance with the famous man, have her life splattered across the media, her privacy gone and truth distorted, ignored even, in the pursuit of a sensational story that made newspaper owners and publishers rich men. What, if in a perverse twist of human nature, she became a suspect? Ellie frowned. She turned and looked in the direction of the cave where Farley's last breath of Highland air had been taken. Why had he not gone to Ben Hope? Or had he returned early? Who had hated him so much to end his life?

The blue of the sky and the bright clear sunshine seemed as if they were mocking her, the God-given day no longer a treasure. It was so peaceful. If she believed in the folklore of the locals, she might have heard the whispering of the stones and the sweet singing of the invisible ones who some believed lived in the caves. Instead, the wind sang its mournful tune as it flowed around and across the Knobbles. Ellie waited, remembering Farley as the passionate photographer and lover of wild places, a determined protector of Scotland's wild places.

Kipp suddenly stood up, growling, and Ellie instinctively looked towards where the path entered the Knobbles. Just appearing were Jack Kennart and, to her dismay, Byron Oakes. For several minutes she watched without moving. There was no sign of Tim Ashby. She supposed he had the job of leading the hikers back to the village and taking statements.

The two men stopped and looked around, probably for her, but she remained still, watching. Unexpectedly, she thought what a fine-looking man Byron was and the way he held himself spoke of toughness and vigour. The tiniest shiver curtailed her thoughts. Stupid thinking. She put it away.

Then she stood up. "Go on, Kipp."

He raced ahead of her, stopping only when he reached the sergeant who bent down and made a fuss of him. Drawing closer she saw Byron's surprised expression as Kipp capered round the policeman. No doubt Jack had dealt the blunt side of his nature to the visitor.

"Ah, there you are, Ellie," Jack said when she was within a few yards.

"Hello, Jack.

"Mr Oakes has given me his version of what happened up here. Are you okay to take me to Farley?"

"Of course. Why wouldn't I be?" she asked, annoyed that Byron seemed to have given the impression she had not coped well in the cave.

Jack did not respond directly. "He'll not be sorry his end came up here. Okay, lass, let's take a look at him."

It was no easier the second time, but Byron, who she'd damned in her heart as another nosy tourist, was standing right behind her in the cave that resembled the shape and size, she thought, of a nutshell. Whether he was aware of it or not, his presence gave her strength and she drew on it as Jack approached the body, bent over and asked whether either of them had touched it.

"No," they said in unison, the sound strangely loud and inappropriate.

The sergeant turned his head and looked from one to the other. Ellie kept her eyes on him, but she could see the dark bloodstain on the anorak and Farley's head tipped forward. A scream of denial began rising in her throat. Her body stiffened and, swallowing, she thrust the scream down. These two men could not be allowed into her private closet of emotions. Then, as if a feather had floated past, she felt the lightest of touches on her back. She did not move.

"The forensic lads'll be up here soon. When d'you last see him alive, Ellie?" Jack asked, straightening up and tugging a notebook and pen out of his jacket pocket.

"Ten days ago."

"And did he seem okay to you?"

"Yes, fine. He was off to do what he loved best, photograph wild places."

"Where was he going?" Jack scribbled on the unlined page.

"Ben Hope."

He glanced up, frowning, and studied her for a moment. "Are you sure? He's a long way from his destination."

Ellie sighed, annoyance creeping into her voice. "Yes, I'm sure. Ben Hope doesn't sound anything like the Knobbles and he made no mention of coming here."

"And where's Ben Hope?" Byron interrupted, stepping forward alongside her.

"Almost twenty miles north," Jack Kennart said curtly. "And I'll ask the questions."

Despite herself, a low chuckle escaped Ellie. "Mr Oakes can't help himself, Jack. I think he was born with questions running out of his mouth."

Jack scowled at the Englishman. "For the time being keep them to yourself."

A shrug of Byron's shoulders quickly followed the frown creasing his forehead and Ellie supposed he did not really care about the sergeant's attitude. She watched as he walked closer to the body, wondering why he would want to do that. After all, Byron had no connection whatsoever with Farley.

Again, Jack snapped at him, keeping him under his control. "Don't touch him or anything else. This is a crime scene and the forensic people won't like anyone poking around."

The other man turned his head and stared at him briefly before continuing his study of the body.

***

It was over an hour before two men and a woman from forensics arrived, descending from a helicopter that had landed with some difficulty, buffeted as it was by the wind, about fifty yards away. The men immediately cordoned off the cave and several yards outside. Byron watched them at their work, photographing, measuring, collecting samples of dried blood, going through Farley's pockets and clothing, and making notes. It seemed orderly and methodical, something he appreciated, and infinitely more interesting than his job as an architect. They were at the forefront of unravelling mysteries. The only mystery left to him these days was whether the client would be happy and pay up.

However, as it seemed this collecting of evidence might take a long time, Byron wandered off, walking towards what he hoped would be a stunning view across the Highlands. It beckoned, beguiling him with what he could not yet see in full, his heart beating in anticipation of something special. Nor was he disappointed as he was embraced by the wind and seductive beauty of the Highlands. For what seemed an age he simply looked, absorbed in the lush green of the hills, the royal cloaks of purple heather, the burbling of an unseen stream and the shrill cries of birds for which he had no names. People would pay a great deal of money for a room with such a view and the Mayfair Hotels Group was relying on him for a good report. Dragging out the notebook and pen from a jacket pocket, he scribbled down his thoughts and a general description of the view.

"Perhaps I'll build myself a house up here," he said wistfully before a chuckle rumbled in his throat. "Not with the Iron Musketeer around."

For a few minutes he was preoccupied taking photos and wondering what madness possessed him to think he could recommend building up here. It was sacrilege.

Ellie's voice crashed in upon his thoughts; he had not heard her approach. "Thought you could escape, I suppose."

He lowered his camera and turned to face her.

"I suppose so. Has Jack Kennart gone?"

"No. He's talking with those people." She looked troubled. "I don't like them going over Farley like that."

"They haven't any choice if they want to find out what happened to him."

"But couldn't they do it at the lab? They'll dissect him there anyway," she said, a hard note in her voice. The green-brown eyes were hurt and angry.

"No doubt, but they need evidence from here." He paused, taking in her stance, arms folded across her chest and her chin thrust forward, before asking, "You were fond of Farley, weren't you?"

In her eyes a trace of fear appeared, but fled instantly, and Byron considered if it hadn't been his imagination.

"We were friends. He and his wife were very good to me when I first arrived here. They drew me in as part of their family."

To his ears the response was stilted and guarded. Still, it was none of his business.

"I'm sorry you've lost your friend. Is there anything I can do?"

"No," she said quickly. "You're a stranger here. We've just experienced a situation together, that's all. You'll leave here and that'll be the end of our brief encounter."

"Well, that puts me in my place." He returned the camera to its bag as Kipp bounded up. In the distance he saw Jack Kennart beckoning. "I think we'd better go. The sergeant appears to want us back."

She turned around to where he was looking and immediately tapped her leg. "Come on, Kipp. Let's go home."

Byron followed several yards behind. She intrigued him. At once confident, blunt, determined and yet, glimpses of fear and deep pain, offered him a woman of complex emotions. Perhaps, there were, after all, chinks in the armour.

Chapter 2

Three days later the phone shrilled in the gloom of a wet Thursday morning. Raindrops thudded on the slate roof and slapped at the windows as Ellie pulled herself reluctantly from cosy warmth beneath the quilt and padded across the carpet and downstairs.

"Ellie Madison." A yawn almost cut off the last syllable of her surname. She glanced at the clock on the wall. It was after eight – she'd slept in.

"He was murdered. I suppose you already know that."

The last trace of sleep vanished at the sound of twenty-six-year-old Fenella Orman's voice and Ellie didn't think twice about her response.

"Any half-wit who'd seen your father at the Knobbles would've worked that out, but as you weren't there I expect Jack's told you. Get a report from Inspector Carter, did he?"

Ellie could imagine her expression – exquisite features screwed to resemble a dried apple, mouth pinched and thin. It would last less than half a minute, then she'd give herself a mental shake and put her face back the way it had been made.

"To this day I don't know what my father saw in you. You've got the temperament of a shrew. You won't…"

"Your father didn't *see* anything in me. He was married to Alice first then the Highlands. There wasn't much room for anyone else. Is there any point to this phone call, Fenella?"

There was a moment's hesitation before the young woman answered.

"You won't get anything of his."

The moment she hung up Ellie remembered what she'd said about Farley's lack of parenting skills. It was, she conceded, somewhat unkind. Despite her own tense relationship with Fenella, she'd always hoped Farley would see what he was doing to his family by being away so often. He hadn't.

Her hand had barely left the phone when it rang again. This time it was Jack. She told him about her brief conversation with Fenella.

"Aye, she's right," the policeman said. "They're almost certain he was murdered. Shot in the chest at close range."

"Oh," was all she said.

Jack's blunt statement of the facts shocked her.

"I'm sorry, Ellie. We'll not rest 'til we get whoever did this."

With difficulty she swallowed the tears. "I know you won't, Jack. Just make sure it's soon."

"We'll do our best."

"You'd better. If Alice turns up you'll want a good reason why not." She heard the intake of his breath. "Sorry, Jack. I shouldn't have said that." She changed the subject without waiting for him to respond. "Did the group all go yesterday?"

"Aye, in the afternoon."

"Doesn't that make it hard to follow things up?"

"Ellie, stick to painting and hiking. Let me do the policing."

Mildly rebuked, Ellie sighed. "Thanks for ringing, Jack. I appreciate it."

"You take care, Ellie girl. Oh, and mind how you go with that Byron Oakes."

"Is he a suspect?" she asked, frowning.

"Everyone is until we find the murderer. Even you, Ellie."

He hung up and she stood in the cold hallway shivering, but not entirely from the temperature. Alone with her thoughts, they came rushing in like a crowd of tattle-tales, each one wanting to give their version of the truth. Padding back to her bedroom, Ellie reminded herself that she was neither policewoman nor super sleuth and she should, as Jack said, get on with life and leave the investigating to the experts. It was no good letting her mind entertain every possibility. Whatever had happened to Farley in the last days of his life the professionals would eventually work out.

The rain had eased by the time she pulled the old door closed behind her and walked down the puddle-dotted path. The cottage was late seventeenth century and she loved it. Nodding rose heads, hollyhocks and delphiniums had fared better than their lower growing companions; white and purple alyssum, lambs' ears, petunias and a few late pansies were bowed to the ground, looking sodden and sorry. As Ellie shut the gate she looked back at her two-storey home and smiled, pleased she had allowed old Fred from next door to re-paint the window sills and frames. Completed a month ago, she still couldn't help looking at them. Dormer windows peeped out from beneath the overhanging slate roof and the lower front windows looked cheerful with potted plants on the inside sills. Fred and his wife, Esther, were the best of neighbours and with their children grown and producing offspring of their own, they were only too happy to have her as a substitute daughter next door.

Her house, on an acre of land, backed onto farmland. Across the fields and beyond, the farmhouse hills rose gently, protectors against the winds that came rushing towards the village from wilder, higher peaks a few miles away.

Ellie knew she had been meant to have the property. It had all been in the timing of her arrival seven years earlier when she'd come from another village four miles south. The previous owners had packed up and left after only a year's residence and returned to England. It was, they'd told her on their one meeting, too lonely, too much hard work, not what they had imagined and glad to get rid of it. The price had been less than Ellie expected and settlement could hardly have been speedier. She had never tired of living in the house or working in the garden. A large and thriving vegetable plot was one of her great successes, thanks to her neighbours' help and advice.

At the village post office she met, as she knew she would, the first of the 'are there any details of Farley's death?' clan. The postmistress, a woman in her late forties and who had taken over the position when her mother died three years earlier, was dabbing her eyes with a damp, pink handkerchief when Ellie went to collect her post. She had put it off for as long as she could and had not set foot in the building since last Friday.

"He was such a kind wee man," she said in a reedy voice as Ellie took her letters. "Always asking how I was and so considerate about my poor health. The shock won't do me any good at all."

"He was not a *wee* man at all, Carrie, as you well know. Farley was six feet tall and a strapping, well-built man," Ellie said with a touch of asperity. She had little patience with the woman at the best of times. Everyone in Kilcomb knew all there was to know about the state of Carrie's health, and most agreed it took up too much of her thinking. No one was quite sure how her husband, a mild-mannered man, put up with her.

"Aye, well. It's just a turn of phrase. Must've given you a shock seeing him like that, Ellie, especially as you knew him better than most. I mean, you did a lot of work together."

As always the underlying probing was on her tongue. Ellie ignored it. "It wasn't pleasant. It was a shock for everyone on the hike."

"No doubt. A nice woman came in here. Moira, I think her name was, and said Farley's poor body was all twisted and blood had squirted..."

"That's enough, Carrie! That woman did *not* see Farley's body and would have no clue as to its state. The best thing you can do for him, as you seem to admire him so much, is keep your mouth shut about things you can't possibly know! And spare a thought for his family while you're busy gossiping."

She turned away, furious, and almost collided with Reverend Shepley. She mumbled an apology and strode noisily to the door.

"Well, the nerve of Ellie Madison! She always thinks she's right. I could tell her a thing or two!"

"She *is* right, Carrie," said Paul Shepley firmly. "Don't gossip about things of which you have no knowledge."

An indignant bleat echoed round the small room.

Ellie, who had been about to step outside and close the door with a resounding bang, turned slightly and caught Paul's eye. He winked and her lips twitched in acknowledgement and thanks. She left the building with quiet dignity.

Whatever people in the parish said about Reverend Paul Shepley, an Englishman with Scottish roots, there was no doubt in her mind that his sense of humour, honesty and gentle manner had brought life to the village. And God, in His wisdom, must have known they needed an injection of humour to get them out of religious humdrum that had little meaning. There had been vigorous opposition from some to the appointment of a man in his mid-thirties from those comfortable with tradition and dull preaching. They had written a blistering complaint to the archbishop of the Church of Scotland after Paul had delivered only two sermons and been in the village less than three weeks. The response from the archbishop's office had been short, polite and merely confirmed the fact of Paul's position. He was there to stay whether they liked it or not. Ellie, who did not attend church regularly, was glad he had come and now, after two years, all was going well.

She dropped the letters on the back seat of the Land Rover, left Kipp in charge, and went down the street towards the local store and greengrocer. About once every six weeks she took a trip into

Inverness to buy, as her neighbour Esther put it, fancy things not available in the village. Occasionally, she stayed two or three days, especially in spring and summer when market days hummed with life. Her paintings, prints and cards sold very well in Inverness, so she had a particular fondness for the city. She'd met a lot of people, including a number who owned galleries and now sold her paintings. Late last summer, a gallery-owning couple from York had bought a pastel of Maw's Hearth, returning several weeks later to buy four others. Farley had been very proud of her. She walked on, keeping the sadness to herself.

Inside the general store the radio was playing quietly as usual, and Ellie heard several voices in different conversations. She reached for a basket and proceeded along the aisle containing house-cleaning wares and products, unseen from the counter.

"So, you saw the poor man, then?" said the voice of Mary Nevin, wife of the store owner and a friend of Ellie's.

Ellie stopped with a bottle of washing-up liquid halfway to the basket. She did not need to ask who she was talking about and her pulse quickened. This is just the beginning, she thought, feeling sick in the stomach. However, at the sound of the next voice her body stiffened and anger began pushing its way into the forefront of her emotions.

"No, not exactly. I was left to comfort the woman who did and she just poured out her heart to me. Said 'e was covered in blood. A terrible mess. If you ask me, I'd say someone had it in for him. I mean, how else could 'e have got in that state?"

The woman from Norwich. Someone should have sewn her lips together.

"I expect the police will work it out. Farley Orman was well respected here, though he could be…" The sentence ended abruptly as if, sensible woman that she normally was, realised it was a mistake talking to a stranger about village concerns. "That'll be £2.25 please."

Moira, it seemed, could listen when she wanted to. "Was 'e a bit odd? I mean, no one's perfect are they and them greenie types… Well, they don't live in the real world, do they? More concerned about rocks and things than people. Look at Ellie Madison. She's a hard case if ever there was one. Couldn't have cared tuppence I had an injured foot."

Injured foot indeed!

"Were you planning to pay? There are customers waiting to be served." Mary's voice was sharp.

"Someone's hiding somethin' you can be sure of that. Here's your money. And don't think just because I'm an outsider I can't work things out," she said defiantly, her shoes rapping on the lino as she headed for the door and left the shop.

"Well, I never!" exclaimed Mary.

"We can do wi'out her sort. They know how to twist a tale until it has no truth left in it," said the voice of an old woman Ellie knew a little and whose path she rarely crossed. She was a woman who, according to Farley, could tell you the colours of the socks in your drawer and the dates your parents were busy making their next child. That, Ellie did not believe.

"Aye, and no doubt the story'll have acquired more gruesome details by the time she gets home."

"Have you seen his children?"

"Only Fenella, but not to speak. She was getting into her car."

"Poor things. It'll be hard on them. And what about Ellie Madison?"

Ellie heard the clang of the register. "D'you want to pay now, Olga, or next time you're in?"

"How much?"

"That's £1.05."

"I'll pay now."

"Thank you. As for Ellie, I haven't seen her for a few days."

It was time to make her presence known while she was the main subject matter and before other customers got caught up in the conversation. Ellie quickly lifted the other items she needed off the shelves and proceeded to the counter. Mary had her head down putting items into Olga's dark green shopping cart.

"I heard she was very good friends wi' Farley. Be hard for her too." Mary stood up.

"Aye, it would…" A slight blush tinged her pale cheeks when she saw Ellie, but there was no flustered response to the situation, simply a straightforward, "Good mornin', Ellie. What an awful thing to happen to Farley. Are you all right?"

The woman in front of Ellie turned slowly and for some moments while Ellie verbalised her thanks for Mary's concern, looked up at her, staring, as if trying to memorise every single aspect of her appearance.

"I've seen you about the village often enough, young woman, but never met you. Sad thing for all of us this business wi' Farley. Has that old plod Jack given you or his children any news? I heard the forensic people are involved?"

"Sergeant Kennart only tells who he needs to," Ellie said pointedly, without giving a direct answer. "I imagine he's well aware of the damage and pain caused by misleading stories."

Unexpectedly, Olga's round body began shaking, followed seconds later by hearty laughter that took Ellie, and Mary judging by the sudden arching of her eyebrows, by surprise.

"I think I could get to like you, Ellie Madison. Straight to the point and not afraid to give a warning about pokin' into your affairs. I'm Olga Erskine," she said and held out a fleshy, calloused hand which Ellie shook.

"I've seen you about too, Mrs Erskine."

"I haven't been Missus for over two decades, not since Mister ran away wi' an old flame. I'm Olga, plain an' simple."

A short while later as she was going round the greengrocer's store, Ellie thought about Olga. She wasn't quite sure what to make of her, but liked her forthright manner and unbridled laughter.

"So then, here we are," said a familiar male voice. Its sound filled her with sadness and a strange longing. "I think you've been avoiding me."

She looked up into the smiling face of Byron Oakes, and images of that day at the Knobbles appeared suddenly and with painful intensity. For a moment she could not reply. A frown creased his brow and his eyes clouded with concern.

"Are you all right, Ellie?" he asked quietly. "D'you need some fresh air?"

"No," she said, swallowing. "I hadn't expected to see you."

"I'm not sure if that's a good or bad explanation."

"It brought back Monday."

He nodded. "Sorry. I should've realised. It's the only day in our lives we've had anything to do with one another. Can I buy you a cup of coffee so you have at least one other remembrance of me?"

"What, and have the whole village gossiping?" she said, mustering the traces of a grin.

"There's always another village."

For a few seconds she held his eyes, looking for a flicker of insincerity or mockery, but they remained steady and clear.

"Okay – but definitely not here. There's a good tea shop in Castlebay. If you walk along the Eigg road, I'll pick you up in ten minutes."

"Are you serious?"

"You don't have to live here."

With that she moved along the fruit display, picking up oranges, bananas, a punnet of hothouse strawberries, and a cauliflower. By the time she finished Byron was nowhere in sight, and she presumed he had either begun walking or written her off as a nutcase. Why she'd accepted his invitation she didn't know. It wasn't anything she'd ever done before, gone off for coffee with a stranger. Already the reasons why she should go straight home were filling her head. What insanity had made her say she'd pick him up?

Kipp moved obligingly into the back seat along with the shopping and mail, and Ellie pointed the car in the direction of Eigg. As she set off, Olga Erskine, who was pushing an envelope into the letterbox outside the post office, waved.

Drizzle pattered on the windscreen as the road wound through Kilcomb, a village with its roots in the mid-ninth century, past a short row of houses on the outskirts built two centuries later, and two Iron Age barrows from even earlier times next to the mill. Several miles north, archaeologists had recently discovered an inhumation cemetery from about AD 500. Jack, she recalled, had been thrilled. He loved the history of Scotland.

The mill still functioned, crushing for its owner's use and providing flour to local bakers. The Mill, as Bob Caraway insisted it be known and not by a fancy name, was also a living museum. Visitors were often lured to it, not only by the tourist brochures, but by the deep, rhythmic drumming of the water wheel slapping and churning the clear river water. Much of the bread Bob made went to bakeries in the local and surrounding districts. He used old Scottish recipes as much as possible. Bob employed two millers, one his nephew, and an older man from Kilcomb who had spent his childhood years watching and learning the craft of the miller from his father.

Before Bob's return to Kilcomb, the mill had suffered a succession of owners, none of whom were very successful. When Bob, now forty-eight, took ownership he'd spent seven months restoring it, hiring experienced builders, historians and architects to get it right. What helped his success, she'd teased him once, was his reputation as a great chef, although there were those in the village who'd questioned why he'd come back after working in some of Britain's and Europe's finest restaurants. It was simple, he'd told Ellie. He missed Scotland.

Ellie slowed down and drew into the The Mill's car park. The queue inside was longer than she'd hoped – two customers were agonising over whether they wanted wholemeal or linseed and pumpkin seed, spicy sticky buns or Bob's oat cakes. Eventually, purchases made, the next customers had books on Kilcomb's history in their hands, but they too dithered over what to get. Ellie peeked at her watch. Fifteen minutes had already gone by. She tapped her foot on the wooden floor, glancing around the old stone walls, the big oven set in the back wall around the corner. Behind her was the tea room with windows and French doors facing into the garden, and a fireplace kept burning during the colder months. She'd spent a lot of time in that room, sometimes drawing, sometimes reading, and sometimes sharing tea and cake with friends.

Ellie sighed – loudly. How long did it take to decide on a loaf of bread? Well, she would have to come back later. Time was up. As she turned, she heard her name called and saw Bob carrying out a tray of her favourite strong, whole-wheat bread. He put it down on the bench behind the counter and then beckoned her to the end of the counter.

"Want the usual, Ellie?" he said, grinning. "Looks like you're on a mission."

"Why? Have I got the 'can't they hurry up' look?" She chuckled.

"Aye, you have."

He came back with two loaves and took her money. "Bad news about Farley," he said quietly, sadly, returning with her change. "I'll miss him. He was a good friend despite…"

Ellie reached out and touched his arm. "Yes, he was, Bob," she said, stopping him. He'd never approved of Farley's frequent absences from his family and had often castigated him about it.

"Sorry, Ellie." He shook his head. "Any idea what happened to him? It must've been an awful shock."

"I don't really want to talk about it, Bob. And not here."

"I understand," he said gently, grasping her hand. "You know I'm here for you."

She nodded and looked into his compassionate blue eyes. Eight years ago he'd lost his wife in a car crash and had turned all his energy and focus into building a successful business. He missed her more than he ever said. Of his four children, two lived in Scotland, one in south-west England and another in Australia.

"I must go. Thanks for rescuing me out of the queue. We'll talk soon."

Almost twenty-five minutes. She clambered quickly into the Land Rover and raced off down the road, narrowly avoiding a collision with a yellow sports car on a bend. That would never have done, especially as she recognised the Earl of Strathvern's middle son in the driver's seat. Several minutes later she spotted Byron perched on a seat in a bus shelter.

"I'm sorry, Byron. I got held up in the baker's," she said, glancing at him as he climbed into the passenger's seat. "Tourists who couldn't make up their minds."

"I was beginning to think you'd changed *your* mind."

"I nearly did."

"So, how far to Castlebay and is it actually on a bay?"

"Tell me, Byron, are you a quiz host in your other life?"

"Oh, very good, very good indeed," he replied, chuckling. "Actually, I'm an architect."

"That's a bit hard to believe. You look like the outdoor educator or sportsman sort."

"Really? What gave you that idea?"

"Your looks if you must know." It just came out.

They turned, glancing at one another – she straight-faced and reddening and he with raised eyebrows and an amused expression.

"Look out!" he cried suddenly.

Her eyes shot back to the road as her right foot hit the brakes. Kipp yelped as he slid off the back seat and landed awkwardly on the floor. Metres ahead a flock of black-faced sheep filled the road, followed by a startled, fist-shaking herder who was trying to get them into a field.

She wound down the window. "Sorry," she said loudly above the bleating.

"Did you no see the signs or can you no read? 'Slow down, sheep ahead' it says. You should hand in your licence drivin' like a maniac on these roads," said the middle-aged man with a weathered face and blond-red hair, grey starting to encroach at the sides.

Giving a final wag of his finger, he turned his back on them and, with the help of a sheepdog at the rear of the flock, ushered the sheep through a gate into the field. Ellie got out and opened the door behind her to ensure Kipp was all right. A few groceries had spilled onto the seat and floor and she shoved them back into bags.

"My *looks*," Byron said, emphasising the second word in a tone she could only describe as faintly cynical.

"Yes," she said as she shut her door and waited for the road to clear. "You're very fit and it looked to me as if the climb up to the Knobbles was an easy walk for you. Didn't think you'd have a desk job."

"Well, I do, at least some of the time. Love hiking and climbing though."

"And do you do a lot of that?"

"A fair bit. It's a passion of mine, always has been. Both my parents were mad about camping and exploring, so we kids went too. I was the only one who enjoyed it. Still am."

"You have brothers and sisters?"

"Two sisters, both younger. And you?"

She hesitated. Questions about her life. Out of the corner of her eye she could see he was watching her, waiting. Farley never asked as many questions about her past life as this man did.

Reluctantly, she said, "My father died a few years ago in an accident at sea. He was in the Navy, one of those career men. I've got two older brothers and a younger sister."

He looked past her. Someone was tapping on the window beside her. She wound it down.

"Road's clear now," said the herder. "Mind how ye go. Personally, I think your man should be drivin'."

"Thank you," she said, a faint blush creeping into her cheeks, but he was already turning away and she had no idea if he heard.

Beside her, Byron was grinning. "I always was of the persuasion that women made better passengers. It seems my view is shared even in the middle of nowhere."

She gave him a withering look and drove on. The conversation turned to local sights and history, and a little later there were glimpses through the trees of a castle. Close by it a dark loch and its protective hills curved around in a shape resembling a crescent, and Ellie told Byron about the walks near the water's edge and up over the hills to Maw's Hearth.

"Now there's a place for a ho... house. And what a house," he said, staring out the window.

Ellie frowned. Was it her imagination or had he been going to say something else? However, he turned and looked at her as if the hesitation hadn't occurred. She chose to ignore it.

"The Earl of Strathvern owns it, the loch, and much of the land you see. He spends a reasonable amount of time here, but has another home near Edinburgh and jets off to the Continent often enough. His oldest son Michael lives here with his wife. The castle was built in 1252 and has an impressive history of murders, illegitimate children, visits by Scottish and English royalty, German hierarchy in the last world war, and a place for the rich to stay in hunting and fishing seasons. That's the brief overview."

"Impressive."

"Like many landed families he knows his family's history in greater detail than most of us wee ordinary people know our own. It's documented in estate logs, diaries, letters, books and paintings."

"Can't complain about the view or lousy neighbours, so why doesn't he spend more time here?"

"Depends on who you talk to. He's a busy man with friends and enemies. There's also son number two, Jamie. You probably got sprayed by a yellow sports car while you were waiting for me. He'd have thought it a great joke."

"I didn't."

"No, most don't. He can be a bit wild at times – he's twenty-four – but he's a talented painter and poet. Son number three is quiet, rarely seen as he's away at uni."

"You're a fount of knowledge, Ellie."

"I take people hiking and painting. They want to know more than the trees, mountains and glens. The people and history are important too. Anyway, Jamie's done a number of paintings of the area around Maw's Hearth, sold them and donated the money to a Highland preservation trust set up by Farley."

"Very generous of him."

"That's how he is."

"And the rest of the Strathverns? What kind of people are they?'

"Why d'you want to know?"

"I'm a tourist remember. Curiosity, interest in local history."

"They're much like most families, albeit they're well off and live in a very big house. They have their problems. I don't know who doesn't."

"I heard the current earl's father was a Nazi supporter in the war."

She turned her head and looked at him briefly. "So I've heard, but don't know how true it is."

"I see," he said and stared out of the side window.

They were almost in Castlebay and he did not speak again until she pulled into the car park outside the café.

"Is this all right?" she asked brightly, though a little disturbed by his sudden quietness. "It overlooks water."

"Wonderful."

They stood outside for a few minutes in a stiff breeze that penetrated their thin jackets and made their ears tingle. Ellie wished she had worn a warmer jumper. She pointed out the landmarks and told him they were overlooking Loch Linguay, which found its way round an island or two and joined the Firth of Lorn.

"Come on, Byron, I'm very cold. Let's go and have coffee and cake."

"I thought you were a Highlander!" he teased, laughing.

"Not me. And the locals certainly don't think that. I haven't been here for a century or more."

Warmth wrapped itself around Ellie as they sat in an alcove with a view across the loch, its shoreline drawing a border between houses and shops huddled as close to the water as possible, and the water itself. Farther away the mottled mauve, white and emerald slopes of cloud-topped hills disappeared into the dark loch, divided from smoother, rounded cousins near Castlebay by a narrow stretch of water. Rain was now coming down in sheets and Ellie watched boats being tossed about like flotsam as the wind increased in its strength.

She turned her head to make a comment to Byron about the unpredictable Highland weather and found him studying her intently.

"You don't like my wind-blown hair?" she asked jauntily, yet disconcerted by his intense gaze. She had taught herself not to be concerned when people looked or stared at her. She'd had to.

"Why did you come to the Highlands, Ellie?" His voice was quiet, strong. It reminded her of Farley.

It was her turn to examine his features and she took her time. Eventually she said, "A change of scenery."

"Did it have anything to do with your father's death?"

Ellie frowned and said a little sharply, "I don't wish to discuss my reasons for coming here, Byron. Let's talk about something else, like the sorts of buildings you design."

Leaning back in his chair, Byron's mouth stretched slowly into a smile that unexpectedly set her heart pounding. Don't be fooled, she told herself.

"You are, without a doubt, the most forthright woman I've ever known," he said in a half-playful voice. "I can see why you and Farley Orman had such a formidable reputation."

"I think you mean him and perhaps you'd explain the 'why'." Somehow, she felt she'd been fobbed off.

"From what I've heard and read he was strong-headed, determined and didn't give in to pressure. Perhaps someone didn't like that. And before you ask why I'd be reading about him," he said, as she opened her mouth, "photography's an interest of mine and I admire his work."

"Is that why you came up here, to meet Farley?"

He was careful in his answer. "I hoped to," he said. Not exactly a lie. "I've been in the Highlands before, but I wouldn't have passed up an opportunity to meet him."

"No, I'm sure you wouldn't." She gazed out the window, watching dark clouds lowering themselves over the hills and waves becoming more frenzied as the wind increased. Then she said, studying him again, "I think you're the sort of person who designs ultra-modern buildings that stick out like a Picasso amongst all the Constables."

"So that's how you see me. I did wonder."

"Am I right?"

"Partly. We're a bit alike really, not quite misfits, but definitely not conformists. I think I was fairly young when I realised that being stuffed into the same mould as everyone else wasn't for me," Byron said, with a wry grin.

The coffee and cake arrived and he reached out to take a slice and sugar his drink. Ellie watched him. As she poured milk into her coffee, she said quietly, "A lot of people do think I'm a misfit."

He did not respond straight away, but took a mouthful of coffee, looking at her over the rim of the mug. When he put the mug down he reached out, his fingers tightening gently and briefly around her wrist as if he could see into her soul and empathised. The gesture was not unwelcome, but she slowly moved her arm away; his expression gave no indication of how he felt about her withdrawal, but he let go and resumed drinking his coffee.

"So, d'you work for one of those big city companies?" It came out more loudly than she intended. Two children at the next table stared at her.

For a split second the spoon stopped stirring, at least she thought it did.

"I work for myself, but if someone's paying well enough I'll do contract jobs."

"I suppose that's big office buildings, all glass and steel poles."

"Not always."

"Give me the Highlands any day."

"Well, at least the air's cleaner."

Stilted conversation she supposed he no more liked than she did. It was a dumb idea having coffee with a man she barely knew. They were strangers and were unlikely to ever meet again after this day. They finished their cake and coffee in silence, an island amongst laughter and chatter, chinking china and the whoosh of the cappuccino machine behind the counter.

Byron paid the bill and they hurried as best they could across the car park to the Land Rover pelted by heavy rain and wind that seemed determined to dispossess them of their clothing. The windows misted up almost immediately Ellie started the vehicle and put the heater on. She shivered, longing for warmth. Without asking, Byron reached across and turned the knob to demist. Ellie looked at him, mildly annoyed at the familiarity.

"You can't possibly see where you're going and I don't want to end up in the water," he said, sounding irritated.

"Well, I'm freezing and I thought the window could wait a few minutes."

"You're supposed to be used to this kind of weather."

"That doesn't mean I don't feel the cold and, though you might find it difficult to believe, I do."

"So, how d'you manage in the winter?"

"I rug up and keep the heater running."

"Hard to do when you're outside."

"That's different."

"Really? Tell me how."

Ellie stared at him. Was he being deliberately exasperating? "Why are we having this stupid conversation?"

"Because neither of us wants to talk about things we really want to."

She blinked, digesting the sentence. He was right. "You mean Farley."

"Yes. We haven't seen each other since we... saw him and neither of us have the guts to bring the subject up," he said with some acerbity. "You, because you knew him very well and me because I happened to be there when his body was found and it seemed obvious he'd been the victim of foul play."

"A tearoom's not exactly the place to discuss, as you put it, 'foul play'."

"Maybe not. Any other suggestions?"

"Yes, now, on the way back to Kilcomb," she said bluntly and began negotiating her way out of the car park.

Even so, it was another ten minutes of winding upwards along narrow roads before either of them broached the subject.

"So, tell me why you think he was murdered," Ellie asked, feeling less aggressive now she was warmer.

Byron looked at her. "You did too. I saw it in your expression. The only other explanation is that he committed suicide."

She almost ran the car off the road as her head snapped round to stare at him. "How dare you say such a thing! He would never do that!"

"I'm not saying he did, but..."

"Farley would never take his own life. Life was precious to him. You have no right to speak like that!"

"Ellie, it seems clear someone took his life. I was just making a comparison about the situation."

"I'd rather you didn't say anything else. You didn't know him."

Without thinking beyond her anger at this man she sped around the corner and up the next hill. Anger turned a key and grief asserted itself, spilling down her cheeks in salty tears as the car breeched the crest. The storm was unleashing its power on the shrouded valley below. The clouds were low. Again, there was a gentle pressure on her arm.

"Pull over, Ellie," Byron said with quiet authority.

She did not argue, there was no will in her to do so, and drew to the side of the road and turned the ignition off. The pain of loss grew in her belly until she could not contain it and the sound of her sobbing filled the car. Byron put his arm around her shoulders and pulled her against him. Immediately, without even thinking about it, Ellie stiffened and pulled away.

"Please… don't." she said thickly.

He did not speak, withdrew his arm and sat regarding her. She didn't know what to say, so said nothing.

A cocoon. That's what they were in, while the rain continued its determined outpouring, drumming on the metal roof and bonnet that shielded them from its wet coldness. Strangely, and slowly, Ellie realised that Byron, whether he was aware of it or not, was instilling in her a measure of peace by his silent presence. The raging emotions subsided and she began wiping her face and blowing her nose. He got out and went around to the driver's door and opened it. Still he said nothing. She, like a meek lamb, got out and went and sat in the passenger's seat and he, as if it was what he'd always done, settled into the driver's seat.

He turned to her then. "I didn't mean to upset you, Ellie," he said quietly. "I'm sorry."

Ellie sighed and looked at him, her eyes hot and puffy. "I was shocked. I hadn't even thought he… about suicide. He just wouldn't. And I can't get away from him. Everywhere I go there are memories."

"I know you're tough, but grieving *is* allowed. Don't let anyone tell you it's not."

Dabbing her eyes, she stuffed the handkerchief in her jacket pocket. "Can you drive this thing?"

The unexpected burst of laughter caught her unawares and she stared at him.

"I drove a tank once, so I think I'll be all right."

The wind pushed at the Land Rover as they journeyed across the hilltops. Rain kept the windscreen wipers busy. Several miles later, at a crossroads, she told him to go right and they began winding their way down past crofts and fields with shaggy, brown Highland cattle. In the warmth of the car, and her head against the seat, Ellie dozed. She awoke with a start, hearing her name.

"What?" she said loudly.

"Sorry to wake you, but which way – left or right?"

She saw the old milestone. "Oh, left."

"Are you sure? You haven't got your eyes open properly."

"It's left," she said drowsily.

"You're the local."

It seemed only a few minutes before Byron stopped again. "Are you sure we haven't gone in the wrong direction?"

This time she came fully awake and looked out the windows at the madly waving branches and an ornate gate opening to a long avenue of oak trees.

"Not *wrong* exactly, a bit out of the way, but we're not too far from my house. A few yards up the road there's another road into Kilcomb. Just keep going for a couple of minutes."

They passed an ancient barrow in a copse, and a quarter of a mile later a few people and a couple of tents in a field.

"Archaeological dig?" Byron asked.

"Yes," she said, nodding. "It's a village dating back to the first century A.D. A farmer unearthed it when he was ploughing and found bits of pottery and a few bones. Jack's a bit of a history buff and got in touch with Edinburgh University. So, there they are. They've been at it for about two months. People from the National Trust are also involved."

In the back Kipp barked, his wagging tale thumping against the seat.

"He knows he's nearly home," Ellie said, "and when we go walking there a couple of the archaeologists always manage to find him a biscuit."

"I'd be interested in having a look."

"Too wet and they don't like people tramping over it when they're not there."

"I can wait."

"I thought you'd be leaving. Actually, I'm surprised you didn't leave when the rest of the group did."

"My holiday's barely started and I intend to finish it."

"I see. How long will you be around?" Ellie asked, half wishing he'd go.

"A week or so. I still want to get to Maw's Hearth."

"Let's hope for better weather then. It gets very slippery and the last climb is over rocks. I only take more experienced hikers in the wet."

"I'm surprised you'd go up there again with me," he said, slowing the vehicle as they rounded a bend.

"There's another group coming tomorrow."

"Ah. Safety in numbers then," he said and peered through the windscreen. "Where's this road you were talking about?"

"My house is round this bend and the road to Kilcomb is just past it on the right."

Byron steered the vehicle around the corner. Beside him, Ellie stiffened in her seat. There was a car parked outside her gate and a man walking down the path.

"Stop the car."

"Sure. Something the matter?"

Ellie did not answer but got out the minute he pulled up in front of the fence. This was one man she did not want to see. It was Camden Orman, Farley's eldest son.

Chapter 3

The noise of the crowded pub that evening suited Byron as he sat at a corner table with a pint of bitter after finishing a plate of steak, chips and vegetables. The publican, a plump, tall man with a neat beard and moustache, wandered over to collect the plate.

"Enjoyed that did you?" Andrew Stewart said, eyes twinkling.

"Certainly did. My compliments to the chef. Your wife again?"

"Aye. And she'll be well pleased you enjoyed it. Thinks you need feeding up if you're going climbing."

Byron grinned as the other man raised his eyebrows and picked up the plate, collected two glasses on the next table and headed towards the kitchen. The pub owners had taken pity on him, noticing he ate alone. He'd got used to being alone.

Most of the people in the pub were locals according to Andrew, but there were also a number of tourists, including three Americans whose accents filtered through the Scottish brogue. The laughter and conversations washed over and around him. He was part of the scene, yet separate. Here in the corner he could mull over the day's events without too much distraction.

He'd decided not to try and work Ellie out. There wasn't any need yet, but he was intrigued by her and she had known Farley. Earlier that day he'd watched through her rain-splattered windscreen as she engaged the man at her gate, clearly not welcome, in heated conversation. He had waved his fist once or twice, face contorted with anger, and she'd responded with equal energy, stabbing the air with her finger and pointing at him. Only once had Byron opened the vehicle's door when Kipp began growling behind him. The man had stepped towards Ellie. However, she'd turned and shaken her head. Soon afterwards the visitor strode to his car and sped off down the road.

To Byron's surprise, Ellie, rattled and angry, had asked him in for a cup of tea. She'd told him little of the conversation, only that it was Camden Orman, intent on blaming her for his father's death. When Byron asked whether he resented her place as his father's co-worker, she'd retorted that Camden Orman was like a spoilt child, very odd, unpredictable, aggressive, and his mother's darling. That had effectively brought the conversation to an end. It had become clear that Ellie Madison allowed no one to probe into her personal life, particularly where relationships were concerned.

"So, you're still here then, Mr Oakes."

The voice of Jack Kennart crashed in on his thoughts. He had a pint of bitter in his hand. "Mind if I join you?"

He could hardly say no and indicated a chair.

"Thought you'd have been only too pleased to go," the sergeant continued. "The others were."

"I like to finish things."

"Oh? And what might they be?"

"My hiking holiday."

He nodded and took a sip of his beer. "I did some checking on you. Seems you were in the army for quite a spell."

Byron regarded him intently for a few seconds. "That's right."

"Why d'you leave?"

"Time was up. Decided to try something less demanding." Where, he wondered, was this going?

"Must've been a tough decision. You were one of their best they said. Did jobs no one else could. What sort of jobs?"

"You know I can't tell you that."

"When there's been a murder on my patch I expect you to tell me everything I want to know."

"And be tried for breaching the Secrecy Act? Don't be ridiculous, man."

"Don't get smart wi' me. I can be stubborn too, especially when it's my brother-in-law lying in the morgue." He stood up, his thick eyebrows drawn together and his expression resentful. "And stay away from Ellie Madison. She's enough on her plate wi'out you complicating things."

"Farley Orman was your brother-in-law? Why didn't you say so at the Knobbles?"

"Because it's none of your business and I'll thank you not to speak about it."

Byron watched him wend his way between tables until he was lost to sight on the other side of the bar. Odd Ellie hadn't mentioned it either.

Swallowing the last of the beer, Byron left the pub and walked outside into a cold, damp evening. The storm had passed an hour or so earlier leaving everything dripping wet and puddles brimming in all the dips and holes. Clouds were moving slowly across the sky and he caught a glimpse of blue as they broke up. The air was clean and sweet and he drew it deep into his city lungs. In the middle of the village he stopped and looked around as he had on his first day, then beyond the old stone buildings to the mountains, their presence at once forbidding and majestic. It took little effort to imagine the peaks laden with snow, everything shorter than trees smothered until the thaw began.

The potential for year-round business and substantial profit in a hotel designed and built to fit snugly into the surrounds could not be underestimated. At least that was Mayfair's way of thinking. Byron sighed. He was beginning to question his wisdom in taking on the contract. The uniqueness of the Highlands was getting into his heart in a big way. Tomorrow morning the owner's son was due in Kilcomb to discuss with him the probabilities of two sites the company favoured. He suspected the hotel company's board would not welcome anything other than energetic endorsement of its ideas, though the owner, John Thorley, seemed a reasonable man.

For a moment he stood and looked up and down the road. Cars lined the main street and there were a number of people abroad. Two young couples spilled out from the other pub, The Highlander, and judging by their ebullient behaviour had enjoyed themselves immensely. There were others out walking, studying the buildings, peering in shop windows, while an older man cut roses and chatted to anyone who cared to stop and ask him about his garden.

The patch of blue in the sky widened as Byron neared the narrow street where his accommodation stood, a bed and breakfast in a house that had once been a school. Its doors had closed thirty years ago after almost two centuries of children's feet crossing its threshold. He went on down the road, passing the post office. The door opened and closed.

A female voice said, "That's the man I saw wi' Ellie, pet. He was in the party that went away up to the Knobbles when poor Farley was found. I don't understand why he's still here."

Byron stopped and looked through the gift shop window next door.

"On holiday, I expect, Carrie love. Come on, we'll be late."

"And Farley not buried."

"What're you talking about?"

They began walking across the road. "You don't know Ellie like I do, love. Best you don't."

44

The gossiping postmistress, who Byron doubted knew Ellie well at all, slipped her arm through her husband's as they disappeared down a lane. He had heard the woman in full verbal flow when he queued for overseas stamps for postcards to friends, waiting less than patiently for her to finish a conversation with a female customer. Between them they had dissected the life of some poor chap who lived in the next village. If it hadn't been for an even less patient local man behind him who told her to quit carving up a chap who was too old to defend himself, he would have left and posted the cards back in London. He sighed. London seemed an alien land and he was in no hurry to get back to its temperamental moods.

Still, his curiosity was aroused by the postmistress' remark. Ellie was an almost unknown epistle to him; he had read a page or two of her life and knew the mystery had no simple solution. In different circumstances, and if there was more time, he would have enjoyed unravelling it and finding what was at the heart of her.

Early next morning, Byron woke to shafts of sunlight fingering the quilt and dappling the flower-patterned carpet. Thoughts of Ellie striding the moors had occupied his dreams. Stretching his body on the firm mattress and yawning into the coolness, he thought with pleasure of the next day's hike to Maw's Hearth. First, however, there was Glenn Thorley. His smile disappeared.

Savouring every mouthful of sausages, fried egg, bacon and toast, Byron glanced through the newspaper with mild interest. There were others in the dining room: a young married couple casting shy smiles at one another, two women at separate tables, and an elderly couple chuckling over something to which only they were privy. None were seated near him, which was just as well. He was feeling neither sociable nor in the mood for toast-munching tourists sitting too close.

"Tea or coffee, Mr Oakes?" said a quiet female voice.

He looked up into the face of the owner's nineteen-year-old daughter.

"Tea. A pot please."

A faint blush tinged her fresh complexion. "Be about five minutes."

"That's fine." His polite smile deepened the colour in her cheeks. She turned and hurried away.

Byron returned to the paper, his attention captured by a headline on the next page. 'Was Farley Orman Betrayed?' headed a two-column piece which, as he read on, contained a diatribe on Mayfair Hotels that made Byron smart. The informant, 'who wished to remain anonymous', made it quite clear things could get very uncomfortable for the company if it attempted any further destruction of the Highlands that 'Farley Orman had lived and died for'. Towards the end of the piece was a veiled suggestion that Ellie Madison had turned her back on preservation for her thirty pieces of silver.

He read the article again over a second cup of tea before folding the newspaper and leaving with it, returning to his room briefly for his jacket. Almost two hours of freedom before Glenn Thorley arrived, time he spent walking along the river outside the village. A patchy blue sky with ragged clouds cast a gloomy, almost eerie, light over the land where deep shadows made low, rounded hills uninviting. However, he walked on up a gentle slope and sat on a boulder surveying the landscape stretched out like a patchwork quilt of pink heather, tough green bracken, quaint cottages, farms and the river. Beyond the quilt towered higher peaks.

Somewhere was an anonymous and angry talebearer, perhaps someone known to Ellie. He was beginning to realise that Mayfair was not as popular as he'd believed. At least, not in Scotland. A young company compared to others, John Thorley had built a very successful business in a short span of time, surpassing at least two of the bigger players in the south. It seemed he hadn't counted on the determination of the Scots around Kilcomb to keep their Highlands free of what they deemed chain hotels. At least that was one opinion. Others he'd spoken to in the village and out walking didn't think a hotel in the hills would do any harm, especially if it brought money into the region.

The stillness and sparse beauty of the scene spread before him captivated Byron and a muted, internal voice questioned the wisdom of being involved in designing a hotel for this environment. He thought of Ellie and her love for the Highlands, saw the brightness in her eyes and the intensity of her expression as she told of the struggles and victories she and the Ormans had seen. He envied her passion and the deep conviction that this was her place. It stirred a buried need inside him and, as always, he pushed it down until the intensity of it dulled.

Yet there was another unknown side to her, one he'd glimpsed yesterday. In her expression, for a brief moment, she'd fled a thousand miles away from him and he could only assume he'd overstepped the mark. No use dwelling on one minor incident. She'd have forgotten about it by now. He looked up at the sky, still cloudy, and slowly made his way back to the village.

By the time he reached The Mill just after ten o'clock he was ready for his meeting. Glenn Thorley was waiting. They shook hands.

"I've ordered for us," Glenn said as Byron sat down. "The Highland air suits you, Byron. You look relaxed."

"It's that kind of place."

"So, what did you think of the two sites we have in mind?"

As he had been in their two other meetings, he was forthright. Personal greetings and chat were kept to a minimum, much like his father, though the senior Thorley was more relaxed.

"Both exceptional, as you already know, but not for building hotels."

"Really. And what alternative d'you have in mind?"

"It's about two miles west of here overlooking a loch, a couple of peaks nearby and views of an old castle or two. Should keep the tourists happy. I saw it from the Knobbles and went to have a look on Wednesday."

"We didn't ask you to look at another site. Where the hotel is built isn't your decision. Did you sketch up the designs as we asked?" Glenn's voice and expression had lost their earlier civility. He had not, Byron thought, inherited his father's charm.

"I've drawn up two plans, yes."

"May I see them?"

Byron passed a leather folder across the table and saw a glint of suspicion in the thirty-seven-year old man's grey-blue eyes as he opened it and took out the papers. For several minutes he studied the drawings in silence while Byron drank coffee and watched him. Impassive, single-minded, driven by success and money, and ruthless in dealing with employees or business associates who did not shape up, about summed up what Byron thought of him. What he was like with his wife and two children he had no idea; he had heard a whisper she'd left him.

"I can see why my father hired you, Byron. There's no doubting your creative ideas and talent. However, they're not quite what *I* had in mind."

"And what did you have in mind?"

"These concepts do not fit the Mayfair mould. I gave you clear guidelines."

"You did, but they don't fit the Highlands' image. If your company wants any chance at all of convincing local authorities and the people who live here that the hotel will benefit the region, the 'Mayfair mould' has to be flexible. Does your father agree with your ideas on this?"

An immediate response was not forthcoming. The drawings were placed back inside the leather folder and handed to Byron. The silence continued while Glenn finished his coffee. Only then did he speak.

"Your comments are noted. However..."

A shadow fell across the table and Byron looked up expecting to see a waitress. Instead he saw Ellie, observing him with a hard, cold expression.

"You left this in my car," she snapped and slapped a card down on the table in front of him. "Don't bother joining the hike tomorrow. You won't be welcome."

Without waiting for his response, she turned and walked quickly towards the door, ignoring the owner's friendly greeting and dodging incoming clients. She disappeared through the door into the pale sunlight outside.

Byron knew without looking at the card that it was one of John Thorley's. It must have fallen out of his pocket. Frowning, and inwardly cursing his stupidity, he slipped the card into his wallet.

"I didn't know you knew Ellie Madison," said Glenn with a hint of amusement in his eyes.

"I was in her hiking group the day Farley Orman's body was found."

"Ah, yes, the famous defender of all things Highland. Only one fighter left to pursue his cause. She's much better looking in the flesh than in tabloid photographs don't you think? Passionate too, but she won't win."

"You think money and force will woo her over?"

"That and a little... persuasion from you."

Byron looked at him. "Then you don't know Ellie Madison."

"But I do. She and the Ormans are one of the reasons we haven't been able to build up here yet. Anyway, all women can be bought in some way or other. She just needs a different sort of cajoling than most," Glenn Thorley said quietly, eyes half closed.

The man's demeanour made Byron think of Machiavelli, who cared nothing for morality and actively pursued deceit and treachery in his political career.

Glenn peered at him over the rim of his cup. "I doubt you know her really. Or do you?" A lascivious smile accompanied the latter.

"Have you read Dumas' book *The Three Musketeers*?"

The other man's expression closed. He snapped, "What's that got to do with our discussion?"

"Everything. They fought for their cause with single-minded loyalty. Only death could separate them from their cause. If you'd bothered to do any research you'd know that Ellie and the Ormans were called 'The Iron Musketeers'."

"Oh, that. Media hype. Break through her armour. It can't be difficult, not with all the army training you've had."

Byron stood up, put money for the coffee on the table and said, "You're more of a fool than I thought."

He was glad of the walk back to his lodgings, the clear air doing its job of rescuing his mind from Glenn Thorley's muck. By the time he put the drawings back in his bag and retrieved his camera he had a clear idea of his position and the decisions needed.

Out on the hills once again and away from civilisation, Byron pulled his mobile phone from his jacket pocket and pushed the buttons. Reception was not great, but good enough and a few seconds later he heard John Thorley's voice.

***

Ellie chose a different route to Maw's Hearth, skirting the Knobbles by a lower path. She could not face being up there, not yet, perhaps not for a long while. The path would lead them over Cuttingstone Hill, through Glen Erc and up the western side of Maw's Hearth. Steeper and more demanding, it was not a path she'd have taken with the previous group, but these eight hikers, all from the same club in Norfolk except one of them, were experienced walkers and fit.

Though she did not want to think of Byron, her thoughts kept drifting to him whenever she was not occupied with conversation. Finding a Mayfair Hotels' card on the driver's seat had infuriated and wounded her. She should have listened to her earliest instincts on first meeting him, and not allowed his charm and good looks to bewitch her. All that photo taking and writing – what a deceiver! Farley was right; they could not trust anyone, especially outsiders. From deep inside, the pain of Farley's death and his separation from her rose like a tormentor. She wanted to run away into the wildest, remotest part of the Highlands and stay there. How could she and those who were left carry on the fight, *his* fight, without him? She didn't have the expertise or knowledge he and Alice had between them.

"...magnificent scenery. Is that the Isle of Skye in the distance?"

The middle-aged man's voice intruded into her pain and she wanted to shout at him, tell him she wasn't capable of enjoying beauty right at this minute.

With difficulty she said, "Yes. It's worth a visit."

"We're off there next week."

Ellie nodded, struggling to squash the inner turmoil and get on with the job. Grief was allowed, yes, but she would never show anyone how much churned away inside. She was good at hiding it. After all, she'd had plenty of practice.

"All right everyone, we'll get to the top of Cuttingstone Hill and stop for a rest."

Once there, like other groups before them, they wanted to know where the hill had got its name.

"In the middle of the eighteenth century there was a sect that worshipped the moon. Not much is known about them, but it's believed they came up here at every full moon with offerings of food – and blood. The blood was their own. They would make cuts in their arms with stones and let the blood run onto the earth."

"Did they really think the moon was a living entity?" piped up a young man in his mid-twenties.

"I don't know," Ellie said, "but why would they worship it if they didn't think it could help them in some way?"

An older man, a historian, offered an answer. "They wouldn't have, but deception's long been part of such things. And the blood offering's common to lots of religions, making it legitimate for them. People need to believe in something," he added, with a slight lift of his shoulders.

"Does the sect still exist?" asked the young man's girlfriend.

Ellie shook her head. "Not that I know of. Still, this is far enough from civilisation for any number of weird things to take place, but I don't know anyone who'd venture up here at night, full moon or not."

"Not your thing, then?"

"No. I believe in the living. Now then," she said before that was pursued any further, "have a rest, look at the view and then we'll begin going down through Glen Erc."

It was two months since Ellie had been on the hill and she wandered across the flat top buffeted by a stiff breeze. The great jutting rocks of Maw's Hearth rose from the treeless heights like a sentinel, drawing Ellie by their sheer size and dominance. Facing her, a dark and ominous rock rose from the base of the Hearth almost straight up, its face smooth except for one or two narrow ledges – The Chimney.

"You're looking across there intensely. I'm beginning to think that's where we're going," said Jenny Browne, a slender, attractive young woman in her early twenties who'd moved to Inverness nine months earlier from Carlisle.

They'd met several times at meetings in village halls. Ellie thought she made herself too familiar with certain people, including Farley, and wasn't keen for a close association with her. She had not long finished her studies to become a journalist and Farley thought she would be an asset to their cause. That wasn't Ellie's opinion.

"We are," Ellie replied, turning to her, "but not up The Chimney."

"Aptly named. Do people climb it?"

"A few. Mountaineers and rock climbers. Interested?"

Jenny laughed, a loud, almost harsh sound that jarred on Ellie's nerves. "Just the thought of it makes me dizzy," she said, getting her camera out of its bag. "Did you read the article in the paper about Farley being betrayed?"

Ellie looked at her.

"No, I didn't."

"Somebody hinted it might've been you."

"What rot. D'you know who it was?"

Jenny shrugged. "No one at the paper is saying."

Her answer sounded non-committal and Ellie wondered whether it wasn't Jenny herself who'd written it. Or maybe the woman from Norwich had phoned the newspaper. Well, she wasn't going to waste time brooding over that snippet.

The others drifted across to them and the conversation came to an end.

"Right, let's go. We're heading towards that," she said pointing across the glen, watching the faces of her group grow serious.

"Don't worry. It's The Chimney at Maw's Hearth. None of us will be climbing it."

A collective sigh and the smiles returned – they were ready for the next stretch. If the views alone weren't enough, a little farther on were remains of a medieval village. However, she knew that from Maw's Hearth they would gaze in wonder across high, bleak moors and hills that had long ago captivated Ellie's heart.

For a while the path allowed single file only and, sheltered in the lee of the hill and warmed by the walk, the bright chatter and laughter picked up again. Ellie drew on it; she had no time for gossip in newspapers and didn't want any thought of it intruding upon her thoughts. It also helped that the walkers were an inquisitive lot who asked intelligent questions about the history and environment of Glen Erc and Maw's Hearth.

"So, they came from Ireland then," Jenny said, walking by her side as soon as it was wide enough.

Ellie had to cast her mind back to general conversation begun after leaving Kilcomb earlier on, but which had got lost in the wonders of heather, bird song and a burbling stream under a humped, stone bridge.

"Well, it's been a matter of dispute for many years. From what I've read and heard, some historians have Scots coming from Scandinavia or Spain. A university history professor told me he believed the Scots are connected to the Scyths and that's where the name came from. But I've also read that traditions from Ireland seem to point to a woman called Scota. Apparently, she was a Pharoah's daughter," Ellie said raising her brows in a 'who knows' expression.

"So, they could've come over well before the birth of Christ – if you believe in all that," she said and Ellie heard a note of condescension in her voice.

Irked, she replied firmly, "Christ's birth is a well-established fact. And, according to that author, those early Scots arrived here about a thousand years beforehand."

"So, I was right then. The interesting thing about ancient history is that a lot of it can't be proved. Still, I suppose that's part of its fascination."

She smiled, an insincere twitch, and Ellie had little doubt it was to put her in her place – wherever that was.

"You're young, Jenny. I imagine a few more years and a lot more reading will improve you. Now then everyone," she said loudly, turning and speaking to the group, "don't forget to keep an eye out for osprey and stone kilns just outside the medieval village."

Sunshine poured out its warmth and brightness, butterflies fluttered in profusion amongst the heather and wildflowers and birds twittered and called. They saw a small herd of deer browsing near a copse some distance away, the animals staring at them, nervous. Ellie led the hikers away quietly.

They stayed longer at the village than she usually allowed, unless it was the reason for the journey. All except Jenny begged for time to photograph and study it. The historian's wife sat down and began drawing. She was a fine artist and Ellie couldn't bring herself to snatch her away from it. Jenny was talking with one of the other women who looked as if she would rather be left alone to explore the stone walls and remains of the tiny church.

By the time they left, they were making arrangements with her for another trip in spring to spend decent time in the old village and at the kilns. They did not stop again, other than to take photos, until Maw's Hearth and The Chimney loomed above, 1casting their shadows down the length of the hill.

"Okay everyone. It's almost half past one. We've two options – we stop here and eat, or go on up. It's about forty-five minutes to the Hearth. Normally I decide, but you're fit and keen and a great bunch, so your choice today."

In less than a minute there was a unanimous decision to carry on. Ellie was pleased – more time for bird watching. They stopped to look at the small, dark loch and marvel at its stillness in the clear, bright air. Jenny spotted an osprey, though she didn't know what it was until Ellie told her. It was noted down in the little book she had in her pocket. She told Ellie she planned to write an article about the walk, with emphasis on Farley's life and work. Ellie asked if she'd be able to read it before it went to print, but doubted that would happen despite the promise.

As they drew closer to Maw's Hearth and craned their necks to try and take in the immensity of the rocks towering above them, the looming face of The Chimney dominated. Ellie began to hum quietly, smiling. Every time she brought people up here she had a little bet with herself about their reactions when they stepped onto the Hearth. Except for one particularly grumpy group she had always won. Nor was she disappointed this time.

The last mile was uphill, some of it steep and over rocks, but the remaining yards were particularly testing and everyone was breathing hard as they rounded the end of the rocks and stepped onto the relatively flat floor of Maw's Hearth. They stood, almost as one entity, eyes wide open staring at a view that stretched north, east and west as far as they could see. Ellie chuckled.

"Wow!"

"I've never seen anything like it."

"This is absolutely stunning."

"Praise God!"

"This is so beautiful."

"I think I'll stay here forever."

They turned to look at Ellie.

"You should see your faces," she said, laughing. Then, looking northwards, "Not bad for a view I think."

"Not bad?" said the historian, "There's not a human on earth who could create anything like this."

"No," she responded, regarding him thoughtfully, "I don't think there is."

He smiled and was about to speak again when his wife exclaimed loudly, "Oh, my!"

Everyone looked at her and followed her gaze – up and up, enormous stacks of sheer, dark grey rock rising high behind them. The first time Ellie had stood there she had stepped back in fright, the dark dominance and its lower shoulders overwhelming. Two of the group did the same.

"Perhaps you can see now why whoever it was who named it, thought this outcrop resembled his nice warm hearth at home," she said.

"I'm not sure about the 'nice warm'," said the historian's wife. "If anything, it's a bit sinister."

"Lots of people have said that. Someone even wrote a novel and used Maw's Hearth as the place where evil things happened on The Chimney, but I don't know if anything of the kind has ever occurred here," Ellie said, smiling with what she hoped was reassurance.

"How long have we got?" a middle-aged woman asked brightly.

"No more than two hours. Be careful near the edges and *do not* try and climb The Chimney, not even the lower ledge. It's too dangerous if you're not an experienced rock climber and properly equipped."

After finishing sandwiches, cake and tea supplied by the Stewarts at The Hart, they began dispersing across the breadth of the Hearth. Cameras appeared and two people retrieved small sketching pads and pencils to draw The Chimney, while another couple in their fifties walked towards the southern end where a path led away to a neighbouring hill.

Ellie wandered the familiar, loved place with its small rocks scattered about like pale coal on a bed of sparse, coarse grass, and eventually perched on the western side in the sunshine. The shores of the Isle of Skye were the clearest she had seen them in a long time, reminding her she should visit friends who lived there. Pulling out her sketch pad and a pencil, she stared at the untouched page. How often she had found perches at Maw's Hearth while Farley photographed and jotted in his notebook, returning to peer over her shoulder and enthuse about her work. Her heart remembered as her mind did. She closed the pad and put it back in her pack. Another time.

Footsteps fell softly on the grass behind her.

"D'you ever get sick of hiking and painting with bunches of strangers?" asked Jenny, suddenly beside her.

"No. I see something different every time, learn new things, meet new people. And what I really love is the weather and the light. They keep places interesting and unpredictable."

"Unpredictable," she mused. "Have unpredictable things happened to you?"

For a moment Ellie studied her. What was she after?

"Yes, a few times," she said, keeping her expression unemotional.

"I quite like the unpredictable," Jenny said, grinning, and looking beyond Ellie. "In fact, it keeps life very interesting indeed."

"But not always pleasant."

Jenny did not respond, but the smile did not leave her face and Ellie turned around to see what had caught so much of her attention. What she saw did not cause her to smile. Without hurry she pushed herself off the rock and began walking towards Byron Oakes. When they were within a few yards of one another, she stopped and watched him approach, like a mistress waiting for a servant who had not done well at a given task. He barely acknowledged her presence until he was much closer, almost within touching distance, and then he, too, stopped.

"Why are you here?" she demanded coldly, forcing herself not to shout. She did not want Jenny to hear their conversation.

"I would've thought that was obvious – to see Maw's Hearth." His tone was even, without emotion.

"You knew I was bringing a group up here today."

"This is not private property as far as I know, especially yours."

It was a clever answer and it rattled her.

"Don't even think of sticking one of your fancy hotels up here. In fact, don't think of anywhere in the Highlands. We'll fight you and that arrogant, sleazy Glenn Thorley everywhere you turn. You look surprised."

"Only about your description of Thorley." Byron's eyes studied her face giving no indication that he had seen the beautiful, blonde Jenny in the background.

"I've met him before," she said bluntly.

"Before this morning?" Now he looked surprised.

"Want some advice, Byron Oakes? Stay away from him. He's full of lies and deceit and will let nothing, and I mean *nothing*, prevent him getting what he wants. He..." She stopped and glanced past him at a slice of Glen Erc, now bathed in brilliant sunshine.

"He what?"

Swinging her attention back to him, the anger gained momentum and she glared at him. "If you stick with him I'll see to it that you *never* get employment as an architect again! He's a pig! And stay out of my way up here."

Ellie spun on her heel and strode past Jenny, who seemed bemused, and across Maw's Hearth.

Byron watched her go and wondered how many other people had upset her in the crusade to save the Highlands from developers and entrepreneurs. The threat to end his career did not disturb him. However, he doubted that Ellie Madison rarely, if ever, said anything she did not mean.

Sighing, he turned his attention to Maw's Hearth. It was fantastic. Even Farley Orman's photographs had not prepared him for the dramatic rise of The Chimney or the almost irresistible pull to climb its ragged ends. Today would be perfect though it could be windy higher up. An old chap he'd met out on the moor a few days earlier had told him there was a secret tunnel in it somewhere, where men in days past had hidden their women and children when Nordic raiders had come. Interesting stories and no doubt nothing more than local fancy.

A voice crashed in on his thoughts and he turned to find the young woman he had noticed briefly whilst receiving Ellie's verbal battering.

"It's awesome, isn't it?" she said, blue eyes sparkling.

"Yes. And the view from the top would be worth the climb."

She blinked. "I can't think why anyone would be mad enough to climb up there. Or are you one of those eccentric types who can't resist challenging the odds?"

Byron laughed. "Eccentric I'm not. A rock climber, yes."

"Aren't you afraid of falling?"

"Always."

"I suppose you'll tell me it keeps you alert."

"That's right."

She stuck out her right hand. "Jenny Browne."

He shook the fine-boned hand and recognised the searching in her eyes. "Byron Oakes."

"Are you joining us? You seem to know Ellie."

"A little. And no, I'm not joining your group," he said, easing the back pack off his shoulders and onto the ground.

"She didn't look too happy."

Byron squatted on his haunches, retrieved the camera from its pocket and then glanced up at her. "No, she wasn't."

"I hope it wasn't anything I said."

"I doubt it." He fixed the wide-angle lens on the camera.

"Are you always so thrifty with your conversation?"

There was a change in her tone; it was lower, almost throaty. It was time to go.

"No, but I don't know you and I've things to do," he said without warmth, standing up and regarding her coolly. "Perhaps you should go and explore with the rest of them."

"I like getting to know new people, especially interesting people who do things like climbing impossible rocks. I haven't been up here before. I'm new to the area. Inverness actually."

She stepped towards him as Byron bent down, picked up the back pack and shrugged it onto his shoulders.

"Go and join them, Jenny." It was a command, not a request.

"I like strong men," she said, tilting her head and looking down the length of his body. "I'm sure we'll meet again."

She turned and walked off. Byron took a deep breath. "Not if I can help it," he said quietly.

Within seconds he had put her out of his mind and begun exploring the rocks around The Chimney, taking photographs of the glen and the views beyond. Without climbing gear, he was unable to go far for, though the lower section was safe enough near the ends, the central rocks were wide and sheer in the middle. If there was any tunnel, the entrance would not be there unless those who had used it had supernatural abilities. Byron shook his head, but he could not rid himself of the thought that the stories might be rooted in truth.

Content to take photographs and gaze at the views he was, for a time, unfettered by thoughts of Mayfair Hotels and Glenn Thorley. The lure of the Highlands was strong; his mother's parents had lived in Oban for many years, their Scottish lineage stretching back to the mid-sixteenth century, so his mother, the family history buff, had discovered thus far. He wondered why he had waited until the last couple of years to explore Scotland, particularly the uncrowded north, but knew the years in the army, and lately the energy required to establish himself as an architect, had absorbed his life. There was no reason, however, why he shouldn't pack up and move across the border, away from the madness of London and the insistence of his friends that if he wasn't continually asserting his place in the world of architects, he might as well go back into the army.

They lived lives striving for the next big break, the next promotion, a new job with higher wages, holidays abroad with like-minded people. Surrounded by it day after day and trying to get a clear perspective on where his life was going, was like swimming in a pond with dozens of other fish and people looking on to see what choices he made. If the choices didn't meet their expectations, there was a distinct possibility he might end up in a pond all of his own.

Byron shook his head and watched a hawk soaring over the glen. Freedom – that's what he wanted. It was one of the things that had driven Ellie north. Sighing, he packed his camera into its pocket in the backpack. Unless he made amends with the 'Iron Musketeer', not only could his time with Mayfair Hotels come to an abrupt end and potentially have devastating effects on his business, but Ellie might cut him off completely. That would have other consequences for which he'd need very good answers.

All around him lay the glory of the Highlands and countless lives that did not need the pressure of lucrative contracts and unpredictable employers. A long sigh, unheard by any other living thing, sailed into the air. What did he really want?

He picked his way carefully over the rocks, taking a different route closer to the mass rising above him. There was in its sheer dominance something that spoke to him of strength and endurance, something that lifted his soul out of its rut and made it sing. He enjoyed the physical exertion and realised how much he had missed rock climbing and hiking in remote places in the past year. Clambering over a square-shaped boulder, he glanced around, and in that split second of lost concentration he slipped and landed in loose scree. The ground beneath him began sliding away and he heard small rocks and stones beating a tattoo as they tumbled towards the glen.

***

They had spent almost two hours on Maw's Hearth and though most were loath to leave, Ellie knew from experience that the long hike back to the village would challenge them.

Surprised she had seen no further sign of Byron, she hoped he had not been foolish enough to attempt climbing The Chimney. He'd certainly looked up at it with the yearning she saw in other rock climbers who'd thought about it, and the few who had succeeded. That he was an experienced climber she didn't doubt. He was also alone. However, he had deceived her and if she had not found the card in her car who knows to what lengths he would have gone to steal her trust. Still, she hoped The Chimney did not claim him.

Later, on the return journey, while they were negotiating a narrow path between hills, Jenny slipped and twisted her ankle, necessitating a twenty-minute stop while the historian's wife, first aid trained, strapped it up. The pace was slower now with Jenny unable to place full weight on her ankle. No one seemed to mind helping her over rough or boggy patches and keeping up cheerful chatter. Ellie, thinking more about her encounter with Byron found the slowness frustrating and contributed less to the conversations than on the way up. The group was still buzzing with all they'd seen and didn't seem to mind that it took almost three hours to reach Kilcomb. She was relieved to arrive at the pub, where the publican's wife produced a meal that satisfied and filled Ellie and her hungry charges. With her frustration at the crawl back to Kilcomb thawing as white wine found its way round her system, Ellie enjoyed the banter and recounting of the day's outing. They were an entertaining and enthusiastic group.

Towards the end of the meal Jenny, who was sitting next to her, leaned closer and said in a low voice, "Are you and Byron Oakes a pair?"

Ellie almost dropped her glass. "No, we are not. Where did you get that idea from?" she demanded, louder than she intended.

The historians looked briefly at her from across the table and then continued their conversation with two locals sitting behind them.

"Observation."

"Of what?"

"You two arguing."

"And exactly what were we arguing about to make you jump to that ludicrous conclusion?"

"I didn't need to hear anything. How you both stood and the way he looked at you told a better story," Jenny said lightly, sipping beer.

Ellie's eyes narrowed. "You have an over-active imagination. I'd be careful it doesn't dump you in trouble."

"My imagination is lively, yes, but definitely not over-active. Keep him in your sights, Ellie. It's not every day a man of that calibre pops up. A smart woman will map out a route into his life."

"Then you have a narrow view of 'calibre' if that's what five minutes in his company has deluded you into thinking," Ellie snapped and pushed back her chair. Kipp, who had been asleep nearby, came instantly awake. "You might want to get to know a person before making such an arrogant assumption."

She did not wait for the other woman's response, stopping briefly only to wish the others well before leaving the pub and stepping out onto the street with Kipp beside her. Instinctively, she looked in the direction of Maw's Hearth, though it could not be seen from Kilcomb. A faint shiver ran down her spine. Where was Byron? Even Andrew had asked. Could he have been foolish enough to attempt a climb of The Chimney without proper equipment and another climber? Despite her anger at his deception, she was worried. In the short time she'd known him it was obvious he had strength and determination to achieve significantly in life, but there was always the risk of over confidence in such people.

Without thinking about what direction her steps took her, ten minutes later she turned the corner into the lane leading to The Mill. Much of the anxiety over Byron altered course and travelled the route of suspicion. What was he *really* doing up at Maw's Hearth?

At its feet, Glen Erc had been at the heart of a bitter legal battle seven years earlier, when an American consortium wanted to build a health resort. It had taken almost three years for a group of locals, including two lawyers, and a number of members of three prominent heritage associations, to get the thing quashed and new regulations put in place. Farley Orman, articulate and unafraid of authority, had been the main spokesman, delivering the facts with passion. He was not one who'd cared much what people thought of him. For him it had been both a public and personal triumph.

However, on the other side of Maw's Hearth were some five thousand acres that remained privately owned land. The owner, Isabella Donaldson, only child of a wealthy laird, had been left the entire estate after his death two years earlier. While she had publicly declared that the land would remain in its relatively pristine state, and her sixth generation roots would not allow her to cut ties with it, Ellie knew she spent less time there than she liked as she was married to a Scottish businessman who was often in either New York or London. At times there had been rumours the business was under financial pressure, the most recent of which had been less than a year ago. It had worried Farley. Now it worried Ellie and her friends, one of whom was attempting to contact the owner after several people from one of Scotland's most prestigious land development businesses were seen there as guests of Isabella's husband. There had been no sign of Isabella. Adding to that concern was Glenn Thorley's presence in Kilcomb and a rumour that he'd also been there.

"Why did you have to die now, Farley?" she said loudly, resentful and hurting. "I need you! How could you leave me with Glenn Thorley sniffing around like a pig in muck? And then there's Byron Oakes. You don't know him, but he's turned out to be a traitor. Who will take your place, Farley? Who will fill the hole you and Alice have left?"

Tears pooled in her eyes and spilled over onto her cheeks. She wiped them away, angry and not knowing what to do with the pain. The well was inside and needed emptying, but she wasn't used to letting it do so. The way ahead blurry, she sat down on a log barely fifty yards from the bakery and sobbed. Kipp put his head on her knee and looked up at her with mournful eyes, whimpering quietly once or twice. His unquestioning love for her touched a deeper level of pain; the pressure of the emotion squeezed her chest and her face and head began aching. Feeling utterly alone and wondering if there was anyone who truly cared about her, and to whom she could go for understanding and counsel, she stroked Kipp's head and mourned her lost ones.

Footsteps crunched on the gravel and she hastily wiped her wet face with a handkerchief, embarrassed to be seen in such a state.

["Lost your way?" said the gentle voice of Bob Caraway.]

Unable to answer or look up she simply nodded as he sat down. She allowed him to hug her, his warmth and tenderness releasing a fresh flow of tears.

He stroked her hair. "It'll be hard for a while, Ellie, quite a while probably, but even Iron Musketeers need people."

"Some people here think I don't care much about people," she said thickly.

"*Some* people don't know you, but your friends do and we're here for you. You're too self-sufficient," Bob said softly, lifting her chin with his hand. "Don't be afraid to ask for help, Ellie. Being a strong person doesn't mean your weak times are signs of failure. Quite the opposite. We weren't meant to do life alone you know."

"It's less painful that way," she said.

"Is it? And is there as much joy?"

Ellie gazed at him through hot eyes and saw understanding. Her heart melted and her lips quivered.

"What's happening to me? I feel so… so alone," she whispered, leaning against him.

"You're grieving, Ellie. Only you know the depth of it and only you know exactly what you're feeling, but there are those of us who've been through grief. We're here for you."

"Thank you, Bob," she whispered, wiping her eyes.

"Come on inside and I'll get you a cuppa. Have you eaten?"

"Yes, at the pub with a group of hikers."

They began walking up the lane to Bob's house just beyond the mill.

"Up to Maw's Hearth wasn't it? Beautiful day for it."

"Mostly, yes," Ellie said, not as enthusiastic as she usually was about a magnificent summer's day. The joy of it had been diminished by Byron Oakes' appearance and Jenny Browne's presence.

"What d'you mean 'mostly'? It was actually summer today! That high-altitude air's affected your brain, Ellie Madison."

She looked up at him and saw merriment dancing in his eyes.

"I don't think Maw's Hearth qualifies as high altitude, Bob."

"Well, you've been trekking up there such a long time now you probably don't need to go too high to be affected," he said plainly, and glanced at her as she dodged the end of an overhanging branch.

Ellie stopped, turned, took hold of the straw broom leaning against the back wall of the mill and began chasing him up the path, brushing at his heels as he ran. Their laughter disturbed a pair of blackbirds that flew off chip-chipping into the trees. Kipp loped alongside Bob, barking. Near the door to the house, a rambling building Bob had rescued from its run-down state, he slowed and eventually came to a halt. He bent over, hands on knees, as if puffed.

"It's about time you came up the mountains again, Bob Caraway. You're getting out of condition," Ellie said, grinning.

"Oh, am I now?" he said and stood up, caught her up in his arms, and whirled her around in a jig, laughing at her surprised expression.

Kipp pranced about them until they finally stopped. Bob took Ellie's hand and they went inside to the familiar and comfortable kitchen with its big, scrubbed wooden table. Pots and baking tins hung from the ceiling above the table, and large pottery jugs and old tin storage containers stood around the walls on the floor. It was a chef's kitchen. Before taking on The Mill, Bob had been head chef at Edinburgh's most prestigious hotel for five years. Occasionally, he'd found himself flitting off to various destinations in Britain because there were those who valued his considerable skills for important functions. Such, he had frequently said, were the whims of the wealthy. After almost thirty years in frantic kitchens preparing perfectly cooked and presented food, he'd decided it was time for a venture of his own. Eight months later he'd found himself the happy owner of the Mill Bakery.

The long Highland evening brought chill air and a translucent sky splashed with pink and lilac. They sat outside in the back garden where their conversations were broken with periods of silence which neither minded. Through a gap in the trees they could see reflections of the hills in a loch, its waters still and dark. Ellie shivered.

"Cold?" Bob asked. "We can go inside."

Ellie frowned. "I'm worried about Byron Oakes. Not that I should be."

"Care to explain those two statements?" he said, looking at her with a quizzical expression.

"I found a Mayfair Hotel's business card in my car this morning, one of John Thorley's. It must've fallen out of Byron's pocket. A bit later I found him having coffee in The Mill with Glenn Thorley."

"Forgive my lapse of memory, but is this Byron the one who was with you when Farley was found?"

"Yes," Ellie said, nodding. "I thought he was okay, someone genuinely interested in the Highlands, but I was wrong."

"Sorry, I don't quite see the connection."

"Mayfair Hotels have been nosing around here for a couple of years trying to get one of their posh hotel complexes built. Byron Oakes is an architect."

"Ah, I see. And you think he's working for Mayfair."

"Why else would he have one of their cards and be having cosy cups of coffee with the owner's son and heir?" she said, the pitch rising in her voice and tension mounting in her body.

Bob reached out and pressed her hand. "You might be right, Ellie, but it could be that Byron Oakes is being pursued by Mayfair and hasn't actually signed on the dotted line."

"I doubt it. He didn't say anything then or on Maw's Hearth."

"Maw's Hearth?"

"I'd told him he wasn't welcome on the hike, but he came up anyway on his own."

"No law against that."

Ellie looked at him, frowning. "Whose side are you on, Bob Caraway?"

"This isn't about sides, Ellie. Sometimes you jump to conclusions. You don't know for sure that this Oakes fellow is working for Mayfair and the least you can do is hear his side of the story."

"If I ever see him again you mean. The last I saw of him he was looking up at The Chimney."

"Is that why you're worried? You think he might've tried *climbing* it?" Bob asked, eyebrows arching below his fair hair.

"Yes, and he was on his own. I couldn't see any climbing gear on him, but he's a very fit man. He spent time in the army."

"Did you warn him about the dangers?"

"No. He didn't actually tell me he was going climbing and I didn't see him heading that way, but I saw no sign of him in the last hour or so I was there with the group."

"Perhaps he didn't stay long. He's probably at the pub having a beer."

Ellie sighed and nodded. "I hope so. Not a good place to be stuck overnight."

"No," Bob said quietly, "it isn't."

Chapter 4

Weighted down by scree, Byron sat up slowly, groaning. His right leg was throbbing and, fearing a break, he carefully explored the lower part for exposed bone. Relieved, he found none. Both his hands were stinging, bleeding. He touched his aching face and found wetness and a tender lump on his cheek.

Like a bundle of clothes in a dryer he had tumbled over and over, pelted by stones, and eventually landed on what he hoped was a flat surface. Peering into the gloom towards the point of his sudden entry, pale rays of light were finding their way through the dust raised by the disturbed scree. He sensed, rather than saw, that he was in a biggish space.

Moving as little as possible until he could better see where he was, he eased the pack off his shoulders. The thought that a few feet away might be a yawning crevice, wasn't thrilling. He winced as he reached into the side pocket, his knuckles scraping against the material. With relief he found the torch in one piece and switched it on, its powerful beam revealing no crevice waiting like a hungry monster to claim him, instead a cave with a sandy, mostly flat floor.

Above was an overhang supporting a rock wall that had narrow openings at either end, through one of which he had fallen. With difficulty he stood up, pushing through the scree and gritting his teeth as he put weight on the injured leg. Once on firm ground he looked up again at the opening and realised how close he had come to serious injury. Had his body been the other way around, his head would have hit the rock wall with force. Not a pleasant thought and he switched it off.

Rolling up the right trouser leg he inspected his shin. Although it was badly bruised and swollen, blood soaking into the sock, there was no reason to think he wouldn't be able to make it back to Kilcomb. A handkerchief made an adequate bandage as he tied it round the most damaged section and then carefully pulled the trouser leg back down over it.

The drop from the overhang was perhaps fifteen feet, but he could not yet see anything on which to hook the rope in his pack. He had been in worse scrapes than this and always managed to get out. Eventually, he'd find a way, whether it was up or somewhere else.

Swinging the torch beam around the cave he saw a tall, wide gap in the rock. As he approached it he realised the sandy floor bore traces of footprints. Frowning, and bending to have a closer look, he was surprised that some of them seemed recent. They were quite big, probably made by a man. He looked around and studied the cave again. Where had the footprint owner been going? Byron could see no way out here. Perhaps he'd missed it

He peered into all the dark nooks he could find. After years in the army spent getting out of dangerous, sometimes almost impossible situations, his instincts would not allow him to leave the cave until he had explored it as thoroughly as possible. His patience bore fruit. In a corner about three feet above a flat-topped rock, was a hole. It was big enough for a largish person to get through. Byron pulled himself up with difficulty, pain shooting up his right leg. However, once up he was inside a tunnel that led, a couple of minutes later, to the outside. Hidden behind a huge boulder and trees, the entrance led out to a narrow grassy verge that ended abruptly and dropped straight down into the glen below. It would be impossible to see the gap from either down there or farther along the base of The Chimney.

Byron looked at his watch. Five o'clock – the weather was still bright and sunny. Plenty of daylight hours left, though the sensible thing was to get back down to Kilcomb, rest his leg for a day or two then return. The adventurer in him argued. What if a storm came in and the weather didn't clear for days, weeks even? Then there was Glenn Thorley. He might call him back to London, demanding plans according to his directions or no payment and no job. It wouldn't be the end of the world, but he'd prefer not to leave on Thorley's terms. There was always John Thorley. If he did what he said he would, then son and heir would soon be hearing how his father had no desire to upset the authorities in Scotland.

Byron stepped into the sunshine, planting his right foot more heavily than he intended. He grimaced. Yes, the sensible thing was to get back to the village or at least to the nearest house and get a ride into Kilcomb.

Looking behind him, then up at The Chimney, the temptation to stay grew. He'd be fine. He turned and headed towards the cave, slipped through the hole and began retracing his steps, passing the scree and approaching an opening that was several feet wide and at least eight high. As he stepped through and torchlight penetrated the darkness, Byron stared at an astounding sight. He could almost believe he'd been transported to another time.

The cave was wide and high with ledges of varying widths, hollows, nooks and shadows. It was a school boy's delight, reminding him of the countless books he'd read of treasures and crooks, rescuers and rewards. Yet it wasn't the cave that caused him to wonder if he was imagining things, rather the remnants of people's lives. It was no orderly or ordinary collection: clay pots were upturned or on their sides, there were baskets of all shapes and sizes, blackened circles where once had been fires, rudimentary apparatus on which a pot might have once hung and a woman cooked the family's meal. A small hand-pulled cart was on its side nearby.

Byron was no historian, but he was fascinated. Why had no one discovered this and done something about preserving it in a museum? Surely, in all this time at least one hiker, climber or caver had stumbled across it. Or perhaps this one was still awaiting its turn to enter the annals of historical discoveries.

In the limited light he picked his way carefully amongst what had been other people's belongings, trying not to disturb anything. Whoever had been there seemed to have left a lot behind – or hidden it. Fascinated, he moved towards the back of the cave where, in a small trunk, he found several books, some in Latin and others in perhaps ancient Gaelic. He recognised them from his studies at a private school his parents had insisted he attend to 'polish him up'. He'd rarely used either and remembered little. He pocketed the smallest book and also a scroll, a rudimentary map of Scotland.

Lost in another world where people had left their valuable belongings, he wondered what Ellie would make of it all. A few books, bits of jewellery and beads in a plain wooden box, oddments of wooden furniture, it all seemed curious to him.

He sighed and glanced at his watch. It was six-thirty. He'd spent longer than he intended and his leg was now throbbing painfully. As he made his way towards the entrance to the outer cave he caught a glimpse in the torchlight of something shiny, partly hidden behind a curve in the rock wall. Curious, he walked towards it and found a camera lens poking out of a bag. Stuffed behind it were three other similar bags. There was only one man he knew who was missing his camera equipment – Farley Orman.

Without hesitating Byron undid all the bags and carefully inspected their contents. In the last bag were half a dozen rolls of film, one of Farley's books and a wide-angle lens. Pocketing the rolls of film, Byron turned to look again at the camera in the first bag. He stopped. Voices.

He switched off the torch, closed the bag and slid quietly into a recess several feet behind him.

Light burst into the cave.

"Come on, let's grab the stuff and get out of here. It gives me the creeps," said a young man's voice.

"You're nothing but a softie, Bran."

Byron stiffened. It was Jack Kennart.

"Maybe, but it's like a great big tomb. I don't like it."

"Well, you don't have to. Just help me get…"

"What's the matter? Seen a ghost?" Bran said, chuckling.

"Dinna be daft. Someone else's been here."

"Now you're the daft one. No one else knows about this place."

"The dust's been scuffed up and the footprints aren't mine."

"Is that all? I had different shoes on last time. Probably mine."

"Only if they're the same size as the footprints," Kennart snapped. "Measure your foot against that one."

There was a pause in the conversation. Byron's heart raced and his hand moved towards his breast pocket. He could not be discovered. There was work to do.

"Yea, I reckon they're mine."

"Are you sure?"

"Sure as I can be in this gloomy place."

"I hope you're right. Let's get the bags and go."

The two men walked towards Byron's hiding-place and he pushed himself tightly against the rock.

"You sure they were your footprints, Bran? There're more here. Look fresh to me."

"You're the policeman, but don't know what you're worried about. No one knows about this place. It's our secret, remember?"

"Aye, I remember all right." Byron heard him open a lid. "What's your dad doing dead, Bran?"

Byron heard a loud sigh.

"I don't know. I wish I did. Come on, let's get out of here. It's making us gloomy as death."

The lid was shut. "Get on with it then."

Byron had nowhere else in which to squeeze and hoped Bran remained as careless about observation as in the last minutes.

Within minutes the camera bags were pulled from their niche and Byron was again alone in the dark silence. He stayed where he was until he could no longer hear voices. By now his right leg was throbbing painfully and, in unfolding himself from the cramped position, sharp pains shot up into his hip. His cheek, too, was aching. All he wanted was to get out of the cave into fresh air and back to Kilcomb. Jack Kennart had given new meaning to the words 'undercover cop'. He wondered how they'd got into the cave.

***

"Keep driving," Byron said as the farm truck slowed down.

He peered through the windscreen, pale morning sunshine brightening the dull red of the bonnet.

"Well, this is Ellie Madison's hoose," said Charlie Adamson, a thin, ancient farmer with a thick brogue.

"I know, but her car's not there. Can you drop me in the village?"

"Aye," he said chirpily. "The missus will no mind if I take a drop of something at the pub to keep the cold out."

"No, I don't suppose she will," Byron responded absentmindedly.

He stared at the property as they continued on. Who owned the dark blue car parked around the back of the house, the tip of its bonnet poking out beyond the wall?

"Ellie will miss young Farley. Terrible tragedy his passing. He were a well-liked man and did a lot o' guid for the area. Mind you, he ruffled a few feathers in his time. Didna stand for any nonsense from big companies wantin' to mess up our hills. Some people here didna like him much, either."

"Why was that?" Byron's mind was still on what was happening at Ellie's.

"Stood in the way o' progress, laddie. Aye, some here had their hearts set on becoming very rich. Fools!"

The truck, almost as old as his last night's host, Byron thought, groaned and jerked through the gears until they reached a reasonable speed. This lasted all of thirty seconds before they slowed for the corner and the knobbly hand guided the lever down a gear. So it had been for most of the eight mile journey. While his patience had worn thin at times, Byron mostly found Charlie a man of quick humour and generous disposition. His wife Betty was the same and he had spent a night being tended to and told stories about the family, neighbours and the Strathverns. That guests were not as common as they would like, they had made plain. Their five children had long since left, turning up for holidays or presentation of the latest grandchild.

"Wanting change and making money isn't a crime, Charlie."

"It is if someone gets killed. And it is if they're aboot destroying what can't be replaced. Ellie Madison's alone now. I hope the guid Lord's watchin' over her," he said raising his eyes towards the roof.

Byron studied the old man's profile for a few seconds and saw a slight tremor on his lips, a moistening in his eyes. He reached out and patted his arm.

"I hope so too, Charlie."

He swallowed. "She's an ootsider, but she's been guid to us. Me and the missus love her like she was one of our own."

Byron nodded. During the story telling Ellie's name had cropped up several times, always with affection and respect. However, Byron was annoyed with himself. All those years in the SAS and it had taken an old man to remind him that Ellie could be in danger.

Charlie dropped him off at the end of a lane near the bed and breakfast, making him promise to visit before he left for London.

There was no doubt that between soaking in a hot bath and Betty's ministrations to his leg, he had been saved from prolonged pain and an extended period of restrictive movement. If he was careful he would be back to normal in a few days.

Rain pattered steadily on the window as he peered out, frowning. There were a few small breaks in the clouds, but from experience he knew that in some situations observation, when not wanting to be seen, was better done in the rain. Sunshine had a way of glinting off metal and glasses even when you thought you were well hidden. Turning back into the cold room he shoved a few things into a bag, left the room and got into his hire car. On the way out of the village he passed Glenn Thorley going into the pub. Surprised, Byron wondered why he had not returned to London. When he had spoken to John Thorley the previous morning he had been told that Glenn would be called back that day. While Mayfair's owner was a hard businessman, he was not lacking wisdom and did not share many of his son's views on how to deal with people. Byron had told him he would not continue working for the company if he had to deal with Glenn and explained why.

It took him almost forty minutes to reach Inverness and another ten minutes to find a car park. He looked at his watch – two o'clock.

Five years had passed since his last visit to the city; the centre had changed little and he soon found a camera shop that processed film in an hour. To fill in time he looked for a bookshop. He did not have to go far or search the interior; the window display was predominantly of books by, or about, Farley Örman. Byron bought three, all written by Farley. Two contained many of his photographs, and the other was a history of the Kilcomb region and the efforts to preserve its uniqueness. The sales girl told him Orman's books had been selling 'like wee hot cakes' since his death.

He found a tea shop and sat drinking coffee and flicking through the books. Drawn into the photographs, Byron forgot about the roll of film at the camera shop and it was not until the waitress asked if he wanted anything else that he looked at his watch. He declined, put money in her hand and walked quickly across the road, collected the photographs and headed back to the car in watery sunshine. Underneath the windscreen wiper was a piece of paper which he retrieved. When he saw it was a parking fine he swore and an elderly lady who was passing looked at him. Expecting a rebuke, he shut his mouth.

"I know how you feel, young man. There was one on my car as well. I just screwed it up and tossed it in the gutter. That's where it belongs if you ask me!"

Byron grinned. "You're right, but there's a bin next to my car. It can go in there. I don't want a fine for littering as well."

She waved her walking stick at him, laughing, and went on her way as he got into the car.

However, he forgot all about the parking fine when he pulled the photographs out of their packet. The first few were evening shots across a loch, pink and mauve pearl clouds crowning the hills behind, a world wrapped in the softness of a lover's embrace. In contrast, the remaining shots were taken in the morning. The purity of the light was startling in its colour and clarity and he fancied he could smell the damp earth of early morning and feel the bite of the chill air. Why he'd settled in London he didn't know and a familiar restlessness stirred in his bones.

72

Slipping the photos back in their packet, he retrieved the next one. He was confronted by a black and white world in a different era, the bleak time of the Second World War, where Nazi flags flew and people saluted Hitler. There were photos of German radio equipment, a Nazi flag hanging behind an antique wooden desk, a framed photo of Hitler, and a map of Britain with markers stuck on it at various locations. Other pictures depicted men and women in uniform, domestic scenes of a family on a lawn, a man with his head under the bonnet of an Austin, and young children helping herd cows into a farmyard. But it was the last photo in the packet which intrigued him the most – a woman was standing next to a wooden chair on which lay a pair of leather gloves, a pair of spectacles, a pistol, and a blue scarf with thistles embroidered around its edges and draped over the back of the chair. In the woman's hand was a small Nazi flag. The whole scene seemed like a clue for a 'Who Did It?' game.

He went through the pile again, noting details he'd missed the first time, and was so engrossed in the old photos that a tap on the window made him jump. He reached immediately for the ignition key and looked up with a ready response about just leaving. It was the elderly lady smiling at him.

Byron wound down the window.

"I'd get a move on if I was you," she said perkily. "There's an inspector on his way, tickets at the ready to slap on windscreens. Mightn't get away with chucking out a second one."

"Thanks for the warning."

He had just started winding up the window when he heard a sharp intake of breath.

"Where did you get that photo?" the woman asked almost whispering, her tone urgent.

The question caught him completely unawares, and when he looked up a pair of fear-filled eyes were studying the photo.

"On a roll of film I've just had developed," he said, not quite answering the question.

"Yes, but *where* did you get the original photo?"

"I can't say."

"What d'you mean you can't say? I haven't..."

She broke off in mid-sentence and hurried around the front of the car, opened the passenger side door and eased into the seat.

"Young man, I haven't seen that photo for forty-odd years. Where did you get it?"

73

Byron began sliding the photographs back inside the packet, but she reached out and put her hand on top of his. He picked up the photograph she had seen, slipped the others away and said, "D'you know this woman?"

There was a second's hesitation. "It's my sister."

"Are you sure?"

"I may be old, but my brain's in perfectly good working order. Have you shown this to anyone else?"

"No." He had no idea who she was and the entire thing could be an attention-seeking act; loneliness pushing her to relay an extraordinary and false story for a few minutes in someone's company.

Yet, as they sat there in silence, she no doubt weighing him up, he had a feeling she was telling the truth. It was doubtful she could have summoned up the depth of fear he had seen in her eyes when she first saw the photo. She was well dressed and her honey-coloured hair was permed. The rings on her left hand did not look cheap and she was articulate.

"Have you come to any conclusions about me yet?" she asked.

Byron chuckled. "You're an observant woman. We could have done with you in my army unit."

"Ah, a man after my own heart. I was in the army during the war – signals. That's where I met my darling husband. He was an officer and I a lowly corporal, but after the war, once I was a civilian, they couldn't keep us apart. What about you?"

"SAS. Love life – nil."

She looked surprised. "I've heard about the SAS. That's a tough life, I believe. Shame about your love life though. I should've thought a good-looking man like you would be hounded by the fairer sex."

Byron shook his head. He did not wish to talk about that side of his life to anyone.

"Now then, why don't you come home with me and have a cup of tea? My husband, who hasn't been too well lately, would love some army talk."

"And will you tell me about this photo?" he asked, looking at her intently.

"A little." She held out her hand in greeting and he took it. "My name's Ruth Lawford."

"Byron Oakes."

74

He followed Ruth through the ancient trading port city, declared a royal burgh in 1150, and not far from the centre in a leafy street of old houses, they drew into a driveway hidden from neighbours by an impressive row of rhododendrons. When Byron got out of his car he was immediately set upon by two golden retrievers, overjoyed it seemed, to have a visitor. Ruth laughed.

His leg was paining him and he limped alongside her.

"What did you do to your leg? You look like you're in a lot of pain, young man."

"I had a bit of a fall when I was climbing the other day."

"A bit of a fall? Your expression tells another story."

Byron did not respond and she asked no further questions.

The dogs followed Ruth and Byron up the front path before bounding away across a large expanse of lawn bordered by wide garden beds crammed with shrubs and flowers. Big trees, oaks and chestnuts, and the more slender silver birches stood like royalty in their domain.

"Beautiful garden," he said as they went up half a dozen stone steps to the front door.

"Yes, it is. The house was built in 1753 and until we bought it nearly forty years ago, it had been owned by the same family, handed down the generations. Sadly, the last surviving member had no children and none of the other family members wanted it. Good for us though," she added with a smile and lift of her fine eyebrows.

The colonel was watching a cricket match on television when they entered the sitting room, its two bay windows overlooking the front garden. Ruth introduced them and told of the unexpected meeting over parking tickets. She did not mention the photograph. While she was off making tea, Byron found himself engaged in a lively conversation about the army, the Second World War and its impact on the modern army. Byron was relieved that he was not subject to a tedious re-telling of war stories. The colonel, it seemed, had been a career man, and his expertise in the intelligence arena had meant that the army – and the government – continued to call on his help even after retirement.

"I still have contacts in both institutions, though most of the old boys have either retired or decided it was time to feed the grass – from below you understand. No doubt I'll be doing the same before many more years go by. Not a happy thought," he said with a wry grin.

Byron enjoyed the man's keen sense of humour and the room was filled with laughter when Ruth returned with the tea and coffee.

"I see Hugh's been keeping you entertained. Tea or coffee, Byron?"

"Coffee please."

They had abandoned formality coming up the front steps.

"Have you shown Hugh the photograph?" she asked, handing him a china mug and offering the sugar. He shook his head at the latter.

"No. I take it you'd like me to."

"Of course. Hugh and I have no secrets from one another."

The smile they exchanged touched a vulnerable spot in Byron and he looked down into the mug in his hands. One day perhaps there would be a woman who looked at him with such love and trust. One day he might allow himself to be loved again and give love in return.

"You meet a stranger, a young man at that, and already you're looking at his photographs. Really, Ruth, to what depths have you sunk?" Hugh said, his eyes round with exaggerated horror.

"Oh, the lowest, darling. I even got into his car uninvited, but with good reason."

For a few seconds Byron let the banter soak into his soul like a warm bath relieving tense muscles. One day he wanted this.

"So then, what's this photograph of?" Hugh asked, putting his glasses on.

Byron hesitated and glanced at Ruth who was watching him with an intensity he had not expected. Neither by expression or a nod of the head did she try to influence him. It was as if she was waiting to see what he would do. If he wanted to start digging around and find out why Farley had an old roll of film, he might as well start here. He pulled the photo out of the packet, leaving the rest inside. Do it one spadeful at a time.

When Hugh looked at it, his hand shook.

"Where did you get this, Byron?" His voice was quiet and steadier than his hand.

"That I can't tell you. We've just met and that's hardly a basis for the kind of trust needed here."

Hugh nodded. "There speaks a soldier."

"Former soldier. I'm an architect now. Run my own business in London."

"So, what're you doing up here?

"Hiking, visiting the sights." Hugh looked unconvinced. "You'll just have to believe me," Byron added.

Hugh looked at his wife. "Have you told him who it is?"

Ruth nodded.

"This woman," he continued coldly, "was stupid enough to think that Nazi Germany had the answers for the rest of the world."

"Only because she was in love, Hugh darling."

"In love with Nazi ideals and a Nazi who filled her head with propaganda. So far as I could ever make out, he spent the entire time of their relationship lying to her and flitting off back to Germany whenever the whim took him or Hitler whistled!" He handed the photograph back. "Sorry, Byron – some old wounds haven't properly healed."

"I can understand that," Byron said, his own memories often whispering and reminding him of painful episodes. "Is your sister still alive, Ruth?"

"I don't know," she said, her expression sad. "Marian disappeared in 1950. We tried to find her, but every trail led to a dead end. The only thing we do know is that her lover was caught leaving England in early 1949, tried for spying and went off to prison. He died there ten years later."

"You're sure about that?"

"Yes," Hugh said emphatically. "I saw his body. Wanted to make sure it wasn't a story someone in MI6 had concocted to cover up a trade."

"And Marian never turned up?"

"No," they said together, glancing at one another.

"Was she a spy, d'you think?" Byron asked carefully.

Ruth laughed, embarrassed. "No. She was too busy having a good time, although we didn't know until after the war just who she was having a good time with!"

"The unfortunate thing is that we came to the conclusion a long time ago that Marian knew too much, or the Germans assumed she did, and had her killed," Hugh said, and took a sip of his tea.

"We'll never know really what happened to her," Ruth said quietly. "My father never got over the loss."

Hugh glanced at her, an odd look, Byron thought, of cynicism and impatience. Ruth reached out and squeezed her husband's hand.

Chapter 5

"So then, Ellie Madison, how're you farin'?" came the unmistakable voice of Olga Erskine.

Ellie, who'd caught sight of her group from yesterday heading off in cars not five minutes earlier, looked up from the newspaper, her sandwich halfway to her mouth. The tables outside the pub were almost full; people did like to make the most of sunny days.

"Hello, Mrs Erskine. There's a pot of tea coming – unless you fancy something stronger," she said, jesting, knowing somehow this woman wouldn't mind.

Olga's eyes twinkled. "It's Olga. And tea'll be fine. Cheeky, too. Mary didn't tell me that!"

"And just what did she tell you?" Ellie said, as the older woman sat down.

"That you kept to yourself."

Ellie nodded, looking thoughtfully at the other woman. She must be at least seventy-five. Mary's bit of gossip about her being given to roaming around at night with badgers and foxes at her heels seemed implausible in the bright sun. Dabbling in herbal teas and remedies she could believe.

"You don't want tae believe everything you hear," Olga said quietly, regarding her with something akin to sadness. "People aren't always very kind."

The words shocked Ellie, not what they were, but that Olga seemed to have read her thoughts.

"Somebody told me you had what she called 'the gift'. I didn't have a clue what she meant. Did you just read my mind then?"

Olga smiled and reached across the table, patting her hand. "Let's just say your expression gave you away."

"You're evading the answer."

"A little. We don't know one another well."

The landlord's wife appeared with the tea. As she put it on the table, she looked at Ellie and said, "Is this woman wanting a drink?"

Frowning, Ellie replied, "Another cup would be good, Pauline. There's enough tea in the pot for both of us."

"So long as she pays."

"I'm paying," Ellie said firmly.

"You should mind the company you keep, Ellie Madison."

The solid, middle-aged woman turned abruptly away and was gone before Ellie could think of an apt response. When she looked at Olga she saw anger in her eyes, but it seemed to Ellie that she put it away as if it shouldn't be seen. Sadness took its place.

"What's the matter?" she asked.

"Nothing tae concern you, m'dear."

"Maybe not, but you're upset."

"Old memories, that's all."

"So what on earth got into Pauline? She was downright rude to you."

"She's a woman in pain, Ellie. The past… it can be a millstone sometimes, but it does no one any guid to hang on tae it."

Silent on the matter and aware of the battles waged in her own heart and mind, she poured the tea, listening as it gurgled into the cups. There was another chapter of grief now, Farley, though unlike the others in her past.

"Pain's part o' life," Olga said, slowly stirring in a teaspoon of sugar.

Ellie stared at her. This woman *was* reading her mind. She wasn't sure she liked it.

Without looking at her, and still stirring, Olga continued quietly, "Pauline's youngest son died nearly twenty years ago. He was eighteen. I found him in the woods. Poison. Pauline said I'd done it, but the inquiry's verdict was accidental death. She never believed them."

"I don't know what to say. How awful."

"Aye. He had a guid mind, should have been at university. I tried to warn Pauline, but she wouldn't listen."

"Warn her about what?" Ellie blurted out, forgetting for an instance that it was none of her business.

"Don't worry your head about it. It was before your time. You've enough grief o' your own."

They drank the rest of their tea in silence before Olga stood up to leave. Ellie did likewise. On the path outside the pub, Ellie turned towards the Land Rover parked down the road. Olga put a hand on her arm.

"Be careful who you trust, Ellie."

"Is this a friendly warning or a way of telling me something without saying anything?" The words sounded sharp and she wasn't sure Olga deserved that.

"Don't judge so quickly. I mean you no harm. Familiarity can be deceptive."

With that she went her way, leaving Ellie staring after her, wondering about the parting remark.

During the rest of the afternoon as she took a group of Americans on a gentle hike around a loch owned by the Earl of Strathvern, Ellie's thoughts kept straying. Unsettled as the waves lapping on the shore's edge, they hopped from one thing to another until she was so frustrated she snapped at a man who wanted to know about the castle on the other side of the loch. The group had stopped to take photographs.

"I'm sorry, Mr Chesterton," she said, swallowing her pride under the affronted stare. "Too much going on in my head."

"Then sort it out. I haven't paid you to snipe at me. Now, tell me about that castle."

Behind him his wife raised her brows. "Don't take on so, Mike. Miss Madison's apologised. We all have our moments."

Ellie gave her a quick smile then launched into Strathvern Castle's history before he could reply. By the end of it his mood had returned to the earlier unemotional, though pleasant, state and his questions inspired her to a broader history lesson that included Castlebay. An image of Byron sitting across the table in the tearooms interrupted the flow of historical stories and data.

"Are you all right, Ellie?" asked one of the younger women.

"What? Yes, sorry," She frowned, annoyed with Byron for intruding into her thoughts. That it was irrational to blame him, she knew, but it helped. "Now, as I was saying, the quay at Castlebay was used by smugglers for unloading contraband. The only reason they got away with it for so long was that most of the people in the town were in on it, or relied on it, to some degree or other."

She stretched out the lesson for another five minutes then moved the group along. They had a long walk around the loch to reach the castle by the appointed tour time. Earlier in the year, the earl had organised with her several dates for tours of the castle during the summer, on the proviso that his housekeeper, a spinster in her fifties who had taken over from her mother after her death, conducted the tour. The woman, with her dual role, seemed to have the Strathvern archives in her head.

A few clouds bustled across the sky as the group walked, stopped for views, listened to her recount snippets of historical interest and talk about the uniqueness of Scotland's Highland region. Once or twice when she mentioned Farley and his wife, or their work together with her as the 'Three Iron Musketeers', her throat constricted. Ellie did not apologise, but swallowed and said he had recently died. There was a lot of sympathy and one person keen on photography said he had read about it in the newspapers, but he did not elaborate and for that she was grateful.

The image of Byron resurfaced, but annoyance was replaced by a sudden, intense injection of fear. How could she have forgotten? What if he had gone up The Chimney, had fallen, and was lying injured? She hadn't even thought about alerting anyone to the fact that he could be stuck there alone. Bob knew, but with the business of the bakery, thoughts of Byron Oakes probably hadn't entered his head.

She could not get the group to the castle quick enough. However, the weather was changing and they needed little encouragement to pick up speed. By the time they reached the solid front door, fat raindrops were targeting her cheeks and forehead. Kipp sat dutifully outside the door under the portico as they trooped inside.

Ellie left her group in the housekeeper's care, explaining she needed to make a phone call, and went back outside. Mobile reception was not the best at the castle. The distorted, slightly off-key ringing seemed to go on forever, but eventually she heard Agnes' voice.

"He's not here, pet," she said in response to Ellie's request to speak to Bob. "He's away off to Inverness to see his mother. She had a fall this morning and Bob's sister's in London just now. Can I take a message?"

"No, but thank you, Agnes."

"Any time, pet. Bye."

"Bye, Agnes."

Now what? She looked down at the phone; reception was deteriorating, only one bar showed. There was always Jack Kennart. After all, his role included the safety of persons within his district.

"Who's this?" The familiar voice seemed a long way off.

"It's Ellie," she said loudly.

"Oh, Ellie. You on the moon, girl?"

"No, Strathvern Castle. Jack, have you seen Byron Oakes today?"

"Seen who? It's an awful bad line."

"Byron Oakes," she said slowly, loudly.

"I canna hear you, Ellie. Get to a landline."

He hung up.

She frowned at the phone, hit the off button and went back inside. It took her a few minutes to find the group, ask the housekeeper's permission to use a phone, and another several minutes to reach the kitchen. A maid was peeling potatoes. She looked up, expressionless, and without a word to the visitor, went back to the peeling. While Ellie dialled the police station then waited for Jack or his constable to answer, she watched the girl, wondering what kind of life had produced such a defeated attitude, dour expression and hunched posture.

"Jack Kennart."

"It's Ellie."

"At least I can hear you now. What was it you were saying?"

"Have you seen Byron Oakes today?"

"No. You lookin' for him?"

"Not exactly."

"So, why d'you want to know if I've seen him?"

"Because he was out hiking on his own yesterday. I saw him at Maw's Hearth." For a few seconds she heard only breathing.

"Are you all right, Jack?"

"Aye. What time did you see him?"

"About two. I was up there with a group when he arrived."

"How well d'you know him, Ellie?"

The question was unforeseen and it rattled her. "I don't think that's any of your business, Jack."

"It is if he's up to no good."

"And what makes you think he might be?" Unaccountably she was annoyed.

"He's hung around here long after the rest of that group's gone home. He's not your average tourist and he's spent years in a specialist army unit."

"Define 'average tourist', Jack. From my experience they're as diverse as the fish in the sea. Let's face it, you just don't like him."

A snort of laughter came down the line. "I heard about your visit to the bakery the other morning. Not exactly friendly I was told."

Ice ran down her spine and she slammed the phone on its cradle. The maid barely glanced at her, plainly indifferent to the emotion of the stranger. She got up slowly with the bowl of peeled potatoes and went to the sink. Ellie stared at her, eyes blazing, though the girl was not the object of her anger. Glenn Thorley!

The housekeeper was warding off questions she clearly perceived as prying into the Strathvern family's privacy, and was moving the group towards the turret wing when Ellie caught up with them. She hoped Jack's eardrum had not suffered too much damage. It wasn't his fault that Glenn Thorley was an ugly man in every respect.

From the room at the top of the turret a view of the loch, the gardens and hills brought out cameras and a recitation by the housekeeper of a poem written by the earl's great-great-great-grandfather. It told of victory over a marauding clan from beyond the range of hills, and Strathvern's laird taking the beautiful daughter of his foe as wife. There was no doubt the normally serious housekeeper knew how to tell a good story and, once again, Ellie found herself caught up in the emotions and triumph of that long ago event.

They eventually reached the conservatory where afternoon tea was prepared and the last piece of Strathvern history imparted. There was a good half an hour's walk to the village in cold, heavy rain which none of the hikers seemed to mind. One lady even remarked it was a good excuse to have a hot bath then relax with a sherry and a good book by the fire.

At crossroads a hundred yards along the road, Ellie caught a glimpse of the signpost: Eigg, 2 miles. How many times had she driven there to see the Ormans? A dull cloak of pain draped itself over her; she missed him, and she missed the warm and lively Alice.

Halfway back to Kilcomb the phone in her pocket burst into tune, dragging her out of dullness.

"Hello, Ellie Madison."

"Where on earth are you? I've been trying to phone you."

It was Bob.

"About fifteen minutes' walk from the village. What's the matter? You sound agitated. Is it your mother? Agnes told me she'd had a fall."

"Mum's okay. My cousin Jane's with her. I'd just got back here when Camden Orman turned up. He was looking for you. They've found Farley's photographic stuff."

"Where?"

"In the old barn at your place."

"What!?"

The hikers' heads snapped around as if a button had been pushed.

"Get here as soon you can. See you, Ellie."

For some moments she stared at the rain-spattered phone dumbfounded, unable to think a single thought.

"Miss Madison, are you all right?" Mrs Chesterton asked.

"Yes, fine, thanks. If we can just keep going, but I will have to leave you at the Mill Bakery."

Ellie was livid. What were they doing on her property without permission? Whatever was Farley's gear doing in her barn?

***

Ellie was not impressed to find either a police car or Camden Orman's car parked outside her house. She was grateful for Bob's presence as she marched straight past the constable, down the driveway and across the back garden to the barn.

"What are you doing here?" she demanded of Jack Kennart. "I don't remember giving you or anyone else permission to invade my property."

"I have a warrant to search your place, Ellie."

"I'm supposed to be here. You're out of line, Jack."

"Perhaps, but what I'd like to know is why Farley's photography gear is in your barn."

"When you find out let me know," she snapped, and then turned to Camden Orman. "I want you to leave."

"Dad's stuff's in there. I have a right to see it's not tampered with," Camden said, folding his arms across his chest. Not a very impressive chest at that, Ellie thought unkindly. She looked him up and down. His thinning, reddish blond hair, pale skin left slightly marked after adolescent acne, and blue eyes that reminded her of his mother, did not endear him to her.

"But you don't have a right to be in my garden. Please go. Or do I have to ask Sergeant Kennart to escort you off?"

"You can't order me around, Ellie Madison. You're nothing without Dad."

Ellie ignored the spiteful remark and glared at him. "This is *my* property, Camden. Just go."

"Or what?"

The querulous boy had never grown up.

"For goodness sake, Camden!" Bob said impatiently. "Act like a man and do as you're asked. You're trespassing."

Farley's eldest son, twenty-five-years old, spun round to face the baker.

"She's got you hoodwinked, too! I don't know what any of you see in her. She's a witch – and an ugly one at that! And I want Dad's stuff back – soon."

He walked off and a couple of minutes later they heard his car start up and roar off down the road. Jack Kennart was shaking his head when Ellie looked at him.

"He just canna get out o' the shadow of his father," the sergeant said.

"You mean he's resentful and vindictive and was jealous of his father succeeding while he, so far, hasn't amounted to much," Bob retorted.

"You've not been around much to be making such remarks, Bob Caraway," Jack said, his eyes narrowing.

"The trouble with you, Jack, is you're so entrenched in this area you can't see the wood for the trees. Duty in another part of the country would do you good."

"Has no one ever told you that local knowledge solves crime, especially in a case like this?"

Bob snorted. "And keep hidden what you don't want known. Is the truth ever revealed in your cases, Jack?"

"My record stands for itself and I dinna need to prove myself to you or anyone else," he snapped, his face colouring as he took a step toward Bob.

"Stop it you two," Ellie said loudly. "Farley's dead, his bags are in my barn and Camden, prig though he is, might be grieving."

"Could've fooled me," Bob said, raising his brows.

She gave him a withering look then turned to Jack. "There were no bags in my barn yesterday morning. Someone must've put them there since then."

"So what time did you come up here?" Jack asked, taking a notebook and pen out of his jacket pocket.

"Just after seven. I came to get some firewood."

"And were you at home yesterday?"

"No. I left here about eight-thirty and didn't get back until just after ten in the evening."

"So, you didn't notice the bags when you parked the car?" Jack said, frowning.

"I parked the car inside the front gate last night."

"So where were you all that time?"

"I took a group up to Maw's Hearth, then went to see Bob."

"Oh, aye. And I suppose you'll vouch for this?" He looked at the baker.

Bob nodded and said pointedly, "It's the truth, Jack."

"That remains to be seen." For a few seconds he scribbled busily in his notebook. "And what about today, Ellie?"

"I didn't come up here at all. Had lunch at the pub with Olga Erskine, took a group hiking to Strathvern – you can check with them and the housekeeper at the castle – and then back here now." She was getting cold and impatient. "Can I see the bags? I'll know if they're Farley's."

"Camden's already identified them," Jack said, flipping the notebook shut.

"I'd like to see them, Jack. They are on my property and as far as I can tell I have a right to go wherever I like."

There was no doubt that the bags were Farley's and the last time she had seen them they had been in his hands. She stared at the bags; it was incomprehensible that Farley would never again tote them into the mountains and wild places, or retrieve his precious photographic equipment to take photos.

She folded her arms over her stomach and let the tears run down her cheeks. There was no sound, just a gentle shaking of her shoulders as she allowed the pain of his absence to rise. It did not seem possible that anything would ever repair the hole he had left.

"Are you all right, Ellie?" Jack asked behind her.

Without responding she nodded and he left the barn. It was five minutes before she emerged, not caring what they thought of her puffy, red eyes still fresh with pain. Kipp came up behind and nudged her hand; she stroked his head, comforted by his faithful presence.

"So, what are you doing about finding Farley's murderer?" she said bluntly, looking intently at the sergeant.

"Everything I can. It's not easy, Ellie, and finding those bags in your barn complicates matters."

"And just how did you know to look in my barn?"

"A man phoned in this morning. Wouldn't say who he was."

"Oh, how convenient. I suppose he also said he'd seen me with a gun in my hand leaving the scene of the crime!"

"No, he didn't," Jack said gently, "but you do have a gun."

"You know I do, Jack, but I didn't kill him. Someone else ended his life and that makes me very angry."

"Spare a thought for his children then. They've lost their father and their mother's missing. That's not easy."

His expression of mild rebuke challenged her and she slowly realised hers was not the greatest loss. She'd been so wrapped up in her sorrow, she'd almost forgotten about the Orman offspring – and Jack.

"Sorry, Jack. You've lost both as well," she said, her expression softening. "Whoever did it must've known him."

"Or his movements," Bob said as he stepped closer to the pair.

"Aye," Jack said, sighing.

Ellie stared at the ground. The brutality of Farley's death made her shudder. How could anyone do such a thing? Had the sadist, taking a sick, deluded pleasure in his handiwork, watched while his victim sucked in his last breaths?

"We'll have tae search your house, Ellie."

"Not without a warrant," Bob said before she could speak.

Jack shook his head. "No, but I'll be back in the morning. And Inspector Carter will be here, too."

"Whatever for?" Ellie said, dragging herself out of her imagination where Farley lay dying.

"It's a murder investigation and that's his territory."

Jack turned and called the constable and, without another word to her, they collected Farley's bags and left. When they had gone, Ellie looked up at Bob.

"I feel as if I'm on trial already."

"Don't be daft," he said while they walked towards the house.

"But who would put Farley's stuff in my barn?"

"Someone who doesn't like you opposing them probably. You and Farley aren't popular in some circles. People with lots of pounds to invest and even more to make don't like it when their plans are obstructed."

"And if I'm in prison I'll be out of the way."

Bob stopped and stared at her. A fleeting expression of fear showed in his eyes and Ellie caught her breath.

"I want you to come and stay at The Mill," he said, searching her face.

"You think I'm next, don't you?"

"It's a possibility and until they've found Farley's murderer you shouldn't stay on your own."

"But I've got Kipp and he'd warn me if anyone came onto the property."

"And what would you do if they got into the house?"

"I'd shoot and ask questions later."

"This is no time for that wacky humour of yours, Ellie. Think about it. What would be better than to have all three of you out of the way – permanently?"

"Now, hang on a minute. We don't know that Alice is permanently out of the way. She disappeared and there was no sign of any kind of violence. She hadn't been all that well and she *was* worried about something, but I don't think she's dead. Your imagination's got the better of you, Bob Caraway," she said, unlocking the back door and stepping into the kitchen.

"Has it? She'd been fine a couple of weeks beforehand. If I remember rightly, the doctors weren't exactly sure what she had."

"That's not uncommon," she said, putting the kettle on and retrieving mugs from the cupboard. "I think you need a holiday."

"And leave you here alone? Not a chance. Ellie, I'm serious about this. You could be in danger. It's a wonder Jack Plod hasn't thought about it."

"Perhaps he has and doesn't think there's any threat."

"You can be as stubborn as a blockage in a drain sometimes!"

Ellie turned from reaching for the coffee jar and looked at him, her lips twitching. Suddenly she burst out laughing.

"And do I come shooting out the other end eventually?"

Chuckling, Bob nodded. "Always. Now get on with that coffee. I'm cold."

Chapter 6

During the last few days Byron discovered he had become something of an eavesdropper. At the local pub he was kept abreast of village life and its diverse, multi-level goings on. What sounded like a continuing difference of opinions about tourists had kept several older locals occupied for the last half an hour, and an intense interest in Farley Orman's death was popping up around him. Everyone was an authority on the matter and he had heard more than one robust argument about who had popped him off and why. His death also seemed to have revived interest in Alice Orman's disappearance.

Sitting quietly with a pint of bitter, he remembered Ellie referring briefly to Alice the day Farley's body was found, and two couples were airing their varied views on this at the next table. However, despite one of the men's assertions that Farley was a man with a mission and 'he was bloody good at it', the general opinions he'd heard in the post office, the pub and the garage, were that Alice had simply had enough of Farley's peculiarities and gone off to find someone who loved her more than hills, glens and taking photographs. (Carrie Ross, heard across the head of a balding man, knew someone who'd had a postcard from Alice happily re-settled) in Australia.

Byron had not been back long from Inverness, having promised to visit the Lawfords before he left for London, and he was enjoying the sounds of Scottish voices, some deep and strong, some higher and lilting like a song. He listened to the laughter, the tinkle of it from near the bar, and shouts and guffaws from across the room. Mingling with these were a few English voices. Such contrast, such diversity, and he soaked in it.

Mulling over the unexpected afternoon in Inverness, he was beginning to feel his stay in Scotland was going to be longer than planned. Tomorrow he'd have to phone his assistant, Ray, and let him know he wouldn't be heading south in the next couple of days as originally planned. He had a feeling about that, too. Ray, though trustworthy and mostly thorough, wasn't one to pursue work and could make a job last longer than was required. It was not good for business and Byron knew he'd have to make a decision about whether or not to keep him by the time he got back to London.

He took another mouthful of beer and thought again about Inverness. Before leaving it altogether, and out of sight of the Lawford's house, he'd sat in his car looking through the rest of the photographs. He'd found them compelling and surprising: a photographic collection of wartime artefacts, items of clothing draped over the lid of a trunk, a painting on someone's wall, a cottage in the country. These were in colour as were those of the Highlands, several of which featured Ellie, and a couple of Farley beside a stream setting up camera equipment. One of the last photos was of Ellie in a deep blue evening dress. He'd stared at it for a long time.

Yet it was a set of black and white photos in a packet he'd stuffed into his bag when at Charlie and Betty Adamson's farm that captivated him. One of the shots showed guests at a party, several of whom were in German army officer uniforms, mingling with men and women in evening dress. The army uniforms were Second World War issue and from what he'd seen in books and films, the women's hair and dresses belonged to the same era. Another showed several women seated in a radio hut and wearing headsets, their heads bent as they listened. Four photos showed equipment: a cipher unit, teletype machines, a field radio with an anxious-looking corporal, and armoured vehicles bearing German insignia. The last three were of dockyards, although Byron didn't recognise them. He phoned his friend, Colin, an expert in historical research who promised to do some digging into archives.

Byron could only speculate about why Farley Orman's bags were in a cave beneath The Chimney and what Jack Kennart's involvement was in retrieving them. Farley could have left them there, intending to photograph the historic collection. What was odd was the lack of lighting equipment. A man of Farley's experience wouldn't have gone up there without it. Perhaps he had never been in the cave and it was all Jack Kennart's doing. Byron sighed. That wasn't logical. Why go to all that trouble when he could've hidden the bags much closer to home?

Despite trying to avoid thinking about it, he wondered about the nature of Ellie and Farley's relationship. His wife had disappeared, Ellie was single, and they shared a passion for the wilderness. They must have spent a lot of time together, two lonely people exploring the Highlands, in love with the land and perhaps each other. The village was whispering; there was gossip and suggestion.

He studied the crowd over the rim of the glass. An interesting lot tonight, he thought idly; a family of Americans in the corner, a number of English, Spanish and German tourists, three old Scotsmen who had been at the same table by the fireplace every evening he'd been there, and a sprinkling of assorted locals. Byron was the only one by himself and he didn't like it. He was not good at being alone. Why didn't he just go home and forget all about Farley Orman and Ellie Madison? And do what with the photographs and the Lawfords, not to mention the unfinished job? There would be consequences if he ran south. He'd never run from a job, no matter how hard or dangerous. Anyway, it wouldn't be for much longer and by then Scotland would be shedding its summer colours and preparing for the cold months ahead.

One of the old men by the fireplace reminded him of Hugh Lawford. Now there was an interesting man – an interesting couple if he was honest. Their involvement with the woman in the photograph had stirred a need to dig deeper. A need? Odd he should think that. He'd left his army life behind – mostly. He was supposed to be finding out about Farley.

He stared at a painting hanging above the fireplace on the opposite wall – Kilcomb crouching, resplendent in autumn's yellows, rusts and oranges, fading greens, beneath its mountainous protectors.

He was no one's protector and it wasn't his responsibility to meddle in police matters, but he had never been satisfied until he had got to the heart of a problem and *this* one was no different. Others were waiting for information. In the army his persistence and determination had taken him quickly through the ranks and earned him high respect. In civilian life he was an architect with no authority whatsoever. How they thought he would find out anything useful was a mystery to him. It wasn't exactly the same as being on an army mission.

"Hi there, Ellie, Bob," he heard the publican's wife call out as she picked up empty glasses from a nearby table. "Here for a meal?"

A male voice responded. "Not tonight, Pauline. Just a quiet drink."

Byron glanced up and recognised the man from The Mill. Ellie sat down opposite him, shrugging off a light brown jacket and

91

draping it over the back of the chair. She looked tired. Their conversation seemed intense and, unlike most of his fellow imbibers whose voices carried across the room, theirs did not. With her head tilted to one side, listening, the light fell across her face and he found himself holding his breath, not wanting her to move. He wanted to touch her cheek, feel its softness, and kiss the lips opening to speak.

"Another one, Byron?" It was Andrew.

Reluctantly, he drew his gaze away.

"Yes, thanks," he said, as the other man picked up the glass and quirked an eyebrow. Byron didn't really want another drink. It was an excuse to stay.

Pulling the local paper left behind by someone else towards him, he noticed Ellie move her head and glance around the room. When she saw him she blinked, then stared, frowning. Bob must have spoken to her because she nodded, said something to him and got up, heading for his table.

"Hello, Byron. You got back all right from Maw's Hearth then," she said, pulling out a chair and sitting down.

"As you can see. Were you worried I was going to climb up The Chimney alone?" he asked lightly.

"Yes, as a matter of fact I was." She sounded cross, though he found it difficult to read her expression. "I didn't fancy explaining to Jack Kennart why someone else I know was found dead in an isolated place."

"Well, you're spared that."

Ellie nodded, gazing at him as if deciding whether to speak what was on her mind. Then out it came.

"How well d'you know Glenn Thorley?"

It was not what he'd expected. "We're not close."

"D'you work for him?"

"Depends on what you mean by 'work for'." Where, he wondered, was she going with this?

"You're being obtuse. Why were you having a cosy chat with him over coffee?"

"It's not really any of your business, Ellie."

"It is if you're about to destroy an area around here by building a monstrous hotel."

"I'm not a builder. I design buildings."

"Oh, so that's some sort of salve to your conscience, I suppose."

"I don't have a guilty conscience."

"Being linked with Glenn Thorley should give you a very guilty conscience. Did you bother to do any checking on him before you got yourself involved?"

Byron studied her features, intense in their interrogation of him, and wondered how he could penetrate the iron plating she'd put around her life.

"Mayfair Hotels is a respected company. Besides, John Thorley's the owner not Glenn."

Leaning forward in her seat and putting her elbows on the table she rested her chin in cupped hands and said, "You didn't answer my question, Byron Oakes."

"No, I didn't."

"You're one of the most infuriating people I've ever met!" she whispered furiously. "Is that, no you didn't check, or no you didn't answer my question?"

"Both."

"You must've driven your army masters insane. Either questions upon questions or you're tighter than a submarine under water."

He raised his eyebrows at this, a corner of his lips twitching upwards. "That's very good, Ellie, and original, too."

For a second he thought she was going to bang her fist on the table and shout at him, but she did neither. Whether it was his expression or approval of her phrase he didn't know, but she sighed and shook her head.

"You're an unpredictable man, Byron. Maybe that's why I like you."

For a few seconds they gazed at each other across the table. He ignored the bleating of his mobile phone, but the words forming in his mind never came out as Bob got up from his chair and walked towards them. A few seconds later he was seated at the table and Byron could think only of strangling him. However, he found himself taking a liking to the baker as the evening became absorbed in banter about their livelihoods, snippets from the past and a few comments regarding Farley's absence. Ellie did not contribute to the latter. Her expression was closed, tight. Byron had known such pain.

It was not until he got back to the bed and breakfast house and was standing under a hot shower feeling a little woozy from too many Highland beers that he realised there was a new reason he

93

wanted continued involvement in finding Farley Orman's murderer – Ellie Madison.

However, there was pressure from London. Ray had phoned wanting to know exactly how long he planned to stay in Scotland. The workload was too much for him, he'd said. Byron, resenting his attitude, had said if he was so overloaded he should've faxed the papers to the number he'd given him. That aside, the thought of returning to his sterile world in London left him cold.

"Ellie Madison," he murmured.

She was outspoken, wilful, determined, energetic, bursting with life, and he wanted to be part of her world.

As he towelled dry in front of the warm radiator he began thinking seriously about the possibilities of relocating the business to Scotland, even if it had to be Edinburgh. Not that Ray would budge from the confines of the city he'd grown up in and thought was the best place in the world to live, but for Byron it was a serious consideration. Besides, Ray would probably be happier in a larger business.

Byron frowned. It was true he had not checked out Glenn Thorley during the initial contact with Mayfair Hotels despite uneasy feelings about the man when they first met. He hadn't thought it necessary. They were a well-respected company and he knew other architects who'd been waiting a long time for a chance to get in with them. He had not mentioned to Ellie his conversation with John Thorley telling him he would no longer have any dealings with his son if he didn't change his attitude. Even if Bob hadn't arrived at the table it would have made no difference. He knew too little about her.

His leg was throbbing again. He'd bumped it against the end of the bed as he was walking towards the en-suite bathroom. Easing himself into an upright chair, he stretched the leg out in front of him. When things like this had happened on army assignments, and they had on a number of occasions, he'd taken little notice. As long as the injury was bearable the outcome of the assignment took first priority. There had been men in his teams over the years who found his personal expectations too high and, in trying to match them, nursed resentment and envy. Not once had he ever asked anyone to live up to his own personal standards, but he did expect them to excel. They might think differently of him now sitting wincing over what he knew was a minor injury compared to some of the things he had suffered. He shook his head, rueful and a little disgusted at how softness was creeping into his civilian life.

Poking out of the top of his bag was one of the envelopes containing Farley Orman's photographs. He pushed himself out of the chair and retrieved four packets of photographs. Withdrawing the contents of one, Byron spread them out on the bed; several shots were taken in Kilcomb and Ellie featured in two taken in the wilds somewhere. He fanned the rest out and found himself staring at images of Hugh and Ruth Lawford about town, in their garden, and coming out of The Mill. From the lack of interaction with the camera Byron guessed the couple had no idea they were being photographed. What on earth had Farley been up to?

A light tap-tap on the door surprised him and he quickly shuffled the photos together and threw a jumper over them. When he opened the door he stared at the visitor.

"That is the first time I've seen you stuck for words. Are you going to let me in?" Ellie, looking pleased she'd sprung such a surprise, stepped past him as he opened the door wider.

Byron shook his head. "How on earth did you get in? The landlady has a thing about visitors in the evenings."

"I know. I stayed here when I first arrived."

"And I suppose you told her some story about having important information that couldn't wait until morning," he said, cocking an eyebrow.

"That's about it." A faint rose tinted her cheeks.

Suddenly conscious he was in his dressing gown, he wondered what she had told the perky landlady. He closed the door and, excusing himself, went into the bathroom and put his clothes back on. When he came out she frowned.

"You're limping."

"Slipped on the hike yesterday."

She raised her eyebrows and opened her mouth, but closed it again. As he looked at her he felt a rush of longing he hadn't known since he'd lost Ena, a longing that went beyond physical intimacy. She was so close.

"So why are you here?" he asked with difficulty.

She looked at him, searching. It almost took his breath away.

"I don't... trust easily," she said, halting, as if uncertain about saying anything to him, "and I don't think you do either. I want to trust you, but if you're working for Glenn Thorley then it's impossible."

"I work for the company, Ellie. I'm not Glenn's confidante. I don't even like the man."

He reached out and touched her cheek; it was soft and warm. For a moment, she stiffened and then she closed her eyes. Leaning towards her, his lips touched hers and he felt a little shudder pass through her. Every other aspect of his life disappeared, but it was transitory, a hope unfulfilled. She put the palm of her hand against his chest and stepped away. It triggered anger and disappointment in him and he fought to control his tongue as she spoke.

"I can't. You'll... I'll regret..." The words trailed off, her expression guarded.

Regret was the last thing on his mind, but if he wanted to win her trust venting his frustration would only strengthen her reasons for not trusting him.

Instead, he asked, "Are you afraid, Ellie?"

An expression, fleeting, and one he couldn't define, passed like a shadow across her face.

She said tartly, "Don't be ridiculous. I hardly know you, Byron. On top of that, Farley's dead – murdered – and they haven't released his body yet. His children can't give a date for the funeral and people in the village are speculating on how much of his supposed fortune I'm going to get. So, forgive me for not being romantic!"

They were valid reasons and he could believe her or not, but he had to gain her trust or he may as well pack up and return to London. He looked at her. He *wanted* to know her better, *wanted* to be trusted. An emotion he did not immediately recognise pushed its way into his heart. It was too long since he'd felt it, compassion, and it seemed an odd thing to follow his frustration over her rejection of his nearness.

Eventually he said, "I like you, Ellie. I..."

He got no further, the moment interrupted by the abrupt bleeping of his mobile phone and he almost swore at it out loud.

"Not very considerate to ring at this time of night," Ellie remarked. "I'd ignore it."

"I can't." He picked the phone up off the dressing table. "Byron Oakes."

"It's Colin. You're going to have to give me more info about those photos. Any chance you could stick them in the post?"

Byron turned away from Ellie. "Copies do?"

"As long as they're clear."

"I'll do it tomorrow."

Ellie sneezed.

"Got company?" Colin asked, his tone bright and inquisitive.

"It's past your bed time."

"A sleuth never sleeps, but got the message. I await your package."

When he returned he found her bending down to pick up a photograph beside the bed. It must have slipped off in his hurry to hide them.

"Your children?" she asked, without looking up. He knew she wasn't referring to the photo.

Another question lay behind it, but he left it unchallenged and said, "No. A friend."

Straightening up, she turned around looking puzzled. "Where did you take this?" She held the photo up for him to see.

"I didn't. D'you know who these people are?"

"Yes, it's Hugh and Ruth Lawford, Bob's aunt and her husband."

Byron frowned. "Bob's aunt and uncle?"

"Of course. I've known them for years." She stopped and studied him. "Where did you get the photograph, Byron?"

In answer he stepped towards the bed and uncovered the rest of the photographs. "They were taken by Farley Orman."

Ellie stared, astonishment plain. She picked up two photographs, panoramas across hilltops draped in snow. "These were taken in March when we were up near Ben Nevis. They were going to be used in a National Geographic article, but they changed their minds and took different ones. Farley was disappointed. He thought these were two of his best shots."

"I'm not surprised. They're fantastic. Wish I could take pictures like that."

"Time and practice he used to say."

"Hmm. Natural ability would help."

A cloud drifted into her expression and he wanted to hold her and say it would be all right. But he knew it wouldn't, not for a long time. "Don't try and do this grieving thing on your own, Ellie."

The cloud disappeared, replaced by anger. "I've been a fool coming here. My mother always said I was too impetuous for my own good."

"Not for me, Ellie," Byron said, catching her hand. "Anyway, I've been thinking about moving up here for a while."

97

"If this has anything to do with me, don't be too rash."

"Maybe once in my life I'd like to try it."

"I don't recommend it."

She moved away from him and stood near the window.

"Did you know Jack Kennart found Farley's photographic bags in my barn?" she asked.

Unprepared for the question, he felt unexpectedly awkward and hoped she didn't notice as he said, "No. When was this?"

"Today." She looked at him, frowning. "I'm missing something here. Jack seems to think I'm involved with Farley's death, even though I haven't a clue how those bags got in my barn. And now you've got a whole pile of Farley's photos. What's going on, Byron?"

"I don't know, but if Jack Kennart didn't put those bags in your barn then maybe his offsider did."

She stared at him, frowning. "What on earth are you talking about?"

"After you left Maw's Hearth I was working my way round the base of The Chimney. There was some loose scree and I lost my footing, fell through a hole and ended up in a cave. That's how I banged my leg up. Fortunately, I had a torch with me. I found a few interesting things, including Farley's bags."

"And where does Jack fit into this?"

"I was looking through the bags to find out whose they were when I heard voices. I grabbed the rolls of film and hid."

Ellie's eyes narrowed. "Rolls?"

Nodding, Byron continued. "I'd just crawled into a crevice when they came into the cave with torches. Kennart's not a fool. He figured out someone else had been there, but thanks to his spooked offsider they didn't bother looking. They were gone in minutes."

"Who was with Jack?"

"Someone called Bran." He cocked an eyebrow. "I thought that was a breakfast cereal."

Ellie didn't laugh; her expression was troubled. "Bran – it's a Celtic name meaning raven – and the only person I know called that is Farley's youngest son. He's not the most dynamic of the Orman offspring, but he's got more of his father's qualities than the other two. He works on the Strathvern estate."

"You're not keen on Farley's children then?"

"Huh! Camden's greedy, arrogant, very odd and self-serving, and Fenella's so haughty it's a wonder her nose isn't permanently stuck to the ceiling. As for me, I'm the harlot who took their mother's place, or so they think."

"Did you?"

For a long moment she studied his face. "In a way. People always imagine they *know*," she said emphasising the word and raising eyebrows above resentful eyes, "but few do. I've had people ask me ridiculous questions. Village life has its drawbacks."

"So, why don't you leave? London's a great place to live if you want anonymity."

"A minute ago, you were talking of leaving it behind. Anyway, it's not for me. I've survived village gossip this long. They'll find someone else to talk about."

"Not while Farley's death is still unsolved. To some you'll be the prime suspect."

"D'you think I am?"

"No." Did he really believe that? He barely knew her.

"I hope that's true."

"I can't imagine you killing anyone." He smiled. It wasn't exactly reassuring her, but her life was mostly closed to him. He changed the subject.

"How well d'you know the Lawfords?"

She blinked, looking surprised. "What an odd question when you've never met them. You're a man of deep secrets, Byron Oakes. But, in answer, I've visited them a few times with Bob and they come to Kilcomb occasionally. Ruth doesn't like it here much."

"She's not a country lass then?" He did not tell her of his meeting with them.

"Not really. I think it has painful memories for her, though she's never said anything to me. I know Hugh was in Army Intelligence during the war, so maybe it has something to do with that. Could make a good story if only I knew what it was," she said with a quirky smile. "I painted them once with their two magnificent golden retrievers."

"I'd like to see your paintings."

"Perhaps you will one day."

Byron smiled, but didn't respond. His mind was elsewhere. Was it possible that Bob knew nothing about his other aunt's involvement with a German army officer? Ruth, he suspected, wouldn't want knowledge of that shameful episode passed to the next generation.

"Where have you gone, Byron? Recalling some army escapade no doubt."

He smiled, tucking the thoughts away for another time. "Have lunch with me tomorrow."

"Can't sorry. I'm taking ten Glaswegian artists to do a bit of painting and a bit of walking around a fishing village."

"You're abandoning me?"

Ellie tilted her head to one side, giving him a quizzical look. "Just saying no to the invite. It's the artists I can't abandon."

"Care for an assistant? I could help put easels up or something."

She shook her head. "There is something you could do for me – keep an eye on my house. After what you said about Bran and Jack I don't trust the police not to *find* other incriminating things. Then there's Camden. Oh, and Fenella." She picked up her bag. "Can I trust you, Byron?"

"I'm not in the habit of abusing people's trust."

Her eyes searched his, intense. "I hope not. Tell me, why did you ask about the Lawfords?"

"I thought you'd be able to tell me why Farley took the photos of them."

"What does it matter to you?"

He shrugged. Caution was deeply imbedded in his nature. "I'm just curious."

"And I don't believe you, but if I ever get on your need-to-know list, no doubt you'll tell me."

With a sudden smile she disappeared into the hallway and Byron found himself pondering her perceptiveness. Divulging too much information wasn't a risk he could take. Besides, what bits he had were a few jigsaw pieces that he wasn't sure belonged to the same puzzle. Farley was dead and he had taken the shots of the Lawfords who were connected to the Second World War photos, but that didn't mean his death had anything to do with either. Jack Kennart was another piece connected with Farley, but how had the bags got into the cave and into Ellie's barn? Then there were the Orman siblings, no doubt waiting for the will to be read so they could get on with their lives. And last, but definitely not least, there was Ellie. Who *had* she been in Farley's life? If they had been lovers and not simply friends, why hadn't she said so?

For a long while after he flicked off the light switch and pulled the quilt cover over him, Byron stared into the gloomy room. A sliver of moonlight pointed to a spot on the bed near his feet and he thought again of the cave and the belongings of a people long gone from the earth concealed in its thick blackness. Why had no one ever moved them to a museum? Another thing that made no sense was why anyone would go to such lengths to hide Farley Orman's bags in a cave that was all but inaccessible and miles from anywhere. Byron frowned. Perhaps it wasn't miles from anywhere. He couldn't imagine Jack Kennart taking the route he had to Maw's Hearth and, more to the point, carting Farley's bags all the way back to Kilcomb on foot.

Switching on the bedside lamp Byron climbed out of bed and retrieved a map of the Maw's Hearth area from his backpack. At the base of the massive hill and way below The Chimney, a thin line indicating a dirt road threaded its way west until it joined the main coast road. About five miles from where Maw's Hearth rose out of the land were tiny black letters, the name of a small village. It would have been easy enough for Jack to take the coast road back to Kilcomb, though it looked to be about fifteen miles.

None of it made sense. Frustrated, he got back into bed, turned the light off and castigated himself for trying to work it out. Let the police do it, it's their job. Still, he thought, if they're all like Jack Kennart the truth might be buried deep.

And who made you the local private investigator? You don't even live in Scotland. You just happened to be in the wrong place at the wrong time. Well, not exactly the wrong place or time.

***

"Don't you take that tone with me, young woman."

"You're in my way."

"Really. I believe I was here first."

"You can wait, I can't."

"Manners like yours don't intimidate me."

"Perhaps, but they always get me what I want."

Byron, still tired from his restless night, looked up from the magazine article he was reading about Farley Orman's career. It was a few seconds before he realised that he recognised the voice; the older woman had her back to him. Facing Ruth Lawford was a tall, dark-haired woman in, he guessed, her mid-twenties. The black skirt and jacket fitted her like a glove, and on a plum-coloured blouse beneath the jacket a single strand of pearls rested on the soft material. She wore low-heeled, black shoes. The entire outfit looked expensive. She was what film, television and modelling agencies would call beautiful. If she was married, he pitied the husband.

Byron watched them; two women from two different generations having a public altercation at the counter in The Mill. Neither seemed embarrassed. Looking around the room he saw Hugh talking with Bob at a table near the fireplace. However, Bob rose from his chair during the last snappy comment by the younger woman.

Hugh caught Byron's eye and waved, indicating that Byron should join him.

"Not on this occasion, Fenella," Bob said, and looked at the other woman. "What can I get you, Aunt Ruth?"

"Two white coffees and two Eccles cakes please," she replied, ignoring her sparring partner.

"Well, no wonder you served her first! D'you do that to all the people you're related to – serve them before everyone else?"

"Only if they arrived first. Millie's free now and she'll be happy to serve you. Thank you, Aunt Ruth. Here's your change."

"I don't think I'll recommend this place to any of my friends again," said Fenella petulantly. "My father would never have approved of you treating me this way."

To Byron's astonishment, as he sat down next to Hugh, Bob laughed out loud.

"Then you didn't know Farley Orman very well!"

She snatched her purchase out of Millie's hand and stormed out of the building. Conversations in the café, hushed during the spat, increased in volume and Byron had little doubt the Orman family and Farley's death were now favoured topics.

"Well!" said Ruth as she sat down. "What a little upstart she is. And to find out she's Farley Orman's daughter. We met him recently at a fundraising function in Edinburgh. He wasn't a bit like that." She turned to Byron. "How nice to see you again, Byron. I apologise for letting off steam before greeting you. It's not often I meet anyone like her and it's upset me a little. When d'you return to London?"

"I haven't decided yet, but I can't stay away too much longer. My business won't last long if I'm not there," he said, sighing.

"Well, you must come and have lunch with us before you head home," Hugh said, exchanging a glance with his wife, who nodded.

"Yes, do."

"Thanks, I'd like that."

"And," Hugh continued, leaning towards him and lowering his voice, "I might have some information for you."

Byron's internal antenna switched on. "About?"

"One of the matters we discussed when we met. The photos sparked off a lot of long forgotten memories."

The antenna buzzed, but he said, "We hardly know one another. Shouldn't you be talking to Bob or your family?"

"No," Ruth said quietly and emphatically. "We rather like you, Byron Oakes, and think we can trust you not to go blabbing to anyone."

Byron looked from one to the other. How much did he trust *them*? "You hardly know me."

"True," Hugh agreed, nodding, "but you were in the army and that means something to us."

"So, lunch the day after tomorrow suit you?" Ruth asked, smiling.

"Great." There was one thing he wanted to know. "I'm surprised you don't know the Ormans. Bob was quite good friends with Farley."

"We know *of* them, but have met only Farley on that one occasion," Ruth said.

"Can't say we've missed anything if that daughter of his is anything to go by," Hugh said, stirring his coffee. "I know Bob's never thought much of the offspring."

Ruth leaned forward and said quietly, "Perhaps it was one of them."

"One of them what, darling?"

"Who killed him."

The two men looked at her, Hugh as if she had gone mad.

"Really, Ruth. You don't know them at all to be making such a statement."

"It's only a thought, Hugh. Don't get uptight. In cases like this it's often someone the victim knows, or so I've read. And she strikes me as being capable of such a thing."

"She certainly knows how to fire off the words, but the other two might be okay," Byron said lightly, although his thoughts were more serious. Ellie certainly didn't think much of them, especially Camden. It was a possibility. From the scant knowledge he had of the family, there seemed to be little loyalty between them and a lot of self-serving.

Hugh shook his head, looked from one to the other, and then patted his wife's hand. "Leave the detective work to the police, you two."

"I'm an armchair detective, my love, as you well know. What about you, Byron?" Ruth looked at him, her eyes probing beyond the question.

"This is work for the police. I'll let them sort it out. And there is my business."

"You could always move. I should think a business like yours is fairly portable," Hugh said, his voice conveying some of his old authority and certainty. "I'm sure we could help you make connections."

"That's very generous of you. If I get back there and find I can't stand it any longer, I'll let you know."

It was time to make a move if he wanted to explore along the coastline. He'd hired a car for a few days and intended to make the most of the weather while it remained fine; he also had it in mind to check his hunch about Jack Kennart's route from Maw's Hearth back to Kilcomb. The Lawfords were discussing their day which seemed to include lunch with Bob, whose cheerful voice carried from a nearby table where he was delivering a tray of tea and scones. For a moment Byron found himself absorbed in the sounds of the café: chatter, laughter; the chinking of cutlery on china, and the hiss of the cappuccino machine.

Bringing his thoughts back to his two companions, he saw a quick look of surprise on Ruth's face before Ellie slid into the chair beside him.

"Hello, Hugh, Ruth," she said, and then turned, smiling at him. "I see you've met Byron. Has he asked you a million questions?"

Hugh laughed. "Just a few, and yes, we met a few days ago when he was in Inverness."

Byron sensed Ellie's body tense and a second later, though she kept her voice under control, knew she was not pleased he hadn't told her about meeting them.

"I see. Did Bob introduce you?"

"No," Ruth said with a twinkle in her eyes. Before Byron could answer she added, "We met when we discovered parking infringement notices on our windscreens. To say Byron wasn't impressed is probably an understatement."

"You weren't too happy, either," he said in self-defence. "Will I tell her what you did with yours?"

"Ellie knows me well enough. I threw it in the gutter, my dear."

In case Ruth intended going on to mention that Byron had been in their house, he said to Ellie, "I thought you were taking a bunch of painters out this morning."

"I was, but it's been delayed until tomorrow. Two cousins were on their way by train to Edinburgh, but engineering works on the line delayed them so they won't be here until late this afternoon. The group's agreed to wait."

"How very nice of them," Ruth said, cutting her Eccles cake in half.

The younger woman nodded, then turned to Byron and said, "Have you got a minute?"

"Sure." He pushed back his chair, stood up and said to the Lawfords, "Thanks for your company. See you again."

"Yes, that'll be nice," Ruth said.

A cool breeze fingered Byron's face as they stepped outside and he pulled his jacket collar up. Grateful that neither Hugh nor Ruth had mentioned afternoon tea at their house or lunch tomorrow, he realised he might have to tell Ellie, but he was cautious. She was a woman he wanted to know, yet too much was unknown about Farley's relationship with her and the circumstances of his death. Perhaps he was being too cautious. Perhaps his instincts, usually reliable, were letting him down.

They walked in silence until they were away from the building and almost at Ellie's Land Rover. Kipp was watching out the passenger window.

"Why did you lie to me about not knowing Hugh and Ruth?" Ellie said in a cool voice.

"I didn't. You assumed I hadn't met them."

"But you didn't correct me."

"The conversation went on. I would've told you. It's not important, Ellie. Don't get stewed up about it."

For a long moment she gazed at him intently and he had the distinct feeling she was weighing up his worth as a man, friend, and perhaps lover.

"You're right," she said, letting out a sigh. "I'm sorry. Let's start the morning again."

Relieved, he nodded, and reached for her hand. She moved away. He should've known better.

"I don't know you well enough," she said. "Besides, people will be watching."

"Worried someone might think I killed Farley to get you? Or that we both did it?"

"That's not funny."

"It's not meant to be."

"Why would anyone think that? We're hardly more than acquaintances."

"They don't know that."

"Jack Kennart does."

"Does he? Your sergeant strikes me as a man interested only in local affairs, self-interest, and bending or hiding the truth if necessary."

There was no immediate response. Instead, as if needing time to think, Ellie walked round to the driver's door and opened it.

"If you're right, then Farley's murderer might never be found." Her voice was small and sad. "Follow me home."

***

Ellie straightened the mat on which sat a vase of roses in the middle of the kitchen table. It was a 1600's piece made of oak which had been in her father's family for at least two hundred years. Her mother had never liked it and had always kept it covered with a dark green velvet cloth. When Ellie moved north the table had gone with her.

Byron's opinion of Jack Kennart worried her, although not because she thought he had misjudged the man. Over the years she had been puzzled by the way Jack had handled certain cases related to the work the Ormans did, and on more than one occasion discovered he had interpreted facts and information not entirely as the law stated. She had dismissed her thoughts as lack of understanding. Now, Byron's words stirred latent doubts that she had not shared with anyone.

In all her life she had never met a man like him; his strength, underlying passion for life, assurance of who he was, and confidence in his abilities, roused dormant feelings. He was, she thought, a bit of a rarity.

The sound of a car drew her attention to the window and she looked up, an unexpected gladness at having him to herself for a while. However, it wasn't Byron. Only Camden Orman could keep his car gleaming in all weather and today the sun glinted off the shiny red bonnet. Ellie was not pleased to see him and wished Byron would hurry up. Where on earth had he got to?

Not wanting Camden in the house, she went outside and met him halfway along the path to the front door.

"What d'you want, Camden?" she asked without preamble.

"Not a nice way to greet an old friend," he said, his lips turned upwards, twitching in a smile that wasn't quite one.

"We've never been friends."

"*You've* never tried. Never treated me like I was there. You only cared about Dad. He looked after you. Oh, yes," he said, nodding. "Even when Mum was still here. You haven't got a clue, have you?"

"About what?" She glared at him, her lips drawn in a tight, thin line. He was a peculiar man, not to be trusted.

"Dad got you all those painting jobs."

"Oh, grow up, Camden!"

He continued as if she hadn't spoken. "Useful you were. That's all. He nearly messed up his career because of you."

"What are you wittering about? You've never cared tuppence about your dad's career," Ellie snapped, feeling something close to hatred for this infantile man.

His eyes narrowed and his voice, when he spoke, was filled with loathing. "You wanted to take him away from us so you could have his money."

Ellie stared at him, more certain than ever there was madness in his genes. "Don't be stupid."

"Stupid? No. I watched you with him"

She chose to ignore the comment. "What *is* your point, Camden?"

"You should show some loyalty to us"

"Give me one good reason."

He walked closer. "Us – me and Bran and Fen. We know he put you in his will, but all the money's ours. We'll make you give it to us."

"Don't get above yourself, Camden. You're not the local laird and I'm not going to get anything, so you can stop going on about it."

He drew near and it was all she could do to repress a shudder, but she refused to move and show him either fear or repulsion.

"You think you know all about me, but you don't," he almost hissed. "Women like you don't know what loyalty is, but you should find out."

Arrogant twit, she thought.

"Your dad wanted to be proud of you, Camden. The sad thing is he didn't find much to be proud of. You let him down more than anyone else, but your poor mum just couldn't see it."

His body tensed and she saw his hands curl into hard fists, the knuckles white.

"That's a lie! You... you're jealous. A jealous slut! That's what Fen says."

"Why *are* you here?" she said impatiently, interrupting him and refusing to take the bait. He could believe what he wanted. *Where* was Byron?

"To get what's mine."

"I have nothing of yours."

"The stuff you took from Dad's bags. It belongs to me. I'm the eldest."

For a second she was back in Byron's room looking at photos and listening to details of his adventure on Maw's Hearth.

Camden's eyes gleamed. He hadn't missed the hesitation.

"You *have* got it! Your eyes give you away, always have."

"You're deluded, Camden. You were here when I came home and found you and your Uncle Jack on my property. I didn't even know the bags were there until then."

"Liar. There're things missing."

"What things?"

"Uncle Jack's not as stupid as he makes out. He looked before you got there."

"So why don't you ask him?"

"Because he hasn't got them – more rolls of film and stuff."

"Well, neither have I. Perhaps you took them. Anyway, how d'you know there were more rolls of film?"

"His notebook. He always wrote down what was on the films." He cocked his head to one side. "You've forgotten already. Fen says you're shallow, like a..." He paused, looking thoughtful, and then brightening said, "... like a tide that's gone out. When Mum's back you won't be welcome at our house."

"I never was. Not when you and Fenella were there."

Ellie stepped back and began to turn away, but he grabbed her arm and twisted it behind her back. She could feel his breath on the back of her neck and a shudder ran down her spine. His voice was low, menacing and something cold and hard was pressed into the side of her neck.

"You think I'm stupid. Other people made that mistake. They got hurt. I get what I want. Give me the films."

"Let her go right now."

Byron! How on earth had he turned up so silently? She'd heard no car, no footsteps.

Camden did not release her.

"And if I don't?"

"I'll shoot you," Byron said coldly.

"You'll hit Ellie. I know how much you... *like* her. If you shoot her she won't get any of dad's money."

"I said, let her go."

"I'll shoot off her ear."

"You'll be dead before then."

"Uncle Jack'll lock you up and you'll be out of the way, too."

There was no response other than the sound of a click and Ellie was suddenly pushed away. Grimacing, rubbing her arm, she turned and saw Byron pointing a gun at Camden.

"Get off this property. You're trespassing."

"And don't come back," Ellie said.

"He won't be here forever," Camden said, looking at her. "Then you won't have anyone to protect you. You never know when or where I'll turn up."

They watched him stride off, chuckling, get into his car and drive away without looking back. The tension in Ellie's muscles eased and she looked at Byron with a mixture of relief, anger and frustration.

"Where *were* you?" she demanded, as they walked towards one another. "I thought he was going to kill me!"

"He wouldn't have. He's someone who likes to play games. Anyway, the publicity over your death so soon after Farley's would have driven him insane."

"How d'you know? You haven't got a clue about him."

"I know his sort." Byron tucked the gun away inside his jacket. Silently, she watched.

"Who are you, Byron Oakes?"

He looked up and in his eyes she saw a challenge. "This kind."

He cupped her face in his hands and kissed her with a passion she had never experienced. Unprepared and affronted by his boldness her mind told him to back off, but she neither struggled nor spoke the angry words. In a room almost lost in her heart, she heard a cry for intimacy, a need to be loved and held, but past

109

memories were stronger and a few seconds later she pulled away from him.

"Whatever mission you're on, I hope I'm not one of the pawns," Ellie said, looking into his eyes, searching for a flicker that would give him away. There was no flicker.

"You're not," he said, and she thought she heard a faint sadness in his tone.

"So, what're you doing with a gun? I didn't think it was the sort of implement architects needed."

"It depends where you live."

For a moment she gazed over the hedge to the hills beyond. He was not going to tell her no matter how much she questioned.

"Okay, no more interrogation. I need a good strong coffee after that visit."

They sat outside the back door in the sunshine and for several minutes silently watched Kipp nosing about the garden. Several blackbirds were busily flicking leaves and soil in the vegetable patch. In the fields behind the house a horse whinnied.

"So," Byron said, breaking the quietude, "what did Camden want?"

"The photos you've got. He knows some are missing from his father's bag."

That he was looking at her intently she was aware even before turning to him. His voice held a note of probing suspicion. "How does he know I've got them?"

"He doesn't," she said, disallowing an inner taunt to react. "He thinks I have them. He also thinks I was after money from his father."

"So, how does he know films are missing?"

She told him about Farley's notebooks and the fastidious way he had of keeping track of what was on each film, when it was processed, where the films were developed, what prints and negatives went where, and what articles he needed to write using which photos.

Byron was silent and contemplative. She wondered where his thoughts had gone. There was in his expression a warning not to intrude.

A soft breeze was stirring in the treetops and in the sunshine a hint of warmth. These were the summer days Ellie loved and she hoped the weather would hold for the trip to the fishing village. She was glad it was only one day with the painters; her soul was restless to be tramping over the high peaks away from speculation and nosey villagers who thought they knew her better than she did herself – especially Carrie the postmistress. Two days ago, the spiteful woman had told Olga Erskine she had heard from a member of the Orman family that Ellie Madison was contesting the will. Ridiculous when it hadn't been read yet due to some legal hold up. The whole thing was maddening, but people who wanted to would believe any lies told them.

"I wonder why he's so interested in Farley's photos," she said, not consciously including Byron in her puzzle.

"Because there'll be something in them that concerns him."

Surprised to hear an answer, she glanced at him. His brows were drawn together in an expression of foreboding; a knot twisted in her stomach.

"What makes you say that? Anyway, you should give them to Jack."

"Why?"

"Because Farley was... was murdered and..." She had difficulty continuing. What did it really matter who had the photographs? Farley was gone and she'd never see him again – that mattered.

Byron's hand closed over hers. In his eyes she saw understanding.

"I won't be giving them to anyone, Ellie," he said gently. "I think Farley found out somebody's secret or saw what he shouldn't have and paid with his life."

"You don't think Jack will dig deep enough, do you?"

He shook his head.

"Nor do I," she said, and related to him the incidents that had seemed unsatisfactorily resolved over the past few years.

Once or twice he asked a question, but mostly gazed into the distance listening without making a comment. In a way, he reminded her of her father who, though he could be solemn and given to outbursts of anger, was also a man who loved and who had a great capacity for unravelling problems and fixing them.

She left him sitting there while she went and made more coffee. When she sat down, he watched her for a moment and then asked,

"Ellie, were you and Farley lovers?"

The question was so unexpected and intimate that she retorted, "It's none of your business. I thought you were above listening to village gossip."

Turning away from him, she took a gulp of coffee and almost burned her mouth.

"This has nothing to do with village gossip. Your life could be in danger."

"Have you been colluding with Bob?"

"No, why d'you say that?"

"Because he said the same thing a few days ago. Still, that little episode with Camden shook me up a bit."

A pair of dark brown eyes studied her. Then in a quiet, intense voice, Byron said, "Were you and Farley lovers, Ellie?"

She couldn't look at him, a dullness settling on her heart. Any hopes regarding Byron withered.

"No. Just a one-off thing after his wife disappeared," she said in a lifeless tone, ashamed. "It was stupid, meaningless and I was ashamed. Farley's work absorbed his life."

There was silence between them until the last drop of coffee had been drunk.

"I have to go to London and see what's happening with my business," Byron said, no trace of emotion in his voice. "It could be in trouble."

"Will you be back?"

Lifting her chin so that she had to look at him, he said, "Don't doubt me, Ellie."

Chapter 7

"You don't want to listen to Carrie, Ellie," Mary Nevin said as they left the post office together. "How Dan puts up wi' her is beyond me. She's nothing but a gossip intent on making trouble for everyone."

Ellie raised her eyebrows and sighed. "I know, but hearing her moaning about how the Orman darlings have been short-changed by that 'loose Madison woman' is hard to take. Most of the villagers probably agree."

"No, Ellie, *most* don't," Mary said grasping her hand. "What on earth's got into you these last couple of weeks? Where's the warrior woman I know?"

"She's having a holiday," Ellie replied, touched by her friend's concern. "I had no idea Farley put me in his will, Mary. Anyway, most of it's in trust for the projects we were working on with the SNH. I only heard about the will reading a few days ago. Farley's solicitor rang after Bob and I got back from a meeting with the council about the hotel Glenn Thorley wants to put up. I didn't have that wretched new gadget they call a mobile phone that Farley insisted I keep with me. So, I didn't get his calls and he blasted me for being out of contact. Stuck up prig! And how did Carrie hear about Farley's will being read? Is she psychic as well?"

Incensed, as always, by the postmistress' vindictive tongue, she would have liked to cut it out and hang it up to dry. The warrior wasn't totally on holiday it seemed.

"Heaven forbid! It was probably the cleaning lady listening outside the solicitor's door. She's Carrie's second cousin and almost as bad as she is," Mary said with some asperity. "Who knows? You've got tae be strong. You haven't lost the support of anyone who believes in the work you and Farley were doing. You can't stop now. You've plenty of friends and contacts who'll help."

"I hope so, but it needs someone like Farley to take charge. I can stand up and make a noise, but I'm just a painter and I take people walking. All right on the local level, but nationally? That was Farley's forte. Anyway, I need time to get used to not having him or… not having Farley around."

Ellie riffled through her mail, hoping Mary hadn't noticed the hiccup in the sentence.

"Ah, so that's it."

"What's it?" she asked lightly, looking up.

Mary's expression conveyed all that Ellie sensed she was going to hear.

"I'm nae daft, Ellie Madison. I've known you since you arrived here. Farley's only part of the reason you're 'on holiday'. You're missing someone else as well."

"Is that so? When you know who it is, let me know," she said, determined to keep her feelings to herself. That Byron's two-week absence was disturbing her more than she liked or wanted to admit, she was not about to share with anyone.

On the other side of the street, she spotted Reverend Paul Shipley and Olga Erskine walking towards the baker's shop, deep in conversation.

Mary saw them too, and said, "We'll talk about this later, Ellie. I've tae get back or Mark will think I've posted myself to somewhere exotic."

Ellie grinned and her friend nodded approvingly before giving her a quick hug. Long ago she had discovered in Mary a friend who wouldn't hesitate to speak her mind if it was needed, but one who also gave of her heart. There were few in the village who hadn't known meals to land on their table, had washing hung out to dry, ironing folded or put away, or a trip in Mary's car to the hospital in Castlebay. Though she liked a good chin-wag when time permitted, Ellie had never known her to betray a confidence or spread malicious gossip. Ellie often thought Mary's perception of people and situations could be uncannily accurate. During one of Ellie's first encounters with Carrie, the postmistress had told her to beware of Mary Nevin because the little folk were constantly whispering in her ears about everyone's business. It wasn't long before Ellie decided that was more applicable to Carrie.

Feeling lighter in spirit after talking with Mary, Ellie crossed the road and went into the baker's. The clergyman and the old woman were in front of her.

"Morning, Paul, Olga."

"Ellie, how are you?" Paul said, retrieving a loaf of bread from the shelf. "I hear you had an interesting group last week."

"Business folk who didn't know a sheep from a cow, I heard!" piped up Olga who was paying for her purchase.

114

"That about sums them up," Ellie said, grinning. "They were sent by their company for personal and team-building development and the hike was part of it. Most of them made it very clear they didn't want to be there. Even Kipp got fed up with them!"

Ellie made her lunch purchase and the three of them left the bakery together.

"I'm taking Olga down to the river at Cuilean's Bridge. D'you want to join us? I've got a flask in the car and there's enough for three."

"I'd love to, but I've promised myself I'd finish a painting someone's commissioned. She's coming to collect it in two days and it's not ready."

"C'mon, Ellie. It'll do you the world of good," Olga said. "It's one o' my favourite places and it's too long since I've been there."

"We won't be all afternoon," Paul said, smiling, "and then you can get on with the painting, refreshed and inspired. By the way, where's Kipp?"

They stood looking at her, Olga's eyes twinkling.

"All right! But don't forget, I've got a deadline. Kipp's at home. I was only coming into the village for a few minutes!"

Cuilean's Bridge had reached over the winding, energetic river since the sixteenth century. According to local history books, it had been preceded by a wooden bridge washed away during a storm, sweeping a father and his son who had been crossing, to their deaths. Ellie had been told that if you listen carefully on stormy nights you can hear the father calling for his son. On an autumn evening last year, Farley had taken her there and they'd leaned over the stone wall watching the turbulent water rushing by beneath. Thunderous skies had shut out the moon and the howling, powerful wind rushed up the valley and over the moors. There had been an excitement and majesty in such might and she'd wondered about God.

The sun disappeared behind a lone cloud as Paul stopped the car on a flat piece of ground near the river. Ellie felt a momentary chill, as if a warning of potential danger. Closing her eyes, she waited until it passed. Fanciful was not a word she applied to herself, yet the anxiety was real enough. In the rear-vision mirror she caught a glimpse of Paul's eyes, concerned, she supposed by her expression. To reassure him, she smiled and then got out of the back of the car to help Olga who was in the front, but the older woman mostly got herself out.

"You're a wise young woman, Ellie," she said as they stood together watching the river. "You keep fit. That's what I've done all my life and when you get to my age of seventy-five, every ounce of energy counts!"

Paul, who was retrieving a blanket and a box with picnic items from the boot, stuck his head around the end of the car and said, "She even chased off a would-be burglar a fortnight ago. Waved a brass poker at him and prodded him with it until he left, promising never to return!"

"Och, that was nothing. He was only a lad."

"How d'you know that? You said he had a balaclava pulled over his face."

"Compared to me he was only a lad. Anyway, he went. I don't think he trusted me wi' the poker," she said, winking at Ellie.

Ellie chuckled. "You're a brave woman, Olga. Does Jack Kennart know about it?"

Olga frowned. "I wouldn't waste any energy telling him. The last time he just shrugged. Nothing much he could do about it, he said. Didn't take hardly any notes. No," she said, shaking her head, "he's not what I call a good policeman."

"What d'you mean 'last time'?" Paul asked, as Ellie relieved him of the rug and a folded chair.

"It was about six months ago. I chased him off, too, but he got away wi' a silver locket that meant a lot to me."

She looked away to the mountains behind them, but Ellie could see her chin quivering and put an arm around her shoulders. Neither of them spoke. Paul touched her shoulder as he walked across the grass and put the picnic box on top of a flat rock.

For a while they sat in silence, Olga on the chair, Paul and Ellie on the rug, gazing at the mountains and rushing river. Though Ellie had enjoyed many picnics by the river over the years she never tired of this spot. Great craggy rock outcrops rose beyond lower, smoother hills, and across the river were hills clothed in trees, grass and bracken at their feet. As the seasons changed, so the colours, too, changed; bracken that was bright green in spring turned bronze in autumn, jutting grey rock outcrops became softer in winter under blankets of snow. The sky could be black and turbulent, loud, and ominous, or translucent and quiet with rose, salmon and lilac streaks of cloud. It didn't matter to Ellie; her passion to paint it and help others see the beauty and diversity of the area never dimmed, neither did her desire to help keep it safe from greedy developers like Glenn Thorley.

"It's so beautiful here," Paul said, sighing. "I don't know how I lived anywhere else."

"Nor me," Ellie said. "I can't imagine living anywhere else now. I envy the locals having all this as their heritage."

"Don't," Olga said emphatically, shaking her head. "The environment's one thing, but it's the people who make a place and they're not as beautiful as the mountains."

Ellie studied the intensity on the older woman's face, eyes dark with secret emotions and her lips pinched together as if suppressing great anger. It surprised Ellie. She'd always found it hard to imagine old people as once young and having great passions and dreams, collecting life's baggage along the way. Yet, stored inside Olga Erskine was a wealth of history, both personal and of the decades of change she had survived.

"I've been reading about Kilcomb's history this last month," Paul said as he handed Olga a sandwich and offered Ellie one. She declined, indicating her own packet. "One of the old boys in my congregation made an interesting comment about World War Two, so I went to the newspaper office in Castlebay to see if I could find anything in the papers."

"So, you do have interests besides shepherding your flock," Ellie said, grinning. "Does God mind?"

Paul laughed. "The Almighty has more interests than we do, so why should He mind? What He objects to is disobedience and doing things we know we're not supposed to and aren't good for us – now that's a sermon in itself. How long have you got?"

"Not that long today, Vicar," Ellie said, smiling but feeling mildly uncomfortable. She didn't consider herself a bad person, but she hadn't always done the right thing either.

"Anyway, back to what I found in the papers," he said, although his gaze remained on her for a moment and Ellie saw in his eyes a depth of understanding that disconcerted and moved her. "There were rumours that German spies were living in the region during the last two or three years of the war. I couldn't find any article that named anyone or whether locals were connected in some way. Funny thing though, in one of the papers from 1944, a great chunk had been cut out of a page focussed on 'evidence' of local German activity. I bet the archivists don't know it's missing!"

"Someone with a school project to do probably," Ellie said. "Nothing like a bit of authentic material to get good marks."

"Could be. We'll never know." Paul turned to Olga. "Did you hear about the spies, Olga?"

There was no response and Ellie thought she must have dozed off over her sandwich; her head was bowed. Ellie was about to suggest that she and Paul finish their lunch and go for a walk when Olga slowly lifted her head.

"I came to Kilcomb in 1947," she said quietly, "but I knew about the spy stories. Everyone did."

There was in her expression what Ellie could only describe as guarded sadness.

"What brought you here, Olga?" Paul asked.

She looked at him for a long moment as if weighing up what was safe to reveal. After all, thought Ellie, the consequences of the war years were still fraught with danger and grief for some.

"Actually," Olga said, the beginning of a smile turning the corner of her lips, "it was a man."

"Love is a good reason," Paul said, nodding, "especially when he came from a magnificent part of Britain."

"Aye, it started out that way, but men can be untrustworthy creatures, though. Given tae fanciful notions. Wouldn't you agree, Ellie?"

"Good at betrayal and untrue statements, I'd say."

In her tone was more heat than she intended and the other two regarded her, briefly, with some intensity.

"And in our defence, we're not all like that, thankfully," Paul said, after he'd swallowed a mouthful of sandwich. "If you'd counselled husbands whose wives have up and left them for someone else, you'd know that it's not the sole domain of men to betray and lie. We're all capable of doing these things. And, getting back to the war, look at how many men *and* women were spies."

"That's a bit different, though," Ellie said.

"Is it?"

"Yes, it was wartime."

"So, are you saying that lying and betrayal are okay in some situations, but not others? It's still men and women causing great pain and grief to other human beings. I'm not sure the distinction is as clear as you think."

"But in war we're talking about the future of entire nations."

Paul gazed at the hills, his eyes troubled. Then he said gently, "And what if your husband slept with another woman – or perhaps more than one – in his duty to the nation? Would your pain be any less because it was for the war effort?"

There was a muffled sound from Olga, but Ellie could only look away and stare at the river, trying to quell anguish from the past and a growing belief that Byron *had* lied to her and returned to his old life – and perhaps, wife – in London. After all, what did she know about him? The reverend was right; betrayal of any sort caused pain so deep it was impossible to adequately describe. She ought to know.

A minute or two later when she brought her attention back to the others, Paul was handing Olga, who was dabbing her eyes with a handkerchief, a cup of water.

"Olga?" Ellie said, scrambling up and going to her side. "What's the matter?"

"I'm all right, lass, but talking about the war... well, some wounds never really heal." She sighed, then almost to herself said, "There's no one who can heal my wounds."

Paul and Ellie glanced at one another and he opened his mouth to answer, but Ellie shook her head thinking this was not the time for a theological answer. Then, she wondered if she'd had the right to interfere.

When Olga finished the water, they walked along slowly by the river and up to the bridge. It wasn't far and Olga, who was fitter than she looked, insisted they cross to the other side where there was an old tree trunk she had perched on happily in the past. Ellie knew it well, but could not make her feet follow them. Paul and Olga were over the river before they realised she was not with them, and Ellie saw Olga put a restraining hand on Paul's arm as he was about to call out to her. Poor man with two women keeping him from doing what he knew so well how to do – include and comfort others.

On that tree trunk she and Farley had shared their dreams and hopes, and it was there, four months ago, he had asked her to marry him. The proposal had shocked her.

She watched the water swirling around and over a jumble of smooth rocks below her, reminding her of Farley's anguish when she told him it was impossible. Not only was Alice probably still alive, but she'd never thought of him that way. She would never forget his distress nor forgive herself for being the cause of it. It had

119

not occurred to her that he would consider her as his wife; she had been content with their relationship with no intention of changing it. Besides, his offspring made it clear they would never recognise her as a family member. Friendship with their father was all they would tolerate. Farley had often brushed off their loutish, cold behaviour as understandable since their mother had disappeared without a word, but Ellie perceived it as a far more complicated and destructive thing. Once, Camden and Fenella had sent her a card with a picture of a heart thrust through with a dagger. Inside, one of them had written, 'Destroyer'. The message was clear and, Camden's visit just before Byron left, renewed her belief in their intent to allow her nothing of their father.

After the day Farley had proposed, she'd hardly seen him; he had plunged himself into his work, waiting for her to change her mind. Three days before his body was found, Ellie, despite Farley's second proposal, knew that marriage with him would never work; his love for her was entwined with their passion for the Highlands and not for her solely. He could go off for days, even weeks at a time, and not contact her other than for work reasons. It had been the same for Alice. Remembering that his wife's heart needed him, too, simply went out of his mind.

Ellie mourned his loss. Whenever life had pressed its ugliness on her, Farley always found a way to make her laugh or cry; sometimes he had simply held her.

The sound of an approaching car made her look up. It was Jack Kennart. He stopped next to her and wound down the window.

"Hello, Ellie. What brings you up here?"

"Not that's it really any of your business, Jack, but I'm here with Reverend Shepley and Olga Erskine. They're over there in case you don't believe me," she said, pointing in the general direction.

"No need to get testy, girl. By the way, have you found the photographs I was askin' for a fortnight ago?"

Ellie glared at him. She was in no mood for police questioning. "I think you're going deaf, Jack. I've already told you – and Camden Orman – that I don't have them."

"You can say what you want, but I've got a search warrant for your house. Expect us tomorrow."

"You've suddenly become very efficient, though there's a bit of a time lag I'd have thought. Is someone in authority putting the pressure on?"

The sergeant's eyes narrowed. "You're too smart for your own good, Ellie. Things aren't lookin' up for you at present, so I'd mind my manners if I were you."

"I've got a meeting at home in the morning with people from Edinburgh. Don't come then," she said bluntly and began turning away.

"Are you threatening me?"

"I've known you too long to do that, Jack. Searching my house won't help you find Farley's murderer. The photographs, whatever they are, are not there."

"They're not lookin' just for photos, Ellie. The murder investigation squad's from Edinburgh, too – and they've got their own agenda."

"I know. They visited a week ago, which I'm sure you know about. Camden told them I was hiding evidence." She glared at the three stripes on his sleeve. "The man's a toad. How on earth did Farley manage to produce him?"

"He's a lot of hot air, Ellie."

"No, Jack, he's not," she said firmly, looking up. "About three weeks ago he came to my house and threatened me with a gun, grabbed me and would've done who knows what if Byron hadn't turned up."

"Why on earth didn't you tell me?" Jack said, getting out of the car.

"I never thought about it."

"What did he want?"

She gave what sounded a bit like a snort. "Actually, the same thing you do – the photos. I wish someone would find them and leave me alone. You know," she said sadly, "I don't know why anyone would think I killed Farley. He meant a lot to me."

Jack sighed. "I know, Ellie, but…"

"But what?" she said, frustrated by policemen, investigations and bullies. "You think we had a lover's tiff? Or, perhaps like Camden, you think I was after his money!"

"I didn't say that. You have to remember that I'm not in charge of this investigation. Farley was an important man and people in high places want tae know what happened to him."

"And so do the rest of us, Jack. Some of us loved him."

Jack nodded, and then said quietly, "But not everyone, Ellie."

She watched him drive off down the narrow, winding road until the vehicle was lost to sight behind a hill. There was no guessing where Jack's loyalties lay. For a man who espoused little interest in the environment, he had, at times, been a vocal supporter of Farley's work regarding protection of the Highlands, while grumbling with other like-minded locals about the obstacle Farley was to progress. Once, he had clapped him in a cell at the police station for 'obstructing the cause of justice'. Farley had simply been reprimanding Glenn Thorley for walking on land he had no right to be on in the first place.

Ellie turned her gaze to Paul and Olga who were perched on the fallen tree trunk like two birds, seemingly engrossed in animated conversation.

It wasn't much good staying there on the bridge; the only journey to freedom from the grief was to confront each hurdle, mountain, or valley, go over or through it, and continue walking on the other side. With this in mind, and knowing she had conquered before, Ellie walked towards them, pushing down a strong desire to turn and run the other way.

"… the most outrageous parties!" Olga declared.

"Were you there often?" Paul asked.

"I suppose I was. His wife liked me and we became friends. I tried to stay out of his way though. He was too familiar at times. I'm nae fond o' that behaviour." Olga looked up and smiled. "Ah, there you are, Ellie. Was that Jack the Plod?"

Ellie nodded, but she did not want to discuss Jack. Besides, she was curious who they had been talking about. "So, whose outrageous parties were you at?"

There was a faint upward movement of Olga's eyebrows as if she detected the avoidance of discussing police activity. "The late Earl of Strathvern's. He knew how to throw a good party. During the war as well so I heard," she added, too quickly Ellie thought. "They continued after the war. Pity the present earl hasn't, in my opinion, inherited his father's panache. Still, there are signs of it in one of his grandsons."

"Jamie," Ellie said, studying Olga.

There was a brief hardening in the older woman's expression, but before Ellie could ask her about the parties, Olga said brightly,

"Aye. You know him, then?"

"A little." She put Olga's words aside for now. "Farley and I found him once or twice up in the hills, painting. He told us he liked the lonely places. He couldn't have been much more isolated than where he was! The only other visitors he'd have had were birds.

Actually, when we saw him a couple of months later he said an odd thing about not wanting to be a coward like his father. Farley asked him what he meant, but he just shrugged and got on with his painting."

Paul made a wry face. "Might just be disgruntled with his lot in life. Perhaps he fancies himself as the next earl."

"I don't know," she said, shrugging. "He didn't seem to have an over-sized grudge against his father when Farley and I took him to dinner. Jamie sold several of his paintings and donated the money to a fundraiser we had to save the old church outside Kilcomb from demolition. He was good fun."

"Pity his father's not the same," Olga said, beginning to get off the tree trunk. "There's a man who could do with gettin' his head out of the bank books!"

"Oh, he does," Paul piped up. "He's been generous to the church."

"Huh! Probably thinks he can buy a place in heaven."

"Now, Olga, that's a bit unfair. If you ask around you'll find he's done a lot to help people in the village."

"That man doesn't do anything wi'out a reason – profit for his own coffers."

The afternoon sun was warm and clear as they headed off towards the bridge. Halfway across they stopped to watch the water going downstream towards the village and beyond. Olga leaned against the wall and closed her eyes.

"I love the music o' the water," she said, and her voice held an almost sensual, yearning note. "Oh, to be young again."

Ellie and Paul glanced at one another and, by silent consent, did not respond. It seemed inappropriate to crash in upon her memories.

By the time they reached the village it was almost three o'clock and Ellie, after she thanked them for including her in their picnic, hurried home to finish the painting. There were also newspaper articles and a report to read, concerning a proposition to put up a telecommunications tower for a television company a few miles from Kilcomb. This, she hoped, would be the last time she'd have to be involved in this as it had been going on for two years. Surely, they'd got the message by now!

The flowers in the front garden stood bright and colourful in the sunshine, roses and delphiniums nodding amongst their low-growing companions of alyssum, lavender and nasturtiums.

Against the wall of the house, hollyhocks stood tall and proud displaying pink and yellow blooms to the entire garden. Ellie smiled, pleased that her efforts had been rewarded.

She wondered where Kipp was as he liked to sprawl on the front porch on warm, sunny days. However, all thoughts of the garden fled when she began walking down the drive. On the ground splodges of blood coloured the stones. Her heart pounded and she began running towards the back garden. There was no sign of Kipp and she called out several times before there was a whimper from the shed. She ran towards it and found him inside near the door.

"Kipp!"

Kneeling down beside him, tears ran down her cheeks as she gently touched his leg and stared at the gashes on his head and shoulder, blood oozing and matting his white hair.

"Lord, please don't let him die, please don't let him die!" Reluctant to leave him, she raced towards the house, picked up the phone in the kitchen and dialled the vet's number. Her heart was thumping. "Come on! Answer the phone!"

Seconds later she heard a vet nurse's voice and Ellie gabbled out that Kipp was badly injured. She was instructed to bring him in as quickly as possible.

She phoned Bob and within ten minutes he arrived, helping her lift the dog into the Land Rover. Ellie sat in the back with Kipp while Bob drove. There was little talk during what seemed an interminable journey. It wasn't until they were inside the veterinary clinic and Kipp in the capable hands of vet, Jim Plowden, that a little of Ellie's fear ebbed.

During the examination, Ellie and Bob hovered in the background. Once or twice Kipp yelped and Jim's calm, gentle voice flowed into the room, its sound soothing Ellie's heightened tension. After what seemed an age, the vet looked up and nodded.

"He'll be okay, Ellie. The young chap needs quite a lot of stitches. We'll keep him in for a couple of days to make sure there's nothing more serious lurking underneath all this hair."

"Thank goodness." She closed her eyes and took a deep breath, letting it out in a long sigh. "I hadn't intended being out so long. While Kipp was being attacked I was on an unexpected picnic. I knew I shouldn't have gone!"

"Don't, Ellie. Condemning yourself makes no difference to the circumstance and you know that. Kipp's not a small dog and wouldn't have taken kindly to strangers at your house. Check with Owen if anyone's been in with bite wounds."

Ellie nodded. Owen Garnock, the doctor for Kilcomb and several other villages, hamlets and isolated farms, had set up three years ago and, though sometimes taciturn, had proved himself to be an excellent diagnostician and doctor.

She leaned down and gently fondled Kipp's ears. "You'll be fine, boy. Jim said so."

"That's better," the tall, blond man said, smiling. "He'll be well looked after."

"I know that. I wouldn't have brought him here otherwise."

Jim nodded his thanks and Ellie returned to the waiting area where Bob had already gone.

"Come on, Ellie, let's get you a cup of strong tea at the café," he said, giving her a quick hug as they walked to the Land Rover. "I could do with one as well."

"How about a drink at the pub down the road?" she suggested.

"Even better. Who's driving home?"

"Let's worry about that later."

Bob drove down the road past the café where she had last sat with Byron. How stupid to have trusted him. He'd had years of army training and she knew enough about him, although he had never specifically said what he did, to understand that much of his work involved subterfuge and secrecy. What an easy target she was after the loss of Farley! Perhaps Byron – if that was his real name – hadn't just been a hiker on holidays. And what, she thought with a jolt, if Farley had been up to things he shouldn't have? Why had he taken photos of the Lawfords through their hedge? That *was* very odd. She sighed, leaving a misty patch on the window, and remembered Byron's last words to her, "Don't doubt me, Ellie."

There was always a chance, of course, that he was telling the truth.

"Are you okay, Ellie?"

"I will be after a drink. Sorry, Bob. I didn't mean to ignore you."

"I didn't think you were. Kipp's in a bit of a state, but he'll be fine with Jim. It's not the first time he's been patched up."

"I know, but if I'd taken him with me it wouldn't have happened. I got waylaid by Paul Shepley and Olga Erskine. They were going on a picnic down by the river and convinced me I needed a break. I did, but…"

"Olga Erskine? I didn't know she was a friend of yours."

"More of an acquaintance."

"Well, mind how you go. She's on my oldies' run when she can't get out of the house and she's crotchety at being cooped up, to say the least."

"D'you think she's a witch and poisoned Andrew and Pauline's son?"

"She's a bit odd. Witch? I doubt it. Why the sudden interest in her?"

"I wouldn't call it 'sudden interest'. Bumped into her recently and we got talking. I've seen her a bit over the years, heard quite a few stories, but never had a conversation with her until the other week. Someone told me she doesn't like people much and lives a fairly solitary life, but so far I've found her quite friendly and interesting."

"Maybe because you're not from these parts."

"And why should that make any difference?" she retorted. "You locals can be so frustratingly bogged down in ancient feuds and myths. Come on, let's get that drink."

It was too early for the after-work drinkers, but there were other patrons and Bob and Ellie found a table near a bay window overlooking the pub's orderly gardens. There was something enchanting about the smell of beer and old pubs that appealed to Ellie's sense of homeliness. It soothed her taut emotions.

"Sorry, Bob. I shouldn't have sounded off like that," she said, looking at him across the table apologetically.

"Well, I shouldn't have said what I did about locals. Anyway, who am I to talk? I've lived away from here for two decades!"

"Ah, but you were born here."

Bob nodded. "Close by, yes."

The juke box burst into life with Tom Jones' 'Delilah' as three boisterous young men entered the pub and took up seats at the bar. They seemed well known to the publican who engaged them in a lively conversation about football.

"I should be at home finishing a painting," Ellie said, lifting the wine glass.

"Someone waiting for it, is there?" Bob remarked, raising his eyebrows above mischievous eyes.

"You know me too well, Bob Caraway. Tomorrow, actually. If I'd gone straight home I'd have it done by now and Kipp and I would be enjoying a walk."

She looked out the window. The street was busy with people going in and out of shops, or hurrying along with bulging bags, push chairs and sleeping infants. Three teenage girls were stopped looking in a shop window opposite. A queue was forming at the bus stop.

Bob didn't respond for a little while, but then he said quietly, "And what if Kipp was a substitute target because you weren't there?"

Her head snapped round and she stared at him. "That's ridiculous!"

"Why? Is anything missing from the house? Windows broken?"

"I haven't checked. Kipp was all I could think about."

"If you'd been in the way of a thief you might be in hospital now," Bob said bluntly. "Ellie, I warned you earlier that you shouldn't be staying alone. Until Farley's killer is found, and especially now his will's been read, it's not safe. Come and stay at The Mill. If you don't like that idea, surely Mary would put you up."

She reached out and grasped his hand. "You're such a good friend, Bob. Maybe you're right, but what if Farley's death becomes a Highland mystery that goes on for decades? I can't stay away from home forever."

"Just come for a while, then," he said, concern in his eyes.

For a long moment she studied his familiar features, and then slowly nodded. "All right."

Evening sunlight was draping warm, golden fingers over Ellie's house when they arrived to collect what she needed. There were no indications of forced entry. In a way she wished there was, because now there were other reasons to consider, reasons she did not want to think about.

On the way out the back door, Bob stopped and bent down, picking up an envelope from the slate floor.

"You dropped this," he said, handing it to Ellie.

Frowning, she looked at the unfamiliar writing. "No, I didn't."

Ellie wasn't sure she wanted to know what was in the envelope, but she tore the end off and pulled out a single sheet of folded paper. On it was a typed note.

'It was the dog this time. You're an easier target. We know you've got the photos, so do what you're told and you'll stay in good health. Put the photos in an unmarked envelope and leave in The Chimney nook at the old

farmhouse by Jimmy's Tarn. You've got until Wed midday. Do it alone and don't tell anyone.'

It was now late Monday.

Without worrying about the threat, Ellie handed the note to Bob. "I wouldn't be surprised if this is Camden's handiwork. He doesn't know the truth when he hears it!" she said angrily.

Bob finished reading and looked up. "What photos?"

"Some of Farley's, but which ones I don't know. Jack Kennart and Camden think I've got them – and now this! I'm sick of hearing about Farley's photos!"

"I presume they were in the bags found in your barn."

"So Camden and Jack say. I never looked in those bags. They were put there without my knowledge." Her voice was hard. "Someone's determined to blame his death on me and I don't like it. If the police don't find the murderer soon, then I will!"

Flint-faced, Ellie stared at the barn and wished that she'd never got to know Farley so well. Perhaps, then, the pain wouldn't be so bad and no one would be hounding her for things she didn't have. As for Jack, she didn't believe for one minute he would solve the case. The CID chaps had been thorough, professional, and detached, but she preferred that to the local policeman who undoubtedly had too much knowledge of local affairs.

"Leave it to them, Ellie," Bob said mildly, touching her arm and handing back the note. "For a start, they have back-up, you don't. At the moment we have to decide what to do about this note."

"Not show it to Jack, that's for sure!"

"What about the CID inspector? He seems to know what he's doing and he seems approachable."

"Given that I haven't anything to leave at the old farmhouse, it's probably the sensible thing to do. Except for one thing – what if whoever sent it finds out and the next time you see me, I'm lying on a mortuary slab?" Ellie said, folding the note and putting it back in its envelope.

"No doubt you'll have police protection."

"And then they'll know I've blabbed."

"About what? The note? CID will already know about Farley's missing photos."

She looked at him for a long moment before saying thoughtfully, "I bet they don't."

"That's impossible. You would've told them when they interviewed you."

"It didn't come up. They weren't mentioned and I was so upset about Farley that I never gave them a thought. It was just photos."

"Not 'just' to someone."

"I'm beginning to realise that."

Momentarily, Ellie was in Byron's room again gazing at the pictures on the bed. What else had been on those rolls of film? And had he, by sheer chance, snatched up the ones that others desperately wanted or had Byron known exactly what he was looking for?

"Something you're not telling me?" Bob asked.

Re-focussing her attention, Ellie sighed, and shook her head. Whoever Byron was, she was not willing to reveal the secret about finding himself under The Chimney.

***

It was not the first time Ellie had stayed at The Mill. The room she occupied, situated along the hallway from Bob's, looked from its upstairs window into the back garden, and beyond to the hills. It was a comfortable room. The bed was covered in a quilt, made by Bob's mother, of yellow and blue with embroidered flowers in the centre of every second square. A soft, velvet cream armchair occupied a corner by the window and within hand's reach was a small bookcase crammed with books. She had spent a few hours in that chair, warmed by summer sun and a riveting story. For her the room had been a place of retreat when life had become, briefly, too much. Bob had protected her, fed her, and spent long hours talking with her. Not once had he intruded where he was not invited.

The rain woke her next morning, hard drops rapping against the window, and she peered over the quilt to see dark grey clouds glowering in the sky. Suddenly, she sat up. The painting! It was still unfinished.

Scrambling out of bed, she hurried down the hallway to the bathroom, had a quick shower and then, still pulling on her jumper, went quickly downstairs. The smell of toast and bacon greeted her before she reached the kitchen and she smiled. On cold days at Bob's there was often bacon, eggs and toast for breakfast.

"Morning, Ellie," he said as she entered. He put the lid on the teapot and turned towards her. "Hope you slept okay."

"Mostly. I'd still be up there if I hadn't remembered the painting."

He handed her a steaming cup of strong tea. "Just tell the buyer you've had an unexpected problem to deal with and you'll phone them in a day or two. You should be used to explanations like that by now," he said jauntily.

She threw a cork coaster at him, catching him on the shoulder. "And you're very cheeky for this time of the morning."

A few minutes later Bob put two plates with toast, bacon and eggs on the table, and sat down opposite his guest. After the first mouthful, he said, "Are you going to do anything about that note you got?"

"I suppose I'll have to, but I can't decide what."

"Give it to CID, Ellie. What else can you do? Trying to do this alone isn't smart."

It was the right thing to do, but there was a resistance inside her about following through with it that, if she was truthful, had everything to do with Byron.

"I know, but what if Jack's got a hand in it?" she asked, watching him cut a piece of bacon.

"He can be slack, misled and lazy, but he's not violent and I doubt very much if he'd help anyone bent on harming you."

"Oh?"

"Though I'm not that keen on the man at times, I will say that he's done more 'undercover' work to keep you and Farley out of trouble than anyone else in the village."

The forkful of food stopped halfway to her mouth and she lowered it to the plate. "That's a bit of a surprise considering how often he's grumbled about us."

"In *public*," Bob said, emphasising the second word. "It wouldn't be seen to be giving an outsider too much encouragement, would it?"

Ellie shook her head, indicating her understanding, but said, "I still don't trust him."

"Nor do I."

Chapter 8

Frustrated and cold, Byron came out of the tunnel from below The Chimney to be met by a blustery September wind rushing at him. It pushed him close to the edge of the precipitous rock face that fell down into the glen. Stinging rain hit his face as if he was the recipient of target practice and it occurred to him that perhaps he should have taken his old colonel's advice and begun leading a sensible civilian life. Well, he'd never done that and couldn't imagine starting now. Besides, there was Ellie. He doubted she'd be interested in him if he was a 'sensible' man.

After three weeks' absence, Byron had returned to the area on Tuesday, two days earlier. The time in London had not gone well. Two contracts sitting on Byron's desk awaiting his signature had not been posted to him as he'd requested and the date of acceptance had passed a week and a half earlier. Ray's response when asked about them resulted in Byron shouting at him for the first time. Had the fool not realised his job was at risk along with the ongoing existence of Oakes Architectural Designs? Thousands of pounds of business had gone to someone else, thousands of pounds Byron needed to survive. On top of that, Ray, an excellent draftsman, had completed drawings for a well-known and wealthy actor completely ignoring the man's specifications. He'd further insulted the man by saying that he, Ray Johnson, was the expert and the client should keep his opinions to himself. Byron had given Ray notice and he'd finished working for Oakes Architectural Designs a week ago.

There was little doubt it would take months to rebuild the company's reputation and restore the bank's faith in the business. He'd spent hours mulling over how to do it, calling close friends and colleagues for advice, and growing more disgruntled and less enthusiastic as each day passed. Two days after Ray's departure, he knew that half the problem was he no longer had much interest in keeping the business going. His heart was elsewhere.

So, with the business just in the black and taking with him what he needed, he'd returned to Scotland and rented a cottage on the outskirts of Kilcomb. The cottage was about half a mile from Ellie's house. Whether she would welcome or reject him was something he didn't dwell on. He could only hope it hadn't caused permanent damage. The silence had been unavoidable and necessary.

Tucked away from any snooping eyes were all the photographs, now developed and occupying plastic pockets. He'd sent copies of the negatives to the man who'd sent him north and another set to Colin in London.

How long before he let Ellie know he was back he hadn't decided. It depended on what he discovered in the next few days. The photographs, which had sent Colin into whoops of delight, contained images he said were connected to a World War Two mystery never fully solved. He'd rubbed his hands in glee and opened a bottle of wine to celebrate what he called 'his most-looked-forward-to piece of war sleuthing'.

Secrets concerning ships being built on the Clyde had got out of Scotland undetected during the war for at least two years, or so modern war experts surmised. However, even they had been unable to uncover much of any use regarding the Kilcomb area according to Colin. What they did know, he'd said, was that the day the discovery was made by a signalman in Edinburgh who'd tuned into an obscure channel by mistake, the signals had stopped. Who had sent them and to whom, despite intense and prolonged investigations, remained unknown. Suspicion had centred on a number of Scottish nobles and high-ranking officers, but nothing had ever been proved.

Before Byron had returned to London he'd visited Hugh and Ruth, who had been less forthcoming than on the first visit, and he had not pursued it. He'd thought it strange in light of their conversation at The Mill. However, Hugh had told him the name of Marian's German lover, Otto Herrik, to which Byron had shown nothing more than polite interest. On his return to London, he'd begun researching Otto Herrik who, he discovered, turned out to be a colonel and a spy infiltrating elite British troops in England and gaining access to sensitive information which he'd passed to Germany. During the trial in September 1949 his love affair with Marian MacAdam had unfolded, but no one had been able to find her. In the summer of 1950 a shallow grave was found in woods outside Kilcomb, not far from where she lived, but it had never been conclusively proved that it held Marian's remains. Whoever it was had been savagely attacked.

Following a narrow, almost indiscernible path, Byron made his way back down. It was an easier route than the known track to Maw's Hearth and led into the extensive property of a wealthy family whose enormous house was about a mile and a half from its base. The path hadn't been easy to find. However, intrigued by how Jack Kennart had managed to reach The Chimney's base and then back down with Farley's bags, he'd gone hunting for old maps. In Inverness yesterday he'd found a small shop specialising in maps, old and new, and history books of Scotland. On a shelf near the front window had been the Ordinance Survey maps and, a few feet away, a number of books on the history and stories of the Maw's Hearth area. With one of two maps he'd purchased spread out on the passenger's seat of his car, it hadn't taken long to work out roughly where the path began.

This morning, he'd parked where he thought Jack had and then scouted round for signs of the way up. It had taken twenty minutes before he saw bits of broken foliage and bruised grass in amongst a clump of trees, but when he'd pushed through them a jumble of big rocks offered no clues. He'd clambered over them, looking for possibilities and, wondering how Jack would have even got up the first rock, he'd jumped off and begun investigating the thickly wooded area. A few minutes later, to the left of a wide-girthed tree and deep in shadow, he noticed two small blocks covered in moss and bits of leaves sticking out from a vertical bank. At least, that's what he'd thought it was at first. The bank turned out to be part of a wall hidden by years of fallen leaf matter, moss, and low-growing, dark-loving plants. After he'd checked the steps were still secure enough to stand on, he'd gone up them and onto a flat area from which he saw the remains of another stone wall and part of a chimney. Hidden from view and lost to people's memories, he'd wondered what it had once been to be pressed so close to the foot of Maw's Hearth.

A few feet ahead lay an ill-defined path with vague footprints pressed into patches of soil. This he'd followed, twisting and turning around trees, crossing a narrow stream, and finding his way up as much by instinct as occasional marks of man's presence. Some thirty minutes later he'd found himself on the ledge where the tunnel entrance was hidden.

However, it was not the Middle Age artefacts that had drawn him back to the caves. It made no sense that Farley Orman's bags had been there or, more particularly, that Jack Kennart knew exactly where they were and had gone to collect them with Bran Orman. If Farley had put the bags there what was the reason?

Better equipped than on his first and unexpected encounter with the caves below The Chimney, Byron had taken his time exploring. Most of the artefacts were in good condition and he was undecided about what to do with the knowledge of their existence. They should be in a museum. Why had no archaeologist or historian ordered them catalogued and removed?

He had turned from them and begun searching for deeper recesses and tunnels that might indicate a link with the property at the base of Maw's Hearth. A stream ran through part of its base, eventually emptying itself into a body of water that flowed away towards the Isle of Skye. In London he had scoured every report and document he had been allowed to see, eyes and mind focused and tuned to discern the most innocuous statements as pointers to critical pieces of information. Although much of the reading had been laborious, he had not allowed himself to gloss over details and risk missing words and phrases of importance. His diligence had rewarded him. While the information he now had could not be said to be earth shattering, it was enough for him to search out that which had been hidden for so long.

Smiling, he unzipped one of his jacket pockets and slid his hand inside. His fingers touched a roll of film he'd found on the ground close to where Farley's bags had been, and a signet ring embossed with the eagle of the Third Reich. It had been in a little leather purse, half buried in the dust against the wall of the cave on the far side, perhaps dropped by someone in a hurry to leave.

He'd found nothing else, not even a tunnel or gap in the rock. Needing light and fresh air, he'd come to the surface. If there was a link with the big house below, as his old colonel and one of the documents suggested, it was not revealing itself today.

By the time he reached the foot of Maw's Hearth the rain had eased, but the cold wind persisted. There was a flask of coffee and a packet of sandwiches waiting in his car and Byron was ready for them. He spread out the map on the passenger seat, studying it while he sipped the hot liquid. There weren't a lot houses in the area and, as he had discovered, few roads.

The faint sound of a vehicle made him look up. It was getting louder. He folded the map and slid it into a pocket inside his jacket, hoping whoever it was wouldn't turn in. There were 'Keep Out, Private Property' signs near the open gate. It hadn't deterred him, but he hoped the driver of the oncoming vehicle had other places to go. He'd parked as unobtrusively as possible and knew the car could not be seen from the road. Stuffing anything in the car that would identify him, and the map, into his pockets, Byron got out and disappeared into the woods. From behind a boulder and tufts of bracken he could see enough of the car park should anyone turn in.

Less than a minute later he stared in disbelief as a familiar vehicle drove slowly into the clearing. It was Ellie. Of all the people in the district he had not expected to see her. He was unprepared. When she stepped out of the Land Rover his heart set off at a gallop. He'd missed her, thought of her every day, but this wasn't the way he'd planned their reunion. This was not the right time.

Well, she didn't know the car belonged to him so the fact of his return could remain secret a while longer. He hadn't been into the village or made any one of the few locals he knew aware that he was back.

As he watched her, he suddenly realised Kipp wasn't there. A faint alarm rang; he'd never seen Ellie without him.

She looked towards his car, studying it, and then walked over to it, peering through the front and back windows. He hoped he hadn't carelessly left anything behind she'd recognise. The road was not on the tourist route, so perhaps it was nothing more than her vibrant curiosity at work.

When she walked away, he breathed a sigh of relief. Yet, the longer he watched her, the deeper grew the yearning to be near her, to hear her voice, and to hold her. The army years were over; this was not a military assignment or any other mission requiring subterfuge. There was no logical reason why he shouldn't simply stand up and walk into the clearing as if he had been out exploring the woods. Before his mind could give him every reason why he shouldn't, Byron eased out of the crouched position. Looking across the small clearing he saw her bend over and pick up something off the ground. It looked like a business card.

He took a deep breath. It was now or not at all this morning. The words were prepared in his mind, but by the time he was two feet out of the bushes they seemed trite and contrived.

At the sound of footsteps crunching on the ground, Ellie stood up and spun round, fear in her eyes. Byron frowned, wondering if she had been expecting someone else. She stared at him and the small card in her hand floated to the ground. Then she began walking towards him. Her expression changed. He didn't know what to make of it. He prepared himself for an angry rebuke and whatever else was stewing in her heart. She would be, he felt, justified in her anger.

Stopping just out of arm's reach, he watched as she stood silently before him. Suddenly, he didn't know what to say, even though he thought he should be the first to speak. While he was still getting his words into order, Ellie said in a tight voice,

"I didn't expect to see you back in Kilcomb, Byron Oakes. How long have you been here?"

"A few days."

"Were you going to tell me?"

"Yes. I'm sorry. I couldn't contact you," he said, less gently than he intended.

Ellie stepped close to him and looked into his eyes. Quietly, without any emotion evident in her voice, she said, "Have you come to tell me that you forgot you have a wife and children in London?"

"No. There's no wife, children, ex-wife or girlfriend in London or anywhere else," he said firmly, and while he wanted to pull her against himself, he knew it would be a mistake.

"You could be lying, Byron. I really don't know much about you."

"Nor I about you, Ellie."

"So, why did you go to London?"

"Business. I told you."

She gave a curt nod. "So you did. You could've phoned."

"Difficult."

"Really? Then a note in the mail would've been fine. Why is it men are always full of excuses?" she said, and Byron detected a note of taunting.

He rose to it and replied, "Perhaps it's you women who're too suspicious of their men. Whether you believe it or not, I had legitimate reasons to go. By the way, where's Kipp?"

"At the vet's. Somebody tried to kill him."

"I'm so sorry, Ellie." His tone softened. "Any idea who?"

"Do you care?"

"Now you're being ridiculous. Of course, I care. You know that."

Unexpectedly, she looked at her watch.

"I have to go."

"In the middle of a conversation?" His voice rose in disbelief.

"Business," she snapped, turning her back on him and walking away.

The arrogance of the woman!

"Ellie!"

She spun round, her expression as impassive as The Chimney's great stack, but in her voice he heard an urgency borne of something very familiar – fear.

"I've no choice. I have to go."

"At least let me walk with you."

"No!" It came out like a shot from a gun, lodging deep in his belly. Something wasn't right. "Anyway," she said, with a little less aggression, "I've managed without you these last few weeks. In fact, I've survived a long time without you. Go back to your life in London, Byron."

Coldness crept into his being, the coldness of dismissal without being given time for redress. The saving of their fledgling love urged him to run after her, but instead he stood still and watched as she crossed the road and began disappearing into the woods opposite. Whatever her 'business' was about it was no concern of his, but he didn't believe she really wanted him to go back to London.

Sighing, Byron turned around and walked towards his car – Ellie was too independent by far. He pulled the electronic car door control out of his coat pocket and was about to push the button when he remembered the small white card on the ground. He returned to where Ellie had been standing and found it, grubby with mud, face down. Cleaning the front of it with his thumb, he looked at the expensive print and logo – *Glenn Thorley, Property Development Manager, Mayfair Hotels.*

His head jerked up. There was no sign of Ellie.

Chapter 9

It was quiet and eerie at Jimmy's Tarn, the old farmhouse looking forlorn in the grey dampness. It still had its roof and a few windows; the front door was sagging and leaning peculiarly and partly open just as it had on her last visit almost a year ago with a group of students from Edinburgh University. They had dallied there too long for her liking, but they were history buffs, sketching their passion, and the farm had been on their 'must visit' list. She couldn't imagine why. Even the locals knew little about its past. At least, so they said. Several of the group's questions had challenged her knowledge and she had undertaken some research for them. A couple of the students had been particularly interested in the Second World War era for a research grant they had been awarded, but so far she had found very little and had advised them it could be a lengthy process, even fruitless. Now she was here again, staring belligerently at the house. She'd never liked the place.

The former farm was in a small valley surrounded on three sides by low, bumpy hills. Woodland was encroaching across what had been pasture in its life as a farm. Looking down the valley, Ellie could just see the river tumbling over a rock face before continuing its journey towards Kilcomb. The road to town was on the other side of the river. There was a bridge about three hundred yards away, some of its wooden planks rotting and in need of replacing. Travel by car across it was now prohibited and the gates were locked at either end. She could have parked and walked over, but trekking across the open ground to the house did not seem like a good idea.

About a hundred yards behind the house the still water of Jimmy's Tarn was dark and unwelcoming. She turned and looked across at it and shuddered. The stories about it were numerous and varied, the oldest from the sixteenth century. It told of the disappearance of a local laird and two of his sons, supposedly lured to the tarn by the farm's tenant who couldn't pay the rent. Last year four campers had hurried back to Kilcomb claiming they'd been visited by a ghost with a sword, bent on harming them because they were trespassing – which they were.

She had never seen any ghosts and had no intention of being there long enough to see one. As it was, entering the house was daring enough, and if it hadn't been for the second letter yesterday threatening to kill Kipp and burn her house to the ground, she wouldn't have come. She'd not told Bob she'd ignored the first letter and chucked it in the bin. The second contained the same instructions.

This would be a good time for Byron to appear she thought with a degree of frustration. Why had he come back? Did he know about the note demanding Farley's photographs be delivered here? Perhaps he'd sent it. The thought evaporated as quickly as it had come. She was angry, yes, but she couldn't believe he'd lure her to Jimmy's Tarn. He'd probably never even heard of it.

Strange how he came to be at the back of Maw's Hearth today though.

There was a sudden bird cry behind her and she spun round, staring at the house, heart pounding, but there was no sign of anything other than the bird flying off from the roof. More than anything she wished Byron would come striding out of the woods towards her, but there was no human movement in any direction. Why were men never around when you needed them?

Pulling the envelope containing the photographs out of her jacket pocket, Ellie took a deep breath and strode towards the farmhouse door. She hesitated on the worn doorstep, staring into the gloomy interior with mounting trepidation.

"Thirty seconds and you'll be out, girl," she muttered, stepping quickly into the kitchen.

The old range was still there, covered in cobwebs and dust, tucked into The Chimney nook. She put the envelope in a niche in the bricks and, relieved she'd done it, turned around to leave. Her heart almost stopped.

"Hello, Ellie. I don't suppose you were expecting me," said Glenn Thorley, his mouth curled in a smile that mocked and lusted at the same time.

The sight of him, the sound of his voice repulsed her. Fear reared out of a dark room she'd locked long ago and began wrapping its chill tentacles around her body. She would *not* give in to it!

"What're you doing here?" she demanded.

He looked her up and down. "Looking at property – for a hotel, of course. What're you doing here?"

"None of your business."

"You always were an obstinate bitch. And, if I recall correctly, it got you into a lot of trouble."

Ellie glared at him, the old, complicated fear-rage wanting to dominate, but she was wiser now and did not take the bait. She forced her thoughts away from the past.

He grinned and stepped towards her. "You've got some spark. Where's the other Ellie, the one I knew?"

"None of your business."

His eyes narrowed as he came closer. "She won't be far away. People like you don't change. What were you putting behind The Chimney?"

"Also, none of your business. Or maybe it is. Maybe you're the one who sent me the note."

"I don't send notes. Go and get what you've hidden."

"Get it yourself. I've done my bit."

She could see the vein in his neck throbbing, a sign that anger was asserting itself.

"I'm sure you haven't forgotten what disobedience means."

She hadn't. Though she wanted to slap his face, she turned without acknowledging his statement and retrieved the envelope. When she gave it to him, their fingers touched briefly and she shuddered. He smiled.

"I'm glad I haven't lost my touch, Ellie. I wouldn't want you to forget those days in Somerset," he said smirking, and began pulling the envelope open.

"You made that impossible. Fortunately, most men aren't like you."

"Oh, quite the expert now. Byron Oakes next in the queue, is he? Didn't think he'd be your type."

"You're a warped, sick man," she said, wishing she had the courage to spit him in the face. Instead, she stepped away towards the door. She wanted to be out of the house.

"What game are you playing at?" he said. Anger glinted in his eyes.

"I don't play games, Glenn. It's too dangerous. You taught me that."

"Where did you get these photos?"

"I found them."

"Don't be smart with me, Ellie." His face was pinched and cold.

"They were taken by Farley. Look on the backs. He always wrote on them."

"What was he doing taking these?"

He held up three, fanned out.

Ellie stared at them. They were of Glenn and Bob at Isabella Donaldson's, her property fanning out from the feet of Maw's Hearth.

"I've no idea. I didn't look at them all." She frowned at the photos, then at Glenn. "What were you and Bob doing there?"

"Seeing the sights."

"Bob maybe, but I doubt you're the sightseeing sort." She took a step closer to the door. "How did you coerce Bob into going with you?"

There was almost no expression in his eyes. He spoke slowly. "Where did you get these photos?"

"I've told you. I found them. In a drawer in my study if you must know."

"How convenient. Left there by your dead lover, were they?"

"You're an ignorant lout, Glenn."

The vein in his neck was throbbing rapidly, and in his eyes was that peculiar mixture of hatred and arrogance that even now chilled her. Every feeling of repulsion she felt towards him began surfacing.

"You'd better go home and check he hasn't left any others like this lying around. You've got until tomorrow afternoon."

"I told Jack Kennart and Camden Orman, and now I'm telling you – I don't have any packets of Farley's photos!"

"What're you talking about?"

She stared at him, angry with herself for speaking about Jack and Camden. She assumed he knew. Now she'd have to tell him.

"Jack Kennart said he found Farley's camera bag in my barn. I didn't know it was there and I never saw inside it. Jack Kennart took it."

"Then you'd better get it back."

"I don't run errands for bullies."

He struck her hard across the face with the back of his hand. She reeled under the force of it, staggering backwards, her eyes filling with tears of pain and shock. Rage contorted his features and she turned and stumbled towards the door, but he was too quick and caught her upper arm, twisting her around to face him. Burning pain shot down her arm and back and she thought he

141

would tear her arm out of its socket. She swallowed down the cry that came from deep inside.

"Don't *ever* think you can outsmart me, Ellie. Remember what used to happen when you tried it. You didn't win then and you won't win now. If you don't get those photos, there'll be more of this."

In his voice, the malevolence that had terrorised almost all her childhood had not diminished, nor had her hatred of him, but she was older and stronger now and would not quench her anger. She wrenched her arm free.

"At least I'll be rid of you for good! You're the worst of the scum on the earth!"

The moment the words left her mouth he slammed her head against the wall and began tearing at her clothes. She could feel blood trickling down the back of her head, and for a moment thought she was going to lose consciousness.

"You think it was bad before, but you can't talk to me like that, Ellie," he hissed in her ear.

He hauled her away from the wall and threw her onto the floor. The middle of her back and shoulder blades hit the hard boards, but she let out no sound. It was instinctive – no noise, less brutality. For a second, she wished she was dead. Her body and mind responded as they had in the past, with numbness and absence.

But there was a difference this time, *she* was different, and when he knelt over her, revulsion fuelled fury and a strange new strength. She shoved herself away from him, kicking and screaming at him. He pulled her back and one of her arms flung out behind her onto a piece of wood as he leaned down towards her. Her fingers curled around the wood and she swung it at him.

It hit his hand and he let out a yell, whether in pain or rage Ellie did not care. In those few seconds she pulled herself up and stumbled towards the door, but he grabbed her by the hair and her head and body jerked sideways. The pain spread its searing tentacles through her head and shot down her neck into her shoulders. For a second she thought she was going to faint. He laughed as he released her and reached out to grasp her beneath the chin.

Ellie's eyes narrowed. Anger took on a life of its own, intense and forceful, and she hit him with the lump of wood. As it connected with his body, her rage, kept hidden for so long, now vented and she attacked him without mercy, striking him hard.

Once, twice it thumped into him and then she missed and hit the wall. He caught hold of the wood and tried to wrench it out of her hands, but she yanked it back. There was blood on him – his hands, his face. Tears were streaming down her face.

"I hate you! I hate you! I hope you die!" she screamed, and raised the lump of wood, swinging it towards his head.

He moved sideways and it thudded into his neck.

"Aagh!"

Stumbling backwards, clutching his shoulder, he landed hard on the floorboards. For a second she stared at him, uncaring about the agony she saw in his eyes. She raised the wood like a baseball bat and brought it down on his left leg below the knee.

His yell of pain filled the room and she stayed no longer, fleeing out the door.

The fresh air and rising wind were like welcoming friends and she ran, stumbling across the open land. Her head was pounding and her neck and back were throbbing with pain.

For a moment she slowed down and looked back, but there was no sign of him. However, when she reached the edge of the woods, gasping for air, she turned and gazed at the house, a forlorn and isolated building. She shivered. Perhaps he was watching her, creased into the shadows of the building, wounded and savage, plotting revenge.

Pain was increasing, and energy was seeping out of her body like water out of a ruptured container. She moved into trees where there was greater protection. All she wanted was to sit down until the throbbing went away and her head stopped swimming. In tentative exploration, she felt the back of her head and met a sticky, wet tangle of hair. Blood, red and warm, covered her fingers. The sight of it provoked an anger that had its roots deep in her past, kept safely locked away because she had always been afraid of what she might do. The desire to vent the anger and grief was still so great a cry began to leave her mouth. It was quickly shut off when she glimpsed movement near the house. Even from that distance she knew it was Glenn. He was hobbling and hunched. A strange pleasure stirred inside her. The wounder now wounded. What did *he* feel like to be a victim?

For a while he stood, moving little, as if deciding what to do. She watched and waited.

He lifted his head, looking across the neglected ground. A disjointed cry came across the clearing, startling her, affronting her.

"… sorry!"

Was he asking for *forgiveness*? His face was in his hands now; she felt nothing – no pity, no compassion, no sorrow. She would never forgive him.

Moments later he began walking slowly, limping, towards the woods. It was a ploy, all that crying out. Revenge, that's what he wanted. Ellie turned and walked deeper into the trees, pushing down rising fear of what he'd do if he caught her.

Think of something else, Ellie Madison! Watching where you're going would a good start. Don't draw attention to yourself by making a racket. Byron – perhaps he was still near Maw's Hearth. She hadn't been gone all that long. If only she'd bought one of those cumbersome new mobile phones she disliked. Right now, it seemed like a lifeline – one she didn't have. She stepped over a log and looked back. Trees blocked most of the view across the clearing to the house. Losing sight of Glenn worried her.

Forcing herself to jog, she found the faint trail she'd used earlier and turned onto it. There was a sound behind her. She turned, her heart beating frantically, but it was only a squirrel moving through the branches.

"Why can't you just appear, Byron!"

Her whisper was louder than she meant it to be. Why had she been *so* stupid? She'd known going alone wasn't sensible, but she was strong now and the remaining Iron Musketeer. What a lot of rubbish that was! She hadn't counted on Glenn arriving and turning her resolve upside down. Her body was hurting now, pain slowed her down.

She shouldn't have got on her high horse with Byron. *Stupid!* Glancing around, she listened. No sound of anyone walking towards her, but making assumptions because Glenn was a city boy was a mistake. Who knew what kind of stalking skills he'd acquired in all the years she'd seen nothing of him.

The woods and glens of the Highlands, for so long safe and welcoming sanctuaries, were now breached by acts of violence. It was over a month since Farley's death and the police seemed to have few clues about where to go with the investigation. Jack and Tim had local things to deal with besides Farley's death, and now she'd been attacked by Glenn Thorley over a few photographs.

She shuddered and suddenly doubled over. Nausea rose like an evil tide and her stomach rid itself of its contents onto the ground. Turning away, she fell to her knees, tears running over her cheeks, silent. Mustn't make any sound. Don't want to draw attention to herself. They'd know then she'd been a bad girl. It wasn't my fault, it *wasn't!*

A bird flew out of a tree, startling her, drawing her back into the present. Her head snapped round. He must've heard her. He wouldn't give up until he found her. Sit still, be silent. But there was no sound of human movement. Perhaps, for once, he was the beaten one, unable to follow.

She desperately wanted to see Byron appear through the foliage, Kipp by his side. Safety.

Forcing her thoughts elsewhere she wondered what was in the photos in Farley's bags. Others seemed keen to get their hands on them. They couldn't all be of the Donaldson property and she was convinced Byron knew more than he'd said. There was little doubt he had more photos. She had to get hold of them.

It took Ellie another ten minutes to reach the clearing beneath Maw's Hearth. Hers was the only vehicle parked there, unseen from the road behind trees. Dismayed, she stared at the spot where Byron's car had been. It hadn't occurred to her that he'd leave.

She climbed into the Land Rover, pulled the door closed and sat with her face in her hands. There were no tears. A heavy weariness and aching, a wounded body sapped of energy. Her mind could not decide what to do next. Everything that had happened at the farmhouse came together like a movie, unedited and raw, full of brutality and hatred. She wanted to stop it running, but couldn't and a dull, empty ache emerged from its hiding place rekindling memories she had long put away.

She'd heard people say that time heals, but it wasn't true. Time was a measure of passing minutes, days, years. At their passing the pain lessened, but that didn't mean the wound was healed. Ellie knew hers wasn't.

By now her head was pounding. Turning the rear-vision mirror towards her, she looked at her face – bruising and drying blood covered almost one side. It was time she went home.

As she put the key in the ignition the sound of a vehicle travelling slowly along the road restrained her from starting the engine. Instead, she sat very still hoping that whoever it was would keep going. As the vehicle got nearer it began slowing, then pulled off the road and parked across the clearing's entrance. She could just see it and wound down the window a little. The car's engine was still running and through the front passenger window she saw the outline of a man in a brown jacket hunched over – Glenn. He was talking into a phone.

She wound up the window, slid down in the seat and prayed he wouldn't get out or decide to drive into the clearing. For several minutes she stared at the vehicle, her eyes aching and a peculiar, disembodied wooziness creeping over her.

On finishing the call Glenn lit a cigarette, staring out through the windscreen. He looked round and her heart almost stopped, but a few minutes later he drove off in the direction she would take. It was fifteen minutes before she drove slowly out of the clearing and down the road, wary of finding Glenn parked along the way. How he was driving at all she didn't know.

"I hope you're suffering," she said loudly, but a minute later she wondered how she was going to get home. Her body was suffering too.

About halfway to Kilcomb, Ellie's concentration began waning and she found it difficult to focus. The loud blare of a car horn shocked her back into reality; she had swerved across the other side of the road as someone was pulling out from a farm gate. Her speed was erratic. All she could think about was getting to Kilcomb and the doctor. Less than two miles from the small town she heard a strange wailing sound behind her. Forcing herself to look in the rear vision mirror she saw a blue flashing light. An instant later her body jerked backwards and forwards as her vehicle slid off the road into a ditch. She was in so much pain she didn't care.

When Constable Ashby opened the door, she saw his surprised expression, but she had no energy to speak and sat there, eyes closed, oblivious to anything that was going on around her. As if from afar came the sound of his voice and then his feet running back to the police car.

Slow tears slid down her cheeks. She wished Byron had followed her.

***

In the late afternoon her eyes flickered open. Where was she? She frowned, grimacing as sharp pain shot across her forehead and into her cheek. Her head felt funny, tight, and for a few seconds she couldn't focus. What had happened? Where was she? Then it came back, brazen in its detail. She shuddered.

"Hello, there," said a familiar voice gently.

146

Barely moving her head, Ellie saw Bob smiling at her and beside him was Mary.

"We've been *so* worried about you, Ellie," she said, squeezing her hand. "Young Tim Ashby said you'd had a car accident."

"Now, Mary, all in good time," Bob said. "She needs rest."

Ellie gave a little smile; it hurt. Gingerly she touched her cheek, around her eyes and her forehead and then her head. It was bandaged.

"How long have I been here?" she asked weakly.

"About four hours," Mary said. "The doctor gave you something to make you sleep. Is there much pain?"

"Some." Her eyelids drooped. Drowsily, she said, "Bob, can you find out how Kipp is. Won't like being at the vet's."

"Of course."

"Is there anything you need?" Mary's voice seemed a long way off.

"Don't... know. Where... where's my car?"

"At the garage. Jack wants to make sure it's safe for you to drive."

For a moment she didn't answer. He'd look through it, she was sure. Her brain was so foggy she couldn't remember what was in the glove box and seat pockets.

"We'll be away now, Ellie," Mary said quietly. "Just ring if you think of anything you want or need doing. I'll pop in tomorrow. 'Bye, love." She bent down and kissed her on the forehead.

Bob took her hand and leaned close. "Don't worry about Jack," he whispered. "I'll take care of the Land Rover."

Ellie squeezed his hand in response and was asleep by the time they were in the corridor.

It seemed only minutes later that she woke up, but the hands on the wall clock were pointing to quarter-past six. Was it evening or morning? And what day was it? While she was still trying to work it out a nurse came in.

"Hello, Ellie. I'm Deirdre and you're stuck with me this evening," she said brightly as she picked up the chart at the end of the bed. "Are you hungry?"

"No, but I'd love a cup of tea."

"Right you are. How's the pain?"

"Okay. Will I be in long?"

"That's for the doc to say. He'll be in to see you a bit later."

With that she disappeared through the door and ten minutes later one of the kitchen ladies arrived with tea and a piece of cake. Things were a bit unconventional at Castlebay Hospital.

Ellie wondered how long it would take Glenn to find out where she was and come to visit. She closed her eyes and found herself back in the woods, watching him cry out. She'd never forgive him – never! If he limped for the rest of his life she didn't care. He deserved far more than that. Perhaps he'd leave Kilcomb for a while, give his body time to heal and return when he was fit enough to take his revenge. One thing was certain – he wouldn't be keen for anyone to know how he got his injuries.

Was he the one who'd attacked Kipp? She certainly wouldn't put it past him. He had little respect for human life, and an animal meant nothing to him other than a means to cause people anguish. She frowned then. There was something lurking in her memories that would not come forward. Had he lied about sending the notes? She hated him. She wished she'd killed him!

Memories were beginning to surface like sewage kept too long in a cesspit that couldn't take any more in. She didn't want to remember! It was too much. Groans rose from deep in her heart, rising to her throat. She leaned forward, closing her eyes. Everything was submerged beneath the pain and the fight to stop entwined memories of the past and present tormenting her.

Then she heard his voice, the softest vapour reaching her troubled heart. His hand covered hers, and gently, so gently, he drew her against himself and held her close until the lid closed over the cesspit. How long she leaned against him, at times shivering, she neither knew nor cared, but he was there and that was all that mattered.

When she slowly drew away Ellie looked up into Byron's face and saw such sadness that she almost burst into tears.

"I saw Bob in the street. He told me you were in a car accident," he said, squeezing her hand, not intruding into those tender places.

"The Land Rover went into a ditch."

"Was that before or after you got those injuries?"

"It's none of your business. Anyway, what kind of question is that?" she said, but there was no bite in her voice.

"A serious one. And yes, it is my business."

She stared at his wristwatch. Had it been all that time ago since she'd run from the farmhouse? "After," she said quietly.

When she looked up he seemed to be hesitating. He let go of her hand, stood up, and retrieved his wallet from his back trouser pocket. Out of the wallet he withdrew a card, glancing at it for a moment before handing it to her.

"You dropped this in the clearing. I found it after you'd disappeared into the trees."

When Ellie saw Glenn Thorley's name she screwed the card up and hurled it across the room. The scenes at Jimmy's Tarn began replaying; her body tensed and she glared at the image of him in her mind, hating him and wishing he was dead in Farley's place. If she'd found him at Maw's Hearth instead of Farley, there would have been rejoicing instead of grief.

"Ellie?"

Her head snapped round, eyes blazing, and she opened her mouth to pour out contempt and hatred. Pain shot through her head and down the length of her body, and the wounds on her cheek stretched and bled, but the eyes that met hers did not belong to Glenn Thorley nor were they filled with mockery and arrogance. The rage subsided.

She reached out and touched Byron's hand. "I'm sorry about what I said in the clearing, but I was so mad at you for disappearing. I don't want you to go back to London."

"I'm glad," he said, yet his eyes were troubled. "Why did you go off on your own? I would've gone with you."

"I know that now, but I thought I'd only be half an hour. I was hoping no one would be there. Thought I could handle it even if there was."

"Was it Thorley?"

She glanced away, swallowing. "Yes. He was at Jimmy's Tarn."

"I saw that on the map. Looks isolated," Byron said, frowning, disturbed that she was there alone with Glenn, but he said nothing about his fears. "Isn't it a farm?"

"Used to be. It's been abandoned for years. I don't like the place. It's eerie and lonely."

"So, what made you go there?"

Ellie wasn't sure she wanted to tell him. "I've never known anyone to ask as many questions as you do. Is that all they taught you in the army?"

He shook his head and she knew by his expression he would not be put off by female delay tactics.

"Just tell me, Ellie."

For a second she hesitated. "I got a note." She didn't say it was the second one. "It said I had until three o'clock today to put the photos from Farley's bag in an envelope and leave them in the fireplace nook in the kitchen."

"All of them?"

"I don't know. I found a fat-ish packet of his photos in my desk and took them. Only looked at the first two and assumed Farley left them there ages ago. Jack Kennart and Camden think I've got whatever it is they want," she said, studying his face. "You've got photos that were in the bags."

He nodded. "Some."

"Have you got them all developed?"

Byron nodded, but she sensed he was reluctant to confide in her. He said, "Did Thorley open the packet while you were there?"

"Yes. He showed me three with him and Bob. They were taken at the Donaldson property."

"Bob? I wouldn't have thought Glenn was his kind of friend. And what's the Donaldson property?"

"Isabella Donaldson owns the land at the foot of Maw's Hearth. It goes all the way to the sea. She inherited it from her father. There've been rumours of financial difficulties. Her husband's in business – big business – and he's not what you'd call a friend of the environment. She is – and she's on the board of Scottish Natural Heritage."

"Does Bob do business with them?"

"Yes. Caters for all their important functions."

"Then maybe they were just there at the same time."

"Maybe. Glenn wasn't very pleased when he saw the photos."

She kept her tone bland, showing no emotion in her voice or eyes; he didn't seem to notice.

"Being spied on isn't everyone's idea of fun."

"You don't know if that's what Farley was doing!" she snapped, defending him, affronted by Byron's summation of the situation.

"I'd say if Glenn wasn't happy about it, then it's a possibility. Wouldn't you?"

"I've no idea."

There was an awkward silence between them. The thought of Farley spying on anyone was ludicrous, but then she remembered the photos of the Lawsons. Had they known he was photographing them?

"Promise me you won't go off on such crazy errands again."

"I've been doing it a long time, but I'll do my best. It's just…"

"You're impetuous. Your mother told you so," he said with a resigned smile, shaking his head. "Look, Ellie, this is serious stuff. I wasn't in London twiddling my thumbs and I didn't like what I found. You have to be more careful."

"But what're they, whoever 'they' are, after? What's so important about Farley's photos of wild places and lochs?"

"That's not all he took photos of," he said, lowering his voice.

"What then?" However, before he could reply, she said, "Hello, Jack. Come to ask me about my little accident, have you?"

Byron turned around without hurry and Ellie thought the policeman looked less than pleased to see him there.

"Aye, I have. Nasty bumps you've got there. Hit your head on the steering wheel, did you? One day you'll take my advice, Ellie, and wear your seat belt," he said, standing at the end of the bed. "How long they keeping you in?"

"Don't know. I'm waiting for the doctor to come. Hopefully they'll let me out in the morning."

"D'you want to tell me how you ended up in the ditch?"

For a second she hesitated. "I dozed off."

"Unlike you," he said with some scepticism. "Any other vehicles involved?"

"Hasn't Tim Ashby given you a report?"

"I'm asking you, Ellie."

"No, there weren't. It's very simple – I dozed. The Land Rover went into the ditch," she said, and leaned too heavily against the pillow. The pain that encased her head shocked her and she sat upright, eyes closed, until it ebbed.

"I'm guessing you've got more than a bump to the back of your head," Jack said. "What happened?"

"I hit it against the door. Jack, it's a piffling incident. You don't need to get the pilliwinks out to make me say someone ran me off the road when they didn't," she said, frustrated with him and the pain. "It's not a police matter."

"It will be if I find it has any connection wi' Farley Orman."

He snapped his notebook closed, put the pen back in his pocket and with a nod towards Byron left the room.

"Pilliwinks?" asked Byron, eyebrows arched.

"Medieval torture instruments. They were used for squeezing fingers and thumbs. Jack told me. He studied medieval history at university."

"That's interesting. I wonder why…"

"What?"

There was no answer.

"Byron, are you here?"

He nodded slowly, deep in contemplation. Eventually, he said, "Farley Orman's bags weren't the only things in that cave. There were a lot of historical artefacts that looked to me as if they were from the Middle Ages."

"What!" she exclaimed, and then lowered her voice as a nurse poked her head around the corner of the door and told them visiting hours were finishing. "What're you talking about? How come I've never heard about this?"

"I don't know. I wonder if Farley knew about them, or maybe someone took his bags there after he was killed. Odd thing to do though," he said, the frown deepening the furrows across his brow and fine lines like bicycle spokes branching out from the corner of his eyes. He looked at her thoughtfully. "We can't talk about this here. I'll come and get you when you're discharged. Ring me on the mobile when you're about to leave."

"Okay," she said, not wanting him to go.

Outside in the corridor the bell rang as a last warning for visitors. In parting, Byron touched her cheek, his eyes searching hers.

"I'm for you, Ellie, not against you."

Chapter 10

The garage owner, a tall, solid man with bright copper hair and beard, was not pleased when he found Byron looking over the Land Rover next morning.

"Hey, you! What d'you think you're doing?"

The man's Scottish accent was so strong it took Byron a few seconds to work out what he'd said.

"Checking Ellie Madison's vehicle. I'm a friend of hers."

"Never seen you before. Besides, it's involved in a police enquiry."

"Oh? She only ran into a ditch. A bit of panel beating and a wheel balance and it'll be fine."

"An expert in mechanics, are you?"

"Expert no, but I've driven a few different kinds of vehicles," Byron said in an off-hand manner. "When will it be ready?"

"None of your business. I'll speak to Ellie when she comes."

"Who brought it in?"

The man glared at him. "Who'd you think? The police."

"Driven here, was it?"

"No, it came by itself! Now, get on your way. I've work to do."

Without waiting to see if his unwanted visitor left, the big man returned to the vehicle he was working on. Byron had no doubt that the minute he was gone he'd be on the phone to Jack Kennart.

He took one last look at the damaged left front, peered in through the windows and left. There had been no obvious evidence underneath the vehicle that it had been tampered with and, for the moment at least, he believed Ellie that she had dozed off at the wheel.

He was tempted to go and see Jimmy's Tarn for himself. It was an odd place to pick up photos, but then Thorley was not an ordinary man even though the comments he'd made about Ellie at The Mill were of the sort men of arrogance, and often little self-respect, made. Ellie didn't seem the sort to keep quiet if a man approached her with unwanted attention, but no one would hear a woman's screams out there and if she died, she might never be found.

From across the road he heard a voice hail him and he looked up to see an older woman waving. She stepped off the kerb and walked over to him. She looked vaguely familiar and he supposed he had seen her about the village.

"Hello, young man," she said, puffing slightly as she reached him and held out her hand. "I'm Olga Erskine. I've seen you about with Ellie Madison and I've just heard she's in hospital. Is she all right?"

"I'm Byron Oakes," he said, shaking her hand. "Ellie should be out today."

"What's the matter wi' her?"

"Her vehicle went into a ditch. She banged her head against the door."

Olga peered at him through half closed eyes. "And?"

"There's no 'and'."

"Young man, I wasn't born yesterday. Ellie's not the sort of person to drive off the road into a ditch, and a wee bump doesn't usually land you in hospital. Did the car have a puncture?"

"No."

She looked at him with some exasperation. "Are you sworn to secrecy or are you being plain obstinate?"

"Neither. I don't know you."

"A good answer. You're not a military man, are you?"

"No."

"Hmm. I'd say you probably have been. You've got officer bearing. I was in the army during the war and rarely get it wrong."

He smiled at this and was about to respond when his phone rang. "Excuse me. Hello, this is Byron. Hi, Ellie. Fine, I'll be there then. Bye."

When he looked at the woman again faded blue eyes were watching him intently. It seemed as if she was weighing him up, whether to ascertain his worthiness as Ellie's friend or his stamina as a man, he couldn't decide.

"Tell Ellie I was asking after her," she said, still peering at him. "Some folk did not like what she and Farley were doing. And there are things about Farley…"

She closed her mouth and although her expression gave little away, he had no doubt she'd deliberately used those words.

"What things?" he asked.

"That Ellie doesn't know about."

It was his turn to study her. Portly, dressed in a long red skirt, red, blue and green jumper with a white cotton collar popping up above it around her neck, the intelligence and sharpness in her eyes didn't go with what she was wearing. Stupid thing to think. Passing her on the street, Byron would have thought little about her other than she was another old woman trying to get through the day.

He decided to be as direct as she had been. "Is there a reason you've said this to me and not to Ellie?"

"Ah," she responded, nodding and smiling. "An astute man. Attached, but not ruled by emotion. I like that."

"What is it you want to tell me, Mrs Erskine?"

"Farley Orman didn't only take pictures of trees and pretty Highland country. He was digging around about the war and some people here don't like it. A newspaper was going to pay him a lot of money."

"How d'you know?"

"No one takes any notice of an old woman in a pub corner, Mr Oakes," she said, patting his arm. "Now then, I've to be off."

"Have you told the police about Farley?"

"No doubt they already know," she said, frowning. "Take my advice, young man, and don't meddle in matters that are nothing to do wi' you."

"But I am involved, Mrs Erskine. I was with Ellie when Farley's body was found. You'll know that, of course," he said pointedly, annoyed by her manner. "That's probably why you've told me."

"Just look after Ellie, Mr Oakes."

As she turned and walked back across the road there was a car hoot behind him, but he took no notice until the car stopped beside him. It was Bob Caraway.

"Hello, Byron," he said, as he got out of the car. "Did you go and see Ellie?"

They shook hands as Bob joined him. "Yes. She's just phoned. They're releasing her in an hour."

"And you're going to get her." A faint shadow crossed his face.

Byron made no comment and nodded. "D'you know Olga Erskine?" he asked, changing the subject.

"Yes. She comes to The Mill every now and then and I drop bread off to her if she can't get out. She's a bit of a loner. A few people around here don't like or trust her. There's a rumour she poisoned the pub owner's son some years back, but apparently no one could prove it," he said, waving a hand to someone out of Byron's view. "I saw her walking across the road just now."

"She wanted to know what'd happened to Ellie."

He frowned, looking peeved. "Sometimes this village really gets on my nerves. News goes around almost before it's happened. How on earth could Olga have heard about Ellie? She barely knows her – or you. What did you tell her?"

"That the Land Rover went into a ditch and Ellie bumped her head. Olga's not the shy kind."

"Far from it. She's a bit strange, but she's not daft as some villagers think."

"What's her husband like?"

"From what I've heard, Mr Erskine found the secretary more to his liking than his wife and went off with her decades ago," he said, raising his eyebrows. "Olga's lived alone since then. Never had any children to my knowledge and never mentions family. I've heard she grew up in Edinburgh." He shrugged. "We're all odd in our own way I suppose."

"I guess so." Byron hesitated. "Did you want to go and fetch Ellie, Bob?"

Byron wasn't sure what to make of the bemused expression on the baker's face when he answered.

"Would love to, but I've got a couple of deliveries to make. You can tell her that Kipp will be able to go home in a couple of days. I know she's worried about him." He half turned towards his car. "Try and make her see sense about staying on her own at the house. I don't think it's safe for her, but she won't listen to me."

"I'll do my best."

He watched as the other man got in the car and drove away. In the short time he'd known him Bob had been friendly, helpful and seemed the sort anyone could rely on in times of crisis. A genuine, decent bloke, he thought as he crossed the road and walked along the pavement towards the post office. And he was probably right – Ellie shouldn't be alone in her house. Perhaps her friend Mary Nevin would put her up for a bit. If he was truthful, he couldn't see Ellie taking his advice any more than she'd taken Bob's.

Neither the postmistress, Carrie Ross, nor her only other customer, a smartly dressed, slim woman with her back to him, heard him enter. The postmistress was behind a partition. Byron made himself scarce behind a tall row of shelves filled with Post Office materials.

"If you continue your slanderous gossip about my father I'll take you to court!" said the well-spoken customer.

Byron had heard the voice before.

"Just you try it. There's more than one wee skeleton in the Orman cupboard," said Carrie, her voice hard.

Of course – Fenella Orman.

"My father was a decent human being trying to preserve our heritage. All you're capable of is spreading rumours and destroying lives. You're pathetic! Look at you – going to fat, dressed from a charity shop, and wearing cheap, sluttish lipstick."

"I would not be casting such a slur on me. I know all about your little affair wi' that southerner Glenn Thorley. And he a married man from what I've heard. No doubt it's the money you're after," Carrie said caustically.

Byron cringed at the tone.

"The trouble with people like you," Fenella snapped, "is that you dig your muck out of the pigsty and then smear it over the whole village. Even Ellie Madison has more breeding than you!"

"And I imagine you've got to know her quite well, her being so close to your father. It's not a secret. And you can't be happy about him leavin' all that money to her. She was only his wee bit o' baggage, wasn't she? Not so much left for you and your brothers."

For a second there was no response.

"That's because he had to pay you to keep your mouth shut about something. You're a greedy, malevolent woman who ought to be hung, drawn and quartered. In fact, I could arrange that!"

She marched out of the post office, slamming the door behind her. Before Byron had taken a step to move from behind the shelving, he heard Carrie scuttle across the floor. Seconds later she was on the phone.

"It's me. Guess who's just been in? Fenella Orman. She threatened…"

She stopped as Byron stepped into view, a posting bag from the shelf in his hand. "I have to go. I'll call you later."

"I've come to get my mail and post this," he said, looking straight at her as he put a small padded bag and the new one on the counter.

In her eyes he saw uncertainty.

"I did not hear you come in. Have you been here long?"

"A couple of minutes."

"Don't take our local quibblings too seriously." She attempted a smile, but looked instead as if she had eaten something unsavoury.

"I'd like my mail, thanks."

She glared at him, turned away and disappeared into another room. A few seconds later she returned with several envelopes, one of which required his signature. "It's from London. Government business," she said.

"And mine," Byron said pointedly as he paid first-class postage, stuck the stamps on the bag and began walking towards the door.

"I wouldn't go repeating any of what you heard," the postmistress said to his back.

With a hand on the doorknob, Byron turned his head and looked at her intently without speaking. She quickly busied herself with paperwork on the counter.

"You certainly will and I'm making no such promise."

Her head snapped up, but he was already halfway out of the door by the time she opened her mouth to reply.

Outside in the fresh air Byron took a deep breath. The woman was a menace to society, a viper waiting to strike at any moment. How much of what she said was true was beyond his knowing, but he hated the way she'd talked about Ellie. The thought of the countless lives she had damaged through her loose and loquacious tongue infuriated him. When he glanced through the window, he wasn't in the least surprised to see her on the phone. He turned away in disgust and shoved the bag of photos into the letterbox.

Ahead of him, and standing outside the bank, Byron saw Camden Orman with his sister. Fenella was jabbing him in the shoulder with her finger. Not particularly wanting to be seen by them, Byron stepped off the pavement between two parked cars ready to cross the road and head in the direction of his car parked near the garage. As he looked for traffic, Camden grabbed Fenella's wrist and just as quickly let it go, turning suddenly and getting into his car. Without checking if anything was coming he drove off, narrowly missing a motorcyclist who swerved out of the way and almost ran into a butcher's truck coming the other way. Fenella was still standing on the pavement, taking no notice of her brother's dangerous behaviour, more concerned it seemed to Byron with straightening her jacket.

The snippet of conversation about Glenn Thorley came to the forefront of his thoughts, and he admitted to a certain amount of admiration for the way Fenella had handled the woman's sniping. At no point had she denied or confirmed Carrie's suspicions about Thorley.

Ellie was waiting for him in the foyer of the Castlebay Hospital and her eyes lit up when she saw him. His heart beat with pleasure.

"Sorry I'm late," he said, "I got held up in the post office."

"Carrie Ross?"

Byron nodded. "Has she always been like that?"

"So I've been told."

He took her hand and together they walked out into the pale sunshine. A breeze came in off the water riffling through their hair, the salt in the air depositing its tangy, unseen crystals on lips and skin. When they reached the car, Byron gently brushed her bruised face with the tips of his fingers.

"Let's walk for a bit if you're up to it," he said.

"I'm fine, Byron. Don't fuss. I'm not used to it."

"No one's ever accused me of fussing before. Are you sure you've got the right word?"

"Yes."

Byron laughed and they set off towards the water.

Seagulls screeched above and around them, wheeling and turning in the buoyant air, while boats bobbed on the water. There were men and a few boys sitting on the end of the wharf with their fishing lines flung out into the water, and boats came and went across the bay. A number of people, perhaps holidaymakers, were walking along the shore, their children dashing in and out of the water's edge.

Suddenly remembering Bob's message, Byron said, "I saw Bob this morning and he said to tell you that Kipp can go home in a couple of days."

"Two days! I can't not see him for that long! Will you take me to the vet's before heading back to Kilcomb?"

"Of course."

Ellie did not walk as boldly as she usually did, and Byron noticed that at times her expression was tinged with pain. Anger stirred in him and he opened his mouth to ask how a bump on the head could affect her walking. He wasn't quick enough.

"How d'you know the stuff you saw under The Chimney is from the Middle Ages?" she asked unexpectedly.

The question surprised him.

"I double checked with a friend in London. He's a lecturer in medieval history."

"You told him what you found?" There was incredulity in her voice.

"Not the precise details, no."

"It should all be in a museum."

"Should it?" Though he'd wondered the same thing.

"Yes. It's part of Scotland's history. I'd like to see it."

"You've only just come out of hospital. And don't tell me you feel fine."

"I'm not going to, but I want to go up there."

"That's plain. Give it a few days, a week maybe."

"Were you this hard on people in the army?"

Byron studied her for a moment. "That was a different life, Ellie. I couldn't afford to be soft when people's lives depended on me."

The words seemed to sober her and she nodded slowly, her brown eyes thoughtful.

"That's where you found Farley's bags," she said. "Perhaps if I go there something will make sense about his death. I know he wasn't always popular, but he was one of my best friends and I want to know why he was killed."

"So do I."

"I miss him, Byron. We were close and talked about lots of things. I miss the sound of his voice and his determination to see injustice righted. He was a fighter, but he loved the little things as well – the first snowdrop, the scent of the heather. Other people didn't see that side of him often." She took a deep breath as if she didn't want to cry and began walking again.

They continued on without speaking, a vague uneasiness between them. When he was in London, Byron had questioned himself repeatedly about the sanity of pursuing a relationship with Ellie Madison when Farley's death was so recent. There was nothing he could do about that. He would have to be patient. He knew little about her and he had to remember why he was there.

Sunshine suddenly poured out over the town as the blanket of cloud slipped slowly away across the bay to cast its shadow over the valleys and lonely, rugged higher peaks. Indomitable, strong guardians of a precious treasure they were unwilling to relinquish, Byron regarded them with considerable respect. Their crevices and folds, dark and deep caves and little-known valleys, concealed secrets of unknowable joys and disasters lost long ago in history.

The water looked bluer and more inviting in the brightness as it lapped at the shore, leaving evidence of its presence in the darker, damp sand. Seagulls, busy and squabbling, argued in the air above the waves or on the beach where they left dozens of thin footprints in the sand. Others, bobbing about on the water, seemed disinterested, as if they were part of another family.

"An Olga Erskine was asking after you," Byron said, dispersing the silence between them. "She bailed me up on the pavement."

Ellie chuckled. "She did the same to me. She's quite a character."

"That's one way of putting it. How well d'you know her?"

"Hardly at all. I've seen her around, but the first conversation I had with her was right after Farley's death. Why d'you ask?"

"Just curious. She wanted to know why you were in hospital. I got the distinct impression she didn't believe you just had a bump on the head. That's what I told her," he added when she glanced at him, eyebrows raised.

"Odd she disbelieved you."

"She thought I was fobbing her off – which I was. In fact, she said so."

"I went on a picnic with her and the local vicar, Paul Shepley, when you were in London. I think she must've been a feisty young woman."

"How long has she been here?"

"She said she'd come sometime after the war. I forget when."

"Well, she seems to like you. She told me to look after you."

Ellie stopped and studied him. There was, he thought, a strange mixture of fear and hope in her eyes, like a deer that wanted to trust but didn't quite know how. Unexpectedly, he felt a rush of protectiveness for her that made him take her hand. He half expected she would pull away, but she did not.

They stood without speaking as waves lapped behind them and the cries of children and gulls filled the air. The sun warmed his back, stirring distant memories of another beach and another life where nothing was certain, especially the safety of his men.

There didn't seem the need for words as they walked up the steps at the other end of the beach, and back towards the car along a street where shops and cafés facing the bay were doing lively business. They stopped and had coffee at a small place Ellie liked before returning to the car and heading off to the vet's.

Once the vet had finished quizzing Ellie about the state of her health, she introduced Byron to Jim Plowden. He was a tall, lanky man with a mop of blond hair, greying at the temples, and a pair of eyes that were so blue Byron couldn't help wondering how many women had made more trips than necessary to the animal hospital. He looked about sixty, but was still a handsome man.

His attention wandered from the conversation between Ellie and Jim about Kipp's well-being to the paintings on one of the walls. They were so exquisite in detail and colour he thought he would feel the feathers, the fur, and the silky ears beneath his fingertips if he touched the canvases.

"Amazing, aren't they?" said Jim's deep voice behind him. "They liven up the old place no end. Never would've been allowed in my younger days."

"They're fantastic. Who's the artist?" He glanced at the life-like litter of fox cubs and in the corner of the painting was a small signature. He turned around to find Ellie looking strangely sheepish. "They're magnificent, Ellie. Why aren't you famous?"

She laughed and, if he wasn't mistaken, a faint blush tinged her cheeks.

"Don't be daft."

"He's not," said a woman sitting in the waiting area, a cat box by her feet. "I bet the queen would have you paint her corgis in a flash if she could see these."

"That's kind, thank you."

"Kind? Pah! You don't know your worth, girl!"

"Mrs Thurlow's right there. It's time you were noticed, Ellie," Jim said, hooking his arm around hers. "Now, come and see your boy. He's been pining away and wasting my good food."

Byron followed them into the 'ward' as Jim called it. The second Kipp saw Ellie his eyes lit up and his tail thumped on the floor of the pen, his whimpers and barks filling the room. When Ellie knelt down beside him he leaned against her.

"It's so good to see you, boy," she said, smiling, kissing the top of his head and stroking his back. "You'll be home soon."

"Just a couple more days, old boy, then you can go home to junk food," Jim said, rolling his eyes, a smile beginning.

"I'll ignore that," Ellie said, shaking her head. "Right now I'd like to beat the living daylights out of whoever hurt Kipp."

Byron and Jim exchanged glances.

"Against the law I'm afraid, though it's somewhat lax in these parts," the vet said, scowling. "Any idea who could've done it?"

"Maybe."

"Don't do anything rash, Ellie. Last time…"

He stopped. She looked up, glaring at him. Byron glanced from one to the other; neither seemed to notice him.

"Those louts would've destroyed the remains of the medieval village and that poor animal would've died – as you well know. I could tell a few stories about you and Farley the council haven't a clue about, so don't come the squeaky-clean vet with me."

"Wouldn't dream of it. But let the police have a go at earning the money we pay them – isn't that what our taxes do? – and *you* stay out of trouble."

"If we waited for the authorities to get off their backsides any historic remains would be vandalised or completely destroyed. Not to mention the loss of wildlife," Ellie said sharply.

Jim sighed. "I know, but *be* careful – and call me if you need help. You're too independent by far."

"I've had to be. Not many people in my life have proved trustworthy."

"There are good people on the council, Ellie, and you've friends at SNH – me for one."

Ellie nodded. "I've been asked to speak at the meeting next week. Mayfair Hotels are putting in another proposal for a conference centre near Maw's Hearth." She glanced at Byron. "D'you know anything about that?"

There was a surprised look from the vet, but Byron ignored it. "A bit."

"Care to enlighten me?" Jim said, a hand on the door to reception.

"Maybe."

"I'll be in Kilcomb on Friday night. Have a drink with me in the pub."

"I'll let you know."

Jim studied him for a moment, nodded, and opened the door for his visitors. As they went through, a man and a boy with two Saint Bernard puppies came into the reception area.

"Hi, you two. This the latest litter?" Ellie asked, walking across the room to speak with the puppies' owners.

"Good timing," said Jim quietly to Byron. "She needs to look after herself, not go off trying to right the wrongs of Scotland."

"Sounds like you both do a bit of that."

Jim's expression hardened. "I can't abide cruelty and neither can she. Was it a rescue mission that landed her in hospital?"

"No. The Land Rover went into a ditch."

"Brakes fail?"

"Not sure."

"I wouldn't be surprised if that lot from Mayfair are involved in this."

The new customers and Ellie turned towards them and began walking across the floor in their direction.

"Have to keep going, Byron. See you in a couple of days, I hope."

Out in the fresh air again Ellie and Byron took a different route to Kilcomb than he'd been on before, she directing him down narrow lanes, over an ancient bridge above clear flowing waters, and up roads that followed the curves of hills and fields, eventually flattening out across the top of the hills. Bracken, its summer green turned bronze, swept across the landscape. They passed a few black-faced sheep nibbling grass, their wool a startling white against the rich-coloured bracken. A few minutes later he drove into a lookout, a semi-circular stone wall protecting distracted drivers from disappearing over the rim into the valley below.

"This is magnificent," he said, reaching for the binoculars in the glove box.

"Yes, it is." She opened the door and got out. She had been quiet during the drive, thinking about Kipp he supposed.

Byron walked towards the wall and raised the binoculars to his eyes, engrossed in the peaks and glens, the lochs, a mansion in a wide valley, and a farm near a bridge. It was a full couple of minutes before he realised that Ellie was not giving a commentary on what he was seeing. In fact, she wasn't beside him at all.

He looked around. She was sitting on a wooden seat several yards away, staring into the distance. When he reached her she did not look up.

"Do you want to talk?" he asked, sitting down beside her, but not touching.

"Talk?" she almost shouted, not turning to face him.

"Yes – about what happened at Jimmy's Tarn."

Her head snapped round, eyes blazing. Intense, like a volcano before it erupts, the lava flow gushed out of her mouth, red hot and scorching. "I want to beat him to pulp! I want to beat him to nothingness. I want him to know what it feels like to be nothing, to crawl away every time anyone looks at him because he's so afraid. D'you *know* what it's like to be nothing, Byron?"

"No," he said, shaking his head. A great heaviness came over him, thick and numbing. He did not know what to say to a woman in such great distress. He never had.

"Well, let me enlighten you." She stood up and pointed out over the valley in front of them. "Can you see the smallest blade of grass down there? No, of course not! That's what it's like – insignificant, vulnerable, trampled on, spat on, trapped. And you stay *so* quiet. Don't dare say a word."

"What did he do to you, Ellie?"

"You know what he did," she said, an edge to her voice. "You're not stupid. I saw it in your eyes when you came into the hospital room." She turned towards him, pointing to her head. "A little bump on the head? He shoved me against the wall. Then he threw me on the floor. Are you getting the picture, Byron Oakes? Have you ever seen rage and hatred in a man's eyes?"

He nodded slowly and said in a low voice, "Too many times."

Her eyes narrowed, scrutinising him, looking him up and down. "Have you ever raped a woman?"

The question shocked him and his heart pounded. He swallowed. "No."

"Then you know nothing of the kind of rage and lust Glenn Thorley's capable of!" She turned away from him. "Anyway, who cares? Who believes you?"

He got up and stood near her and she turned her questioning, angry eyes upon him, stirring his heart out of its heaviness into a place of deep shame.

"I believe you," he said quietly.

For a split second he thought she was going to vent more of her anger – this time at him.

"I'd put a bullet between Glenn Thorley's eyes if I had the chance and be glad the world was safe from at least one piece of filth."

"I'm so sorry, Ellie."

"What for? It wasn't you." She was still angry.

"I should've followed you."

165

"You didn't."

A wall came down between them.

"No, but you were determined I wasn't to come."

"So, now it's my fault."

Byron closed his eyes, silently groaning. He'd just added another row of stones to the wall.

"That's not what I meant."

"Then what did you mean?"

"You had something to do, alone, but I could have ignored what you said and followed anyway."

She looked at him then, distant and cold.

"Too late, Byron. You wouldn't have let a soldier go off like that."

This time he was irked by her response. How on earth was he meant to answer that?

"Now you're being bloody-minded. A military offensive's a completely different situation."

"It didn't feel like it to me." Before he could respond, she said, "What made you get mixed up with him?"

"I wouldn't say *mixed up* exactly."

"What would you call it then – friendly business banter?"

"No," he said keeping his voice even. "I responded to an ad regarding a project in Scotland with Mayfair Hotels and won the contract. Glenn was the one overseeing the project."

"I thought a man of your calibre would've recognised Glenn Thorley for what he is."

It was a challenge and he knew it. He remained silent for perhaps a full minute. She would wait as long as it took, of that he was certain. As certain as he was that she expected him to make a mess of his answer and give her an excuse not to trust him.

"No, not at first. That he was a bully became clear in the first week or so. I stayed for the money and connection because my business needed it. I don't trust him and I don't like him."

He sensed, rather than saw, an easing of the tension in her body, but she wasn't willing to let go yet.

"So why are you still working for him?"

"I'm not. I quit when I was in London."

"That was noble of you. What about the money?"

"I'll survive. Other matters cropped up."

"Such as?"

There wasn't much he could tell her. "Farley's death."

"I'm surprised you're still interested in that. Anyway, it's police responsibility." She studied him, he thought, as one would an insect under a microscope. "You're a man of deep waters, Byron. I think Jack Kennart's afraid of you."

"And I think you're afraid of asking me why I really returned," he said, stepping closer to her.

"Don't be ridiculous!"

"So, ask me."

Arms folded, she looked away, her expression closed.

He'd seen it before, not in her, but in battle-hardened men who'd witnessed and, in a few cases, been perpetrators of atrocities that no man could ever forget. Anger and fear rooted in pain so deep they didn't know how to deal with it, festered for years.

He was not surprised when she asked no question about his return.

"If Glenn Thorley's involved in Farley's death..." Her voice trailed away and a chill ran down his spine.

His eyes did not leave her face. "How long have you known him, Ellie?"

Her features were drawn and chestnut strands of hair touched skin that had lost its colour. In the green-brown eyes were darkness and pain. He wondered if she'd flee, shut him out, and never speak about it again.

The air was cold, sailing across the hills and moors, and she turned away from him and went over to the wall. He gave her a minute before walking towards her, standing two or three feet away. Part of him was certain she would change the subject and he didn't want that. He wanted her trust.

There was no answer for a long time. When the words came out they were stilted, hard and brittle, as if she didn't really want to speak them, to hear the words from her mouth.

"All my... my life." She turned her head slowly and looked at him. "He's my... cousin."

Time seemed to stand still. Anger burned in his heart and it came out, controlled and clipped, in his voice. He hoped he was wrong.

"Up on Maw's Hearth you called him an arrogant, sleazy pig. You also said he stops at nothing to get what he wants. Were you something he wanted?"

She nodded. "This time I got away. He won't be happy about that."

"Did he...?"

"No," she said sharply, interrupting. "I hit him with a chunk of wood."

Somehow it had been easier dealing with his men.

"When did all this start?" The question shot out, sounding more brutal than he meant.

She opened her mouth to speak, but no sound followed. She swallowed and the words came out in a rush as if of their own volition. "When I was about ten. He was sixteen."

A groan struggled from deep within him and he glanced away so she wouldn't see the revulsion and mistake it for her. Never would he get used to hearing these stories.

"Have you spoken to anyone about it?" he asked with difficulty, looking at her.

"No." Her expression was hard. "In case you hadn't realised, it's not the sort of thing you bring up in conversation."

Well, he'd botched that one. He tried again. "Was there no one?"

"No."

Bird calls carried on the breeze as it danced across the hill tops. Away in the distance Byron saw another car winding its way up from the valley floor. Several dots on a higher peak were moving across the face of a rock and he remembered the time he had fallen from a more precipitous place, damaging much of his body.

Without speaking he stepped close to her but not touching. For a fleeting second he thought she was going to run, but then she leaned against his arm.

Quietly, he said, "You're not alone with this any more, Ellie."

The tears came in a great wrenching flood and he held her, not too tightly and not speaking. What could he say when she needed to empty the well of pain?

The climbers eventually left the rock face and disappeared into trees, appearing a little while later higher up. The car had vanished. He could see a pair of birds gliding on the wind, but had no idea what breed they were. Birds weren't his strong point.

Ellie withdrew from him, turning aside to blow her nose and wipe her eyes. They were red and puffy when she faced him.

"I've never met anyone like you." Her voice was hoarse and strained.

"Is that good?"

"I think so. I haven't cried like this in anyone's presence." Her smile was half-hearted, but the anger had gone from her eyes.

"You need to talk about it, Ellie."

"I know that now, but not yet."

Byron nodded slowly, put his arm around her shoulders, and together they walked back to the car.

"Did Thorley follow you when you left the farmhouse?" he asked as he unlocked the car door.

"I saw him come out when I got to the woods, then at the turn-in to the clearing, but he didn't see me." There was a momentary hesitation. "No one here knows about my connection with Glenn."

"I won't be telling anyone, Ellie."

"If you do..."

"I won't."

"I don't even know why I said any of this. Years ago I decided I'd *never* talk about it."

"Well, perhaps you trust me, just a little. I'm very good at keeping secrets. I've been doing it for so long it's part of my DNA." He took hold of her hands. "I won't tell you what I'd like to do to Thorley. I'm ashamed of what's happened to you."

Ellie touched his cheek and said softly, "He's not worth the trouble, Byron."

"What if he's done it to others?" The anger was back in his voice.

"What can I say? I don't know much about his adult life. I've spent all those years avoiding him. It was only when he came up here with the hotel business that I saw him again."

"Did Farley know about him?"

"No, I couldn't tell him. Neither of us was much good with deep emotional stuff and he wouldn't have coped with that," she said, looking across the valley. "His greatest love was the wilderness. Sometimes I wonder whether his wife Alice left him because of a broken heart."

"And you?"

"Despite what his darling children say, I'd never have married him. Did you know he left me a sizeable sum of money and funds for some of the projects he'd been working on? Quite a bit went to the SNH and his children got the rest."

"No, I didn't. You look troubled about it."

"Only because the Orman clan will do everything they can to get their hands on every single penny that went to anyone except them. I've already had a letter from their solicitor informing me they're contesting the will. I wouldn't care too much except for the projects and for SNH. Without more funds some areas are in great danger of being lost to developers. Mayfair is only one company after slices of the Highlands."

Ellie shook her head, sighed, and got into the car. On the journey towards Kilcomb, she told him about a man who had managed to convince an entire village that the health clinic he proposed to build on the shores of their pristine lake would not only blend into the very earth itself, but bring in money to boost the local economy. The plans were accepted by the local council, but a few weeks after work commenced one villager, a retired construction engineer, noticed that the buildings didn't look quite like a health clinic. They were in fact building a water plant. The owner was planning to take the water from their lake and surrounding springs and sell it to overseas markets. There would be no money or employment for the local community. Workers would be brought in from countries where any wage was better than the poverty they were used to. The council and locals were outraged and they were now engaged in a bitter legal struggle.

She told him of areas of ravaged forests, habitats lost, hotels and tourist ventures turned into miserable failures which now stood mostly empty and ugly against the backdrop of the hills, and ancient sites robbed and desecrated.

As they neared Kilcomb, she rested her head against the seat and closed her eyes. Byron glanced at her once or twice wondering what she was thinking about. During the last two days she had come face-to-face not only with her violent childhood perpetrator, but also the memories of those dark days. What that was doing to her he could not imagine. While his childhood and youth had been peppered with disappointments and pain, they had been times in which he'd known his parents' love and support, and there had been no devastating events such as Ellie experienced.

When he stopped the car in the driveway to her house, Ellie opened her eyes. She stared at it; so did he.

"I can't leave you here by yourself," he said, looking at her.

"That's more or less what Bob said after Kipp was attacked."

"Did you listen to him?"

"As a matter of fact I did. I stayed in one of his spare rooms."

Byron's heart skipped a beat and, despite himself, he doubted, but said, "Good. So what about this time? Mary would take you in.

Or d'you trust me enough to stay in my spare room, or for me to come here?"

Ellie nodded, but her eyes told him she wasn't sure.

"I'd like to be at home."

"Fine. I'll go and get some things and come back. Don't think about skipping off to solve the world's problems while I'm gone."

She gave him a withering look as she got out of the car and headed towards the back door. Before driving off, Byron followed her inside to satisfy himself no one else was there. All was clear.

It took him only a few minutes to throw what he needed into a bag and check the photographs and negatives were where he had hidden them. Relieved to see them, he picked up the bag. He had taken two steps towards the front door when he stopped. Someone was outside the back door. Quietly putting the bag back on the floor, he stepped into the hallway as a man turned away from the kitchen window and walked to the side of the cottage where there was no neighbour. Beyond the other hedge lived an older, retired couple who seemed to spend a lot of time in their picture-book garden and had been pottering about when Byron came in.

There was a rattle at the window of a small room off the sitting room, but after a few seconds it stopped and Byron slipped quickly, silently out of sight of all windows and into the shadow of a corner in the hallway. Out of habit he had locked the front door when he entered the cottage. Seconds later he heard the knob being slowly turned. The would-be-intruder was being careful not to disturb the neighbours. Byron eased the gun from its holster under his jacket.

Silence. Byron did not move for perhaps thirty seconds before peering into the front room. The man was limping away from the cottage towards Byron's car and, in the time it took him to reach it, Byron was beside the window watching through the net curtains. It was as the man turned away from peering through the driver's window that Byron recognised him – Glenn Thorley, with an ugly swelling on his temple. A tide of anger, disgust, and shame that this man had done what he had, rose out of the depths of his belly. Justice, even illegal justice, begged for release and Byron raised the gun until it was pointed at the man outside.

Glenn turned and took a last look at the cottage and car before walking slowly towards the road and disappearing out of sight. A minute or so later Byron heard a car engine fire up and watched as Thorley drove past in the direction of the village centre. It would take him near Ellie's house.

He went to the phone on the hall table and dialled Ellie's home number. There was no answer.

Agitated, he picked up his bag and went out the front door. He made sure it was locked and quickly went around the house checking the windows and the back door. They were all secure.

As he started the car engine he tried Ellie's number again, but it just kept ringing. Where was she? He put his finger over the disconnect button.

"Hello, this is Ellie Madison."

"Ellie, it's Byron. Where've you been?"

"In the barn collecting chicken eggs if you must know. Did you think I'd run off?"

"No. I thought something had happened to you."

There was a faint, indistinguishable sound on the end of the phone. Then she said, "Oh, Byron, you amazing man. I'm fine."

"Lock the doors. I'll be there in a minute."

"What..."

"Just do it, Ellie. And don't answer unless you hear my voice."

At the top of the road, he had to wait while a slow-moving tractor towing a trailer of hay bales followed by four cars went past.

"Come on," he muttered irritably, tapping his fingers on the steering wheel.

The last car had barely gone by when he shot across the road and sped off, narrowly missing an old man on a bicycle. There was no sign of Thorley's vehicle as Byron went around corners faster than care required. When he turned into the lane leading to Ellie's, he slowed down as he drew nearer, expecting to find Thorley parked out of sight of the house. However, the only vehicle in the vicinity was the one he was in. Relieved, but wary, he pulled into the driveway and parked. He sat for a minute, his eyes scanning the back garden and the barn and hedges. There was no movement.

He got out and walked down to the barn, missing no corner as he checked for unwanted visitors. For several minutes he stood without moving, listening for sounds out of tune with what he expected to hear, but there was nothing. Halfway back to the house he saw Ellie standing in the doorway.

"What's going on?" she asked as he drew closer.

"Glenn Thorley was snooping around my place and trying to get in," he said grimly. "He drove off in this direction."

Ellie frowned. "No one's been here since you left. You don't seriously think he'd come here, do you?"

"He might if he wants revenge. He was limping and had a bump the size of a football on his forehead. Then there're the photos."

"For goodness sake! I'm sick of hearing about photos. I'd give them to the first one who asked if I had them."

"No you wouldn't. Anyway, I think he's after something different."

"Oh? And are you going to tell me why? I'm beginning to think you're as mixed up in all this as Glenn, Jack, the Ormans, and CID!"

"And what about Farley? Where he does he fit into the picture?"

"He's the innocent one here, Byron. It's his photos everyone's fighting over. Remember?"

"That doesn't automatically make him an innocent party. What if you didn't know him as well as you thought?"

"Don't be absurd. I probably knew him better than most."

"Of course you'd think that."

They stood staring at one another like a pair of sparring blackbirds, neither willing to give in, neither quite trusting the other.

"I know you've got some of Farley's photos. They're the ones they want, aren't they?" she said unexpectedly.

"I haven't a clue what they want."

"I don't believe you. I'm sure your time in London wasn't all spent checking business was still running smoothly. Who d'you really work for, Byron?"

"Me – mostly. And business isn't running smoothly." This was getting difficult.

"You are the most irritating, secretive man I've ever known. If you've always been like this I pity your parents, but I suspect the army's to blame," she said, and turned to go inside.

The crack of a rifle shot shattered the air and, before Byron had time to cover Ellie, the bullet ripped between them and smashed through a pane in the kitchen window.

"Inside now!" he shouted, but no more shots followed as he slammed the door shut behind them.

They stayed out of sight of all windows in a nook underneath the stairs. There, amongst a pile of magazines and books that Ellie told him she couldn't bring herself to throw out, he held her close. Her arm fell across his legs, her hand curling around one of his knees; he felt a profound sense of belonging that caught him unawares.

She looked up at him, opening her mouth to speak, but he put a finger to his lips and shook his head. Allowing a couple of minutes to go by, he whispered, "Stay here."

Although he had done this many times in his life, he couldn't help thinking he was caught in some kind of vortex, replaying the actions of half an hour ago. However, he could not assume the rifleman was Glenn Thorley. It didn't seem his style. It took Byron ten minutes to get around the house, peering out of windows.

"I'm going outside," he said to Ellie. "Stay here until I get back – and keep the door locked."

"I'm coming with you."

"No, you're not. I want you alive."

"And what if you get shot?"

"I won't."

Before she could protest further he was out the back door. He heard the lock turn as he ran quickly towards the back of the property in the shelter of the hedge. The shot had come from near the barn.

In the lane beyond the property's boundary there were fresh footprints in the damp soil. A man's boot tread had trampled grass on the verge, continuing to the thick trunk of an oak tree which he had climbed. There was fresh mud on the lower limbs and a little higher up, just out of reach, Byron could see a piece of ragged material caught on the end of a branch. Using another limb to get into the tree, Byron hoisted himself up and retrieved the material which he put in his pocket. He continued on up until he was almost in the same place he guessed the rifleman had been. There was a clear view of the back door and part of the house. The rest was obscured by an old, gnarled apple tree and two walls of the vegetable garden.

Byron climbed back down and walked along the lane until he found tyre tracks of a car. A small, fresh puddle of oil had been deposited on the ground. The lane continued past Ellie's house, disappearing round bends to unknown destinations – at least to him. He walked to the junction with the lane running down the side of the hedge. The car had gone straight on.

Back inside the house he told Ellie about the footprints and tyre marks and where the rifleman had fired from. He pulled the piece of dark green material out of his pocket.

"This was caught in a branch of the oak. Know anyone with a jacket this colour?"

"It looks familiar," Ellie said, taking it from him. "Common colour around here, but not the pattern. I've seen it before. Hanging in someone's hallway."

He sighed and put it back in his pocket. "Let me know if you remember. Any chance of a strong cuppa?"

Ellie raised an eyebrow. "Not Scottish whisky then?"

He shook his head. "Too early in the day for me."

While she made tea, Byron looked for the bullet; he found it lodged in the side of a cupboard.

"One of us could be dead," she said quietly, standing beside him as he held the bullet in his fingers and studied it.

"Yes, but we're not. Might've been a warning. We were easy targets."

"But someone was waiting up that tree. I wonder how many times he's sat there watching." Ellie shuddered. "It makes me feel sick. D'you think he'll be back?"

He looked at her intently. "I don't know."

Chapter 11

Ellie watched Byron walk towards the back lane with the sergeant. The weather had turned cold and wet during the night, and she stood shivering in the doorway waiting for Inspector Carter who was trudging towards her. He had interviewed her the day after Farley's death. He was a tall, thin man, English like herself, who had moved to Scotland two decades earlier. His temperament hadn't improved much since their first interview, not helped, she supposed, by standing out in the rain.

"Shall we go inside?" he said in a clipped tone. "I'm sure my man will take good care of your friend."

A little condescending this morning as well, she thought, peeved.

Slightly behind him, Jack Kennart raised his eyebrows and said in a friendlier tone, "And you're sure you didn't see anyone hanging about before that bullet landed in your kitchen?"

"Positive. I wasn't looking at the back hedge, only Byron coming up from the barn."

"And why had he gone down there?" the inspector asked.

"Byron's already told you."

"And I'm asking you now."

Boorish man.

"It was a precaution. As you've pointed out, I was close to Farley and he'd left me and his projects quite a lot of money."

The kitchen table still had breakfast plates and cups and a pot of tea on it. She began clearing them away.

"Where did you get those bruises, Ellie?" he asked in a rather more kindly tone.

The change of direction was unexpected and she put the plates and cups down with more force than intended. When she turned to retrieve the teapot he was watching her intently.

She picked up the teapot and held his gaze. Two could play at this game.

"I don't doubt for a minute that Jack's already told you what happened."

"I'd like you to tell me."

176

"There's nothing really to tell, Inspector. It was all very simple. The Land Rover went off the road into the ditch and I hit my head against the headrest and my face against the window. Nothing more, nothing less," she said sharply and turned away to the bench. Lying was not her best asset.

"You fell asleep at the wheel."

"Something like that."

"Either you did or you didn't."

"Yes, I dozed off."

"You weren't hit by… someone?"

The pause was, she knew, deliberate. Ellie faced him slowly.

"Why on earth would you think that?"

"Let's just say that I heard your friend Byron Oakes has a bit of a temper. Likes to wave a gun about. I hope it's licensed," he said, putting a hand in his jacket pocket and pulling out a packet of cigarettes. "D'you mind if I smoke?"

"Yes, I do!" she snapped, her eyes glinting. "And Byron does not have 'a bit of a temper' as you so absurdly put it."

He looked mildly offended by the force of her answer, but put the cigarettes back in his pocket.

"You haven't known him long enough, Ellie, to be making such a statement," Jack said in a tone she knew was meant to calm her down.

"I know him well enough."

"You only met him the day Farley was found. How d'you know he'd not been in the area for a while before then?"

Ellie stared at him. She couldn't believe her ears. "Are you suggesting that Byron had something to do with Farley's death?"

"The timing of his arrival is interesting," Carter piped up.

"And what's that supposed to mean? The other hikers arrived at different times."

"They're not in the same category as your Mr Oakes. We've done extensive checking on him. He had quite a career in the army: an elite soldier, not the average foot slogger. He could kill a man in seconds."

He watched her, waiting for her reaction. Ellie took her time.

"So could I, Inspector Carter," she said quietly, holding his gaze. "That doesn't mean I killed Farley or anyone else."

He blinked. Her answer, she thought with satisfaction, was not what he'd expected.

Great gusts of wind suddenly rattled the latches and back door, heavy rain drummed loudly against the windows. The bit of cardboard over the broken pane was looking soggy. Grey clouds, darkening as they passed over Kilcomb, deepened the gloom in the house. In the distance there were rumbles of thunder.

"While Byron Oakes was in London he contacted a researcher known for his brilliant, but eccentric abilities as an historical researcher. He also met with a high-ranking army officer, albeit retired," Carter said, as Ellie switched on the light. "Now, why would he do that?"

"I would've thought that was obvious," she said with a tinge of sarcasm. "My father was in the Navy for many years and he always called on his military friends when he was in London. Byron has a right to see his friends."

"You're very keen to defend this man, Ellie. I can understand you grievin' over Farley's loss, but to replace him with someone like Byron Oakes isn't wise." Jack pursed his lips and looked at her, his expression dubious. "He's no alibi for the day before Farley's murder, he was an expert in covert operations and he could still be working for the MOD."

"And how did you get that information?" she said, ignoring the remark about replacement.

"This is a murder enquiry." he said, not answering her question.

"I imagine he's told you he's here for the hiking or fishing," Carter said, standing up. "However, we know that he met Farley Orman earlier this year in Edinburgh. We're after a murderer, Ellie, and I don't appreciate it when people play games. Your co-operation would be to your benefit. Until this investigation's over, or I can prove it otherwise, you're a suspect as well as Byron Oakes."

A cold, wet gust blew in when he opened the door; the calendar on the wall fluttered and a page of the newspaper still lying open on the table flew onto the floor. Jack, pulling the door closed, turned briefly to look at her; she couldn't decide whether it was with pity or concern.

Before she had time to think about whether the inspector's information was true, Byron, huddled in his jacket, opened the back door and came into the kitchen. He took off his shoes and hung his wet jacket over the back of a chair near the combustion stove. For a few minutes he stood in front of it absorbing the warmth into his body. She turned away and put the kettle on. Having him in the house was challenging her emotions and after yesterday's revelation to him about Glenn she felt peculiarly vulnerable, something she had not experienced for a long time. For years she had kept everything hidden away and now this man had come along and changed all that. She knew it was a doorway to freedom, but if the inspector was right perhaps she shouldn't have trusted him with her past at all. The loneliness of distrust descended upon her as it frequently had all her adult life and she busied herself with washing up mugs.

"Ellie?" he said from across the room. "Are you all right?"

"Fine."

"Were you grilled while we were out there getting drenched?"

"A bit."

"What did Carter say?"

His hands were warm on her shoulders and she wanted to lean against him, but she couldn't. Instead, she turned with soapy hands and wiped them on a towel hanging near the stove. He gazed at her, silent, waiting.

"Why didn't you tell me you'd met Farley before?" she asked bluntly.

His expression lost its warmth and became guarded. "I haven't."

"Are you lying to me?"

"No. I was supposed to meet with him, but couldn't at the last minute. Somebody else went."

"Why didn't you tell me?"

"It wasn't a social meeting with Farley."

"I know that. Carter told me they'd investigated your army career. You were an elite soldier. He thinks you had something to do with Farley's murder." She looked at him with a mixture of sadness and anger, and said more evenly, "He said you met some top-notch army officer and an eccentric researcher. Jack thinks you're still working for the MOD. Why couldn't you tell me this?"

"I promised not to. I agreed to look into some things about Farley, but I don't work for the MOD. Farley had sensitive information he wanted someone to hear."

A loud clap of thunder made her jump. The wind was now howling round the house and somewhere upstairs a door slammed shut.

"Is that why he died?"

"We think so."

By 'we' she assumed that meant whoever had sent him, and the researcher. She didn't ask because she knew he wouldn't tell her.

"Farley mixed up in secret stuff. It doesn't go with the man I knew."

"He barely got started, Ellie."

"The inspector was right then in saying you hadn't come here for the hiking."

"Actually, he wasn't," he said with a lift of his eyebrows. His beautiful eyes, full of confidence, rested on her. "That *is* why I came, but also to see Farley. When he'd been met in Edinburgh it was at his instigation. Even then he changed his mind and said very little. We had no contact from him after that date. I was coming up here hiking and was asked to seek him out. I didn't know about the photos until I stumbled on them in the cave."

"Are they important?" she asked, leaning forwards.

"Very – at least some of them are. They're connected with the Second World War."

Ellie stared at him. "You're serious, aren't you? But where does Farley fit in?"

"Not sure yet. He found several rolls of old film and developed them. He also took a number of photos, but where they were taken I've no idea."

"Did he tell anyone where he found the film?"

"No." There was a hesitation, as momentary as a blink. When he spoke, she knew he'd decided not to reveal whatever it was that was in his mind. "There are still a lot of missing bits of the puzzle."

"And you're not going to tell me any more than you have to," she said, frowning. Lack of trust, it seemed, was embedded in them both. "I don't think Glenn put the pictures in the nook, but someone must've told him I'd be at Jimmy's Tarn."

He reached out and touched her hand, but she drew it away.

"If he's up to anything illegal the police will have to do something about him," he said in a hard voice. "He's not exempt from the law, no matter what he thinks."

"My cousin has his own laws. He's not interested in anybody else's."

The loathing rose suddenly in her throat like polluted river water and she ran out of the kitchen and into the bathroom, retching over the toilet bowl. It seemed her body was trying to eject the perpetrator as much as her emotions were and waves of shame and uncleanness washed over her. She thought she would drown in them.

She did not hear Byron come in and when he gently said her name, her reaction came out of the past.

Glaring at him, still half bent over the toilet, she yelled. "Don't come near me! You just… stay over there!"

"It's all right, Ellie."

"It's not all right! How can you even think that? Can't you see the muck he's left behind?"

"No." His voice was quiet. "There's no muck."

"I'm not good enough for you, Byron. Not good enough for any man."

"That's not what I think, Ellie. What happened wasn't your fault."

"How d'you know? I could've teased him. I could've made him angry," she shouted.

"At sixteen he was old enough to know exactly what he wanted and what he was doing. There're no excuses for what he did. Don't take on blame that's his."

She barely heard him. Snap shots of the past popped up one after the other. "He liked it when I was angry. Made him feel like a man to put me in my place. I hated him! He stole my life."

"But he doesn't have to keep on stealing it. You can change the locks on the door of your mind and keep him out."

"You've no idea, have you? If you did you wouldn't say that so easily."

"Not what you've been through," he said, shaking his head, "but I know about torment and months of sleepless nights. I had to learn to stop the voices in my head and shut off the pictures or men would've died."

There was anger and frustration in his voice, but she knew it was not towards her. She also knew he was right. For some years she'd had a measure of relief from bad dreams and replaying memories, but Glenn's arrival in Kilcomb had changed that. The last few days had been like a crazy emotional roller coaster ride that had plunged her into deep valleys and then up to the highest curve ready to throw her over the edge. There was no fun at this fair. She wanted it all to stop.

Standing up, she ran water into a glass and drank it down, its clean taste refreshing. When she turned around, Byron was

181

watching her. Without speaking, she stepped towards him and took his face in her hands, looking intently into his eyes.

"You've managed to frustrate me with your never-ending questions," she said quietly, "make me angry for leaving, and get me caught up in a war mystery. I've been shot at and attacked. I've slipped into a bleak place because of Glenn's presence here and I nearly killed him at Jimmy's Tarn. On top of all that I find myself talking to you about my past and not once have you shown any disgust or disbelief." She removed her hands and stepped back. "You are unique, Byron Oakes."

She saw the disappointment in his eyes as she moved away, but she was not capable of reviving the moment. There was nothing in her ready for that yet.

"I wouldn't want to be ordinary for you. I've never lived an ordinary life and I'll do everything I can to…"

A sudden hammering on the front door stopped Byron in mid-sentence.

"Most people come to the back door," Ellie said, wary.

"Let me go."

"No. This is my house, Byron, and people here expect me to answer the door."

The door knocking increased in tempo and Ellie squeezed past him and walked up the hallway to the door. It was Paul Shepley.

"Hello, Paul. Come in or you'll be soaked."

"Thanks, Ellie. I'm sorry I couldn't get in to see you at the hospital," he said when he stepped inside. "How are you feeling?"

"Fine thanks. And you did ring, which was kind. What brings you out in this weather?"

"Olga Erskine was knocked over by a car driver yesterday evening. Apparently, it was a young man in a hurry. Jack said he was devastated by what he'd done. She's in Castlebay Hospital and is asking to see you."

"Is she all right?" Ellie was surprised by Olga's request. They barely knew one another.

"Yes, she's… Oh, sorry," he said, looking beyond her. "I did wonder if you had visitors. Saw the car in the driveway."

"Of course, you two probably haven't met," she said, turning as Byron joined them.

Paul held out his hand. "I'm Paul Shepley, local minister."

"Byron Oakes, here for the hiking."

"Pleased to meet you, Byron."

"Likewise," he responded, smiling.

"As I was saying, Ellie," Paul continued, "Olga's all right in herself, but her left wrist's got a hairline fracture and one of her legs is badly grazed. And I think her back's painful. She didn't say much."

"How did it happen?" Byron asked. "I met her yesterday when she introduced herself."

"According to Olga she was on her way home after a drink at the pub – and she only ever has one stout – and had just stepped onto the path in her lane when she was hit from behind. The car wasn't going very fast she said. Carrie Ross and her husband found her not long afterwards. All Olga could remember was that the car was a brown colour," he said, shaking his head.

"Strange the driver didn't stop." Byron's face expressed his puzzlement.

"Drunk, perhaps," Ellie said.

"Don't know," Paul said. "The police are investigating. Anyway, I must go. She'd really appreciate it if you have time to see her. I think the doctor's keeping her there for a few days."

"I'll try and go tomorrow when I pick Kipp up."

The minister thanked her, nodded to Byron, and then ran to his car, buffeted by a vigorous wind. Ellie shut the door as he disappeared inside the vehicle, then followed Byron into the front room. He was deep in thought, hands in his pockets, staring out the window.

"Has Olga ever talked to you about Farley?" he said, turning as she sat down on the settee.

It seemed a strange question. "Only a day or so after he was found on Maw's Hearth. That was the first time I'd ever spoken with her. Why d'you ask?"

"She knows something about the photos."

Ellie frowned. "She used to go hiking with Farley and Alice until about ten or so years ago. I think it was Olga who came up with the idea for some sort of preservation group, but they had a falling out. And before you ask, I don't know what about. He never told me. Farley rarely talked of her."

"Weren't you curious?"

"Of course. But Farley was tighter than a bung in a barrel when it came to things he didn't want to talk about."

Byron looked at her with a quirky grin. "Did your interesting words and phrases amuse him as much as they do me?"

"Not always," she said, pleased he liked them. It had begun in childhood, a game using unusual words and phrases to hide her feelings and keep unwanted images of Glenn Thorley at bay. Later, she had used them to impress teachers and friends. At times it had backfired, but she'd never lost the knack or interest.

"I'd like to visit Olga with you if that's okay," Byron said, sitting down opposite her.

"Fine with me. She'll soon tell you if you're not wanted. She intrigues me. I think she's made the most of her life, including friendship with the Earl of Strathvern's family."

In the study across the hallway the telephone rang, its persistent sound competing for attention with the rain. Ellie got up to answer it.

"Hello, this is Ellie Madison."

"It's Andy at the garage. Your Land Rover's ready. A few scratches and a dent in the bumper bar. Jono's fixed that. I checked the steering, axle, brakes, and undercarriage. All fine."

"Thanks, Andy. I'll be there this afternoon."

"Oh, and that police inspector was here yesterday afternoon looking at it."

"Whatever for?"

"Don't know. Told me to mind my own business. Went over it inside and out."

"Thanks for telling me."

"No worries."

The storm's ferocity was lessening as she gazed out the window, her hand still on the telephone. She wondered why Carter had thought it necessary to inspect her vehicle, and an uncomfortable niggle suggested he was looking for something to link her with Farley's death or possession of the wretched photographs.

Outside the black clouds moved on, leaving grey ones in their stead. Everything looked dreary and cold; the flowers were nodding in the wind, bowed with the weight of raindrops, and the hedge looked forbidding and bruised. Beyond it, a car sped by too fast, she thought, for the conditions. Thunder rumbled in the distance reminding her of times she and Farley had been caught in storms high up in the mountains, on occasions with little shelter other than an overhanging rock. There had been times of closeness and of anger in those wild places, and over the years she had realised that Farley's mood was often linked with the weather.

"Everything okay?" Byron said behind her.

She nodded slowly, sighed, and drew herself away from the memories. She missed Farley, most likely would for a long time, but her life had to continue. They went back into the front room.

"The Land Rover's ready. I told Andy I'd get it this afternoon. He said Carter's been all over it."

"Hardly surprising. Did he find anything?"

"Don't know. Bob retrieved all my personal stuff. There'd only be maps and the usual car things left in it, unless he took out everything."

The contemplative expression returned to his countenance and for a moment she studied it. There seemed added strength to his character, as if behind the strong features was a fortress that few weapons could penetrate. He would not be easily fooled or manipulated. Where his thoughts had gone she could not imagine. When he spoke his words surprised her.

"Had you marked Jimmy's Tarn on any of those maps?"

His eyes were sharp, searching hers.

"No. I know where it is, so..." But she had. It was so long ago she'd forgotten all about it. "It's marked on an old map I bought when I first moved here. It's always lived in the glove box, an old friend I couldn't part with."

"Any idea who owns Jimmy's Tarn?"

"A descendent of the last family. They've owned it for several generations. I've no idea who because he or she doesn't live in the area as far as I know."

"D'you know much about its history?"

Ellie nodded. "I've done quite a bit of research for my own interest and for some uni students I took there. They'd heard about it from a local and wanted to paint it as well as soak up its history. A couple of them were doing research for a project and wanted to know about the Second World War era. I spent a while searching that out, but couldn't find much. Jimmy's Tarn wasn't important to anyone," she said, looking at his hands. They were fine, strong, well-shaped hands. "It's not on tourist maps or routes, but is on a few maps used by hikers. It's not far from Kilcomb or Castlebay."

She went on to tell him that the earliest record of inhabitants was from the late fifteenth century, tenant farmers who farmed the land for a hundred or more years for a local laird. A short time after the incident when the laird and two of his sons disappeared, the Earl of Strathvern claimed ownership by paying the widow a small sum. In the records in Strathvern's library a note stated she was *'glad to be purged of that accursed place'*. The tenant farmer was convicted of the murders of the three men and hanged on gallows in Castlebay. During the next two hundred years there were a number of tenants, who variously farmed sheep, Highland cattle, and grew crops. Success depended on the weather, the earl's generosity, and whether or not diseases were present. In the first few years of the twentieth century a single man bought Jimmy's Tarn from the Strathverns. Times were tough. The man, Douglas Bromley, had been on the Klondyke Goldfields in the Yukon and returned home with a substantial amount of money. He'd built the farmhouse and improved the pasture and for a few decades Jimmy's Tarn prospered.

"When was it abandoned?" Byron asked.

"The family left in the early seventies. During the war the husband and his eldest son worked in the Clyde shipyards. A couple of the oldies in Kilcomb remembered the family, but couldn't tell me a lot. It seems they weren't the most sociable people, and after the war the farm struggled for a few years before it did any good," Ellie said as the phone rang again and she got up. "I believe the offspring didn't want to farm. It was one of those farm stays for a while, but that didn't last."

The rain had almost stopped when she picked up the phone and spoke into the receiver. Glenn's voice sent a chill down the length of her body.

"You've made me very angry, Ellie. A little bird's told me there are more photos I should see. Get them for me or next time I won't be so... merciful."

"Neither will I. You'll wish I'd killed you," she said coldly.

"You haven't got the courage. And keep your mouth shut about Jimmy's Tarn."

"I'm not playing that game any more."

"You stupid woman! Get the photos."

"You'll have to be more specific. I've got a lot of photos."

"Don't be smart with me, whore. You know what I'm talking about."

Ellie cringed, but her anger increased.

"Actually, I don't. You're so arrogant, Glenn, the truth wouldn't come anywhere near you because it'd feel too dirty."

"Just do what I say, Ellie. Leave them in the saddlebags hanging up in your barn by ten o'clock tomorrow morning or I'll..."

She hung up, shaking with anger, and picked up the nearest thing, hurling it across the room. Bits of paper fell out of the diary as it flew through the air and hit the wall with a loud thud. It landed, open, the cover facing upwards, half on the floorboards and half on the rug that covered most of the floor. She stood staring at it, every muscle in her body taut, wishing it was her cousin. So much for his 'sorry' sailing across the field. It was, as she'd known, no more than wind without power. Seconds later Byron appeared in the doorway. He looked across the room at the diary.

"I'll never give him any photos! I'm not a little girl any more and he doesn't control my life."

"Thorley." Byron's voice was harsh. "He wanted you to go to Jimmy's Tarn again?"

"No – to my barn tomorrow morning. I hung up on him."

"Don't suppose he'll like that."

"No, but I won't allow him to control me, Byron. He did it for too long. Now he knows. You were right. I have to stop him getting into my head every time I take a breath."

"I'm glad, Ellie," he said, as if proud of her, "but be careful. He might take it as a challenge to get you back under his control. Don't be alone and mind where you go."

She nodded. "Farley hated him. When Glenn first came here last December, he had his eye on Fenella. She played up to him to spite Farley, but she's not stupid and I think she dumped him earlier this year. Found out he was married, although his wife's left him," Ellie said, drawing her brows together thoughtfully. "But with Fenella you never know. Money and position mean a lot to her and she'll trample over people to get them. She and Camden have conceived a few dodgy schemes, but he hasn't got the same mental abilities she has and they didn't come to much. She owns a successful temping agency in Inverness with a branch in Castlebay. Won't let him near it which peeves him no end."

"She was in the post office yesterday morning defending her father – and you. She accused Carrie Ross of blackmailing Farley."

Ellie looked down at a pile of books on her desk. It was a secret she had kept for twelve years; even Alice hadn't known.

"She was. Had been for years." She looked up at him. His expression gave nothing away. "When Farley's photographs first began being seriously noticed twenty-five years ago, he organised two exhibitions in Castlebay and Edinburgh. What no one knew was that many of the photos weren't taken by him, but by a dead,

187

obscure yet brilliant photographer. Unfortunately for him, Carrie Ross went to the exhibition in Castlebay and recognised them. The obscure man was her father who'd taken the pictures a decade earlier just before he died. She saw a way to make money and began blackmailing him."

"I'm surprised she's managed to keep that to herself. How did Farley get hold of the photos?"

"He knew her father and envied his skill with the camera. He stole a few packets of negatives," she said, remembering Farley's expression when he told her – defiant, yet tinged with guilt. "He couldn't bring himself to admit what he'd done because those photographs had a lot to do with his initial success. He never did it again. I promised I wouldn't tell anyone and I haven't until now."

A bright beam of sunshine suddenly brought golden light into the room, touching her cheek like a warm caress. It tapped on Byron's shoulder and the side of his head on its way to a spot on the wall behind him. What he thought of her revelation wasn't immediately obvious, but she did begin considering telling Farley's two obnoxious offspring. It'd be good to put a dent in Camden and Fenella's oversized egos. Bran probably wouldn't care.

"After all this time I shouldn't think it'd matter much if people knew, especially now he's... Sorry, Ellie," he said with an apologetic smile. "Carrie was on the phone to someone about Fenella's visit the second she was out the door, but I interrupted the conversation when I appeared from behind the shelves."

"So, eavesdropping as well. Is that how you get all your information?" she asked, teasing him.

"I wish it was that easy. She warned me not to talk to anyone about what I'd heard. I said she would, so I would."

Ellie laughed. "I bet she didn't like that. She's a spiteful piece of work, so don't be surprised what you hear about yourself."

"I'm more interested in who she was talking to on the phone. It could be she'll try and blackmail Fenella."

"She'd probably regret that. Fenella's a fighter with plenty of courage. Carrie wouldn't be a match for her in full battle mode."

"I thought you didn't like her."

"I don't much, but I admire her fighting spirit even if it's misplaced and misdirected," she said, vaguely surprised at her defence of a woman who'd belittled and attacked her more times than she wanted to remember. "Jack says all the Ormans have solid alibis for the time of Farley's death, but Fenella's very clever at avoiding blame."

He was studying her, but she supposed the analytical cells in his mind were already digesting the information and sorting it out. "I suppose Jack told you where they were."

"Yes – she was in Inverness shopping with a friend. Camden was supposedly in Edinburgh, while Bran was tucked up in bed at home with the flu." Ellie sighed and stared forlornly at her diary still lying on the floor. "I can't imagine why anyone would want to kill him – not even them."

Byron picked up the diary and the papers that had escaped from its confines and gave them to her. A folded scrappy piece of paper slipped out of his hand, fluttering to the floor and lying open when he picked it up. It was a receipt. He looked at her and there was profound silence between them as she held his eyes; he seemed as unwilling as she to break it.

"Why didn't you tell me about this?" His voice had a hard note to it.

"It never occurred to me," she said, which was true, though she doubted he'd believe her.

"How long have you had it?"

"Years. I bought it in case Glenn ever turned up," she said in a bland tone. "You look surprised."

He was, in fact, staring at her. There was a subtle change in his expression, and for a brief moment she saw a mixture of fear and sadness. By the time he spoke a second later a shield had drawn over his features as if he was protecting himself.

"Killing him won't erase the past or heal your future, Ellie."

"No, but it'd keep him out of my life. Don't worry, Byron. I won't kill him, even though I'd like to."

"Where's the gun?"

"In my bedroom."

He followed her up wooden stairs carpeted down the middle in a flower pattern and worn on several steps. One day she'd need to replace it. The wood creaked and groaned in spots, and in the gloomy light she heard Byron trip up one of the steps. She was so used to them she hadn't thought to switch on the light.

On the landing she turned right and half a dozen steps later went into the main bedroom. It was a big airy room with two large windows, one overlooking the front garden and the road with the spire of a church poking up through trees in the distance, and the other peering out over the neighbour's field and vegetable patch. Their house was just beyond the flourishing beans, marrows, and lettuces, and partly obscured by two gnarled apple trees.

Ellie went to the bedside table, opened the bottom drawer and reached for the metal box hidden beneath pillow cases and hand towels. The gun was kept locked away inside it.

There was an unnerving lightness about the box. It was unlocked and her heart gave a flutter of panic. Refusing to peek at Byron, she lifted the lid and looked inside. It was empty.

The master rope maker, fear, began tying her stomach in knots. Reaching beneath the bed she found the key secured in its usual place.

Had she left the box unlocked and a burglar broken in and taken the gun? There wasn't anything else missing as far as she knew and there was no sign of a forced entry, but if she'd left this unlocked perhaps she'd done the same with the back door. Or had she put it in the Land Rover recently because of Glenn's appearance in Kilcomb? No, she couldn't have or Jack Kennart or Carter would have brought it back and questioned what it was doing in there.

"Perhaps you put it down in the house somewhere," Byron said, studying her a little reprovingly, she thought.

"I wouldn't do that," she snapped, angry with her own carelessness and with his disapproval. "Even if the phone had rung or someone had come to the door, I'd have locked it away before answering."

"Have you taken it out anywhere?"

Ellie shook her head.

"Maybe someone knew where you kept it and took it."

"That's impossible. I've only told Farley and Mary. Jack knows too."

"Then maybe it's in the house. When was the last time you saw it?"

"On mid-summer day. I caught a glimpse of Glenn in Castlebay. That's why I remember."

Byron fell silent, looking away and out of the window. Ellie wished she'd imprisoned the words within her. For all those years she had rarely mentioned her cousin's name, but now she had spoken of his violations of her, there was release to say more in the presence of a trusted one – the only trusted one. Yet Byron's silence caused her to rebuke herself for the almost casual remark about seeing Glenn.

As if dragging himself out of a box full of memories, Byron's gaze came back to her and she waited for an admonition about the evil of murder and retribution rarely solving or changing anything.

"I once caught one of my men attempting to rape a teenage girl. He didn't see or hear me coming," he said in a hard voice. His eyes glittered with anger. "I got my gun out, aimed it at his head from the other side of the barn and pulled the trigger." Ellie gasped, shocked. "All I wanted was to see his blood pouring out of his body, but as I squeezed the trigger, I re-aimed and the bullet went over his head. It's not the same, Ellie, but don't think I don't understand."

He drew her close to him and they stood in each other's embrace in a secret place of shared pain and understanding.

After some minutes he took her hand and said, "Come on, let's see if the gun's got a new abode, then decide what photos to leave Glenn."

Chapter 12

It was clear from the moment they arrived at the garage, when Andy shot out an expletive on sighting Byron, that the mechanic would need convincing he was her friend. He turned his back on Byron in a defiant gesture and began conversing with Ellie about the Land Rover. Byron, arms folded across his chest, merely raised his eyebrows.

"It's no good talking to me about all that, Andy," she said, annoyed by his attitude. "You know mechanical things and I don't get on. I can vouch for this man."

"Maybe you can, Ellie, but he's a stranger to me. And I don't trust strangers that go poking about in other people's vehicles."

"But it's *my* vehicle, Andy, and Byron has my permission. Now, stop behaving like an adolescent and tell us, especially him, what you've done."

He glowered at her, then shrugged his shoulders and turned around to face Byron.

"Come on, then. Let's see if you can understand anything I've been doing."

As he marched off, Byron grinned at her, winked, and followed the mechanic. Ellie stood nearby, listening and occasionally asking a question, but they became engrossed in technical talk as Andy seemed to gain some respect for Byron's questions. Her thoughts returned to the morning's events.

They had not found the gun; it was not in the house, the barn or even the gardening shed. The house, she thought, had not had such a thorough going over since the day she'd moved in. No nook or cranny had escaped scrutiny. In a dark back corner beneath a pile of dusty sacks covered in bits of straw and bird droppings, Byron had found an old hedger's staking mallet and butter churn she'd long forgotten about. He'd chastised her for being so neglectful of history.

That someone had been in her house, rummaging through and peering into her life without her knowledge or permission, disturbed and angered her. She went outside, staring at bright yellow flowers in a window box across the road, and wondered who could have known about the gun's location. Or had she been stupid enough to leave it out, distracted perhaps, and then left the house? The puzzle was that nothing else seemed to be missing and of the few people who knew she had a gun one was now dead. Mary had no clue as to where it was kept and Jack had told her to move it into a locked cupboard, but she'd never got around to it.

The wind was still keen and Ellie zipped up her jacket and stuffed her hands into her pockets. Flowers across the road were bobbing madly and a shower of leaves fluttered onto the pavement, sticking like collages on the cars parked beneath the trees. She shivered and was about to go inside the garage when three people came out of the post office up the road. Carrie and Glenn seemed locked in an agitated conversation, with Paul Shepley hurrying out behind them.

The sound of Carrie's sharp voice carried, although the words were lost in the wind. Ellie made do trying to decipher gestures and expressions. Carrie was pointing at Glenn, jabbing her finger like the staccato of a machine gun while Paul seemed to be, as always, the mediator, though not very successful on this occasion judging by the way they ignored him. Of Glenn's expression Ellie could see little as he was half turned away from her, but from the erect and stiff way in which he held his body, she knew he was angry. It made her think of a big cat waiting to pounce and devour its prey, but unlike that creature it wasn't a matter of survival. Glenn's purpose was always to humiliate and conquer. How he achieved that didn't matter. The only thing of importance was Glenn Thorley.

Carrie's verbal assault continued unabated until he grabbed her arm and yanked it away from him. The force of his action made her take a step backwards. The flow out of her mouth ceased, replaced by the deep, authoritative voice of a man used to getting his way. Ellie couldn't help wondering which of them had goaded the other; it was a speciality they had both honed, using it to inflict discomfort and distress on others whenever the opportunity arose.

Suddenly, Glenn's voice was drowned out by a piercing scream. Across and down the road people turned and looked. With a quick, downward movement he let go of Carrie's arm and she held it to her as if it was wrenched from its socket. If only it had been, Ellie thought without any twinge of remorse.

Footsteps sounded behind her as Paul stepped between Glenn and Carrie. Glenn brushed him aside and walked off towards the library three doors along from the garage. Across his features passed shadows from a dark abyss.

"Did I hear a scream?" Byron asked, reaching her.

"Yes – Carrie. She and Glenn were arguing."

"He doesn't look too happy."

"I don't think he ever is or ever has been," she said coldly and turned away from the sight of her cousin. "Is my Land Rover ready to go?"

He nodded, held up the keys and they headed towards the vehicle. As she and Byron were looking along the road before turning into the traffic, there was a loud thump on the window next to her. It so startled them that Byron slammed on the brakes, jolting them in their seats.

There was a grunt of surprise from Byron. Her heart pounding, Ellie turned towards her window expecting to see a wounded bird on the ground. Instead, Glenn was glaring in at them, motioning for her to wind down her window.

"You idiot!" she yelled, when she had it halfway down. "You could've caused a serious accident."

"Not me, Ellie. Your... *friend's* driving," Glenn said. He looked past her in Byron's direction. "You just can't find the right man, can you? I wouldn't put your hopes in this one either. You should come back to what you know."

Rage surged through Ellie and she opened her mouth to pour it out over him, but Byron was quicker.

"What d'you want, Thorley?" he demanded.

"She knows."

"I'm asking."

"It's none of your business, Oakes. Ellie knows her place. She won't tell you. She's good at keeping secrets."

The bitter gall of repugnance at his unrelenting arrogance rose in Ellie's throat, and her hands curled into a ball. He was so close she could break his nose with one hard punch. Instead, she changed the subject.

"What were you and Carrie arguing about?"

"You're a nosey pair, but she's worse than this whole village put together. The stupid cow opened a package sent to me thinking I wouldn't notice. I told her if I found out she's told anyone I'd cut her devilish tongue out." He grinned. "That shut her up. The parson didn't know what do."

For all her abhorrence of him she felt no sympathy for Carrie.

"Did you kill Farley Orman to get Ellie back?" Byron said without emotion.

Ellie's head snapped round and a sharp pain shot down her neck; she was not mended yet. She stared at him, her mouth partly open, shocked by the question.

"You don't know what you're talking about, Oakes," Glenn said derisively. "Keep out of it. Orman was a fool."

"I'd say he knew exactly what he was doing. You didn't seriously think he'd try and persuade the authorities to lease you land at the foot of Maw's Hearth, did you?"

"What!?" exclaimed Ellie. "Is this true, Glenn?"

The big man snorted. "And upset the 'delicate balance of the Highland environment'? You know, I heard that phrase from Farley often enough to make me want to vomit. The only delicate balance was what he was raking off for his photographs. Farley could've made a lot of money out of it if he'd just done what I asked."

"You don't ask, you tell," Ellie snapped and began winding up the window. Her head was aching and she wanted to be rid of the cause. He put his hand on the top of it.

"Don't think we'll stop. In fact, with him out of the way it'll be a lot easier to get things moving. Our new architect's got no interest in emotional environmental issues. And he's a damned sight better than you, Oakes. Maw's Hearth Grand Hotel will be one of the best in the world, with some very... shall we say... *interesting* features."

There was in his voice a hint of malice, as if he was taking pleasure in taunting her and waiting eagerly for the retaliation, the battle even.

"The only interesting feature at the foot of Maw's Hearth will be your gravestone. *"Here lies an enemy of Scotland, whose lust for money ensured his demise. Mourned by no one."*

With that she continued winding up the window and he withdrew his hand.

"You can't win, Ellie," he shouted as he was shut out. "The Musketeers are finished and you haven't the clout Farley had. Get the photos!"

Refusing to look at him, she glanced at Byron who put his foot on the accelerator and headed off down the main road. If Glenn thought he had put a stop to the fight...

Byron was staring, deep in thought, out through the windscreen.

"D'you really think Glenn could've killed Farley?" she asked him as she massaged the back of her neck. The headache was worse and her cheek was aching.

"Maybe," he said, frowning. "Farley was determined to stop him. He lied when he agreed to do some furtive persuasion, to gain time. His idea, I gather, was also to feed Glenn's plans to the SNH. He'd been pinning his hopes on greater support from the environmental convention you attended last year."

"Is there anything you don't know about all this?"

"More than I do know, Ellie. I had only the report of that one meeting with Farley to go on, but it was enough to convince a friend we needed to get involved."

"The mysterious 'we'," she said, raising her eyebrows. "Glenn will pursue this hotel thing like an army general on the battlefield. And he won't expect to lose."

"Neither do you, do you?"

"No, nor will my conservation friends. My father was a tough man and he taught me to stand on my own two feet, but I'm not Farley."

"Then do it. I can help."

She glanced at him, thoughtful. "I could almost believe you were sent to me."

"And you don't mean by the 'mysterious we', I suppose."

She shook her head and changed the subject. "I wonder if Glenn's got my gun."

"Someone like him probably has one or two of his own."

"I suppose Jack Kennart will charge me with negligent care of a weapon or giving criminals access to dangerous weapons," she said rather morosely.

They reached the outskirts of Kilcomb as the sun disappeared behind another bank of clouds. The breeze picked up momentum, gusting through tree tops.

"Depends if you tell him or not," Byron said casually.

Ellie glanced at him, not a little surprised by his remark. "I thought you were a law-abiding citizen, Byron Oakes."

"I am – mostly. Don't you speed occasionally?"

"That's not quite in the same league as losing your gun. Anyway, what if he finds out?"

"Then we'd better find it first."

***

During the night another squall blew in from the sea, disturbing Ellie's sleep and sending her downstairs just after one o'clock to check there wasn't a puddle trying to creep in under the back door. There wasn't, but she put the sausage-shaped draft excluder and a towel down anyway. Window latches were rattling, and out in the dark garden she heard the loud crack of a big branch as it broke off a tree and, from the noise, crashed onto an outbuilding before thudding into the ground. It was followed by another thud. There was a faint and momentary sound, too indistinct to discern.

Changing her mind about going back up to bed, she switched on the light in the scullery, pulled on her gum boots and retrieved the torch from the alcove behind her. She winced as she shoved her arms into the jacket hanging behind the door. Bruises were appearing on the upper part of her right arm. Pushing aside the excluder and towel, Ellie stepped out into the porch. A cold wind slapped at her violently and rain swirled in, leaving its dampness on her. The light from the kitchen was muted, shut as it was behind a blind pulled halfway down; the porch light offered only a dim yellow. It was about time she changed the bulb.

In the garden the torch's light opened a narrow pathway in the darkness, making the black night around seem even darker. Beyond the borders of her garden she heard glass splintering and several dogs barking; twigs and leaves flew about her as if demented, catching in her hair and flicking her face.

This was madness, but she had to find out whether the ancient barn was damaged and the chickens safe. The night seemed thick and impenetrable, eerie, the wind disguising any sounds of mischief by men, and a shiver of fear ran down her spine.

"Don't be silly. This is my garden."

Already, she was chilled to the bone. Before checking the barn, she had a quick look at the garden shed and saw a branch resting on the corner of its roof. She couldn't tell how much damage there was and had no desire to investigate in the awful conditions.

Ellie veered away from the sound of the thud that had brought her out and went to check the chickens. She was glad to reach the coop and find the building and its occupants intact – as far as she could see. Inside, there was some respite from the wind and rain, but the birds were restless atop their chicks nestled in close; a few hens were protecting eggs.

By now the wind was howling. Somewhere, a door banged shut, making her jump and she inadvertently switched off the torch. She frowned, straining to hear what she thought was a groan, but it was gone, if it had existed at all. The door to the coop rattled behind her, and she was immediately back in her childhood bedroom on the first night Glenn Thorley had visited her. The knob on that door had a particular rattle which, from that night on, had caused her heart to fear and her trust of adult males cease to exist. The dread of darkness came rushing back.

What if he was creeping about, bedded down in the barn even, waiting, willing her to come? He could've been watching her make her way down the garden, that lascivious grin on his face. The thought of it made her want to vomit.

She was in the chicken coop, in the dark, alone. If he came in she would not be able to get past him.

Fumbling with the torch, she found the switch and glorious light flooded the coop once again. She said good night to the chickens, got out of their house, and decided she'd had enough of damage assessment. The best place was bed. However, as she turned towards the house, she heard a sharp cry.

She swung the torchlight in the direction of the sound and saw a mess of leaves and branches.

"Hello! Is there anyone there?" she shouted, nervous.

In response came a man's weak voice. *"Help me."*

Ellie hesitated. What if it was Glenn and the cries a ploy to trap her? Leaves thrashed about, striking her body as she stepped over a branch. On the other side, she found a tangled mess of smaller branches with almost no room to put her feet. It reminded her of a painting she had done, a silent cry of pain, an expression of the torment from which there were only brief episodes of freedom.

"I can't see you," she shouted suddenly.

"Help... me."

The voice was thin and snatched away in the wind. She pointed the torch into the tangle and between two substantial branches was a glimpse of legs in jeans. This was no trick of Glenn's even if it was him under there. Turning back the way she'd come, she went round the other way and tried to get in closer, but it was blocked by a partly destroyed apple tree.

"I have to get help!" she yelled. "Don't move."

There was no response and she scrambled out of the mess and ran, stumbling, back to the house. Without stopping to take off her muddy wet boots she ran up the stairs, banged on Byron's door and charged in. He was sitting bolt upright with a gun pointed at her. For a second she stared at the dark blue of his tee-shirt and at the gun. It was like a scene from a movie. He lowered the gun.

"There's a man pinned under a tree near the barn," she said plainly, stirred even at this late hour and in such uninviting circumstances by Byron's unpretentious and commanding presence.

He was immediately out of bed pulling on jeans and jacket and asking who it was.

"I don't know. I could only see part of his legs. He was barely conscious by the sound of his voice."

"Get some trousers on," he said as he zipped up his jacket.

"There isn't time!"

"You'll be no help in your dressing gown if you get hooked up and badly injured when I need you. Now, go!"

She wanted to argue, but didn't and within a couple of minutes joined him in the kitchen where he was tying his boot laces; another torch lay by his feet.

"I'll phone for an ambulance," she said picking up the handset – the line was dead. She dialled the number on the mobile phone, but after a few hesitant rings it dropped out.

"Try again later," Byron said. "That man needs us right now."

The rain was heavy and relentless, driven into their faces by the wind and stinging their eyes.

"Over this way," she shouted, directing the torchlight towards the fence with her neighbours.

The wind buffeted and pushed, getting inside their jackets and slowing their progress. There was another loud crack as they reached the fallen branches, but it was farther away, in the lane behind or in the neighbour's paddock beyond it. Byron shone his torch into the tangle of branches where Ellie indicated she had seen the man's legs. A piece of stick grazed the side of Ellie's head as it whipped past on its dark journey. She grunted.

"Are you all right?" Byron said, quickly beside her.

"Yes. I'll be fine. We need rope. I'll get it from the barn."

He squeezed her arm and nodded. "Be careful! When you get back, try pulling some of these branches out of the way. And try the ambulance again."

Ellie nodded, but she was not feeling well and trekked heavily against the wind and through the vegetable patch, much of it flattened or covered in leaf and twig litter. A sodden and frightened chicken was cowering amongst the runner beans; she picked it up and put it on a straw bale in the barn. It was noisy but dry inside, except where there were holes in the roof, and little puddles were forming on the cobblestones and on the packed earth floor. Rope was hanging up in one of the stalls. For a second she paused and drew a deep breath; her head was pounding. Retrieving the rope from the hook, she trudged back to Byron and the unknown man.

Byron was calling him. "Can you hear me?"

There was no answer.

"Hello!" he shouted.

Nothing.

Flashing the torchlight around, Byron began scrambling through a curtain of leaves, popping up seconds later on the other side before suddenly bending down. Seconds later he stood up and peered through the rain at her. Even the shadows of the night could not disguise his anxiety.

"I've found him, but he's half buried under the tree. Try the ambulance people again."

This time she had more success with the phone and after what seemed forever listening to the tone strengthen, weaken, and almost drop out, the call was answered.

"Yes, it is an emergency," Ellie said when a woman answered. "There's a man trapped and unconscious under a big branch."

"D'you... kind of injuries he has?"

The line was breaking up.

"No. We've only just found him. How long before an ambulance gets here?"

"... about forty-five minutes," came the partial answer as the mobile signal ebbed. "It's... busy night... of traffic accidents."

"That's too long!"

"I'll do my best. If you can get... off... yourself... help. The Emergency Services are flat... roads and rescuing people."

There was no sign of Byron as Ellie dropped the mobile into her pocket and began pulling at small branches. Pain burned in her right shoulder blade and arm. It wasn't the first time she'd been injured and had to pretend it wasn't hurting, so she could do it again. Slipping the rope around a larger branch, she tugged at it, but it resisted. She strained harder. Suddenly the branch lurched and shifted bringing smaller ones with it and Ellie found herself on her hands and knees on the sodden grass. Pain exploded in her head; she thought she was going to faint. Rain, persistent and cold, blew into her face and down her neck. She had to sit, just for a few seconds, to stop feeling sick. Behind her she heard Byron snapping branches. Wiping her hands on her jeans, she got up.

"This is no time to be fragile," she muttered, and began clearing the smaller bits out of the way. A minute or two later she saw Byron bending down again and she went closer.

"How is he?"

He turned around slowly, frowning, his expression pensive below wet hair flattened against his forehead. The jacket he had put on in the kitchen was covering the man on the ground, and his tee-shirt was sopping and sticking to his upper torso as if it was part of him.

"Still alive." There was a pause. "It's Camden Orman."

"Camden? What on earth's he doing here at this time of night? Let me see. Are you sure it's him?"

Without waiting for him to respond she clambered over the boughs. As she stepped into the small arena of cleared space, Byron held out his hand to steady her. She stood close to him and looked down at the face of the man who had threatened to kill her. Yet, for all that, he was still Farley's son.

Byron squeezed her hand. "Did you get through to the ambulance?"

Ellie nodded. "Could be forty-five minutes."

"Damn! I think he's got a broken leg. There's a biggish branch across him. I've moved it off as much as I dare, but I can't risk shifting him."

"Don't we have to try and keep him conscious? Let me talk to him," Ellie said. "He might respond to my voice."

She knelt down beside Camden, took off her jacket, and went to lift his head.

"Don't! He might have neck or spine injuries."

Byron's sharp tone made her jump and she gave him a quick, displeased look, but he was right. It hadn't occurred to her. She bent her head close to Camden's.

"It's Ellie, Camden. Can you hear me?"

The response was so faint she could barely hear him. "Yes."

"Ask him if he can feel his legs," Byron said, retrieving his mobile phone from his pocket and pushing buttons.

Camden's hand moved slowly.

"Is that yes?" she asked.

The response was slower in coming, but eventually his fingers moved.

"Byron, I think he's losing consciousness."

"Keep talking to him," Byron said, and then spoke into the mouthpiece. "We need an ambulance immediately. We've got a…"

Ellie returned her attention to Camden, talking to him about Edinburgh and London, two cities he knew and loved. Behind her she caught snatches of Byron's conversation, his voice one of authority and persuasion.

"No, we can't move him. He could have spinal and internal injuries."

By now she was very cold and wet, and the wind persistently blowing strands of hair across her face did nothing to help the creeping feeling of doom. She was tired and just wanted to get back into her warm bed preferably after a cup of piping hot tea and maybe a swig or two of brandy.

"Camden, can you hear me?" she shouted, afraid he was slipping away.

"… dead by then. No, I'm sure you don't," Byron said.

A leafy twig brushed her face and she pushed it aside impatiently. Despite her dislike of Camden, she could not leave him.

"Are they coming or not?" she called.

Byron held up a hand and she realised he was having difficulty hearing the voice on the phone. All around in the dark night were sounds of crashing, banging, splintering and thunder cracking through the air. Beyond the house, sheet lightning intruded into the blackness, giving the building a ghostly appearance.

Byron squatted down beside her and touched Camden's wrist.

"His pulse is very faint. Has he said anything?"

"No. What did the ambulance people say?"

"Fifteen minutes."

"How did you manage that?"

"A truck turned over about a mile away and they've just about finished. They'll come here next."

His expression was troubled. Ellie swallowed.

"D'you think…?"

Byron put a finger to his lips. "Talk to him. I'm going to the road in case they're here sooner."

He was gone quickly across the dark garden, a shadowy shape in the meagre light from the windows. Left alone with Farley's son, the weight of his situation crushed in upon her and she bent close to his ear, her hand upon his arm, talking about whatever came into her mind. It was a jumble of words: memories of the past; Fenella and Bran; Farley and Alice; his new car.

If he survived, would he think better of her having played a part in keeping him alive? Or would he feel beholden to her and his hatred and resentment increase? If only Farley was here, she thought sadly. Whatever she thought of Camden, he was part of a life she had loved and missed very much.

"D'you remember the bright orange car you bought that your father said could be seen a mile away, so no speeding?" she asked him, but there was no reply this time and she slid her hand to his wrist. It took her a few seconds to find the pulse beating faint and erratic. "Camden – say something!"

It came, the merest whisper, like an almost imperceptible breeze. "Fenella... secrets."

The whisper died away.

"Camden! Wake up! What're you talking about?"

He was so still and quiet. Where *was* that ambulance? As she lifted her head to call Byron, Camden's lips moved and she bent down again, but she could barely hear him.

"She knows... family... knows..."

"Knows what, Camden? Come on, stay awake. I can hear the ambulance."

There was no answer. She talked on about all the things he could do after he was out of hospital, but she doubted he was going to recover. There was no sign of Byron. The dark, noisy night encompassed them and Ellie remembered another stormy night hiding in her father's potting shed, in a long-forgotten little room behind old stuff and big bags of soil and terracotta pots. She'd stayed all night. It had been her safe place. Even Glenn had never found it. He knew she had a place to hide, but no matter what he did to her she never told him.

Men's voices reached her down the years and she looked round, dragging herself back to the present as Byron and the ambulance men pushed through the leaves and branches to reach them.

They tended to Camden and, with Byron's help, lifted the branch across Camden before moving him onto a stretcher and carrying him away to the ambulance. Byron and Ellie followed, watching and anxious as the man they'd found in the garden disappeared behind the closed doors of the vehicle.

The senior officer spoke to them briefly.

"He's lost blood. Been punctured by a sharp bit of branch. Left leg's not broken, but badly banged up. Might have internal injuries."

He hurried away and climbed into the front of the ambulance. Seconds later they were gone from sight towards Castlebay.

"I'd better phone Fenella," Ellie said without enthusiasm as they took off their boots in the old scullery, and hung sopping jackets over the capacious enamel sink.

The conversation with Farley's daughter was brief and intense, Fenella demanding to know why Camden had been there at all. When Ellie told her she had no idea, and that Camden hadn't been in any fit state to explain, Fenella hung up.

Ellie put the phone down, disappointed by the Orman woman's reaction. Whether it was from habit or distress at her brother's plight Ellie could not guess. Byron touched her lightly on the back and she turned around to find him regarding her with a respectful expression. It surprised her.

"You were fantastic out there tonight, Ellie. I know you were hurting, but you ploughed on. Thanks."

The words went into her heart, nestling in a deep place. They were true words and honouring, no hint of mockery or lie was in them.

"He's Farley's son, but I think I did it more for you than him. You've brought something into my life that no one else ever has."

A sound like a soft moan came from his throat and she saw in his eyes that her words had pleased him, but he made no move towards her.

"And you're bringing life back to me." His voice was quiet, touching her, wooing her.

Opposing emotions jostled inside, each clamouring to be chosen. The arguments began. If she gave in to him she would regret it long before morning. Her need of warmth and love was so deep she didn't know what to do with it, other than ignore it. What would it matter if she went to him? Who would know? I barely know the man. Anyway, I don't feel comfortable about it. She fled into what she knew – practical response.

"I'll sleep like a baby after all that, so I'm off back to bed."

They parted on the landing and Ellie knew he was frustrated and despondent, but she just couldn't do it. She knew she was also testing the strength of his attachment to her, and whether he really wanted to be with her long past the present situations with Farley's death and Glenn Thorley's unpredictable presence in Kilcomb. Trust grew slowly with her.

**

The phone rang just after eight the next morning. Ellie stumbled down the stairs, barely awake, lifting the receiver and mumbling into it.

"It's Jack, Ellie. Camden's in a bad way. I've been told he lost quite a bit of blood. He's going into surgery now."

"Oh," was all she could say.

"Are you all right?"

"Yes. Can't say I'm surprised. He was barely breathing when they got him into the ambulance. It was a huge branch he was under when we found him."

"Aye, so I've heard. You did a grand job."

"He's Farley's son."

She stared at a painting of a serene nineteenth century Scottish cottage scene.

"Have you told Fenella and Bran?" she asked as Byron came down the stairs. He halted beside her.

"Aye. They're not taking it too well. Farley's sister and husband are on their way from Edinburgh," he said, and then excused himself, coughing away from the mouthpiece. When he came back his tone was almost apologetic. "Ellie, I'm sorry, but I'll be around with Tim in an hour to ask you some questions. And you said 'we'. Who was there with you?"

"Byron," she said stiffly.

"Right. Make sure he's there as well."

He hung up as if he didn't want to pursue what Byron was doing at her house at that time of night.

"I'm guessing that was Jack," Byron said.

Ellie nodded. "Camden's on his way to surgery. Lost a bit of blood apparently."

He pursed his lips and momentarily withdrew into his place of deep contemplation.

"Strange place for him to be in the middle of the night," he said and went to turn into the kitchen. He stopped. "Are you okay, Ellie?"

"Perhaps it was him."

"Him what?"

"Who shot at us yesterday. Maybe he came back to kill me. You interrupted him last time."

"Maybe he did, but there was no gun on him."

"Could be under all those leaves," she said, frowning. "Oh, I've just remembered something. Before he lost consciousness, he said, "Fenella, secrets. She knows family, knows..." Doesn't make much sense. Anyway, he and Fenella are full of secrets."

Byron wrote the words down on a piece of paper. "Seems to me the village is full of them."

"Maybe. Camden's unlikely to remember what he said and, as I'm not his favourite person, I haven't a hope of finding out even if he survives. Still, I wouldn't put it past him to miraculously recover to spite everyone." She looked at her watch. "Jack'll be here in forty minutes. I don't think I'll tell him what Camden said. Anyway, he probably suspects you or I had a hand in Camden's accident."

At this he raised his eyebrows. "In your back garden?"

Ellie shrugged. She was too tired to think logically. At least the wind had ceased howling and contented itself with a soft soughing. The rain had stopped altogether.

Jack and Constable Ashby didn't stay long. They asked their questions, looked at the mess of fallen branches and the spot where Camden had lain and were gone by nine thirty.

The garden was a mess. Much of her vegetable patch was squashed, juiced and ground beneath the fallen branches. Only half of the trellised beans were left standing and the apple tree looked a little misshapen. Except for a few roof tiles which were now lying smashed on the ground the house was intact, but her small greenhouse needed about a quarter of the glass replaced. The roof on the garden shed would require repairing along with one wall. To her great relief, the barn was untouched except by a thick carpet of leaves and twigs on the roof. Out the front, plant pots were lying on their sides and two had been bowled onto the lawn.

She found her closest neighbours surveying their house from the road, and she joined them to find out if they were all right. Several panes of an upstairs front window lay in a shattered state on the lawn along with the contents from the window's ledge. Their eldest son was looking forlornly at his car; a branch had hit the roof and left a sizeable dent.

As she headed back down her driveway, thinking there was at least bringing Kipp home to look forward to, she saw Byron walking towards his car. The photos!

"Byron!" she cried, beckoning him. "It's nearly ten o'clock!"

He nodded and she thought that in all the mayhem of the night he'd forgotten as well.

"It's okay, Ellie."

"Glenn…"

"I've taken care of it."

"And if they're not what he wants?" she asked, presuming he'd left photos in the barn.

"Then we'll find out what it is he's really after. In the meantime, let's go and get Kipp."

"That's the best thing I've heard in days."

Kipp's bright eyes, wagging tail and attempts at prancing around Byron and Ellie, restored to her a measure of contentment lost in the last days. A veterinary nurse and several people in the waiting room looked on as Ellie led Kipp out of the animal hospital. Jim Plowden and Byron lifted the big dog into the Land Rover.

"He's mending well, but you'll need to keep him quiet for a week," Jim said as he handed Ellie a packet of pills. "One, twice a day with food. He can have some exercise in the garden, but don't take him for a walk until after he's had his check-up next week."

"Thank you, Jim. You're a marvel," Ellie said and gave him a peck on the cheek.

"It's good to see him happy again. By the way, I heard Camden Orman's in hospital. He was due to pick up his cat, but his sister rang asking if we could keep it a few days longer," he said, sighing.

"We heard, too." She didn't know what else to say.

"Can't say I'm overly fond of Camden," Jim continued, "but he loves animals. He even nursed a sparrow back to health once. Sometimes I thought he was two people in one body. Was he in an accident?"

"He was hit by a falling branch as far as we know," Byron said, glancing at her.

"Well, it was a wild night. We've had a number of injured animals in here this morning and farmers have been ringing since late last night."

"Any wild birds or animals?" Ellie asked.

"A few. Don't worry, I'll let you know if I need you to take any and nurse – mollycoddle more like," he added with a grin.

They bought lunch and headed out of town and along the coast for a few miles until they reached a small horseshoe cove. It was surrounded by rocks and hills that led up to higher areas where Farley had, ten years earlier, found remains of an ancient burial site. It had since been excavated by archaeologists who'd uncovered further evidence of several buildings. Farley had captured their progress in photographs that were displayed with artefacts in a permanent display in Castlebay Museum.

Almost four months had gone by since Ellie's last visit to the cove, when she had taken a group of fifteen French schoolgirls and their teacher up to the village site for two hours of drawing and photographing. There she had smiled at their delight, for France had many higher and grander peaks and views than Scotland, but the Highlands were unique, a special treasure in Great Britain. She had watched the girls trying to capture the lochs lying still and dark in the valleys, and the grand house and manicured gardens of a family with its roots deep in Scottish soil. Beyond, where the hills crept lower towards the sea, inlets of water tapped at the shores of one or two fishing villages, their boats bobbing on the low swell. Giggles had arisen amongst a group of four girls who were peering through binoculars. They had spied a couple lower down in a grassy nook exchanging a kiss in what they thought a private moment.

Ellie and Byron ate lunch on the sand, sheltered from the breeze by the low hills. Sunshine was struggling through scuttling clouds and at times it was warm on their backs. Evidence of the storm's ferocity lay in the piles of seaweed, bits of wood and several dead seabirds. Farther round the curve of the beach they could see a large wooden box. Byron went to investigate while Ellie stayed with Kipp. He came back grinning with a sealed tin of chocolates in his hand.

"Booty," he said, handing her the tin. "The box is broken open and about half full. It's also unmarked. Smugglers?"

"Maybe. I doubt it'll ever die out. It's a lucrative market from what I've been told."

Byron cocked an eyebrow. "Pub tales?"

"Of course, but the old timers have passed down their stories and knowledge to their sons," she said lightly. "They know the secret paths in the hills and around the coast. Some are known and trekked by the public, but others are still secret. They were used in the Second World War."

"D'you know any of them?"

Ellie hesitated, gazing for a few moments across the cove to a cluster of boulders at the far tip. Several seagulls stood like sentries, squealing at newcomers. Farley had shared his love of the area with her, a receptive and keen listener, and at times she wondered if he had said more than he meant to, but he also knew she was trustworthy. He was dead now, yet she struggled with the right and wrong of speaking what had so long been kept quiet. Strange how her life had been full of secret-keeping. It was a burden.

"Ellie?"

She blinked and turned towards him. "Sorry. Caught up in the past. I know one or two."

There was in his eyes, she thought, a hint of caution or guardedness.

"Is Maw's Hearth on one of the routes?"

"If it is, no one's told me," she said carefully. She waited, studying him, aware of more than a fleeting admiration of his features, unexpectedly wanting to kiss him rather than discuss an old war.

"You're not comfortable with this, are you?" he asked.

"No, but I'm so used to keeping secrets I don't know how not to. It's important though, I can tell by your expression. It's got that guarded look."

"Ah. You're getting to know me too well, Ellie Madison," he said and moved closer to her, their knees touching. This time she did not move away.

She smiled. "Only a little really."

"You have my permission to learn more."

Did she want to? The truth was she was uncertain of him; the little girl still had a long way to go.

"Don't be afraid of me, Ellie."

In the tenseness of his tone she heard a hint of something else. Fear, or perhaps despair. It stirred her and she touched his cheek gently with her fingers.

"Are you afraid I'll never want to be close to you, Byron?"

He drew in a deep breath and clenched his teeth, looking beyond her. How familiar she was with keeping emotions under tight control. What was in the closet of his past? He did not answer the question.

There was awkwardness between them while they packed away the remnants of their lunch. Leaving Kipp asleep in the Land Rover, they walked along the beach picking up shells and surveying the debris swept in by last night's turbulent sea. By the time they reached the broken crate, Byron had caught her hand in his and sent awkwardness fleeing.

The sun was out, making diamonds dance on the crests of low waves and scuttling shadows from all but the most inaccessible hollows and dints upon the hills. A small plane buzzed overhead on its downward path to Castlebay's small airstrip. It could hardly be classed as an airport, as the only building was a hangar incorporating a small office built during the war.

Ellie drew out several tins of expensive Belgian and Swiss chocolates, bottles of whisky, and jars of caviar.

"Bound for the gentry," she said, raising her eyebrows. "Or a local shop. We'll have to report it."

Ellie rang the police in Castlebay who advised them to stay with the find until they arrived. When they did, twenty minutes later, Ellie watched while they checked the Land Rover for stolen goods. She wasn't happy and told them. Just doing their job, they said.

An hour later than planned they arrived at Castlebay Hospital and found Olga in conversation with Bob. It was Olga who spoke first.

"So, Ellie, how're you mending? I heard you'd had a wee accident. Your poor face doesn't look too good."

"I'm doing fine, Olga. How're you? Paul told us you were hit by a car."

"Aye. And the blighter didn't stop. Of course, it had to be that gossipy Carrie Ross who found me. Still, I'm grateful for her and her husband's help. He's a nice man. Pity he got stuck wi' her," she said, looking then at Byron. "I'm glad you've brought the handsome Mr Oakes with you."

Ellie glanced at Byron, his expression without emotion. Bob was watching him and she wondered what he was thinking. Since Byron's arrival in Kilcomb she saw less of him.

"I guess you've heard Camden's in hospital," Bob said.

"Yes," she and Byron replied together.

"What a thing to happen," Olga said, frowning and shaking her head. "Just as well poor Alice isn't here. She wouldn't have coped very well." She paused and looked at Ellie. "Bob said he was in your garden. What was he doing there?"

"I haven't a clue. He certainly wasn't invited," she said, peeved by the question.

"I know you don't like him, but he is Farley's son and deserves some respect for that."

"Does he?" Ellie retorted. "He did everything he could to undermine his father and make his life hell. Not once did he thank Farley for all the money and opportunities he gave him. I'm sorry he's had such a horrible thing happen, but he's still an ungrateful lout."

"Then perhaps you didn't know him as well as you thought. Perhaps it was Farley you were listening to about his son and heir."

"Have you ever seen Camden in full war cry, shaking his fist at Farley because he couldn't have what he wanted? Little boys can change, Olga, but he didn't. Camden's a violent man, with a violent and ugly mouth. And he's creepy. A few weeks ago he threatened to kill me. Why would I want to honour such a man?"

"Aye, I can understand why you wouldn't. Perhaps Camden has too much fighting blood in him from his ancestors."

The latter words fell empty and without merit upon Ellie's ears.

Silence, like the heavy oppression of a hot day, enveloped them and sounds in the corridor seemed far away and disconnected. Olga held Ellie's gaze for long seconds before she looked out of the window at the clouds playing hide-and-seek with the sun.

Ellie glanced at Bob and Byron; both were studying her.

"Why didn't you tell me, Ellie?" Bob asked quietly, frowning.

"I didn't tell anyone."

He glanced at Byron and for the first time Ellie wondered whether Bob resented the other man's presence in Kilcomb.

"I happened to turn up at the right time," Byron said. She could have kicked him. "It could easily have been anyone else."

"Maybe. I hope for Ellie's sake, friendship with you isn't misplaced."

"Bob!" Ellie exclaimed. "What's got into you?"

The baker stood up. "It's time I was going. I hope you're up and about soon, Olga."

He pecked Ellie on the cheek, nodded briefly to Byron and vanished into the busy corridor.

"Well, Byron Oakes," Olga said with amusement in her eyes, "you do seem to be making an impact in our wee village."

"Bob will be fine, Olga," Ellie said firmly. "No doubt he's got a lot on his mind. Now, what did you want to see me about?"

"Did I? I don't remember saying I did."

"Paul Shepley stopped by yesterday and said you were asking to see me."

The old woman looked thoughtful, but Ellie did not believe she had forgotten.

"Perhaps you'd rather talk to Ellie in private," Byron said.

Ellie could not read his expression. It was closed, hard even.

"I'm not sure whether I trust you, Mr Oakes, but there's no need for you to leave. Ellie," she said, turning to her and patting the edge of the bed, "sit here for a bit. I've remembered what it was."

I'm sure you have, Ellie thought uncharitably, and glanced at Byron who sat down in a chair several feet away.

"Well, that's good," she said, allowing a reserved smile.

"You'll not be forgetting the picnic with the reverend. You seemed interested in the Earl of Strathvern that was in the seat during and after the war."

"Oh, yes," she said vaguely, drawing her brows together. "It was something Jamie said about his father."

"There's not much hope for your memory by the time you get to my age!" Olga said, chuckling. "Traitors, Ellie girl. You said Jamie told you and Farley he didn't want to be a traitor like his father."

Out of the corner of her eye, Ellie saw Byron lean slightly forwards.

"That's right, but at the picnic…"

"What I've remembered," Olga said, interrupting, "is that I read somewhere Jamie's grandfather was questioned about some of the guests he had staying during 1944 and '45. Two of them I think were high-ranking German army officers. The MOD couldn't prove the earl was a spy, but villagers have long memories and rumours went around for years that he was a Nazi supporter giving away our secrets. I heard he continued doing that even after the war, indoctrinating his son along the way."

"I don't know if it's all true. You said at the picnic you'd been to parties at the castle after the war. Did the subject ever come up?" Ellie was not convinced of the reliability of Olga's memory. She had heard all kinds of stories about the earls of Strathvern.

Olga shrugged. "Canna remember. It's not the sort of thing guests discussed. Very disloyal, not to mention rude."

"Not as disloyal as being a German spy," Byron said bluntly. "What was he accused of doing exactly?"

"Nothing was proven and I put it all out o' my mind. Ships, perhaps. I don't know. The war was a long time ago and I'm tired." She closed her eyes and folded her hands over her stomach.

"We'll go," Ellie said, looking at Byron who nodded and stood up, his expression stern. "See you another time, Olga."

There was no response. Ellie was certain Olga Erskine was not only wide awake, but regretting the entire conversation.

Several minutes later they were out of the hospital, but didn't speak until they were in the Land Rover.

"I bet," Ellie said after she'd checked Kipp was all right, "that was a story with little truth. I've heard the present earl's father was convicted, but somebody high up got him out of it and it was all hushed up. There're rumours that Ross is a Nazi sympathiser, but I don't believe it."

"Ross?"

"The current Earl of Strathvern. True he goes to Europe a lot, but he's a business man. Very successful antiques dealer and restorer of old buildings."

"Could've turned him the other way. Things like that don't always pass down." He looked thoughtful. "Olga's line about not discussing spying at those parties doesn't wash with me. It would've been a hot topic after the war, especially if the host's got Germans as guests. What d'you know about her?"

"Nothing other than what I've told you, although I don't know if she's telling the truth about when she was at the parties. At the picnic with Paul – you were in London – Olga said that the earl used to throw good parties *during* the war. She quickly added, 'so I heard'. Maybe she had 'heard', but what if she was *here* during the war?"

"Might be her memory, or lack of it. Still, it's an odd thing to lie about unless you're afraid."

"Or you've got a secret."

"Any idea if the Strathverns had connections with the people at Jimmy's Tarn."

Ellie pursed her lips. "Shouldn't think so. From what I've heard about Ross' father he didn't mix with anyone of common birth. He barely talked to his servants." Then she recollected an earlier conversation with Byron. "You're thinking about the man who owned Jimmy's Tarn during the war – he and his son worked at the Clyde Shipyards."

Byron nodded. "Farley was on to something, but he was afraid."

"Is that why he died? He knew too much?" she said quietly.

"I don't know. Did Farley keep a diary?"

"He had one for his work, but if he kept a personal one he never told me."

Byron started the Land Rover and drove out of the car park, turning the vehicle towards Kilcomb.

"It's possible Camden's found out what his father was up to. If so, he could've been in your garden on his way to see you, not hurt you."

Ellie blinked and stared out the windscreen. Years of Camden as a destructive influence left no room to consider him as anything else.

She felt a light touch on her arm. Byron was looking at her with a quizzical expression.

"Why would he come in the middle of the night?" she asked. "If he wanted to speak to me he'd just come and say it."

"What if it was too important? What if he was scared? Or maybe he thinks you know something. You shouldn't be alone, Ellie."

"You've already said that."

"And you keep going off by yourself. You and Camden could've both been out there – dead."

They left the outskirts of Castlebay, followed the curve of the bay for half a mile or so, and then wound round the bottoms of curved hills before the land flattened. Ellie locked herself into her thoughts, annoyed with Byron for ordering her about once again. For years she'd escaped such dominance and hoped he wasn't going to prove a disciplinarian like her father, though to be fair, he never hit her.

They began climbing and Ellie maintained her silence for several minutes. No one was going to make a prisoner of her again. Then she said, "I'm not going to stay closeted inside my house like a nun! I've got work to do. Anyway, that'll tell whoever it is that I know what Farley found – and I haven't."

Byron pulled suddenly off the road into a farm gateway. A car shot past.

"I'm not asking you to be a nun."

"What then? Anywhere outside I'm a target and you can't be with me every second of the day and night."

"Someone else then."

"Like who? One of your old army cronies? Oh, I know – she'll have to be a long-lost female cousin or school friend. Isn't that how it works?"

He turned to her, taking her face in his hands. His eyes were blazing.

"And what if it's Glenn Thorley? He's not going to kill you outright, is he? Think about it, Ellie. He'll make your last hours worse than they've ever been, or he'll leave you so maimed you won't have a life!" he said, angry and intense. "And neither will I."

She couldn't take her eyes off him. The truth of his words sank deep into her inner being. He let go of her face, but did not turn away and she could see a vein throbbing in his neck.

"Then I have no choice," she said, touching the vein.

"I want you alive, Ellie. There is little meaning or hope in my life without you."

He kissed her hungrily and this time there were no intruding images of her cousin. Vaguely, she heard a couple of cars go past and, for a fleeting moment, Ellie hoped it was no one she knew, but then decided it didn't matter. They were doing nothing wrong. Byron was her...

The windscreen shattered with a violent and loud crack, there was a grunt from Byron and she saw blood on his fingers after he'd touched his ear.

"Byron!"

"I'm okay," he said, pulling the gun out of its shoulder holster.

In the back seat, Kipp whimpered; he was uninjured and Ellie turned again to Byron.

Suddenly, the doors were wrenched open. She was dragged from the vehicle, her arms pinioned by her sides, and before she could kick out behind her, a foul-smelling cloth was clamped over her mouth and nose. Seconds later the world had vanished.

Chapter 13

Byron slowly recovered consciousness on the grass verge, the smell of a warm engine almost suffocating. His head was throbbing, his mind slow and muggy. Groaning, he rolled onto his side and sat up slowly, opening and closing his eyes several times to clear his vision. What was he doing lying next to the front wheel of the Land Rover?

Barking – it was familiar. Byron frowned. Kipp – where was he?

"Ellie," he murmured, pushing himself upright to lean against the vehicle. When he took a step, he tripped, put his arm out, and caught hold of the open door. "Ellie!"

Staggering round to the other side of the vehicle he saw footprints and flattened grass as if something had been dragged. There was no sign of Ellie. Weaving back down the road Byron studied the verge for tyre marks and footprints. They were there in the damp earth, clear and fresh.

A wave of nausea rushed into his throat and he vomited into the bushes. Pain exploded in his head with renewed vigour and he was forced to sit down, eyes closed, waiting until it subsided. It seemed an age he sat there while his thoughts began collecting themselves. Images emerged: a shot, windscreen shattered, the door wrenched open behind him. A cold tremor ran the length of his body; if he'd moved half an inch, he'd have been dead. It was odd. Anyone adequate with a gun could have killed him. Shoving a cloth over his face and rendering him insensible seemed ludicrous in the quiet Scottish countryside.

He got up carefully, standing still for several moments while his head cleared. Walking slowly, he searched along the verge. Amongst trampled grass and bracken he spotted a pen belonging to Ellie, given to her, she'd said, by Farley on her last birthday.

"Where are you now, Ellie?" he murmured, turning it over in his hand.

A quiet dread lurched in his gut, sending unwanted images to his mind. He shut them off. He knew what they could do to a man.

From down the road Byron heard barking and remembered Kipp. He turned back and saw, on approaching the vehicle, the round hole where the bullet had entered. He pulled open the back door and, to his relief, Kipp was sitting up, his tail wagging when he saw Byron. Patting the big dog's head, Byron mumbled thanks to God though he hadn't quite decided whether he believed in Him or not.

Lodged in the back of the seat was the bullet. Remembering seeing a first aid kit in the glove box, he retrieved it. Inside was a pair of tweezers with which he extracted the bullet and, emptying cotton buds from a small plastic bag, dropped it into it, sealed the top and put the bag in one of his trouser pockets. The first aid kit went back into the glove box. Still in the passenger's seat, Byron pondered what to do next.

He had to get back to Kilcomb, but it was a long walk and Kipp certainly wasn't up to it. A couple of cars from the Castlebay direction went by without slowing down. He glanced at the steering wheel and on the other side of it noticed the keys still in the ignition. Frowning, he got out and climbed into the driver's seat.

Why had the keys been left? Who had left them? Was it supposed to look like an accident? Or maybe the keys had been left to implicate him in a crime he hadn't committed. Ellie – he *had* to find her.

A bright yellow sports car pulled off the road in front of him. He had seen it before, a little too close for comfort as it rushed past him on a wet day shortly after Farley's body was found.

"Hi there," said the cheerful voice of a slender man in his mid-twenties. He had blond hair tapping his shoulders, a blond-red beard and blue eyes. Dressed in baggy brown trousers, a patterned shirt in bright colours and a well-worn brown jacket, his clothing didn't quite match the car. "You look as if you could do with some help. I'm Jamie, by the way."

He held out his hand which Byron shook.

"Byron Oakes. Help would be welcome. The windscreen's shattered."

"Not to mention the mess on the side of your head. D'you want me to call an ambulance?"

"No. I'll be fine."

"You don't look it." He studied him for a moment then glanced away. "Isn't this Ellie Madison's Land Rover?"

217

"That's right. And I'm guessing you're the Earl of Strathvern's son."

"You're well informed."

"I know Ellie and I know your car. It nearly collected me a few weeks ago."

Jamie made a face. "Sorry. I've got a thing about speed. Can't help myself." He looked round. "Is Ellie here?"

"No. Are you going to Kilcomb?"

Jamie nodded.

"I'll follow you," Byron said, pulling a handkerchief from his pocket and holding it to his head.

"Sure. To the garage?"

Byron shook his head and regretted it. "Ellie's will be fine. Her dog's in the back. Just picked him up from the vet's, so I need to get him home."

He looked at Byron, curiosity sparking in his eyes. "Is Ellie okay?"

As Byron opened his mouth to answer, the passenger door of the yellow car opened. A pair of trousered legs swung out, followed by the rest of Fenella Orman.

"Is there a problem, Jamie?" she asked, walking towards the two men. "I've got an appointment with the solicitor in half an hour."

"This is Byron Oakes, a friend of Ellie Madison's I believe," he said. "Byron, this is Fenella Orman."

Byron held out his hand a second time. "How's your brother doing?"

She took his hand briefly, looking him in the eyes, bold and authoritative. "I take it you mean Camden. He'll be fine," she said, a shadow flitting across her expression before she changed the subject. "You don't look so good though. And where's the unconventional Ellie?"

"At another appointment." He was rewarded with a tiny smile and another bold look.

"A man of wit. I like that," she said, her eyes roving over him with speed and precision. "I don't believe I've seen you before, Byron Oakes. I'd certainly have remembered, even without all the blood."

"We haven't met, but I've seen you in Kilcomb."

"Not the shy, retiring type, our Fenella," Jamie said, grinning. "However, Fen's right, we have to be going. So, if you're ready, I'll try to drive at a more sedate speed."

He turned and began walking over to his car. Fenella, however, lingered a moment longer.

"Ellie and I aren't what you'd call friends, but you and I might be. I need to see to family things in the next few days. Perhaps we can meet for coffee next week."

"Perhaps," he said, holding her gaze. "I saw you in the post office a few days ago. Carrie Ross was firing poisonous darts at you."

There was a sharp, indrawn breath. "How much did you hear?"

"Don't know. Enough."

"She's a cow of a woman."

"Worse, I'd say." He looked up and waved.

"Come on, Fen!" Jamie called. "You're going to be late."

"Coming! Till next week then, Byron Oakes. I'd appreciate it if you didn't tell anyone what you heard."

She walked quickly away and slid back into the yellow car. As he went back to the Land Rover, he thought about the conversation between the two women and Ellie's revelation about the reason. It would certainly have put a dint in Farley's reputation.

Jamie waited while Byron punched out enough of the shattered glass to see the road, before continuing on towards Kilcomb. When they reached Ellie's house, he stopped and got out, ascertained Byron was all right, got back in his car and sped off down the road. Fenella neither looked nor waved.

Before doing anything about Ellie's Land Rover, Byron washed his face and tentatively dabbed where the bullet had grazed his ear. Rummaging in her bathroom cupboard he patched himself up. Now he needed to find a temporary home for Kipp. The dog wasn't fit for active duty yet. All the way back to Kilcomb he'd argued with himself about telling Bob what had happened. Part of him didn't want to share Ellie.

It was stupid. He was the newcomer. Ellie and Bob were close friends and he'd work out something was wrong before long. How Bob would receive him he had no idea. The comment at the hospital about misplaced friendship didn't give Byron much confidence. He had been surprised to see him at Olga's bedside, but perhaps he'd merely been delivering her favourite cakes as there had been a paper bag bearing The Mill logo on the table near her bed.

He put Kipp into the back of his car along with dog food and basket. It wasn't until he was almost in Kilcomb that he remembered the photos in the barn. They would have to wait. Either Glenn Thorley would make a personal call or he had what he wanted.

When Mary saw Byron her eyes clouded and she shook her head.

"What's happened to you, you poor man?" she asked, leaving a young girl, her granddaughter as it turned out, in charge behind the counter.

"A bump on the head that's all. Have you got a minute, Mary?"

She nodded and followed him outside.

"I know we've only met once or twice, but I've come to ask a favour. Ellie's not well and it's best if she doesn't have to worry about Kipp right now. She told me you're the kindest person in Kilcomb."

He had a feeling, as he looked into the clear brown eyes, that she was no dunce.

"Flattery's lost on me, Byron," she said with a lift of her finely plucked eyebrows. "She must be bad if she can't look after Kipp. D'you want me to go round and see to her or are you doing that?"

He was right.

"I'll call you if I need help," he said.

"Aye, you do that."

"Thanks, Mary."

"I'll come wi' you to my house and settle in the patient. Just give me a few minutes."

It was a three-minute drive to her house and Mary spent most it talking of her friendship with Ellie. They had, it seemed, formed a bond the first day Ellie had come into the store.

"So, Byron, are her injuries worse than the doctor thought?"

"She just needs time to rest and heal."

"Rest and Ellie don't go together. Now, don't get me wrong, but I'm missing something here. Oh, here's my house."

He stopped the car outside an old house. "No, Mary," he said as he took the keys out of the ignition, "I don't think you're missing anything."

Between them they got Kipp and his belongings into the big kitchen. She put down a bowl of water near his basket, patted his head and stood up. She looked directly into Byron's eyes.

"Ellie's not there is she?" she asked bluntly.

He didn't answer immediately. Anything other than the truth would not be accepted by this woman. He had to trust her.

"No."

Tears started in her eyes. "Where she is?"

He shook his head, glad in a way of her perception. "I don't know, but I'll find her. You have to keep this to yourself, Mary."

She nodded. "I will. You can trust me. Ellie's my closest friend and I'll do whatever I can to help you find her – even if it means scaling the heights of Ben Nevis. And I'm not fond of heights much!"

"I'll do the risk taking, but I might need your help in other ways. Okay?"

"Yes," she said as he bent down to pat Kipp. "You've been good for Ellie, Byron. She's different somehow, just a bit. Farley was not for her. He was too much a loner. Has this got anything to do with his death?"

"I don't know." He didn't want to say more. "Look after Kipp. I'll be in touch."

"There's gossip in the village that Ellie killed Farley because of the money, and some will say she had a go at getting rid of Camden, too. Aye, it's no secret where he was last night."

He didn't comment, but wrote down his mobile number on a piece of paper. "Ring me if you need me, or hear or see anything you think I should know."

Mary nodded. "I'll do that." She folded the paper and put it in her purse.

When he got back to Ellie's he went straight to the barn. It was quiet, apart from the chickens clucking in their run and, with caution long ago written into his wiring, he walked over to the sack and opened it.

He frowned. The envelope with its photos was still there. He looked at the floor and could see only his and Ellie's footprints in the dust. Why hadn't Glenn collected the photos? He couldn't have known they were going to Castlebay unless he'd followed them. So why bother with demanding the photos?

Deep in thought, he left the barn and walked up the garden towards the house, his mind turning to Mary. His instincts told him she could be trusted, but her life as a store owner was not preparation for the rough games some people played. He hoped he hadn't put her at risk. He thought over every aspect of his visit to the store and her house, searching his memory for any missed and unwanted other presence. There was nothing.

The sound of a car pulling into the driveway made him look out the window and he saw Jamie's yellow sports car coming to a stop behind his car.

"I wasn't expecting to see you again so soon," he said as the two men approached one another in the driveway.

"How's your head?"

Byron, surprised by the lack of response to his observation, kept a neutral expression. "Okay now I'm stuffed with headache pills."

He waited, curious about the younger man's visit.

Jamie glanced at the house before speaking.

"Ellie's the only one who understands why I have to paint. She's a brilliant artist. We had an exhibition together back in the spring. It got me on my feet. Gave me the courage to stand up to my father," he said, and ran his fingers through his hair.

Still no explanation.

"Let's go inside," Byron said. "Ellie's out, but she won't mind."

It was quiet and cool in the house and there was an emptiness that drew on his fear for Ellie's safety.

"Tea or coffee?" he asked, heading towards the kettle.

"No, thanks. Don't drink the stuff."

Byron sat down opposite him.

"I gather you don't get on with your father."

"Not very well. He thinks I'm wasting my time. He can be a bully and a..."

He seemed to remember he was talking with a stranger and his expression closed like a cloud sliding over the sun and casting shadows upon the earth.

"A what, Jamie?"

"You must've heard village talk." He sounded impatient.

"Not always reliable."

"No, but people around here like to keep rumours and myths alive and well. Our family's not exactly held in high regard by all the local populace because of the war, because of my grandfather.

People have long memories and some people think muck sticks forever."

Byron studied the anger in his expression. "Is that why you paint?"

"It's one reason. My father thinks I'm lazy and rebellious. The most disappointing of his offspring he says, but he's often away so how would he know?" His pitch had risen. "He wants me to spend time at the house in Germany. Says it'll expand my horizons. There's no way! The only one who goes is Michael, eldest son and heir, and only so Father won't pass him over in favour of Leith – he's the youngest."

"Is that likely?"

"I doubt it, but Michael's got a thing about it and says if Father thought he was being disloyal he might make Leith his heir. When Father found out…" He stopped and looked with penetrating eyes at Byron. "I don't know you. I just heard you met Ellie on one of her hikes and were there when they found Farley."

"I think you've been wondering what I was doing in her Land Rover when she was nowhere to be seen."

Jamie nodded. "Another thing I heard is that you're smart. Had you really been to the vet's?"

"Yes. And are you going to tell me what your father found out? Anything to do with the lady who was in the car with you?"

"We've been friends for years. She teases me about not being much of an earl's son. Spending her life with someone who slaps paint on a canvas for a living has zero appeal. She's not interested in a toy boy either – her words. She's two years older than me. Wants a real man, she says." He shrugged. "Beautiful, yes. We have fun, yes. That's it. Anyway, about three years ago Farley came up to us in the pub and started in on me about being the son of a Nazi-lover. Told Fen to stop seeing me. It was weird. We didn't take any notice, of course."

Byron cocked an eyebrow. So much for Jamie's reticence to talk. He seemed to have changed his mind.

"I've heard he was a bit of a loner."

"He was. Bad tempered sometimes too." The young man frowned. "He went a bit strange in the last year. Fen said he was missing her mother and under a lot of pressure. She didn't say what. You ever been married?"

"No, but I doubt it's much fun having your wife vanish."

"That's if she did vanish." Jamie gave him a sidelong glance.

For a second, Byron regarded his youthful features in which two blue eyes flicked back and forth between attempts at challenging him and resisting him.

"I've never lived in a village. I was born in Portsmouth and then moved around in the army before doing a couple of years in London. I've come to the conclusion that there are different sorts of secrets. There's the one which almost the whole village knows except outsiders or visitors. Another kind is reserved for a few people, and then there's the kind that gnaws away at families or between friends. Ellie is an outsider in village terms and I certainly am. There are people in this village who have a secret and know what happened to Farley." He let a few seconds silence go by before asking, "Why are you really here, Jamie?"

A moment's pause was followed by an observation. "I don't think much gets past you."

"I wouldn't have survived if it did."

Jamie did not respond to the statement. Instead he answered Byron's question.

"I'm here because Ellie didn't know Farley as well as she thinks she did. And Fen told me in the car that Camden was found injured in Ellie's garden. Is that true?"

Byron nodded. "He was hit by a big branch."

He wasn't sure they were getting to the point of the visit. The conversation was hopping from one bit of information to another.

"What was he doing there?"

"No idea."

"Not sure I believe you, Byron, but Camden's odd. Has a lousy temper. Fen always defends him. Don't know why." He tapped a finger on the table. "You know, I think Ellie's in danger because she was close to Farley. He knew lots about what went on this district. He made enemies and he didn't forgive easily. My father's the same. A few days before Farley died I heard him and Father arguing."

"Anyone know about this?"

"No," he said, a flicker of resentment in his eyes. "It wasn't anyone else's business. I mightn't like my father much, but I don't make a habit of bringing more shame on our family. Anyway, I couldn't hear everything they were saying because it was windy and they had their backs to me. I was reading in the rose garden on the other side of the hedge. Farley said something about my grandfather and his cronies sabotaging ships on the Clyde during

224

the war and sending the Germans plans of ships being built there. He said he had evidence."

Byron shifted in his seat. "Did he say what it was?"

"It was too hard to hear. I didn't want to move closer in case they saw me, but Father was furious. Threatened to shut Farley up. But Farley was no coward I'll give him that. Said he'd give the newspapers names. Then there was something about a special room. Father went ballistic and punched him. Farley swore at him and hit back. Suddenly it was over. Farley went and I saw Father heading toward the castle."

Byron sensed he was being tested. Or perhaps, challenged, was a more apt word.

"Special room?"

"I haven't a clue what he was talking about." He looked down at his watch. "I'd better be going. Have to pick Fen up."

"Rather conspicuous in that car of yours."

"Not in the next road," he said, with a quick, cheeky smirk. "Anyway, Farley's dead."

"What about your father?"

"He doesn't like it, but never says anything."

They walked out of the house and Byron watched him back the sports car out the driveway. The richness of the engine reminded him of his reckless driving days. Nearly killed himself once. Seconds later there was no sight or sound of the yellow car.

He returned to the kitchen and made coffee. For a long time he sat pondering the conversation. It was useful stuff, but why had Jamie given him all that information?

Restless, he got up and went into Ellie's study where he scanned two large bookcases, looking for books that might have information on Clydebank shipping. There wasn't much, especially about the Second World War. However, he did learn that during the six-year period about two thousand ships were built on the Clyde and over twenty-three thousand repaired. Each day some thirteen new or refurbished ships had gone down the slipways. He was impressed and could see why an enemy might want to stop or hinder such productivity. With so many men working there it would have been easy to slip in a few who weren't as patriotic to Scotland and its allies as their workmates. He wondered where Farley's wartime photos had been taken.

Pushing his hands into his trouser pockets, his fingers came into contact with the plastic bag containing the bullet. Pulling the bag out, Byron studied the bullet with its trace of blood.

"Who fired you?"

He put it back in his pocket, left Ellie's house, and drove to his rented cottage. Tomorrow he'd go to Castlebay and post the bullet off to London for analysis. He had no intention of giving Carrie Ross another chapter for her gossip column.

As he put the key in the lock and opened the front door he sensed that someone else had been there. It all looked the same in the hallway, but then he went from one disturbed room to another. Cushions were pulled out and on the floor, cupboard doors were open and contents moved around, shelves partly emptied, books on the floor, pictures askew on the walls. There was soot in the front room fireplace where the intruder had apparently poked up the Chimney. The cupboard under the stairs was in a shambles, and in the scullery wet clothes had been thrown out of the washing machine. Upstairs in his bedroom the linen was off the bed and the mattress not square on its base, the wardrobe door was open and items of clothing tossed carelessly on the floor, along with the contents of the bedside cupboard. Whoever had trespassed had been thorough.

Byron went back downstairs and drew all the curtains. In a dark corner in the ceiling of the front room he removed a panel next to a rafter. He groped inside the opening and his fingers found the packet of photos he had hidden. He left it there, replaced the panel, climbed down and put the stool back in its place and on its side as he'd found it. If anyone intended returning hoping for clues in moved furniture they would find he had not obliged them.

While part of him wanted to put everything back in its place, another part needed escape from the intrusion into his life. He was glad he'd brought little paperwork and no mementoes with him. It was too early for that.

Byron pulled the front door shut behind him and got back into the car. As he turned into the road a familiar car went by and a honk of the horn made him look up. It was Bob, who waved and pulled up in front of him. Byron wound down the window as the other man got out and approached him.

"What on earth happened to you?" Bob asked, looking at the bandage.

"Almost in the path of someone out hunting."

Bob's pale blue eyes widened.

"Are you joking?"

"Not a bit."

"Well, be careful! You're not in the army now. Next time you go wandering about in the wilds of Scotland, take a local with you."

"I'll remember."

Bob did not look convinced, sighed, and shook his head.

"The reason I was coming to see you was to apologise for what I said at the hospital."

"Thanks. No offence taken."

He nodded. "Ellie and I have known each other a long time, Byron. It's not easy watching her affections pass to a stranger."

"I don't think they've *passed* anywhere, Bob."

Bob looked at him as if considering how to arrange his next words. "Maybe not. Ellie doesn't give her heart easily. At least, not all of it."

"Do any of us?"

The other man shrugged. "I did – once. Don't know if I could do it again. Ellie's the closest I've come. I lost my wife in a car accident eight years ago."

"I'm very sorry, Bob. I didn't know. Children?"

"Four. All grown and away from home. Ellie's filled a gap."

"Yea. I think she'd be good at that." And that, he knew, was what she was doing for him. He changed the subject. "Any idea why Farley died, Bob?

"Hmm?" He looked up. "Oh, I think he got too much in the way of a property developer. A couple of them really hate him."

"Hate's a strong word. Is that how you felt about him? It couldn't have been easy knowing Ellie was spending so much time with him."

The change in Bob was instant and Byron regretted the way he'd spoken.

Bob's eyes narrowed. "I don't hate anyone," he snapped. "You don't know her and Farley didn't either. She needs an anchor in her life. Farley had some great qualities, but stability wasn't one of them. They'd never have lasted the distance."

"Want to enlighten me?"

"No, I don't. Just tell Ellie I still need to see her about the petition for William's Loch – the sooner the better."

"Might be difficult," he said.

"What's difficult about such a simple message?" Bob asked, still angry.

In the short time Byron had known Bob Caraway he'd never seen him so uptight.

"Ellie's disappeared."

Bob stared at him. "What d'you mean, 'disappeared'?"

Byron told him briefly what had happened, leaving out the argument he and Ellie had been engaged in. Bob looked as if a bomb had exploded beside him taking other lives but not his, while he was left in a state of unbelief that such a thing could happen.

"Who was it?"

"I don't know."

"You must've got a description of someone!"

"No. All I remember is a bullet coming through the windscreen, doors being yanked open behind and a dark blue arm hauling Ellie out of her seat."

"Have you told Jack Kennart?"

"No. I'm considering it."

"Considering it!" Bob said vehemently. "She could be dead by now!"

Byron snapped. "I want her back, too, Bob – in one piece."

"Then do something about it and tell Jack. He'll not thank you for withholding this information."

"The problem in this village is that too many people have too many secrets and will keep them no matter who gets hurt. D'you want to tell me who could've done this or is this another thing about Farley you don't want to talk about?"

"Ellie's disliked by developers almost as much as Farley was. Start by looking there – especially Glenn Thorley."

"I'm beginning to think it's someone closer to home and nothing to do with Farley or Ellie's work."

He watched Bob closely, but there wasn't a flicker of concern. A steely silence came between them for half a minute.

"If any harm comes to her, I'll be the one asking questions."

With that he turned and walked towards his car, leaving Byron to ponder the relationship between Ellie Madison and Bob Caraway. It seemed Ellie liked to have men around her, but the stop signs were up as far as anything deeper than friendship. With a past like hers, he could hardly blame her, but had she told Bob or Mary about it? Such a thought gave him no comfort. Was Ellie to be trusted?

Bob did not drive off immediately and when Byron passed him he noticed he was talking on his mobile phone. It reminded him to turn his on. It beeped; a message was waiting, but he put the phone in the cup holder beside him. As he reached the top of the road and began turning right, Bob came up the road behind him. Glancing in his rear-view mirror, he saw Bob turn left and quietly breathed a sigh of relief. He thought the other man would follow him.

A few minutes later his mobile phone rang. Pulling off the road, he picked it up. "Byron Oakes," he said, as several cars went by in both directions.

"And this is Jack Kennart," barked the sergeant. "At least you're alive."

Byron's body stiffened and he became very still, every nerve and sense heightened. "Meaning?"

"Don't play games with me, laddie. Why the hell haven't you called me about Ellie? You know damn well she's gone missing – and you're supposed to be dead according to the anonymous caller. You should've reported to me straight away."

Byron's eyes narrowed. Had Bob called him?

"Difficult when I was unconscious and had blood oozing out of my head from a close shave with a bullet. Anyone meant to kill me wouldn't have bothered knocking me out with chloroform or whatever it was. Check with Jamie Strathvern if you don't believe me. He found me. When did you get the call?"

"Over an hour ago. Where've you been? I've been ringing you. I thought a man like you would've had his phone on twenty-four hours a day."

"I don't. Did you recognise the voice on the phone?"

"Constable Ashby took the call. He said the voice was muffled, but it was male. Get yourself to the station."

"Later. Here's what I know," he said and launched into an abbreviated version of the circumstances before Jack could protest.

When he finished a few minutes later, he heard a long whoosh of air from the sergeant.

"Inspector Carter's going to love this. Get away down the station now. You're his favourite suspect and you'll soon be mine."

"Give me two hours. There's something I want to check."

"You've not got two minutes! The inspector's on his way."

"Two hours, Sergeant."

He hung up and switched his phone off.

Fifteen minutes later he was parked on the opposite side of the road to where the attackers' car had stopped. He sketched the patterns of the tyre marks and shoe prints, and examined the narrow verge for other signs of the perpetrators' presence.

A bit farther along the road, where he and Ellie had been parked, he scanned the grass and mud and looked amongst the bushes for anything they might have dropped. The only thing he found lay close to where the back of the Land Rover had been. It was a Styrofoam cup bearing 'The Mill' stamp on the bottom. He scooped it into a plastic bag and walked back to his car with it, sitting inside and staring at the road ahead. Once or twice his glance rested on the Styrofoam cup. He looked back across the road. The only thing he could do was try and find where the other car had gone, though it would be more guesswork than anything else. It was a long while since he'd done any tracking, but it was better than doing nothing. He pulled the map of the local area out of the glove box and studied it; roads and tracks like veins in a man's arm stretched and wriggled across the paper. He knew too little about the district.

About a mile along he turned into a thin road that, according to the map, headed vaguely in the direction of Maw's Hearth after skirting round the edges of a loch and an inlet from the sea. About two miles from the road was the Earl of Strathvern's castle. There was little logic in why he'd chosen the road he had, other than Jamie's visit earlier. It was odd... the assault was odd. In fact, the whole damn day was odd.

When he noticed fresh tyre marks on the muddy roadside he stopped and compared them to the sketches. They didn't match. It was nothing more than a fool's hope of finding a pot of gold buried under a tree in the forest.

Frustrated, he pushed his foot down hard on the accelerator and skidded back onto the road. Ten minutes later the road came to a dead end at a farm gate hanging on its rusty hinges. Part of the bottom wooden slat was embedded in the earth. On the gatepost was a sign warning trespassers about prosecution. Byron looked around and some thirty yards away, with the land rising gently behind it, a croft stood crumbling under a bowed roof, alone in its old age. A small area of woodland had crept close to one of the field's broken fences. Byron, with binoculars around his neck, traipsed across the soggy land, but there was no evidence that anyone had been near the croft in a long time. The front door was gone and inside it was damp, dirty and sad.

Back outside in the early evening light he looked through binoculars hoping to find a trace of a track leading from the gate, but it had long been obliterated by bog and heath. Birds cried on the wing and he saw them flying towards the loch, while somewhere beyond the rise behind the croft came the distant sound of dogs barking. Quite a way off, though looming close through the binoculars, were several cottages on the shores of a loch that seemed to correlate with the one marked on the map. Maw's Hearth and The Chimney were shrouded in clouds.

Somewhere between the loch and Maw's Hearth squatted the lonely farmhouse of Jimmy's Tarn. A chill ran down his spine. Why had Glenn Thorley not claimed the photos in Ellie's barn? He peered through the binoculars seeking the farmhouse, but a long low hill hid it from view. Had Thorley taken her there?

Fear and anger, both determined and ferocious, locked him in an internal battle. Tears filled his eyes. He'd been a hardened soldier who'd seen atrocities that could send a man mad. Their images were kept locked away in a room somewhere in his mind. If he could survive all that, then losing Ellie shouldn't matter. He barely knew her. Yet, he knew enough. Who would see him out here? From deep down inside a cry rose that pierced the cold air and sailed across the empty land.

"Ellie!"

The intensity of his emotions subdued the sounds and blurred the scenery around him. It didn't matter. Ellie mattered.

"You won't find her here."

The voice crashed into Byron's space, slamming shut the door on his emotions. He spun round, his heart pounding. Angry now for allowing himself to let his guard slip, he stared at the man and two English setters sitting beside him. They were about five yards away. How could he have not heard them?

"Sorry to startle you and sorry to intrude, but Ellie Madison isn't here. I assume that's the Ellie you were calling," said the man, coming towards him. The dogs waited. "I'm the Earl of Strathvern. You're either a lost tourist or you're new around here. This is my land you're on."

Chapter 14

The air was chill and there was a musty smell of old wine and over-ripe fruit. A strange and uneasy feeling crept into Ellie's heart as she struggled awake. The dull heaviness that troubled her mind did not want to shift and it was a slow process getting her eyes open. When they did, it was to a dimly lit room of undefined shapes that wobbled before her blurred vision. Slowly, the fogginess lifted. To her dismay she realised she was in a cellar.

What on earth had happened? All she could remember was sitting in the Land Rover with Byron. Where *was* he? She looked around, but there was no sign of him – or Kipp. In her mind she saw images of Byron and Kipp, unmoving, in pools of blood.

"No!" she said sharply, loudly, "that's not real. I didn't see that. Don't think it."

She was lying on her side on an old, dark green settee with carved wooden armrests and legs. Large stone slabs covered the floor, stretching away to a set of steps which marched upwards and disappeared behind a wall. Vaguely, she supposed a door was up there somewhere, a locked door.

A single bulb, its cord entwined with cobwebs, was the only significant light. High up in the wall was a grate through which limited light filtered into the cellar. Easing herself onto her elbow, she glanced at her watch. Seven-fifteen, but was that evening or morning? She listened – there wasn't a sound.

Pushing herself upright, the room gradually gained depth and definition. Behind her was a wall, and near the settee stood a desk which had on it a number of large ledger books between bookends, an ink pot and a couple of bottles of wine. A swivel chair was pushed neatly against it, its legs tucked underneath the body of the desk. At the end of the desk the room opened out; rows of wine racks stood silently in the gloom. A film of dust covered the desk and its contents as well as the arms and legs of the sofa and chair. Against the wall on her right was an assortment of wooden tea chests, several chairs, a tall cabinet with its doors closed, and a trolley. Two long cases were propped against the wall on her left.

The cellar was sadly neglected.

Tentatively easing herself off the settee, she leaned for a moment against the desk and waited for a wave of dizziness to pass. When it had gone she looked at the things on the desk, retrieved one of the fat ledgers and opened it. Row after row of entries in ink recorded prices and quantities of wine, brandy, whisky and continental food. Over the page was a comment on when the next shipment was expected. An historian would love this, she thought, as she turned to the page inside the front cover and hoped the clerk had written something more than a date. And he had: Strathvern Castle Cellar 1, April 1894 – August 1896.

Ellie frowned. On a couple of occasions, the earl had allowed her and a painting group she organised at odd times in the year, to spend a day at the castle. Once, Michael had taken them on a tour that included an old cellar near the kitchens. The size of it had astonished her, but it wasn't as big as this one.

Pulling out the end ledger on the far right, Ellie flipped open the cover: Strathvern Castle Cellar 1, June 1942 – there was no end date. Entries finished about halfway through the volume, the last one in September 1943. It was a large order, taking up almost three whole pages, and included suppliers from Scotland, France and Germany.

There was something about September 1943 that Ellie thought she should remember, but couldn't. She shut the dusty volume and placed both it and the earlier one back in their respective places. The drawers had few things in them: an assortment of papers, a bottle of ink, leaves of blank, yellowed paper, bills addressed to Strathvern Castle dating back to the war, and two slightly tarnished, gold cartridge pens.

She walked across the floor towards the steps, reached the bottom and looked up. It was gloomy near the top, but there was a door. She went slowly up to it and tried the knob. As she'd suspected, the door, a solid piece of wood with a substantial lock, did not budge and she went back down, deciding to investigate the area where the wine racks stood.

On the other side of the wall to where the sofa was located, she found three light switches, only one of which produced action when a single bulb down the far end threw its dim glow across rows of dusty racks. Much of the room was hidden in shadow and Ellie's spine tingled with apprehension as she walked towards the lit area. She had no idea whether anyone was watching her, absorbed into the darkness and waiting. Convincing herself it was a silly idea, when they could have bumped her off while she was out cold, she moved steadily onwards.

Some of the racks were empty, others held a few dusty bottles, and several were almost full. She knew little about the value of wine, but she supposed a lot of money was sitting here in the dark. Not that the earl was poor, quite the opposite she'd heard.

Where the light was brightest, Ellie lifted one of the bottles from its home and read the label, 'Clos de Myglands, Bourgogne 1915, Nuits St Georges'. It sounded impressive and expensive, but it was so old she wondered if it had turned to vinegar. She pulled out several more, brushing away years of dust and cobwebs with a deepening sense of undisturbed history that she was now troubling.

Interesting and mysterious though it was, the thing foremost in her mind was escape from the cellar. Walking to the end of the row, she glanced left and right. There seemed to be an indent in the wall farther along and so she went right into an area of shadow. It was eerie. She thought she heard a sound behind her and froze. Absolute silence.

Reaching the indent Ellie found an iron gate and beyond it what might be a tunnel, but it was devoured in darkness and she had no idea whether it came to a dead end a few feet on or was a way out. The gate was locked and though she shook it, it remained solid and uncompromising. However, if the cellar was under the castle, then the tunnel must lead to the living quarters. Where it was under the castle was a puzzle.

She was halfway across the cellar to the room in which she'd first found herself, when she heard the noise again. It was louder and closer, a key turning in a lock. Hurrying, she switched off the light and waited in the dark between two rows of bottles. The footsteps of one person rapped on the stone steps – then stopped. Silence. Had whoever they belonged to reached the bottom and noticed her missing? Ellie's heart was thudding; a headache began. Straining to hear the merest movement, she reached out and grasped the neck of a bottle.

The silence stretched on until a man's voice suddenly erupted into it.

"It's no good hiding, Ellie! The only way out is up these steps."

Bran! The quiet one who hated violence. He had always been the most approachable and trustworthy of Farley's offspring. What was he doing here? Had someone convinced him she had killed his father to get the family's money?

Ellie did not respond. Let him wait.

"Come on, Ellie," he said, cajoling. She'd heard the tone often enough before in Farley. "I've brought you something to eat, but I can't wait for you all night."

She kept quiet, but now she knew it was evening. As gently as she could, she pulled the wine bottle out and crept down the row towards the back, walked along the end of three rows until, still hidden in the shadows, she could see Bran. He seemed to be on his own, holding only a container and a flask in his hands. There was no sign of a gun nor, as she'd dreaded, of Glenn Thorley.

For another minute he did not move and then she saw a frown gather across his forehead, his dark eyebrows drawn together, before he walked across the floor and disappeared out of sight. Seconds later, without the container, he was standing in the entrance surveying the rows of racks. He looked worried.

"Ellie? Where are you?"

It occurred to her then that Bran might construe her silence as more than a desire not to be found. In his often uncomplicated way of thinking, he might believe someone had either killed her or moved her to another location without telling him. He seemed hesitant, but then moved quickly towards the light switches. Ellie slipped into the next row. If anyone else was with him, they would surely show themselves now.

The cellar was filled again with eerie shadows as the dull yellow light spread its glow as far as it could.

"Ellie, for pity's sake! Answer me!"

There was no mistaking the panic in his voice and despite her reservations she could not contribute to his torment any longer. She'd always liked him. Moving quickly and quietly along the row she stepped out into half shadow. He spun round and she saw relief on his face, but it was instantly replaced by fear and suspicion.

"Is that you, Ellie?"

"Yes, Bran, it is," she said, moving into the light whilst keeping her distance. "Who did you think it was?"

"You just gave me a start that's all. Why didn't you come out when I first called?"

"I wanted to make sure you were on your own."

"Well, I am. I've brought you food. Best eat it. You'll be here for a while."

Ellie didn't move. "Why? Where are Byron and Kipp?"

He shrugged. "I've to look after you. That's all I know."

"Who's put you up to this, Bran? I didn't think you were the type to get yourself mixed up in violent company."

An expressionless shield came down over his countenance, one she'd seen many times before when he did not want anyone to know his feelings. How like his father he looked.

"Don't waste the food," he said and began turning into the other room. "And don't think you can get out of here, because you can't. You're locked in tight with the ghost."

Ellie walked up to him and stood close, annoyed by the juvenile tactic. "And whose ghost might that be?" she asked abruptly.

He looked surprised as he took a step back from her. "His Lordship's mother. She topped herself down here just after the war ended. You must've heard about it."

Ellie nodded slowly. "Of course, but I didn't know where it happened. It's been kept a secret and you can never believe rumours."

"Well," he said with an unexpected grin, "you can chat to her all night. She's the only company you'll have."

"And how d'you know that?"

He looked at her as if she was stupid.

"Because no one else knows you're here except Mr." He snapped his mouth shut. "My dad thought you were the smartest woman he'd ever met, but you'll not find a way out." He pointed towards the back of the wine racks. "The gate's locked. No one's been through it since *she* killed herself."

He turned on his heel and walked away.

"Why were you afraid when I didn't answer your calls, Bran?" she said loudly to his back.

The young man stopped, but he did not turn around. After a few moments he said quietly, "Because Dad loved you."

Then he continued across the floor, ran up the steps, opened the door, and shut it behind him. The key clunked in its lock and once again she was on her own.

For a long time she sat on the couch and thought about Bran's unexpected parting statement. All the feelings she'd had for Farley in their early years of friendship came rushing back. She had kept her emotions under lock and key, but Farley somehow recognised them. He wanted her and told her so, but Alice was his wife. Feeling guilty for even feeling the need for a man's strength and love, her emotions would swing violently the other way, her mind rejecting any kind of physical connection with Farley or any man. Her past had invaded her thoughts vigorously and hatred of Glenn had increased during those first years in Kilcomb. However, there had been a time shortly before Alice's disappearance when Ellie had given in to her need. Guilt had twisted inside her for a long time afterwards and she had told Farley she would never do it again. Their relationship had altered after that and she'd shoved her need for love away, directing all her passion into her painting and supporting the Ormans in the fight to keep out developers. Whether Alice ever knew what had happened, Ellie still did not know.

The cold and silence, the uncertainty of her future past this night, were soil for distressing thoughts and questions. Even supposing Byron and she survived, and she had no clue what had happened to him or Kipp, how could she trust her emotions? There was no evidence in her past of any ability to maintain a long-term relationship with a man without the past marching in and destroying it. And yet, Byron was different to any man she'd met. He was the kind of person she'd always hoped would arrive in her life, but never believed would, and she did feel different, stronger about her part in their relationship. Whether it was love or an inherent need to be needed and cared for, was another thing. Dwelling on it now in this gloomy place wasn't a good idea.

Looking around the room, she saw the flask and container of food on the desk and got up. If she didn't eat she wouldn't be able to think properly and she certainly wouldn't have any energy to attempt escape. If Bran thought she was going to be a good girl, eat her dinner, and then go to sleep, he was misguided and mistaken.

The food was still warm and the strong tea piping hot. Just what she needed as she turned her focus on the situation and what she was going to do about it. She'd read too many stories about people escaping from apparently impossible situations not to believe she couldn't do the same. Apart from that, she had no intention of being there when Bran, or the kidnapper, returned in the morning.

"Well, Countess Strathvern," she said to the empty cellar, "looks like we'll just have to get along."

The story of the countess' death was so little talked about that few, if anyone now living, knew what had happened or what had

237

caused her to make such a devastating end to her life. It had occurred on the night of birthday celebrations in her honour. The earl, sixth in his line, was known to have been a hard man. His wife, a gentle woman passionate about Scotland, could not abide his Nazism and some said that, along with this treatment of her, became too much to bear. Others said the earl had a mistress on whom he secretly lavished affection, money and gifts at the expense of his family, and who had been present on the birthday night. There were even rumours of a child by the mistress. No evidence of a mistress or child had ever been proven. If he had been involved with another woman, she had not come forward after the countess' death and he had never acknowledged the existence of a mistress. Nor had the earl publicly disclosed the location in which his wife had died. Bran, however, had worked on the estate since leaving school and she supposed he might have overheard something about it.

Returning to the iron gate she stood staring at it, contemplating how she was going to get it open. It was a testimony to men from another century of solid workmanship and durability, but she had all night and was not giving in when all she had done so far was rattle it. She bent down and looked at the lock. It was firmly in place and not about to come loose no matter how much she shook and tugged it. At the other end of the gate the hinges were solid and forbidding, a challenge greater than the lock.

Attempting it with bare hands was a waste of time and Ellie went off in search of tools. Workers must have left some behind. She started in the first room. The gun cases were empty and the tall cabinet contained only a decanter, several wine and brandy glasses, and someone's spectacles covered in dust and long-deceased moths. She spent some while looking inside tea chests, but they were empty. Others were still nailed shut.

By now, Ellie was covered in dust and grime and the night was creeping on. Every noise seemed loud enough to wake the entire population of Kilcomb three miles down the road. Hands on hips, she gazed around the room. There had to be tools somewhere.

Moving along to a pile of cardboard boxes she had not noticed earlier, she tentatively lifted the unsealed flap of the nearest one and found it filled with tins of imported French food. All the boxes bore the same company name, but different contents; she wondered how long they had been there. One of the boxes was labelled with the name of her favourite jam and she couldn't resist opening it.

However, when she lifted up the top flap she found herself looking at boxes of bullets. She quickly opened the remaining boxes; half contained the same contents. In two others she found hand guns packed inside biscuit tins. She stacked all the boxes back up, hoping Bran wouldn't notice they had been shifted.

The find was disturbing.

Ellie returned to where the wine was stored and walked cautiously past the rows of bottles towards the back. Her thoughts were crowded with pictures of Glenn's hand suddenly grabbing her out of the deep shadows, his strength overpowering her and she being left half dead where no one would ever find her.

"Stop it!" she said, annoyed with the way she was allowing fear to govern her mind.

If he was there he would have made his presence known before now; that was his way and such was his arrogance. Nevertheless, her heart was pounding and her hands were clammy.

It was then she remembered the pencil torch in one of her jacket pockets. She hadn't used it in a long while, quite forgotten about it, and she hoped the batteries still had life in them.

The torch flickered on and off, then stayed on, but its light was still quite good. Fear receded, but lay crouching in a corner of her heart as the light revealed each row empty of human life. She wished Byron was there. In the quiet isolation she yearned for the sound of his voice and his reassurance that there was a way out.

Suddenly, she froze. What was that noise? A long silence followed, her ears straining to hear the slightest sound. She switched off the torch and stood vulnerable and fearful in the shadows. Then she heard it, a scuttling on the other side of the rack. Turning the torch back on, she peered around the end into the next aisle and saw the tail of a rat disappearing underneath the wine rack. Ellie breathed a sigh of relief and continued the search for a tool.

Scattered about in various piles and in one or two small wooden boxes were numbers of rusty tools about which she had little clue to their use, except for the hammer and a saw. However, one item in particular looked useful; it had long handles, wooden on the ends, and a rounded end like a metal mouth that might do sufficient damage to the lock so she could get it off.

With the implement in her hands Ellie reached the gate with determination. She had no intention of sitting docilely waiting for whoever might arrive next. It did not seem logical to her that the one who had planned and executed the whole event would leave Bran in charge of her. If she was a valuable commodity then eventually someone would come and claim their bargaining object. There were hours left of the night, but she did not know when her abductor would turn up. A sense of urgency pushed her on though she was uncertain whether she'd be able to get the gate open. Even if there was success, she had no clue where the passage led or whether there was an exit at the other end.

The first attempt at breaking the lock resulted in little more than a slight dent on it as she squeezed the implement, her muscles burning in protest. She continued for another fifteen minutes, applying pressure and hoping the metal would weaken sufficiently for her to break it open. It remained obstinate and unmoving.

Ellie stared at it, frowning in frustration. Byron would have had it off in seconds. What would he do?

She stared through the gate and then, putting the tool on the ground, she returned to the other room. For a few indecisive minutes she studied the crates from France. All she knew about guns defeating stubborn locks was from the movies, but if it worked she would save a lot of time.

The only other thing to do was to wait until Bran or the mysterious man he'd alluded to turned up. That wasn't the choice she preferred and so, with doubts about the wisdom of her decision, Ellie retrieved one of the hand guns and a box of bullets. She hoped they went together. They did, and she returned to the gate.

The most worrying factor about using a gun was the sound of the shot carrying along the tunnel, and if she was in old cellars directly beneath the castle there was a distinct possibility it would be heard.

It was almost ten thirty. People might still be about; it was a risk she had to take. If she waited much longer and dozed off, the opportunity would be lost and she the hapless pawn in someone's sick game.

Taking aim, Ellie stood almost motionless, concentrating on hitting the lock. The silence of the cellars wrapped around her like a cold blanket and the dread of pulling the trigger increased.

"Captivity or freedom?" she murmured, glaring at the lock.

Without another delaying thought, Ellie pulled the trigger. In a split second the bullet left the chamber, hit the lock and exited into the tunnel beyond. The sound of its firing exploded in her ears, ricocheted around the cellar and into the passageway. She hurried into the shadows where, for almost ten minutes, she stood listening for any sounds other than the tattoo of her own heart. She was shaking and her eardrums were ringing.

No one came, either from the tunnel or down the steps in the adjoining room. Slowly, her body calmed down and her mind came out of its stupefied state. She approached the gate. Putting the gun on the ground, Ellie pulled the gate hard towards her. It did not open, but the lock was loose and as she rattled it she realised that the gate opened into the tunnel not into the cellar. Shoving at it with her shoulder, it suddenly flew open and she tumbled into the tunnel.

Ellie's shout of triumph was abruptly cut off as hot, sharp pain shot from her neck into her head and down her back. The violence at Jimmy's Tarn replayed in graphic detail.

"No! No!"

She shut it off, thinking of Byron, Mary, Kipp. They were faithful, true and kind. They would never hurt her! Several minutes passed in waiting, the images fading as she thought of the good things in her life.

Getting up, she went back along one of the rows of bottles and switched off the light, returning in dim torchlight to the tunnel entrance. If anyone came in the night to fetch her she hoped darkness would slow their search.

Before beginning her journey to what she hoped was freedom, Ellie picked up the gun and the long-handled tool from the floor and stepped into the passage, pushing the gate closed behind her. The darkness seemed denser in the narrower space; the tunnel was about ten feet wide and the roof, she thought, almost the same across. A few minutes later the tunnel curved and on her left-hand side was a door. Tentatively, she turned the knob. The door was locked.

Pointing the torch ahead she could see no end to the tunnel. Thick cobwebs hanging from the ceiling caught at her hair and face, making her shudder and brush them frantically away. The journey was slow. Her boot touched something soft and her heart lurched. Hands tightening round the implement and the empty gun, she looked down. It was a dead rat.

She had taken no note of the time she'd entered the tunnel and could not tell how long she'd been walking. It seemed no more than ten minutes, but of that she could not be certain. Weariness was beginning to make a claim on her. She peered at her watch – just after eleven thirty. A few feet ahead a dark shadow loomed in the wall and as she drew slowly closer, it revealed itself as another tunnel, wider than the one she was in. Her tunnel took another curve several yards ahead.

Ellie was about to walk past the branching tunnel when she heard a faint sound whispering along its length. It was too indistinct to be clear about its identity and she decided to keep going. Perhaps it was a main route to the cellars she had left behind.

A minute or so later, her torchlight slowly dimming, a set of stone steps loomed suddenly out of the darkness. At the top she could just make out a wooden door, rounded at the top and with a black metal strip running from top to bottom and from side to side. Near the foot of the steps the tunnel continued on until it too, as she discovered a minute later, came to an end at another door. The knob turned easily in her hand and she pushed the door open to find a small room containing boxes, pieces of furniture, half a dozen paintings leaning against the wall and several more stacked in a pile on an old desk, and two filing cabinets. She shut the door, leaving history to itself, and began back-tracking to the stairs. Ellie was about to begin climbing the stone steps when she stopped. Someone was unlocking the door at the top. She spun round and ran as quietly as she could to where the second tunnel appeared. As she reached it, dim light filtered into the darkness and she heard footsteps tapping quickly on the steps. Ellie fled around the corner and did not stop. The sound she'd heard earlier drew her on and the indistinct whispering became a distinct and gentle lapping of waves.

Behind her the footsteps grew louder and although they were in no hurry they had the characteristic of a man's footfall. She went on, almost careless of the soft patter of her rubber soles on the flagstones. She had to get as far along as she could. If he turned into the tunnel and switched on a light she might escape notice if she could make herself small in the shadows.

Ahead, to her relief, Ellie saw several wine racks lining the walls. Quickening her pace, she reached the end of the first rack when, without warning, light burst into the passage. She switched off her torch, her heart pounding. Her mouth had gone dry. Without turning around, she slid between the ends of two racks and flattened herself against the wall.

There was no yell behind her, no hurrying of footsteps to warn her she'd been seen. She sent up a silent prayer of thanks.

The light was bobbing up and down; he was carrying a torch and perhaps that had saved her. However, a minute or so later he was feet away. His pace did not alter. The light caught the end of her boots and Ellie's stomach churned. Every muscle was as tight as the strings on a violin bow, her breath held captive within her.

The torchlight shone away. The man was so close she could almost touch him. His expression was one of intense concentration. He did not notice her. In his hand was a bunch of keys.

It was the Earl of Strathvern.

He began walking towards a cupboard on the opposite wall. Ellie frowned. What a strange time of night to come all the way down here to get a bottle of wine.

But it wasn't wine he was interested in. Astonished, Ellie watched as he hung the torch on the wine rack and began pulling the cupboard out from the wall, grunting once or twice with the effort. Although he pulled it open only wide enough for him to get by, Ellie stared at the door revealed in the wall.

For a few seconds the earl hesitated, staring at the bunch of keys in his hand.

"Damn you, Father!" he hissed.

The unexpected exclamation shocked Ellie; her mouth fell open and she wanted to ask what was troubling him. His father had been dead a long time.

He shoved a key into the lock and turned it, grasped the doorknob and shoved the door open. There was no doubt he was angry.

He swung the torchlight into the room and the smallest of gasps escaped Ellie's lips as she stared in disbelief at what was before her eyes – a large Nazi flag on the wall above a desk. He stopped and stood very still, but he did not turn around. Ellie clamped her lips shut and let no breath out of them. He stood for so long, her head began thumping and she thought she was going to pass out, but suddenly he stepped through the doorway and went into the room. Ellie released her breath, relieved he had not turned around. The door stood slightly ajar; part of Ross was in view, but he had his back to her looking at something on the desk. He moved out of her sight for a few minutes and she could hear papers being shuffled and drawers opened and closed.

On the desk she saw a small statue of Hitler and several framed photographs too far away to make out details. On the right was a short stack of books.

About to step out of the cramped space, Ellie froze as Ross came back into view and through the doorway. He closed the door quickly and for a few moments he leaned against the cupboard, his head bowed, and then Ellie heard the unmistakable sound of crying. Tears pricked her eyes.

Should I make myself known? Don't be daft. What if he's behind my abduction?

Yet, here he was in deep distress. She could not ignore it, but as she was about to reveal her presence the tears stopped. He pulled a handkerchief from his pocket, wiped his eyes, blew his nose and pushed the cupboard against the wall. As he turned to walk back along the passage, Ellie caught a glimpse of pain-filled eyes and jaw tightly clenched as if forbidding the distress to voice itself again.

He hurried away, blending into the gloom, until the eerie tap of his shoes was all that remained to remind her of his presence. What, she thought, had all that been about? A hidden room filled with treasures or things people didn't want disturbed or remembered was the stuff of movies and books. Strange Jamie had never mentioned it. Perhaps he didn't know. Perhaps none of the family except Ross knew.

Any doubts she might have had of him being a Nazi-lover were quenched.

Ellie left her confined spot and went across to the cupboard. No one would ever know there was a room behind it. She looked along the row of wine racks and cupboards, shaking her head in amazement. Had Farley been in the room and taken something of such importance that Ross, or somebody working for him, had killed him to keep the secret safe?

A shiver ran down her spine. It was time to get out of Strathvern Castle and find Byron – but which way to go? Towards the sound of the water which she hoped was the loch? If she followed Ross it was doubtful he'd leave the door at the top of the stairs unlocked. Besides, it was too risky throwing herself on his mercy, though he had always been polite and listened to her on matters of the history and environment of the region. He'd also bought two of her paintings.

So, that left the unknown.

Suddenly, the passage lights went out and she fumbled in her pocket for her torch. Its light was feebler and the darkness blanketed itself around her, thick and threatening.

Chapter 15

Byron regarded the earl with interest. He had expected him to be well-rounded, shorter, and with a shock of red hair, but here was a man with black hair and neat beard, both showing tinges of grey, who was tall and thin.

"Byron Oakes. And you're right about the lost tourist."

"A tourist who seems to care about one of our local artists judging by that cry," the man said, his expression suggesting he did not entirely believe Byron was lost.

"We're friends," Byron said. He indicated the dogs, still sitting, watching their master. "Nice animals."

The other man, probably mid-fifties he guessed, looked at him intently for a second. A shrewd man used to weighing people up.

"The best. You like animals?"

Byron nodded. The earl called them and they bounded over the ground, tails and breeches flying, and their wavy liver-and-white coats telling of good diet and grooming. They capered around Byron after he patted their heads, then they were off, racing across the field after birds that fluttered up from the ground.

"They rarely catch anything. I don't encourage it, much to the dismay of my friends who think I should shoot anything and everything that flies," the landowner said with a wry grin. "Even so, the dogs once did a very good job of catching two burglars who were after our family silver. Bailed them up in the corner of the dining room and barked the whole castle out their beds."

"Better than an alarm," Byron said, but thinking more about the activities of the man's father in hindering the British war effort and whether the current owner of the castle was of the same mindset.

"So, what brings you up this road, Oakes?"

"I wanted to see where it went. According to the map it should go all the way to the loch and on to Maw's Hearth."

"It used to, but it was just a farm track. I closed it off about fifteen years ago."

"To keep out unwanted tourists?"

"You could say that. A group of campers almost set fire to the place. I don't like strangers traipsing over my land unless they're with one of my staff or out painting with Ellie."

Byron studied him for a moment. This didn't sound like a man who hated artists. He had strong features and an upright stance, and an expression that advised the world he carried his authority as a matter of right.

"Are you here by coincidence, Lord Strathvern, or did you know I was on my way up the road? I think you know who I am. I'm sure Jack Kennart or someone else has kept you informed."

"Yes, I know a bit about you, but not from Kennart. I have little to do with him. He's a bumbling policeman who's done little to earn my respect. Just heed my words, Oakes – don't go poking your nose into the community's affairs. Let the dead stay dead."

"I'm more interested in the living," Byron said bluntly. "Did you see Farley Orman on the day he died?"

The controlled expression on the man's face changed and his eyes turned cold and hard.

"You're a presumptuous man. *Tourists* don't ask such questions. I'm often away and rarely saw Orman. We had little in common. You'd do well to keep out of what is none of your business. And if you've ever read the bible, you'll know that sons should not be punished for the sins of their fathers!"

He turned on his heel and marched up the slope, calling the dogs as he went. He did not look back. By the time Byron was turning his car, Lord Strathvern had reached the brow of the slope where he waited for the dogs who still dallied, sniffing round the croft.

On the return journey to the main road Byron saw little of the landscape, his thoughts pre-occupied by the unexpected meeting with Strathvern's owner. On the surface he seemed likeable enough despite the outburst about sins of the fathers. Understandable, if he was innocent.

It was clear he had little affection for Farley Orman, but that did not make him the man's murderer. He was entitled to keep his family secrets. However, Farley had discovered something about the Strathverns that had driven him to contact the MOD.

As he neared the T-junction he caught a glimpse of a dark car coming at speed along a track through the trees on his left. It was heading in his direction.

Thrusting down on the accelerator, Byron's car sped towards the end of the road. The other vehicle disappeared behind a row of densely growing trees, and a few seconds later Byron was close enough to the woodland track to see where it reappeared. The car did not. Byron kept going.

As he reached the end of the road he slowed long enough only to be sure he wouldn't run straight into any passing traffic. In the next second he surged forward across the intersection, pulling the steering wheel sharply to the right, getting over seconds before a dark car shot past him. It did not slow down and quickly vanished round the next bend. Whether or not it was the same car he'd seen on the track he had no idea.

He turned his car around and drove off in the opposite direction. There was no point in taking unnecessary risks. The other car did not reappear. Byron glanced at the clock on the dashboard. It was just gone five thirty and he'd told Jack Kennart to give him two hours. They were almost up and he'd learned nothing of Ellie's whereabouts. The truth was he didn't have a clue where to start. He was a newcomer, still a visitor, and the area vast and unknown to him. How would he ever find her?

Above the treetops the summit of Maw's Hearth was peeking through ragged clouds, its higher companions shrouded in a thick veil. Deep in their shadow squatted the lonely farm of Jimmy's Tarn, but no matter how drawn he was to it because of Glenn Thorley's treatment of Ellie, there was a knot of resistance about going there. It didn't feel right. There was no evidence that Thorley was involved in her kidnapping – or anyone else's. A paper cup from The Mill, unless tested for fingerprints, was no evidence at all. Her abduction had to be connected to Farley.

Byron frowned, frustrated by his lack of knowledge. The more he thought about Farley's photographs and trying to connect them with the information he'd given the MOD guy, the more he wondered about the previous earl's part in the bombing of Clydebank in 1941. Five hundred tons of high explosives had been dropped there, killing over five hundred people and destroying many of the town's tenement buildings, rows of them, like cards in a pack. Those that weren't destroyed were, for the most part, badly damaged. Few escaped.

And then there was Aberdeen. It had started with the bombing in January 1940 of a trawler off the coast followed by other attacks in the spring. In June the first bomb was dropped on land at Nigg on the outskirts of Inverness. While Aberdeen wasn't subject to the same mass bombing that occurred at Clydebank, it suffered more raids upon it than any other Scottish city.

Byron never could understand why anyone would betray their own country, and live with the knowledge that they were as responsible as those who had dropped the bombs that killed and destroyed, and feel little or no remorse.

When Churchill had become Prime Minister in 1940 he'd promptly removed the Scots in government and sent them to various parts of the land and, in one case, to India. To make his point even clearer he'd then appointed an English MP as Secretary of State for Scotland.

It was no secret that during the war many of the Scottish aristocracy had connections with, or at least leanings towards, Hitler's regime. Byron mulled over how many had entertained Nazi spies, whether of German or British stock, without anyone knowing. Had some of them, too, sent their estate workers off to steal, leave doors open, tamper with equipment so it failed, and a myriad other things that would hinder the British war effort? As most of the Scottish working population had scant knowledge of the purposes of war, an aristocratic employer determined to help the enemy could have exerted considerable influence over those dependent on him for their livelihood. Had the Earl of Strathvern done that? Were there villagers living with terrible memories of the part they had played in the Clydebank bombing raids? Or perhaps their offspring now carried the guilt.

Alone in his car, the weight of responsibility for Ellie heavy on his heart, Byron turned into a road that led to Strathvern Castle less than two miles away. When he arrived, he found big iron gates standing open and a long, tree-lined driveway curving to the right and over a short bridge.

Byron drove slowly between the trees, stopping a little way from the bridge. The evening light was deepening and the dark stone of the castle peeked through the foliage like a shy child, as if wanting to keep its secrets a little longer. He drove on, stopping on the other side and listening for a moment at the water rushing past below him. He reached for his binoculars and peered through them at the castle. It was a big building with gardens full of shrubs, flower beds and statues bordering the terrace; a man and woman, late twenties he guessed, were walking hand-in-hand along one of the paths towards the castle.

Another man approached them, inclined his head in a subservient manner, spoke, and handed the younger man an envelope. The exchange was over in a couple of minutes and the servant walked away, but as the young man read the piece of paper he'd withdrawn from the envelope, he looked up and called out. The servant turned around, shook his head, and kept walking as the couple embraced, standing together for several minutes as if afraid to let go. A bit farther along the path the other man stood looking at them. On his face was an expression of deep sadness. Then he turned, walking quickly away and disappearing round the end of the castle.

The couple drew apart and were quickly engaged in earnest conversation. As they walked back the way they'd come, the woman stopped and pointed in Byron's direction. He doubted they could see the car, but when the man began walking down the stone steps leading to a lower garden, Byron slowly backed across the bridge and turned the car towards the gate. A minute later he was outside the estate and parked nearby hidden down a narrow lane. He got out the car, reaching the road as Glenn Thorley drove onto the estate.

As soon as Thorley was out of sight, he ran across the road and slipped through the sparse hedge onto Strathvern land. Keeping away from the driveway, he moved quickly amongst the conifers and deciduous trees beginning to don their autumn coats. Voices brought him to a halt behind an ancient oak. He could not hear clearly what was being said and risked peering round the thick girth of the tree. Foliage hid him and he reached a tall fir several yards away without being noticed. From there he could see the side of Thorley's face, but the other man was facing Byron. He looked a lot like Lord Strathvern; he was tall, though stockier, and had thick brown hair.

"You're not the Earl of Strathvern yet, Michael," Thorley said, his face in the open car window and his arm crooked over the edge of the door. "And until you are, I don't take orders from you or any other minions on this estate. My business is with your father."

"I rather think, Thorley, that you're the minion. You may have a lot of money, but you certainly don't have good breeding. The trouble with people like you is that you always have an inflated idea of your standing in society. Believe me, around here, that standing isn't much higher than the wall around a pig sty."

There was a second's silence.

"This estate needs my money, so I'd be careful with that mouth of yours."

"Strathvern doesn't need *your* money, Thorley."

"I don't see anyone else sticking up their hand to help Nazi informants."

He laughed then, withdrew inside and made to drive on. However, Michael grabbed his arm and banged it down onto the narrow ledge of the opening. Thorley's laughter disappeared.

In Michael's eyes Byron saw hatred he hadn't encountered since his days of active service. He wouldn't blame the man if he leaned in, strangled Thorley and threw his body into the loch.

"That's in the past!" Michael hissed. "You, on the other hand, have a present and ugly pastime, so I'd be careful about how much mud you go slinging around."

Glenn threw off Michael's grip, jerked open the door and slammed him against the bonnet of the vehicle. They were of almost equal height, but Glenn was bigger and anger fuelled his strength.

"You inbred worm! You don't know a thing about me. You spread any gossip and you'll be a bloody mess smeared all over the road!"

Byron's hand folded over the gun in its holster underneath his jacket. One bullet, one arrogant, vicious man destroyed.

Fear exposed itself for a split second in Michael's features and then it was gone. He pushed his assailant away, eyes blazing, hands clenched.

"I've been asking questions about you. It's amazing how many people love chatting to a real aristocrat. Does your wife know about the young women? Oh, I forgot, she left you. And threatening to murder me is a lost cause. You'll never get Strathvern!"

Glenn's reaction was immediate. His arm swung up, fist curled in a tight ball. He hit Michael in the face with such force that Strathvern's heir staggered back and fell to the ground, groaning. Blood gushed from his nose. The big man did not hesitate. Picking up a thick broken branch he raised it over his victim.

Byron stepped out from behind the tree and cocked his gun. The click made Thorley spin around.

"You!" he spat, his face contorted with rage. He took a step towards Byron.

"I wouldn't," Byron said. "Get in your car and get off this estate."

"You've no authority to order me anywhere, Oakes," he said, stepping towards him, the branch clenched in his hand.

"Maybe not, but I can put a bullet through your heart and say it was in self-defence. And there'd be a witness. I doubt anyone would miss you, Thorley."

He cocked an eyebrow, his lips curled in an insolent smirk. "What weapon have I got?"

He dropped the piece of wood and took several steps towards Byron who stood still, the gun aimed at the man's chest.

"You think I won't fire this?"

"I don't think you've got it in you."

"Well, you don't know me very well."

Behind him, Michael slowly and quietly pushed himself up and reached for a thick piece of wood. Byron's eyes did not leave the man still approaching him and then, with whatever energy Michael had, he hit the back of one of Glenn's knees.

Yelling with pain, Glenn turned towards Michael, picked up the wood and brought it down across both of the man's shins. Without hesitating, Byron fired his gun, the bullet passing close by Glenn's head and embedding itself in a fir tree trunk.

"I won't be so generous next time, Thorley. I never miss my target. Get in your car and leave – *now!*"

Michael staggered away from Glenn's vehicle and dropped onto the grass.

"You're a marked man, Oakes. No one – *no one* – crosses me and gets away with it."

"You mean like Ellie."

Thorley's body stiffened and he glared at Byron.

"What're you talking about?"

Byron played the game. "I don't think you were too pleased with the relationship she had with Farley Orman. Did you kill him to get her?"

"Don't be stupid!" There was, then, an almost visible relaxation. "I barely know her."

With that he walked off and got into his car. Seconds later he was off the estate. Byron watched and waited until he heard the sound of the engine receding into the distance.

"I don't know who you are, but thank you," Michael said groggily, removing a blood-soaked handkerchief from his nose. "He would've killed me."

Byron studied him. Blood was splattered over his face and shirt.

"I'm Byron Oakes, a friend of Ellie's."

"Michael. Strathvern's heir if you hadn't gathered that. I imagine you heard most of the conversation."

Byron nodded.

"What was all that about Ellie Madison?" Michael asked. "I assume that's who you were talking about. She and Farley Orman, along with the SNH and a local conservation group, opposed Thorley right from the start. D'you really think he might've killed Farley?"

"I'm no policeman, but I'd say he had motive. Wouldn't you?"

"Yes."

"Sit here for a minute. I'll get my car and take you down to the castle."

When he returned Michael was sitting with his head in his hands, elbows resting on his knees. Bruising was appearing on his right cheek and under the eye. Byron helped him up, Michael leaning on him, as they made the few steps to the car. A few minutes later, with directions from Michael, they reached a side door into the castle.

Here the lawn stretched down almost to the shore of the loch. Two small boats were tied to a short jetty. Michael, in considerable pain, allowed Byron to help him across a gravelled area and into a short, narrow corridor that led past the laundry and kitchen. Cheerful voices floated out from the latter, but Michael indicated they were to keep going. Someone was playing a piano, beautifully, exquisitely. They saw no one until they reached the library where Michael rang a bell and a middle-aged manservant appeared within minutes.

The man stared in horror at his master's son.

"What on earth…?"

"Call the doctor, John, and then get Catherine. Is Father in?"

"No. He's away across the estate wi' the dogs."

He looked at Byron with curiosity, but Michael did not introduce him.

"Get along, John."

The man hurried out the door.

"I'd better go," Byron said, not wishing to bump into the earl returning from his walk.

"Can you wait?" He winced and screwed up his eyes. "Catherine – I'd like you to meet her."

Five minutes later the slim young woman he'd seen before on the terrace rushed in and sat down beside her husband, making a great fuss of him.

"Oh, Michael! What's happened to you?"

"Glenn Thorley's what happened. He was coming to see Father, probably to make more threats, but I stopped him when he was up near the bridge."

"And look at you! He could've killed you!"

"He would have if it hadn't been for Byron."

"Who?" Her head snapped round and she looked at their guest. "I'm sorry. I didn't mean to be so rude. I just saw Michael."

"Naturally," Byron said, inclining his head. "I'm Byron Oakes."

"And you have business at Strathvern?" Her fair brows were raised above blue eyes and the beginning of a smile was followed by a little frown. "Ah, now I know. I thought I saw a movement in the trees. It must've been you."

"Perhaps."

"How did you get rid of the odious Glenn Thorley?"

"I can be persuasive at times. He chose to leave but I suspect he'll be back. He won't forget what you said to him, sir."

"I'm Michael not sir to someone who's saved my life. D'you know Thorley?"

"Not well, but he appears to have his eye on Strathvern Castle. I thought he was pushing to get permission for land near Maw's Hearth."

"Who knows what he's really up to, but one thing's certain – he's after our home."

Catherine looked up from smoothing her husband's hair. "I've not seen you before. Are you new to the area?"

"Yes. Came here for the hiking and got delayed."

"Glenn Thorley's an evil man, Byron," she said quietly.

Michael caught her hand. "It's all right, Catherine. I think Byron knows what kind of man he is. Delayed, you said? Rather an odd thing to happen." He closed his eyes and leaned back against the seat. "Hope the doc's not long." He sounded tired.

For a second Byron hesitated and Michael's eyes opened. Truth, Byron decided was the better option.

"I was in the group that found Farley Orman's body."

"Were you now?" Michael perked up, the expression in his eyes somewhat at odds with the bloodied, bruised face. "You haven't had the happiest of acquaintances with the Highland region."

"I've been in the Highlands before, but not to the Kilcomb area. How well did you know Farley Orman?"

"Not well. Father's never approved of the Ormans, especially Farley, so we don't have much to do with them. Except Bran – youngest son. He works here. Father once allowed Farley to take photographs of the estate which were published in a book. It'll be here somewhere. It's been a great help in promoting Strathvern and bringing in tourists and extra money. Seems that's okay," he said, raising his eyebrows.

There was a knock on the door and John appeared with the doctor at his elbow.

"Don't be a stranger, Byron Oakes," Michael said, as Catherine got up to accompany their visitor across the room."

"Thanks, Michael. I'll remember."

Byron and Catherine walked across the polished floorboards of the spacious foyer, a wide staircase with red and blue carpet marching up the centre of it to balconies on either side that disappeared as hallways to unknown rooms. A grandfather clock stood against a panelled wall, its great hands showing just after six o'clock.

A deep, silent groan rose from his heart. *Where* was Ellie?

Almost of their own will, his eyes gazed up at the ceiling, its dark wood intricately carved with animals and birds, mountains, lochs and dwellings.

"It's beautiful, isn't it?" Catherine said, looking up as he was doing. "It's the most amazing ceiling I've ever seen. Michael says it depicts the early history of his family's estate."

"Impressive," he said, his thoughts still on Ellie. Was she on the estate?

"Are you okay, Byron?" Catherine asked.

"Things on my mind," he said, without looking at her.

He pondered, as he often had, whether people who had such strong links to, and knowledge of their heritage, truly appreciated it. He turned to Catherine. "It must be quite something to step into such history."

"Yes," she said, looking at him with interest. "My family's not nearly as illustrious as this one."

"Are they from around here?"

"Yes. Uncle Bob owns the The Mill in Kilcomb. My parents live in Edinburgh now, but my mother was born in Inverness. The rest are spread around the Highlands and out to the east coast."

"I've met your Uncle Bob a few times. And if your great-aunt is Ruth Lawford, I've met her as well."

She inclined her head in acknowledgement, but her lips were a tight line. Byron could not gauge her emotions as she kept her eyes down, long lashes shielding them from his gaze. When she did look up he was surprised by the sadness on her pale and lovely, oval-shaped face.

"Uncle Bob is a darling. He bakes specialty breads for the estate, charging us very little really. Most of the elderly crofters around here get their bread free – and he often delivers it to them."

Byron was not surprised by this information as Ellie had told him much the same. For a second, there was a pang of guilt; he felt a little like a thief stealing another's prized possession. Feelings between him and Ellie were strengthening. He came back to the moment.

"So, why the sad expression?"

"That has nothing to do with Uncle Bob. I've always had to visit my great-aunt Ruth in secret because she and my grandmother had a falling out years ago. I've no idea what about. Some silly thing to do with the war, I think. Why can't people patch things up? I hate rifts," she said, sighing.

"Me too, but they're a fact of life, Catherine. The war's left terrible scars even this far on. One of my uncles, a sergeant, went AWOL from his unit, leaving his mates to battle it out with the Germans. He was found in a nearby village and shot for desertion. No one ever talks about him and the only photos of him are ones I rescued from my grandparents' house. The family wanted to annihilate every memory of him."

"But that guilt or shame shouldn't be put on the next generation," she said, anger in her voice and her cheeks colouring.

"No, but it often is. Maybe something like that happened in your family. I believe one of Ruth's sisters went missing."

"Just one of the many thousands who died an unknown death."

"Probably. D'you know anything about her?"

"No. It's never mentioned. Anyway, I'm not really interested other than I wish Gran and Great-Aunt Ruth would put it behind them. I'd rather live in the present. My life is with Michael and we don't want dark secrets of the war spoiling anything. They've got nothing to do with now."

Byron regarded her and envied her uncomplicated, if unrealistic, viewpoint. He did not have the heart to say that the treachery and devastation of the war and all its secrets would continue to have an effect for years to come. He decided to change the subject.

"D'you know Ellie Madison, Catherine?"

Her face brightened. "Yes, but not well. I grew up in Edinburgh, but my father's English and I was sent to a girl's school in Harrogate. Then I studied music at Edinburgh University. That's where Michael and I met."

"So it was you playing the piano when we came in. You're a gifted musician."

A blush added colour to her cheeks and she smiled. "Thank you. I absolutely *love* music! And I like to draw as well. That's how I met Ellie. I went on one of her outdoor lessons. It was great fun! You will say hello to her for me, won't you? In fact, you could bring her to dinner. I'll talk to Michael about it."

The front door opened and two English setters bounded in ahead of their master. The two men stared at each other.

"I didn't expect to see you so soon, Oakes. What brings you to my house?" Ross asked. The tone was not welcoming.

"Your son Michael was in a bit of trouble and I helped him."

"Michael is never in trouble."

"He is today. The doctor's with him in the study," Catherine said, walking across to him and kissing him on the cheek. "Byron saved his life."

Ross, halfway out of his jacket stopped, his expression ashen. Catherine tugged him out of the sleeve and draped the jacket over her arm.

"What d'you mean – 'saved his life'?"

"Exactly that," Catherine said firmly. "Come on, you need to see him. He can tell you the story himself."

He looked down at his daughter-in-law and Byron saw the affection in his eyes. "You go on, my dear, and tell him I'll be in shortly. I want a chat with Mr Oakes first."

The young woman looked curiously from one to the other, nodded, and walked quickly towards the library. When she disappeared into the room, Ross strode across the floor to Byron.

"We can't talk here. Follow me."

He opened double doors across the hallway and Byron found himself in a long, wide room with large bay windows on two sides looking across the loch from one and over an expanse of lawn and gardens from the other. It was a room with bright coloured furniture, paintings of hills and lochs on the walls, and cabinets filled with books and mementoes. A grand piano stood at the far end of the room.

Ross directed him to a seat and Byron sank into the soft cushions of a royal blue sofa opposite him.

"Was that Catherine's youthful version?"

"No. After I left the croft a car in the woods kept pace with me, but…"

"That would've been one of my groundsmen," Ross said, interrupting. "I saw you at the croft when I came out of the woods. I'm wary of strangers on my land and told him to make sure you left."

"I did, but then decided to come and have a closer look at Strathvern."

"At least you're straightforward. Go on."

"I was parked outside down a lane and saw Glenn Thorley drive in."

"Thorley," he said slowly. His face darkened.

"So I followed on foot and came across him and Michael having a blazing row. Thorley attacked your son and could've killed him."

"But you stepped in."

Byron gave a slight nod. He didn't want anyone giving him hero status.

There was a knock on the door and the manservant informed the earl of the doctor's imminent departure. Ross was gone less than ten minutes. When he returned he scrutinised Byron, weighing him up.

"What were they arguing about?"

"Money and the estate. Your son's got courage. He went for Thorley and it earned him a beating."

Ross got up. "Wait here. I'll be back in a few minutes."

While he was gone Byron wandered around the room. It was a restful place and if Ellie wasn't missing and his innards weren't churning he would have enjoyed it. In the early evening light, scattered clouds of pearly pink and lilac gave the loch and

257

mountains an ethereal presence. Somewhere... somewhere... was Ellie.

The door opened behind him and Byron turned to find Ross coming in, followed by the manservant with a tray which he deposited on a side table. After the latter had gone quietly out Ross said, "I need a drink and you look as if you could do with one as well. Brandy all right?" he said with a lift of his dark brows. Byron nodded. "My son filled me in on what happened. What can I do for you?"

Byron did not hesitate. "Tell me the truth about whether you've got links with any Nazi groups."

For some minutes Ross stared at the glass in his hands, his expression impassive. While Byron waited he took a sip of brandy and watched a flock of birds flying across the loch. The brandy was expensive and excellent.

"The truth," Ross said eventually, his voice quiet. "I wonder what that is sometimes. In my boyhood I thought it meant something to belong whole heartedly to what my father believed in. It wasn't until I went to boarding school that I began to see life differently."

"And now?"

The earl looked at him, pensive.

"I never knew my mother. She committed suicide in early 1946, about a year after I was born. I've often thought how different my life would have been had she lived. D'you have both your parents, Byron?"

"Yes. They live in Staffordshire."

"Then you won't understand what it is to grow up without one of them. By the time I got to my late teens I was questioning Father's views. He threatened to disinherit me, so I kept quiet – self-preservation. I quite liked the idea of being the Earl of Strathvern one day. As far as he was concerned it was just a momentary adolescent hiccup. I stayed out of both the pro- and anti-Nazi camps at university. By the time I had my degree I was passionate, fanatical my friends said, about Scotland. I never told my father, though I think he was suspicious. Every time I was home he would make me swear fealty to the dead Fuhrer and all he stood for. I've never told my sons about that. I *hated* what he stood for, especially when I found out..."

He did not finish, but drank the rest of his brandy and poured another. Byron declined a top up, waiting for him to finish the sentence. He did not.

"I want people to know this is a different household to the one in the war, but some people won't let go of the past, whether they were there or not." He sighed. "I understand betrayal's a big issue. I just wish they'd remember who it was who did the betraying."

Byron considered his next question carefully before speaking. He expected to be chucked out and on the doorstep within minutes.

"Why did your mother commit suicide, Lord Strathvern?"

Ross' eyes narrowed and his expression grew dark.

"For a tourist you ask impertinent questions, Oakes. But then I doubt that's not all you are. When my father was ill and unlikely to live long he felt it his duty to tell me he'd never really loved my mother and that's why I didn't have any brothers or sisters. I walked out and never saw him again. He died a month later on a dreary October day. Apt I thought. My father had an affair, a long one, though he always denied it." He glared at the man opposite. "This is damned painful."

"That's why she…"

"Yes! She couldn't live with it."

"Your father told you that?"

"Don't be absurd. He never admitted to anything that might besmirch his image. He lived a lie. It was my old governess, a substitute mother really. She told me when I came home for the funeral. Felt it was time I knew. I'd turned twenty-one that April."

His face tightened for a moment and he seemed to gather up the memories of the past and release them from his mind in a long, quiet sigh. When he opened his eyes, Byron saw what he thought was relief.

"I haven't talked about any of this for years, and then only to my wife and a trusted cousin. I don't want it bandied about."

"It won't be."

The earl looked at him as if trying to see what was inside his head.

"I hope not. Are you up here on some kind of official business and fell for Ellie Madison in the process?"

"It seems I'm not the only one well informed," Byron said, considering how much to tell the man. One of Ross' eyebrows twitched upwards, but otherwise he did not respond. "A friend of mine in London was contacted by Farley about some World War

Two stuff and wanted to meet. Wouldn't talk on the phone. I was already coming to do some hiking and said I'd be happy to chat with the famous photographer."

"And what did Farley have to say?" The expression in Ross' eyes hardened.

"I never got to meet him. I was in the hiking party with Ellie that found Farley Orman's body. That was the only time I saw him."

"So, his secrets died with him."

"Maybe."

Ross shifted on the seat. "I've heard you were an elite soldier, one of the best. Why did you leave?"

"Had enough. It was a tough life."

"I'm guessing you're not married. Any children?"

Byron shook his head and his mouth, almost of its own volition, said, "My fiancée was killed in combat a few years ago. I lost interest after that."

They sat in silence for several minutes, deep in thought, until Ross glanced at his watch.

"Dinner will be served in half an hour. Stay and share it with us. My wife would be pleased to meet you and I'm sure Michael and Catherine will be glad of your company."

"I would very much like to," Byron said, hesitating, "but…"

He could not finish. Here he was sitting in comfort drinking brandy with the Earl of Strathvern and doing nothing about finding Ellie. Had it been Ena he'd have given every ounce of his energy to find her.

"You're meeting Ellie?"

"No. Ellie's disappeared."

The earl stared at him. "So that's why you cried out near the croft. Why on earth didn't you say earlier, man? We could be out there looking!"

"I know that, but we've only just met and we're not exactly life-time friends. The other thing is I don't know where to start. I've been trying to piece bits of a puzzle together and getting nowhere. Farley's death is only one of them."

"You mentioned the war. Does a piece of the puzzle have to do with my father?"

"It's possible."

Ross turned his head and looked out one of the windows.

"I don't blame you for not trusting me, but I haven't followed in my father's footsteps. No doubt you've heard to the contrary." He shoved his hands into his trouser pockets and glanced at Byron. "While I had no time for Orman, I've always found Ellie to be honest, direct and very good for my middle son Jamie. I've never understood him, but she does, and he's doing well because of her." He stood up. "Come on, I want to show you something."

On the way across the hallway they met the manservant coming from the direction of the kitchen. The earl asked him to delay dinner for twenty minutes. Turning to Byron, he beckoned him to follow. They went up the stairs to the next floor and along a corridor hung with tapestries and paintings. Ross did not stop to explain their history.

He opened an oak door at the end and Byron followed him into a room with a wide bay window overlooking the loch and hills. A big desk stood in front of another window. There was a large bookcase crammed with books, an old chest on which stood a number of photographs – the earl's family Byron supposed – and a small settee and two armchairs in front of the bay window. Beneath his feet was an enormous, intricately woven thick rug which looked expensive. The walls, except for the one facing the loch, were panelled with oak.

"My sanctuary and office," Ross said, walking towards the desk. "What d'you think?"

"I'll swap with you any time you like."

"You'll be waiting a very long time. Have a seat," he said, waving his hand towards the bay window. "Beneath the castle there are a number of tunnels with storage rooms and cellars. Most of them are very old, but parts are more recent. A couple of the cellars were built by my great-great-great-grandfather and are a good step from the castle. Apparently, he built them away from the house because he encouraged smuggling and didn't want anyone knowing what was going on."

"I'd like a tour some time."

"Maybe. We don't take people down there often. It's gloomy. My father wasn't fond of walking and he was impatient, so he had a motorised cart built which either he or his butler would use. The cellars were once stacked with wine, other alcohol and exotic food, but what's left I've no idea. I've rarely been there."

His voice was hard and clipped as if forbidding dark memories to intrude. From an armchair, Byron watched him move towards a chest in the corner of the room nearest the desk. The front of it was covered in carvings of leaves, vines and men on horses. It looked old.

"That's a magnificent piece of furniture. Was it made around here?" he asked as Ross knelt down beside it.

"No. It's American, a dowry chest made about 1700. It's called a Hadley chest. That's where they made them, Hadley, Massachusetts."

For a moment he hesitated. His eyes clouded and he looked ill-at-ease.

"Are you okay, Lord Strathvern?"

He gave a curt nod, bent down and reached underneath the chest. A second later a portion of one panel slid away. Behind it was a narrow door. Shifting the chest, Ross took a key out of his pocket and opened the door revealing half a dozen shelves in a cupboard. They contained items of exquisite silver and china, but also other pieces. Even from where he was sitting, Byron knew they were war relics.

A groan came from Ross and his face was ashen. He stepped away from the chest and turned his back on the cupboard.

"I hated him," he said thickly. "I hated everything he stood for. Look on the top shelf and take out the box."

Byron walked across the room, stepped past Ross and reached into the top shelf. Along with papers, envelopes and their contents, there was a small box which he picked up and took down. Placing it on the desk, he opened it. Inside was a medal – a German Iron Cross – and a card with writing inside. It was in German.

"D'you speak German?" Ross asked.

"No. French and Arabic."

"Impressive. The card reads: *To our brave and noble servant, sixth Earl of Strathvern, for his unfailing love of the German Reich*. It's signed by Hitler. My father was nothing but a traitor. D'you call that brave and noble?" he asked abruptly.

"No, I don't," Byron said, emphatic. His memory flicked up two faces, men under him who had betrayed their movements to the enemy.

"Nor do I. Put it back. No one else has seen it. My family don't know this cupboard or the... exists. My father gave thousands of pounds to the German war effort and was rewarded with several invitations to visit Hitler, which he did, and stolen, priceless artefacts from Italy and France. I've returned them to their owners or their descendants, and some to the German authorities when I couldn't trace any relatives."

Byron looked at him, silent, with mingled respect and pity. He had not missed the momentary halt between words and speculated briefly on Jamie's assertion of a secret room. He retained his thoughts and said, "I'm surprised you haven't destroyed it all."

"I nearly did once, but except for the blatantly Nazi things, I knew the rest had belonged to Hitler's victims. They had a right to have them back."

Ross stood up and retrieved another box, smaller, and handed it to his guest.

"Have a look."

Byron did as he was bid. In the box were a number of photographs. He flicked through them slowly. The top ones were of people at a garden party, but towards the bottom were several of a beautiful young woman. In two she was posing provocatively. Byron studied the photo in his hand, frowning.

"Was this your father's mistress?" he asked.

"I don't know. My governess showed me a picture all those years ago, but I was so angry I threw it in the fire. Look at the inscription on the back. He never put her name, but you don't write such words, no matter how brief, to a family member. Are you shocked by these pictures?"

"I've seen worse."

"Then what's bothering you?"

Byron shook his head and sighed. "There's a vague similarity to a woman in a photo I saw recently."

He tipped the photos onto the desk and spread them out, not speaking as he searched.

Ross came and stood next to him. "D'you know who she is?"

"Not for sure. As I said it's a vague resemblance. It was in a packet of Farley Orman's photos."

"Orman? How would he have a picture of her – and why?"

"I don't know." Byron shuffled through the rest of the photographs. A number of them were taken outside in the hills and beside rivers and lochs, and several at a seaside town. "He discovered something that somebody didn't want him spreading around. Whether it has anything to do with her, I've no idea." He found what he was looking for and gave it and one of the others to the man beside him. "Look closely at the woman – the hair, clothes, her look, all quite different, but the shape of the face and the ring on her right hand... bit of a coincidence to be two different women."

There was no sound from the other man as he studied the photographs; he gripped the corners as if propelling all his anger and hostility into the images. Hatred glittered in his eyes.

"*They* destroyed my family." The words were brittle and hard.

Byron had no need to ask who he meant and he made no remark of his own. The man had endured years of shame and private hell. What could he say?

A long way off, he heard a clock chiming seven o'clock. Ross sat down and continued staring at the photos as if the present world was temporarily on hold. Byron occupied himself with the contents he'd spilled onto the desk, spreading them out to better view. He took out the last few in the box. Two were shots of Hitler with several men in uniform and three women. One of the men was Goering.

"Find out who she was, Byron."

Ross was looking at him, holding up one of the pictures. Bitter resentment tingled round the edges of his words, his body was tense.

"And will you help me find Ellie?" Byron asked.

There was no answer for several seconds. When Ross spoke he sounded tired as if the past had aged him. "Of course. I'll do what I can. And ask Jamie. He's fond of her."

He stood up and went to the desk where he gathered up the photos, put them back in the box, and returned it to the cupboard. "Keep the two you have. Let me know if you need any others."

The decision to trust a stranger was more than a little surprising, Byron thought.

"D'you *really* want to know who she was, Lord Strathvern?" he asked, slipping the photos into his pocket.

"Yes."

"And you really want me to do it?"

"Yes."

Ross bent down again beside the Hadley Chest, reached underneath to the wall and the panel slid back in place.

"You're placing a great deal of trust in someone you don't know. Not sure I'd do the same," Byron said, glancing out the window. The evenings were drawing in now. Soon, the Scottish winter would change the character of the land and people would retreat to their warm burrows.

"I'm a reasonably good judge of a man. You could've slunk away when Michael was in trouble, but you didn't. Strathverns don't take such things lightly." He looked straight at Byron. "I've spent all my adult life trying to keep the past locked away. Lately, I've realised that's been neither wise nor helpful to my family."

Passing the portraits of his ancestors, Ross began telling Byron a little of the history of the Strathvern line. He told of friendship with William Wallace and the shared struggles for a free Scotland, of heroes at Bannockburn, and supporters and enemies of Mary Queen of Scots, and of kin later who became embroiled in the Highland Clearances. One of them, he said, had been a close friend of the Countess of Sutherland who'd evicted some fifteen thousand people from her one million acres of land between 1807 and 1821.

It wasn't often Byron experienced jealousy, but he did then. Drinking in the rich wine of Ross' family history he felt the privilege of such a heritage and of knowing its details. He knew a little of his great-grandparents, but beyond that no one had found time to research.

When they reached the bottom of the stairs, a middle-aged woman met the earl and handed him a portable phone.

"Wouldn't say who it was, M'Lord."

He thanked her and said, "Ross Strathvern."

His expression hardened and a cold light glittered in his eyes. He began walking slowly towards the sitting room Byron and he had been in earlier. Suddenly, he swung round and looked intently at Byron across the space, colour draining from his face.

"What d'you mean you've got Ellie?" he snapped. "Who *is* this?"

Byron stared at him; a cold tremor ran down his spine. He did not move.

"I won't sign any papers with or without my lawyer." He walked slowly back across the floor, frowning. "Don't talk rubbish! If you don't release Ellie I won't even consider signing any papers. Who's that with you?"

He held the phone away from his ear and pushed a button.

"Who was it?" Byron's heart was racing.

"It sounded like Fenella Orman. She hung up." He began pushing buttons. "I'm fairly certain the voice in the background was Thorley's."

Chapter 16

The cold had crept into Ellie's bones during her cramped confinement between wine racks, and she began the journey towards what she hoped was the loch and freedom with slow, stiff steps. Energy was leaking out of her like an invisible stream. She should have brought the flask of tea with her.

As she trudged on in the gloomy tunnel, its musty dampness seeping out of the walls, she felt as if she was in the company of smugglers on their way out of the castle after depositing illicit goods from the Continent into the cellars behind her. Ahead would be a rowing boat waiting to take them safely across the loch.

Her heart skipped a beat or two. It was *so* dark – cloying, thick, and she was alone. What if she couldn't get out? She was no smuggler experienced in out-riding excise men or melting into the countryside. Dread, like one of Pilgrim's tormentors, spoke to her. Who will notice you're missing? Who will care if you've chosen to disappear like poor Alice? You've no roots, no family here. And all these people you call friends – where are they? Farley's dead, Alice has found another, better life, and Mary has her own family. So has Bob. You don't belong to, or with, any of them. Where *do* you belong, Ellie Madison?

The old familiar fear of an empty, lonely future came in a suffocating blanket. Byron would look for her, but she could hear panic in her thoughts. Would he? He had his own agenda. She was a mere provider of information. Why would he bother looking for her?

The torchlight flickered, jerking her thoughts out of dark negativity. She shook the torch and its dim light steadied. She sighed, relieved. She could do this – she *had* to.

Without warning the lights in the tunnel came on and Ellie stopped. Had Ross forgotten something? About to turn around and investigate, she changed her mind – the person was coming in her direction. Walking quickly and quietly, she shielded the end of the torch with her fingers allowing only enough light to touch the ground so she didn't trip over anything.

The tunnel curved and she was again in darkness except for the dim torchlight. Every now and then she passed a packing chest against the wall, but there was no time to decide if she could hide inside one. The footsteps were louder and closer. She could only guess that her escape from the cellar had been discovered. Whether it was Bran in pursuit she had no idea or little care.

By now she was much warmer and, despite fatigue, years of tramping the Highlands with all its challenges and temperamental weather, came to her aid. Her body was fit and strong and she kept going, spurred on by the smell of the water and a fresh stream of air brushing her face. She heard the hoot of an owl.

The torch went out. For a second Ellie faltered, tripping, and she put her arm out towards the wall, grazing her palm on the rough brick. In that brief stop she looked up and saw the end of the tunnel ahead, pale moonlight intruding upon the darkness and revealing a grill over the mouth of the small cave. Dismayed, Ellie forced herself to keep going.

If only Byron was here!

Seconds later, bright torchlight burst into the tunnel and she heard someone breathing hard. It reminded her of her cousin. Without looking behind, she began running towards the cave.

In years past, one of the Strathverns had built a short wooden jetty. About halfway along this a wire fence stretched from side to side of the cave's mouth. At each end of the fence was a gap, big enough for a small child to squeeze through. There was a gate on the jetty with a thick chain and heavy lock securing it to the fence.

There was nowhere to go except into the water, but she hesitated and in those few seconds her pursuer arrived. Ellie turned around into the full beam of the torch. All she could see was a pair of men's training shoes and jeans. The hard breathing slowed and became quieter. There was a hoarse chuckle. It identified him.

"Cowards usually prefer darkness or waiting until no one else is around, Glenn. You haven't changed a bit."

"Your opinion's always been tainted, Ellie, but it doesn't matter now. Give me the gun." He lowered the torch and held out his hand.

"What gun?"

"The one you used to blow the lock apart in the cellar."

"I don't know what you're talking about."

"Don't make me angry, Ellie. You know what'll happen to you if you do."

"And don't threaten me!"

"There's nowhere to run and nowhere to hide. No one knows you're here and no one will hear if you scream."

"You're forgetting Bran," she said, staring at him without expression.

"He's a fool. I've sent him on an errand."

"As you're a compulsive liar…"

"He's not here, but you're coming with me."

"I'm not going anywhere with you."

His eyes narrowed. "You've no choice, Ellie, unless you think you can just walk through that fence."

"I'd rather die than go with you."

"Why are you being so stubborn?" he demanded, stepping towards her. "There's *no* way out. And if you think I'm letting you go when you've turned out to be a surprise golden opportunity, think again! My future as Strathvern's owner is at stake here."

"I couldn't care less about your future! And why would the Strathverns sell their birthright to trash like you?" she snapped, her lips curling with contempt.

"He needs the money."

"I doubt it. He's a very successful businessman."

"And this place sucks up money like a bog. I'll be its saviour whether Strathvern likes it or not. He hasn't got the guts to stand against me. When I've finished with this place it'll be making millions. People will come from all over the world to see the castle and its cellars, stay in its extravagant rooms. Or they might choose the new hotel at the foot of Maw's Hearth."

Ellie glared at him. "You arrogant pig! You're not worth the dignity that Strathvern bestows. The people of Kilcomb will *never* support you."

"They have and they will. Money speaks louder than any loyalty to Nazi aristocracy."

"Really? I think you'll find not everyone believes the rumours about Lord Strathvern's loyalties. You won't win, Glenn, and I won't be part of this any more than Farley was."

"My patience is running out and, like him, you've no choice."

"There's always a choice. Is that why you killed him?"

He gave a derisive laugh. "I wouldn't waste my time killing him, but at least he's out of the way. Now let's move."

Ellie looked him and then said slowly, "Perhaps you didn't hear me. There is *always* a choice."

"Not this time. You belong to me, Ellie, and I have no intention of letting you go now. The fun is only just beginning. I want to see Oakes writhing with jealousy. And Strathvern? Well, he'll be only too happy to negotiate – on my terms. Amazing how luck always turns up at the right time."

Remnants of the past squeezed her heart and nausea stirred in the pit of her stomach. He saw the change in her eyes and began smiling, just as he had as a teenager and young man. He began walking towards her, unhurried and certain of victory, but in those few seconds Ellie realised she could use it to her advantage, though it was risky. As if suddenly nervous, she put her hands in her jacket pockets, her right hand curling around the handle of the pistol. She allowed the fear in her expression to deepen.

"I see you've come to your senses, cousin," Glenn said, taking another step toward her. "Let's be civil about this and it'll be over in no time."

Ellie took a few steps backwards. "You never keep your word. You don't know how. I don't trust you."

"People change, Ellie. You always were my favourite cousin." His voice softened and he moved closer and held out his hand. "It's late and I need your help."

"I wouldn't help if you were lying at my feet in agony begging for mercy. I hate you!"

The switch in him was instantaneous and anger resurfaced with intensity. He swung the torch up and into her face, making it impossible for her to see anything.

"You'll pay for this!"

He lunged at her and she stumbled backwards, almost losing her balance. Flashing the torchlight about to disorient her, Glenn came after her, swinging his fist at her head, but she ducked and half turned away to run. He was quick and grabbed her arm, twisting it. The pain fuelled her anger and she lashed out, catching him across the cheek with her fingernails.

He yelled. "You bitch! You'll pay!"

"And so will you."

She pulled the gun out of her pocket and aimed at his face. Immediately, he relaxed, but she knew that tactic and kept the gun steady.

"You won't use it. You're too soft-hearted. Always were."

A second later the torchlight was in her face and she blinked. He struck out at her, knocking her off her feet. The gun went off and he roared, whether in anger or pain Ellie didn't care. In a moment she was on her feet and running towards the water. Behind her, she heard his heavy footsteps and a stream of vile language. As he ran, the light darted about distorting distance and making objects appear and disappear in a split second of time.

Ellie bumped into a barrel, slowing her down. His hand came down heavily on her shoulder. For a moment she groaned under the weight of it. There was a coarse grunt of victory – the hated sound. Ellie's animosity thrived and she drew on it, twisting round and thrusting the gun's nozzle into his belly.

"Let me go – now! Or I'll fire this thing into you and leave you bleeding to death. It'll be a very long time before anyone finds you."

The grip lessened, but he did not release her and she pushed the gun in harder, cocking the trigger. He let her go and she backed away from him.

Suddenly he grinned, but before she could find out why, she fell over a pile of old rope and landed on the edge of the rough, short wharf where the narrow jetty joined it. The water lapped gently and as she struggled to gain her balance her hand slipped and dipped into the water. It was up high.

Glenn leaned over her, reaching for the gun. There was blood on his cheek and the collar of his jacket. "Get up! There's no choice for you now, Ellie."

"Oh, yes there is."

With that she rolled over and plunged into the dark, cold waters of the loch.

***

Byron woke up with a start, perplexed, and his head throbbing. Unfolding his arms from across the steering wheel, he stared dully out through the windscreen into the moonlit night. Wind was stirring in the trees, whispering and sighing. Where on earth was he?

The sound of a car roused him out of his lethargy and a pair of bright headlights suddenly swung through the trees and down the lane in his direction. He remembered then; he was outside the Strathvern estate. Ducking below the dashboard he heard the car slow down and then turn, disappearing along the road at the head of the lane he was parked on. A string of names passed through his mind; Lord Strathvern, Michael – unlikely, Glenn Thorley, perhaps Bran Orman. Ellie?

Byron's heart sank. He didn't even know where she was and he'd lost valuable time sleeping.

"Stupid!" he said, clenching his fists.

Despite the evening drawing in close, Ross had taken him around the grounds of the castle, into the stables, sheds, and the greenhouses where his wife spent many hours he'd said, tending plants from all over the world. She sold them to raise money for local charities. They'd found nothing to indicate Ellie had been there since her last visit in August to do a water colour painting of the stables. While Ross had been away in Spain at the time, his wife had told him Ellie had come as arranged. The painting was to be a present for her mother who'd been a keen horse woman all her life.

What Byron had not yet decided was whether Ross was genuinely concerned about Ellie or the tour had been a deliberate ruse. Allowing an interested stranger access to the inner sanctum and giving him a glimpse into the owner's heart was, if nothing else, a good way of winning that stranger's confidence. And how could he then want to believe that such an accommodating soul could be the perpetrator of a serious crime? In Ross' case, he had good reasons for not wanting anyone poking around in his private life. Enough muck had already been slung at the family, much of it firmly stuck.

So, why was Byron drawn to this place? He thought he was long past the romantic notion that peerage always had significant black sheep and black deeds to keep suspicion alive and that the sheep would inevitably be caught. And a good number of Scotland's aristocracy had been Nazi sympathisers, among them the previous Earl of Strathvern.

What Farley had discovered had cost him his life. That it concerned the Strathverns, Byron had little doubt, but the connections were still tenuous and buried in history.

In London he'd spent time delving into archives concerning Scotland's involvement in the War and, in particular, the country's spying activity. The sixth earl had been politically active in Scotland and England, taking seriously his responsibility as a member of the House of Lords. He'd maintained close ties with a number of politicians of both main parties. There were hints, but no defining evidence, of undue influence with the most senior politicians in the government.

Farley, in his brief encounter with a staff member of the MOD, had indicated he had evidence of the earl's involvement with the bombings of Glasgow and the Clyde. When questioned about whether he knew the names of any accomplices, the photographer had apparently decided he'd given enough information and ended the conversation.

Byron stared out the windscreen. Had Farley shared anything of his war discoveries with Ellie? He frowned and shook his head. He was making assumptions about why Farley had died. There were, he kept hearing, land developers who would be happy about Farley's death, but he hadn't met any of them other than Glenn Thorley.

He could not allow himself to entertain thoughts that Ellie was dead. Experiences in the past had proved such thinking destructive, futile and leading to inaction. Ellie needed him to be at his best and he could deny her nothing less.

Byron glanced at the clock; it was ten thirty. He'd left Strathvern just after nine and got back to his car ten minutes later. The map on the passenger seat was still open from his poring over it trying to figure out where Ellie might be, before he'd rested his head on his arms and begun going over all the possibilities connected with Farley. So much for that! He'd gone to sleep.

The truth was that she could be anywhere in the hundreds of square miles of the Highlands.

"But where?" he shouted, frustrated and, by now, cold.

The sound of his voice was loud and intrusive in the quietness of the dark countryside. He couldn't sit here for the rest of the night following his thoughts along questionable paths to inconclusive destinations. He *would* find her.

He withdrew his car keys from his pocket. As he did so he remembered the photos Ross had allowed him to take and pulled them out of another pocket. He started the car to warm up the engine, switched on the internal light, and gazed at the pictures. The more he looked at them, the closer he came to deciding the woman was someone other than the one in Farley's photos. After all these years it could well prove impossible to identify her.

It was time to get back to the cottage. He was not achieving anything sitting here mulling over events and wishing for a miracle that would take him to Ellie. Jack Kennart knew the area and its history far better than he did. Already long overdue at the police station, he'd better get himself down there in the morning – early.

Half an hour later he arrived at his cottage. He retrieved Farley's photos from the ceiling and spent an hour studying them and those Ross had given him. There were similarities, but they weren't strong enough for him to say whether or not the photos were of the same woman. He knew many women had visited the castle during and after the war, and fashions with hats half hiding faces over the same curled, bobbed or coiffed hairstyles didn't help. The woman standing in front of the Nazi flag had a bold look in her eyes and stared out from beneath the brim of an army hat bearing German insignia. Her plain dress reinforced the image of a grim regime. Could this shot have been taken in a secret room Jamie had mentioned?

With a cup of strong hot tea and a pizza defrosted and heated, he made a phone call. It was in a cheery holiday tone, but the recipient would understand the true content. Before he went to up to bed he put all the photos in the same packet and secured them in the ceiling cavity.

Tomorrow he'd take a drive to Inverness and visit Hugh and Ruth Lawford.

He'd just reached the landing when his mobile phone rang.

"Byron Oakes," he said without enthusiasm.

"Where've you been, Oakes? I told you to get down to the station this afternoon and I've not seen even a hair of your head! Two hours you said. It's now almost midnight!"

It was Jack Kennart.

"Things came up."

"Was Ellie one o' them?"

Byron sighed and said quietly, "No, she wasn't."

"So what've you been doing? Inspector Carter's not impressed. He's ready to hang you out to dry, but I've convinced him to wait a bit. You owe me, Oakes. And so you don't think I've been sitting around here on my backside, the boys in blue from Castlebay, Ashby and I have been out looking for Ellie. We'll start again in the morning."

"Any sign of her?" he asked, ashamed for assuming Jack was waiting to speak with him before scouring the region.

"One or two, though not much to get excited about. Just make sure you get yourself down to the station first thing – eight o'clock."

"That's barely a civil hour."

"I don't care," he snapped and hung up.

Sleep did not embrace him immediately and he turned from one side to the other finding no comfortable spot on the pillow or rest for his mind. He stared out the window and watched stars peeping from behind passing clouds. The moon, too, poked its face out, beaming down on the earth and exposing the trees near the cottage before they hid in the darkness again as she disappeared for long minutes at a time.

In a castle as big as Strathvern there had to be secret and forgotten rooms and tunnels. That was part of the allure of such places – the mysteries wrapped up in history, rooms discovered, secrets that beckoned. Fathers often passed family secrets to their eldest son. Did Michael know any of his family's?

Byron closed his eyes and turned away from the window. He fell into an uneasy sleep, his mind taking him back into the army and the chaotic days in Ireland. She was there, of course, the one he called his. They belonged together, he and Ena. She was one of the bravest soldiers he had ever known, a true representation of her name – ardent, fiery one. And she, who had loved him with a deep and committed love, was looking at him with such yearning; there were tears in her blue eyes, but her fair hair was tangled and muddy. He called out to her, but she didn't hear and he watched stricken with grief, unable to reach her, as the gunman mowed her down. He felt sluggish, his steps laboured, his cries silent. Bullets and grenades were flying everywhere. She seemed such a long way off. In the next instant he was kneeling on the grass beside her, her breath faint, her heartbeat erratic. The sodden earth around her was drenched in blood. She opened her eyes once when she heard his voice, smiled, and in a second was gone where he could not follow. There was strange gunfire sounding in the distance, but he couldn't move; he felt heavy as if his limbs were being sucked into the muddy field.

Ena! Ena! She didn't respond, but the irritating sound persisted, penetrating the dullness of sleep. He suddenly sat bolt upright and grabbed the mobile phone burring away on the bedside table.

"Byron Oakes," he said in a voice thick from disturbed and troubled sleep. He expected to hear her voice, as if death had not claimed her after all.

"It's Colin. I've got some info for you."

Byron's heart filled with an agony he'd thought long gone. For a few seconds he struggled with it, pushing it down. He glanced at the clock. "Don't you ever sleep, man? It's four o'clock in the morning!"

"And you know if I get the scent of something I'll keep at it until I find whatever it is I'm looking for. I didn't get to be, arguably, Britain's best history snoop by going home at five o'clock. D'you want to know what I've got or will I call back after the sun's up and you've had breakfast? You've got soft, Byron."

Byron chuckled despite the heaviness in his chest, switched on the lamp and reached for a notebook and pen in the bedside drawer. "It's good to hear your sense of humour's still intact, Colin. Tell me what you've found."

"Your friend Ellie – do I detect she's more than a friend?"

"Get on with it." That came out more abruptly than he meant. He was afraid for her. Didn't want to lose her either.

"Sorry, don't mean to be nosy. Anyway, she was right. Jimmy's Tarn was bought by the then unmarried, but wealthy Douglas Bromley, around 1908. However, money wasn't the only thing he brought back from the Klondike. He also had a son of about ten with him. Douglas eventually married and had at least three children, but there could've been more, most likely by other women."

"D'you have names for any of them?"

"A couple, but it's the son's children who've come up with the goodies. Douglas Junior fathered two illegitimate children by the time he was twenty – a son, followed a year later by a daughter. No details about whether they had the same mother. Nothing like carrying on the family habit of philandering," Colin said, chuckling. "And, like his pa, he later married another woman, adding more children to his collection."

"So, was it Douglas Junior's son who worked at Clydeside during the Second World War?"

"Yes. Now, Junior inherited a lot of money from his father and was a great pal of the Earl of Strathvern who was some years younger than him. Loaned him money once. But it was Junior's son Alasdair who became a fervent Nazi supporter. Even went to Germany as a teenager and possibly joined the Hitler Youth movement."

"Is there anything to link Alisdair Bromley with the bombings on Clydeside?"

"Again, yes. He was arrested after an SOE operative found him carrying ciphers detailing positions of the shipyards. Didn't get any further though. Somebody of influence quashed the whole thing. In 1944 Bromley was reported for taking photos of the construction of the pierheads known as Mulberry Harbours. They were used successfully in the invasion of Normandy by the Allies. Alisdair was never even questioned."

"Any idea who covered it up?"

"None. But there's a bit of info I think you'll be interested in. One of Douglas junior's daughters might be the woman in the photo you sent. I stress *'might'*."

Byron's thoughts went to a house in Inverness. "Ruth Lawson?"

"Don't think so, but I'll admit I do make the odd mistake from time-to-time." His tone was matter-of-fact and one Byron knew he used to make sure the listener understood it wasn't a matter for discussion. "Douglas Junior had a daughter called Ruth, born after he married. Marian MacAdam was illegitimate, but there's no record of why she didn't have her father's name."

"The Lawsons think she's dead."

"Probably is," Colin said bluntly.

"So, Ruth, sister of a traitor, joins the army and marries an intelligence officer. *That's* convenient. Maybe the whole family was in on it."

"A possibility. There're two younger sisters. Margaret lives on the outskirts of Inverness and Edith lives in Edinburgh. She did very well for herself."

"So I heard. I met her granddaughter, Catherine. She's the earl's daughter-in-law, and..." he stopped. Another piece of the jigsaw puzzle landed on the board.

"You there, Byron? Not gone to sleep, have you?"

"No," he said quietly. "I've met one of the other relatives as well."

"Sounds like you're getting to know the locals rather well, old chap. Next thing you'll be telling me you're moving up there."

Byron only half listened; he was thinking about Bob Caraway. A few seconds later he asked, "Is there anything to link the previous Earl of Strathvern with the Clydeside bombings?" He ignored the prod to talk of private matters. Colin Farmer, though brilliant at historical detective work and a good pal, was not someone he'd ever confide in.

"Okay, so you don't want to talk about that either," the other man said jovially. "The answer to your question is, not yet. There were hints of involvement in some of the archives, but nothing I'd call evidence. You might have better luck up there. Who knows what's hidden in the family vaults."

More than photos of a beguiling mistress, Byron thought.

"Thanks for your help, Colin."

"I'll let you know when I find anything else."

Byron hung up and turned off the light.

Interesting that Ellie didn't seem to know of the connection Ruth Lawson had with the Bromleys. Perhaps all four daughters had been involved in spying and as a protective measure severed ties with their parents and brother at an early age and disappeared into another society. Or were they innocent? What of the mothers? Colin hadn't mentioned much about them.

The old farm at Jimmy's Tarn was isolated – an ideal place in which to plan and prepare. No one would notice what was going on there.

Then there was Bob. How much did he know about his family's history?

Dawn was approaching as Byron drifted into a light sleep in which Ellie's face came and went, her mouth uttering silent words he knew were important but could not hear. He woke to hear a blackbird chirping in the tree outside his window, joined moments later by others and, farther away, the calls of different species one to another. The night was breaking up, chased away slowly by the rising September sun.

As he stood under a hot shower, he went over the conversation he'd had with Colin Farmer. It stirred what had been dormant in his mind since the fortuitous visit with the Lawsons in August. Aside from Hugh's extensive knowledge of the war and his position in the intelligence area, Byron had nursed a niggling thought that both he and Ruth knew a lot more about her sister's disappearance or death than either were willing to discuss. That was understandable. They knew almost nothing about him other than he had photos of personal interest to them.

Halfway through towelling himself dry, Byron's thoughts turned to Bob. He had to make amends with the man. Despite an underlying rivalry for Ellie's affections, they seemed to get on well and he wasn't willing to let that take an untoward turn and die away. Too many times in the army friends had come and gone, the friendships never rekindled because of either death or postings or misunderstandings. And friends discussed things acquaintances did not.

Downstairs, he put the kettle on, slipped two slices of bread into the toaster, and went into the sitting room, taking a chair with him. He flicked on a lamp. The thick drapes were drawn across the window as he stood on the chair and retrieved the photographs from the ceiling cavity. Clicks from the kitchen told him his toast was done and the kettle boiled.

Sitting down with his notepad and breakfast, he added information from the earlier phone conversation. Apart from the chorus of birds there were no other sounds outside. Thoughts of Bob kept intruding. The baker, everyone's friend, a kind-hearted man who delivered food to those in need, a man whose business gave him access to great and small houses alike.

He glanced at the clock – time to be off. He checked his jacket pockets held all he needed, and into an inner pocket tucked a packet that contained the war photos. The rest he put in a backpack with other essentials, including a flask of coffee.

It was six thirty.

As he was crossing the kitchen floor to return upstairs, he stopped. There was movement outside. An animal perhaps, but he could not be certain. No one could see in; all the curtains and blinds were drawn. For a few moments he listened, but it was not repeated.

Before leaving the cottage, he pulled out his phone and dialled Ellie's home number. He tried several times, but there was no answer. It gave him no comfort.

"Damn!"

He shoved the phone back in his pocket and wished he had some kind of faith to draw on, to believe there was an Almighty Being who cared about individuals and heard their cries for help. Even Ellie had a faith in God. Right now he'd just like to know she was alive and where to find her. If there was a God, He'd know, but Byron preferred to trust his own instincts rather than hope something invisible might come to his aid. He'd managed all right on his own so far. *Liar*, he heard resonating somewhere deep in him.

Fear was seeking to assert itself. The dreams came hurtling into the forefront of his thoughts and the pain of losing Ena entangled itself with the fear of losing Ellie. An odd little thought popped up. Strange how the two women he'd loved most had names beginning with the same letter of the alphabet.

The image of Ena dying in his arms had never gone away nor had the desolation of losing her. Over and over again he'd pushed it back into its box, angry with himself for not getting to her in time and knocking her out the way of the gunfire. Had he been two minutes earlier she would never have died.

There had been no time to grieve his loss, no time to do anything other than defend themselves, and finally secure the area while the militants melted into the darkness to fight another battle another day. They'd taken Ena back with them and she'd been given a military funeral, with honours. As they'd lowered the coffin into the grave, he'd known a desolation that had almost sent him over the edge. It was a long time before the hated and bleak loneliness, the dark grief of loss, shifted.

It would not happen again. Ellie was not a soldier, he was no longer in the army, and the circumstances were nothing alike.

Chapter 17

The dark water closed around Ellie as she began sinking towards the bottom. Do not panic. Get out of his reach and stay down long enough to convince him I've drowned.

Torchlight was dancing over the water; Glenn was shouting her name, cursing her.

Nothing would make her return to him.

Fighting the weight of her clothes, she became momentarily disoriented and turned around seeking the wharf. If she could get underneath it there might be a space near the roof. She had to get air soon. She bumped into rocks and banged her shin. Pain shot up her leg as she tried to focus on the moonlight; it was her best guide. Facing it was the way to the jetty and fence, with it behind her the wharf was ahead. When Glenn had gone she would make her way towards the fence. There *had* to be a way out.

Her heart was pounding and she was beginning to feel light-headed. Glenn flashed the torchlight in her direction and she saw, for a brief moment, the edge of the stone wharf. With a determined push she propelled herself towards it.

There was a shout; he'd seen her. Something landed in the water behind her. Glenn! For a second she flailed, panicking, but it wasn't him. A heavy hook caught one of her knuckles and tore a piece from the sleeve of her jacket. The pain was so intense a cry rose in her throat. Water rushed into her mouth and nostrils, filling her with dread. She closed her mouth, swallowing the water. Out of the corner of her eye she saw a thin trail of blood wriggling like an amoeba under a microscope. A second later there was another splash and the hook landed in the water a few feet away. It hit one of her shoes and she drew her legs up out of its vicious reach.

The reality of her surroundings was fading and she had a vague notion that her cold body was being tumbled over rocks. Byron was lost to her forever. Kipp would pine away, and Bob mourn her loss. Mary would grieve, but the Ormans rejoice in her absence. This, then, was to be the end of her life, escaping from Glenn. She heard his voice as if he was a long way off, disembodied almost. She caught a glimpse of the hook, but the battle was over at last.

Unexpectedly, she came out into air. Spluttering as erratically as her heart was thumping, she didn't care if Glenn heard her. She was still alive.

For several moments she could not focus on anything; her mind seemed to be struggling with the signals it had to send to the rest of her body in order to keep it functioning. She was freezing, shivering violently. Away to her right the hook, that she could now see was a three-pronged monster, was being dragged through the water. Perched on a rock with only her head and shoulders above the water, she watched the hook, thankful it had not sunk itself into her body.

Above, Glenn was pacing. Suddenly, the hook was hauled out of the water, landing with a heavy clang on the brick floor above. He walked away, but not far and more light unexpectedly erupted into the dark, cold cave. He'd found a light switch. Was he intending to sit there waiting, unmoving and hidden in a dark place listening for the faintest sound of her presence? Ellie had no intention of giving him that satisfaction and so she, too, waited.

Numbness crept into her limbs and a calf muscle went into a spasm as she stretched out her leg. She could not stop shivering and she was desperately tired.

Time, she supposed, kept moving although it didn't seem so. Concentration was almost gone. All she could think about was the cold – and Byron. Had their lives touched for nothing? Was the possibility of love nothing more than a joke? Was she *so* bad?

If you're listening, God, I don't like this! You're supposed to be a God of love. Is this a test? What is it I have to prove to be good enough? How come *he* has a family and I don't? Are you going to answer me, God? Please just get me out of here!

She cocked her head on one side. What was that? Ellie clamped her teeth and listened. Footsteps – Glenn's footsteps. Torchlight went to and fro across the water, along the jetty and out through the fence. It came back and she watched its journey along the water near the edge of the wharf. Ellie could almost touch the rays. Glenn stopped once or twice and knelt down; she saw his blurry face in the water.

Not now, she prayed silently, desperately, not now! Let me be free of him.

She heard him stand up, then in an odd voice he said, "Don't do this to me!"

Another minute or two passed before his footsteps rapped across the wharf and along the tunnel away from the cave. Tears of relief flowed down her cheeks.

"Thank You!" she whispered.

Ellie waited until the sound of his footsteps disappeared altogether before she moved slowly and quietly along the overhang of her sanctuary. She would not leave it until she reached the jetty. Her legs were stiff and chilled, her hand throbbing. The skin was torn close to the bone, making it difficult to cling to the bits of jagged concrete above her head as she moved along. Some of it was loose and plopped into the water. Each time, Ellie froze, waiting for and expecting Glenn's sudden and violent appearance. However, there was no sound or sight of him.

At the junction with the jetty, Ellie stopped and listened for several minutes before she made her way beneath the wooden structure towards the fence. It afforded cover from Glenn should he return. As she got closer to the fence visibility improved in the moonlight, but it did not offer immediate encouragement. Even under the jetty the fence was in place.

"There *has* to be a way out," she muttered, reaching the barrier and wanting to kick it in frustration. She stretched out one of her legs to give the metal a tap and register her protest, but her foot met no resistance. Hope rose again. She moved her leg round in a wide circle, her foot touching the top, sides and bottom.

Hesitating no longer, Ellie ducked down into the water. Stretching her arms out in front she touched the sides of the fence and pushed herself through a gap barely wide enough. Her jacket caught and ripped; she tugged herself free and, her frozen legs protesting, kicked out behind and swam until she was clear of the barrier and jetty.

Surfacing a few minutes later, she saw the loch a few yards away and almost gave a shout of joy. Freedom! *And* – she'd escaped Glenn a second time. That thought gave her a boost of energy and she swam towards the bank where it joined the loch.

She hauled herself out of the water and onto the grass, shivering uncontrollably. Energy had deserted her. It had been long hours since the drive from Castlebay with Byron. Was he looking for her?

What now? The wind, though gentle, pierced her wet clothes through to her bones. Wisdom whispered that it wasn't wise to remain where she was, unmoving, and hoping for a miracle that would bring Byron to her. The only person she had to rely on was herself, but she was so tired and sore there was no incentive to do anything. Nor did she know where she was on the estate. Of the cave and its exit to the loch, she had never heard any mention. Perhaps Ross wanted no risk of anyone stumbling on the cave's entrance.

A chill not born of cold ran down her spine. Quite by chance she had been given a glimpse into a world that was alien to her – loyalty to an enemy nation. The Nazi flag, so brazenly hanging over the desk, had challenged her deeply; it offended her and she would like to go back and rip it off the wall, throw it in a fire and watch it burn until there was nothing left except ash.

Farley had hated everything associated with Nazism. His father had suffered in the war and died within ten years of its end. He had been in the Signals Corps, strayed too far from friendly lines in trying to get the field radio to work, and been captured by two German soldiers on patrol. He'd been taken to their headquarters, tortured, and his body later dumped, at night, into the trenches of the nearest allied troops. The experience altered him physically and mentally and he had never fully recovered from it, becoming remote and taciturn. Only once had he alluded to the torture and Farley's hatred of the Nazis had grown and never abated. His mother struggled to keep the family together and Farley had told Ellie he remembered her often going out to work at night as well as keeping up her day job. When she died thirty years later the last word she had spoken was the name of her husband.

Whenever she remembered the story, deep sadness disturbed her, not only for Farley's mother and her children, but for nameless, countless others who had suffered, who still suffered.

She wondered whether Farley had known about the room in the tunnel. Several years ago, he had mentioned that Ross was not an innocent bystander and had been making trips to Germany. When she'd suggested it might be for innocent reasons like business and visits to friends, his reaction had shocked her. He'd been furious and told her she was a fool if she believed that. Ross Strathvern, he said, was as much a traitor and lecher as his father. Those things, he'd shouted, were knit so tightly into their souls they couldn't even recognise the evils of them. He'd not rest until he uncovered the truth and saw justice brought to Kilcomb.

Rustlings underneath nearby bushes set Ellie's heart pounding and she pushed herself off the ground, standing unsteadily on her feet. She began moving away towards a clump of trees. Keeping an eye on the bushes, Ellie reached the trees as a cat emerged from underneath the leaves and followed her, miaowing.

Almost immediately there was another sound – someone running. She slipped behind the nearest tree, an oak, its thick trunk solid and reassuring. The cat brushed against her legs, purring.

Some yards away the unmistakable voice of her cousin burst into the quiet.

"Stop, you fool!" he hissed. "You'll wake the whole castle thumping along like that."

"You told me to hurry." It was Bran, sounding aggrieved.

"Yes, but not… damn you, never mind! Where's the entrance?"

"Somewhere round here."

"Somewhere? I haven't got time for somewhere!"

"And His Lordship wouldn't be happy about you snooping around."

At this, Ellie smiled. Bran wasn't the brightest Orman, but he had inherited almost every ounce of his father's stubbornness.

"I don't care about *His Lordship*. He's finished anyway. I want Ellie Madison found – now!"

"What d'you mean, 'finished'?" Bran asked. "His Lordship's family's been here for centuries."

"That's my business, not yours. Get a move on!"

There was no reply for a few seconds.

"Not until you tell me what you mean."

Ellie heard suspicion and pain in Bran's voice. He had never wanted to work anywhere other than on the Strathvern estate, and his loyalty to the family was unquestionable despite the feuds between his father and his employer.

"I only met your father once or twice," Glenn said slowly, "but I hear he wasn't a favourite of the earl's." Ellie tensed. It was a tone she'd heard many times, one he used before delivering a blow, usually physical and verbal. "And look what happened to him! A bullet in the head. Your friends in the village think he deserved it. So do I. He meddled where he shouldn't have."

"It wasn't in the head. And my father didn't deserve to die like that. His Lordship wouldn't have killed him. He couldn't kill anyone! You're a liar!"

"Really? Well, Bran, I was there when it happened, so I should know," Glenn said.

"No you weren't. You… you're a liar!"

Ellie heard him moving towards his antagonist. She didn't believe Glenn's announcement that he'd been present at Farley's death; the tone of his voice, supercilious and offhand, told her it was purely for Bran's benefit. It was one he used to taunt, without truth in the words.

The cocking of a gun was loud in the cold night air and Ellie's heart missed a beat. He must have found the one she'd had. She had a vague recollection of it falling out of her pocket as she went into the water.

Fear and the dampness of her clothes sent chills running down her body. Near her feet, in its warm, furry coat, the cat was busy washing itself.

"And you'll be next if you don't get me to the entrance. You wouldn't want to deprive your sister of another male member of the family, would you? Still, it would give her more time for me."

Glenn and Fenella – what a pair they were. Unknown to Kilcomb's inhabitants they were yoked together planning ownership of Strathvern. She couldn't see it working long term. Neither of them was the submissive type and, in her opinion, Glenn was too old for her. She wondered if Fenella knew he had a wife and children, albeit absent ones. Besides, most people in and around Kilcomb wouldn't stand for an outsider, especially an arrogant Englishman, usurping the rightful and present owners – whatever the family's murky past. As to Maw's Hearth, it would never be allowed despite what Glenn thought or who he bribed – and that, she knew, he did often.

"She only sees you because she thinks you'll give her everything she wants."

"It's reciprocal. Get moving, Bran, or I *will* use this."

Ellie peeped through the leaves, leaning out slightly from behind the tree trunk, hoping Bran would do what he was told. A twig snapped under her foot.

Glenn spun around and took several paces towards the stand of trees.

Ellie's heart missed several beats. She hadn't endured freezing water and near death to be captured again by Glenn Thorley!

She eased back without moving her feet. If he came any closer and found her, there was little energy in her to fight him. The cat rubbed against her legs and she looked down and smiled. Just the thing. She gave it a little push and with a soft, protesting miaow it ran off in the direction of the two men.

She heard Bran chuckle. "It's one of the countess's cats. Anyway, if you fire that gun someone in the castle will hear you."

"Don't be ridiculous."

"He's not," said another voice. It was Ross. "I'm a light sleeper and I knew you'd be back, especially after the phone call. Put your gun on the ground."

Ellie leaned round the trunk again; she could see their shadowy figures.

Glenn turned to face the other man, but did not let go of the pistol. There was a loud, solid click and a bullet from a shotgun sped past Ellie's cousin and buried itself in a tree trunk a dozen yards from where she was sheltering.

Glenn put the pistol down on the grass. As he stood up, he put a hand to one of his ears. "Nothing will stop me getting Strathvern."

"You have an inflated opinion of yourself, Thorley. Now, get off my land and stay off."

"You'll come running to me soon enough when Ellie Madison's body floats to the surface inside that cavern you've caged up. Who'll believe you're innocent? Everyone knows you hated Farley Orman and killed him."

"What were you doing in the cave? Who told you about it?" Ross snapped. "Bran?"

"No, Your Lordship. I wouldn't tell anyone," Bran said emphatically.

"Don't believe him, Strathvern. He's only a servant."

"That's *Lord* Strathvern to you, Thorley. And my employees know more about loyalty than you'll ever know or get. Now – get off my land!"

"So," Glenn said, not moving, "you're not interested in Ellie Madison's demise then?"

"Ellie's not been here for weeks."

"Go look for yourself. She fell into the water and I haven't seen her since. Apparently, there's no way out. A good solution, I'd say. She's nothing but trouble."

That he would believe her dead, without evidence, seemed more like a ruse to deflect the earl's attention away from himself. He would not dismiss her now when he had divulged his plans, if that's what they were. It was, Ellie thought, careless of him, but then he was assuming she hadn't got out of the past and was still fearful and compliant to avoid the whole sordid thing being revealed. Whenever there had been bruises her parents listened to the lies he told of her bumping into things or falling over. Her mother had always believed him – the charming side of Glenn turned up whenever he had a need to convince anyone that he was utterly good. Yet her father doubted. When he was home he would ask how she was, though she could never tell him. But he knew, of that she was certain. He would often sit on the edge of her bed and tell her sea stories with happy endings. Glenn rarely came when he was home. If she threatened to say anything, he simply laughed. Shame and fear had ruled her life, though few knew it. She had determined that no man – or woman – would ever dominate her life again, and in the process her soul had become stronger and more resilient – most of the time. It had also become untrusting and resistant.

"Get off this estate, Thorley. I won't warn you again," Lord Strathvern said. The cocking of the shotgun echoed in the night air.

"And I'll see you on your knees before the year's out!"

Glenn walked off and Ellie breathed a sigh of relief. She wished Byron was with her. All she wanted was to feel his arms around her, strong and protective. She was shocked by the depth of feeling, almost desperation. It was a long time since she'd allowed herself the need to be held.

She watched as Ross picked up Glenn's gun and wished the two men would move off. Her body was now so cold every joint and muscle ached and her toes seemed barely part of her. She put her hands under her arms in an effort to warm them.

"What's going on, Bran?" Ross demanded. "Is Thorley right about Ellie Madison?"

"Don't know," was the faint response.

"But you know something. If Ellie really is down there and you're keeping silent for some stupid reason, you'll be seen as partly responsible for her death."

"I just put her in the old cellar, that's all. Don't know how she got out," he said, sounding defensive, afraid.

"What? Who told you to go down there? You know those cellars are out of bounds and not to be spoken about – to anyone!"

"I didn't tell anyone, My Lord, and I didn't harm Ellie. Wouldn't harm a fly."

"Then what possessed you to take her down there? Did she ask you to?"

"No."

"Then what was she doing there?"

There was no response.

Ellie's eyes began closing. She was so tired.

"Bran if you're covering up for Thorley, which I think you are, I'll have to re-think your employment here. I don't want to do that. You're an excellent groundsman, but this kind of behaviour won't do. D'you understand?"

"Yes, Lord Strathvern. Please don't sack me. You know I don't want to work anywhere else."

"Then tell me what's going on. How did Thorley know about the cellars?"

"Don't know. He was waiting for me when I came out. Said he'd seen me up to something suspicious and that he'd tell you. He forced me to take him down there."

"What happened then?"

"Ellie was gone."

"Right. Let's get to the cave. You can tell me the rest on the way."

"Yes, M'Lord."

"Strathvern doesn't need another scandal, Bran."

Ellie struggled to her feet, using the tree trunk for support. By the time she was standing upright, the two men were running towards the loch and did not hear her calling out.

At least they wouldn't find her body floating on the water. With that she slid back down, leaned her head against the trunk, and fell into a fitful doze.

***

Ellie stared at the dark water, undecided. Rain was falling steadily, blowing into her face and hitting her damp shirt. Her jacket was hanging up under the eaves of an old garden shed she'd stumbled across amongst trees on her way back to the water's edge. Less encumbered, she could swim faster and reduce the risk of becoming snagged on objects in the water.

It was, of course, madness. Waking up ten minutes earlier, cold and stiff, it had taken her a few moments to recall why she was in a garden in the dark. Her clothes were drier, but she had with no idea of the time or how long she been in a stupor. Her waterlogged watch had stopped. However, though her mind and body were lethargic, recollection of the journey along the tunnel stirred her. She also remembered something else. When Lord Strathvern had come out of the room she had been so preoccupied with his distress and how she was going to get out of the tunnel, she only now remembered with some serious doubts that he had not withdrawn the key from the lock.

Shivering, and forcing herself to walk back towards the loch, she hoped she could find the entrance to the cave. The thought of an unlocked room with its secret collection beckoned; it was impossible to ignore such a moment – *carpe diem* her father always said. Well, she intended to do just that. It was unlikely she'd ever get down to the cellars again.

Farley's death was entwined with stuff that had happened during the war, of that she was certain. She knew Byron had more photos and she had a suspicion he was working for the Ministry of Defence. He'd slid too easily into wanting to help her solve the mystery of Farley's death.

Poor Farley. He hadn't deserved such a horrible end to his life. That anyone would want to deliberately kill another human was incomprehensible to her. Well, almost. In her mind she had collected a room full of ideas on how to humiliate and destroy Glenn. Most of them she had forgotten, but some remained, popping up every now and then to remind her that it was still possible.

He had stolen much of her life, shattered her expectations of love and marriage, and driven her to a place she had never intended to be – childless, unmarried, and unable to fully trust any man. Yet, despite her hatred of him, she had a vague sense that he was a desperately lonely man.

Shutting the memories away, she stared at the cold, dark water. It was decision time. All she had to do was swim to the jetty, climb on top of it, and then slip into the water near the fence and through the gap. The danger lay in the darkness of the cave. Once she was out of the water, how would she find the light switch without a torch?

In the distance she heard dogs barking. Had the earl sent them to make sure Glenn left the estate?

"You've been in worse situations than this, Ellie Madison," she murmured, annoyed at her lack of courage, "and this is an opportunity on a plate."

The sound of the dogs grew louder. If they picked up her scent there would be little hope of evading them, and the water would not put them off from pursuing her. The jacket might keep them occupied for a few minutes, but eventually they'd find the trail down to the water. Bran could be with them. Ellie hesitated no longer. She took her shoes off and flung them wildly behind her towards the shrubs before jumping into the water which wrapped its chill blanket around her once again.

She changed her mind about climbing onto the jetty until she was through the hole in the grill and within minutes she was inside the cavern. Here she kept close to the jetty feeling her way along it in the water, all the while listening for the sound of the dogs. There was no fear in her of them and they'd remember her. She just didn't want to get caught – not yet.

Pale moonlight filtered into the cave, but as Ellie got closer to the end of the jetty its impact into the darkness diminished. A few feet ahead she touched the rough edge of the quay and was about to climb out of the water when the noise of barking dogs ricocheted around the cavern. Dimly, Ellie saw one of the earl's setters with its front feet in the water.

There was a shout and a man appeared near the dog, a torch in his hand. In the halo of light his features were drawn and ghostly. It was Bran. He swung the torchlight in a wide arc around the entire entrance and Ellie, taking a deep breath, ducked beneath the water and went down to the bottom. The light swept away the darkness, playing upon the water and seeking any sign, she supposed, of her along the jetty or the back of the cave. When it hovered over where she was, probing into the underbelly of the quay, it seemed impossible that it would not betray her whereabouts.

A few more seconds and she would have to surface. Why didn't he just go? He couldn't see her so there was nothing to keep him there. Go away, Bran, just go away.

The light lingered, moving along the edge of the quay, then back again. It swung up and into the area where the tunnel began.

Ellie's lungs were aching for air and her heart was pounding. There was no choice; she had to get up into the air. Slowly, and as the light swept the whole area, she rose upwards and broke the surface. Without meaning to, she gasped, and a second later the area above her lit up again. She had no idea whether Bran had heard the sound or whether he was being thorough. Her lungs replenished, she bobbed down under the water, but seconds later the cave slipped into darkness and Ellie heard him call the dogs and move off.

As she climbed onto the jetty the wind blew against her wet clothes and tiny cold darts pricked her skin. This wasn't much good for her health.

A fresh burst of animated barking disturbed the night air and she supposed the dogs had found her discarded shoes. They wouldn't be occupied in the bushes for long before finding their way back to the water and the cave.

Padding carefully across the floor in her wet socks, Ellie headed for the wall on which she had a vague recollection of seeing a light switch. She bumped into a wine barrel, stubbing her toe.

Frustrated and tired, she blamed Farley. "If you hadn't meddled in things that were none of your business you'd still be alive and I wouldn't be down here, freezing and hobbling, trying to find out who killed you! I hope you're listening, Farley Orman! You weren't always good at that on earth."

Her voice, though barely above a whisper sounded loud and echoed along the tunnel. Deep inside her heart, as if in a little room by itself, stirred a longing to see the man who had been one of her closest friends.

"I miss you, Farley," she murmured, "I miss you a lot."

Tears, unbidden, filled her eyes and her memories rekindled a picture of him sitting at her kitchen table on the morning of the day she had last seen him. He had on a shirt she had bought him and she remembered watching his animated face as he told of his latest wrangling with the local council about the damage hooligans were doing in one of the nearby glens. She saw his slender hands wrapped around a mug of coffee and felt the warmth of them on her face as he'd kissed her goodbye before going off into the wilds.

"You know I love you, Ellie."

She'd smiled and said quietly, "I know." But his love for her ebbed and flowed like the sea on the shore, sometimes retreating to the horizon where she could not reach him. The driving passion of his life was bound to the Highlands and she knew it would always have first place. She needed more than that if she was ever to give herself to any man in marriage; she needed his undivided love.

He'd got into his car, looked up and waved and then headed down the driveway and out into the road. She had not seen him alive again.

The other image intruded immediately, one of violence and death, seeking to erase any memory that was good. Stark and real, as if she'd stepped back into that scene on Maw's Hearth, she saw his face in death, cold and remote, and his blood congealed and dark on his clothes. He had not deserved such an end, whatever it was he had discovered and whoever it had threatened. It would give her the greatest pleasure to find the murderer and make sure he spent the rest of his days locked away in a dungeon.

Shuffling along trying to not to damage herself on unseen objects lying on the floor, Ellie ran her hands over the wall. This is, she thought, annoyed and frustrated, a ridiculous exercise. Finding a light switch in a cave with only the palest moonlight offering any illumination was the stuff of movies where an immaculate and beautiful blonde heroine just happens to be in the right place. Either that or the tough, handsome hero arrives to save her. Well, that was not going to happen to her. She had no idea where Byron was and, as she wasn't a stunning blonde, she'd have to rely on herself and not a movie script.

A few minutes later Ellie gave up padding her hands up and down the rough wall and walked carefully towards the entrance to the tunnel, her fingers touching the wall to guide her. A couple of minutes later she was there.

"It's *so* dark," she whispered.

Bad things happened in the dark and she fought the intrusion of images long put away. They did not belong in her present or future and she would not allow them to dictate what she must do now, but for a second she was tempted to get back into the water and swim out. She'd rather face Bran and the dogs than her cousin. Long minutes passed while she argued silently about the possibility of Glenn waiting for her in the tunnel. Procrastinating further, she took off her socks and wrung them as dry as possible before putting them back on.

She heard the dogs again and Bran calling after them. While she was still undecided the barking grew louder and without warning a light flashed over the water on the other side of the grill.

Ellie stepped close to the wall and squatted down. As she did so she noticed two light switches, side by side, on the opposite wall.

The dogs were quiet now, but the torchlight was strong enough to reach into the cave and Ellie watched it bobbing about. As it swung towards the tunnel entrance she bent her head to her knees, hiding her face. For some moments the light lingered.

"Ellie! Ellie!" Bran's voice was loud and strong. "Can you hear me?"

The quiet seemed deeper as the cries died away. Part of her wanted to respond, but he had brought her here and she did not trust him. The light dimmed.

"I won't hurt you, Ellie! His Lordship's looking for you. *Please* come out if you're here! I really won't hurt you. My dad *loved* you."

In his voice she heard panic and she believed him, but who else was waiting out of sight not sharing his promise not to hurt her? She felt sad for him; he'd lost both his parents. He was like a lost lamb. Who would be his shepherd now? Fenella wasn't exactly the nurturing sort and Camden was unpredictable and completely self-centred.

She looked up, peering in his direction. The dogs began whimpering. Bran must know she was alive if he'd seen her jacket and boots; she couldn't believe the dogs would miss them. They were of hunting stock even if the earl didn't encourage that in them. One of them barked and the other joined in and seconds later they were both in the water swimming towards the grill.

"Bonnie! Jock! Come here!" They slowed, but did not turn. "Come!" The command held an imperative note and the animals returned to shore, shaking their silky coats near Bran.

He took another long look at the cave's entrance and then slowly walked away, the two dogs bounding ahead of him.

Ellie waited until she guessed he was well away before standing up and walking towards the opposite wall. Seconds after touching the bricks she found the switches and flicked them on, bringing light into the underground world. Relief flowed through her body. She turned off the one lighting the cave and turned into the tunnel, padding along in damp socks. When she saw the spots of blood on the floor, Ellie stopped and stared at them. This time she had won the battle with her enemy. Twice now she had outwitted him. For her there was no going back and she continued on more determined to bring Farley's perpetrator to justice.

It did not take long to reach the row of wine racks and find the cupboard defending the room's entrance. She was not a weakling, but pulling out the rack took all the strength of her tired body. Eventually, it was far enough out to squeeze behind and reach the door knob. It turned begrudgingly, grating in the lock. For a second Ellie thought it was locked, but then it clicked and she pushed the door open.

She stood on the threshold, staring into the darkness, suddenly and acutely aware that she was trespassing into a forbidden world. There was a strange and alien atmosphere about the room, sinister almost, and she switched on the light. For undefined minutes Ellie stared at the scene; it reminded her of a museum display, crammed with artefacts and memorabilia. And yet, this was more. It belonged to a family she knew was still struggling to shake off the taint of a traitorous forebear.

Before closing the door, she turned and looked at the back of the cupboard and found a handle with which to pull it towards the wall. She shut the door and walked towards the desk. Part of her did not want to disturb anything; it was private and no one had given her permission to probe. For a moment she stood glancing round the room, a peculiar mixture of feelings tumbling around in her heart; sadness for the tragedy of war, fascination for the way people lived in those days, a simpler life made complicated by war, and abhorrence of the Nazi regime. Ellie shuddered – such evil in the disregard for a human life.

And yet, in this room so filled with pieces of the enemy's world, she felt as if she was standing in history itself.

Time melted away as she went around the room looking at the collection, wishing now that she'd paid more attention in German classes. A small bookcase crammed with books in German stood near a seamstress' dummy dressed in a Nazi officer's uniform and placed in an alcove. Alongside, was a glass-fronted gun case displaying several rifles and pistols. On all the walls were photographs of ships, German soldiers on tanks, in parades and planes, a couple of Hitler with Nazi hierarchy and others, and one of people being herded through the entrance of Buchenwald and into the camp. The latter so disturbed Ellie she turned away from it.

On the top of the desk she saw a radio and an odd-looking machine she couldn't identify, as well as a number of photographs, writing implements and a large blotter with one or two jottings on it.

Tucked away in a corner and hidden beneath a pile of army blankets she found a trunk. Wrapping one of the blankets around her, grateful for its warmth, she looked at the lock on the trunk. There had to be a key. She opened the top drawer in the desk and found a neatly arranged pile of yellowing envelopes, pads of fine writing paper, several gold pens, a box of cap badges, and a letter opener. There were four drawers on each side and it wasn't until she got to the third one on the opposite side and was bending down to it that she caught a glimpse of a small lever underneath the desk. When she pulled it a cavity opened up. Down on her knees she peered into it and saw four keys hanging on hooks; the second one fitted the trunk's lock and opened it.

Inside she found neatly folded clothes. On the top was a man's dinner suit, complete with a black silk cummerbund and bow tie. Immediately beneath it was a pair of silk stockings, a petticoat and a woman's dress. She lifted the items out one by one and placed them carefully on a stool next to the trunk, wondering, as she touched the softness of the stockings and petticoat, whose they had been and what they were doing buried in the bowels of the castle.

Underneath the clothing was a tray which had kept the items flat and almost creaseless. Lifting it out, she put it on the floor behind her. When she looked back in she found herself staring at articles of baby's clothing: a pink woollen cardigan in an intricate lace pattern, several pairs of knitted bootees, fine lawn white nighties, and two cotton bonnets. Ellie felt a pang of pity for the previous earl. He'd lost his wife to suicide. Was this the reason – a baby daughter who'd survived a short time and was never spoken of again? As with the other clothing, she put the items on the stool.

On the bottom were two wooden boxes, one of which she lifted onto her lap. She opened the lid to find the box stuffed with military signals, documents and photographs. Her heart thumped and for long seconds she hesitated, fearing to disturb what had never been meant for her eyes. Whether it was her father's military influence or an inbuilt respect for national secrets and security, Ellie's inquisitive nature rebelled against breaching the information so long hidden away. The longer she hesitated, the stronger the feeling grew and she had almost decided to put everything back, close the lid and walk away. Yet this was no movie mystery she was in; the written materials were not in a museum nor locked away in a military safe.

"This had better be worth it, Farley Orman," she muttered, and sitting down at the desk, glanced randomly through the box; the papers were in chronological order. Someone had been meticulous.

Some of the signals and documents were in German and indecipherable to her, but others were in English. The earliest ones were dated 1938, the year before the Second World War had begun, and concerned Hitler's political rise which the previous earl applauded in a letter. Two from Berlin were marked Top Secret and mentioned the building of camps for enemies of the new Germany. There were a number from the earl, classified Secret, about the shipping yards on the Clyde and the numbers of ships produced each month. Ellie's ire grew. Even before the war began Ross' father has been feeding information to that Nazi weasel!

There were also detailed travel arrangements to various parts of Scotland, England and Germany, for the earl and a couple of men whose names were vaguely familiar. Politicians, she thought. Handwritten reports outlined the content, and success or failure, of meetings with union leaders, anti-government agitators, community leaders, and known Nazi supporters amongst the Scottish aristocracy.

The signals of 1940 and into 1941 showed Ellie clearly that the earl was a determined and prolific gatherer of information for the Nazi cause. He advised Hitler of Churchill's plans to remove all his pro-German Scottish ministers from government, and continued to relay information regarding Glasgow and Clydebank. He stressed the importance of Glasgow as a centre for the iron, steel and chemical industries and how much damage would be done to the British war effort with these destroyed. Detailed information regarding the shipping yards increased, and she knew he could not have got it without help of trusted people working there.

In an envelope a series of signals to and from Germany were hidden behind a number of photos. On the back of each picture was written the name of the location – Greenock, Paisley, Glasgow. Some were aerial photographs of the shipping yards, but others were of machinery, insides of partly-built ships, and men working in specific areas. One photo showed almost a dozen ships that had recently gone down the slipway and were ready for the war effort. Of Glasgow, the focus was on its industrial sites; someone had taken shots inside a steel factory showing the entire process of rolling out what looked like girders.

A handwritten note from the earl accompanied the photographs.

'Most of these were taken by Alisdair Bromley who risked his life on several occasions to help our friends in Germany with the planning of their air raids. I, and Germany, owe him a debt of gratitude for his unfailing devotion to the tasks he's been given.'

Hearing rumours that someone was a spy was one thing, but seeing the evidence in his own home was, she now realised, a very different matter and with very different emotions. She felt sick in the stomach. Whether the earl hated his homeland or thought the Third Reich the way to greater riches and glory she didn't know and didn't really care, but he had betrayed his country and should have been brought to justice. Instead, he'd lived out his life as a wealthy aristocrat. She wondered whether Alisdair Bromley was related to the Bromley who'd returned from the Klondike with a fortune and bought Jimmy's Tarn.

Several signals during March and April, 1941 made Ellie's heart ache. They detailed the exact locations, dates and hours for the bombings of Clydebank and Glasgow. Others gave numbers of ships and people, shift times on the dockyards, and what convoys were docked at the Tail of the Bank. This, she knew, was a roadstead off Greenock. She also knew it was of significant importance during the war because it had been a strategic assembling point for convoys setting off for the Atlantic.

It was clear the earl had been a keen and significant contributor to the successful bombings on Clydebank. Somehow it seemed more personal because Mary's grandmother had died in the Glasgow bombings and, like so many other Clydesiders, had been buried in a sheet tied with string because coffins were so scarce.

Addressed to someone called Bealach, which Ellie knew was Gaelic for mountain pass, was an urgent directive from the German High Command to obtain information about the Atlantic convoys. It was impossible to tell who the recipient was, but from the response it was clear the spy was willing to do everything humanly possible to ensure success. An outgoing piece of traffic from the unknown spy sought contact with one of their 'friends' at Whitehall. A reply was not amongst the contents of the envelope.

For Ellie, time was forgotten as she delved into the past. There was enough evidence in half a box of signals to have arrested the

Earl of Strathvern. In the last half were directives regarding infiltrating the Scottish Council and the Scottish Council of Industry as significant amounts of war production were shifted back to Scotland. Ellie saw names of prominent Scottish families as friends of the German regime, the earl reporting on their willingness to house visitors from the Continent. In 1944 the signal traffic from Strathvern concerned the Invasion of Normandy. He believed that factories on Clydebank were involved in some way. Two photographs taken inside a factory were clipped to the back of one such signal.

She got to the end, having read many, but not all, of the box's contents. Several signals she had put to one side. She placed the box on the desk and withdrew the second one. This was filled with letters and again Ellie experienced a moment of hesitation. Reading the signal traffic had revealed the extent of the earl's treachery, but they were impersonal and short. The letters were likely to offer far more and she withdrew the first envelope. As her fingers touched the paper inside and she withdrew it, her heart beat a little faster. She carefully unfolded it. Hesitancy fled.

It was from a woman declaring her devotion to the Earl of Strathvern and the cause for which they struggled, pledging her support of him. She understood completely, she said, why he could not leave his wife: '*Indeed, that would be foolish, my darling. So much rests on you that we don't want any attention drawn to you about such an insignificant matter. I will always love you and will always be yours. Don't forget to leave my present in the usual place. I have one for you too. We'll be together soon.*' The letter ended, '*for the glory of the Third Reich*'. There was no signature.

An insignificant matter! The woman had no scruples, no concern that another woman could be suffering because of her! The earl was no better. Ellie wondered whether he'd even cared that his wife had committed suicide. How convenient for him.

Speculation about the earl's indiscretions had come up even in recent times, once when Ellie and Bob had been at Mary's birthday party. Bob, not one for lingering in the past, told them it was too long ago to really care and surely it wasn't anyone's business. However, such things were not forgotten. Ellie pitied the earl's wife. If she'd known about the affair the humiliation and distress must have been excruciating. Loathing for the other woman who, by her words scorned marriage and all that was British, stirred in

Ellie. Driven now by intense curiosity and outrage at the woman's callous feelings, Ellie delved into the box.

The earl's letters were often passionate and demanding, his declarations of love for his mistress frank and bold. He had married his wife, he stated, because his parents had insisted. *"She comes from one of Scotland's finest families, is beautiful and cultured, but she lacks your zest for life which, as you well know, stirs my blood. I have never loved her other than as a friend. You, however, have my heart – totally. In giving me a daughter our love will live on."*

A daughter!

"I wonder what happened to her?" Ellie said into the cold, empty room. "Farmed out to unwitting crofters probably. Or maybe sent to Germany and raised by Nazis."

A note stuffed between two letters and addressed to the earl in the neatest handwriting Ellie thought she'd ever seen, advised him that Jimmy from the Glen was settling in and would be given 'a guided tour of Glasgow and Paisley' the following day to 'become better acquainted with his new job'. It was not signed.

The shipyards, she thought bitterly. Jimmy from the Glen – could be anyone. There were Jimmys by the dozen in the Highlands and more glens than she'd been in.

However, tucked away was a snippet of information concerning Alisdair Bromley that she'd read earlier; he had helped plan the raids on the Clyde. It had to be him. Alisdair Bromley was Jimmy. Jimmy's Tarn. Of course! It was in a glen. The Bromleys, long gone from the area as far as she knew, had, it seemed, been smart and completely eluded suspicion as Nazi sympathizers.

She yawned. The initial emotional energy that had surged when she'd discovered the two boxes and their contents was draining away. She was warmer and drier, but her body was yearning for sleep. Not yet. A few more and she'd go. She had no wish to be locked in or found reading secret family documents.

In 1943 there was a change in the tone of several letters and telegrams. The woman, who was addressed only as *'My Darling'*, had taken up with an army officer. The earl was blunt. One response from the woman was equally blunt.

"You ought to know that the Father's orders are my priority. I cannot deny him, nor will you if you value all that is dear to you. And I hope that includes me. It is my job to do what is necessary. Surely you must know that I would not choose this man and, despite what others in London see, we will never be one. That is not the purpose. Whether you believe me or

not is your choice. I can be many faces, but not to you. I do this for the Father and the Third Reich, not my own desires. Yours forever."

For a while Ellie sat with the letter in her hand. Did spies really trust one another? Was their proclaimed love merely a means to an end? War was full of lies and treachery.

A telegram shared the same envelope. It was a brief reply from the aristocrat.

"You are of the greatest value to me. I'll wait for you. Our next appointment 20 Sep. Usual venue. Ross."

Ellie thought of his wife and wondered how much, if anything, she knew of her husband's involvement with the Nazi regime. Entertaining German officers occasionally might have been acceptable, though Ellie doubted it was broadcast to the local community. Had the countess approved of his liaison with the enemy? Unlikely, she thought.

Ellie sighed and looked at the next piece of paper, a handwritten note from early 1944, jottings for a signal perhaps, in which the earl vented his anger at the bombing of Dresden. He reassured Hitler of his commitment to the Third Reich. There were several short letters between the earl and his mistress, a mixture of terse language reminding M of her commitment to him, M rebuking him for his lack of trust, and words of desperate longing from both.

"Commitment," Ellie said with some force and looking at the neat handwriting of one of his letters. "You didn't care a hoot about your wife."

Ellie's eyes closed. A few seconds rest was all she needed and she stretched out her legs. Her clothing was almost dry underneath the blanket and warmth was reaching her toes. A few more letters and then she'd go.

The next envelope she retrieved was thicker. It was addressed to 'Ross, Wick Cottage, Mulltorr, dated January 1944. Ellie's enthusiasm was waning as she pulled the letter out and unfolded it. She needed sleep.

"My darling Ross, I have the most wonderful news! We, you and I, are going to have another baby!" Ellie's eyes widened and her mind raced off seeking answers. *"And before you get all riled up about 'this new wretched German fellow', I can assure you that I'd never let him father any child of mine, even if I was inclined towards him in that way, which I'm NOT! Besides, I'm almost three months gone, and he was away in the homeland for a number of weeks then on Father's business – as you well know. Do let me know as soon as possible how you feel. I hope you're as ecstatic as I am, for you know how MUCH I love you."*

The tone of the letter switched abruptly to war matters, but Ellie lost interest and put the pages back into their envelope and aside with the others. She was now intrigued to know whether the woman had the baby and she began rummaging through the box. Part of Ellie rebelled against the woman having such warm emotions about motherhood. That should have been the countess' joy, not of this enemy of Scotland!

She soon found letters written in September and October, skimming through them until she found the one she was looking for.

"At last you have seen your son, the bonniest baby at three weeks old. And you were so good with him! I'm sorry you could not spend longer, darling Ross, but I understand the demands of the House of Lords upon your time, and the need to be at Strathvern as well. I'm sure you will be well rewarded for your sacrifices and actions once the victory is won. Look after yourself, my love, for we will not see much of each other in the next few months at least. I'll do as you ask regarding arrangements for our baby. You and I know it's for the best and really the only option we have. Perhaps, one day, you will find a way for our children to live at Strathvern as I never could, but I suppose that is just a dream."

Ellie looked up. The Countess of Strathvern had died in 1946, giving her husband all the opportunities he needed to fulfil his mistress' wish. As a man of wealth and influence used to lying and hiding parts of his life, Ellie thought he would not have had any trouble installing his daughter and son in his home – even unacknowledged. But had he?

She put the letter with the few others. As she was putting the box back into the trunk she noticed a piece of paper sticking out from the bodice of the dress. It must have slipped out when she'd moved the clothing. Ellie carefully withdrew it from the pocket. It was a note from the earl to M in March 1964.

"Dearest M, it's no good arguing over whether or not I will allow the boy to come here. You know it's impossible. Ross is my legitimate heir and I won't let anything hinder him taking up his heritage in due time. I might not like some of his views, and I'm still not entirely convinced he's a true believer in our cause, but as long as he's not hindering it I'll tolerate his attitude. Do not raise the subject again because I'll ignore it. My decision will not change. The boy must remain where he is and we're agreed, as we were with our daughter, that we cannot allow them to ever know who their natural parents are. It would have catastrophic results for both of us. That you and I have somehow managed to fool everyone into believing you're a long lost cousin is a miracle in itself. The situation must remain as it is.

I know it's difficult, but I want to see you again. I miss your spark. Kurt and Hilda are coming over from Germany next month and they are adamant about seeing you. They were bitterly disappointed last time that you couldn't come. My son's at Oxford so it's easier for you to come here. He was determined on going to Cambridge, but I didn't want him tainted by those Communist radicals and forbad it. Eventually, he saw my point of view.

Write soon and make sure you come here in April. Still yours, R.

The change in the tone of the letter offended Ellie. The arrogant assumption of the man that everything he'd written beforehand was law and therefore unchangeable, but that he expected their relationship to continue as always, was outrageous. There were no more letters to give any clue about how M felt or whether their relationship had survived.

If anyone had written to Ellie in that superior tone she would have responded in the strongest words. The earl's indifferent feelings and decisions regarding his offspring by M showed her a man who believed, at least in his mature years, that duty was the highest calling. Perhaps M felt, in part, the same way, although how anyone could willingly give up their children was beyond Ellie's comprehension.

What had happened to the children? Who were they?

Ellie began packing everything back in the trunk and endeavoured to leave it as she'd found it. However, she felt a twinge of guilt in taking – *stealing* – the few letters and signals she'd kept out. It was a long time since she'd stolen anything and memories of her teenage years reminded her that once she would have thought nothing of taking money or things that belonged to someone else.

I'll bring them back, she thought, and stood up. The suddenness of getting off the chair and her body still stiff from the night's activities caused Ellie to wobble and half fall across the desk. A small wooden box fell off and landed on the top of the trunk. Photographs spilled out and onto the floor. Ellie scooped them up, looking at them only briefly, as they meant nothing to her and she was too tired to bother with the inscriptions on the reverse of some of them. As she picked up the box she saw an envelope still in the bottom and took it out. She was curious.

Inside the envelope were four black and white photographs; one of a baby girl, another of a toddler boy; and two taken a few years later. In the last two, in different locations, there was a slender woman. The girl looked around ten or eleven in a plain dress, while

302

the woman wore a fitted tailored suit and hat, her hair pulled into a bun at the back of her neck. She had her head turned towards the girl and was looking down. In the photo with the boy, the woman wore a summer dress and a hat with a wide brim. Pale hair touched her shoulders. In both photos most of her face was hidden.

Ellie stared at the boy's photograph. In his demeanour she detected deep unhappiness; his head was tilted down hiding his eyes and a shadow fell across his shoulder and over his mouth and neck. He was young, about four or five, but Ellie felt she knew him.

Chapter 18

Byron had over an hour before keeping his appointment with Jack Kennart and decided to visit Ellie's house and check it was undisturbed.

Before leaving, he returned upstairs to check he had what he needed and that nothing was lying around that should not be. There were days, he thought grimly, that his life seemed no different to when he was in the army.

As he slipped quietly out the back door and listened for a few seconds, he realised how much he wanted to shrug off and leave in a cupboard somewhere, all the sameness of that military existence. He'd given his country a lot of years and had no intention of being a regular 'adviser'. Next time his pal in London called on his expertise he'd be out – having another life!

In the early morning light Ellie's house was beginning to escape the shadows of night and there was a lonely aspect about it Byron hadn't felt before. Ellie's absence stirred a deeply embedded sadness that had been part of his soul for a long time. He didn't know how to get rid of it. He could bury it beneath work and social activities, yet it never quite disappeared. Even Kipp wasn't there to welcome him.

Down the back of the garden, the tumble of branches and foliage reminded him of his and Ellie's struggle to rescue Camden Orman. It seemed an eon ago. What had the man been up to? Byron couldn't imagine him plunging into history to right the wrongs of the past. Apart from anything else he seemed more than a bit odd.

He walked across the grass to the tangled branches and into the space where Camden had lain. There were a number of drying footprints in and around the area that he supposed belonged to policemen investigating the incident.

In too many such places had Byron stood where men had fallen and died, courageous men not deserving of early deaths far from home. There were a few blotches of dried blood on the ground, reinforcing the pain of their loss. What madness and cruelty had stolen his men and Ena? Had decision-makers been so unable to come to an agreement or had other agendas been on the table?

"I didn't expect to see you here at this time of the morning."

Byron swung round at the sound of Bob's voice.

"Likewise," he said with an inbuilt wariness, but felt immediately abashed as the baker walked towards him, hands in his trouser pockets, his expression open and friendly.

"I just came around to see everything was all right," Bob said.

"Me too. I haven't been inside yet."

"Any news?"

Byron shook his head. "I don't know where she is, Bob, and to be honest I don't know where to start looking. Maybe it's somewhere obvious, but…" He shrugged and joined the other man on the grass.

"In the Highlands you could be hidden without ever being found."

"But Ellie knows the Highlands and she's not the sort to sit around until someone finds her."

"But she doesn't know every inch of the Highlands. I doubt anyone does."

"Then where d'you suggest we start?" Byron snapped. "You know this area better than I do. If you had to hide someone, where would you go?" He looked at the baker then sighed. "Sorry, Bob. I didn't sleep too well."

"No apology needed, and if it's any consolation I didn't get much sleep either," he responded, yawning. "By the way, Olga Erskine's being released from hospital today. She phoned the bakery yesterday to make sure her bread and favourite cakes would be delivered."

"You seem to get on well with her."

"I discovered soon after I opened The Mill that elderly people like to think their milkman, baker and butcher have a special place in their hearts for them – and they often do. The housebound use us as a sort of telegraph line," he said with a grin.

"Did she know Farley Orman well?"

He shrugged. "Don't know. Why d'you ask?"

"Curiosity. He was doing some research about the Second World War and I thought he might've targeted all the elderly in the village."

"What was he researching?"

"Good question. Anyway, it's probably got nothing to do with his death. I thought I'd ring the SNH and find out if they knew anyone who had a particularly vindictive bent towards Farley."

305

Bob snorted. "That could be a longish list – local councillors, builders, farmers, small businesses. Glenn Thorley managed to get quite a few of them worked up when Farley got backing from a number of parliamentarians willing to block any petition to have land at the foot of Maw's Hearth turned into a hotel complex. Thorley's a fool. It's no place for building anything."

"He had me look at it and draw up plans."

Bob's expression clouded. "When was that?"

"It's what he sent me up here for. He didn't mention anything about the application being blocked."

"He wouldn't. Why are you working for him?" He sounded annoyed.

"I'm not. I quit."

Cautious relief eased the tightness of his facial muscles.

"Have you seen our local plods yet?" Bob asked, changing the subject.

"Not since Maws Hearth, but I've been summoned to the station at eight."

Bob glanced at his watch. "Want to check inside the house before you go?"

There was a moment's uncertainty in Byron. He'd anticipated being alone and wasn't sure he wanted to share the experience of wandering through Ellie's home with Bob. Nor did he relish the idea of searching the house for clues and information while he had a companion.

"Sure," he said without enthusiasm, noting Bob's shrewd study of his hesitant response.

"Don't worry, I know you were here on the night Ellie found Camden in her garden," Bob said, with what Byron thought a cynical grin.

Byron couldn't be worried about the other man's feelings now and simply nodded, walking ahead of him to the back door.

It was cold inside and the rooms were gloomy and unwelcoming in the early light.

Bob opted to do the upstairs rooms leaving Byron a few minutes of freedom to investigate Ellie's study. It looked much the same as the last time he'd been in there; papers and magazines were scattered across the desk and a number of books were piled on a small table near the swivel chair. In the corner, one of the filing cabinet drawers was open. Byron frowned. Ellie was pedantic about the security of paperwork relating to the issues she and

Farley had been involved in and said she always kept the cabinet locked when she wasn't home. Skirting round the desk, he went towards it and peered at the lock. There were scratches and a small dent, and the keyhole was bent slightly out of shape. Someone, uninvited, had been in the house.

Inside the drawer and about halfway along, one of the hanging files was gaping and empty – Maw's Hearth.

Byron's eyes narrowed and a chill ran down his spine. Glenn Thorley – a man without boundaries who would consider it his right to appropriate any information he wanted, whether it was his to have or not. He had a particular interest in Maw's Hearth that had nothing to do with preserving it as a natural and national heritage, whatever he told the authorities.

However, there had been no indication of forced entry at the back door. He was about to open the top drawer using a dusting cloth on the edge of the desk, when he heard Bob coming back downstairs. Annoyed and frustrated, he turned as Bob appeared in the doorway. His expression was hard to read.

"Someone's been here," Byron said, without waiting for Bob's report. "The lock's been tampered with."

"Anything missing?" Bob asked, entering the room.

"From this drawer, yes. All the paperwork for Maw's Hearth."

"Why on earth would anyone want to take that?" He stared, eyebrows raised, at Byron. "It's a great lump of a hill with a chimney stuck on top. What about the other drawers?"

"Haven't checked. We'd better look round outside and see if the front door or any of the windows have been tampered with."

"I can do that. Why don't you check the rest of the cabinet – and don't get your fingerprints on it. Jack'd have a thing or two to say about that!"

"Only if we tell him."

"Hmm. I don't think it'd look too good if he finds out later."

"Anything amiss upstairs?" It was too late for him to be worrying about his reputation with the local police.

"No." Bob's answer was blunt and uninviting, but was quickly followed by a cheerier, "Be back soon."

Uneasiness stirred in Byron as he watched Bob disappear down the hallway and into the kitchen. Perhaps the sight of his clothes strewn across the bed in Ellie's spare room had upset him. He'd feel the same.

307

Byron returned to the cabinet and flicked through the hanging files, delving into the paperwork only if the subject tag suggested to him a link with Farley. However, as he progressed through the drawer he realised that Farley was connected to almost every file except ones containing the likes of electricity bills.

He sighed and stared at the crowded drawer. To do a thorough job he'd need all morning. Byron glanced at his watch. He had forty-five minutes, but he could come back – without Bob.

A couple of minutes later, at the back of the drawer, he noticed a thin file titled 'Fenella Orman'. Pulling out the entire contents of about a dozen pages, Byron glanced through them, curious as to why Ellie would have a file on one of Farley's offspring. When he finished reading the top page, a letter dated five months earlier, he stared at the signature on the bottom – Glenn Thorley. How Ellie had come to be in possession of it he had no idea, but there was little doubt from the letter's content that Fenella was involved with Glenn in plans to remove the Earl of Strathvern from the castle and turn it into a luxury hotel. This went way beyond ambition. And was Maw's Hearth a diversion, keeping councillors and the like occupied while Thorley went after a better site?

With the papers in his hand he moved towards a seat near the window and had just bent to move a cushion out of the way when a there was a loud thud, immediately followed by splintering glass behind him. A bottle, flaming at its neck, flew over his head, landing behind him. He dove onto the floor, hands protecting his head. In seconds, the smell of petrol had him on his feet, shoving the papers still clutched in his hand into his jacket pocket. He grabbed a cushion, beating out flames beginning to claim a pile of books on the floor.

"Bob! Bob!" he shouted.

There was no response.

Ejecting flowers in a vase, he threw the water onto the last of the flames licking around the bottom of the settee. The fire was out in minutes, leaving scorch marks on the settee and carpet. Shards of glass littered the floor beneath the window. He had escaped injury, but where was Bob?

Running down the hallway and out the front door he saw him on the lawn, struggling to sit up. He had a hand to his head. Byron crouched down beside him.

"Sit still, Bob. Are you okay?"

"I think so. Somebody whacked me on the head. What's going on?"

"Your 'somebody' threw a bottle of petrol, alight, into Ellie's study."

"What!" he exclaimed, struggling to get up. "We have to put the fire out."

"It's out," Byron said, placing a hand on his shoulder, restraining him. "Did you see anyone?"

Bob shook his head and grimaced. "Heard a car, but I was too busy checking things to take any notice. I think someone's prised the laundry window open."

Byron helped him up. "Let's have a look at your head."

"It's all right. I'll get the doc to check it. Are you sure the fire's out?"

"Yes."

"I've got to get back to the bakery."

"I'll take you. Don't want you having an accident."

"I'm fine. Anyway, don't you have to be at the police station?"

Byron glanced at his watch. "I've a few minutes yet. I'll lock up first."

"Right," Bob said, and began walking slowly towards his car.

Watching him get into his car and back down the driveway, Byron found himself wondering how hard the assailant had hit Bob. He'd managed to get up well enough.

Byron went back into the house and made his way to the laundry. Years ago, it had been a scullery and was a good-sized room with a deep enamel sink and clunky taps, and two terracotta pots of geraniums in the middle of the windowsill. Ellie had painted the walls blue and hung a collection of prints with garden scenes in the middle of the back wall. They'd brought life into what Byron suspected had once been a drab workroom where men tramped through in their work boots and women with baskets of washing.

Byron's gaze returned to the geraniums. He frowned, then went outside and studied the window frame. The window, big enough for a slim person to clamber through, was partly open. Near the latch were scratches in the paint, but what perplexed him were undisturbed pots of geraniums inside.

***

"So, you're still alive then," Jack Kennart announced as Byron walked into the police station.

"Seems so. Any news on Ellie?" he asked, following the sergeant into his office. He nodded to Tim Ashby and another constable who were regarding him with interest.

Jack shut the door behind them, took out a cigarette, seemed to think better of it and seconds later put it back in the packet.

"Not a thing. No threatening phone call or letter, no whispers of someone seeing her somewhere. Are you sure she was kidnapped?"

"Yes. There were signs in the grass near the Land Rover of something being dragged. Who would go to all that trouble?"

"And why?" Jack's tone was subdued. "Any ideas?"

"One or two. The most obvious is her connection with Farley Orman. He upset quite a few people I hear and they'll assume Ellie will step into his shoes, but she won't. Money's a powerful driver and building hotels is big business. Corrupts the best of people, even policemen."

"What're you hinting at, Oakes? I've never taken a bribe in my life and I've no intention of starting at this late stage!"

"Then what or who persuaded you to go up to Maw's Hearth and retrieve Farley Orman's bags? You don't seem the climbing sort to me."

Jack stared at him, the colour retreating from his cheeks. He said bluntly, "I'm not. Haven't been up there for years. Can't stand the place if you must know."

"You might want to re-think that. You were seen."

"The London smog's addled your brains. I only went up as far as the Cobbles because of Farley's body."

"And I thought policemen were always supposed to tell the truth."

"We're human in case you hadn't noticed. This won't find Ellie."

"It might if you tell me what you were doing under The Chimney."

Years of masking his thoughts and feelings came to Jack's aid and his expression remained unchanged, but Byron saw a slight flicker in his eyes.

"The Chimney's a solid lump of rock. Eerie, if you ask me. A place for fools who think rock climbing's fun until they fall. It's people like me who have to collect their battered bodies from the

310

bottom. Ellie found one once, a lad of about fifteen. Took her a while to get over that."

Byron inclined his head in understanding. However, he knew it was an attempt to draw him away from the subject.

"I saw you, Jack," he said quietly.

There was no immediate reaction other than a greater intensity in his expression. Byron shifted in his seat, waiting.

"Okay," Jack said, nodding slowly, "I was there. I'll give you credit, Byron Oakes. You hid yourself well. So much for Bran's tracking abilities. I'll stick to my instincts in future."

"I've had plenty of practice in hiding, Jack. Seems an odd place for Farley to have left his photographic equipment."

"He was planning to come back. You've seen what's up there. It's one of the greatest finds in Scottish medieval history and we were going to make good money out of it. All legal," he added quickly when Byron raised his eyebrows. "I studied medieval history at Edinburgh University, but couldna find a job after I finished. Joined the police instead." He shook his head. "Should've kept looking."

"And that's it?"

"Aye. Didn't count on anyone putting an end to it by killing him," he said, and reached for his cigarettes, holding them up. "Okay with you?"

"Sure. Did Camden know what you two were up to?"

"Not unless Farley told him, which I doubt. He's a jealous lad that one and a wee bit odd. Hates anyone doing better than him including his father. The only reason he wants to get his grubby wee hands on Farley's bags is to stop anyone else making money out of the rolls of film."

"Well, he's out of action for a while. Strange he turned up in Ellie's garden."

"Aye, but he believed Ellie had taken rolls of film he felt belonged to him. He's a possessive man. And you also have to understand that Camden was very close to his mother. He hates Ellie and did everything he could to destroy the partnership with his father even after Alice disappeared." He shook his head. "Shocked the whole village her disappearing like that. Camden thinks there was something going on between Ellie and his father, but Ellie's not one to do such things. Camden broke her arm once. Attacked her outside the post office. I don't suppose she told you that," he said, tapping his cigarette over an ashtray.

311

Byron watched the ash drop off the end of the cigarette. "No, she didn't."

"Camden's strong-willed, like his father, but Farley wasn't violent. Never even saw him kill a fly. I feel sorry for Camden sometimes though. Farley was often away during the lad's growing up and never had much time for him even when he was home. Don't think they had much in common and Farley had no patience with his peculiar ways." Jack shook his head. "Shame, him being the eldest and least liked. Should nae be that way."

"Fathers shouldn't be absent either."

"No, they shouldn't," Jack said quietly. He looked out the window. "The inspector's none too happy about any of it and he's convinced you're in it up to your neck. Lucky for you the boys in London have warned him off or you'd be locked up in a cell by now."

"All I care about is finding Ellie – alive. Give me a free hand here, Jack."

"And have my backside kicked from here to Edinburgh? You've got a nerve asking." He stubbed out the cigarette, leaned back in his chair and looked at Byron. "On one condition – you keep me informed and call for help when you need it. You're not the law and you're only one man."

"Thanks, Jack. I appreciate it."

"And one more thing – no more switching off your mobile."

Byron laughed. "Deal."

"I can see they're useful, but lugging that great thing around must be a damned nuisance."

"Well, they're useful as you say, but I don't take it everywhere."

"Maybe you should."

The constable came in with a message that one of the local councillors wanted to see the sergeant, but Jack told him he had an urgent matter to deal with and to make an appointment for next week.

"That man's about as useful as a goldfish in a bowl," he said to Byron after the constable had gone. "How he got elected is a village mystery. I don't think anyone here voted for him. The only good thing he's done so far is sign the papers to have a new toilet block built in the park."

He reached out to the shelves behind him and picked up a map which he spread over the desk. They pored over the map, deciding which areas the search would cover and, with Byron's knowledge limited to a few places, Jack directed him to the area around Strathvern Castle.

"If you bump into the earl pretend you're a tourist. He's not too fond of people sticking their noses about his property."

"Too late for that," Byron said, to which Jack raised his bushy eyebrows. "I was following a set of tyre tracks I thought might belong to the vehicle Ellie was in and wandered into a field. The next thing I knew I had the company of two English setters and their owner."

"He keeps a close eye on every square foot of his land with the help of Bran Orman and his outdoor staff. Be careful you don't get caught again."

"I don't think he'll be bothering me, Jack. His son Michael was in a bit of trouble and I just happened along and got him out of it."

The expression on Jack's face made it plain he wanted an explanation.

"Glenn Thorley was playing rough," Byron said, hoping the man across the table wasn't going to press for details.

"You seem to be very good at 'just happening along', Byron Oakes. Thorley's a thug, a rich thug, who's got enough money to be trouble. I don't like the man and wish he'd get away out of the village."

"He's got his eyes on Strathvern."

"And how d'you know that? No," he said, holding up a hand, "I don't think I want to know. But we're no' a bunch of country yokels he can bully."

"Don't underestimate him, Jack."

The other man nodded slowly. "I forgot. You're working for him."

"Not now. I don't like him or his terms and quit. I've met too many of his sort."

"Well, if he is after Strathvern he won't have much success. The villagers might not have forgiven the sixth earl for being a traitor, some don't even like the present one, but we won't give up one of our own."

"I've heard Fenella Orman's mixed up with Thorley," Byron said, probing.

"Fenella!" Jack exclaimed. "That little minx might be full of herself, but she's not a fool. If she's taken up with him, and that I

313

doubt, she'll be leading the dance. Farley's daughter's never played second fiddle to anyone."

"Money might persuade her."

"You know something I don't?"

"Only what I've heard. And I did see a letter with both their names on it."

"Where?"

"At Ellie's."

"Now why am I not surprised? You think they've got something to do with Ellie's disappearance?"

"I don't know. If it is them, where would they take her?"

"The Orman property perhaps. They've got about ten acres with a couple of empty crofts, not to mention their house, built about 1780, with at least one secret passage and a cupboard that takes you into another room. Then there's... Sorry, history lesson can wait."

He outlined his plan for the day, changing his mind about sending Byron to Strathvern, and instead directing him to the Orman property with a constable, while he'd go to Strathvern. He'd organise two constables from Castlebay to scour the countryside around two villages on the Firth.

"Right," he said folding up the map, "let's go and find Ellie."

***

Pale sunshine was spreading its tepid warmth over Kilcomb as Byron walked across the road to his car. The street was busy preparing itself for the day: the post office door swung open and Carrie Ross stepped outside with a small billboard and parked it on the pavement; a few cars were moving slowly down the road, some parking and others making their way out of the village; he could see Mary Nevin through the large windows of the grocery store, tidying a shelf; and outside the bank two uniformed employees were waiting to be let inside. The sound of young children laughing drew Byron's attention and he saw a family dressed in walking clothes, the parents with backpacks strapped on, turning into a lane that led out of the village.

He sighed, envying their joy in the simple pleasure of being together and going for a walk. If only life was really so free and uncomplicated. His trip into the surrounding countryside would be a far different journey of discovery – if there was a discovery. The laughter disappeared down the lane with the family and Byron found himself wondering if he would ever laugh with Ellie again.

"Mr Oakes! Mr Oakes!"

He turned to see Tim Ashby waiting for a car to pass before running across the road.

"Mr Oakes," he said, puffing slightly on reaching him, "Sergeant Kennart wants you back inside. He's had a call from Lord Strathvern."

They walked quickly across the road and, as they were about to enter the police station, Byron caught a glimpse of Ross' middle son, Jamie, driving by in his bright yellow car. Beside him was Fenella Orman. She smiled; he waved.

"His Lordship's just informed me that he believes Ellie was at Strathvern last night," Jack said testily as Byron entered his office. "He said Bran found her jacket and shoes in the grounds this morning – near the loch. Why they've taken so long to inform me I don't know."

"And the rest of her?" Byron's heart was uneasy.

The sergeant pinched his lips together and studied him for a few seconds, his expression softening. "I don't know, Byron, but we're going to find out. Two constables from Castlebay will meet us there. They're divers."

Fear rose in Byron like an evil tide, threatening to choke and immobilise him. "Let's go," he said quietly and left the office.

Byron followed the police car containing Jack and Tim Ashby. A junior constable not long out of training was left in charge of the police station.

Byron's thoughts connected one to another in a stream of possibilities concerning Ellie's whereabouts. She was a survivor and she was smart, but still a cold fog wrapped around his heart.

They had not gone far along the road when Byron's mobile rang. It was Jack.

"You need to get home. Someone's set fire to your house, laddie. Fire Brigade's on its way."

"What d'you mean, *set fire to*? Could've been an electrical fault. The cottage is ancient."

"One of your neighbours said he saw somebody running down your path then onto the road. I think you'll agree that's a wee bit suspicious. I'll keep you posted regarding Ellie."

He hung up without waiting for a response and Byron, frustrated, slowed down and spun the car round. A horn blasted from behind and a car skidded in the dirt on the side of the road before speeding past. There was no mistaking the angry waving of a fist and mouthed words were meant for him.

The firemen were running out the hose as he arrived and by the time he was out of his car and walking towards them, a great spray of water was dousing the cottage.

"Are you the owner?" asked a solid, red-haired man in a fireman's uniform standing at the back of the fire truck.

"Tenant actually. How long's it been going?"

"About fifteen minutes or so."

"Any idea how it started?"

"Too early. Had the electrics tested lately?"

"Don't know. That's up to the owner," he said, watching flames shooting out of the roof.

"Good thing your neighbour noticed or you'd have lost the lot. He called us then came back and broke a window. His wife chucked buckets of water through it."

Byron looked around, but there was no sign of David Masters.

"He went home to change his clothes," the fireman added. "Was there anyone else in there? Pets?"

Byron shook his head, relieved he'd taken Kipp to Mary Nevin's. "How long before it's out?"

"Ten minutes maybe, then we'll check we haven't missed anything. It's a solid enough wee place, but you'll have to find somewhere else to live for a while."

Byron scanned the front of the building and saw a shattered sitting room window. He pointed it out to the fireman.

"Aye, that's your neighbour's handiwork."

"Hey, Don! More water!" yelled one of the men on the hose.

Don turned to the truck and did as he was asked. The radio burst into life and seconds later he was reaching inside the truck's cabin to answer it.

Behind him, Byron heard his name called and turned to find David walking towards him. They'd chatted a few times and he'd found him and his wife friendly and good-humoured with wide ranging interests. He was a tall thin man with a cultured English accent; he and his wife had moved into the big house next door on his retirement from a prosperous banking career.

"I hear you had a bash at firefighting," Byron said, extending his hand. "I owe you at least the best bottle of whisky in Kilcomb, David. Thanks."

"The least I could do, Byron. Besides, it wouldn't do to have the whole neighbourhood burnt to the ground, would it?" he said with a grim expression.

"No, it wouldn't," Byron replied, looking at the firemen who were round the side of the cottage with the hose. "Jack Kennart said you saw someone running away from the place. Any idea who it might've been?"

"Sorry, no. Just saw a medium-sized man in a pair of black trousers and a dark green jacket. Had a tear at the elbow. I think he had a dark hat on, the sort a skier or mountaineer might wear. Not much help, Byron. Let's hope the police catch whoever it is. Why would anyone do such a thing?"

"I don't know. Didn't think I'd been here long enough to make any enemies," he said more light-heartedly than he felt. The runner may or may not have set light to the cottage, but it might be the person who'd taken a pot-shot at him and Ellie. "Anyway, thanks again for your help."

"Glad I could help. By the way, if you need somewhere to stay we've got plenty of room."

Byron was surprised and unexpectedly moved by the man's generosity. "Thank you, David, that's very good of you. I'll let you know if I get stuck."

"That's fine." His attention was distracted by something behind Byron. "I think the firemen want you. See you later."

The flames were subsiding as a ladder was run up the side of the cottage where part of the roof had fallen in. A young fireman climbed up with the hose to douse the area with a heavy shower of water, while two men held onto the hose on the ground. A pall of smoke escaped into the atmosphere as he watered the roof and attic. A second hose was re-directed from the roof by two men when flames re-ignited in the front room. They were out within a couple of minutes and it seemed to Byron that the fire in the roof was now under control.

Suddenly, the man at the top of the ladder wobbled and clutched at the guttering, water spraying all over the roof and up into the air. He dropped the hose and scrambled down the ladder, water shooting over the neighbour's hedge as the hose slid down the roof. It hit the back of the second fireman as he took hold of the ladder to steady it.

"Watch out, everyone! Keep clear of the hose. What's the matter with you, Seamus?" shouted Don as he ran back to the truck and turned the water off.

"In there... in there..." gasped the wet and shaking Seamus, pointing at the roof, "there's a bo... body. It's, it's..." He could not continue.

"Don't be daft, boy! Have one too many pints at the pub last night, did you? It was downright dangerous what you did. That hose could've caused one of us serious injury. Next time I'll send Robbie up."

"But it's in there! I swear! And I only had a pint last night."

Byron was already on his way towards the ladder.

"Hey, you! Don't go up there!" Don's voice followed Byron as he approached the ladder. "Come away, you fool. It's too dangerous."

Byron ignored him, his heart pounding as he began climbing the ladder. Near the top, his hand on the gutter, he stopped, afraid of peering in, afraid of what he would see. There was a hard lump in his chest. What if...?

"You've never been a coward, Byron Oakes, don't start now," he said not loud enough for anyone else to hear.

He stepped up quickly and the smell of damp, smoke-laden air filled his nostrils as he peered through the ragged hole into the gloomy and charred attic. A couple of seconds later he saw what had terrified the young fireman, but it wasn't a body. Propped up in a rocking chair was a skeleton, partly covered in a sheet. Bits of long hair, or what was left of it, hung from the skull.

Relief flowed down the length of Byron's body. It wasn't Ellie.

"Get down!" came a shout from below. "You're not allowed up there."

Byron ignored Don again and retrieved his mobile, dialling Jack Kennart's number. The sooner he told him the better.

"Come on, come on," Byron muttered impatiently, watching Don striding across the lawn towards him. Seamus and one of the other firemen were there first. He supposed Seamus' find would dominate conversations at the pub by the time he'd finished his first beer. There was no answer on Jack's phone. Byron left a message before climbing down the ladder.

"You shouldn't have gone up there without my permission," Don chided him as Byron reached the last rung. "Have you no idea of danger, man? My job'd be on the line if you'd fallen and broken your neck. Get the ladder down boys then check round the back for smouldering or flare-ups."

"I've been in more dangerous situations than being up that ladder," Byron said bluntly. "And keep this quiet. The police need to see this."

"Who're you to tell me what to do?" Don's cheeks were bright with indignation.

"I work for the government." Just a small lie.

"So what? You could be a nobody. I'll be telling who I like and that includes the police."

Byron stepped towards him. "*I've* told Sergeant Kennart. You stick to fighting fires – and keep your mouth shut." He turned to Seamus who went bright red as the attention switched to him. "It's a skeleton, Seamus, not a body. Probably been there a long time. Just don't go blabbing about it."

Seamus and his companion shook their heads, but Don was less co-operative.

"What's your name and who's your landlord?" he demanded.

"I'm Byron Oakes. Haven't a clue who the landlord is, but I'll make sure the estate agents know the cottage needs repairs."

Don glared at him and wrote his name in a notepad he retrieved from his jacket pocket. When he finished tucking the pad away, he looked up, suspicion in his eyes. "I've heard about you from Andy at the garage. Said you were snooping about Ellie Madison's vehicle when she had that accident. *And* I've heard she's gone missing. Now this. Trouble follows you does it Byron Oakes? *If* that's your real name."

It was the sort of small-minded arrogance that always irritated Byron; he had no time for it.

"I've got things to do," he said and began walking towards the side of the cottage.

"I'll be doing some checking up on you."

"You do that," he said, without turning around.

"I will. You can be sure of that. And don't go upstairs."

Byron raised his eyebrows at this. Don, he thought, was probably like others he had known who insisted on having the last word but rarely ever did anything about their threat or promise.

"I live here, you don't."

"The police won't want you tramping all over it. Anyway," he added less abruptly, "it's bloody dangerous."

The other two firemen were coming out of the back door as Byron approached it. They nodded to him and kept walking.

The smell of smoke and burnt wood and furnishings was strong; there was also a pungent odour of warm dampness. The kitchen was untouched by the flames but filthy with ash and cinders. There was little damage in the hallway, other than wet floorboards and part of the walls near the door to the front room. When he stepped into that room he sighed, glad he had taken all the papers and photos with him. The outer coverings and padding of the settee and its two chairs were burned to the springs, the wooden frames now charred. Against the walls, the dresser, bookcase and a small table were badly burned, as were their contents. Most of the carpet was gone and what was left squelched under his feet. Above him was a hole where the fire had burned through the plaster and wooden ceiling. The curtains were mere remnants and the walls were grubby with soot. On the windowsill, and just below on the floor, lay shards of glass. There were also remains of a bottle. Well, that confirmed David's observation about the window.

He thought of Bob and the strange incident at Ellie's house not two hours earlier. Pulling a handkerchief from his pocket he picked up what was left of the large bottle and sniffed – petrol. He frowned. Few people knew him; he hadn't been in the village long enough to be classified as a resident. What strange purpose was there in tossing petrol-filled bottles through the window?

Leaving the wreckage of the sitting room, Byron went back outside and retrieved the ladder from the old stable down the garden. The firemen were occupied round the front of the cottage. He went upstairs, curious about the skeleton and annoyed that he hadn't bothered to go up into the attic before now. Maybe some of his old habits were slipping away, which wasn't a bad thing, but in this case he wished he'd listened to that small voice. Too late now.

Unfolding the ladder beneath the attic he climbed up and found it bolted shut. He'd forgotten seeing the small padlock just as he'd forgotten the agent's warning about the attic being off limits as it was full of the owner's belongings. Strange belongings. The padlock looked as if it had been there for years and he couldn't help wondering when the owner had last visited. Given the state of the skeleton he guessed it had been a very long time.

He went back down the ladder and out to the stable where he found a rusting axe. It would do. He had no time for protocol or waiting for Jack. Trying to break the padlock would take too long. Using the axe, he gave the attic cover several forceful bashes before the wood suddenly gave way. He wobbled, as did the ladder and his foot slid off the rung. He grabbed the edge of the hole above him, got his foot back on the ladder and pushed himself upwards.

Almost everything was sodden and the acrid smell of the recently doused cottage met him with intensity. Against the farthest wall stood an old chest of drawers and a cradle, mostly untouched by the flames. The remains of two tea chests steamed near the hole in the ceiling and a few paintings leaned against the wall near the chests, bits of scorched canvas hanging from the frame of the front one. A bundle of papers was reduced to a blackened heap.

Almost reluctantly his eyes turned to the skeleton in its saturated sheet, water dripping from its hair. Bits of ash stuck to the sheet and head. It was a pathetic and sad sight.

Treading carefully, testing the floorboards, Byron made his way slowly towards the rocking chair. Who on earth was it? A woman, he guessed from the hair, a woman who'd been there quite a while and now reduced to bones.

He heard a sound on the landing below. Damn! He turned around and a few seconds later Don's head popped up in the opening.

He glared at Byron. "I'm going to report you to the police. You're tampering with evidence."

"Evidence of what? Faulty wiring could be the culprit – as you pointed out."

"You shouldn't be up here touching all this stuff. It's not yours."

"How d'you know? I live here remember."

Don's eyes narrowed. "A skeleton in a rocking chair isn't the sort of thing any normal person carts about."

"I never said I was normal."

"You'll have some explaining to do to the police. Sergeant Kennart won't like this one bit." He stepped back down the ladder. His voice, loud and angry, shot up into the attic. "Bloody English! You're all the same – think you own the whole world! Taking our crofts and turning them into souvenir stores, building hotels where you've no right to. Go back to London where you belong!"

Byron turned his back on the attic entrance and returned to studying the skeleton. Carefully lifting a corner of the sheet, he discovered a faded green-brown tweed jacket and skirt hanging limply on the bones. The legs were covered in sagging woollen stockings, the feet still encased in sturdy walking shoes. It was all good quality. There was nothing cheap about the fabric or cut of the jacket and skirt. Even the buttons were stamped with a pattern. He leaned down and looked more closely. He'd seen it recently, but where? His heart skipped a beat and he reached for his mobile phone.

"Jack, it's Byron Oakes," he said when it was answered.

"We haven't found Ellie yet, but there's no doubt she was at Strathvern – might still be here somewhere."

"I hope so." He paused. "Jack, there's something in the cottage you need to see."

"I don't like the sound of that. What is it?"

Byron told him what had happened. There was silence for several seconds before the sergeant responded.

"You sure?"

"No, but it's possible – isn't it?"

He heard a long sigh. "Aye, it is. I'm on my way. I'll leave the others here. Ellie'll no be far away by my reckoning."

He hoped Jack was right, but if Glenn Thorley had anything to do with it he wasn't sure any good would come of it.

Chapter 19

The fresh morning air met Ellie like the breath of life. She inhaled deeply of its cold sweetness and almost let out a shout of joy. The hours of underground existence and freezing in wet clothes had been challenging enough, but Glenn's presence had unsettled her despite her bravado. The Ellie child was still there, memories still raw.

Now she had to decide what to do with the extraordinary information she'd acquired in the hidden room.

The journey from the room had been in darkness. She had tried staying in the middle of the tunnel, but without light the middle was impossible to follow. Several times she'd tripped over unseen objects, stubbing and bruising her unprotected feet as she hurried as much as possible to get into the open air. Swimming out through the inlet had been impossible because of the papers and photos stuffed into her pockets. She had no intention of keeping them. They belonged to the Earl of Strathvern and nothing would persuade her to hand them over to anyone else, not even the government.

Until she'd walked straight into the wall of the traversing tunnel she'd had no idea how close, or otherwise, she was from the junction of the tunnels. The toes of her right foot, arm and hand had scraped against the concrete, but the damage to her was minimal. She had to get back to the cellar. It was her only hope of getting out despite the locked door awaiting her.

Whether it was her imagination or not, she thought someone else had been in the tunnel, someone who'd come from the direction of the castle. She'd heard no distinct sound to confirm the fear, but she still could not rid herself of the feeling that she'd been followed. Had it been Glenn he would have made himself known.

Once in the cellar, she'd gone along the wall until she found the light switch. Its dull light was as the sun to her. As it permeated the darkness she was certain she'd heard a sigh and had spun round, heart thudding. There wasn't a soul in sight.

A chill had run down her spine and again, now, as she remembered. Ellie did not believe in ghosts, though she knew others who decried her disbelief and had given her full descriptions of their encounters with the departed. Alone in the cellar, Ellie had almost convinced herself that the previous Countess of Strathvern had been there, protecting her, releasing a sigh of relief when her charge reached the cellar. How else, Ellie had asked herself, could the door to the outside have been unlocked?

Now, breathing in the Scottish autumn air, she pushed aside the fanciful notion of Her Ladyship's presence and looked around. The castle was obscured behind a line of trees and the walls of the extensive kitchen garden which the current countess had revitalised and brought to vibrant life. Its espaliered fruit trees and prolific and varied vegetables and herbs were an inspiration to Ellie.

"I never believed you were dead for one minute, Ellie."

Ellie's head jerked up and she stared at the man who'd appeared so suddenly, standing feet from her. Fear flooded into her body taking advantage of her exhaustion. She felt near collapsing. Hope of ever escaping her cousin was trampled under the feet of despair; tears of frustration, anger and pain filled her tired eyes.

"So it was you," she said abruptly, ignoring the tears.

"What're you talking about?" he said, looking at her as if she was a fool.

"You should've killed me while you had the chance. Who would've known?" She was talking loudly now and did not care.

"You've lost your mind, Ellie. I've been waiting for hours. I didn't think you'd fancy another dip in the loch and *knowing* you as well as I do," he said, smirking, "I thought you'd try for the door. I was right – as I usually am."

"You don't know me at all, Glenn. You're stuck in the past."

"And you're stuck with me until I'm finished with you. My business dealings are bigger than your pathetic attempts to save the Highlands and you'll do as I tell you. I didn't go to all the trouble of shattering your windscreen for you to just run off home."

"You're a sick, deluded man."

"And your boyfriend Oakes won't be around to help. I have it on good authority that he's probably toast by now. So…"

Ellie's eyes narrowed and she glared at the man, hating him. "He's a better and smarter man than you'll ever be."

"I doubt it," he said, watching her. "Don't you want to know about his untimely demise? Shame on you, Ellie, for having such shallow feelings. His cottage was set alight."

324

"You're a liar. D'you know what your mother said to me once? That you were incapable of love and chose to abuse and lie instead. Gave you some sort of weird sense of accomplishment, she said, and she didn't know what you'd done to me until years later."

He stared at her, his eyes blazing. "You told her? *You* told her! You bitch, you stupid bitch!"

"I didn't have to, Glenn. She guessed."

"I don't believe you."

"I don't care. You're incapable of knowing what truth and integrity and honesty are. You're the most warped individual I've ever met. I've had no trouble in keeping the fact of our family relationship a secret, apart from your threats, because I don't want anyone knowing I'm related to you. I'm ashamed to admit it," she shouted, shaking with anger.

"Keep your voice down!" he snapped, his brows drawn together under a heavy scowl.

He tried to grab hold of her arm, but she side-stepped out of his way. The truth, so long stuffed away in a deep chamber of her soul, was straining for release.

"I'll be as loud as I want! Your mother told me about the times you hit her because she didn't put the right food in your lunch box or hadn't ironed your shirts on time. You pushed her down the stairs once and left her while you went off to play football. If your sister hadn't come home she'd have been a cripple for life. You even threatened your grandmother once and tried to poison her dog, but your father got there in time. And you know what? They covered up for you, even lied to the police once to protect you. What for? Nothing! You don't deserve anything good, Glenn. You're a destroyer. Everyone who comes into your life you set about demeaning, abusing, and destroying. Is that what you did to your wife? And, d'you want to know something else? When your mother was dying, and you hadn't bothered to visit her in hospital, she said to me that no matter what you'd done she still loved you because you were her son, the first born, and the fruit of an amazing love."

Tears, Ellie barely noticed, were running down her cheeks. In all her words she had discovered something for herself – the love of unconditional love, a mother for her wayward son. Her mother had not loved her that way.

For the first time that Ellie could remember there was no retort from her cousin. In his eyes was an intense expression she could not read, nor did it invite comment. He stared at her for several long seconds before turning and walking away. Just before he disappeared behind the wall, he looked back and said quietly, "I'm not done with you yet, Ellie."

She sank down on a large upturned terracotta pot, exhausted and cold, and wept. Years of painful emotions and memories dropped, tear by tear, onto the gravel path and soaked into the soil underneath.

"I can't carry them any more," she whispered, "I just can't."

There was a footfall on the gravel and her head jerked up.

"My dear! Oh, Ellie! We've been looking *everywhere* for you. Where on earth have you been? Are you hurt? Thank goodness you're safe."

The words rattled out, a conveyor belt of concerned snippets. Seconds later, Caroline, Countess of Strathvern, in Wellington boots and gardening clothes, was sitting beside her on another upturned pot, holding her until the darkness in the ancient chamber dissipated.

Dabbing her eyes, and embarrassed the countess had found her in such a state, Ellie stuttered out thanks for her kindness.

"I'm very glad you're all right, my dear. When you're ready we'll go and let everyone else know. At the moment I'm content to sit here like Bill and Ben the Flowerpot Men at the end of the garden and you can get your thoughts together," she said, smiling in the gentle way the locals knew and loved. She was much admired and respected in the Highlands.

Ellie, drained and wanting only to lie down and sleep, managed a wan smile.

"Do you want to talk about what's causing you so much distress, Ellie?"

She shook her head. "It's my past and it's painful. I can't talk about it. Never have really."

Caroline gave her hand a gentle squeeze and said gently, "I understand, Ellie. Things we'd rather stayed buried and forgotten eventually pop up, and that usually means we have to deal with them. I do know what you're saying."

Ellie looked up at her; she was still a beautiful woman. In her blue eyes was deep sadness. What in her privileged life had given such pain?

Caroline was staring at the gravel. "We have three wonderful sons, but our first born was a girl." She sighed. "It was the happiest moment of my life. I always wanted a daughter. I had dreams of being her confidante and friend, sharing lots of things, but it didn't turn out that way. She had a congenital heart condition and died two months before her fourth birthday." She swallowed and Ellie saw her lips quivering. She reached out and touched her hand which the countess covered with her own. "The pain never quite goes away," she said with a watery smile.

They sat in silence for several minutes, companions of understanding, before Ellie spoke.

"What time is it?"

"Just after eight. The police are here, although Sergeant Kennart left a little while ago. There was a fire in the village. I got the impression there was something odd about it," Caroline said, frown lines creasing the brow of her small oval face.

"Fire?" Ellie said, sitting upright. "D'you know where? I should've listened!"

"Listened to whom, Ellie?"

"It doesn't matter now. Where was it?"

"I'm sorry, I don't know exactly. It's important though, I can see that. Come on. Let's go inside. My husband will be very glad you're safe," she said, and stood up. "My goodness, Ellie! What's happened to your poor feet? Where are your shoes?"

"It's a long story, Lady Strathvern. Perhaps I'll be able to tell you one day."

As they approached the castle Bran came out of the door leading to the kitchen. For a second his expression was like a kaleidoscope and Ellie couldn't decide what he was feeling about her unexpected appearance with his master's wife.

"There you are, Bran," Caroline said, smiling at him. "I was about to tell Ellie how you'd been up half the night looking for her."

"How…? I mean where…? We looked all over," he said, the words stumbling over one another.

"I found her near the potting shed, no shoes on and worn out like a rag. Can you get Anne to rustle up a hot breakfast and a big pot of tea?"

Bran was staring at Ellie and didn't seem to have heard her.

"Bran!"

His head snapped round and he looked at the countess.

"Sorry, Your Ladyship. It's seeing Ellie so suddenly. What did you say?"

327

However, before she could answer, Ellie said, "Lady Strathvern, I *have* to go. I can't sit around eating breakfast when Byron could be in serious trouble."

"I do understand, Ellie, but surely you can wait a few minutes to see my husband. He was up half the night looking for you as well."

"I..." Ellie closed her mouth in time to stop the next word, 'know', slipping out.

Bran's scrutiny of her increased, and she became acutely aware of the precious stolen cargo stowed in the pockets of her trousers.

"Only a minute, Ellie," Caroline said, squeezing her hand as she turned to walk towards the door.

"And what if it was your husband or son lying injured in a burning house? Would you wait?" In the quiet tone of her voice there was challenge.

Bran looked puzzled.

Caroline stopped and turned around. "No," she said softly, shaking her head. "I wouldn't let anyone stop me going to them. I apologise, Ellie. I didn't realise he meant so much to you. I'll let my husband know you had to leave. Bran, please take Ellie to wherever she has to go."

"But what about the people who're coming this afternoon? His Lordship told me to get the boats ready before eleven," he said, protesting.

Ellie wasn't sure about taking a ride with him, but she couldn't decline the offer when she'd emphasised her need to leave.

"I'll tell my husband. You won't be gone long. Now then, please do as I ask. Ellie needs our help. Go and get the car, Bran, and don't be long about it."

After a few seconds hesitating, Farley's son went off in the direction of the garages while the countess hurried inside to find Ellie some shoes. She returned with new-looking trainers and a pair of socks still bearing their maker's tag as Ellie was getting into the passenger seat of one of the estate's cars. The trainers were a little too big, but the socks helped take up some of the space.

Two minutes later she and Bran were through the main gates and on the way to Kilcomb. The silence was awkward, like a damp cloth suffocating the life out of the person beneath it. Ellie's thoughts chased each other around – negotiating, deliberating and arguing.

A mile or so along the road she wondered whether Bran, while he had been fetching the car, had phoned Glenn.

"Stop the car!" she said suddenly, loudly.

"What on earth for?" He glanced at her, frowning.

"Just do it, Bran."

"You heard Her Ladyship. I have to take you where you want to go. You haven't said where yet. It'll be trouble for me if I don't do it."

"You're already in trouble – with me. Why did you put me in that cellar, Bran?"

"Just doing what I was told. I wouldn't have hurt you, Ellie."

"Maybe not, but His Lordship would have you out of his employment if he knew. I heard him telling you you'd lose your job if you were keeping quiet about me."

Ellie was suddenly flung forwards and backwards into her seat as Bran thrust his foot down on the brake. They came to a skidding halt, narrowly missing sliding into a ditch. Bran switched off the engine.

"You heard all that?" he said, looking uncomfortable and staring out through the windscreen. "And… anything else?"

"Yes. If you're tangled up with Glenn Thorley you've made the worst mistake of your life – like your sister."

"She's not tangled up with him," he said, turning worried eyes on her.

"More than you know," she said, watching him.

"You're lying."

Ellie shook her head, looking at him. A strange sensation turned in her stomach. Was the boy in the photo Farley? Could this be the earl's nephew she was sitting next to? Farley had never spoken much about his parents. He'd said they'd had a serious falling out when he was in his early twenties.

"Why're you staring at me, Ellie? Just tell me where you want to go and I can get back to work."

"Did your father ever talk about his parents?"

The question seemed to disconcert him. He looked angry and puzzled.

"What's that got to do with anything?"

"Perhaps his death," she said quietly, and she verbalised what had been sitting in the shadows of her mind since leaving the room beneath the castle. It seemed to make perfect sense.

For a moment they looked at each other. He seemed shocked.

329

"That's ridiculous! You can't say things like that. We had hardly anything to do with them, so it's just... you're guessing because the police haven't found the killer."

"It's a suggestion, Bran, that's all. I want his killer found as well."

He sighed, but didn't look at her. "I know. Fenella and Camden say you had something to do with it, but I don't believe them. It'll be one of those people who want to build all over the Highlands. They hated Dad."

"Yes, they did."

The rain was hitting the windscreen and the passenger windows with greater ferocity and her words were almost lost in the noise.

Between them she and Farley had received copious threats, some of which had been enacted. Most weren't serious, but Farley had been beaten, received hate mail, and once pushed off an escarpment. At one of her exhibitions, someone had got into the gallery at night and destroyed all her paintings and sketches by splashing paint over some and slashing others with a knife. Her friend, who owned the gallery, had told her she thought it was Camden Orman. She'd seen him lurking about, but he'd vanished late in the afternoon. The police had been unable to find any proof and neither he nor anyone else had ever been charged. The police had done what they could over the years, but the reality was that she and the Ormans had learned to live with the fact that not everyone agreed with their views and actions, and threats were to be expected.

"And no, Dad didn't talk about his parents much," Bran said unexpectedly. "We hardly ever saw them."

"What about grandparents, aunts and uncles?"

He stared at her and she noticed a familiar expression. In that moment she could have sworn she was talking with a young Farley, even though she had never known him at Bran's age. The protective film told her Bran was feeling uncomfortable and would give her little or no information.

"No."

"Oh, come on, Bran, you must know something. Surely you visited relatives when you were younger."

"Not Dad's, at least only once or twice. Can't remember who they were."

Ellie reached into one of her pockets and withdrew the photo of the two children with the woman 'M'. She held it up and he took it from her, scrutinising the black and white image.

"D'you recognise anyone in this picture?" she asked, studying his features.

"Where did you get this?" he said, frowning.

"It was in a box of stuff I came across."

"Fenella says Dad gave you too much of ours. I don't think he did," he added quietly, his tone changing, softening, much as Farley's used to.

"Thank you, Bran."

"It looks a bit like Dad when he was a kid. Hard to tell. The woman could be his mother or aunt, and the girl a cousin. I don't know. We've got photos of Dad when he was growing up, but not with these people."

"Not his sister?"

He glanced at her with a slightly puzzled expression. "Dad didn't have any sisters. I thought you'd know that."

"As you said, your dad didn't talk much about his family. He always changed the subject."

"Must've had his reasons. Fenella might know. She's interested in that kind of stuff and could wangle things out of him Camden and I couldn't. But she keeps secrets. Always has. I'm not interested in family stuff. It's just history."

"The thing about history is that it has repercussions on the next generations."

"Not for me. Dad's parents are both dead now. I don't even feel like they're part of me. All I've got is their genes and that doesn't matter to me because I didn't know them."

Bran handed the photos back and Ellie returned them to her pocket. If only you knew where I got this, she thought, as he switched the ignition on.

"I need to go to Tallow Lane," she said, changing the subject, "number five."

"Dad owned some of the cottages down there. Said he inherited them. Guess his old man wasn't too poor. Fenella's been looking after all that stuff," he said and turned his head to glance out the side window. When he looked back to the front, Ellie glimpsed tears in his eyes.

"I'm so sorry, Bran," she said gently, and touched his arm.

"I miss him. I know we didn't always get on, but he was my dad." His words were choked and he wiped the back of his hand across his eyes.

They pulled out into the road and continued on towards the village, each closeted with their own thoughts. The rain eased and in a strange way the steady swishing of the windscreen wipers calmed Ellie's tired and fragile nerves. A car going in the opposite direction went by too fast and a great deluge of water smacked against Bran's side of the car and part of the windscreen, obscuring his view for a second or two and making Ellie jump. For a moment it seemed they might run off the road. Unperturbed, Bran averted danger and kept going.

Ellie had deliberately kept her thoughts from straying to Byron during the conversation with Bran, but couldn't do so in the silence. His face, their times together, filled her mind and nothing within her would allow that he was seriously burned – or dead. She wanted to shout at Bran to put his foot down and get her to Tallow Lane.

However, she managed a calmer, "Bran, can you get a move on. I've been talking too much."

"No you haven't. It keeps you occupied when bad things happen," he said, and suddenly put his foot down on the accelerator. "This fast enough?"

Ellie grasped hold of the hand rest on the door as they shot along the road and round a bend, hugging the inside curve so closely the hedgerow was almost touching the vehicle. She heard a chuckle from her companion. It was a long time since she'd known him to have such a joke. All through his teenage years he had been withdrawn and often sullen, but since working at Strathvern his demeanour had slowly begun to change.

"Camden's been released from hospital," he said unexpectedly.

Puzzled, Ellie said, "I thought he wasn't expected to live."

"Not live?" His head snapped round, his expression showing how ludicrous he considered her words. "Who told you that?"

"Jack Kennart."

There was a pause. When he spoke his voice was more subdued. "Oh. Well, he was wrong."

"Or he was lying."

"He was wrong," he said and touched the brake as the car approached a tight bend.

Once round it he increased speed again and they shot along a straight piece of road, farmland on their left stretching itself towards a range of low, craggy hills. Clouds, draped like a dark shroud, hid their peaks.

"Bran, your father's dead and your brother's been in hospital. What has to happen before you speak up? It could be you or Fenella next."

"I won't let anything happen to her."

"But you're only one person and you work at Strathvern. Anyway, she's good at looking after herself from what I've seen."

"She's had to be. Dad was hardly ever at home. Always off in the hills or on some isolated island. As for Camden, he's got a warped way of thinking. I never know what's going on in his head or what he'll do next. Strange thing is he's quite good at making money when he thinks seriously about it. And me? Quiet and too shy to stand up for myself let alone Fen."

Ellie glanced at him and said lightly, "You did all right with Glenn Thorley last night."

"There wasn't anyone else around – and it was dark. And I hate him."

"He could've killed you."

"No. I knew His Lordship was there before Thorley did."

"You're full of surprises, Bran."

"It's about time."

Without warning they turned into a narrow lane Ellie had taken little notice of in her travels along the road.

"Where are we going?" she snapped.

"It's a short cut to Tallow Lane."

"No it's not. Stop the car, Bran."

"You don't trust me, do you?"

"Give me one reason why I should."

"I'm Farley's son."

"Yes, and look at the other one! Not to mention what you did last night."

"You don't know what I did."

"You locked me in that cellar and left me!"

"I was supposed to stay."

For a moment Ellie's panic subsided. "Why didn't you?"

"I wanted… hoped you'd escape."

"You could've done something about it before you banged me up in that cellar!"

"I was being watched."

"By Glenn Thorley?"

The road narrowed and Bran remained silent. They passed a derelict croft with a camper van parked outside it and a man and a woman wandering around, looking and pointing as they went. More people looking for serenity in the country, Ellie thought, and couldn't blame them. She'd done the same. Half a mile or so farther along on the opposite side of the road was another croft brimming with welcome, the garden abundant in its growth and colour.

Bran had eased off the accelerator and the car slowed down. He glanced at her but didn't speak; apprehension stirred within her again.

The lane they turned into was wide enough for one car and after five minutes of a straight, bumpy section it began twisting and turning around the bases of low hills. At least the rain had stopped and she could see ahead better. There was nothing familiar about the area.

By now she was convinced Bran was lying. They were nowhere near Tallow Lane, of that she was certain. He was taking her somewhere no one would think of looking, where her yells for help would be unheard. There was only one thing to do. The minutes passed and Ellie was beginning to believe the opportunity wouldn't come. Bran seemed in a world of his own, occupied, she supposed, by his next encounter with whoever had ordered him to redeem himself and abduct her a second time.

She almost missed her opportunity as they suddenly left the closely hugged hills and began passing through woodland. The road was straighter, but still bumpy and, at a spot that offered possibilities for cover, Ellie caught hold of the door handle and pushed. The momentum carried her toward the opening and she was about to launch herself out when Bran grabbed her arm and yanked her back in. The car door flew open, but he did not slow down and as they entered the next bend it swung back, latching tentatively onto the catch, rattling.

"What're you trying to do? Kill yourself?" he shouted, letting go of her arm as he pressed down on the accelerator. "You'd have got caught by the back wheels!"

"I'd rather be dead than left to Glenn Thorley!"

"I'm not taking you to him. Tallow Lane's just up ahead. If you don't believe me, I'll drop you off here and you can walk the rest of the way. I'll wait for you at the end of the road," he said, still angry.

"Forgive me for not believing you!" She glared at him.

"Dad always said you did things off-the-cuff. He scowled and grumbled, but he liked that about you," he said, glancing at her. "Only don't go trying to jump out of moving cars again. It's downright dangerous. How'd I explain to His Lordship that you got tangled up under the wheels of *his* car?"

"I don't know and right now I don't care. All I want is to make sure Byron's all right."

She was not ready to believe him and kept hold of the door handle. It was quite possible the altered tone was to seduce her into changing her mind about him, but she was not so gullible.

"Ellie, there's something I have to tell you. It was me who put Dad's bags in your barn."

"Why would you do that?"

"Because I thought they'd be safe there. Besides, they belong more to you than us. You're the one who trekked all over the Highlands with him, not us."

Despite her reticence to believe him, she was touched by the kindness in his voice and she knew in this he was telling the truth.

"Jack said he didn't know who put the bags there."

"He's my uncle. He didn't want me to get into trouble."

Ellie sighed. That, too, she believed.

Less than a minute later he stopped at a T-junction. Directly in front, on the opposite side of the road, was a sign – Tallow Lane.

He did not look at her. "What number did you say?"

"Five."

He turned right. There was no doubt she would have to apologise – later, perhaps much later, depending on how she felt.

She saw Jack's car parked on the road and Bran pulled up behind it. Where was Byron's car?

Ellie pushed the door open, getting out almost before the car stopped. She heard Bran sigh loudly and ignored him, instead staring at the cottage in disbelief. Fear gripped her innards like a steel belt and her heart rate accelerated. For a few moments she scanned the scene, her eyes like camera lenses taking photos and putting them on the film of her mind. The roof had a hole in it and large sections of it were charred. Tattered, scorched curtains were fluttering in the shattered front room windows. Where was Byron?

Behind her she heard the car door shut and she turned as Bran was getting out of the vehicle.

"Wait here," she said.

"Not likely!"

"I said, wait. It isn't appropriate for you to come in," she said bluntly.

"Too bad. I'm coming with you. It could be dangerous in there."

Ellie walked quickly across the lawn, but at the corner of the cottage she began running, her feet slipping in shoes a fraction too big. A constable coming the other way put out a hand to try and stop her, but she evaded him and went on round the back. At the open door she stopped, her nasal passage assaulted by the smell of a burnt house and damp interior. She swallowed, afraid of what she was going to find. There were no sounds other than the wind. Where was Jack?

Inside the kitchen and along the passage to the front room the smell was worse and caught in the back of her throat. It was warm, too. The heat was still in the old cottage walls, timbers and roof. She gazed around the front room wondering how much of Byron's life was gone. And where was he? Had some coward set fire when he was asleep in his bed?

"No!" she yelled at the house. "No! I *won't* accept it!"

She heard the footsteps of someone rapidly descending the stairs and turned, expectant, dreading it would not be him. She sensed Bran was right behind her as Jack appeared in the hallway and came towards them looking tired and worried. A sob caught in her throat and her eyes filled with tears, spilling down over her cheeks. Jack didn't say anything, but walked up to her and gave her an awkward hug which told Ellie more than any words of his would do.

"You're a sight for sore eyes, Ellie Madison, and I'm glad to see you. You've given me a sleepless night, lass," he said gently.

"Where's Byron?" she sputtered, mopping her tears with a damp handkerchief.

"He left about ten minutes ago. Said he had something to do, but didn't say what." He looked suddenly at a loss and his eyes were moist. It disconcerted her. "Thought we might've lost you."

Ellie swallowed. She was uncomfortable with the man's emotion; he'd never shown this side of him before. All she wanted was Byron.

"I need to go home, Jack," was all she could manage.

"I'll take you soon. Have a wee problem to sort out upstairs first."

Jack turned towards the hallway.

"What little problem?"

"There's a skeleton."

"That's your explanation? Surely you can do better than that, Jack."

"Come with me."

She followed him up stairs untouched by flames, onto the landing and up the ladder. Bran was right behind her. The acrid smell of the recent fire increased, but its impact was far less than the sight that met her eyes as she poked her head into the attic.

"Be careful, Ellie. Don't go near the hole. I shouldn't really be letting you up here – or young Bran."

Ellie walked slowly towards the skeleton, Bran close by. She frowned.

"Who on earth is it? Did Byron know this was in the attic when he moved in?"

Jack shook his head. "He hadn't any reason to come up here, so didn't. Besides, the agents told him it was full of the owner's belongings."

Bran came and stood beside her. He leaned forward and reached out to touch the jacket.

"Don't touch it, Bran," Jack said sharply.

The young man glanced back at him, withdrawing his hand. "That's Strathvern's crest on the buttons. This must be Lord Strathvern's mother."

"I don't know, laddie," Jack said, shaking his head, "but we'll get an expert in to find out."

"Strange place for her to be. They said she died in the cellars. D'you think...?"

Jack cut him off. "I don't think we can make any guesses and neither of you is to say anything about this to anyone. I'll be talking to the earl *if* it's necessary. Is that clear?"

They nodded and followed the sergeant across the floor and down the ladder. Outside the cottage Jack went to talk with the constable while Ellie and Bran stood on the front lawn.

"Glad that isn't in our attic," Bran said, giving a little shudder. "I bet it is the old countess you know. I heard she liked to go off on long walks with her dogs. There's a painting of her in trousers and a jacket like that one in the earl's study. Funny though. Who'd put her up there?"

Ellie shook her head, looking at Jack and wondering what he and Tim Ashby were discussing. "No idea and we don't know for certain it's her. Let's leave it to the experts. Can you take me home, Bran?"

There was no answer and she turned back to him. He was staring into space.

"Bran? Are you all right?"

He blinked, swallowing, and glanced at her. Something was upsetting him.

"What… what if it's Mum?" he asked in a hoarse voice.

A tight knot twisted in her stomach. The thought hadn't even occurred to her.

"Oh, Bran! Let's not think of that. She's in the wrong clothes."

"But someone could've put them on her to make it look as if it's a woman from the estate. What am I going to tell Fen and Camden?"

"Nothing. You don't know it's her and you heard what your Uncle Jack said. We have to keep this to ourselves until they identify the… the person. Don't get yourself stewed up."

"Since Mum disappeared things haven't been the same. Dad never did know how to make our family work, not really. But Mum, she loved us all and could get a smile out of you even when you wanted to punch someone's lights out. She was special."

Ellie nodded. "Yes, she was."

"Camden blamed you, but it wasn't you it was us," he said in a pained voice. "We didn't know how to be a family without Mum. Still don't."

His eyes were damp, his face creased with distress and yearning.

For a few seconds Ellie studied his profile and, not for the first time, felt a wave of anger that Alice had gone away when he was in those vulnerable late teen years.

"Who d'you think killed your dad, Bran?" she asked quietly.

He shook his head, but didn't speak and turned away as Jack walked towards them. She watched Bran, his shoulders hunched, get in the car and drive off.

"Let's hope it's old wiring that's the problem. We've enough trouble trying to find out who killed Farley and now there's your abduction. Anyway, who'd want to set the cottage on fire?"

"Try Glenn Thorley," Ellie said coldly.

He looked at her, surprised. "He's a greedy, manipulative man, Ellie, but I don't think he's up to this kind o' thing."

"You don't know him, Jack. He's capable of whatever he sets his mind to. If he wants something he'll go after it no matter what it costs anyone else."

"And how d'you know that? He's no' been coming here that long."

"I just do," she snapped, glaring at him. "Ask the earl's son Michael. Glenn Thorley's business isn't only hotels."

He was looking at her through narrowed, contemplative eyes.

"So, he *was* the cause of your accident in the summer then." His voice rang with confidence.

Ellie held her emotions in check; her expression did not change.

"Go and see Michael, Jack."

The constable was left to watch the cottage and she got in the police car with Jack, vaguely uneasy. As they drove off up the lane she glanced at her companion; his expression gave no indication that he was up to anything unusual.

"Why did you tell me Camden wasn't expected to live?" she asked when they reached the junction with the main road and waited until several cars had gone by.

"Because he wasn't."

"Not according to Bran. He was surprised you thought he was going to die. Camden's been sent home. Did you know?"

A frown creased his brow and he opened his mouth to speak, but a voice came over the radio and he answered it instead. His presence was required at the police station as a matter of urgency. Inspector Carter was waiting for him.

"I'll be there as soon as I've taken Ellie Madison home. Over and out." Jack put the mouthpiece back in its cradle. "Bloody man," he muttered. "Thinks we country police are nothing but plods."

"Find who killed Farley and that'll shut him up." Ellie yawned, her body now groaning for sleep.

"Aye, but he'll take all the credit. I'll be round to get a statement from you later today, Ellie. We want to find whoever did this to you. Where were you for Bran to bring you to Glenn Oakley's place? Why didn't you go straight home?"

"You haven't explained about Camden," she said, evenly.

"I don't think I have to explain to you, Ellie, but," he said, as if conciliation was a favour to her, "when I rang the hospital about

339

the lad, the nurse told me he wasn't doing too well. He must've rallied – or she was mistaken. Then again, perhaps Bran got it wrong."

"I think he'd know if his brother was home or not. He said you'd got it wrong."

Jack sighed. "Bran's not the brightest match in the box, Ellie, you know that."

"I'm not sure about that any more. I'm beginning to think he's had us hoodwinked for a long while."

One of the local farmers went past in the other direction, waving at Jack as they drew level. Jack returned the gesture.

"You're not suggesting he had anything to do wi' your kidnapping, are you? He's not capable of hurting a fly!"

"Who knows what anyone's capable of until they're pushed to it," she said, staring ahead at the entrance to her road, but seeing her struggle with Glenn and the escape from Jimmy's Tarn.

"True enough, but Bran and crime don't go together. I'd still like to know why Bran took you to Tallow Lane, Ellie. Were you shut up in Strathvern Castle?"

Ellie shook her head. "No. Underneath it."

"What!?" They were in Ellie's driveway and he brought the car to a sudden halt behind the Land Rover, twisting in his seat to stare at her. "How did you get there?"

"I've not the faintest idea. I was dragged from the car, had a chloroform-soaked rag clamped over my nose and mouth and woke up in a cellar. And that's..." she had been going to add 'just the start', but changed her mind. "And that's a shock when the last thing you remember is sitting chatting with a friend."

"Who found you? Bran?"

"No. I managed to get out early this morning and the countess found me sitting on a pot near one of the gardening sheds."

Whether he believed her Ellie couldn't tell. There were times when he could keep his thoughts well hidden and unexposed, but they were rare moments. This was one of them.

The voice on the other end of the radio burst into the car a second time wanting to know how long the sergeant would be.

"I'll be there soon, Constable. Canna be in two places at once. And get a constable over to Ellie Madison's house on the double. I don't want her left on her own."

"Right, Sarge," said Tim Ashby. "Over and out."

"I'll be fine, Jack," Ellie said.

340

"For once, you've no choice. He's coming whether you like it or not." His tone was emphatic. "If your kidnapper knows you've escaped, he's not going to be too happy. And I'll wait inside with you until the constable arrives. Inspector Carter can twiddle his thumbs for a wee while. Besides, I could do wi' a hot cuppa."

There seemed something odd about the house. Then she realised she didn't have her keys and got out of the car and went to the Land Rover, trying to remember where she'd last seen them. All the doors of the vehicle were locked.

"Byron obviously thinks Kilcomb's as lawless as London," she quipped, and heard Jack grunt behind her.

"That man's not too good at obeying a directive himself."

"Back in a sec, Jack."

She walked quickly along the back of the house and around the corner, retrieved the spare keys from a cavity behind a brick near the ground, and re-joined the sergeant. He was studying her laundry window.

"Did you leave this open?" he asked, still peering at it.

"No."

"Well, someone's got it open. There're fresh scratch marks in the paint."

Ellie went to where he was standing and looked at the damaged window frame. It had definitely been closed when last she'd left the house. The scratches were new.

Inside the house it was cold and strangely empty as if she'd been gone a long time. A strange smell caused her to frown and behind her she heard Jack closing the back door before making a comment about a gas leak. With some caution, Ellie walked toward the front room from where the odour seemed to be coming. Seconds later she was staring in dismay at burnt books and curtains and cardboard at the window. This explained the strange eeriness.

"I'd say someone's thrown a petrol bomb through your front window," Jack said in a matter-of-fact tone.

Ellie couldn't respond. Her whole life seemed to have turned into a surreal drama of the ilk she'd only ever seen in movies. 'Why' and 'Who' were questions to which there were no immediate answers.

"Someone's been in here," she said abruptly. "The window's been boarded up from inside."

"And your house isn't a pile of rubble," Jack added drily. "Whoever it was either had an accomplice or dashed inside and put the fire out before attending to the window and cleaning up whatever the petrol was in."

She only half heard him as her mind scrambled through a myriad of images and thoughts, including her time under the castle and what Byron had told her about the cave under The Chimney – and Jack's presence there. "I don't like this. Somebody knows something."

He gave her a peculiar look. "Meaning?"

She looked at him, appraising the expression on his face. "Farley discovered…" Again she modified her sentence, "at least I *think* he discovered more about the earl's father's wartime treachery with the Third Reich than anyone realised."

"And how d'you know that, Ellie?"

She shrugged. "A feeling I have."

It was clear he did not believe her and said as much. "If you're trying to protect him, it's a wee bit late. Whatever he knew, he's paid a high price."

"Too high," she murmured, and then drew herself back to the destruction in her front room. "Who would do this?"

"Probably the same person who killed Farley and set fire to Byron's cottage. I'll get forensics to come here as well."

Ellie walked across to the pile of burned and scorched books, squatting down in front of them and reaching out to touch their old covers.

"Don't touch them, Ellie," Jack said quickly. "Fingerprints."

She pulled her hand away and instead looked around the room. On the carpet near the large bookcase was a silver pen she did not recognise. She glanced up at the sergeant; he was walking towards the window. Quietly and unhurriedly she leaned towards it and, mindful of Jack's comment about fingerprints, she picked up the pen with her sleeve pulled over her hand. Ellie was still staring at it when he turned around.

"What've you got there?" he asked.

For a moment she wasn't sure she wanted to answer, but it was difficult to say 'nothing' when she had it in her hand.

"A pen," she said without looking up.

"Strange place to leave it."

Quietly, her stomach churning, she said, "I didn't. It's not mine."

"Can I see it?"

Ellie held it up as he came over and peered at the implement. Neither of them spoke. There was no doubt to whom it belonged; on the barrel Byron's name was etched in fine italics. Had he put the fire out or had he started it?

Chapter 20

Colonel Hugh Lawford, retired, was sitting on the bench in exactly the place a mile out of Inverness he had described to Byron over the phone. A walking stick was propped against his leg. Looking straight down the Moray Firth, where numbers of inhabitants in the fishing village of Avoch on its west coast, claimed descent from Spaniards who found themselves wrecked on its doorstep after the Armada, he seemed oblivious to squabbling seagulls and a young dark-haired woman loudly disciplining a child.

The busy Moray Firth, with its fertile coastline, a population of resident dolphins and entrance to the North Sea, was an area Byron had first visited as a boy on summer holidays with his family. His father had loved watching the dolphins and was still an ardent supporter of protecting their environment, particularly from careless tourist boat operators who disrupted the animals' breeding season.

There was about the ex-army colonel in his tweed jacket and grey trousers, a quiet authority and assurance that Byron suspected would not be easily shaken. He felt he understood him even though they barely knew one another. The common bond of life in the army allowed him to see Hugh in a way many would not; keeping secrets and wariness of strangers asking questions meant being ever watchful and trusting few. It could be an impediment as well as an asset.

Colin Farmer had done a thorough job of researching the colonel's authenticity and credentials. No one could argue Hugh's commitment to the cause of ensuring Britain's victory was anything other than of the highest level. He'd been awarded a DSM. After the war he continued with the army in the Intelligence Branch and had a rapid rise to the rank of colonel. This was followed by a number of senior military positions in London, Washington D.C. and Paris before taking a quieter post in Edinburgh. Colin had been unable to find anything about why he went to Scotland or the work he'd done there. It was the same year the previous Earl of Strathvern died.

Hugh had suggested the outdoor meeting while his wife was shopping with her younger sister, who'd arrived for a visit from her husband's country estate near St Andrews. He was as keen a golfer as his father and grandfather had been.

A thin wind was blowing off the water, making little curled waves bounce towards the shore. Byron shivered inside his jumper as he approached Hugh, but the coldness deep in his belly had little to do with the chilly wind. Ellie's abduction, petrol bombs through their front windows, and Kipp attacked unnerved him. He had no idea whether it was an aggrieved hotel developer, none of whom he'd met except Thorley, or someone desperate to keep family secrets.

"Ah, there you are, Byron," Hugh said, half turning towards him. "I hope you don't mind the venue, but I thought out here was better than some stuffy tea shop where ears could tune into our conversation."

"The venue's great, Hugh," he said, shaking the proffered hand. "I appreciate the time you've taken to see me."

"You know, Ruth made me promise I'd tell her everything we discussed." He chuckled, but the expression in his eyes was more restrained.

They talked for a while about army life, avoiding the precise nature of their roles, and recounting humorous episodes and a few darker moments without divulging specifics. Twenty minutes passed before Byron felt he could begin drawing out information from his companion.

"What made you come up to Scotland?" he asked lightly. "A bit off the beaten track for your career, wasn't it?"

Hugh raised his eyebrows and sighed. "I had to think about retirement. Couldn't stay in the army until I was ready for the wooden box. A couple of younger officers were hinting – *pushing* is a better word – for me to go. They wanted my job. Unfortunately for them the higher authorities didn't agree and so they kept me on. I was more than happy to stay because I loved what I was doing."

"And Ruth didn't mind?"

"We often talked about where we'd end our days and I agreed it was only fair that it be in Scotland. She'd spent decades traipsing around with me and the older she got the more she missed Scotland and her family. Understandable of course. So, eventually I requested a job in Edinburgh and up we came."

"Must've taken you both a while to settle in. Were her parents still alive then?"

"Her mother was. Lived until she was ninety-four, but Ruth's father was wounded in the war and never had good health after that. He died about thirty years ago." Hugh's forehead wrinkled and his neat grey eyebrows drew together, meeting in the middle above his nose like a pair of fine curtains. "Why the interest in them?"

Byron chose his words and tone of voice with care. He let the words slide out almost casually. "It's thought Ruth's father, Douglas Bromley, and his son Alisdair spied for the German government. Sent information about the Clydebank shipping yards."

The colonel stared at him as if he'd suddenly gone mad. "You are joking, aren't you? I mean, I would've known."

"Would you?"

There was a moment's pause. "Well, perhaps not. I wasn't involved in the Scottish side of things." He looked at the younger man intently, doubtful. "Are you *sure* about this?"

"Reasonably. My source is extremely reliable."

"You'll excuse me if I say I've heard that before."

"I'm sure you have, but d'you think Ruth knew about their involvement with Germany?"

"Now that's going a bit too far," the colonel expostulated. "If she'd known, she would've told me! We don't have secrets from each other, Byron. Kept something from her once, she found out, and that was almost the end of our marriage. Never did it again. She's the only woman I've ever loved," he said with a little smile. "Wouldn't have lasted this long without her."

"I envy you, Hugh," but he wondered if Hugh was being truthful. He was a little too blithe about it.

"Never found the right one then?"

"Once." And then he said, almost involuntarily, "She died in combat."

"Oh," Hugh said in a voice that told Byron he understood the impact that would have on one's life. "I'm very sorry."

He did not add, as people tend to do, that there would be someone else one day, and for that Byron was grateful. A brief silence, kept from being embarrassing by the unceasing arguments between seagulls, enabled Byron to re-order his thoughts and get them back to the original subject.

346

"Did you know Ruth's sister Marian well?" he asked and saw Hugh drag himself back from wherever his thoughts had taken him.

"Hmm? Oh, not really. Hardly had anything to do with her. Ruth only saw her a couple of times during the war. From what she's told me, Marian was a pleasure-loving, rebellious girl who always did what she wanted."

"You said in our first meeting that she had an affair with a German officer. Is it possible she could've passed him information, a bit of wartime fun for her?"

Byron watched a small boat leaving its moorings.

"Haven't a clue. Who'd trust a girl of that nature to be serious about such matters, let alone keep the information to herself?"

In his voice Byron heard a hint of annoyance although his expression hadn't changed.

"It would also be the perfect cover-up," he said, watching, waiting, when it seemed as if his interest was held by the comings and goings of boats on the water.

"My wife would never have involved herself with anyone she suspected of fraternising with the enemy – sister or not!" Hugh snapped, glaring at the younger man. "I don't like where this conversation is going, Byron. Are you here to make trouble, or has someone in MOD decided they need to dig up ancient matters because they're bored?"

"There are many unsolved matters from the war, Colonel, as you know," Byron said formally, "and some of them involve the previous Earl of Strathvern."

"Well, that has nothing do with either me or Ruth. I've just told you neither of us was in Scotland during the war."

"So you say…"

"How dare you get me out here to insult me and my wife! You can't possibly know what it was like in the war!"

Byron decided not to respond to the latter. "It isn't my intention to insult either of you, but I believe you have information that will help."

"Help what and who?"

"Those asking the questions."

"That," he said firmly, frowning, "is just the sort of claptrap I used to spout off. Well, I didn't outsmart the enemy and unravel his intelligence reports to end my days under suspicion."

From his shirt pocket, Byron pulled one of the photographs Ross had given him and held it out towards Hugh.

"Have you ever seen this woman?" he asked.

The colonel pinched his lips together in a gesture of impatience and reached for the picture. As he did so his jacket sleeve rose up his arm a little way exposing the cuff of his white shirt. When he held up the photo, Byron caught sight of the cuff link. He looked up at the other man's face as he glanced at the photograph. It had, if he was not mistaken, gone a shade paler and his expression, though well-guarded, could not completely hide apprehension.

"No," Hugh said decisively as he handed back the photo and pulled his jacket sleeve down to his wrist, "I've never seen her before. Who is it?"

"I'm not sure, but I am sure, Hugh, that you're wearing Waffen SS cuff links."

Byron could not help admiring the man's fortitude and rapid recovery.

His face brightened and he chuckled. "A fellow officer in London gave me these after I cracked a persistent code. A bit of a joke really. He was undercover in Germany and pinched them from a German who'd nipped out to the latrine. Took his gun, too. I heard it came in very handy later." He slid forward on the bench and got slowly up, declining help from Byron. "I can still manage the basics of life. The vitality might have gone, but not the determination."

He turned and peered in the direction of the gravel car park.

"Can I drive you home?" Byron asked, wanting more time with him.

"Thank you, no. My wife and sister-in-law are just arriving in the car."

They walked together, not speaking, Hugh leaning heavily on his walking stick. The relationship was tinged with frostiness which Byron thought was a pity, but he knew he'd hit a nerve somewhere in the man's past. Perhaps he was losing his touch in extracting information.

Ruth was getting out of the passenger side of the car when they approached.

"Good morning, Byron," she greeted, smiling. "No doubt you two had a good old army chinwag."

"Not exactly, darling," Hugh said, opening the back passenger door. "Hello, Edith. Get all your shopping done?"

The woman, Edith, who looked little like Ruth except for the smile, Byron thought, told him she'd spent far too much as usual but had thoroughly enjoyed herself.

"You mustn't mind my cranky husband, Byron. Too many memories and wishing he was forty years younger," said Ruth. "He would've enjoyed talking to you though, I'm sure."

"You'll have to ask him that," Byron responded, and then decided it was worth risking Hugh's ire in showing Ruth the photo. He withdrew it from his pocket and held it out. "Do you…?"

"The photo is nothing to do with us, Ruth!" Hugh's voice was sharp and Byron turned his head to find the man glaring at him. "Whoever it is will be long dead. Please get in the car and let Edith take us home."

Ruth's eyes widened with surprise and shock. "I'm sorry, Byron," she said, frowning, glancing at the photo. "I don't know what's got into him. But he is right; she's nothing to do with us. I've no idea who the young woman is."

"D'you think Farley Orman knew who she was?"

"Whatever makes you say that? He wasn't even born then. Really, Byron, you're getting too caught up in all this. Leave it. It's too long ago and no one's interested in raking up what's done with."

"I am and it isn't done with. Farley Orman was murdered because of whatever happened back then."

She swallowed and looked up at him, her eyes glistening with tears.

"Please," she said quietly, laying a hand on his arm, "leave it alone."

"Ruth! Come on. We're going to be late," called her sister, sticking her head out the driver's side window.

Without another word, but gently squeezing his arm, Ruth Lawford walked away and got into the car. Hugh did not look at him.

Byron watched them drive away. They were lying.

***

Back in town, with Inverness Castle dominating its skyline, Byron found a pub near the River Ness and sat next to a window overlooking the river. A waiter arrived with fish and chips and a pint of their best bitter. Byron stared out at the drizzle. The weather summed up his mood – grey, indistinct features in the background, and little idea about what to do next. He was beginning to wonder if the woman in the photographs and Ruth's sister were one and the same – Marian MacAdam.

He raised the beer glass to his lips, thinking about the sixth Earl of Strathvern. He would have had much to lose if anyone snooping around had talked to the wrong people, but had he murdered Marian MacAdam? Had she found out about his unpatriotic activities?

A trip back in time would be very handy right now, he thought. Too many variables, too many possibilities and too many interested parties.

Glancing out the window he watched damp passers-by scurrying along huddled underneath umbrellas, others with hoods pulled over their heads, some allowing the rain to rinse their hair. Puddles formed quickly and, amused, he watched a young boy of about four suddenly let go of an older girl's hand, run ahead a few yards and jump into a little pool of water. Laughing, he turned with glee in his innocent eyes towards the two people to whom he belonged. The older girl and the man, who looked to be his father, burst out laughing. Seconds later they were all on their way, still chuckling, the man pulling the boy's hood back over his head.

Unexpectedly, he wondered whether Ellie had ever had such moments in her young life. And where was she now? No one had phoned to say she was found and his stomach twisted into a hard knot.

He finished his meal and downed the last of the beer before pulling his mobile out of his pocket. While he was listening to the tones ringing away he caught sight of Fenella Orman and Glenn Thorley walking towards a table on the other side of the room. They hadn't seen him.

"Sergeant Kennart."

The voice was suddenly in his ear.

"Jack, it's Byron."

"Oh, nice of you to call. Where are you? I told Constable Ashby to ring you."

"No one's phoned, Jack. Any news on Ellie?"

"Aye. She's alive and well considering what she's been through. Turned up at your cottage with Bran not long after you left and then I took her home. Seems she was at Strathvern Castle all along, but I suppose you know that."

"What's that supposed to mean?"

"I'm beginning to wonder just who you are. How come you weren't abducted with her?"

"I don't know and don't be absurd, Jack! If I'd have wanted Ellie dead or abducted I'd have done it long ago and with more efficiency than you've ever seen."

"Is that so? Well, Ellie's not too pleased wi' you right now and neither am I." He added in a tone with a probing edge, "Her house was broken into. Someone made a mess of her front room."

He watched Fenella and Glenn ordering. "I know and I'm guessing you think it was me."

"You left your pen behind on the carpet, a silver one wi' your name on it. What were you doing there?" His tone was hard.

Byron felt in his pocket where the pen usually lived. He hadn't even noticed its absence. "I was there with Bob early this morning. We both had the same idea of checking everything was okay. It wasn't. Somebody threw a bottle filled with petrol through the window when I was in the front room and Bob was outside checking things. If you don't believe me, ask him. Where's Ellie?"

"Sleeping. I've left a constable at her house. Where are you?"

"Inverness."

"What the...? Never mind," Jack said, sounding exasperated. "Your estate agent's been trying to get hold of you. Says he needs more details than you gave and the owner's in a right state and threatening to sue the tenant."

Byron watched as Fenella Orman took a large envelope out of her bag and withdrew several papers which she handed, except one, to her companion. She leaned towards him, intense in whatever she was saying, and then glanced into the room. Byron turned his back.

"Are you there, Byron?"

There was no doubting the impatience in his voice.

"Yes. The agent will have to wait. At least he still has a home to go to," Byron said, equally annoyed. "D'you know who owns the cottage?"

Other than the sound of Jack's breathing it was quiet for several moments. When he spoke the words came out slowly.

"Aye, I do. Farley Orman, though it'll belong to one or all of his offspring now."

"Well," Byron said, watching Fenella lean back in her seat, "Fenella seems calm and happy enough to me."

"You're with her?" Jack said in a tone that Byron wasn't sure was shock or dismay.

"No. She's having lunch with Glenn Thorley."

"Then you can talk to her in person," Jack said tartly, "but don't go into anything that's police business. And don't get into a brawl with Thorley."

Byron felt like saying, 'No, Dad', but thought Jack wouldn't appreciate it and said instead, "I don't brawl. I fight clean and fair, although I could make an exception with him."

"Don't fight him at all."

"Fine. There are other ways to get rid of vermin," he said and was just turning back to the window when Fenella Orman looked up and saw him. "Have to go, Jack. I've been noticed."

"Stay out of trouble!"

Whatever she said to Glenn, he simply glanced at her, nodded, and continued reading the paperwork as she got up and left the table. She was walking in Byron's direction, so he rose and went to pay his bill without acknowledging that he had seen her. Shoving his wallet back in his jacket's inner pocket, he thanked the cashier and left the dining room, walking down the hallway, its floor covered in thick red carpet. Against a wall stood a large ornate hall stand that would have occupied a considerable space in the sitting room of his London flat.

Once through the heavy oak door Byron stopped in the porch, zipped up his jacket and waited. The rain was heavier and the wind was gaining in strength, causing turmoil amongst the stand of trees on the opposite side of the road.

Half a minute later the door opened behind him.

"Are you waiting for me?" asked Fenella Orman.

"And why would I be doing that?"

"Because," she said, drawing closer, "you haven't seen me since the day Jamie and I stopped to help you. We were supposed to get together."

"I'd forgotten," he said, turning to face her.

She was studying him closely, smiling, determined. "I hadn't. Tell me, how are you getting along with Ellie Madison? I hear she quite likes you."

"Villages are well known for their gossip. Actually, she was abducted yesterday afternoon."

"Abducted! Don't be absurd. Things like that don't happen in Kilcomb. She'll be trudging about in the mountains with her paints and easel. Like she used to with Dad. He took photos, she painted. How dull."

He shook his head. "I was there, Fenella. Haven't you heard any village news in the last day or so?"

"I rarely listen to it. It's gossip on a grand scale usually. Ruins people's lives." She peered at him through half-closed eyes. "You're serious, aren't you? Is that why you were on your own when Jamie and I turned up? You were a bit cagey about why you were in her lump of a vehicle."

"Yes." Was this good acting or genuine lack of knowledge? "But, she's turned up. Didn't Glenn Thorley mention anything?"

Her demeanour changed and for several seconds the expression in her hazel eyes was hard and arrogant.

"No. Why should he? He despises Ellie Madison and has nothing to do with her. You'd think after Dad's death she'd give up, but oh, no, not her! If she's turned up, it'll be one of her little stunts. She and Dad used to do stupid things to get people's attention. It was pathetic."

This was news, but what kind and how true?

"It was no stunt, Fenella. We were shot at, knocked out, and she was taken," he said, and deliberately added, "On top of that someone set fire to my cottage this morning and had a go at Ellie's as well. Know anything about that?"

Her eyes reflected rapid calculations going on in the background. Seconds later she said, "Oh, so you're my tenant. I wish I'd known sooner. I'd have paid inspection visits," she said, smiling. "My agent tells me there's serious damage. No doubt he'll be in touch with you – or I might do it myself. You'll need somewhere to stay. I do have another property that's unoccupied for a couple of months."

No sympathetic response, no reaction to his pointed question. Self-interest reigned and there was little doubt about the reason for the offer of another cottage.

"I have a place to go. So, you and your brothers are the owners now."

"Only me. Took a while to sort out bits of Dad's will, but you probably know that as you're close to Ellie." Her expression became cold and distant and for a moment she stared past him. With a little shake of her head, she added, "He left two of the Tallow Lane cottages to me in his will."

"How many did he have?"

"Three. Bran got the other one. By the way, did you know Camden's home? Seems his little accident wasn't as bad as everyone thought. It's amazing how he always manages to get out of scrapes. He won't say what he was doing in Ellie's garden. Not one for sharing secrets our brother."

"When was he released?"

"You sound surprised and a bit... angry? What's your problem?"

"Someone was busy this morning."

She glared at him. "And you think he lit those fires! He only got out of hospital late yesterday. Anyway, he wouldn't do that sort of thing. You're making this up. In fact, I think you're a troublemaker, telling lies about people you don't even know."

The colour in her cheeks, combined with the blazing hazel eyes, heightened her beauty. Hardly surprising Glenn Thorley was interested in her. Half the men in the Highlands probably had their eyes on her.

"I don't do that," he said, getting his thoughts back to the subject. "You might want to ask your friend Glenn Thorley if he knows anything about why Camden was in Ellie's garden and whether he was down Tallow Lane this morning."

"He wouldn't set my property on fire and he wouldn't harm Camden. Despite what people think he cares about our family – and his own."

"I doubt it. I'll be interested to see what happens to you when the plans you have for Strathvern fall through."

"What d'you know about that? I'm not involved in Glenn's business. I'm making my own. We're just friends."

"In fact, I wouldn't be surprised if you were the one who put the thought into his head. After all, taking over Strathvern would be easier than trying to get a grand hotel built at Maw's Hearth. Too much opposition. And it's unlikely you'll ever marry Jamie. Even if you did, I expect he'd find himself disinherited before you'd said 'I do'."

"I've no plans to marry into *that* family. Besides, His High-and-Mighty Lordship is weak and doesn't deserve what he's got. There are better men than him to run the estate. He's the son of a Nazi sympathiser and he's followed in his father's footsteps," she said coldly.

"You have evidence of this?"

An impatient sigh met the damp air.

"Everyone who *lives* here knows what he is and you must've heard it from Ellie and Bob. Besides, Dad was on to something. The day before he was murdered he went to see the earl and tell him what he'd found out. He was really uptight about going which wasn't like him. Nothing much scared Dad. He loved us you know."

Self-assurance fled and for several moments he studied the face of a young woman who was grieving for her father and trying hard to keep it hidden.

"Did he tell you why he went?" The minute the words were out he knew he sounded too keen.

Her answer was evasive.

"If he did, I probably wrote it down somewhere. If you're looking for Dad's murderer, try the Strathvern lot and leave Glenn alone. He's not perfect, but he wouldn't kill anyone. Bad for business," she added lightly as she turned to go back inside. With her hand on the doorknob, Fenella glanced back at him, her smile seductive. "I still want that date with you."

Not in a million years, he thought when she'd disappeared inside. He looked up at the nearest window and saw Glenn Thorley turning away. Without waiting to be accosted on one of Inverness' popular thoroughfares along the River Ness, Byron hooked his hood over his head and went down the steps.

Crossing the road and walking back to his car parked along the river bank, he noticed a familiar figure approaching the hotel he'd just left. It was Michael Strathvern, limping and walking slowly, holding hands with his wife, Catherine. They walked up the steps and disappeared into the interior.

Byron hesitated. Ellie was alive and whether she was, as Jack stated, annoyed with him, he wanted to be with her and tell her how he felt about her. Admittedly, leaving his pen behind wouldn't look good in any investigation and unless he could prove it had dropped out of his pocket when he'd been there putting out the fire he might find himself a prime suspect. All Jack had to do was check with Bob and it wouldn't be a problem.

A frown tightened across his forehead. Bob was a long-time friend of Ellie's, someone who loved her. How did she really feel about the man? For that matter, what was her concept of love between a man and a woman? He'd never asked, they weren't that close, and he assumed that her understanding of it was the same as his, but was it?

355

As he stared at the hotel door through which Michael and Catherine had gone, his thoughts went back to the wild night Camden had trespassed in Ellie's garden. What mad plot or urgent mission had sent the man out of his warm house into chaotic and dangerous weather? Had he believed he could harm Ellie, even kidnap her, and no one would ever be able to find any hint of his presence there? Perhaps he was right. Paul Shepley had probably thanked God for protecting Ellie and expressed gratitude that Camden had been spared. Whether he deserved sparing was a consideration Byron chose not to dwell on. If he did, he'd have to seriously think about his own worthiness. Sometimes he envied those with faith. A couple of his army comrades were Christians and he'd often envied their certainty of heaven.

Saved by his thoughts wandering off further, he remembered the words Camden had muttered to Ellie. He'd forgotten about them: *Fenella... secrets. She knows... family... knows.*

What did she know? Did she have secrets of her own? Or had Farley confided in her about family matters?

Byron sighed and scooted back across the road, choosing the entrance to the bar rather than the main door into the dining area. The bar was busy; a busload of American tourists had just arrived, most of whom were making their way into the dining room. He merged with the flowing, colourful stream and found himself immediately engaged in a brief conversation with a burly man from Oregon. They were mostly fishing enthusiasts, he told Byron, and were doing a tour of Scotland's coast and a few of its islands. The man invited him to join them for lunch. Byron thanked him and said he'd already eaten.

Once in the room, Byron drifted away from the stream but not immediately out of their shelter. He saw the Strathvern couple walking slowly across the floor towards a table in a booth, a landscape painting on its panelled wall. It was far enough away from Thorley's table for them not to hear what was being discussed.

It seemed to him that Thorley and Fenella were engaged in an intense debate. They weren't shouting, but Fenella kept glancing into the room as if she was expecting someone. Perhaps him. Thorley, he suspected, wouldn't tolerate her interest in another man.

The Americans were descending upon their allotted tables laughing and chatting in a manner that was not the usual perception of Americans abroad, for they were far from being the loud, over-confident bunch they were often perceived to be.

As he turned from studying the tourists, Fenella saw him and frowned. Stuffing his hands in his jeans' pockets, Byron turned his back on her and walked towards the bar. When he glanced around a minute later, he saw that her attention was caught by Michael walking across the room apparently in their direction. Catherine was sitting alone in the booth. Byron's heart sank. This was not the place.

However, before Michael reached Glenn Thorley's table a slender young woman in fitted jeans and tailored jacket, mid-twenties Byron guessed, her expression hard and angry, completely ignored Fenella and began shouting at her companion. There was something vaguely familiar about the newcomer.

"You owe me money, Glenn Thorley! Five hundred pounds to be exact. I didn't keep your rich pals happy for nothing. I'm not one of those sluts you've got working for you."

Michael stopped. For a moment he looked as stunned as other diners, but then, to Byron's surprise, he turned away grinning. He saw Byron, waved and beckoned, and returned to the booth where Catherine was swivelling round in her seat, embarrassed by the scene.

Glenn's response was unheard, but his face showed utter contempt for the woman. Fenella sat quite still, her face as one chiselled from pale stone.

"I almost feel sorry for Fenella," Michael said, picking up the menu. "But she must've known, surely."

"Known what, sweetheart?" Catherine asked.

Exchanging a glance with Byron, he said, "Nothing you need be troubled about, darling. He has..."

A voice charged with indignation and fury erupted into the room. "I will *not* be blackmailed or threatened by you or anyone else! You think you can buy or bully your way out of everything, Glenn Thorley. Not this time!" She turned to Fenella. "If I was you, I'd get shot of this one before he's used you up as well."

Fenella, it seemed, was not to be outdone by anyone, including this intruder. The expression on her face did not change as she looked up at her and raised her voice just enough for it to carry.

"And if I were you I'd leave decent people to eat in peace. Mr Thorley is a respected and influential businessman, which is more than your behaviour shows you to be."

She picked up her glass of wine, took a sip, and engaged Glenn in conversation as if the interruption was nothing more than a single drop of rain on a leaf, sliding off to disappear into the ground.

However, if she thought the young woman would slink off, ashamed, the response made both of them look up sharply.

"You're a fool if you believe that about him," she snapped. "Read Friday's newspaper and you'll find out he's got more than hotels in his pay packet!"

Without waiting for retaliation, she turned on her heel as a security man reached their table and took her elbow. She shook it off, glared at him, and walked away towards the main entrance with her head held high.

"What a terrible scene," Catherine said, her fine brow wrinkled. "Very embarrassing."

"Interesting though," her husband remarked. "Fenella's definitely got some of Farley's fire in her. He wasn't one to be steamrollered either, whether he was right or not."

"But what's Glenn Thorley doing here with Fenella? I thought she and Jamie were going out together," Catherine said.

Michael's expression coloured. "I hope that's finished. Jamie deserves better. I know he's hot-headed at times and definitely a non-conformist in many ways, but he's a Strathvern and, well, I rather like him the way he is. I don't want a woman like Fenella getting her hands on him, especially if she's associated with Thorley!" He looked round at Byron. "Will you join us for lunch?"

"Thanks, but I've eaten," he replied, studying Michael's profile as the other man perused the menu. "What were you going to say to Thorley?"

Michael looked up from the menu and made a sound that resembled half grunt, half laugh.

"My father got another phone call yesterday from someone claiming to be the business manager of Thorley's hotel empire. He's an arrogant man given to standover techniques, badgering and lying. Anyway," he said sighing, "he demanded my father respond to their client's interest in Strathvern, saying it was in the financial interests of both parties. What rot! My father told them he wouldn't deal with them if they were the last two men on earth – and hung up. When I saw Thorley over there I was going to tell him to get his eyes off our home; it wasn't for sale at any price. And, I was tempted to say it loudly."

"Michael! You wouldn't have, would you?" Catherine's eyes were wide and horrified.

"I might have. I laughed when I saw the young woman berating him. She had more courage than I did."

"Yes, but look what he did to you!"

"I haven't forgotten, but he won't win."

"No more heroics, Michael," Byron advised him. "You're the heir remember."

Catherine nodded and reached to grasp Michael's hand. "And I need you too. Keep away from Glenn Thorley. He's bad news."

Byron's mind filled with images of Ellie the day they were up in the hills and she'd told him bits about her childhood and her terror of the encounters with Glenn Thorley. He saw again the pain in her eyes and adrenalin coursed through his body as it had on that day. Just two minutes alone with Thorley… He gave himself a mental shake. Those days were over; he wasn't on a mission to destroy.

"Are you all right, Byron?" Michael asked.

Slowly, Byron turned towards him and saw concern in his eyes.

"Fine, thanks. Catherine's right. He's bad news – more than you know."

"I do know," Michael said quietly. "You must've overheard the other day."

"Yes."

Catherine was watching them and Byron saw a quiet intelligence in her eyes he hadn't noticed before. Moisture was gathering in the blueness and he knew she suspected what they skirted around.

It was time he was going; he had to see Ellie and he had to make some phone calls. Suddenly, his heart lurched. Fenella was alone. Where was Glenn Thorley?

"Did you see Thorley get up?" he asked Michael.

"No. I must've been looking at the menu. What's the…?" But he knew, and troubled eyes searched Byron's. "Be careful."

***

A squall hit Byron as he came out one of the hotel's side doors and he zipped up his jacket and pulled the hood over his head. He shouldn't have taken his eyes off Thorley for one second. Damn!

The man must have slipped out when he and the Strathverns were talking and gone down a back passage.

Which way had he gone? The girl who'd shouted at him had headed out the front door and could have gone in a number of directions, or even got in a car and driven off.

Left would take him along the alley he was in, round the back of the hotel and along one of Inverness' busy streets. Right led up to another main street along the River Ness where he'd parked his car. Byron went right, running up the alley past an elderly man on an equally elderly bicycle, with a fishing rod resting on the handlebars and tied to a basket with a lid behind the saddle. In the front basket Byron glimpsed a tackle box, and a terrier sitting upright with bright eyes scanning the way ahead.

As Byron reached the junction with the road, he almost collided with a woman huddled inside her coat and almost hidden beneath a wide umbrella with a sturdy point angled in his direction. Two teenage girls were hurrying along behind her. A dozen or so others were also making their way up or down the street, including a man who looked as if he was enjoying the inclement weather as he was strolling along with his face up into the rain. Must be from one of those drought-troubled lands like Australia, Byron thought, remembering an excellent holiday there three years earlier visiting a cousin in the Barossa Valley. He hadn't drunk so much excellent wine since.

He saw the back of Glenn about a hundred yards to his right. Suddenly, Glenn darted across the road in a narrow break in the traffic and then stopped, looking up and down. Seconds later, he was off again.

There was a lot of traffic going past at a steady speed, some drivers more impatient than others. A horn blew loud in his ear as he stepped off the kerb between two parked cars and he looked round to see a small car darting in front of a lorry. The break Glenn had did not eventuate for Byron and his impatience threatened to overtake reason. He would lose the man if he didn't get across within the next minute. Already Glenn was becoming more invisible in the driving rain and the muck coming up off the road from the traffic.

"Come on, come on," he muttered as a furniture removal van crawled past, the driver peering out to the left, as if looking for a particular road.

For a second Byron thought he was going to stop and he groaned, but the driver kept going and the view opened up again. There was no sign of Glenn. In that moment of frustration and growing alarm for the girl, the traffic began slowing. Two drivers decided to change lanes and it gave him precious seconds to spurt over to the other side of the road.

The moment his feet hit the pavement he pushed his body hard to make up lost time. Running into the wind and rain did not slow him; it was light stuff compared to some of the gales he'd contended with in years past. He was pleased he'd kept up the high level of fitness.

He came to a foot bridge spanning the River Ness, the wind ruffling its protected waters between the banks. A couple of cyclists in wet weather gear, their bikes loaded with fat rear panniers and one over the handlebars, were walking across the bridge one behind the other. Glenn was nowhere in sight. A few seconds later the man and woman drew near.

"Excuse me," Byron said, "did you see a man in a grey overcoat on the other side of the bridge? Sandy hair, in a hurry."

"Biggish is he?" the man asked in an educated English voice.

"That's him."

"Bit hard to tell in the rain, but we did pass a man with hair about that colour. I think he vanished down a side road over there," he said, pointing.

"Thanks – and happy cycling."

They smiled in their dripping gear and went on their way. Byron ran across the bridge and headed towards the first side road. It was short and seemed a mixture of old, well-attended, narrow houses and a few small businesses. Cars were parked on either side and pedestrians were huddled inside coats and jackets getting along as quickly as possible. Not one of them resembled the man he was after. How could such a big man disappear so quickly?

He stopped, rain dripping off his hood onto his nose and cheeks. There was an answer to that – Glenn knew exactly where he was going. The girl was known to him. If she lived or worked hereabouts Glenn Thorley would know.

Walking quickly down the length of the road, his eyes constantly searching and seeking a sighting of his quarry, Byron turned the corner into a wider, busier road. Half a dozen houses later he turned again and went along a parallel road to the first one.

It was quieter, residential, with similar houses; the sort of area people lived in when proximity to their workplace and social life was high on the priority list. Although small compared to Edinburgh or London, Inverness was the only place with a significant population for a hundred miles. Tourists used it as a base from which to explore the coast and Highlands.

He was almost halfway along the road, walking fast and purposefully, hoping not to attract attention as he looked at every house, glancing through windows, when he saw Glenn. He was coming up steps from a basement flat. Before Byron had time to turn around and behave as if he was a local walking the other way, his mobile phone rang. Glenn's head snapped round and, for a fleeting moment, the two stared at one another with intensity. Then, Glenn tossed his head back and threw out raw laughter into the street. The sound of it set Byron's nerves jangling and, unbidden, he saw in his mind's eyes Ellie as a child, crouching in the corner trying to get away from her cousin. It was only imagery, he hadn't witnessed it, but it was powerful. Byron wanted to shoot him between the eyes, shutting the man down forever.

Without a word, Glenn Thorley turned and walked down the road away from him. He neither glanced back nor slowed his pace. The number on Byron's phone was unknown to him. Tension spread its fingers into the muscles at the back of his neck.

"Five minutes, whoever you are," he said softly, "just give me five minutes."

He ran towards the steps leading down to the flat from which Thorley had emerged and was standing outside the open front door in seconds.

He banged on the door and called out. "Hello! Anyone here?"

There was no answer. Without waiting to be invited in, Byron entered the house. He found the young woman in the kitchen at the back of the building. She was getting up off the floor, bleeding from the mouth and nose, a bruise colouring one of her cheeks. At the sound of his footfall on the tiles, she looked up, anger flaring in her eyes, her mouth opening.

"You..." For a second she stared at him, frowning, before her brow cleared and she attempted a smile. The wound was ugly and red. He wanted to shudder. "Oh, the handsome rock climber," she said with difficulty, dribbling blood.

He remembered her then – the coquette on Maw's Hearth. He wasn't about to reacquaint himself any more than he had to. He helped her up and onto a kitchen chair, found paper towelling on a roll on the wall and gave her a wad of it. She held it to her mouth and nose.

"You need to see a doctor," he said curtly. "D'you have a taxi number somewhere?"

"On the cork board," she mumbled through the paper towelling. "Can't you take me?"

"I'm on foot. I followed Glenn Thorley from the hotel. You made quite a show shouting at him."

"You were in the hotel?"

That was obvious. "How did you know he'd be there?"

"Saw him go in with that woman. He made me phone the newspaper, but he won't win this one." She made a grunting noise which could have been an attempt at a laugh. "He grabbed the phone off me, threatening them. He thinks he's stopped them printing the story, but they'll have told him what he wanted to hear and print it anyway."

"What story?"

"Buy the paper tomorrow and you'll find out."

He did not respond directly and ignored the playful glance she gave him. "D'you always barge into people's lives without being invited?"

"Quite often." She tried to laugh, but couldn't. She winced in pain instead.

"I'm surprised you're still alive then."

"I'm a survivor. Anyway, Glenn's not a murderer. It'd mess up his lifestyle."

Byron dialled the taxi company's number and told the woman on the end of the phone he needed a taxi urgently to the hospital. Ten minutes. He glanced at the hiker. She looked woozy. He hoped the taxi wasn't delayed.

"How'd you get mixed up with Thorley?"

She swallowed and began gagging, but managed a cough and spat blood into the towelling. Byron got more, damped a few sheets and, despite his resolve not to get any further involved, took the bloodied paper, wiped her mouth and gave her a clean tea towel hanging near the fridge.

Her voice was husky when she spoke. "Thank you, Byron." His stomach churned. He'd hoped she'd forgotten his name. "Jenny Browne. I work for Mayfair Hotels."

"And your job is entertaining the guests," he said bluntly, disapproving.

Ignoring his attitude, she said with a measure of dignity, "I'm the office manager at the Crossed Swords Hotel, one of their smaller, prestigious establishments. But I won't be bullied by him. Anyway, it's only temporary."

"And you really think your story will be in the paper tomorrow?"

"Of course! It's going on the third page. The editor positively drooled when I told him what Glenn Thorley was up to."

Studying her, he saw that beneath the blood and bruise, the swelling lip, she had the kind of face that some men liked: fair and smooth, blue-ish eyes, and prominent cheekbones, blonde hair. Dyed probably. Too skinny, though.

"And what is he up to?" he asked casually.

It was her turn to appraise him and she took her time. He wasn't surprised by her answer.

"That depends on how much it's worth to you to know. I gave the editor enough to get him excited, but…"

Byron shrugged. "I'll find out anyway. It's what I'm good at."

"Are you married?"

The question was so unexpected that he almost answered out of reaction with a harsh 'no'. Instead he told her it was none of her business.

"I like mysterious men and I like unravelling the mystery. What's it worth to you… *Byron*?" His name flowed out like honey.

It was a game he knew and how to play. He always won.

"Don't worry, I'll pay."

"I don't want money."

"I didn't expect you would."

"I want a night with you – and a down payment of your phone number and address."

"No address. It's been destroyed."

"Don't be absurd."

"I'm not. Ask Sergeant Kennart in Kilcomb." He wrote phone details on a piece of paper. "Only ring this number if you change your mind."

"I won't," she said, folding the paper and tucking it into a notebook on the table.

Their voices were still for a minute, the only sound that of traffic passing on the street above. Despite the pep in her voice,

Jenny Browne was beginning to show signs of increasing pain and the discolouring on her face was deepening. Lines gathered on her forehead and at the corners of her eyes as swallowing became more difficult.

"The taxi will be here soon," he said, softening at the sight of her distress.

She took a deep breath, but the smile she intended retreated with blood oozing from the split in her lip. Holding the tea towel to it she closed her eyes and shifted slightly on the chair.

"I know your opinion of me isn't very high, Byron, but you wouldn't have followed Glenn if you were his best friend," she said soberly, opening her eyes and looking straight into his. "I'll tell you what I know and hope you can get the mud to stick. He has a way of making it slide off, often onto someone else."

Byron held her gaze without responding. His phone rang. It was a loud and annoying interruption. Without checking the number, he pressed the off button.

"Sorry," he said. "D'you want a glass of water?"

"Yes, thanks. Glasses… in cupboard near the fridge."

When he returned, she took a sip of water and then looked at him with the intense gaze she had used at Maw's Hearth.

"Glenn's been befriending selected locals who sell the best whisky, imported wine, top-notch food, etcetera. He's promised lucrative business with his company. Sounds okay, except that he intends to shut down everyone else who's a threat to his plans. I've got evidence – and no, I'm not telling you what. It'll all be in the paper," she said, putting a hand to her cheek. "Have I gone blue?"

"Mottled," he said, waiting, impatient. The taxi would be here any minute.

She sighed. "Could be worse, I suppose." She looked at him for a moment, pensive. "What I didn't tell the editor was that I told Bob Caraway – he's one of the Highland's famous local chefs – all this weeks ago and he was going to speak with Ellie Madison so she could warn the SNH and organise some kind of protest. I also told him Glenn has someone local working for him – for thousands of pounds – to get plans through council. Glenn's going to destroy Maw's Hearth if he's not stopped."

"How did you get this information?"

"Let's just say that some of Glenn's guests can be quite chatty at times. And yes, it's reliable information from a reliable source."

"Did your… guest… say who it was?"

"No."

Footsteps sounded on the concrete steps down to the flat. The front doorbell rang. "We have to get you to hospital, Jenny." He looked at her intently. "Tell me who you were with. It's important."

He spoke with an urgency that clearly startled her, but as she opened her mouth to reply a man's voice called out saying the taxi was waiting. In the split-second Byron half turned to reply, there was a loud crack and the sound of glass splintering. Jenny jerked forward, sliding off the chair. Byron caught her before she hit the tiles. Behind him there was an exclamation and he saw the taxi driver looking from Byron to a window beyond him.

Chapter 21

Ellie slammed down the phone. He'd hung up on her twice! Where could he be? It was three thirty on a Saturday afternoon. Had he, after all his declarations of care and love, been using her to get the information he needed, and then tossed her away with all the other flotsam and jetsam he'd no doubt had in his life? He was no better than the likes of Glenn Thorley. Physical abuse or emotional abuse, what did it matter? They scarred a soul and left it desperately needing love and acceptance which seemed never to come.

"Damn you! Damn you, Byron Oakes!" she shouted, and sank onto the chair at her desk. Her body was tense with anger.

She would *not* shed any more tears over him. He wasn't worth the energy or the sorrow. As to love, it was a waste of time. It sucked all your energy and often as not yielded poor, or no, dividends. From now on she'd put all her energy into her painting and get involved again in helping keep the Highlands pristine. She'd let it slip with Farley's death and had hardly spoken with any of her SNH or local friends who'd been in the fight for years. Hadn't even had lunches and jaunts to isolated places with her painting pals. In fact, her painting had suffered more than she cared to think about. She'd barely touched the brushes in the last few weeks.

Well, the police could solve Farley's murder, no doubt with Byron's help. It wasn't her job anyway or her responsibility. As to the room beneath Strathvern Castle, it could stay shut up forever as far as she was concerned.

She gazed around the study, grateful that the damage was minimal. The walls, lined with bookshelves, were stuffed with books, magazines, video tapes, folders, photo albums and papers. Their loss would have been devastating. Not only were rare art books gracing its shelves, but also lots of material about the Highlands.

It wasn't just greedy developers who were a problem. Persuading farmers and crofters not already in agri-environment schemes that it was in their best interests to get involved was hard work. Many had already seen the benefits of careful grazing and growing wildflower meadows. Others had also taken up growing special crops for birds. It could be done – running cattle and sheep and growing crops for livestock alongside preserving the landscape and its wildlife. It was a matter of education and landowners and tenants seeing the benefits. They weren't interested in a lot of emotional conservationists demonstrating outside parliament and yelling abuse. It rarely won brownie points. If anything, it did the opposite, making the work of people like Farley and other intelligent and influential conservationists very difficult. Not that she counted herself in that select bunch. Still, she wasn't averse to speaking her mind to incomers wanting to set up what she called lollypop shops in historic buildings. One couple had tried buying a neglected twelfth century church on the outskirts of Castlebay intending to turn it into a nightclub. Mercifully, even members of the local council had been horrified and managed to get the application turned down. It was now being restored by a married couple, historians, who loved the area.

Could she carry on without Farley? The question continued popping up. There were others equally as passionate and keen to help, and had been friends and colleagues of the Ormans long before Ellie had arrived in Scotland. They were still fighting on. Some had been at it for forty years, maintaining vigilance in the campaigns, celebrating successes and consolidating when things weren't going the way they hoped. Sometimes they didn't win at all, but after brief bouts of deep disappointment they remembered their wins and carried on. Fine people who didn't get side-tracked by attractive men – or women – and secret rooms, or troubles that perhaps should stay hidden.

Ellie switched on the computer and began checking emails; she hadn't looked at them in over a week and hoped there was nothing urgent that should have been actioned days ago. She scanned quickly down the list deleting what she loosely called junk. A little over halfway down, there was one from Michael, sent that morning.

Hi Ellie. I hear you've been found, or rather, you escaped! We're so relieved! Sorry Catherine and I didn't see you this morning. Mother says you're in 'reasonable condition', and I hope that means you're not injured in any way. We were very worried. Who on earth put you under our great pile of stones and why? Michael & Catherine.

I wish I knew, Ellie thought, sighing.

She smiled at the names on the bottom. In most emails Michael added his wife's name. She was a nice young woman and perfect for him. A twinge of envy prodded her wounded heart. At

Catherine's age she'd still been struggling with rage, shame, rejection, loneliness, and who she was – or wasn't. She had believed enough lies about how she looked, how she dressed and behaved, that gloom had captured her on more than one occasion. Two things had kept her from sinking into miry depths: a hymn her grandmother had often sung about hiding herself in God, and a conviction that if she died Glenn would always think he had won. He hadn't and never would even though he had changed her life forever.

Rain was drumming against the window panes, released from dark clouds that were shutting out the remaining light. It would be dark early tonight. Autumn was underway. Snow had begun falling on some of the lower peaks and bracken was turning brown. Highlanders who worked the land were warning of a long winter and more snow than they'd had for some years. They didn't need television weather forecasters to tell them – they knew. Not long after she'd arrived in Kilcomb, an old farmer had told her to take notice of the signs nature gave and heed them. She had and still did.

Ellie was feeling better than she had for some days. The hours of sleep after Jack deposited a constable on her doorstep with instructions not to send him away, had been sweet indeed. Not once had she woken until the phone rang and Mary Nevin's voice welcomed her home. Half an hour later, much to Ellie's puzzlement, her friend had delivered Kipp, his delight in seeing his mistress one of delirious joy. When Ellie queried Mary about why Byron hadn't brought Kipp, there had been a vague response about not being sure except that he had things to do. Ellie was not entirely convinced Mary didn't know.

Mary never did anything without good reason and Ellie had put the matter aside. Their friendship was too special to let a small wedge stand between them. Nonetheless, she had said little of what had happened to her during the night, wanting to keep it unspoken until she'd told Byron. Now she wasn't so sure about him and wondered whether she should go and see Mary. Jack would be back tomorrow asking a lot of questions, some of which she would have to answer truthfully. It was reasonable to expect that they had to find out who'd shot at her vehicle and abducted her, and who was responsible for setting fire to the cottages. Yes, Mary's advice would be helpful.

The phone rang and she snatched up the receiver, her heart racing in anticipation.

"Ellie Madison."

"Hello, Ellie. It's Olga Erskine. I'm phoning to find out how you are? Word gets around and I was told you'd been found."

Ellie's heart sank as fast as a piece of lead to the bottom of the ocean. It was almost beyond her to respond, but she managed a reluctant, "I'm fine, Olga. How are you?"

"Canna complain. I'm home now and glad of it, too. They say you and your young man were on the way back to Kilcomb when it happened. Just after you saw me in hospital, was it?"

"Yes. I don't suppose you know anything about it, do you?" she asked, resenting the fact that it was Olga on the end of the phone not Byron – and angry with him.

"Now why would I know about such a thing, Ellie?"

"You've been in the village a long time, Olga and perhaps you've heard something."

"Lots of the natives don't count *me* as a local, lass," she said with a hint of a chuckle. "You know some think I killed the publican's son and they've never forgotten or forgiven. They don't usually include me in their gossip unless it's about me!"

"*Did* you kill him?" Ellie asked bluntly, punishing Olga because of Byron's lack of care.

Ellie thought she heard a sigh; silence followed.

After a few seconds Olga said quietly, "No, Ellie, I didn't. I've not murdered anyone – with or without the help of herbs."

There was no, 'I've told you before', no recrimination in her tone.

"I hope you're right, Olga," she said, though she was finding it hard to discern who was being truthful about Farley.

"What you believe is up to you, but I'm almost certain I know who killed Farley."

Ellie sat bolt upright. The words seemed to come out of nowhere, stunning her with their simple statement of fact.

"You *know* who killed him? Who?"

"I canna say. Take care, Ellie."

And she was gone, the ear piece burring.

The minutes ticked by; Ellie sat staring into the room. Why couldn't Olga tell her? Was she afraid of being knocked over by a car again? Perhaps someone had been warning her – or the driver hadn't done his job properly. Maybe Olga had heard what she wasn't meant to, been noticed and threatened. She was a strong-minded woman not averse to speaking up. She had survived the hit-and-run and was out of hospital. What if she was in danger?

She picked up the phone to call Olga and say she was coming over and would bring her back with her where the constable could mind them both. No, she thought, that won't work. Olga will think I want to pump her for information and she'd be right. Ellie put the phone down.

She could get on with her painting. There was a piece on the easel waiting completion. And there was always paperwork. With Kipp sleeping on the floor at the end of her desk she could almost believe life was returning to normal, but it was false hope in a way. Without Farley normality had shifted into another place.

She knew a number of files in the cabinet needed attention, but her enthusiasm for paperwork had never been high. In the last month, like her painting, it had been neglected. However, she had to tackle the Maw's Hearth and Strathvern Castle issues.

The scene at the garage with Glenn thumping on the passenger window reminded her that he and his plans remained a serious issue. Glenn's ego and his unconcerned way of using whoever and whatever to get what he wanted would prevail if concerned men and women did little or nothing. The Farley Orman she'd known had never been driven by money, but what if Camden had taken up that challenge and pocketed a sizeable lump of money for his efforts? A couple of the councillors were double-minded and could easily be persuaded by the likes of Camden Orman or Glenn.

Then there was Fenella who had partnered with Glenn in the pursuit of riches, trading the heritage of Scotland for money and aiding him in getting Strathvern's incumbents out before turning their ancestral home into a grand hotel for any rich thug to tramp all over. She shuddered.

With that in mind, Ellie got up and went over to the cabinet. Her heart missed a beat as she stared at the lock. There were scratch marks around it and two of the drawers were not completely closed. Why hadn't she noticed this morning?

Anger stirred. Byron! Had it been an opportunity he could not let pass by? He was a man of action and determination, used to making instant decisions. What was a little delving into her filing cabinet going to matter especially if it yielded information useful to the task he'd been given, because she was certain he was still in the pay of the MOD?

Pulling at the top drawer, which was partly open, Ellie went quickly through the files. She did the same in the second drawer. However, in the third it was immediately obvious that the hanging file for Maw's Hearth was empty. She stared at it, dismayed. All the information, so carefully gathered over a number of years, was gone.

She was about to shove the drawer closed with a resounding bang when she noticed that a new file had the same loose and empty look. There was no need to check the plastic tag with its insert to know what it should contain – paperwork about Glenn and Fenella: their plans for Strathvern; letters to Farley and Ellie from the Council for National Parks and Kilcomb's local council about Maw's Hearth; and a detailed report to the government from the Scottish Natural Heritage concerning Maw's Hearth.

Unexpectedly, she thought of Jenny Browne at Maw's. She'd studied journalism somewhere in the north of England and had got to know Farley quite well while writing a number of articles and stories about him for newspapers and magazines. Ellie hoped the woman never discovered her connection with Glenn. There was about her a subtle cunning Ellie did not trust. The look she'd given Byron had not gone unnoticed either. Well, she was welcome to him. Yet, her heart ached with a sense of loss the second the words raced through her mind. He was a man above all those she'd known; strong, yet vulnerable, a man who had arrived in her life and touched deeper depths than she'd allowed anyone else to do. Had it all been a lie?

Her thoughts wandered and she thought of Olga's phone call and her revelation about the murderer. How could she possibly know? She was an old lady who didn't venture far from home, had no family, and whose main interests in life seemed to be herbs and Bob's bread and cakes. Yet, she had been in the village a long time; her mind had to be a storehouse of stories and interesting information, a storehouse Ellie felt she'd like to plunder.

The only problem was the police constable prowling about her garden. He was new. She hadn't seen him before. According to Jack he came from Carlisle, south of the border, had Scottish blood all the way through his father's side and opted to move north and join the fight for justice there. Against the likes of Glenn or Byron he would fall like a matchstick man, but how was she going to get out? She went upstairs and looked out the bedroom window; the police car was parked on the other side of the hedge which, if she could get to the Land Rover meant a quick, clear spurt down the driveway and into the road. All she had to do was wait until he was round the back and then she could go out the front door.

Halfway down the stairs she had a better idea. Ten minutes later she called the young constable into the kitchen for a cup of tea and deposited a plate of Mary's freshly baked biscuits on the table.

"Thanks, Miss Madison," he said, taking off his hat as he sat down. He plonked it on the chair beside him.

"Must be boring marching round and round and I thought you'd like a distraction for a few minutes," she said, pouring two mugs of tea.

"You're right there," he said and, as if he thought better of his words, added, "Not that the duty of protecting such a person as yourself is boring, Miss Madison. I'm a great admirer of your paintings and the work you did with Farley Orman."

Ellie smiled, noting the flush of embarrassment on his fresh cheeks. "Thank you, Constable Ogilvie. He was a great fighter for Scotland's wild places. Not everyone is keen on having national parks or preserving the heritage of this amazing country."

"Then they should move to Edinburgh or London and leave it to those who really appreciate it. Good cuppa."

He took another long mouthful.

"Well, I'll be in the study with mine. Work to do," she said, raising her eyebrows.

"Righto. I'll get back to patrolling the minute I've finished."

"No hurry. Enjoy it."

"Thanks, I will."

Returning to the study, Ellie pushed the door almost closed, took a couple of sips of tea and retrieved spare Land Rover keys from a desk drawer. She pulled on a jacket, slung a bag over her shoulder and quietly opened the unbroken window.

Kipp pulled himself to his feet, sensing another adventure with his mistress.

"Not this time, boy," she said gently, kissing him on the head. "You're not well enough and I won't be long. Keep an eye on our friendly bobby."

She climbed onto the wooden footsteps she used to reach books on the tops of the bookshelves, got onto the window ledge and jumped down into the garden, narrowly missing a rose bush. There was a disappointed whimper from inside before Ellie pulled the window down and made her way to the vehicle.

It was dull outside, a sliver of sky separating ominous clouds. By the time she had fumbled putting the key in the lock, avoiding using the torch in her bag, the clouds had closed ranks. A few fat drops of rain landed on the windscreen as she slid into the driver's seat. Dimly, as the drops rapidly gained in fervency, Ellie heard a telephone ringing and instinctively knew it was the one in her study. If it wasn't answered the 'friendly bobby' would come looking for her to be certain she was safe. Time to go. With any luck he'd think she'd been abducted yet again. However, as she put the Land Rover into reverse and began backing quickly down the driveway, his face appeared in the study window. Then he was gone and so was she – out the gate and down the road.

Half a mile later, Ellie swung into a lane and stopped under a tree, turned off the lights and engine and waited. If the constable was pursuing, he'd pass by soon. However, if he had been told to wait at the house she would have to go the long way round to reach the other end of Kilcomb where Olga lived.

Time ticked by. It was gloomy in the lane and she looked at the trees on the bend ahead. Old Mr Stewart's family had farmed the land there for four generations. Their highland cattle were from a long line of prize winners, and this past summer had produced no less than three champions at the Royal Highland Show.

She'd waited long enough. Turning the key in the ignition, she switched on the headlights and, narrowly missing the water-filled ditch on the other side, headed back towards the main road. Fat drops of rain increased in tempo and hit the windscreen in a steady cascade.

A car rushed past the end of the road, oblivious of her, followed seconds later at a less hasty speed by a local bus, its windows fogging up and giving the strange illusion of bits of people. A little girl was busy drawing a house on the damp window next to her. There was no sign of the police.

Less than ten minutes later, enduring a stop behind the bus on a bend to unload three passengers, Ellie turned right and headed down a narrow strip of tarmac that soon ended. The gravel road was uneven and although the wiper blades were slashing across the windscreen, heavy rain made it difficult to see. A set of headlights appeared suddenly, blindingly, over a rise and Ellie almost slammed her foot on the brake, but she resisted and avoided the ditch. She slowed, continuing with more caution and looked for a spot to pull into, but was saved the trouble. The other vehicle stopped, its lights flashed, and she went on slowly. As she drew closer she recognised the outline of the vehicle and stopped level with the driver's door.

Paul Shepley wound down the window in unison with her.

"Hello, Ellie! What a dark, gloomy afternoon! Very glad to see you alive and well. I hear you've had an awful ordeal," he called out against the sound of the wind and rain. "What on earth are you doing out on this wretched afternoon?"

"I might ask you the same," she replied, grinning. "I'm off to see a friend."

"Likewise. Or at least one of my flock. I saw Olga this morning. Did you know she was released from hospital today?"

"Yes. Mary Nevin told me." Which she had. Ellie wasn't sure why she didn't say Olga had phoned.

He nodded. "She likes you. Thinks you've got spunk – as she put it." He smiled and raised his brows at an octogenarian using such a modern word. "Better keep going, Ellie. Let me know if I can help with anything. I heard Glenn Thorley's increasing pressure on the council about Maw's Hearth."

"Yes, he is. I alerted Maggie Chauncey at SNH a couple of weeks ago. She'll make sure he's watched. I thought I'd call a village meeting at the end of the month and see if we can come up with anything to stop him."

"Good idea. Want me to do some flyers?"

"That'd be great. I'll ring you tomorrow."

He nodded. "Good. We'll discuss the details. Drive carefully."

The windows went up and they continued their separate ways. He'd make some young woman an excellent husband, she thought.

Ellie knew the road well, but the weather warped her perception of the landscape and she found herself misjudging corners, narrowly missing hedges and fences. Eventually, she came to a crossroad and branched left onto tarmac with relief. She had never been to Olga's house; it was close to the other side of the village and she'd found the road name and number in the telephone book.

Several vehicles went past on the other side of the road, one of them careering around a bend, sliding across into her lane and back again as Ellie veered to the left and bounced across a potholed patch of gravel.

"Fool!" she shouted. The little volcano inside was not yet dormant.

It was a good five minutes before she came to Olga's road. Finding the number in the rain and gloom wasn't easy. There were several homes, but letter boxes, front doors and posts with numbers were mostly obscured by trees and shrubs. It was the fourth house along on the left before she knew whether she was on the odds or evens side.

She drove slowly, watching the road and the houses. When she came to number eleven, she stopped and peered at the house. It was bigger than she expected it to be. The curtains were drawn with a narrow gap in the middle of one set allowing an orange-yellow light to escape into the garden. For a few seconds she deliberated about going in. It was the kind of crazy thing Farley used to do, turn up at people's homes without phoning first. He didn't always meet with polite hellos and please come in for a cuppa. Well, she'd come a convoluted route on an abysmal afternoon and she'd risk a frosty reception. Pulling off the road, Ellie parked in front of the hedge. She sat for a minute or two deciding what she was going to say when Olga opened the door. *'I've come about the murderer'* wasn't the best greeting she'd ever invented. Olga, she suspected, would know why she was there the second she opened the door.

Out in the cold rain, walking carefully towards the open gate, she began feeling she shouldn't have come. It wasn't as if they were friends, acquaintances at best, and here she was sneaking into the woman's garden! Not too late to turn back, she told herself. She stopped, frowning. Beside the side of the house in the dark shelter of trees was a car. Probably an old relic from Olga's driving days.

Rain suddenly swept across the garden, slapping her in the face and darting into her eyes. She glanced at the front door – inside was a haven from the weather. However, the presence of the car made her uneasy and she walked quickly towards it. It was Bob's. For reasons she couldn't fathom, the fact that he'd parked it in the shadows disturbed her.

She pulled up her hood over already wet hair and ran towards the front door, relieved to step onto the porch, though the rain drove into it. For a second she hesitated, her finger pointing at the doorbell. This was an intrusion; she should leave. Olga was an old lady no matter how quick-witted and mobile. Unannounced visits to the elderly were not usually welcomed. At least, that had been Ellie's experience with her surviving grandmother who had told her often that it was not polite to call on elderly women without making an appointment. The last time she'd received a sound scolding, not only for simply turning up, but for not bringing biscuits or cake. As on every other visit, she had endured being criticised for the way she dressed, and lectured on not being married. Ellie had not gone again and only attended her funeral two years ago because her mother had wanted her there.

Well, Olga wasn't her grandmother, was nothing like her, and the little she knew of her, *this* elderly lady enjoyed company. Apart from that, Ellie wanted to know why Bob was there. With that she pushed the doorbell and waited.

The door opened more quickly than she expected, but it wasn't Olga's face that gazed at her with a mixture of surprise and misgiving.

"Ellie!" The misgiving slid away as he seemed to gather up his emotions and store them away. "What're you doing here?"

"I could ask you the same, Bob. Isn't it a bit late to be delivering bread and cake?"

"Olga was the last one on my round this afternoon and the weather's rarely stopped me getting food out. She'll be pleased to see you."

"Just as pleased as you are?" she asked, raising her brows in question.

"I was surprised, that's all, Ellie" he replied and, changing the conversation, offered the smile she knew so well. "Are you fit enough to be out?"

"Of course. Robust as a horse."

"Hmm, that I doubt. Your Prince Charming not with you?"

Frowning, and with an impatient sigh, she said, "No. Can I come in, Bob? I'm sopping wet already."

He opened the door wider and she stepped into the hallway. "Let me take your jacket."

She unzipped it and handed it to him. He hung it on a hook on the hallstand. It was a lovely piece of furniture; polished wood with carvings of flowers down two sides.

Following Bob into the spacious sitting room, she found oil paintings and watercolours of woodlands, European castles, and the sea squeezed in wherever there was space. There were big, comfy seats, two china cabinets full of old and expensive-looking wares and a large bookcase crammed with books. On the coffee table in the middle of the seating, was a large bowl of *pot pourri* and a piece of knotted driftwood. The aroma of mixed scents permeated the room.

Olga was sitting on the settee with a cup of tea in one hand and flipping over the page of a book that lay open on her lap with the other. The photographs seemed more vibrant and alive against the black and bronze of her leaf-patterned skirt. Ellie recognised the photographs. They were Farley's, in the last volume of his work published eighteen months ago.

For a moment it seemed Olga was mesmerised by the beauty of the photo she was looking at – Strathvern Castle on a misty autumn day, a ray of sunlight touching the end of one wall and making diamonds of the windows. In the foreground, age-old horse chestnut trees stood proud in their changing colours, the spread of their canopy reaching the edge of rose beds encircling a fountain.

"Conkers," Olga said, without looking up. "It was a wee bit of fun. The last earl didn't think so, but I'd heard his wife loved doing things like that. They said that to see her in her lovely dress and hat holding a conker on a bit o' string helped them to forget the war." She sighed and glanced up at her visitor. "Hello, Ellie. I thought you'd come."

Ellie could feel Bob's eyes on her. She did not look at him.

"I wanted to see for myself that you were all right," she said, which was partly true if not the main reason for the visit. "Hospital staff like to jettison patients the minute they're deemed fit enough to brush their own teeth."

Olga chuckled. "Aye, that's true enough. Come and sit beside me."

She patted the floral cushion next to her and Ellie obediently obliged. Bob sat down in a wing-back armchair covered in the same material as the settee, observing the two women with guarded interest.

"This was Farley's best book," Olga said. "He told me once he had secret places he'd go when he wanted to be alone. D'you know where all these photos were taken, Ellie?"

"Most."

"But not all."

"No. Why would I? He often went off by himself." The conversation peeved her. What was the woman insinuating?

"Perhaps he found something he wasn't meant to."

Olga turned the page of the book, scrutinising the picture with intensity.

"Such as?" Ellie asked bluntly, glancing at Bob.

His expression remained guarded, although his eyebrows twitched upwards for a second and, if she wasn't mistaken, he was sitting straighter in the chair.

"You were the one he confided in. Did he not say anything?"

"*If* he did, I'd be betraying a confidence if I told you – or anyone else. He didn't, but what is it *you* know, Olga?"

The elderly woman looked up, her eyes lively.

"You're a canny lass, Ellie Madison. Everyone seems to think he was killed because he wanted to preserve more of the Highlands than some liked, but I don't believe that. And Jack the Plod can't see past his nose when it comes to investigation. That young man of yours has more ability than him. Where is he?"

"Investigating," she said without putting any further thought into whether or not to share the truth of the situation. It was none of their business, not even Bob's. Instead, she asked, "Who d'you think killed him?"

A slow smile created more wrinkles on Olga's white cheeks and amongst those branching out from the corner of her eyes. Her teeth were white and straight, too white for someone her age, Ellie thought, in a not very complimentary opinion. Probably false.

"Someone who had a lot to gain from his death. A relative or acquaintance, a friend perhaps."

The faded blue eyes were fixed on her face and from across the room Ellie heard a quiet groan.

No one spoke. Then it dawned on her.

"You don't mean… you can't possibly think… *me?*"

"You did benefit from his will."

"Yes, but most of it's for the conservation work! He knew his family would…"

"Would what, lass? Leave you out? Of course! You're an intruder."

Ellie stared at her. When she spoke her voice was cold. "I did not kill Farley. I did not need his money and I certainly didn't encourage him to leave *anything* to me." She stood up. "I'd say you've looked too far from the home fires! I'm sorry I barged in on you. I'll see myself out."

With an icy dart in Bob's direction Ellie strode across the room and had just reached the door leading into the hall when chuckling halted her. She spun round, ready with a sharp retort. She wasn't quick enough.

379

"That's what I like about you, lass – your fire. You'd have made a good resistance fighter in the war. Come back. You didn't kill Farley. Even if you weren't lovers, there was love and respect between you."

"As you seem to know everything," Ellie said with acerbity, "who was it?"

On the mantelpiece, the carriage clock's tick-tock seemed to beat each one of her heartbeats as Olga stared into the middle of the room, her lips pinched firmly together. Did she really know who murdered Farley or was she rummaging around in her mind to find a likely candidate? Whatever the case, Olga Erskine was not going to be hurried, Ellie thought, impatient and annoyed.

Eventually, in a muted tone as if she didn't want to express her answer, Olga said, "One of the earl's sons."

"What! They've no reason to…" Then she remembered what she'd seen in the hidden room beneath the castle – and the photos Byron had, Farley's photos. Had one of them known about the photos and felt threatened enough to silence him? She looked round at Bob who was watching her with his steady, patient gaze. "Bob? Surely you don't agree with this!"

Across the room, and out of the corner of her eye, she saw Olga studying her with intense interest.

"What if they were about to lose everything?"

"Don't be ridiculous! Farley mightn't have had much time for them, but he'd never set about ruining them. The trouble with this village is it's stuck in the past. It would never do to forgive and let the family rebuild their lives, would it? If you're looking for someone to blame, think about the Ormans themselves," she snapped. "The only loyalties Camden and Fenella have are to themselves. Camden's a greedy, violent man with a strange mind. As for Fenella, you know full well she's hooked up with Glenn Thorley because he's got a fortune and she thinks that'll solve all her problems. It won't. He'll dump her the second she's outlived her usefulness."

"Jamie's also hooked up, as you put it, with Fenella," Olga said. "Has it occurred to you that perhaps the three o' them are up to something?"

"I think Jamie's got more sense than to get himself involved with Thorley. The man's a destroyer."

Unexpectedly, Ellie found herself the subject of meticulous scrutiny by a pair of old and perceptive eyes and, with an uncomfortable and sickening lurch in her stomach, wondered if she hadn't said too much. Bob was looking at her oddly. It was time to change the subject and she reached for her bag, pulling from it an envelope. She stood up and, on reaching Olga, took the photograph of the woman and the two children from its confines.

"D'you have any idea who these people are?"

Olga reached for her glasses and took the photo from her. As she stared at it, silent and unmoving, her grip tightened and blue veins stood rigid in her thinning skin.

Eventually, she said with difficulty as if her throat was dry, "Where did you get this?"

"I found it in amongst paperwork."

The other woman's fine, grey eyebrows arched upwards and Ellie was again subject to sharp inspection. Olga lowered the photo.

"It was in some old stuff I had," Ellie added without hesitating. Lying wasn't her natural trait, but it was necessary. She wasn't about to blurt out where she'd spent last night. "Do you know them, Olga?"

"The children, no," she said, her voice returning to normal. "The woman was a guest at the castle several times after the war. I think she was some relation of the earl's, a cousin maybe. It's too long ago. Why're you digging up the past? The war was no romantic novel." She was annoyed and picked up the photo, looking at it again. Bob got up and sat beside Olga, asking to see the photo. Her reluctance to give it to him was obvious as she continued holding it. "It'll not mean anything to you."

"Maybe not, but I'd still like to see it. Is there any reason why I shouldn't?"

"Of course not," she said testily, gave it to him and looked across at Ellie, asking again, "Why *are* you digging up the past? The war had enough pain and grief wi'out it being dragged up again."

"I don't know if it'll do that. I'm just interested, that's all. This might be someone's long lost loved ones. Was the woman the children's mother?"

"I canna remember. I only spoke to her once or twice." She pushed herself forward on the seat and put a hand on the armrest. "I need my bed. It's been a long day. Give Ellie back her photo, Bob."

He did not appear to hear and she repeated the instruction. When he looked up at Ellie, his face was pale and in his eyes she saw an expression akin to disbelief.

"What's the matter, Bob?" she asked as he held out the photo to her.

"Nothing, I thought it looked like..." He shook his head. "Impossible."

With that he stood up and went to help Olga up.

"I can still manage thank you, Bob. I might be old, but not completely helpless. Thank you for coming. You too, lass, but don't bring me any more pictures. I don't want tae be reminded of the war."

Ellie and Bob walked across the room towards the door. There was a loud click behind them and they spun round as if one. Olga was still sitting down, but in her hand and pointing at them was a gun. She was holding it with a handkerchief.

"Olga!" Bob exclaimed. "Don't do anything stupid."

"Oh, don't worry, Bob. I've no intention of that. At my age, the last place I want to be is in gaol." She looked at Ellie and said quietly, "I believe this is yours. It was found near Farley's body."

Chapter 22

Inverness Hospital was busy as Byron walked through the main entrance and out into the cold, blustery late Saturday afternoon. It seemed an age since he'd arrived. Visitors were coming and going, several nurses were heading off after their shifts, and a couple of patients were standing immediately outside the doors puffing on cigarettes. Byron stopped and switched his mobile back on. Two surgeons were conferring behind him, one apparently on his way to an emergency at another hospital. There was another missed call from the unknown number.

One of the emergency nurses who knew Jenny had taken care of contacting her family and within twenty minutes an older sister and a male friend had arrived loudly. The police came five minutes later taking down details of the incident from Byron and the taxi driver. It was a tedious process as far as Byron was concerned, but he couldn't put them off as he had Jack Kennart. He supposed the hospital staff had called the police.

Before leaving London for the second time to head up to Scotland, his old friend in the MOD had told him to keep a low profile. So far, he'd managed to do the exact opposite. In one day his cottage had been set alight, he'd lost contact with Ellie Madison, had a less than satisfactory chat with an ex-army intelligence colonel, and a rock had hurtled through the kitchen window of a house belonging to a young woman while he, Byron Oakes, was with her. Not exactly anybody's idea of a low profile, average day.

Jenny's sister, a few years older, of solid build, dark hair and brooding eyes, had grilled Byron as vigorously as the police constable. It was clear she believed he had more to do with her sister's present state than he was admitting, and had left him abruptly with a withering backward glance when he refused to give in to her bullying. She completely ignored the taxi driver and thanked neither of them for getting Jenny to the hospital. Nor had she introduced herself. The only reason Byron knew her name was in overhearing the friend, harbouring equal animosity towards the two men, addressing her as Angela.

"Can I give you a lift anywhere, mate?" Andrew, the taxi driver, asked. He was a cheerful forty-plus fellow with a lilting Scottish-tinged Yorkshire accent.

"Thanks. Near Ness Bridge would be fine."

Sitting in the front passenger seat he pushed his cold hands into his jacket pockets. Andrew chatted on about how he loved living in Inverness and what a magnificent country Scotland was, especially in the north. If his wife had been agreeable, he'd be living on one of the island, but she said it was a wee bit too remote especially for the kids.

Byron only half listened. He wanted to know who Jenny had been with, but she'd been in no state to talk in the taxi. The rock that had hurtled through the window had hit her on the side of the head and although Andrew raced out the back door and into the matchbox-size garden and looked up and down the lane, there was no sign of anyone. Byron's only suspect was Glenn.

At the hospital Jenny had been whisked off to a cubical in Emergency and Byron had not seen her since. A young doctor, somewhat officious, had told him and Andrew that she was comfortable. Jenny's sister had not enlightened them.

"...the photographer, Farley Orman. Now, he took *the* best photos of Scotland. I learned a lot from him."

Byron's attention jerked back to what Andrew was saying. "Yes, he knew how to take a great picture," he heard himself saying, hoping Andrew hadn't noticed his inattention. "I haven't got the skill he had, though. Studying his books wasn't enough."

"Hah! That's where I have an advantage. Whenever he was in Inverness he used to hire me to drive him about. He liked to *look*. Had quite a bad accident a few years back when he was doing more looking than driving, so he decided to *be* driven. I'd pick him up at the 'Crossed Swords Hotel' and off we'd go," Andrew said, slowing down in the peak hour traffic.

"He stayed at the Crossed Swords?" He was surprised by this news.

"That's right. You know it? It's on the road to Cawdor and is one of the best hotels in the area. Great little restaurant as well. Open three or four nights a week. The head chef used to work in Edinburgh. Lives up this way now."

"Big move," Byron said, but his mind was busy with Farley's jaunts around the Highlands.

"Wanted a better life I suppose. That's why most people move to the north of Scotland. Fresh air and all that."

They turned into Bank Street as the rain eased and Byron wondered whether Ellie knew about Farley's visits to Glenn's hotel outside Inverness. She said he'd often disappeared for days at a time and Inverness was a good place to venture into the remote regions of the Highlands.

"Will this do?" Andrew piped up as he pulled into an empty parking space fifty yards or so from the bridge.

"Just fine. Thanks, Andrew." He reached for his wallet and drew it out of his jeans' pocket.

"This one's my shout, Byron. It's not every day I go innocently to someone's house to find my passenger's had a rock thrown at her. Enjoy your stay in Scotland."

"I will. Take care."

"You bet!"

Andrew was back in the traffic in seconds, merging with the river of metal and headlights and continuing with his life. He'd told Byron he'd ferried men beaten up outside hotels, women expecting babies, and the elderly needing to get to a destination they could no longer undertake without someone else's help. An attack on someone in their own home had added another dimension to his usefulness as a taxi driver.

A few minutes later Byron was in his car scanning the map and finding the road to Cawdor. With only a vague notion about what he expected to see there, or even why he was going, Byron headed out along the road towards Nairn.

Rain swept at the passenger side of the car, driven by a stiff wind off the Moray Firth. In the murk, he almost missed the turnoff to Cawdor; it appeared suddenly on his right. With no other vehicles about, he turned sharply and the car spurted across the road. Before long he saw an up-market sign with a painted pair of gold crossed swords and bold letters announcing that somewhere down the tree-lined driveway was the Crossed Swords Hotel.

Byron decided to drive down the lane he'd just passed and enter the property another way. It was nothing unusual for him; he'd been entering grounds and buildings by unconventional 'back doors' almost all his adult life. Actually, *all* his life. During boyhood he'd always been yearning and looking for the next adventure – battles in empty buildings he and his friends shouldn't have been in; riding at full gallop in pursuit of enemies of the king across his uncle's fields, sneaking into the grounds of a big house built in the fourteenth century in the next village and pretending he was the long-lost heir. Hardly surprising he'd ended up in the army or that he was now considering a different life to that of architect.

He saw the hotel, a Georgian manor, graced by expanses of flower beds at the front and a covered terrace at the back. In the middle of the lawn near the terrace was a fountain. Box hedges surrounded several square garden beds and paths on either side led to a copse. Another path ended at a small summer house and the other continued through a gate to the countryside beyond.

Byron sat in the car longer than he intended, staring at the clouds moving slowly away to the east and watching the evening closing in. The rain had almost stopped.

What was he doing here? Staring out of the windscreen, he could feel agitation stirring. He was getting almost nowhere with Farley's murder, or the reasons hinted at and were buried in the murk of World War Two. All he had were a few snippets: a photo of a young woman who didn't mind posing in flimsy clothing for whoever had taken it; a trip to Lord Strathvern's study where he'd been shown some of the contents lodged in a secret cupboard; motives mounting up like a never-ending staircase; Camden Orman's accident in Ellie's garden; Ellie's disappearance; Olga Erskine who knew more than she was saying; a friendly baker who was in love with Ellie, thirteen years his junior; Thorley, violent and greedy; a local police sergeant who seemed capable of being totally inept as well as fairly efficient, but unlikely to be trustworthy; the Lawfords who had a hoard of secrets; and Farley, whose life was perhaps more complicated than anyone realised.

Had one of these people deliberately killed him? Or had it been an accident?

Frustration grew like a mushroom pushing itself out of the dark earth. He knew where he had to get to – the truth – but he couldn't see where he was going. Muck was being shovelled onto him wherever he turned. And he was fairly certain the fire at the cottage was no accident of faulty electrical wiring – not with the skeleton of a well-dressed lady perched in the attic.

He wasn't convinced Thorley had murdered Farley, and wondered why he'd chosen Fenella as a business associate when he hated the father. That she was young and beautiful would surely somehow be relayed to Thorley's estranged wife. He pitied her.

It was likely Thorley had chucked the rock at Jenny Browne, but as Byron knew little about her the incident could be totally unrelated to her employer.

So, was he, Byron Oakes, a hiker on holidays, here because of Farley or Ellie? Was this about the photographer's murder or a half-formed idea about taking revenge on Thorley because of what he'd done to Ellie? As to the accusations he'd heard about Thorley's other business interests, it was nothing to do with him. If Michael Strathvern had as much information as he hinted, he should take it up with the police.

The lines were becoming blurred and Byron didn't like it. He'd always been a clear and incisive thinker. He needed more history on both Lawfords. As to Olga Erskine, she too knew more than she was telling.

The first thing he had to do was try Ellie's phone again. He picked up his mobile; it was out of signal range.

"Damn!"

He thumped his hand on the steering wheel. Without really thinking about what he was going to do, but needing to do something, Byron got out of the car. The cold, damp air met him like an unwelcome visitor. He shivered. Well he was here now, he might as well check out the hotel.

Walking up the lane he found a place in the hedgerow that faced an end wall of the building with only one window halfway up. Between it and the hedge was a brick garage, separate from the hotel, a wide gravel path, and a garden bed of roses past their peak. Byron pushed through the hedge, checked no one was looking out the window, and ran across to the garage. A car came up the driveway, went past a square garden bed filled with topiary-sculpted shrubs and stopped. When he peered round the end of the garage he saw the Jaguar parked at the front entrance. The driver was still in the car and although Byron couldn't see who was behind the wheel, he knew it was Glenn Thorley.

The man stepped out of the vehicle, strode across the gravel, up the steps and in through the front door. Running across the path to the side of the building, Byron made his way to the terrace. Light was pouring out through the windows. Confident he hadn't been seen, and hearing no chatter of guests, he leaned forward and peered through the glass. Terracotta tiles interspersed with blue, red and yellow sections across the expanse made a complementary floor for wooden tables of various sizes, each surrounded by padded wooden chairs. There was a small bar at the far end and in the middle of the room a large fireplace, blazing. Double doors led out into the garden. As he was about to continue alongside the terrace, Glenn Thorley's voice broke the silence, suddenly and close by. There was a response from someone, the voice muffled by the walls. Seconds later two men stepped into the terrace room from a door about six yards from Byron's position. He ducked smartly behind the brick wall.

"You're late! No, don't explain now, you'll waste more time. And I don't care what that jackass needs, I want a dozen bottles of *Coteaux du Layon Rochefort* tomorrow at the price I said. He's got it stashed away in his cellar. I'm paying him good money."

"Not according to Andrew Stewart."

The other voice, less abrasive and not rising above a normal tone, was familiar, too familiar. Byron went very still. It belonged to Bob.

"Then I'll have his paltry pub closed down for illegally selling alcohol before he lights his next cigarette. The Kilcomb residents won't like that. Let's see what a little pressure can do to change his mind."

"He doesn't deserve that. There are plenty of other good sweet whites on the market and cheaper."

"I'm not after cheap. I want that wine; Caraway and you'll get it for me. If Stewart won't pay the price, he will – with his pub! Tomorrow night's dinner has to be perfect. My guests will expect nothing less. If you ruin this by getting in an inferior wine, you'll regret it. I won't have a village baker and publican messing up my plans!"

"That 'village baker' is your chef. If I don't turn up tomorrow night there won't be any dinner – perfect or otherwise."

There was a noise Byron recognised.

"Don't *ever* threaten me again, Bob. Just remember why you're here. I don't suppose your *friend* – she does get around, doesn't she? – would be too happy to find you working for me. I expect obedience. Got it?"

Footsteps rapped across the tiles, retreating quickly. Risking being seen, and an adverse reaction from Bob, Byron peered into the room. Bob was standing against the back wall, a hand to the back of his head. In that moment, exposed and unguarded, pain and anger glinted in his eyes as if a wounded warrior in the midst of a battle. He looked neither to the left nor the right, staring ahead, his expression darkening. A phone rang, jerking him out of his deep contemplations and he walked across to the bar, snatched up the handset and spoke into the mouthpiece. The conversation lasted less than a minute. The fire in his eyes died down as he returned across the floor. He reached the fireplace before he glanced towards the windows and saw Byron, stopped, and blinked as if seeing an illusion. Byron raised his hand, beckoning.

Bob altered direction and reached the door leading into the garden, only to be halted by the appearance of a woman in her mid-twenties, dressed in a chef's uniform, who called out to him. Half turning towards her, Bob said he was just getting a breath of fresh air and would be back in a few minutes. She hesitated, asked if he was okay and, not looking entirely convinced by his response, went back to the main part of the hotel.

A minute later he took Byron by the arm and pulled him out of sight of the restaurant.

"What *are* you doing here?" he whispered urgently, frowning. "Thorley will have you hung, drawn and quartered if he catches you! How d'you get here?"

"The how isn't important. Are you okay?"

"Yes," he said impatiently. "Now go away before he comes out."

"Not before you tell me why you're working for him. Ellie doesn't know I gather."

He shook his head.

"Anyone in the village know?"

"People from Kilcomb don't have the kind of money to come here. They wouldn't even know it exists."

Byron regarded him intently. "What are *you* doing here?"

"That's my business."

"Sounded like it was Thorley's as well. He threatened you, Bob."

"He threatens everyone. Bullies threaten because they're full of fear."

"Look, I'm not the enemy here," Byron retorted impatiently. "I was asked to find out about Farley Orman and that's what I intend to do. I need your help, not a load of codswallop."

"So," Bob said, his expression relaxing, "the tough man from England isn't just a hiker and is finding the Scottish locals a little too canny for his liking."

389

"Something like that." He held Bob's gaze, unsure whether he could trust him, but he had to throw something into the pond and see what came up. "I don't think Thorley's the murderer, but you might've heard whispers that don't come my way."

"The locals don't entirely trust me either. I've been away half my life."

"But you're a Highlander."

"Aye. One who's lost much of his accent, most of the local habits, and has more friends in Edinburgh, London and Paris than here." It was Bob's turn to do the studying. "Are you going to tell me what you're doing here?"

"Looking. I had no idea this place existed or that Thorley owned it until after lunch. A chance meeting," he said in response to the lift of Bob's eyebrows. Then he tossed in, "Did you know Farley used to stay here regularly? A bit exclusive, isn't it? I wouldn't have thought it was his thing."

Bob pinched his lips together before releasing a reluctant sigh. "Yes, but Ellie never knew. Don't ever doubt Farley's commitment to what he did and what he believed in. The Highlands were his life, but his soul wasn't so full when it came to relationships."

"He told you this?"

"Didn't have to. I knew him well enough to see beneath the zealous contender for Scottish heritage. There were few boundaries in his passion for photography and conservation, but when it came to his personal life he was the best guarded safety deposit box in Great Britain," Bob said, frowning as he felt the back of his head. "Some of the villagers believe he killed Alice so he could marry Ellie."

"D'you think he did?"

Bob shook his head. "No. When Alice disappeared he went to pieces. Vanished for days afterwards. He never said where he went. As to Alice, I think she's out there somewhere. Maybe she did it to punish him for leaving her alone so often."

"Did Ellie ever say where Farley went?"

Bob's eyes narrowed. "No, she didn't know where he was either. There was never anything... intimate... between them – as far as I know. Don't believe the village gossip. It can be ruthless."

Byron changed the subject. "How's your head? Was it Thorley?"

"He shoved me, but my head hit the brick wall," he said, screwing up his face as if he'd taken a mouthful of vinegar. "By the way, I nearly forgot…"

There was a noise from the terrace room – the quick, determined steps of a man walking towards the rear entrance. The two men glanced at one another and Byron was away across the path and into the shelter of the shrubs behind the garage before Bob could open his mouth.

"Caraway! Where the hell are you? Caraway!"

Byron watched Bob walk towards the terrace room as Glenn came around the corner. From where he stood Byron could see and hear them. Bob, holding a hand to his head, told his employer he'd needed fresh air and would now see about dinner.

The rejoinder was out almost before he'd finished speaking. "You might be king pin in your little empire, Caraway, but here you're a servant and you answer to me. There's a dinner waiting to be prepared and taking time-out over a little bump on the head isn't in your job description."

"Nor is being pushed against a wall," Bob said evenly, turning away.

"I heard another voice. Who were you talking to?" the big man demanded.

"No one."

"Don't lie to me. Who was it?" He began looking around. "Is Ross Strathvern here?"

"Why would he come here when he's got a bigger house than you?"

Byron admired the subtle goading in Bob's tone.

"But less money," was the abrupt response. "I'll find him. I want you back in the kitchen. Ellie Madison wouldn't be so enamoured with you if she knew about the deal you made with your pal at the Scottish Natural Heritage."

"She's not enamoured and that was *your* deal not mine, Thorley."

"And you're forgetting why you went to him. Farley Orman would've sacrificed you to whatever Highland god he worshipped if he'd had to. That those plans to make Maw's Hearth a National Park disappeared, served you as well as me."

"I doubt it."

Long moments passed. Byron digested the implications of the entrepreneur's words, but the taste was sour. What *was* Bob up to?

Was he working in opposition to Ellie? Strange way to behave towards a close friend. Byron wondered what the deal was with the 'pal' at SNH.

"Strathvern's days are done," Thorley said. "The heir apparent won't have a kingdom soon." Then, as if his thoughts had turned a sharp corner and shown him a different view, he suddenly shouted, "Oakes! It's you!"

The shout was followed by the sound of footsteps crunching on the gravel and Byron peered cautiously around the corner of the garage. Glenn was walking across the path. The light was beginning to fade.

Moving towards the hedge, Byron · was aware of his adversary's movements. Thorley was not a battle tactician and he moved like a charging rhinoceros. If he had to, Byron would outrun him and lose him in the countryside. Stepping slowly and deliberately, avoiding sticks or leaves, he came to a gap in the shrubbery and slid through. Glenn was advancing towards him, more cautious now than Byron expected of him, perhaps waiting for the ex-army boy to make a mistake and show himself.

"This is my land, Oakes, and you're trespassing!"

And you've trespassed where you shouldn't have – in Ellie's life. I'd kill you now if I thought I'd get away with it.

Byron moved quietly away from the shrubs towards the front of the garage. He tossed a stick, aiming so that it brushed the leaves. Beyond the shield of greenery, Glenn, patchy through the foliage, increased his pace across the lawn.

Time to move. Soft-shoed, Byron fled across the grass. He'd almost reached its perimeter when his phone rang. He cursed it silently. Still running, he shoved his hand into his pocket and pressed the 'off' button. There was hardly a better 'here I am!' signal.

Glancing behind him, he saw Glenn approaching the gap between the shrubs with great strides. The dark material of his suit made his features seem more forbidding, his fair eyebrows drawn together over intense blue eyes filled with purpose and revenge. He had not yet seen Byron, nor did he, for he suddenly stopped and spun round as Bob shouted out, "Ellie's gun was found near Farley's body!"

In those seconds of reprieve Byron ran back a few feet and took refuge amongst a pile of discarded objects at the back of the garage. Glenn seemed undecided about which was more important –

listening to Bob who was walking towards him or pursuing the trespasser.

"What's that got to do with me?" he said loudly, looking away from Bob and resuming his pursuit.

Byron ducked down behind an old range, its days of turning out fare for the gentry over and no doubt replaced by an upmarket commercial oven. Along the garage's length were discarded tyres, a bathroom cupboard, several piles of bricks, two tall stacks of roofing tiles, and a few planks of varying lengths. It wasn't much protection from determined eyes.

"Everything when they find your fingerprints on it. You took it from her house."

The man did not respond, but Byron could hear his heavy breathing. Then Glenn was on the move, twigs snapping beneath his shoes, and in seconds he was close to Byron's hiding place.

In a way he wasn't surprised to hear the accusation against the man, but would he have gone into Ellie's house, up to her bedroom and taken the weapon? He couldn't have known where she kept it. His gut lurched and a sickening churning distracted him. Had Thorley been there with Ellie, against her wishes? Had she fought and screamed and no one heard? Hatred swelled deep inside, its force greater than he'd felt in years, not since Ena's death. It erupted out of his heart and rose in his throat as a roar of war against the perpetrator. Beyond the piles of bricks, he could see one of Glenn's legs and the heel of a well-polished, expensive leather shoe. Byron reached out, grabbed the short plank nearest him, and charged at Glenn with a cry of rage.

"You're filth, Thorley! I'll kill you!"

Glenn turned around, but the plank thudded into his midriff before he had time to speak. The force of the blow pushed him backwards, a loud grunt coming out of his mouth. His heel caught in a tussock and he stumbled, landing heavily on the ground. Byron raised the plank, watching without mercy as Glenn tried to sit up. He waited until he was up far enough before he delivered another blow.

"No!" shouted Bob, catching hold of Byron's arm. "He's not worth it!"

Byron turned on him. "Stay out of the way, Bob. This has nothing to do with you."

He lifted the plank high, but Bob stepped in front of him.

"This is madness! You might've treated people in the army like this, but you don't do it here," Bob said angrily. "This kind of justice serves no purpose. If you kill him, you'll be the one locked away for life. I'll be left to tell Jack and Ellie. Just get back in your car and go back to Kilcomb – or London."

"And that'd solve everything you think?"

"No, of course not, but you killing him will make things worse. Much worse."

"If he's dead Ellie's..." He didn't finish. She'd told him in confidence. He couldn't betray her.

"Ellie's what?" Bob's eyes glittered, seeming to drill right into his soul.

"She's safe... safer. She's the only one left of the Iron Musketeers," he said, and then looked at Glenn who was holding his midriff and taking gulps of air. "It'd serve your purposes to have her out of the way."

"But not... dead!" he wheezed. "She's my..." He took another deep breath, labouring.

"Your *what*?" demanded a clear, brittle female voice.

The three men's heads snapped around as if one. It was Fenella Orman. A cold shiver ran down Byron's spine. There was an added dimension to her at that moment: secret, determined and hard.

She was wearing a tight fitting, peacock blue dress, its hem just above the knees. Over her shoulder a long black and blue silk shawl, pinned at the collarbone with a sapphire brooch, fell to the waist. She was a priceless jewel amongst stones, a slender sapling robed in the finest foliage – and she knew it.

"Your *what*?" she repeated, walking towards them. Her expression was cold and forbidding.

Glenn was trying to get on his feet. He looked up at her almost, Byron thought, defiantly.

"She's my cousin."

In the silence of their gathering, Byron's heart thumped. No one moved. All the attention was on Glenn who tried to straighten and couldn't. He stood, hunched over, his arm around his middle. *That* secret was out now. Byron glanced from one to the other and sensed the ravens gathering, ready to wreak havoc and make Ellie's world more unstable and unpleasant than it was now. Glenn looked directly at him, ignoring the shocked expression on the other two faces.

"You knew," he said bluntly.

Byron quirked his eyebrows, but didn't speak.

"Why didn't you tell me she was your cousin?" Fenella demanded, glaring at Glenn. She stood over him, hands on her hips.

"It wasn't necessary."

"Not necessary?" she snapped. "The woman's a threat. If this becomes public knowledge it could destroy what we're working for!"

"Don't be shy, Fenella," Bob said, a hint of sarcasm in his tone. "I'd be surprised if most of the village don't know you and Glenn are... *partners*."

"Shut up," Glenn growled. "It'll only become public knowledge if one of you says anything. Ellie's kept her mouth shut, why can't you?"

Bob chimed in. "The only reason Ellie would've kept quiet is so she doesn't have people thinking what runs in your tainted blood is in her."

Top marks, Bob, Byron thought. Not the entirety of it, but still true.

The hotel owner ignored him and looked at Byron.

"Did she tell you?" There was an edge to Glenn's voice that sent a chill along the back of Byron's neck. Ellie, strong as the hills she climbed except for the bits where the snow melted and left the rock bare.

"I don't think you need to know."

The man bristled, his blue eyes reminding Byron of a turbulent sea.

"I have a right to..."

"To what?" Bob interjected, looking from one man to the other. "I'm one of her closest friends and she's never said a word about being related to you, Thorley. Between you, you've managed to stir up more trouble than Kilcomb's seen in decades!"

He turned and walked off towards the hotel. Unexpectedly, Byron felt a shadow of pain. Bob loved Ellie and he, professing mere tourist status, had turned up in Kilcomb, made an impression on the painter and stepped in between them. Unwittingly, but nevertheless that's what had happened. And Glenn? He was the bully who set out to hurt her.

"What other sources d'you have except Ellie?" Glenn said, giving a dismissive glance at Bob's back and stepping awkwardly towards Byron who didn't move. Intimidation did not work on him these days.

"That's my secret. You've kept yours long enough."

Glenn's body tensed as he straightened up. Byron was ready for whatever he intended doing, but it was Fenella who surprised him. She walked up and stood between them, looking straight into Byron's eyes. There were barely six inches on either side of her. Her perfume washed over him, reminding him of the scents of a tropical evening.

"I thought you were a man, a *real* man," she said, her voice brittle, eyes testy, "but you're only a puppet. You dance when they, whoever they are, tell you to. They've probably written out the script as well." It was a challenge. He ignored it and kept silent. "This is Glenn's land and you've no right here. I think Inspector Carter would be very interested in hearing about your latest transgressions of the law. Trespassing's still a crime. He and my father were old school chums and he's keen to find who killed him. He rather fancies you're the killer, probably with Ellie's help. You could both be in prison for a very long time."

Byron stepped back, studying her. It wasn't the same self-assured spouting he'd heard at other times, more like a show for the grand master as if she had to stake her place. He decided not to comment and turned to Glenn.

"By the way, I hear you tried to stop a story going to press about you closing down your competitors in Inverness."

Glenn glared at him. "There won't be a story. She made the whole thing up and the editor's smart enough to know that printing slanderous material isn't good for his business or his health. Did she tell you I fired her last week? She's an incompetent cow."

"Good enough to keep some of your guests happy though," he said, with an oblique look.

"That's her side of the story."

"Did you know someone lobbed a rock at her through her window this afternoon? Didn't see who it was I suppose?"

He withheld mention of the rush to hospital.

"No." There was no emotion in either Glenn's voice or eyes.

Byron cocked an eyebrow, ignoring an impatient noise from Fenella.

"I think you'll be hearing about the bruises though."

With that he turned away and walked without hurry across the lawn towards the driveway. He could hear them talking, tones lowered. As he reached the driveway, Fenella's voice grew louder.

"No," she said sharply. "There's too much at stake. We have to stick with your plan. I'm sorry, but it's all right. I don't really care that you didn't tell me. It doesn't make any difference to us, does it?"

Whatever response Glenn gave was lost in the strengthening wind. Byron glanced behind him as the pair reached the shrubs and she, as if knowing that's what he would do, turned briefly towards him. Her smile was gone in a blink, but it conveyed to him an absolute belief in the course she had chosen and in her own importance.

***

Next morning Ellie sat staring at the gun lying on the kitchen table for a long time. There was no doubt it was hers. It looked innocent on the red damask napkin Olga had wrapped it in. There were no bullets in it to do harm, but there had been – two. A tremor, barely discernible, crept down her spine. She shoved an unwelcome thought aside.

Who had taken the gun? If she went to Jack he'd be in high dudgeon that she'd failed to notify him of its loss simply because she hadn't noticed its disappearance. Nor did she have any clue when it had disappeared. It sounded trite. Off it would go to forensics and eventually they'd tell Jack what they discovered. She wondered if hers were the only fingerprints on it.

Olga had told her and Bob she'd gone out to fetch in the milk two mornings earlier and found a gun in a plastic bag with a note asking her to have it returned to its owner – Ellie Madison. Why she had not left it in the plastic bag with the note instead of taking it out and giving her and Bob a fright by clicking the hammer, she did not know. Olga hadn't said, and she had cleverly avoided answering why she said it had been found near Farley's body. The gun had not been there when she and Byron had been at the awful scene and as far as she knew the police hadn't found a weapon at Maw's. At least, no one had said so.

Glenn loathed Farley, but it had been reciprocated, flowing regularly, a tide of bitter arguments and rebuttals. Glenn was surely capable of devising a dozen ways of having Farley killed and with no obvious connection to him. Was his mind so warped he didn't know how to behave any other way? Or were they always deliberate choices?

A male blackbird flew past the window, twittering. She envied its freedom. Rain was splattering against the panes, though less ferociously than earlier, and its rhythm pleased her, calming taut nerves. She'd always liked the rain.

Glenn had been in her house once or twice when he'd begun investigating the area. He had not got past the kitchen. She hadn't let him sit down and hadn't left him alone. The gun had not been missing that long.

A tucked-away memory caused an unpleasant flutter in her stomach. He had come more recently, back in the spring when the snow was still about. He'd arrived at the back, unannounced and unwelcome. The phone had rung, a call she'd been waiting for, and she'd gone to the study, leaving her cousin on the doorstep. When she got back she found him inside, standing near the sink and looking out the window. Kipp was growling in the doorway, blocking Glenn's exit. Glenn didn't like dogs. She remembered looking at the clock above the fridge thinking she'd left him alone for too long. The call had taken longer than expected and he'd had five minutes or more out of her sight. In that time, he could have gone upstairs, rifled about and found the gun. The box wasn't always locked. Surely she'd have heard the stairs creaking.

She looked at the clock. Just after eleven. Plenty of daylight left.

Half an hour later, dressed for hiking, backpack containing food, flask, and the things always in it – first aid kit, torch, maps, extra socks and thermal polar neck – Ellie, with Kipp in the passenger seat, drove off down the road. She dropped Kipp off at Mary's because she didn't feel he was fit enough yet, and then headed towards the Knobbles. At a property owned by friends and less than a mile from the footpath, Ellie parked and stepped out into the damp wind.

Undaunted by the weather, she began the climb in drizzle. She strode with strong, sure steps along the familiar footpath, her thoughts drifting to Byron. Where was he? He hadn't answered her calls. Once again, she was on her own. She should never have trusted him, but kept him at arm's length as she had almost all other males in her life. So far, Bob was the only one who'd never lied to her, had turned up when he said he would, never minded her mood swings, respected her boundaries, and taken a genuine interest in her welfare without intruding and without wanting anything in return. At least she knew where *he* was – baking or serving at The Mill. Even at this time of the year tourists still came and Sunday was often a very busy day.

The higher peaks were covered in cloud and above her, Maw's Hearth looked much as if it had a woolly hat on and wasn't too pleased about it. All around, as far as she could see in the misty rain, was the richness of colour that was absent on bright sunny days – greens and yellows of grass and bushes and turning leaves, the bronze of ferns. It was a beauty that surpassed the gleam of gold and jewels, a beauty that fed her soul and reminded her over and over again why she stayed in the Highlands. She loved it – in every season, in all kinds of weather. It had its own way of talking, revealing secrets, and showing off. Still, no matter how much she loved it, it could not take away the bouts of loneliness and the fear of being alone for the rest of her life.

Ellie shook her head and sighed. For today, this was enough. If Byron had chosen to go on with his life as if she had been a mere short spring season, then she too would continue on her path. Before long the emerging feelings she had for him would dissipate and any pain attached to the relationship lie deeply buried and forgotten.

Ten minutes later the wind began in earnest, driving heavy rain across the face of Maw's Hearth and shoving the clouds upwards, sideways and downwards. The rain smacked against Ellie's jacket and flew into her face, making it harder to see where she was going. Water was running down the track in places, making it slippery. The only sounds she could hear were the wind and the raindrops hitting her jacket. It was nothing unusual. She had been out in much worse weather. Once, she and Farley had survived a night when late snow had caught them high up in the peaks. They'd found a hollow, the smallest cave he'd ever seen, Farley said, and with enough food and hot tea to keep them going for the night, they'd huddled together and spent most of the time talking. She missed such times. Stumbling, she went down on one knee.

"Pay attention!" she chastised herself.

Farley had taught her never to make familiarity an excuse for not always being alert. Even the most experienced hikers had suffered serious accidents because of inattention. He'd broken his leg once and his fellow hikers had then to get him down which meant, for most of them, abandoning the hike altogether. It was a lesson he'd never forgotten.

Limping slightly, Ellie looked along the path. She was almost at the Knobbles. She remembered the Norfolk woman groaning and moaning about a stone in her shoe and how no one had told her how hard the climb was going to be. On the scale of difficulty, this wasn't much more than dawdling. Ellie chuckled. Rain and mud would have got her hackles up.

The laughter subsided. That was a day she would never forget: a day of contrasts and challenges, of death and of beginnings, of despair and of comfort, of old things passed away and hoping joy would return. She'd lost one of the best friends she'd ever had; no one could replace him. Farley was dedicated, controversial, and often misunderstood. Yet he'd had a knack of making people feel special. Anyone who approached him with a genuine interest in photography would find themselves the centre of his attention. Over the years he'd had a number of students, some of whom had become highly successful.

When she and Farley had gone off on exploratory hikes all over the north of Scotland, the rest of the world ceased to exist. She missed him more than she could express to anyone. Even Byron could never replace him. Nor should he, for he was a unique individual. Her father had often told her every human being was a unique, special creation, but it had been many years before she would even consider there might be some truth in what he'd said. It had been him who'd encouraged her artistic bent despite her mother's determination that she should become a lawyer or a doctor, a proper *professional*. She'd tried. Even went to university and enrolled in a law degree, but at the end of the first year she'd given up. Fury – her mother had become the embodiment of it and hadn't spoken to her for months. By the time her father had returned from an extended sea trip, Ellie was struggling to cope. He'd got himself a shore posting then and spent a lot of time sorting out his family and insisting that Ellie get herself well and then enrol in a course of her choice. Even now, the emotion of those long months and the slow acceptance of her father's care welled up. He'd saved her life and told her God loved her more than any person could, but the rift between her and her mother had never fully healed.

She gazed at the rain-drenched land. Like rain, her father's unconditional love had soaked into her soul and she would always be grateful. His death had shocked her. She missed him still.

Byron's arrival in her life had stirred the cauldron of past events, things she'd never allowed herself to dwell upon. And what of hope? It had come alive, though neither beckoned nor invited to stay, but she had begun to like its presence. Yet now she was beginning to chastise herself for allowing hope to probe those dark places and offer life.

Standing in the rain, its cold drops washing her face, shame rose like the enemy it was and berated her for being such a fool as to tell Byron about Glenn's treatment of her. What if he told someone? What if he told it in such a way that he described himself as having had a narrow escape from a woman with a load of problems that made it impossible to have a future with her? What if…?

"Stop!" she shouted across the hills. "Stop! I don't have to listen to this!"

She went on up, fighting the voice of doom.

"Even if he has finished with me, he's not like that. I *know* he isn't." She pushed the words out, speaking conviction to herself, but adding quietly, "I don't want him to be finished with me."

Where *is* he? We should be doing this together, finding Farley's killer, not two lonely people driven by separate needs and ideas.

Reaching the narrower, steeper section, Ellie stepped up onto a boulder and glanced up. Not much farther. She was looking forward to a hot cuppa. About to take another step, she halted and peered through the rain and wispy cloud. What was that? A shiver ran down her spine. Some of the locals believed that wraiths guarded special places in the Highlands in the form of long dead inhabitants who'd fought in Scottish and Highland battles and skirmishes, warriors who'd given their lives in the pursuit of freedom.

She, a modern woman and familiar with the Highlands, did not dwell on such things and tried not to believe in them, but on a murky day one's beliefs could be challenged. Anyway, the mist loved to play tricks, forming all kinds of shapes and illusions that a fearful mind was well able to imagine things not there. The mist, accompanied by its mate the wind, even if little more than a whisper, could form a ghostly shape into a tormented soul moaning for a lost loved one. Even the toughest Highlanders had tales of scooting back down to a warm hearth and flesh and blood people. Bob, too, sensible and well-travelled, had a story or two of his own.

Whatever she'd seen had gone.

Several minutes later, Ellie was at the Knobbles, its mysterious atmosphere heightened by the shifting cloud bank being blown higher by the noisy wind. She'd shaken off the fear of bumping into an angry Scottish wraith who should, after all, know she was on their side.

However, as she stood looking around, peering through the mist and watching puddles forming on the rocky ground, the horror of seeing Farley's body returned. Folding her arms around her middle, she bent over, groaning.

"Farley, Farley," she cried softly, her tears mingling with the raindrops. "I miss you! Why did you have to go? I want to see you, hear your voice again. the Knobbles and Maw's Hearth won't be a National Park without you. It was your baby. *Farley*! We need you *I need...*"

She jerked upright, tears and words cut off. What was that? It had sounded like a footfall. She looked around, peering, listening – nothing. The cave, keeper of Farley's body, was veiled in a thin cloud, but there was nothing and no one to be seen. Away to the right, where domineering rocks stood guardian over the valley beyond, the mist was thicker and shifting slowly. It revealed neither human nor animal.

Finding shelter from the wind in one of her favourite niches, and often with a view over nearby hills, Ellie unscrewed the flask and poured herself a cup of coffee. Delving into her pack she unwrapped a piece of gingerbread and bit into its rich, full texture. She was in familiar, well-loved territory and she was not going to let anything else disturb her. After all these years she should be used to the vagaries of Highland sounds.

The hot coffee warmed her on the inside, physically and emotionally, and twenty minutes later she was ready for what she had come to do – investigate the place where Farley had been found. Lacking any kind of rationality, the idea had birthed itself in her mind on the drive home from Olga's the afternoon before. It had interrupted her sleep and when morning dawned she'd got up knowing it was something she had to do. Whether it reaped anything of significance was another matter. Yet it seemed as if a memory was lurking, buried deep after the shock of seeing Farley's body.

A piece of orange security tape, caught between two small rocks, fluttered in the wind. Ellie stared at it, remembering the policeman who'd cordoned off the area. She'd wondered then if the nightmare would ever end. There was no answer – yet.

"We have to find out who did this to you, Farley," she said quietly. "The police are taking too long."

She stepped inside the cave and immediately saw bloodstains, Farley's blood, dried and dark, left on the landscape he loved so much.

"You always said you wanted to die somewhere up here. But not this way, Farley, not this way! Even for you it was too unconventional."

Ellie sighed and stepped past where his body had lain. A shiver ran down the bumps of her spine as if on a rollercoaster ride. The police had searched the area and found nothing to suggest the identity of the perpetrator. Even the best could miss things – or they weren't saying.

She got out her torch and crouched down, looking under ledges and rocks, reaching with her hand and exploring crevices that were impossible to see into. Climbing over a rock into the dark recess away from where Farley died, she landed awkwardly, her foot turning on its side. It was a small space, enough for about six people of her size. Towards the back the ceiling was higher and slightly rounded and the walls were decorated with lichen. Bits of moss were sprouting from nooks and crannies.

Ellie shone her torch into each crevice, wanting to find something. Outside she could hear the wind increasing and the low mournful cry it made as it blew between the sentinels over the valley. There was an old tale attached to that too. It was said that women and children had sheltered at the Knobbles one awful day in the late 1290s, during the English King Edward Longshanks' reign when his soldiers had descended on their village and killed many of their menfolk. The women had sat keening long into the night. When they went down to the village the next morning they found most of their husbands, sons, and brothers slaughtered. As the years passed and the women died, it was said that the others would take the body up to the Knobbles and bind it to one of the stones so their mourning would be heard and the bloodshed never forgotten. The sound had been heard ever since.

Down on her hands and knees, Ellie continued her search, although she was beginning to believe that if there had been anything, the police had found it. So far all she'd come into contact with were a few bones from small animals.

It was almost time to go. The weather was getting worse and the journey down would be slippery.

Then, sliding her hand into a narrow gap between the earth floor and the end of the rock wall, her fingers touched something small, flat and metal. Drawing it out, she brushed off specks of dirt from the silver case, but she knew what it was and what she'd find inside.

Her heart was pounding. She sat, crouched and cold, staring at what was in her hand.

Slowly, she stood up. It was a slim business card holder, one she'd seen many times. It belonged to Bob.

Suddenly, she froze.

"Ellie," said a familiar voice, "I thought you'd get around to doing your own snooping. I'm surprised it's taken you so long."

Chapter 23

Ellie twisted round, staring at Jamie standing inside the cave.

"You gave me the fright of my life, Jamie Strathvern! How long have you been there?" She slipped the card holder into her pocket.

"Sorry," he said with a lopsided grin. "Not long. Needed shelter and then heard a noise. I camped in here once or twice."

"Recently?"

"No. It lost its appeal after Farley's body was found. He always encouraged me, even if we did have the odd disagreement."

Ellie swallowed.

"Yes, he was good at that," she said and changed the subject. "Did you see me coming up the track?"

He shook his head. Damp wisps of hair peeking out from his jacket hood were stuck to his forehead. "No. I came across from Ruadh Suidhe. It got too blowy up there for sketching so I decided to head home. Why d'you ask?"

"Oh, myths and legends, shifting mist and odd shapes."

"Well, I'm not a ghost from the past," he said, giving her a peculiar look. "Find anything in there?"

She studied him for a moment, doubting the truth of his words. She wondered how he could have heard the insubstantial noises she had made above the moaning wind and heavy rain.

"A few bones – animals." She shrugged. "The police would've taken anything and everything that was in here. Still, I had to be sure."

"Who knows what they might've missed," he said – too carefully, she thought. "I suppose it gives you some kind of closure, as they say."

"That won't happen until his murderer is found," she said abruptly. "I know the police are doing their very best to sort it out, but sometimes it's us locals who have more knowledge."

Ellie stepped over the rocks and gazed through the curtain of rivulets falling from the top lip of the cave's entrance to the inside of its mouth. Outside, heavy slanting rain was smacking onto the rocky floor and against the huge boulders making up part of the

Knobbles' wall. Water was gushing down it and disappearing over the edge into the valley below.

How could Jamie possibly have heard her? The weather was too noisy. He was lying. So, what was he doing here?

"Want some coffee?" she heard herself asking affably. "You can show me your sketches while we warm up."

"Coffee would be great."

She poured the steaming liquid into one of the cups that screwed on to the flask, studying the earl's son as she held the cup out to him. She poured one for herself.

"Thanks," he said, troubled eyes gazing out at the rain.

"So, what did you draw at Ruadh Suidhe?" She used her best personable tone in an effort to persuade him that she really did want to look at them. "I took a group of wildflower nuts up there in the spring and fortunately the flowers were blooming lustily. Last year they didn't bother much."

She gave a little laugh, but his expression told her he wasn't really listening and that his thoughts were elsewhere. When he spoke he was in another time zone.

"I never knew my grandfather. He died before I was born. I heard Ruadh Suidhe was one of his favourite places. They say he used to take his German friends up there and toast Hitler's victory over Scotland." His lips tightened into a thin line. "He tainted our country and my family with his treachery and his... his... *whoring!*"

Ellie blinked, shocked by the force of his words; she regarded him with renewed interest. This was a side of him she had seen only in outbursts of artistic frustration, when the picture would not come to life as he wished it. What most surprised her was the mention of his grandfather's unpatriotic behaviour and betrayal of family. She'd never heard him mention the man. It was as if the truth was so painful he'd never been able to utter the word 'grandfather' or acknowledge that he even had one. Why it came spurting out now, she had no idea.

"What d'you know about that, Jamie?" she asked, swallowing a mouthful of coffee, its river warming the tributaries of her blood vessels.

"What do *I* know!?" he said loudly, his eyes lively with anger, "I know he was the cause of my grandmother's death. He might as well have killed her himself. He couldn't keep his hands off other women and at least one of them was a *German!* I even found an old article in the newspaper archives in Castlebay hinting at his depravity. I cut it out and burned it so no one else would see it." He put the plastic cup down. "D'you know what it's like to live with that every day of your life? To have people whispering behind your back or reminding you of it to your face."

Ellie shook her head, remembering the skeleton in the attic at number five Tallow Lane. "No, but I can imagine…"

He wasn't listening.

"D'you know why Michael was refused that important position in the Foreign Ministry, a position he was perfect for? Even the prime minister wanted him in it. But no! Because our grandfather was a traitor and our father stupidly keeps going to Germany, Michael was considered too high a risk to be trusted."

"I don't think you should put your father in the same category as your grandfather," Ellie said, frowning.

Jamie's expression darkened. "He's clever. Shows one face to the public, but he's as much a follower of Hitler as his father."

For a few moments Ellie studied him as she tipped out the dregs of her coffee. Then she asked, "What makes you say that?"

"Because he goes to Germany on business. Says it's to do with antiques, but he's never explained exactly what he does. And he hates talking about his childhood, at least the times at Strathvern."

"Well, that's understandable when he grew up with a man who'd betrayed his country. Can't imagine he'd want to talk about it much. You want to forget about things like that, not dredge them up and go through all the pain again," she said snappishly.

"And what would you know about that?" he demanded as a cold blast of air rushed into the cave. More than you do, she thought. "Grieving over someone who's died isn't the same as this!"

Jamie's blue eyes dared her to match his level of shame, but she would not be drawn into a debate about it. He was too young and inexperienced in life for her to take offence over the outburst, meant, she knew, to wound.

"Were you there when Farley was killed, Jamie?" she asked, quietly provoking him, watching as a cat watches a mouse, waiting to see which way he'd move.

Outside as the wind exerted its superiority and declared its position across the hilltops, moaning and howling and attempting to beat all in its way into submission, Jamie did not move.

Ellie screwed the cups back on the flask, aware of him and sensing a battle going on inside that he did not know how to win.

There was about this bright, highly creative man, a lost-ness that reminded her of a fawn she'd once seen separated from its mother. Only when it was reunited with her did its fear subside. She realised then that Jamie, second son of the Earl of Strathvern, was afraid.

Without looking at her, he got up, opened his backpack and gave her a small sketchpad.

"I'll have it back when you've looked at it," he said with almost no intonation as he hoisted the pack onto his back.

The usual 'see you later' smile was absent and without a glance he stepped towards the mouth of the cave.

"You were here, weren't you? You know who killed Farley."

He stopped, the rain rat-a-tatting on his jacket, and slowly turned around. In the gloom of the early afternoon storm, his eyes were dark blue and for a moment fear and anger mixed together. Several drips let go of the rim of his hood, landing on his cheeks like tears and rolling down and off his chin. Beyond him the great boulders of the Knobbles stood grim and silent, waiting, watching. The rain had changed; it was hard and intentional, slanting daggers diving in their thousands onto the lumpy ground. Here and there tussocks of grass, bright in all the grey, were flattened by the onslaught.

"He deserved what happened to him."

Before she could respond, he was striding away, bending into the wind, his feet splashing through puddles.

The words appalled her and she stared at his back. It couldn't be him. It *couldn't!* Farley had been a great encourager of his work even if he hadn't understood it.

A notion came to her that Jamie might know about the room in the tunnel. He was an inquisitive young man and his paintings revealed this in their imaginative and colourful depictions of life as he saw it. What if he knew about his grandfather's other children and believed Farley was the boy in the photos? A scene rolled out in her mind of Farley and Jamie arguing. Had Farley believed he was the earl's half-brother and threatened to expose the whole mess, perhaps claim inheritance rights? What *did* Jamie know – the whole of it or part? And, for that matter, what about his brother Michael?

"Jamie! Wait!"

Whether he heard or not he did not stop and was soon gone through the gap and down the track. A few minutes later Ellie followed, struggling against the insistent wind and glad it was not pushing her from behind and down the slippery track. Jamie was already well ahead, walking too quickly for the conditions. She lost sight of him altogether five minutes later when she slipped and landed amongst the heather.

She was not in the mood to sit and contemplate the beauty, even in the rain, of such an afternoon: the depth of colour in the greens and yellows against dark grey clouds, the leaves washed clean and diamond raindrops clinging to their edges. Briefly, she bemoaned the rarity of the Scots pine, heavily replaced by the Sitka spruce across most of the country. Once, forests of birch, oak, ash, elm, willow and alder as well at the Scots pine had adorned Scotland like a glorious tapestry, but now less than one percent of that ancient beauty remained.

Pushing herself off the heather and giving the fading pink cushion a quick fluffing up, Ellie continued her journey back to her vehicle.

If Jamie had not killed Farley, he had witnessed it – of that she was convinced. Was family honour greater than allowing a man to live because he had discovered a dark truth about another? Even if Farley did believe his true parents were aristocrats, she doubted he would ever have spoken of it to anyone. *That* secret, she thought, would have been safe with him. He could be unpredictable, but he was intensely private and protective about family matters. Yet, a tiny doubt nibbled away at such conviction.

Whether Jamie had pulled the trigger or stood by and done nothing to stop the perpetrator committing the crime, a measure of guilt was his portion. He had drunk of a cup that would poison his life, but she hoped it would not destroy the creativity and vibrancy of a young man whose future was full of promise. Deep sadness grew in her heart. That one man's treachery continued infecting and impacting lives unrelentingly decades later was anathema to her. This, too, would be Glenn's legacy.

By the time she arrived back in Kilcomb the weather had closed in, clouds hanging over the village like a grey shroud and heavy rain causing streams to rush along gutters. An inadequate drainage system blocked up and overflowed forcing great puddles to form and ooze over the roads. Ellie noticed with some glee that Carrie Michael was outside the post office, bedraggled in a light coat, no hat, and sodden shoes, trying to sweep the water away before it invaded her premises. No doubt it would affect her 'puir health' and the village hear all about it.

Parking near the grocer's, Ellie ran inside and found Mary stacking tins of soup on a shelf.

"Thank goodness you're back," her friend said, looking relieved. "I was beginning to think..."

"Think what, Mary? I only went hiking," she responded, lifting her brows, irked by the fatalistic outlook.

The doorbell jangled and several people came in chatting and laughing. Tourists, Ellie supposed. She did not look round.

Mary's focus flicked away momentarily beyond Ellie and she supposed the vigilant eye of the shopkeeper had noticed the lipsticks were uncoordinated or the customers untidying the shelves. It irritated her.

"I was beginning to think," Mary said, putting the can she had in her hand on the shelf, "you'd be late for tea."

"What?" Ellie frowned. This was nonsensical. Mary had not invited her to tea and she didn't have time for banal chatter. "It's only quarter to five. I just dropped in to see if I could borrow your mobile. I'll bring it back tomorrow."

Mary was staring at her without expression, unmoving. Slowly, Ellie understood. There was someone in the shop Mary did not want privy to their conversation.

"Hello, Ellie. Good to see you've recovered from your ordeal," Michael said above the noisy group who were disappearing down the aisles. "I can lend you a mobile if Mrs Nevin's isn't available. I've a spare one in the car."

"She doesn't need it. She can have mine," Mary said in the snappish tone she reserved for the Strathvern family, although she made an exception for the countess who was not, as she said, of *that* blood.

"Well, the offer's there." He gave a half smile, accompanied by an impatient hand motion as if he'd had enough of such feelings.

Mary ignored it and went off to fetch the phone. When she returned, a couple of people were standing at the counter and, after giving Ellie the phone and with a quick glance at Michael, she went to serve them.

"I saw your friend Byron Oakes yesterday afternoon," he said as Ellie turned to leave.

"Where?"

The word shot out like a bullet as she about-faced. Michael's eyebrows tweaked upwards, but he did not comment.

"Inverness. He came into the hotel where Catherine and I were having lunch. The only blight on the scene was Glenn Thorley and Fenella Orman on the other side of the room."

Involuntarily, Ellie shuddered. In Michael's eyes she saw a look of guarded surprise and searching.

"What was Byron doing there?"

"Having lunch." He regarded her quizzically. "What's the matter, Ellie? Didn't you know where he was?"

The question touched a raw nerve. "No."

She walked away and went out the door before he could probe any deeper. No doubt half the customers and Mary had heard. A lovers' tiff, they'd think. It was unlikely she and Byron would ever be that.

"Ellie, wait!"

It was Michael, limping along the pavement towards her and pulling his jacket hood over his head. She stopped, waiting for him.

"Look, I'm sorry. I shouldn't have brought that up in the shop. It was inappropriate." His face was pinched against the driving rain, remorse in his eyes.

Ellie swallowed and nodded her acceptance of his apology. "The truth is I haven't seen him or spoken to him since we were attacked. I don't have a mobile and when I finally got home and rang he hung up on me – twice! I've been a fool, Michael."

"No, I don't think you have. A fool doesn't try and escape from underneath a castle and succeed. That takes courage." He took her arm and drew her underneath the porch outside the library, a shelter from the rain. "But what's this about being attacked? Who attacked you?"

"I don't know. We were stopped on the side of the road talking when a bullet came through the windscreen. Someone wrenched open my door, grabbed me from behind and shoved a cloth over my face. The next thing I remember is waking up in a Strathvern cellar, although it was a few minutes before I found out *whose* cellar I was in. An old ledger from 1894," she said, in response to the question in his eyes.

"This is appalling, Ellie! Why on earth would anyone want to attack you and then deposit you in our cellars?" He stared at her and she could almost see him delving into his mind, searching. "They've been locked for years and no one's allowed down there

411

except the family and John. But that's rare because we store our wine closer to the kitchen now and don't need to traipse all the way along the tunnel."

Part of her wanted to quip what a waste of good wine, but she restrained herself. What she was tempted to tell him was of Bran's involvement in her abduction and her belief that Glenn had arranged it to make it look as if it had been the Strathvern family's doing. Another wedge between the region's inhabitants and the tainted pro-Nazi aristocrats who no longer deserved the privileges they had and should be moved out.

Instead, she said, "There's some interesting stuff there – and not just the wine. You should have a look."

"One day, maybe. How did you get out?"

"Through the door near your mother's potting sheds. It was a bit overgrown."

He frowned, nodding. "Strange. I'd almost forgotten it was there. No idea when it was last opened. Years probably. I expect there's a key somewhere."

"Well, it wasn't locked when I got back there."

"*Back* there?" The frown intensified. "Care to explain?"

Ellie sighed, studying him closely. This wasn't a conversation she had ever imagined having with him.

"I broke the lock on the gate that leads into the tunnels. I found a gun in the cellar. In fact, there's a whole crate of them – with bullets," she said, more emphatically that she meant to. "I don't know much about guns, but I'd say they were old. Luckily for me the one I picked still worked."

"You shot the lock?"

He sounded and looked even more astonished than before.

"Of course! I wasn't going to wait until whoever dumped me in the cellar came back. I don't like the dark much, but..." She stopped, not wanting to mention his father, and went on quickly as he opened his mouth. "I had a little torch in my pocket, though the battery wasn't much good. Anyway, when I smelled water I guessed the tunnel went to the loch and I hoped it was a way out."

"That gate's padlocked too."

"So I discovered, but..."

He wasn't listening. Apart from the wind jostling the cloth of his jacket, Michael was very still. His eyes were fixed on something behind her, intense and worried. The silence between them lingered; he was lost in another world.

412

"Are you afraid I might've uncovered family secrets, Michael? That's the stuff of stories, isn't it? You know, hidden caches, ancient diaries, locked rooms." Half jesting, half probing she waited for his response.

Slowly, his gaze settled upon her again.

"Room? What room? There're only storerooms down there." Without waiting for clarification, he said hesitantly, swallowing, "There was blood, blood near the end of the tunnel. Was it yours?"

She shook her head.

"Then whose?"

Ellie did not want to tell him, distress him further.

"Tell me!" he said, demanding and yet pleading.

The sudden loudness caught her unawares and she jumped.

"Glenn Thorley's. I shot him, but didn't do much damage. Pity."

"Thorley. I should've guessed." Michael shoved his hands in his pockets and looked at her, appraising her. "He wanted it to look as if we'd kidnapped you. I bet he'd have somehow got the story into the papers. Anything to discredit us and get his hands on our lands. I wish Byron had killed him."

"Care to explain that?"

Michael stared at her for a moment. The question verged on abruptness, but it seemed Byron had plenty of time for everyone else, but couldn't – or wouldn't – answer her calls.

"Thorley showed up at Strathvern a day or so ago," Michael said, his expression impenitent. "I'd had enough of his bullying and boorish, arrogant behaviour. He was going on about how he'd turn us out of Strathvern. He didn't like it when I stood up to him. I'm ashamed to admit I'm a bit of a coward normally. When I told him I knew about his penchant for younger women and wondered if his wife knew, he was really angry."

A chilling fear clutched Ellie's heart and she saw by Michael's expression that he thought he had shocked her. He hadn't. Fear of Glenn's retaliation rose, tormenting and mocking, and for a second she closed her eyes.

"I'm sorry. I didn't mean to…"

"What happened then?" she said, interrupting, pushing the words out with effort and cutting off where her mind would have her go.

"Ellie, has he… do you know…?" The emotion in his voice stirred a deep longing in her to admit her pain, but she kept silent

413

and he continued. "I told police in Inverness weeks ago that his hotel caters to tourists and possibly men looking for special attention. I've no proof, but they're investigating. That's why I was in Inverness today, helping with a certain situation."

Kindness, as soft as a perfect summer's evening, glimmered in his eyes, and Ellie found herself moved and strangely strengthened by his vulnerability and tenderness. If only someone like him had found his way into her young adult life.

"I hope Catherine knows how blessed she is," she said quietly.

"I think it's rather the other way around. She's very special."

The wind blew the rain in under the porch and they stepped closer to the wall. The library door opened and two elderly women came out, umbrellas in hand. They nodded to Michael and Ellie and commented on the 'bit o' rain'. They watched as they walked determinedly down the path, arm in arm, chuckling over their wayward umbrellas.

"What happened, Michael?" she asked again.

"Thorley attacked me. Came at me with a lump of wood and would've smashed my brains in if Byron hadn't appeared. I have to say, he was magnificent. Didn't miss a beat. Eventually Thorley got in his car and drove off."

Across the road, Ellie saw Catherine waving from inside the comfort of their car. She waved back. Michael turned his head, smiled and blew her a kiss. Ellie stifled a jealous sigh.

"I'd better go. It's my mother's birthday and we're having a party for her tonight. Catherine's organised almost everything. Why don't you come? It might take your mind off things a bit. You'd be very welcome."

"Thanks, Michael, but I'm not up to parties just yet."

"Well, you're a very courageous woman. You found your way in the dark from the loch and…"

Squeezing his eyes closed, he took a deep breath and then looked at her, waiting.

Ellie stared at him. "It was you," she said almost breathlessly. "You were in the tunnel behind me."

He gave a slow nod as if reluctant to acknowledge her revelation. "Thought I'd given myself away a few minutes ago."

"I missed it."

There was a moment's quiet between them and Ellie watched Strathvern's heir gathering his words together as he gazed out at the insistent rain.

414

"I was in the library reading and had gone to the kitchen to make cocoa. I'd just turned out the light and was about to step into the passage when I saw my father coming from the entrance to the cellars. He hasn't been down there in years as far as I know. I thought it was odd, but I was tired, so I went on up to bed."

"Why didn't you ask him what he'd been doing?"

Michael gave a half laugh. "It's not what we do. My father isn't one to be questioned about such things. I dozed off, but woke up not much later and heard voices in the garden, so I looked out the window and saw someone on the lawn near the stand of oak trees. The dogs were outside barking which was strange because they're always in at night. I got dressed and went outside, but all I saw was Bran and the dogs. I supposed they were after poachers. It was then I decided to have a look in the cellars. I was curious about my father being down there. When I reached the cave tunnel, I heard someone coming and turned off the torch."

"Didn't you see it was me? I could've done with help."

"I'm sorry, Ellie. I was afraid it was Thorley or some other thug bent on violence. I know it was cowardly, but I didn't want another beating. I have little of the fighting blood of my ancestors in my veins."

She persisted. "I heard a sigh."

The expression on his face remained unchanged. "I thought it was you at first, but it was so dark. I didn't say anything in case it wasn't. Look, I really have to go. Think about coming tonight. We'd love to see you there."

He turned into the wind and rain before she could respond. Had he lied? She had no idea. One thing was certain, if Farley was the earl's half-brother she would not let time bury it under a mound of history and rumour so that it became indistinguishable from fiction. Maybe more recent shame had come to the Strathvern household.

Her hand tightened over Bob's card holder. Who had put it in the cave?

***

Byron's mobile phone rang as he was wondering how far off track he'd got himself regarding Farley Orman. Nothing was bleeping on the Glenn Thorley radar to indicate he was involved. Nor could he prove he'd hurled the rock at Jenny Browne. He pulled off the road and answered the phone.

"Colin here, Byron. I've done some rummaging around for you. Be careful where you're going with this. I almost got my fingers singed."

"Then be more careful. You're supposed to be an expert in unobtrusive snooping. You won't be much good if you're put out to pasture," Byron said, only half joking. "What've you found out?"

"Okay, don't get snappy. Colonel Hugh Lawford was one of those model soldiers – exceptional at his work, spic and span in appearance, a stickler for rules and regs without the brutality, and happily married. Squeaky clean, you could say. Not at all like you, old boy," Colin added chirpily. "Still, *looking* like a spit-polished shoe every day doesn't mean you are one."

Byron's inner antenna went up. "And?"

"Well, it's possible *your* Colonel Lawford is someone else."

"An agent for the German cause." The half-murmured words were more for him than Colin, the result of a stirring during the morning's conversation with Hugh.

"Um, not exactly. More your German type."

Byron stared at the outline of hills huddled together above a loch and dappled by the encroaching twilight. The cuff links. Then an earlier memory of his first meeting with the Lawfords; the way they'd looked at one another when they'd said Marian had never turned up after the war, followed by Hugh's declaration that her son had never got over the loss. Byron had forgotten about it until now. A son – what had happened to him?

"Byron?"

"Still here. Find out more about Hugh Lawford of Inverness, Colin."

"Not sure I'll get any closer than that. I'm an historian not a researcher for the Ministry of Defence. They don't like other people poking about in their business."

"Try. It's important. Find out if he ever had a son."

"What?"

"You heard. Hugh Lawford told me that Marian MacAdam's son never got over the loss of his mother. He might still be in the area."

"You don't pay me enough for this. I could end up in prison. Or worse – deported to some deserted island."

"I don't pay you at all. Think of it as a service to Great Britain. And don't be slow."

"No, master. By the way, another little snippet I discovered. Farley Orman had a lot of shares – quite a few in John Thorley's hotel company. There's one near Inverness. It's…"

"The Crossed Swords."

"Keeping ahead of you is like trying to outrun a cheetah. But – did you know he was using income from his shares to invest in another project?"

Byron did not like the sound of this. "Maw's Hearth."

"Wrong this time. Strathvern Castle."

"What! Are you sure?"

"Absolutely. It's amazing how much information a person will give you if you woo them with a posh dinner, champagne, and chocolates."

"And the rest."

"Not at all. She thought I was a high-flying magazine publisher and was interested in taking her on as a full-time investigative writer. Her passion? Unearthing the misdeeds of corporations. She said she'd worked for Mayfair Hotels as an accountant."

Byron's heart thumped. "What's her name?"

"Jenny Browne. She's a freelance writer based in London, but doing some work in Scotland."

"She's got a flat in Inverness. I took her to hospital yesterday afternoon. Someone threw a rock through her window. And that's after Glenn Thorley roughed her up."

"You must be kidding! Are you sure it's the same person?"

"Yes, and thanks for the info. As to her profession, that's debatable. She's trouble."

"Want me to dig deeper with this?"

"The colonel's more pressing. Thorley can wait. And be careful."

"Singed, I said, not burned. I'll see what I can do."

In between the clouds the remnants of a rich tapestry of red, lilac and burnt orange were deepening into night and for several minutes Byron watched the display disappear. Was there a God behind it all, revelling in His masterly touch and in delighting the creatures He'd made? Or was it just matter and gases doing what they'd done since some called The Big Bang, and he, Byron Oakes, a product of a long line of evolving creatures admiring another element of nature? He wasn't sure he liked the latter, a product of

417

a blob with no emotions or intelligence. A creative and all-knowing God was far preferable and, if he was honest, more credible. Well, whichever had produced this beauty, the masterpiece was priceless.

Drawing himself out of introspection, Byron drove off down the road towards Kilcomb, now only five miles away. Ellie had not answered his calls to her home number. Just out of Inverness, he'd tried Castlebay Hospital and Mary Nevin. No luck at either.

His phone rang again and he pulled off the road. It was Mary.

"Mary! Any news?"

"Aye. Ellie was in here a little while ago to borrow my mobile. She needs to get one."

"I know. She's not answering her home phone. D'you know where she is?"

"Not a clue. She'd been up to the Knobbles, but she didn't say why. She left Kipp here. Lord Strathvern's son Michael came in to the shop and she left wi' him. I hope she hasn't been blethering on to him."

Byron ignored the comment about Michael, took down the mobile number and thanked her for ringing.

As he dialled the number he frowned. Why had Ellie gone to the Knobbles in this weather? What was she trying to prove? That she didn't need him? He'd got too close and was now ostracized?

The phone rang several times before Mary's voice asked him to leave a message. He ended the call and stared moodily out the windscreen. If Ellie was in trouble he had no way of helping her. What on earth had possessed his heart to fall for such a stubborn and independent woman?

"Damn! This isn't getting me anywhere. You're on your own, Ellie. I hope you know what you're doing."

In spite of his frustration he stopped by Ellie's house. There was no Land Rover parked in the driveway and no sign anyone was home. He banged on the door several times, but there was no answer.

"Well, that's it. I've tried," he muttered.

Driving away, feeling he was leaving something of himself behind, an unwelcome fear seeped into his heart. Could she have discovered the identity of Farley's killer and gone off in mad pursuit? The thought made his blood run cold. Without really knowing why, he rang Bob's mobile. Half expecting to get a recording he was ready to hang up when the phone was answered.

418

"Bob Caraway."

"It's Byron. I thought you'd be busy cooking."

"Not tonight. I quit."

"What?"

"You heard. Thorley can find another chef. I was a fool to get involved with him. I'm on my way back to Kilcomb."

"What d'you mean 'get involved'?" Byron asked, turning into Tallow Lane.

"Friends who can influence. Friends who agreed to help put Maw's Hearth on the map, as they put it. For a price."

"You might be the one paying the price. Ellie will think you've betrayed her. Why on earth did you do it?"

"I have betrayed her," Bob snapped. "More than you know. I'm not proud of it, but it's done. I only hope I can undo it."

Alarm stirred deep inside Byron. "Care to elaborate?"

"Not on the phone. Where are you?"

"Kilcomb, looking at my charred cottage."

"This isn't a time for jokes, Byron. D'you know the pub at Glen Ayr just off the main road?"

"I've seen it. And it isn't a joke. Someone set fire to the cottage."

Not a sound came along the line for several seconds.

"We need to talk," Bob said in a matter-of-fact tone. "I think I know who it was."

"I'll be there in twenty minutes. What else d'you know?"

"Just get yourself there. No saving the world on the way."

He hung up and Byron headed back along the main road to Inverness.

The night curtains were almost completely drawn over the day as Byron neared Glen Ayr. Beyond the shadowy buildings of the village, vague shapes of hills loomed like protective giants and Byron had a vague understanding about why people came to believe in myths.

He almost missed the turn off the main road as a bicyclist suddenly shot across in front of him, the flickering dull yellow light on the handlebars barely discernible. The cyclist waved his fist, wobbling dangerously into the other lane before disappearing out of sight as a car from the other direction whipped around the corner.

Byron drove slowly along a narrow road between cottages for a couple of minutes before coming to the pub. There were a number of vehicles parked outside it; across the road in a small car park he found a spot. A fresh wind was stirring, bringing the smell of salt water and the sound of lapping of waves. The village was snuggled around the edge of an inlet. Near a lamp post he saw Bob's car.

From across the road music seeped out from the pub and inside it was packed and noisy. A middle-aged trio was whipping up a jig, accompanied by hand-clapping patrons and encouraging shouts of enjoyment. Another reason he loved Scotland – its music.

He almost forgot why he was there until he saw Bob waving from a corner of the room, mobile phone to his ear. Byron got himself a drink and joined the baker who was well down his glass of beer.

"You found the place, then," Bob said, putting the phone on the table. "I hope you don't mind the noise. I'm addicted to Highland music and this is one of the best places for it."

"It's great. I like it," Byron said, sipping his drink and glancing around. "How's your head?"

"Fine. Nothing to worry about. Still, two whacks on the head isn't to be recommended."

"Glad you're okay," he said, still doubtful of the morning's circumstances. He changed the subject. "At least we can talk without being overheard."

Bob nodded, but a shadow cast itself over his expression as if he was having second thoughts about their meeting, but in this Byron soon discovered he was mistaken.

"So, tell me about your involvement with Thorley," he said.

A tall man got up and spoke with the musicians and for a few minutes laughter and boisterous conversations filled the space.

"I haven't told anyone about all this. Couldn't. But you're an outsider and for some strange reason I want to tell you," Bob said, giving someone a wave. "Thorley threatened to ruin me. Said all I had to do was help him persuade the locals that his hotels would be the best thing that had ever happened to the area. By locals he meant council members and select businessmen." Bob sighed. "I refused. Next thing I know he's written to the health authorities and I had to prove that I was a fit individual to run healthy and legal bakeries. *I've* baked for royalty. The gall of the man! I should've stood my ground with him. If I'd known then he was Ellie's cousin, I'd have fought him even if it cost me everything."

Byron regarded him. "I'm sorry you found out from him, Bob. I don't know why Ellie told me, but she did and I can't change that."

"I'm not a fool, Byron. She loves you in a way she's never loved me. I've only got so close. There was always a barrier. She's a faithful and caring friend, but it's as if she doesn't know how to let people in. I've often wondered about her past."

Byron studied him. "I don't think you meant to betray her, Bob."

"It's not the word I thought of, but I knew I'd lose her friendship if she ever found out. Thorley threatened to tell her a number of times. Anyway, I went to a couple of men I know on the local council. Crooked as a dog's hind leg the pair of them, but I thought I could do it in a way that'd hurt Thorley more than Ellie. I've heard his father's a better man, but he seems to let his son get on with it. I don't understand that."

"I doubt he knows half of what Glenn gets up to. What did these contacts of yours do? For a price I'm guessing."

Bob nodded. "They sold Thorley's ideas for an environmentally-sound hotel and convinced the council that big money would come into the region without damaging or detracting from the Highland beauty." He looked at Byron. "Believe that? No, neither do I – not now. To be honest I thought it was possible. The plans looked good, but a few weeks ago I found out that Thorley's intentions were to incorporate only the minimum requirements of the law. Maw's Hearth, if it goes ahead, will be made to suit him, not the other way around."

"So, where's the council with this?"

"Slow, as usual, but the pressure is on for economic reasons. People with more weight to toss about have got in on it. That's the problem. I've started something I don't know how to stop. Thorley's a powerful and persuasive man. He's got half the best of the catering trade from Edinburgh to Inverness doing his bidding."

"Did Farley know about this?"

Bob shrugged. "I don't know. Possibly."

The music started up, a melody and tempo the whole pub seemed to know, as a beautiful, slender middle-aged lady with dark hair and lively eyes got up to dance with the man who'd spoken with the musicians.

Bob suddenly began clapping in time to the beat and let out a hoot of approval as the pair performed to the rowdy delight of the crowd.

"They used to be professionals," Bob shouted. "Were the darlings of Scottish dancing for years. Live near here now."

They danced as if one, so in tune to one another's moves that Byron envied them. For a few minutes he watched, riveted, and enjoying the engagement of the pub's patrons with the music and dancers.

Then a discordant note struck at his pleasure. Across the room, partly in the shadows, partly obscured by other people, Byron thought he saw a familiar face watching them. He glanced at Bob, but he hadn't noticed. When he looked back the man was gone. A vague unease settled upon him.

The dancers finished to an uproar of applause and a standing ovation. Community, Byron thought suddenly, that's what it's about – belonging somewhere with people you know.

When he turned to Bob, he found the man regarding him.

"I'd never have guessed you enjoyed this sort of music. Maybe there's Scottish blood in you somewhere."

"Maybe."

"There's… something else you should know," Bob said, sounding reluctant. "It's about Olga Erskine."

Byron took a mouthful of beer, observing his companion over the rim of the glass.

"How is she?"

"Mostly recovered." He stared into the bottom of his empty glass then looked up. "The day you and Ellie visited her in hospital she called me and asked me to bring her favourite cake. I don't usually do deliveries to hospitals, but she insisted I come. She said she knows what happened to my mother's eldest sister, Marian. Well, half-sister, I think. I don't know much about that side of the family. No one ever talks about them. And I don't know if I believe Olga."

Byron leaned forward. "What did she say?"

"That Marian's alive and well in Germany, married a Nazi who became a very rich industrialist and raised neo-Nazi children. She and Marian apparently met during the war and stayed in touch. Says she's been back to Kilcomb quite a few times, but no one's ever recognised her. Seems a bit odd."

"Unless there was something here she wanted."

"Like what?"

"Evidence about what she'd been up to in the war and terrified somebody would find out."

A long pause, as if Bob needed to thoroughly digest what he was thinking before he spoke. When he did the words were spoken quietly, deliberately. "Somebody like Farley."

"Maybe. He'd been digging around trying to find out stuff from the war for quite a while I gather."

Bob sat upright. "How d'you know that?"

Byron told him about Farley's approach to the MOD and how he, Byron, had been asked to quietly look into the snippets the photographer had given them. He didn't mention Colin.

Shifting in his seat, Bob frowned and gave Byron a long, appraising look. "I don't think I want to know about it. Farley could be very secretive when it suited him. A simple question or remark sometimes shut him down for days. Olga thinks he knew where his wife went. He certainly became less reliable after she disappeared."

"Grief could do that."

"True. I don't think he did know. He was devastated. Anyway, to get back to Olga, I went to see Aunt Ruth after visiting her."

Inside Byron there was a stirring, like the faint whisper of a leaf lifting on a gentle breeze.

"Find out anything useful?" Byron asked, watching him.

"Not really. Didn't get much of a chance. Hugh was there. He was in quite a bit of pain and not in a good mood. Told me my Aunt Marian was a slut of the lowest kind who'd preyed on the vulnerability of wartime soldiers and others further up the pecking order. Said she was the most untrustworthy person he'd ever met in his life. Actually, I've never seen him so worked up." His brow wrinkled. "He asked if you'd sent me to try and wheedle more information out of him. Any idea what he meant?"

"Our last meeting didn't go too well. Has he ever mentioned German friends?"

"Hugh? He hates them. Aunt Ruth told me once that when Marian took up with a German soldier and began..." He stopped and stared at Byron. "You think Olga Erskine is Aunt Ruth's sister."

"I don't know. There are too many inconsistencies." The conversation had turned. He'd have to approach the subject of Hugh later. "Did your aunt say anything?"

"Only that she agreed with Hugh and *if* Marian was still alive she'd never be welcome in their house. She's convinced hers was the body in the woods and killed by her German lover. Yes," he said, as Byron opened his mouth, "most of the family know that, but not much else."

"If Marian was as headstrong as Hugh and Ruth say, faking her own disappearance at the end of the war and then reappearing as someone completely different with a husband and an invented life history, wouldn't have been difficult for her," Byron said, thinking then about the photos Ross had shown him of the young woman. But was it Olga?

"Aunt Ruth walked out to the car with me and said there were things about the war she wanted to forget, mostly did. Her sister was one of them. I asked if it was possible Marian was still alive and living in the area. She said, 'If she is, I'd kill her myself. She brought us nothing but shame and almost ruined Hugh's life and career. She was a traitor in *every* sense of the word. I'd *know* if my sister was alive, nephew, and she isn't!' Then she turned and walked away. That's not like her."

"A traitor in the family wouldn't be much fun," Byron said as his phone rang. "And Hugh may not be as anti-German as you think."

Bob frowned. "Not possible. I told you, he hates Germans."

"Byron Oakes," he said, speaking into the mouthpiece. Then he fell silent, listening.

Bob got up from the table, picked up the glasses and indicated he was going to fetch more drinks.

"Are you sure?" Byron said, sitting upright as Bob wandered off to the bar.

"No doubt about it, old son," Colin responded with his usual chirpiness. "My contact got interested to the point of obsession and found this snippet buried in a dusty box a week ago. She had to do some more research and came around just after I phoned you earlier. She left five minutes ago."

"I think Farley unearthed more than anyone realised."

"Maybe. Be careful. I don't want my next sight of you to be in a wooden box."

"And I don't want anyone else to die because of a World War Two spy! Keep in touch and keep quiet about this."

"Don't insult me, Byron."

"I'm not. But the man getting my next drink is Ruth Lawford's nephew."

For a second there was silence. "Be careful what you say."

Byron was tempted to use the words his friend had, but refrained. They had, he knew, been spoken out of concern.

As he slipped the phone back in his pocket, he turned around and looked towards the bar, then scanned the room, not all of which he could see as it was L-shaped.

Byron got up and walked between the tables to the other side and then into a side room.

"Lookin' for the gents?" asked an elderly man at the table Byron was passing.

"Uh, yes," he said.

"Over there, behind the partition."

"Thanks."

He gave the man a nod and headed towards it. There was no one in the lavatory.

At the bar he asked the barman if his companion had ordered another round of drinks. He hadn't. He knew Bob and said he'd seen him go out the door to the car park. Byron thanked him, collected his jacket and walked out into the cold evening air.

Bob's car was still parked where Byron had seen it an hour earlier. There was no sign of Bob.

Chapter 24

"I thought you were coming over here," Michael said behind her, "but you won't get far without a key."

Ellie's heart thumped at the unexpected sound of his voice. No one had been in the entrance hall when she'd left the ballroom. She turned towards him, annoyed with herself that she hadn't heard him approach – they were far enough from the cacophony of laughter, conversation and the music played by a small orchestra.

"Why did you think that?"

"Because it's the kind of thing you do – out of the ordinary, unexpected. You've always struck me as a woman who pursues what she wants, knows what she wants, and doesn't always think about whether it's dangerous or untimely. Am I right?" he asked, glancing behind him as he opened the door.

"Partly. You left out unwise and foolhardy. Did you see me leave the ballroom?"

"Of course. I was expecting you would. Come," he said and stepped through the door, flicking the light switch on. "You may as well return what I imagine you've got in your bag. I promise I won't tell my father."

Ellie stared at his back; she did not move. Michael went down the steps, turning only when he was at the bottom. Still she hesitated and half turned, uncertain. To her dismay Ross was standing near the kitchen door, partly in shadow, the light cast upon his features defining them in a way that almost shocked her. Perhaps it was a trick of the light. However, in those moments before he shifted, he could almost have been another man. He held her gaze; there was stillness between them. Then, without a word, he went into the kitchen.

"The lights are on, Ellie. There's no need to be afraid this time," said Michael. "Close the door behind you."

He might not have seen his father, but she had an uncomfortable feeling Ross knew his son was in the cellars. How much had he heard of their conversation? Hesitating, she stood with her hand on the door knob; she did not want to shut the door, enclosing her in the gloom and in the past. This was madness.

"Come on, Ellie. It really is safe."

"Who for? Me or you?"

"Both of us," he said, sounding hurt that she mistrusted him. "Anyway, we should hurry before anyone notices we're missing."

She knew she had to go and, shutting the door behind her, went quickly down the steps. They didn't talk for several minutes and Ellie's misgivings grew.

"What is it you think I've got in my bag, Michael?" she asked, her voice echoing quietly, an accompaniment to the tap of their shoes.

"I don't know *exactly*, except that it's from the secret room that doesn't exist," he said without looking at her as they turned into the tunnel leading to the loch. The smell of the water was not so strong tonight. "My father has no idea I know about it. He thinks he's the only one in our family who does, but he's wrong."

"Does... Jamie know?" she asked, hesitating before mentioning his name.

"Yes."

"How long ago did he find out?"

"In the spring. He didn't say how, but it terrified him. I don't think he went in."

"I think he did."

Michael stopped and stared at her. "And how do you know that?"

"Because he was up on Maw's Hearth today, very angry and very unhappy." She watched suspicion creep into his expression. "He had a lot to say about your grandfather and his German spy mistress."

"There's no proof of that." His response was clipped.

"Then *you* haven't been in there. She even had two children by him!"

He stared at her. "You're lying."

"No, I'm not. The proof is in that room and in these," she said, pulling the stolen documents out of her handbag.

He didn't answer nor did he look at what she held in her hand. He strode ahead, leaving her to follow, but his shoulders were not as square as usual. Ellie sighed and unexpectedly felt a tinge of sadness for him. He was heir to a beautiful estate and a long, unbroken lineage, occupiers of the castle for hundreds of years. Yet, he carried a burden of dishonour.

427

The lights were dimmer than in the main tunnel and the fears of that recent night rushed in to claim territory. She did not want to go any farther with Michael. She should never have come with him. If Farley really had been the earl's half-brother, might Michael not have considered him a threat or a troublemaker he'd rather not have around? She would have if she'd been the heiress.

"You take the papers and put them back," she said, reaching into her bag.

"No."

"It won't take you a minute. We've been gone too long already."

"What're you afraid of, Ellie? That I might lock you in? You got out before."

"It wasn't locked then."

"My father always keeps it locked."

"Well, it wasn't then. Anyway, how d'you know that if you've only just found out it exists?"

"Jamie told me."

Ellie restrained a snappish response about not being surprised and said without much emotion, "He knows something about Farley's death."

"Don't be ridiculous."

"I'm not. How many keys are there?" she asked, deliberate in her words. "Your father's not the sort to strew them around the castle. Not the kind of room he'd want anyone seeing."

"Perhaps that's half the trouble. We should've opened up the cellars and tunnels years ago for the tourists. The money would've been useful."

"You can't seriously think of displaying *everything* in that room to the public!"

"Yes – I do."

"Then you haven't had a good look. Some of it's…"

"Some of it's what?"

"Not the sort of thing I'd want displayed for everyone to see if it was my family." She changed her mind about him mid-stream. If he'd ever been in the room he'd know there was top secret stuff in there and, perhaps more painful, intimate letters belonging to his grandfather.

He didn't answer. However, when they reached the cupboards and shelves lining the wall Ellie knew she was right. Michael walked straight past the ones covering his grandfather's room. His steps slowed when he reached the last one.

"You've gone too far, Michael," she said softly.

He turned around without hurry, but did not immediately begin walking towards her.

"Have I?" he said, sounding surprised. "I don't make a habit of coming down here."

"Not even to decide what the public should see and what they shouldn't?"

"My father's likely to be around for many years yet. He'd never agree – at least, not yet."

Ellie studied him; his eyes kept darting away from her. This was not like him. "You've never been in there, have you?"

Michael shook his head. "I came down with Jamie once, but when I saw the bloody great Nazi flag hanging on the wall, I walked away. Haven't been back since."

"But you knew I'd been in there."

"Yes. What I said yesterday was true, but I saw you go in and waited until you came out. I hoped... I hoped you had more courage than I did and had found something that could bring an end to all the guessing and secrecy. You checked your pocket when you came out so I knew you had taken things. I was glad."

"That was the sigh I heard later."

Michael nodded. "Does Byron know what you've got?"

"No."

"Anyone else?"

Ellie did not answer. Alone with Michael in Strathvern's depths made her feel uncomfortable, nor, in this dark place, did she completely trust him.

"Come on, let's get it over with," she said, shivering. A cold breeze travelled along the passage from the loch, reminding her far too clearly for her liking of the situation she'd been in a few days earlier. "I don't like being down here."

He opened his mouth and then closed it without saying anything. From his pocket he took a key. A few minutes later they were standing in front of the door. It was locked. She said nothing as he opened the door.

Michael flicked on the light and Ellie stared in dismay at the papers and clothing scattered around the trunk as if they were meaningless trinkets.

"Bloody hell!" Michael exclaimed, walking towards the desk. "You could at least have put it all back."

"I did!" Ellie said, staring at him. She'd never heard him swear. "You know I wouldn't leave any place like this and besides, d'you think I'd want anyone to know the sanctum had been violated? Don't be stupid, Michael!"

"Then who?"

"Perhaps you should ask Jamie."

"Now *you're* being ridiculous. He's a painter. He never had any interest in our family's history." He held her bold stare and said, frowning, "If he was at Maw's Hearth going on about our grandfather…"

They spun round in unison and stared at the door. It had clicked shut behind them.

***

Byron walked around the car park, listening, peering into the shadows and into Bob's car. There was no one in it. Why had Bob come out here and where was he? If someone had called when he was at the bar and he'd had to leave, the least he could have done was let him know. But why leave his car parked outside a pub miles from home?

"If you're looking for the chap you were drinking with, he's gone off with another chap in a car," said a man's voice nearby.

Byron turned to find a middle-aged couple holding hands, he in cardigan and trousers and she in cardigan and skirt, regarding him with curiosity.

"What kind of car?" he asked.

The man shrugged. "Brown and smallish."

"No, it wasn't, darling," said the woman, shaking her head, before looking up at Byron. "You'd think a man'd know something about cars, but not him. Ask him about fish and he could tell you the colour of their eyes. The car was a dark blue BMW, new-ish, probably last year's model, with fancy spokes and a sun roof. Though why you'd want one of those here I don't know. Only good for counting the number of raindrops landing on your roof."

"Thanks. You're very perceptive," Byron said. "Which way did they go?"

"South, and in a bit of a hurry," the man told him. "Nearly collected the gate."

"I don't suppose you could describe the person he was with?"

The woman peered at him. "Is your friend in some kind of trouble?"

"I hope not."

"It was a man. Bit shorter than you maybe, younger. Not sure about the hair. It wasn't black, but lighter, sort of." She sighed. "Sorry, it was all very quick and it's dark."

"You've been a great help. Thanks."

They walked at a leisurely pace towards the loch and got into the Jaguar parked next to his car. Byron raised his eyebrows. No guesses as to who chose the car. By the time they backed the vehicle out of its parking spot, Byron had his phone to his ear. The couple waved as they passed him.

"Jack, it's Byron."

"Where are you? No," he added quickly, "I don't want to know. I've had the inspector on the phone not ten minutes ago wanting more information on Farley's background. You're to be here first thing tomorrow morning."

"He'll have to wait. There's no time."

Jack's splutter erupted in his ear. "You'll have to *make* time. He's ready to charge you wi' wasting police time and failing to appear for interrogation – his word not mine."

"Tell him I'm lost in the Highlands," Byron said impatiently as he got into his car. "Jack, d'you know anyone who owns a dark blue BMW?"

"Why d'you want to know?"

"Just answer the question." He was tired and his old army authority pushed aside the more equitable civilian he was becoming. It was a long process.

"*I* don't have to answer any questions from you, especially if they're about Farley's death."

Byron drove out of the car park and headed in the direction the couple had indicated.

"If you don't tell me, Jack, then Bob Caraway might well be in serious trouble. D'you know who owns a dark blue BMW?"

"Bob! What kind of trouble?"

"You've got ten seconds, Jack."

"You've got a lot of explaining to do, Oakes. And who'd want to harm our local baker?" he said, sounding peeved. "The only BMW I know of is Farley Orman's. And, yes, it's dark blue."

"Who drives it now?"

"It's been in their garage since he died as far as I know. The Orman offspring would have access to the keys. Well, it can't be…"

Byron cut him off in mid-flow. "I'll be in touch."

He hung up before Jack could begin another long dialogue. There was little hope of finding the BMW; too much time had passed and there were too many lanes and minor roads leading to who-knew-where.

His mind went to the driver. The Orman siblings all had auburn hair in various shades, Camden's the lightest and least abundant. He was still in hospital. Or was he? The face in the crowd – had it been him? Frowning, Byron cornered too sharply and almost ran off the road into a signpost.

It didn't fit. Bob disliked Camden intensely. Why go off in a car with him? His thoughts wandered back over the weeks since he'd arrived in Kilcomb. There were a few things about Bob that didn't add up. The petrol bomb through Ellie's study window had happened when Bob was outside; he'd been none too keen to have his head wound checked. Had he even been hit? And the scullery window with its pot plants still in place on the sill seemed ludicrous when the latch was so badly scratched and the window forced open. No intruder would bother to clean up the mess or put the pots back. Perhaps it was meant to look like a break-in when it hadn't been. The trouble was he'd only noticed it after the petrol bomb and after he'd helped Bob up. He'd been so engrossed in Ellie's filing cabinet contents he might have missed any sounds from outside the scullery. It *could* have been Bob.

For the first time, Byron began wondering whether he had anything to do with Farley's death. Jealousy was a powerful force, but it didn't really fit either. Nevertheless, he'd seen what humans were capable of and they rarely made sense.

It was just after eight o'clock. Where would Bob, and whoever was with him, be going? He pulled into a car park in the next village and dialled Mary Nevin's home number. Something was wrong. Even if Ellie was angry with him, he could not believe she'd ignore his calls for this long. When Mary answered she told him she hadn't heard from her.

Light rain pattered against the windscreen as he drew out into the road. About fifteen minutes later he passed a huddle of cottages on the water's edge and realised he'd missed a turn. He got out the map, cursing his lack of attention, and discovered he was on a pencil-thin road that skirted Jimmy's Tarn by three or four miles and eventually came out less than two miles from Strathvern Castle.

Strathvern. He got the number from a BT operator, rang it, and waited while someone called David went off to get Ross.

"Byron. You're missing a great party. Where are you?"

He'd forgotten all about it.

"Sorry, something came up. I'm not far away. Got a bit lost on your winding roads."

"Well, we'll be going for a good while yet and we'd be glad to see you."

"Thanks," he said, not at all in a party mood. Then he had a thought. "Is Ellie there?"

"Yes."

Byron released a silent sigh.

"I'll be there if I can."

He continued along the road more slowly than he liked because of its unknown contours. It wasn't long before he discovered sharp bends and a narrow bridge. At least he would see Ellie soon and have a chance to explain why he hadn't answered her calls and find out why she had remained unresponsive. It seemed an eternity since he'd last seen her. He smiled, remembering the night she'd turned up outside his room, wanting something of him but not able to reach out far enough. The memory of that visit increased his longing to see her and to put things right between them. Not since Ena had he been so stirred by a woman, to know about her, to love her, to just be...

Suddenly, he slammed on the brakes and skidded across the road as a car with only its parking lights on, shot out at high speed in front of him from a lane on his right. He banged his head on the side window, his car sliding sideways into a bush and stopping with its front wheels in the lane. The driver had ignored the stop sign and Byron, engrossed with his thoughts, hadn't noticed the glimmer of lights. His heart was thumping. Another second and someone might have been dead.

Already the car had disappeared, but its make he knew – BMW.

He looked at the weather-worn road sign, almost overgrown by the hedge and on a tilt – Jimmy's Tarn $2^1/_2$ miles. Byron re-started his car and turned into the lane. A knot, twisting in his gut, dictated the direction he should go – he'd glimpsed only one person in the BMW.

The lane was riddled with dips and puddles and clumps of grass, but it ran mostly in a straight line, until a long curve brought him almost to the river. Fifty yards ahead he saw another bridge, wooden, the gates at either end open. A chunky padlock hung on a heavy chain.

Slowing down, Byron stopped at the end of the bridge and peered through the rain at the shadowy planks. It *looked* safe enough, although a local council sign attached to the end post stated to the contrary – 'Bridge Under Repair'. In bigger letters was 'Private Property – Keep Out'. Whether they were kin or strangers, whoever had unlocked the gates had taken no notice of the sign.

Byron backed up a few feet and drove at speed across wood that clanked under the wheels, one of the back ones hitting a loose section, sending the car skidding over the wet wood and jerking him in his seat. The local council, it seemed, had not been lying after all. In seconds the car was shooting across the remaining length of the bridge without further incidence before bumping along the little-used track to the farmhouse.

Taking his torch out of the glove box, Byron got out of the car and waited in the gloom, watching, listening. It was eerie, as if overshadowed by grief and violence, a house in decay protecting its secrets and unwelcoming of visitors. He could not see the tarn. A cold shiver ran down his spine as if trying to escape the evil of the place. He touched the gun strapped to his side under his jacket. He was beginning to understand why Ellie hated the place.

Walking slowly across the uneven ground, peering into the darkness and fully aware he may already have announced his arrival, Byron got to the corner of the building without incident. The back door was half open and looked as if had been that way for years. It did not invite entry and he was not keen to go in. It reminded him of a night raid on bombed-out houses in Lebanon. The guilt, even though they had not been responsible for the devastation, had taken a long time to go. He remembered the pain and agony of loss in the young woman's eyes. She was kneeling on the floor, but it was her sudden screams as she hovered, arms stretched out over her children, one of them dead, that had seared his soldier's heart. Grief had almost overwhelmed him and that incident had changed him irrevocably.

Byron blinked and brought himself back into the present, pushing away the traumatic memories. He looked around. Except for the range, dusty and strewn with cobwebs, there were only a few lumps of wood on the floor, and an old bucket and short pipe in a corner. A piece of material, once a curtain he supposed, hung ragged and dusty from the rail above a window. He stared at the wood. Was it one of these Ellie had used to hit Thorley? Anger quenched a growing coldness and he swore under his breath.

Suddenly, his ears tingled and he became very still, listening. Never assume anything he reminded himself – and concentrate. Yes, there it was again: could be rats or mice. He waited. Then, a different sound, a scuffing, but it was slow and unhurried coming from beyond a door leading into another part of the house. Byron put his hand over the end of the torch, limiting the amount of light, yet enough to see where to put his feet.

Watching where he trod and going quietly over the tatty remnants of a hallway runner, Byron stopped outside the second door on his left. The first was shut. There was no sound now. Again, he waited.

The sound, a loud whimper, was unexpected and Byron snapped on the torch, shining it into the room. Lying prone on the floor, his back to the door, was a dishevelled figure trying to twist around. The man's hands were tied behind his back, his feet at the ankles. It was Bob.

"Bob, it's Byron," he said more loudly than he meant, kneeling in front of him. The baker's mouth was sealed shut behind a strip of black tape. "Hold still. I'll get the tape off."

There was a grunt. Bob rubbed his mouth and stretched his lips in almost comical fashion.

"You're a welcome sight, Byron Oakes. I thought my days were up."

"They might've been. Jimmy's Tarn wasn't on my route."

Byron untied the rope around his wrists and ankles and helped him sit up.

"How d'you wind up here then?" Bob asked, frowning.

"Missed a turn. A BMW shot out in front of me. It was a close thing."

"But I left you in the pub. You were on the phone."

"I'll tell you in the car. Come on. Let's get out of here."

"No. In the next room there's a box… Olga says there's a box under the floorboards. She wants it."

"She can send someone else. Let's get out of here."

"You go if you have to, but I'm taking the box."

"Olga Erskine's got to you, Bob, but I'm not leaving you here on your own."

Byron studied him for a moment. He changed the subject.

"Who was driving the BMW?"

"How d'you know I got into a BMW?"

"Friendly patrons at the pub saw you. Who was driving it, Bob?"

The other man did not answer straight away. He leaned against the wall, studying his rescuer. "I can't say."

"Well, let me guess. The car was Farley Orman's. Camden's still in hospital as far as I know. Fenella was in Inverness – she could've come and got you, except that she wasn't driving a blue BMW when I saw her. So, that leaves Bran."

"It's complicated."

"Then unravel it for me. Was Bran driving the car?"

"Yes. He phoned me when I was leaving Inverness and I told him I was meeting you. He said he'd come and get me, there was something we had to do."

"What?"

"He didn't say."

"So, he brought you here, tied you up and disappeared into the night, almost wiping me out in the process. What for? Come on, Bob. There's a link here and I'm not seeing it."

"He didn't do anything to me. He couldn't hurt a fly."

"There was someone else here, waiting?"

"No," Bob said, shaking his head, wincing. "Camden was in the back of the car when I got in."

"Are you sure?"

The expression in Bob's eyes was one of disdain. "I'm not going to bother answering that question. He was released from hospital a couple of days ago."

"But he was in a coma."

"Well, someone misunderstood."

"Or lied." But why would they? It would have to wait. "Any idea where the Ormans were going?"

"They didn't tell me."

Bob closed his eyes, screwing them up.

"Are you all right?"

"Bit of a headache, that's all."

"Let's get out of here," Byron said.

"Not without the box. It's supposed to be under the boards in the corner near the window. Olga was very specific and said not to bother digging about because it should be right there."

"We haven't got time for this."

"I promised. Don't ask me why, I just did. She's an old lady and said it had childhood memories in it. You know what it means, don't you?"

Byron hesitated. "That she knew this place when she was a child. It doesn't mean she lived here, Bob."

"Maybe, but it's an odd place to leave it if she didn't."

The thought did not seem to please him; his expression warned Byron not to comment.

Byron's mind wandered and he realised that once again Ellie had slid down his priority list. In fact, it convicted him of neglect and that he had chosen duty over love. At least she was safe at the party. He couldn't leave Bob here alone.

"Five minutes. If we haven't found it by then, we're leaving."

He did not wait for Bob to answer, leaving him alone in the dark. He headed back to the kitchen and picked up the piece of pipe. A couple of minutes later he located the corner of the next room and began hacking away at the floorboard. The farmhouse had stood empty for twenty years and the flooring was rotting and sagging in spots. Here and there bits were completely gone. However, in the corner the wood was still solid and it took him longer than expected to break through and lever the end of the board butting against the wall. A piece of board next to it came up more easily.

Intent on what he was doing, Byron didn't notice Bob standing inside the door until he picked up the torch and shone it into the hole, catching him in the sweep of its light. However, he didn't say anything and Bob, who lowered himself to the floor nearby, sat down and watched.

The torchlight revealed the earth beneath, cobwebs and dead spiders, clumps of dried grass and leaves and a few rusty nails. There was no sign of a box. This was a waste of time.

"Nothing here, Bob. Are you sure about it?"

"To be honest, no. But she was."

Byron stared down into the hole, frowning. "When did she tell you about the box?"

He sighed. "About a week ago. I didn't believe her and didn't have time to come anyway. I've never liked the place even when

437

the family still lived here. Mum and Dad only brought us here once or twice and I was very young then."

"I think she's sent you on a fool's errand."

"Just have another look."

Byron lay down on the floor and felt it sag under his weight. With reluctance he slid his arm into the cavity. Groping around in the dark hole his fingers were at the mercy of whatever was down there. He tried not to think about it.

Then he found it, wedged under a brick in the wall in a canvas bag, and covered by dried leaves. He pulled it out and withdrew it from the bag. It was about the size of a thick hard-back novel, but not as heavy. It was plain, perhaps oak, and it was locked.

"Did she give you the key?" Byron asked, reaching Bob and squatting down beside him.

"No," he said quietly, his face pale and drawn in the torchlight. "She said it was girl's things and of no interest to anyone except her."

While he was talking, Byron took out his pocket knife with all its attachments neatly tucked into the casing and within seconds unlocked the box. The two men looked at one another.

"Go on," Bob said, "let's see what's in there."

The lid, shut for so many years, opened reluctantly. When it did they stared into its interior and at Olga's mementoes, but they were not those that would belong to a child.

Bob picked up a signet ring embossed with the eagles of the Third Reich and turned it over. There were two letters, *MM*, inscribed on the underside. He frowned.

"I wonder who MM was?"

"Marian MacAdam," Byron said, thinking of the ring he'd found at The Chimney. Had Farley discovered it there? "Marian was illegitimate, Bob. Douglas Bromley junior, like his father, wasn't content with just a wife. His son and Marian were born to other women, but Ruth, your mother Margaret, and Edith were born to his wife. Marian, as far as we know, took her mother's name."

The expression on Bob's face told Byron much about the man's character. He was not a liar, at least not a compulsive or willing one.

"I didn't know," he eventually said quietly. "But how did you? And who're 'we'?"

"It's a long story for a night at the pub."

There was a pair of wedding rings, Waffen SS shoulder boards and a cap badge, two locks of hair, one dark and the other pale brown wrapped in separate plain handkerchiefs, and several envelopes with letters and photos. As Bob looked at each of the half dozen pictures, his expression became deeply troubled. He put them down without speaking and opened one of the letters. It was written in German. He read both pages of scrappy handwriting and then another one quickly, silently.

When he looked up he said hoarsely, "Let's go."

"You read German?" Byron asked, surprised.

"Used to read, write and speak fluently, but I'm a bit rusty. My parents insisted I learn a language at school and I always thought French and Spanish too flowery."

"Did you understand anything in the letter?"

"Yes," he said, looking grave, "I did."

Suddenly, Byron's ears tingled and he stood up, putting a finger to his lips. He switched off the torch and went quietly and carefully towards the window. He peered out into the dark, listening, but the sound he'd heard did not repeat itself. As he turned around his foot went through a floorboard and, losing his balance, he came down heavily, crashing through several rotten boards. The torch landed somewhere nearby.

He was largely undamaged except for a sharp pain in his ankle and a splinter in one of his hands. However, as he extricated his foot from the hole, he lost his balance and fell backwards. He put an arm out behind him and his hand came to rest on fragments of board and something hard. Bob was moving slowly towards him.

In the pale moonlight, Byron saw the torch a few feet away. Bob reached down, picked it up and switched it on.

Moving with care, Byron turned himself around and began pulling up the floorboards. There was a sharp intake of breath from Bob, who, without saying a word, began helping. They worked in silence until the entire skeleton was uncovered. It had not been there many years as the clothes, though faded and covered in dust, were only partly rotted.

He glanced up at Bob. Tears were glistening in his eyes as he reached out and touched a toggle of the brown duffle coat. Byron knew then whose grave this had become. He waited for Bob to speak, not willing to disturb him.

"It's Alice," he said, wiping his eyes with a handkerchief. "Farley's wife."

"Are you sure? A brown duffle coat's common."

"It's her. See that little finger on her left hand. It's bent. She broke it when she was a child and the doctor just bandaged it up and sent her on her way. Said it would mend on its own. It never did."

"We'll have to tell Jack."

"It won't be easy for him. I never believed all the claptrap about her wandering off because she was losing her mind. She did have memory lapses in the year before she disappeared, but otherwise she seemed fine to me. It never occurred to me someone might've killed her."

"What about Farley? How was he when she disappeared?"

"He was devastated. I told you that before. Yes," he said, nodding, "he was often an absent husband and father, but he was devoted to Alice. She was a kind, gentle woman. I don't know anyone who disliked her."

"I'm sorry it's her, Bob." He clasped the man's arm for a moment and then pulled out his mobile phone. There was no signal.

As there was nothing else they could do, the two men left the farmhouse and Bob got into the car. He asked for the torch and proceeded to read the remaining three letters while Byron walked away with only intermittent moonlight to help him see where he was going. He wasn't far from the house before he came into signal range and yet, he hesitated. It was not a call he wished to make.

"Jack Kennart."

The television was on.

"It's Byron."

"You keep the strangest hours, laddie. I'm guessing this is important. If not, you've interrupted my favourite programme."

Still, Byron hesitated.

"Come on. You're irritating me already."

The words came out sounding brittle. "Jack, we've found Alice."

Disjointed voices coming from the television gave Byron no clue as to what the programme might be though he listened for what seemed an inordinate amount of time before Jack responded.

"Where?" he asked, the word clipped and half-choked.

"Jimmy's Tarn."

"You said 'we'. Who's with you?"

"Bob Caraway. He identified her."

"Put him on."

"I'm away from the car where he is. There's no signal there. We'll call back."

"You'd better."

Byron reached the car. "Jack wants to talk to you, but you'll have to get out. There's no signal here."

A couple of minutes later Bob was on the phone listening to the policeman. Byron stood nearby hoping for a revelation of some kind that would tell him what Alice Orman was doing at Jimmy's Tarn.

"Yes, Jack. It's definitely her. I'm sorry. No," he said in response to the other half of the conversation, "we weren't there looking for anything. It's a long story. We'll fill you in later. Bye, Jack." He handed Byron the phone. "He's hung up. Said he'll be here as fast as he can and not to touch anything. He loved Alice. Never wanted her to marry Farley. Thought she was too good for him."

As they waited for the policeman to arrive, Bob finished reading the letters.

"You can have the box and everything that's in it. I'll tell you what's in the letters. The photos I can't help with much. I think they're all Germans."

"Who wrote the letters?"

"Marian MacAdam and a Helmut Bercht. One letter was written in 1943 by him reminding her that the Reich expected them to behave as husband and wife even if they weren't and cautioning her not to trust the Scottish aristocracy. The others were written in 1944 by someone called Otto. One gave instructions to carry out further observations of the shipping yards on the Clyde, and the other a command to return to Germany."

"And?" Byron asked, hearing reluctance in his voice.

"He told her if she didn't come back she'd be found and killed."

Chapter 25

The door would not open. Michael knelt on the floor and peered into the keyhole.

"There's a key in there. Someone's locked us in." He settled back on his haunches and looked up at Ellie. "I need something long and thin to poke in there and push the key out or we'll be here for a long time. Who would know we're down here? It's not exactly on the guests' route."

Ellie pinched her lips and looked down at the woman's dress, stockings and petticoat, and the man's dinner suit which had been neatly folded inside the trunk. She could feel no sorrow for the earl's father and his mistress. They were traitors.

"Ellie?"

She sighed and turned towards Michael. "Someone did know we were coming down here."

"Who?"

She hesitated, as if in some strange way she was betraying the earl. "Your father."

His face crinkled in a frown and his greenish-brown eyes clouded. "I left him in the ballroom talking with one of his cousins."

"It was definitely him standing at the kitchen door."

"Are you sure he saw you?"

Ellie nodded. "Yes, but he didn't say anything and went on into the kitchen."

"Then followed us and locked us in. What on earth for?"

"It mightn't have been him."

"But who...?" He looked at her intently. "Jamie?"

"Maybe."

"D'you think he had anything to do with Farley's death?"

Ellie shrugged. "I don't know. Farley helped him a lot, so it makes no sense. But I feel Jamie knows more than we do."

"I don't understand why people keep trying to connect us with Orman's death." Michael's eyes and mouth showed his annoyance. "I know he and Father didn't get on, but Orman persisted in traipsing across our land without asking permission. He could be incredibly arrogant and downright insolent when he didn't get his way."

"He was passionate about preserving the Highlands." Ellie, like others, had forgiven that arrogance more often than she liked to admit.

"And you think we'd let developers destroy it? You know that's not true, Ellie. Anyway," he said, drawing in a breath, "with Thorley breathing down our necks trying to throw us out, I haven't had time to think about much else. Jamie can be a bit wild at times, but murder? That's too hard. Why would he get involved?"

Ellie unzipped her bag and took out the photos, letters and signals she had purloined and handed them to him.

"I think you'd better look at these."

He stared at the bundle she held out to him. Apprehension slid over the anger in his eyes, but he didn't move.

"You do *need* to read them, Michael, or you'll never understand."

"Digging up the past doesn't do any good."

"How d'you know that when you won't bother to find out?" she snapped, frustrated by his attitude. "You're the heir apparent. You should know what's going on. You can't just bury your head in the sand and hope everything will turn out all right. It won't. This thing will never go away now. I think Farley stumbled across your family's secrets and that's why he died. I don't believe it had anything to do with hotel development."

He glanced up at her and took what was in her hand without speaking. By the time she bent down to the disarray behind her, Michael was seated in the chair near the desk. To give him privacy, she turned away and sorted the clothes, folding them along their decades-old creases. She began putting letters back in their envelopes and in doing so realised there were no signals scattered amongst the paperwork. A cold shiver ran down her spine. She glanced at Michael as she stepped across to the trunk. He was sitting quite still, his face ashen, and a wave of compassion rose in her heart. It should never be that a grandson should bear the depth of pain she saw in his eyes. She went back to her task.

Inside the trunk, nestled on the bottom where she'd left them, were the two wooden boxes. Without hesitating Ellie opened them. They were full of signal traffic and looked undisturbed. She sighed, relieved, though not sure why when she had helped herself. About to put the suit back in, she noticed a small white box with a silver

443

rim nestled between the two wooden boxes. She withdrew it from the trunk and looked at it intently. It had not been in there before. On the top was the silver crest of the Strathvern family. She opened the box and inside, on a black velvet cushion, was a silver locket with an intricate Celtic pattern. It was beautiful. She turned it over. The initials MM were inscribed in ornate fashion. When she undid the clasp the photo of a young woman stared back, a bold smile on her face. The hair was different and darker, and she was slimmer, but Ellie believed it to be the same woman in the photograph with the two children.

Closing the locket, she sat gazing at it. She felt she should know about it, but whatever sliver of knowledge was tucked away in her mind wasn't coming forth.

There was a sound behind her and she turned, finding Michael with tears running down his cheeks. She gazed at him, uncomfortable, not knowing what to do or say. None of the men in her life had been given to tears. The only one in her family she had seen crying openly and unashamedly was her Uncle John, Glenn's father, when his wife died. She could not comfort this man, though her heart wanted her to at least say something. She couldn't. It was he who spoke first.

"I'm sorry, Ellie," he said, as he pulled a handkerchief from his pocket and wiped his eyes. "Heirs are supposed to be strong and resilient, all-knowing and wise, but I'm none of those things."

There was a little nudge on the inside and she heard herself saying, "But you are, Michael. Well, perhaps not *all*-knowing and *all*-wise – I think God lays claim to that – but you are strong and resilient. It's not every day a man will cry in front of anyone, even those he's closest to. That's courage. At least, I think so."

He gave a little laugh. "I hope you're right." He looked down at what he'd been reading and then picked up the photograph. "I've suspected, but never allowed myself to think about Grandfather having other children. I managed to persuade myself it was ridiculous. But it wasn't. It's Farley isn't it?"

"I'm not sure."

"They're a bit alike, my father and him. At least if you look hard enough. But the girl? I've no idea."

"Neither have I."

Michael ran a hand across one of his eyes and brow. "My father, for all his faults, has never treated human beings the way this man – my grandfather – did. Are the rest of the letters in the same vein?"

"I've only read a few, but yes, they are."

"I'm glad I didn't know him. I understand much better now why he's never spoken about in this house and why my father hates him. It's not only that he betrayed his country, it's the callous disregard he had for his *family*!" Then he said quietly, "It explains why my grandmother committed suicide. No one's *ever* spoken about it."

For a moment Ellie didn't know what to say. The skeleton in Byron's attic might tell a different story. She chose to say nothing of it.

"Betrayal and violation make us into people we were never meant to be and to do things we were never meant to do," Ellie said, turning back to the trunk. She changed the subject. "There are two boxes of signals in here as well, a history lesson in themselves, but maybe not for public airing. I'd check with the Ministry of Defence if I was you. D'you want to take all the letters with you?"

He was quiet and she supposed it wasn't easy raking through all the muck of your predecessor.

"What did Thorley do to you, Ellie?"

The question, so unexpected and yet asked so gently, hit her like a bolt from a crossbow. She turned towards him unable to speak or believe he cared. His expression told her otherwise.

"Ellie?"

"I was just a child." She shook her head, looking away from him. "What defence does a young girl have against a boy who's almost a man? Where does she go for help? How does she stop it happening over and over again?"

She turned back to him, watching shock tighten his features, then anger, followed by deep sorrow.

"I don't know what to say, Ellie. I never do. It's incomprehensible to me."

"You don't need to say anything, Michael."

"Was he a boy at your school?"

"No. He's my cousin."

He stared at her, his mouth open. Looking shocked, he said, "I don't suppose that's well known."

"Of course not. I hated him. I've hated him for years! I never wanted to see him again, that's why I moved to Scotland. When he came here I wanted to run away, but I couldn't. It's my home. I had

445

to stay and fight with Farley. You think I want people to know I'm related to Glenn? He's the last person on earth I'd choose to be part of my family."

"Have you told anyone?"

"Yes, just one."

"Farley?"

"No. Don't ask me, Michael. I won't tell you. And I don't want you to tell anyone either. This is my burden and it's my past. I'd rather people didn't know."

"I understand. I promise I'll keep it to myself. I *am* trustworthy, Ellie. I know that must be hard for you to believe, but such people – such men – do exist." He regarded her intently and added quietly, "I'm so sorry."

Ellie bit her lip, nodded once and looked at the trunk. "My life's been a bit like that trunk, all locked away and full of awful secrets that would cause others pain."

"But you're not at fault, Ellie. You didn't choose to cause pain and you didn't betray. You've unpacked this Strathvern trunk and now I'll do it too. So will others in time. There are people who love you. Let them help you unpack your trunk."

Ellie could hardly believe what she was hearing. No condemnation, no disbelief, no revulsion.

"No wonder Catherine loves you so much," she said with a mixture of awkwardness and gratitude as tears filled her eyes.

"She's helped me unpack my trunk," he said, smiling and looking brighter. He glanced at what was in her hand.

"It's a locket." She held it out to him. "It was in a box at the bottom of the trunk."

"I've seen this. At least, I've seen it in a painting of my grandmother that hangs above the dining room fireplace." He turned it over and nodded. "Yes. These are her initials – Maria Monmouth."

"There's a picture inside." She watched him as he opened it.

He frowned. "That's not her. It's the other woman, isn't it?"

"If it's not your grandmother, then, yes, it probably is. Her initials are MM, too. Are you sure that's not your grandmother's picture?"

"Yes," he snapped. "Father said the locket disappeared from her room just before she died."

"I don't know what to say, Michael."

"There's nothing to say." He changed the subject. "Now, while we're stuck in here, show me what you've found. After that we'll see if we can get out."

"I hope your father starts getting worried and comes to find us. Catherine will be missing you."

"Not yet. She'll think I've wandered off to the library with a relative."

"I don't suppose there's another way out," Ellie said, handing him one of the boxes of World War Two signals.

"I doubt it."

***

There was little hope now, Byron thought, as he stared across the dark, eerie landscape of Jimmy's Tarn, of Ellie still being at Strathvern. She was, she had told him soon after they met, not a creature who indulged in parties and one who always had an excuse to leave early. It was nearly ten o'clock. He phoned Mary's number but there was no answer.

"Women!" he said, glaring at the phone, angry and frustrated. "I've got things to do too, Ellie."

Shoving the phone into his pocket he turned back towards the farmhouse, frowning. For now, he could do nothing. He could not leave Jimmy's Tarn and go sauntering off to a posh party at a castle while the local policeman dealt with a skeleton that had once been his sister.

The three men ahead of him were about to go inside the farmhouse. Bob had promised to say nothing to Jack or anyone else of the box and its contents. It was, he'd said, for other experts to sort out, not a sergeant grieving for his sister. After all, it was unlikely her death and the box were connected – wasn't it?

Byron hadn't commented. Alice was Farley's wife and the fact that she was buried, and perhaps murdered, at Jimmy's Tarn where Marian MacAdam had spent her childhood, seemed too much of a coincidence. His ideas on who might have done it were limited. He knew little about Alice and the first one, in his mind, who ought to be interrogated, was Farley. Perhaps he'd watched too many police shows, but Byron wondered about the man's long absences from home.

However, if Alice had thought Olga the presumed-dead Marian MacAdam, and threatened to tell Jack and Farley, she might

447

have been permanently silenced. Yet, the portly, elderly Olga Erskine was an unlikely candidate. How could she have killed a younger, fitter woman, lifted floorboards, pushed the body in, and put the boards back?

A bank of clouds slid by, leaving a patch of velvet sky patterned with countless stars and a moon half hidden behind the end of the bank. Its light was weak and barely penetrated tree canopies in their autumnal phase. Another four weeks and barely a deciduous leaf would be left.

Byron found Bob, Jack, and Tim Ashby entering the room where Alice's remains were partly uncovered. The light from the policemen's torches chased much of the darkness from the room and the skeleton was exposed in what seemed to Byron an almost irreverent manner.

The constable stood inside the door and Byron put his hand on the man's torch and pushed it down so its beam was directed more towards the floor. Bob stopped behind Jack and remained there as the sergeant knelt down and looked into the cavity. For some minutes he did not move.

"Go outside, Constable Ashby," Byron said to the constable quietly, "and stay by the back door. If you see signs of any visitors, let me know. D'you understand me?"

The man nodded and turned.

"And keep your torch off outside," Byron added.

Almost the second the constable disappeared down the hallway, Jack's shoulders began to shake and Bob squatted beside him, a hand on the other man's back. Not wanting to intrude, Byron stood a little behind and to the side.

"Oh, Alice! What happened to you, lass? Who did this to you?" Jack leaned forward and touched the duffle coat covered in dust and dirt.

The agony in Jack's voice touched a deep chord in Byron. When Jack gently touched the crooked finger bones Byron clenched his teeth. Jack's pain was almost tangible. Seconds later an image from the battlefield – he had not expected a reminder of Ena in another man's grief.

He looked up and found Bob studying him, pushed his feelings back into the chamber they'd emerged from, and turned his attention to Jack. This was no time to display weakness.

One of the pockets of Alice's coat had a slight bulge in it and Jack carefully delved into it, withdrawing a dusty, crunched-up handkerchief.

"If either of you says anything about this, I'll make life hell for you," he said without looking at them.

"Just unfold it, Jack," Bob said, voicing Byron's thoughts.

With slow, methodical movements he unfolded the handkerchief. On the once white material lay a gold ring. Jack held it up, without touching it. The initials, DB, were engraved on its top.

"No prizes for guessing who that belonged to," Bob said in a matter-of-fact tone, raising his eyebrows.

"Really? Then why don't you tell us as you seem to know so much," Jack invited, though his tone was sharp.

Bob caught Byron's eyes briefly before he responded.

"Douglas Bromley."

"Douglas Bromley?" Jack turned to Byron. "I suppose you're going to tell me you knew that as well, even though you're a visitor. A troublesome one at that."

"We're in the Bromley farmhouse, Jack. Makes sense. She might've found it when she was rummaging around." Or more likely somewhere else, he thought.

"My sister wasn't in the habit of rummaging around Jimmy's Tarn. This place has nothing to do with us."

"Maybe not," Bob said, "but there're still connections in the area. Probably more than you know."

Careful, Byron thought, glancing at him.

"Who?" Jack demanded. "Because I'm going to find out who did this to Alice and I'll make sure they never see light of day again!"

"Well, there's me for a start. My niece Catherine. In Inverness there's…"

"I know all that." Jack waved his hand dismissively. "But the rest are long gone from the area."

"Are they?"

Jack's eyes narrowed. "Who?"

Bob did not speak for a few seconds, glancing from Jack to Byron and back again.

"Farley."

There wasn't a sound in the room.

Byron stared at Alice's skull instead, his expression impassive. Was it possible? Could Farley be descended from the Bromleys?

449

Why hadn't Ellie mentioned it? It seemed so ridiculous that the only sense of it was that Bob was telling the truth. He remembered something Ellie had said about Farley, that he never talked about his parents. Byron looked at Bob, but he was gazing at the fireplace. How had he found out about Farley?

A sound outside – a car – distant but getting closer, encroached upon the intense and private conversation. Byron heard Tim Ashby enter the kitchen.

The three men stood up.

Jack's voice broke quietly into the shadowy, cold room as he turned to Byron and gave him the handkerchief and key.

"I'll delay them as long as possible. Do what you have to here, Byron, but make sure it looks undisturbed when you leave. Then go. Bob, best if you stay. Tell them what you told me."

Strathvern's heir rested several signals he'd been reading on his lap and picked up photos of the Clydebank shipyards.

"I had no idea of the extent of my grandfather's involvement. We heard only that he was a traitor. No one actually said what he'd done, although we did hear a few rumours from villagers. It's worse than I imagined," he said, looking up at Ellie who'd been reading other pieces of paper.

"Here're a couple more letters. Any idea who Charlie was?"

Michael screwed up his face. "The only one I've heard about was a cousin of grandfather's. Had a post in government and did a lot of work helping improve the lot of poor people in England. He was born in London and lived there most of his life I believe. His descendants were – are – very wealthy. Why d'you ask?"

"Could be he saved your grandfather a trip to the gallows," she said, handing him another letter.

"He shouldn't have bothered," Michael said bluntly without emotion. "Grandfather was as responsible for all those deaths in Glasgow as if he'd dropped the bombs himself. And then to involve himself with that German woman…" He shook his head. "Why didn't Father *ever* tell me?"

"Ask him. Perhaps he'll be glad to finally talk to you about it. Imagine the burden he's carried all these years."

"He didn't have to."

"Yes he did! He doesn't seem to have many on his side from what I've heard. His father was a traitor so he must be too? What rot!"

"You're not part of this family, Ellie, so how could you know. He's made a lot of visits to Germany and only ever said it's for business. What're we supposed to think? Oh, I know he trades a lot in antiques, but I'm sure there are other reasons he goes there. You've no idea what it's like being tarnished with the same brush. Three generations of traitors that's what some locals think."

"Then do something about it. One day you'll have children. What're you going to tell them? Or will you be like your father and keep it hidden so another generation has to grapple with it? Come on, Michael, you're a Strathvern of Scotland! Be proud of it. Most of us don't have the privilege of known heritage and intricate family history trees, but you do. Make something of it."

For a second she thought he was going to castigate her and say she was an ignorant peasant who didn't have a clue, but he surprised her.

"You're right. I can't keep blaming my father. I'm going to ask him what he's been doing in Germany. I suppose he could've been there trying to make sense of the whole thing. I've never thought about that before."

Ellie regarded him with interest. "Perhaps he didn't want it to be anyone else's burden."

"Yes," he said quietly, "it could be that. I've gone along with condemning him, but never had the courage to ask what was really going on. He should have my support, not my reluctance."

"You'll be a good Earl of Strathvern one day, Michael."

"D'you think so? I suppose time will tell." He glanced at the papers she had given him and read them quickly. "I'll never understand how anyone can betray their country, or why people in authority cover up to save their own backsides. They have to take some of the responsibility."

"Are politicians any good at that?"

A frown wrinkled his brow and his eyes became troubled. "I've just realised that this affects Catherine as well. Her grandmother was a Bromley, a sister of this Alisdair who got the information on the shipyards and passed it to my grandfather. What on earth am I going to tell her?"

"The truth." Ellie gave him a hard look. "She's your wife! If you want your marriage to last into old age, I suggest you try it. And we have to get out of here or you'll never have the chance."

He was taken aback by her acerbity; it showed in his eyes, but she wasn't about to apologise.

"You've never been married, Ellie. Don't lecture me. I'm not in the mood."

"The truth doesn't seem to come easily to the men in your family. Good at hiding it and protecting their loved ones, yes, but truth has a way of revealing itself. Keep one secret from her and there'll be more. Eventually, it'll eat its way into your relationship and you'll be another statistic. Just because I'm not married doesn't mean I don't know what lying and covering up does to people. Believe me, it stinks!" she said, glaring at him. How quickly the atmosphere had changed.

"And I'm not Glenn Thorley!"

"Deception comes disguised in many ways. Don't think you're above the consequences because you're an aristocrat. Catherine's a wife in a million. She's worth the truth, Michael."

"And you're an expert on telling the truth, I suppose," he said with sarcasm.

"Of course not. I'd be happily married with a dozen children, my emotions and past dealt with to the point where I could help others, and I wouldn't be having this argument with you. You have someone who'll listen without judgement. I never had that."

"You had Farley."

A deeply buried button slipped into active mode. Ellie bristled. "I did not *have* Farley! This village made up its own mind about us and how poor Alice couldn't stand it any longer and wandered off never to be seen again. Well, I hope she's having a jolly nice life somewhere warm, but Farley and I never had an affair – *never!*" Her heart was thumping and she felt her face growing warm, probably glowing, as she regarded Michael. Without meaning to she said, "No man's touched me since Glenn."

The silence was profound. Even their breathing was quiet as she watched the animosity retreat from his eyes and felt her heart become quieter. She had never uttered those last words to another human being and she felt a twinge about lying. The one regretted hour with Farley was insignificant. Why to Michael and not Byron? She had no answer to that, but she felt strangely unburdened.

There was such stillness between them that she did not know what to do with it and so remained unmoving, waiting for him to speak. It was the oddest feeling and the oddest circumstance and yet it seemed to be all right, as if he was safe and her words were safe with him. There appeared to be no need for him to hurry with a response and though every second meant a delay in getting out

452

of the room, Ellie, unaccustomed as she was to dawdling, for once did not mind. When he did speak, with his head tilted slightly to one side, he was smiling.

"I don't think you realise, Ellie Madison, what you've just done."

"Then you'd better tell me, but spare me the psychological jargon." Part of her was squirming inside; this was foreign territory. "And don't be long-winded. I want to get out of here before I'm ancient."

It took him less than ten minutes, with a few interjections from her.

"You mean I've been my own prison warden," she said, sitting down on the chair by the desk. He nodded. "I thought I was protecting myself."

"You were… partly. Hiding is a form of self-protection and it's healthy, but not if it keeps you in your fear and grows that fear."

Ellie nodded. She'd never seen it before, at least, not to this degree. Fear of speaking up, fear of being judged, fear of being alone, fear of being unwanted, unloved, fear of… And on it went. A captor that was rigorous, relentless and unwilling to yield.

"Come on," she said in a lively tone, stirring herself, "let's get a move on. Your wife will be worried by now."

There would be time enough to get herself sorted out later.

Michael looked at his watch. "It's almost eleven. Poor Catherine. I hope she's too busy enjoying the party to notice my absence."

"I doubt it."

"As you're so sure about that, d'you have any clue about getting us out of here? That key isn't budging."

It was said jovially and Ellie knew they had come to a place of respect and understanding.

"No, other than trying to batter the door down. Still, I got out of that cellar and, I might add, survived quite a while in the frigid water under your jetty down the end of the tunnel. That's another story," she added, watching with cheeky delight his eyes widening and his eyebrows shooting up underneath the chestnut waves.

"When you get married you'd better choose a man keen on risky adventures."

Ellie laughed.

Michael went back to the door and Ellie decided to find out if there was anything behind the furniture. Nothing of interest revealed itself so she turned her attention to three flags hanging on the walls in an alcove where the seamstress' dummy stood clothed in a Nazi army uniform. Whether the influence of Enid Blyton's stories read long ago and occasionally still delved into, or her vivid imagination, she couldn't help thinking about secret passages. After all, she was in a castle. Why not one leading from this room? She disappeared behind the first flag bearing the German nation's emblems and found a wooden panel carved with horses and flowers. She ran her hands over each carving, including the centre piece of a horse rearing on its hind legs in a bed of flowers. Around the edge of the panel was a trail of leaves. She moved on to the next one. The middle and third panels were identical except for the animals. The middle panel sported eagles, and the third, the one on her right, stags. They were the work of a master craftsman.

She had once painted a stag standing alone on a hill. Trailing over the hills on her own one day, she had spotted him and been filled with wonder at his majesty, his power and beauty. In her sketchbook she had quickly drawn him and, as if waiting until she had captured all of him, he suddenly turned and trotted away. With him went part of her, the yearning for freedom.

Sighing, Ellie brought her attention back to the present. Studying the antlers of the stag in the middle panel, she heard Michael opening the doors to the cabinet displaying guns, swords and instruments. She had no desire to know their purpose.

"I've had a better idea about getting us out," he said, as she peeked out from behind the flag. He had a sturdy knife in his hand. "I'll try and get the lock off."

"Be careful with that thing," she told him, shuddering at the sight of the knife.

"That's what I intend. Any escape route yet?"

"No. Might not be either."

"Pity Jamie or Leith isn't here. They were always disappearing when they were children. Hunting for hidden rooms and passages took up a lot of their holidays, especially Leith's."

"Did they find any?"

"Oh, yes. They and Father put together a number of drawings of where they were and then locked them away in a safe in Father's study. The stuff of stories really."

"Except they aren't only that, are they? Not if they were found."

"No. But there weren't any near the cellars as far as I know."

"Well, that's encouraging," Ellie said drolly.

Disappearing back behind a flag, Elllie frowned at the middle wooden panel.

"This is going to take a while," she heard Michael say, sounding frustrated.

"Then get on with it. It's the only hope we've got."

What a waste to hide such beauty, she thought, gazing at the carvings and allocating Michael and the lock a less prominent place in her mind. Almost reverently, Ellie ran her hands over the flowers, leaves, and eagles. In the centre piece the eagle was at rest, its head turned towards the room, while the other four eagles were in flight.

Identical design except for the creatures. She pursed her lips and studied the eagle, symbol of freedom and majesty – at least it was to her. Michael was still chipping away at the door. Reaching out and flipping aside the flag on her left, Ellie studied the panel again. There *was* something different, but the figures of the horses distracted her. She went back to the panel on her right.

"Ellie!" Michael's loud whisper made her jump, but she didn't turn around. "Ellie! There's someone in the tunnel."

"Probably your father and Catherine," she said with little interest. The centre panel now had her full attention.

Come on, she told herself, *look* at it. It's here – somewhere – it has to be.

From beyond the door she heard the scraping of the cupboard on the hard floor. Michael was walking quickly and quietly across the room towards her, but still she didn't move.

"Ellie," he whispered behind her. "I'm going to turn the light out."

"No, wait. I think I've found it."

However, she thought he mustn't have heard her because as she peered at the little flower poking out from under a leaf, the light went out. In total blackness, her fear of the dark ignited and she swung around, becoming entangled in the flag. Fear accelerated. The sound of the cupboard being moved loud, threatening. Someone meant them harm.

Stay calm, she told herself, Michael's nearby.

"Michael," she whispered.

There was no answer and her heart responded with strong, anxious beats. Where was he? She was still behind the flag, its musty material surrounding her like a shroud. Turning to face into the room, she stumbled and fell against the wall, her elbow hitting a knobbly carving, jabbing the tender spot of her arm where the bones of the elbow met, sending tingles down to her hand.

She grunted, but before she could consider whether Michael had heard or not, the panel suddenly slid open like a silent, gaping mouth and swallowed her. Losing balance, Ellie tumbled down several steps, bumping into a wall and landing on her side. Her right shin caught the edge of a step sending a sharp pain up her leg.

Slowly, she felt her way back up the steps, five of them, sensing before reaching the top that the panel had closed as silently as it had opened. It was a stalwart guardian of the room and wherever she was now and she could not cry out for Michael to rescue her. For all she knew he was dead or injured, but he did have a knife. What would he do with it? Even quiet men were capable of murder in extreme circumstances.

It was pitch black. No matter how hard she stared, she could see nothing. Desperately wanting to shout and make somebody hear, she resisted. Whoever was in the room with Michael might come and finish her off.

It's all right. *We'll* be all right. He's not far away, but fear took no notice and rose like a thick, suffocating mass within her. Ellie clamped her hand over her mouth to stop from screaming, even as her eyes widened seeking a point of light, a point of sanity, of calm. But there was no light, nothing to calm the pounding of her heart, and she felt herself sliding into the terror of her childhood. Out of the dark came evil, determined to harm her, telling her she had to be quiet because bad girls went to hell and hell was darker than her room. It was filled with wicked moaning and screaming without end.

"No, no," she whispered, "I'm not bad. I wasn't strong enough. He just… he just…"

Ellie sobbed, deep wrenching almost silent sobs of the child without a voice, who dared not tell because no one would believe her. Wicked, they would say. *She* was wicked. Glenn was her cousin. He'd never hurt her. But he had and still it haunted her.

Then, in that dark place that was to be her tomb, the last Iron Musketeer silenced at last, she thought of Byron and the compassion she'd seen in his eyes. He believed her. At least, he said he did.

Gone was the chance to say sorry and ask if they could start again. She could trust him if she tried, if she really wanted to, but it was too late. No one would ever find her. They'd think she'd gone away, just like Alice.

Her hands and legs were already getting cold as they always did when she was extremely anxious, her blood focussing on keeping her heart warm and beating. Life, she still had life. She'd got out of tough spots before and, she told herself firmly, she *had* begun to walk away from the past. Whoever said getting out of prison was easy.

Pull yourself together, think about something else. You have to get out. Besides, Michael must have an idea where I am. I was there one minute and gone the next! Surely he'd work it out and investigate.

Far away she heard the distinctive sound of a door opening and seconds later what might have been a thud. All sounds were dulled by the solid wood door she'd stumbled through.

Ellie frowned. There were noises, scuffling and groaning, followed by a faint click. Had the light been turned on? Then, muffled voices, but she could not hear whose they were. It went very quiet and Ellie's pulse quickened. Had they gone? Surely Michael wouldn't leave her here. He wasn't the sort to abandon people.

The blackness was engulfing, demanding, and claiming her attention. I don't think I can do this. She had no idea what was beyond the bottom of the stairs. Death might be feet away. Or escape. No, it was far too risky.

From somewhere came a waft of air. In fact, it was more like a feeble breeze. Yet, she was reluctant to go back down the steps.

"God, if you're there watching, I need help! I can't see a thing and…" she didn't want to say it out loud, but *He* was God and knew anyway, "I'm scared. You know how much I hate the dark."

She didn't expect to hear a voice, but she was disappointed that she didn't. That His ways were mysterious she knew only too well, but the tiniest whisper would have done.

Ellie stood up. There had to be a knob, lever, or button on this side and she ran her hands over the wood, finding nothing resembling any of them. Perhaps Michael's grandfather had removed it to prevent anyone stumbling into his secret room. That didn't help. In fact, it angered her.

A soft touch of air made her consider the other option – finding the source of the air flow. She took a deep breath, shuddering as she let it out.

Ellie reached the bottom of the steps and stopped, thrusting her hands into her trouser pockets. Decision time, she thought, absently fiddling with the Land Rover's keys. She never left them in her bag, not since she'd had a bag stolen at a party in Edinburgh years ago and, consequently, her car as well. Neither ever turned up.

She took a deep breath. It was now or never. She had to trust her instincts and not do anything rash. One slow step at a time, keeping a hand on the wall and hoping nothing nasty turned up.

Keys! She pulled them out of her pocket. Fear had made her forget everything except the suddenness of suffocating darkness, crushing all rational thinking. For, hanging on the key ring was a gadget the insurance company had sent her when she'd re-insured the vehicle six weeks earlier. The gadget, a personal alarm, included a tiny torch.

Ellie switched it on and swung its narrow, penetrating beam around her. The relief of having light caused her to give a whoop of delight. Perhaps God hadn't forgotten her after all.

Above her a low convex ceiling met stone walls, damp in spots. There was a niche halfway up both walls in which sat old lamps covered in cobwebs. Cobwebs also trailed down walls and hung in thick clumps in crevices.

Directly ahead of her were two potential exits. The one on her left showed a wooden door, rounded at the top, its latch big and heavy with a twisted iron ring as a handle. She walked towards it, grasping the ring and turning it. The latch lifted, sticking briefly at the top before jerking free. Inching open the heavy door she saw stone steps winding upwards a few feet behind it. Where did they lead to?

Leaving the door open, she turned to the tunnel which went straight ahead before veering slightly right several feet farther along. It was down this tunnel the air travelled, beckoning her, for it promised the much-desired outside and freedom from ancient darkness.

Yet, the stone steps aroused her curiosity. The old earl would far more likely have come down those from inside the castle than traipse along the tunnels. And, it could have been that his mistress used the same route.

Had Farley?

She reached the bend in the tunnel and stopped, staring ahead. There were puddles in places, but that didn't concern her for she could see the entrance. Ellie went right up to it; its wire cover was askew and there was a gap large enough for her to slip through. Shining the light outside, she knew where she was – underneath the terrace. It opened to a garden bed, overflowing with shrubs and perennial flowers.

With that she turned around and retraced her steps along the tunnel, wondering whether the Strathvern sons had discovered it during one of their school holiday explorations. The thin beam of her torch lighted on a shiny object. It was a compass, but not one that belonged to the Strathverns. It was Farley's. She'd seen it many times, although not recently. Lost, he'd told her, and resting peacefully somewhere in the mountains. It hadn't been important at the time.

Ellie stopped, holding the compass tightly in her hand before turning it over. *To darling Farley, love Alice.* Shoving it in her pocket, Ellie walked slowly on. Poor Alice. Farley wouldn't have been an easy man to live with despite his passionate nature. Trouble was, it was mostly directed towards the mountains he so loved. She sometimes felt he'd considered people necessary for survival and he did love, but on a cry or whim from his mistress, the Highlands, he forsook those who wanted more of his presence. She'd never heard Alice complain or bemoan the fact that her days of going off with him had ebbed when the children began arriving, but Ellie had seen the sadness in her eyes whenever he left.

Now she was certain Farley had known about the circumstances of the previous earl's hidden life, perhaps even considered his own birth as part of them. Although he rarely spoke about his parents, she knew there had been serious arguments at some point and he'd not spoken to them since.

His death had nothing to do with developers wanting to carve up the Highlands. She was sure it *was* Farley in the photo. He must've believed his real father was the previous Earl of Strathvern. Farley had never been afraid of speaking his mind. Had he spoken it once too often to Ross?

And there was still Jamie. Could he have stumbled on Farley's relationship to his grandfather? He was unlikely to become the next Earl of Stravern, but underneath all that artistic ability and casual attitude there was a young man who was passionate about his heritage. That's why he painted what he did: mountains and lochs, bays and villages, crofts and wild animals, and his home.

Ellie came out of the tunnel and turned towards the stairwell still deep in thought. She was certain Farley had died because he believed the old earl was his father. Someone else also knew and had decided to silence him.

There was the slightest of sounds and Ellie halted abruptly, swinging the torch's beam to the right. Her heart almost stopped. There was a man standing near the bottom of the steps, his face in shadow.

Chapter 26

"Come on, man, hurry up," Bob whispered urgently. "The police are making a crowd outside the back door."

"Another minute," Byron said, lifting the skull with care and peering at its back. "Whoever did this made sure she never woke up. There's nothing accidental about this."

Bob leaned over and Byron pointed to the untidy hole in the back of the skull.

"She was shot?" There was shock and disbelief in Bob's voice.

"More like a very heavy blow."

"What an awful thing to do to her! Poor Alice."

Byron glanced at him; his lips were pinched together and his face seemed to grow older as he stared at the remains of Alice Orman.

Raised voices from outside carried on the still air and, sensing Bob's heightened agitation, Byron carefully put the skull back down in its resting place.

"Now don't forget to go right at the rickety barn or you'll end up miles out of your way," the baker said.

"And you're sure about this ring?"

"Yes. Now go!"

Jack's voice, loud and defensive, tore into the decaying farmhouse; the police were in the kitchen. "I know my own sister!"

"That's enough, Sergeant Kennart!" was the sharp reply from Inspector Carter. "You'd better not have disturbed the remains."

"She's been dead too long to be disturbed."

"Don't get smart."

By the time the exchange was finished, Byron was walking softly along the hallway towards the other end of the house. Intermittent moonlight allowed him to make out where the next door was, but he wanted to make the end room where he'd noticed a broken window.

Reaching the doorway of a room halfway along, he heard footsteps rapping on the kitchen floorboards and heading towards the hallway. He ducked into the room.

"Check the rest of this dump, Sergeant, and make sure there's no one else here. Not you, Jack. You stay with me while we take a look at what you've found," Carter ordered.

"What's been found is *my* sister!" Jack snapped.

"So you say."

Footsteps came in Byron's direction. There was nowhere to hide except behind the door and he knew he'd be discovered when the sergeant shone his torch into the room. The policeman was in no hurry and, as he went into the room opposite, Byron heard him muttering to himself.

"Creepy, horrible place. Full of ghosts and bones. Ugh!"

Byron smiled. Seconds later the sergeant was on his way back up the hallway, the soft, unearthly moaning apparently confirming his belief in ghosts – or perhaps something worse.

As he hurried away, Byron went silently in the opposite direction and squeezed out through the broken window. His sleeve caught on the nail.

"Watch your step, sir," the sergeant told his superior. They were nearer. "The floor's rotten just here."

"Did you check all the rooms?" Carter asked.

"Uh, not at the very end." He sounded embarrassed.

Byron, astride the windowsill, smiled again.

"Then do it. Don't ever take anything for granted."

The man came back down the hallway as the other two men entered the room where Alice Orman was buried. The wool of Byron's jumper was tightly caught and he tugged at it, watching out of the corner of his eye as the torchlight grew brighter.

This time there was no muttering. The man was in a hurry. There was a quiet plucking sound as the wool suddenly pulled free of the rusty nail. His elbow hit the window frame. The steps in the hallway faltered. Byron did not move; he could hear the other man's heavy breathing. He was afraid. He'd heard the sound many times before. Whether spurred on by fear of Inspector Carter's wrath or his own curiosity, the sergeant continued on, though less energetically.

Sliding slowly off the windowsill, Byron put his feet carefully on the ground, ignorant of what he might step on. A sharp snap announced the presence of glass. Byron bent down. Once again, the other man stopped. He was close to the door.

Suddenly there was a shout somewhere in the dark behind him. There wasn't a soul in sight.

"Hey, sergeant! Over here. There's someone running towards the trees."

Byron recognised Bob's voice and nodded. Good man.

The sergeant, it seemed, needed no further persuasion, turning and walking along the hallway with more haste than he'd done on the mission given by Carter.

Byron ran across the grass to his car. He got into the driver's seat and pulled the door towards him, closing it quietly. He released the hand brake. The farmhouse was on a slight rise, but he knew the car would not run silently downhill for more than a few feet before he'd need to start the engine.

Bob was still making a noise at the other end of the house as Byron started the car and pushed down hard on the accelerator. He was halfway to the gate, bouncing over uneven ground before there was any movement behind him. A torch beam flashed across the land. As he approached the bridge, going at high speed, he was certain Carter wouldn't waste time sending the sergeant after the culprit. However, he was wrong. Byron's car clattered heavily over the bridge, wheels sliding on the slippery wood. He prayed they wouldn't drop into gaps and get stuck. He turned left and slammed on the brakes. A car was speeding towards him. Running back to the gate, he shut it. Back in the car, he drove fast into the corner leading to the lane as he heard the police car ram into the gate. Byron didn't stop, hurtling along the lane until he reached the road. Another left turn and he began repeating Bob's directions out loud to himself. He couldn't afford to become lost or disoriented. He'd had years of night manoeuvres, but his sharpness wasn't quite so sharp any more. However, Bob's instructions were clear and he made good time, back-tracking only once when a turn came up more quickly than he'd anticipated.

Veering right at the tumbledown barn as he'd been told, he found himself on a narrow road winding along the edge of a loch. The blackness of the water, watched over by voiceless, shadowy hills sent a shiver down his spine. He turned up the heating. He thought of Ellie and wondered if she was having such a good time at the countess' party that she hadn't bothered trying to phone him.

At the end of the loch a hamlet, its few buildings clustered together, appeared in the brightness of his headlights. They were drab, unlovely dwellings and ramshackle sheds, leftovers, he thought, from a time when it had been a more prosperous village.

This hadn't been in Bob's directions. Where on earth was he? Had he missed the telephone box?

Byron pulled off the road and stared at the unmoving blackness of the water. Desolate, was the word that came to mind. Odd it felt that way. He shouldn't be more than a couple of miles from Kilcomb – if he was where he was supposed to be.

He was sure he hadn't missed any of Bob's descriptions of what to look for, so he got out of the car and went in search of the telephone box. It took no more than two minutes to find – a box on a lean, its door slightly askew, red paint patchy and faded. Unable to resist, he lifted the telephone and put it to his ear. To his surprise it burred happily.

As he replaced the phone in its cradle a car approached at a speed well below the limit. He waited in the shadows for it to pass. Across the road he watched a fox trot silently by a building of indeterminate origins, and behind him an owl gave a couple of loud hoots. Over the loch a bank of clouds slid away to the south and the moon graced the loveless place with its light. The water, bathed in pale cream, relinquished a portion of its forbidding atmosphere and became almost romantic.

A small brown car crept by not six feet away. To his astonishment, he saw Mary Nevin at the wheel and in the passenger seat a plump shape, a woman, who seemed to be talking. Byron frowned. Even before she turned towards the driver, Byron knew who it was – Olga Erskine. The car sped up a little and a minute later it was out of sight around a corner.

The clouds enclosed the moon once more and the loch became a forbidding and lonely body of water. Byron got in his car and drove off.

***

"Ellie! What're you doing down here?" the young man asked, descending the last two steps and switching on a torch more powerful than hers.

There was about him a secrecy she hadn't noticed before, a touch of hardness even.

"I'm a guest at the birthday party and… got lost. How about you, Bran?"

"I don't need an invitation. I work here. What're you looking for?"

"A way out."

"No Prince Charming to help you this time. We passed his car near Jimmy's Tarn. Didn't have time to stop and see if he was all right."

"We?" she asked abruptly, angered by his offhand, uncaring manner.

Bran nodded. "Me and Camden."

"So he's all right then. Who told you he was in a coma?"

"A nurse Camden knows – quite well."

"What on earth for?" Exasperated, she couldn't see any point to it.

"Because Camden wanted everyone to believe it was your fault. You stole Dad, he said. He wanted to punish you."

"A whacking great branch fell on him, Bran! Hardly my doing. And I didn't steal your mother."

"I know," he said, shrugging, and more like the Bran she knew. A wave of pity washed over her, but she pushed it aside. "A decoy, that's what it was."

Ellie frowned. "For what?"

His expression changed, as if realising he'd said too much. Instead, she got, "We dropped Bob Caraway off at Jimmy's Tarn and left him with all the Bromley ghosts."

"He's not afraid of ghosts. Besides, he's family," she said sharply. "But why did he want to go there with you? He could've driven himself."

So, it *was* true.

"No idea."

She followed this with a pointed question. "You know who killed your dad, don't you?"

For a second there was fear in his eyes. Then it was gone. "If I do, I won't be telling you or your Prince Charming. Although he won't hear if he's dead."

"He's not my Prince Charming and he isn't dead."

"You don't know that."

"Yes, I do. He sent me a phone message."

"Show me."

"I can't. My phone's gone flat."

"Liar."

"See for yourself."

She gave him the phone and watched him pushing the buttons. There was no life in it.

"What did he say?" he demanded, handing it back.

"I can tell you anything I like, Bran, and you won't know if it's the truth or not." She watched his expression flick from anger to suspicion to apprehension and back to anger.

He stepped closer to her and a shudder ran down her spine. In the gloomy light, he reminded her of Camden.

"Tell me what he said." His eyes were cold, his body tense. This was a side of him she didn't know.

"He found Bob tied up and some papers under the floorboards." She kept her eyes on his, not wavering. She was not the one to tell him.

"What papers?"

"I don't know. Why would I tell you anyway?"

"Because if you don't..." he began, then stopped. "Things happen in castle tunnels. What papers?"

"German papers, that's all I know."

He stepped right up to her, a head taller than her.

"Maybe Camden's right. Maybe you are a liar. Mum never deserved how Dad treated her!" Tears started in his eyes.

Ellie stared at him. A pit opened in her belly and filled with the muck of pollution.

"What're you talking about, Bran?" she asked hoarsely, her mouth dry.

For a few moments he didn't look at her, pressing his lips together. She watched the muscles in his face tighten.

"You must've known. Bob would've told you. You're best friends."

"Told me what?" Pressure was building inside her.

"Inverness. He used to go to Inverness. Stayed in a hotel there. Told Mum Inverness was close to where he was photographing." He couldn't look at her. Tears were running down his cheeks and Ellie's heart filled with sorrow. "He... he... met a woman there. He stayed in Inverness more than anywhere else. He lied to us. He cheated on my mum! And she knew! Never said a word. She loved him." He shook his head. "I hated him for what he did."

He sat down abruptly on the cold flagstones and Ellie crouched beside him, her arm around his shoulders, her heart shattered by his words, and her friendship with his father tainted. She couldn't tell him, not now.

"It was an accident," he murmured, "an accident."

466

***

The road had long since turned away from Kilcomb as Byron followed the brown car over hills and along winding, narrow lanes before coming to a wider road. Several times he'd had to stop, and once, turn in the opposite direction Mary had taken after coming upon them suddenly round a bend stopped at crossroads. He had no idea if they knew they were being followed.

After a couple of miles along the wider road, on which there was some traffic, he passed the entrance to the Crossed Swords Hotel. He was close to Inverness, though approaching from a different direction, and almost lost them near the city centre as they suddenly swung left and disappeared down a road away from the river. Although there wasn't a lot of traffic he found himself peering ahead with an intensity that made his eyes and head ache. It had been a long day with little to eat.

As he sat at a set of traffic lights in the right lane, he could see the back of Mary's head two cars ahead in the left lane. The lights turned green and he scooted into their lane behind an old Morris as the lights changed. There was a loud hoot from the van behind. Seconds later he shot off to the left after Mary, incurring another blast of disapproval.

The streets grew quieter, shops and businesses giving way to houses and gardens of the more affluent. Ahead, Mary stopped at the end of a road waiting for traffic to pass and Byron pulled up several yards behind. When the car went right he allowed a car to turn into the street he was leaving. As he followed Mary's car, it became plain as a pikestaff where she was heading. The German letters found at Jimmy's Tarn. He nearly closed his eyes in frustration. Why hadn't he worked it out before?

Olga Erskine *must* be Marian MacAdam. Was she, after all these years, going to confront Ruth and her husband, a man who may have had a hand in sending Olga's wartime lover to the gallows? Mary, good-hearted and caring, was doing what she'd probably done for years, giving her elderly customer a lift.

He picked up his mobile and dialled a London number.

***

Ellie followed Bran up the stone steps which did not, as she expected from reading countless historical novels and watching movies, wind upwards in a circular fashion. He had not spoken since he'd got up from the floor and told her to follow him. Nor had she voiced her questions. They agitated like a washing machine thrashing clothes. His silence only fuelled her imagination. Whether the reference to 'it' being an accident that had to do with Farley's death he refused to say.

If the boy in the photo was Farley, and he'd been making noises about exposing the whole wartime mess of an affair and a child, perhaps Jamie had wanted to silence him. But would he? Outwardly he showed little regard for his heritage, yet his love for it was obvious in his paintings and sketches.

The stairwell was narrow. She wanted to get out of it.

To distract herself from the lack of space, Ellie wondered whether Bob knew about his treacherous forebears. His mother had been a Bromley before her marriage. And what of Catherine, also with Bromley blood? Did she and Michael know?

Her thoughts turned to Bran. Was it him who'd locked them in? No. He'd have had something to say about what was in the room. Then who had? A shiver travelled down her spine and apprehension made little knots in her stomach. Only one person had seen them at the door to the cellars – Ross.

Ellie, engrossed in examination of events, bumped into the back of Bran, who'd stopped. She clutched at his jacket to keep from falling and his hand suddenly grasped her arm, his fingers strong. As she steadied herself she saw they had stopped at a door, but Bran ignored it and raised his arms, shifting what looked like a solid block of stone and sliding it forwards. There was a gap big enough for them to get through and he went up quickly, using the crossbeams and bolts on the door to clamber up. With his help Ellie went up and found herself in a small room. Bran slid the flagstone back into place.

Standing up and looking around, she could almost believe she'd been transported back through the centuries. Bran shone his torch slowly around the walls, exposing several bits of furniture. Three old, leather-bound books occupied a niche in the wall and in another a candle holder. A narrow bed with sacking stretched over the wooden frame, was covered in a deer's hide. As her eyes went around the room, she noticed there was no sign of an exit to the stairwell.

A cold draught wrapped around the back of Ellie's neck and touched her cheeks. She turned, casting the thin beam of her torch towards the wall behind her and there, about two feet above her head were three slits in the stonework. A wooden stool and small table stood against the opposite wall. Across the room was a door.

"Where does the door go to?" she asked.

Bran shrugged. "Don't know. Maybe nowhere. Doubt this room's been touched since the last Jesuit priest hid here three hundred years or more ago," he said, and she remembered that, like his Uncle Jack, he'd long had an interest in history. "Let's go."

"Wait a minute." Frowning, she looked at the furniture. Walking over to the books, Ellie stared at them and ran her finger down the spine of the end one. "There's no dust, no cobwebs. Unless your last Jesuit's returned in the guise of a house-proud maid, someone's been here recently."

"Don't be ridiculous. No one knows about this room."

"How d'you know that? Strathverns have been here for hundreds of years." She looked at him suspiciously. "It's you, isn't it? You come down when no one's around and pretend you belong here."

She felt his reproach, saw it in his eyes and regretted the words.

"I don't need anyone to tell me I don't belong here – I know it!" He turned his back on her and walked towards the door.

"Your father didn't deserve to die the way he did, Bran," she said, turning off her torch and suddenly fed up with secret rooms, secret tunnels and men who were never what they portrayed. "If you're right about Farley seeing other women, then his life was a lie, but so is yours. Not to mention Jamie, his father and his brothers. Maybe half of Kilcomb as well! Why is it so hard to tell the truth? Tell me what happened at the Knobbles."

Bran opened the door then turned back towards her, a yawning dark space behind him.

"What d'you mean about Jamie and His Lordship?"

She hadn't expected that. "I know Jamie was at the Knobbles the day Farley died. He's hiding the same thing you are – the truth about what happened. For goodness sake, Bran! If it was an accident tell the police."

Well, she didn't *know* for sure, or what Jamie was hiding, but she had little doubt the pair of them knew quite a lot about how Farley's life ended.

"Bob said we…" He stopped abruptly, swallowing, and stared at her.

A strange and awful tingle ran the length of her body. Her throat was not so much dry as frozen. She could not move. Eventually she said,

"What... what did he say, Bran?"

"Nothing. Now let's go."

"No," she said quietly. "Your father is dead, my friend is dead, and all you can say is, 'it was an *accident*'! If you don't tell me what happened, I'll call the police myself. Inspector Carter's not as easy-going as your uncle. Tell me what Bob was doing there."

He bowed his head and stared at the floor, the only sound that of the soughing of the wind outside. Shadows and dark corners deepened as Bran lowered the torch, its beam shining on the flagstones. Ellie, needing a momentary distraction, thought how awful it would have been for the priests or those out of favour with the ruling sovereign, perhaps spies, being cooped up there.

Then, from another dark night, Camden's strained and disjointed words from beneath the tumble of branches came to her. Was it some kind of awful family pact and Bob learned about it?

She felt sick and forced the next words out. "Was Camden there?"

Bran shook his head. "He hates walking on the hills."

"Then how does he know what happened?"

His head jerked up and he blurted out, "What did he tell you? He lied, just like he always lies and twists things. I've told Fenella he can't keep his mouth shut about anything! She said I was being stupid, that family have to stick together." He stared at her, his expression intense.

"I didn't say he told me anything about being at the Knobbles."

"Then what?"

"When he was pinned under a branch in my garden, he said, 'Fenella... secrets... she knows family... secrets.' Any clues?"

"No. Our father didn't talk about his past. I've told you that before. Perhaps she found out something, but she didn't tell me. And she'd never tell Camden. He can be cruel. Taunts people. You've seen him. He joked about taking a pot shot at you and Byron in your back garden just for fun."

So that's who it was. "I should've guessed," was all she said.

"He used to tell Dad we'd be better off without him."

Ellie's heart skipped a beat and her skin went cold. "Did he kill him, Bran?"

He made a sound in his throat. "No, he's a coward. Picks on the weak. Dad was never weak. He was the strongest of all of us. Always did what he wanted."

"Who was it?"

"It was an accident."

"I don't believe you, Bran."

He turned away abruptly.

Ellie felt as if she was drowning in the darkness and switched on her torch, following Farley's youngest son.

"How d'you know about the room and tunnel?"

"Came across the end of the tunnel when one of the dogs got its collar caught in the wire. Went back later to find out where it went," he said, sounding relieved she'd changed the subject. "What about you? Get bored with the birthday bash and go for a moonlit walk?"

"You could say that."

"You're up to something, Ellie."

"The only thing I'm up to is finding out what happened to your father. Is he dead because he found out he was someone else's son?"

"You're talking rubbish."

He stopped in front of a semi-circular wall with several niches. Stepping to the left, he reached into one and part of the wall began moving. She faced him.

"No, I'm not."

"I don't care. Like I told you, I don't care a fig about family history."

"Well, you should. Your grandfather could be the seventh Earl of Strathvern."

His face went ashen and he stared at her as if what she'd said was so outrageous it either had to be scandalous or true. However, no word left his mouth. Nearby was a sound that caught her unawares.

It was the Earl of Strathvern, the glass in his hand slipping and landing on the carpet, spilling its contents onto the Axminster carpet. Behind him, Michael, who was staring at Ellie, stood up and walked towards the gaping hole in the library's wall. He looked relieved to see her.

Ross didn't move.

***

471

"How dare you come here and push your way into my house! And who's this other woman?" shouted Ruth Lawford, indignant in a primrose yellow dressing gown, her grey hair loose about her shoulders. She was standing just inside the sitting room door. "Call the police, Hugh. This... this awful woman's deranged – *and* trespassing."

"Trespassing, maybe, deranged no," said Olga evenly with little expression on her face. Byron, crouched outside the corner of the sitting room window, its curtains tied back, watched her plump down on the sofa as if she owned it, sliding a hand into a pocket. From her other pocket she withdrew a handkerchief and blew her nose. "And don't bother calling the police. You must know who I am, Ruth. Hugh does."

Ruth looked at her husband and for a moment there was uncertainty in her eyes, quickly followed by indignity.

"This is outrageous! Hugh, please do as I ask and call the police."

The elderly man stayed seated on the piano stool, dignified even in dark blue pyjamas and dressing gown. His expression, stern and without emotion, made him seem as if he wasn't really there.

"I'm surprised at you, Ruth," Olga said, folding her hands on her ample lap. "Surely you didn't think I'd just vanish or get myself murdered. That poor woman in the woods..."

Byron wondered what Olga was up to at this hour of the night. She was shaking her head, sighing, as her last words trailed into silence. With a view only of her profile, he stared at her as if he'd never seen her before. Without announcing they even existed, scattered pieces of the jigsaw were suddenly slotting into their respective places and he began to understand the extent of Olga Erskine's ability to manipulate and destroy. This was no OAP content to revisit her memories, potter in the garden and wander slowly down to the village and enjoy idle chatter with anyone she met.

"That 'poor woman' as you call her," Ruth snapped, "was most likely my sister. She was a traitor. Traitor's deserve death."

There was no response from Olga; she sat motionless looking at Ruth who did not meet her eyes, but seemed engrossed in something beyond the woman sitting on her settee. Hugh was staring at the floor, while Mary, who'd been glancing from one to the other of the three, sat down in a wingback chair next to the piano. Reflected in her eyes was growing anger, smouldering like a bonfire that's quiet and burned down to ash, but fed fresh fuel will burst into scorching, devouring life. Byron fingered the ring. More than a minute ticked by on the clock above the fireplace before Olga spoke.

"An interesting opinion," she said, as if Ruth's words were of no account, "but it all depends on perspective. I prefer tae call it service to another wee country whose ideals were worth fighting for. Our daddy and brother were good workers for the Fatherland, but I proved to Hitler that this Scottish woman was more faithful than all my countrymen who followed him."

Byron's mobile vibrated in his jacket pocket and he ducked down below the windowsill. It was Colin.

"Call you back," Byron whispered and pressed the disconnect button. As he stood up the end of a branch jabbed him in the back of the neck causing him to stumble against the wall.

"You've got a warped sense of 'service', Olga, if you turned your back on Scotland in the war," Mary piped up unexpectedly. "Don't expect me to help…"

"Quiet!" Olga said sharply.

Astonished she'd heard his whisper or collision with the wall, Byron crept away from the garden bed. Olga's bulk loomed in the window as he ducked behind a leafy shrub. She peered out, down and up, her expression stern.

"It'll be one of the dogs," Ruth said loudly, before adding with a note of disparagement, "Pity they weren't out when you arrived. They don't like strangers in the grounds."

"Dogs are not a problem for me. I have a way wi' them."

"Don't tell me what that is."

"I've no intention of doing that. You wouldn't understand."

Byron, though reluctant to move away and miss the drama in the Lawfords' sitting room, did so, slipping behind an oak tree several feet away. He could hear drifts of words, indistinct and disjointed. Peering round the tree trunk he could see everyone except Ruth.

He dialled Colin's number. "What've you got?"

"Hugh Lawford went to Germany on a number of covert operations during the war, but on a trip in late 1944 he was late back by a week. Caused a stir amongst the hierarchy because he was one of the best snoops they had. Now, this gets even more interesting."

"Hurry it up, Colin. I'm outside the Lawfords. Followed Olga Erskine here." He left Mary's name out; Colin had no knowledge of her.

"You did what?"

"You heard. Come on, man. This is serious."

"You're right, it is. There's a note on a file I've found – don't ask how or whose – which states, and I quote, 'I strongly recommend that an investigation be undertaken into Colonel Lawford's latest mission. It's true his account of the reasons for his delay have been verified by a reliable source in Germany, but I've known Hugh Lawford for a long time and he's not once come on duty with anything other than perfect dress, including highly polished shoes or boots. He is fanatical about his military appearance. When questioned by me rather humorously about the unpolished state of his shoes, he looked me straight in the eye, apologised and said, 'A bad habit I picked up'. He does *not* pick up bad dress habits. You may not think this important, but in this climate of war and with Hitler using every opportunity to infiltrate, I have to question who we have in our midst."

Byron shifted his gaze from Mary to Hugh who was still sitting on the piano stool. He was looking at Ruth.

"Anything else?"

"You're a hard man to please, old son," Colin said. Byron heard him sigh and shuffle papers. A few seconds later his friend said, "There was no investigation, but the chap who wrote the note said he went to Germany himself some years after the war and found out that one of Germany's elite soldiers had gone missing around the time Hugh Lawford was supposedly delayed there for a week."

"You met this man?" Byron asked, astounded once more by Colin's ingenuity.

"Of course. Go to the source if you can, that's always been my motto as you well know. Anyway, this chap, who I cannot name, says the hanging of the German spy that Hugh Lawford told you was Marian MacAdam's lover was a lie. Colonel Lawford – who wasn't Colonel Lawford – oversaw the whole thing. They just hanged another spy instead."

"So, the man I can see in the Lawfords' sitting room is Helmut Bercht."

"How did you know that?" Colin asked, his voice a decibel or two higher.

"Found some letters tonight. They were written in German by Marian MacAdam and Helmut Bercht."

"You don't read or speak German."

"Bob Caraway does. It's a long story. It seems our two spies are not only alive and well, but in 1944 she was told if she didn't come back to Germany she'd be found and killed."

There was silence on the other end of the phone.

"You still there, Colin?"

"Yes, just thinking. Where does our Bob fit in?"

"He knows a lot more than he's saying, but I doubt he's either murderer or keeper of all the family secrets."

"You hope. So, what's going on in there? Confrontation time d'you think?"

"Could be."

He saw Mary stand up, shouting at Olga. Tears were running down her cheeks and Ruth went across to her, but was brushed off. However, the figure who captured Byron's greatest interest was Hugh. He was watching Mary with an intensity that brought life to his eyes and drove age from his face.

Colin's voice interrupted him. "Want me to call anyone?"

"I have to go. Something's happened in there. Not yet. I'll let you know."

"Be careful, Byron. No heroics – you're too old for that kind of thing."

He was gone before Byron could tell him his cheek was misdirected considering who was the eldest of the two. Less than two minutes later he was inside the house.

"You've kept this from me all these years! Why didn't you tell me? Why didn't you tell Mary? It's a pity it isn't you in that grave!"

It was Hugh, his voice filled with anger and pain.

"Well, Hugh – perhaps I'll call you Helmut now that Ruth knows she wasn't the first woman in your life," Olga said, reaching into the pocket again. "Aye, you'd scratch out my eyes if you could, Ruth. You never liked me. Was not good enough because our Dad didn't marry my mother. Well, you've had your reward – no bairns. I had four – two boys in Germany, a boy and girl here. I didn't tell you, *Helmut*, because I preferred a man with a title and money. He was my life insurance and he went to the grave believing the children were his. Left me a nice wee sum."

"You're lying," Mary said, but there was a hollow sound in her voice.

"Nae, lass. I'm not. You're my daughter sure as I'm sitting here. And that man, Hugh Lawford – or to give his right name, Helmut Bercht – is your father."

Mary shook her head. "No, you can't be. Mum and Dad would've told me. They didn't keep secrets."

"They kept this one. And I promised not to tell a soul." Olga shrugged. "I certainly didn't want anyone knowing."

"Why didn't you let me be with my father then?"

"He wouldn't have wanted you then, Mary. He wasn't the grandfatherly man you see now, or I a village widow. Oh, no. We had only one love then and his name was Hitler. Our business didn't include children. You were adopted by good people. Be grateful for that. Many weren't. One of your half-brothers wasn't quite as lucky as you."

"So… so you're telling me that I'm the product of two people who worked for Hitler?" The anger in her came out in restrained, hard tones. Byron wondered why she hadn't asked about the half-brother.

"That's putting it bluntly."

"What other way would you like it?" Ruth snapped before Mary could speak.

"You're a wicked woman, Olga Erskine," Mary said. "Pauline Stewart was right about you. I never believed her about you killing her son, but now I do. I think you'd be capable of getting rid of anyone and anything that stood in your way."

"Don't be stupid now, Mary. You've never been that. The boy died because of his own foolishness. He and one of his pals were mixing alcohol and what they thought were herbs and got it all wrong. The friend waited to see what would happen. He was soon at my door begging for help. It was too late. When I got to him in the woods the other boy was dead."

"You don't know how to distinguish lies from truth, Olga," Hugh said tersely. "You twist and turn things until they become your truth and you've forgotten what really happened. And now look at you. I suppose you really think you're Olga Erskine. You've had so many disguises I'd be surprised if you know who you really are."

"Aye, I do, but I'll never forget," she said quietly. "When the war came I was important to somebody for the first time in my life."

"If you expect sympathy, look elsewhere." Ruth's voice was cold and detached, and before Byron could move, she stormed out of the room, slammed the door behind her and marched down the hallway into the kitchen. She did not see him. Byron moved closer to the door to hear. He'd speak with Ruth soon.

"Well, here we are," Olga said, "a family together."

"Don't be ridiculous!" Hugh said. "We're not a family, never will be. You made certain of that in every way. Why are you here, Marian? That's her real name, Mary. Marian MacAdam, daughter of Alisdair Bromley, mother – who knows!"

"I do," the older woman said, "and who it is I'll tell Mary all in good time, but not now."

"Don't bother. I've got very good parents as you pointed out. I don't want to know anything else about you, Olga Erskine. Or whoever you are. I don't want to be tainted by... by your blood, Bromley blood!" Mary's voice rose as she spoke. "I was glad when Alice took the ring away."

"What ring?" Olga's voice was tense.

"The Bromley ring. I've no idea how my mother got it, but she gave it to me years ago saying it was handed down the generations. I assumed it was her family line."

So that's how Alice got it, Byron thought. What else went to the grave with her?

"When did you give it to her?"

"Five or six years ago. If you want it back," Mary said sharply, "you'll have to find her."

There was no response. It was Hugh who broke the silence.

"Why *are* you here, Marian?"

"I'm leaving Kilcomb and couldn't go without saying goodbye. And I wanted to see the look on your face when I turned up with your daughter. It was worth it. But I'm sorry for you, Mary. You've always been good to me."

"Haven't you learned anything since the war?" Hugh barked. "Your life's all about revenge, isn't it? Mary would've had a good home with us."

"You were supposed to return to Germany."

"No," Hugh said quietly, "I wasn't. You were told that, but it was never the intention. Besides, I love Ruth – and I love Scotland."

"Don't give me that rubbish. You could nae stand the sight of her and all you wanted was Britain to be a vassal of Germany!"

"That didn't last long. I didn't tell you or anyone else. It's amazing how you can seem to still be loyal without being so. You could still have given us the child."

"Never! I'd never have given Mary or the boy to Ruth, not if she was the last woman on earth. Now I'm dying and I don't want tae be buried here. I've made it clear in my will. I still have friends in Germany, loyal friends."

"Who is he, the boy?" Mary piped up.

"Just a boy. Went off to a family as a baby, same as you."

"And what about your other bairns in Germany? I suppose they're just by-products of your affairs like I am," Mary said brusquely.

"You could put it that way. They don't know anything about me, just as you didn't. They went to good families…"

"Nazi sympathisers I suppose."

Olga did not respond and went on as if the interruption had not occurred. "And all have families of their own. My first child was an accident – he's dead – but after his birth I thought, one day I'll tell Ruth and watch her squirm. The wait's been worth it. I was nae the motherly sort, but I'm glad I had them."

"Who's my brother?" Mary said, insistent.

"It doesn't matter and it'll do you no good to know."

"Not to you maybe. You're a heartless trollop!"

"I learned at an early age that if life doesn't give you what you need, then you take out of it what you want."

"Does my brother know about you?"

"No."

"I'm glad you won't be buried in decent Scottish soil. The ground would spit you up!"

At that moment Ruth came out of the kitchen carrying a tray with a teapot, mugs, milk jug, and sugar bowl. Byron was halfway standing up, his finger to his lips when she saw him, but it was too late for one of the china mugs as she gave a gasp and it wobbled off the tray onto the wooden floor, milk slopping out of the jug onto the tray and floor.

Chapter 27

"So," Ross said quietly, "you've discovered my secret."

"Which one is that, Lord Strathvern?" Ellie asked, watching as he captured his emotions and put them away out of sight. She glanced at Bran, but if he noticed his master's moist eyes he gave no indication.

Michael rose from where he was sitting and stood near his father. He had said nothing about who'd unlocked the door in the tunnel, though he was clearly relieved to see her.

"It's true, I have many. I'm talking about the room you've come through."

"What room?" Michael asked beside him.

Ross turned towards him and spoke as if Michael was his only audience, the recipient of a confidence. "I used to escape from him there. No one knew about it. It was my safe place, my hiding place. I could disappear for hours on end, although not always there. The castle's full of secret nooks and crannies, but the priest's hole was… is… special."

There was a note of yearning in his voice that touched the hiding place in Ellie's heart. Michael gazed at his father as if enlightenment had come upon him and he didn't know what to do with it.

"Why didn't you tell me?"

Ross put a hand on his son's shoulder. "There's a lot I should've told you, Michael, but I was too busy being ashamed of my father and the heritage he left me to realise how I appeared to my sons. I wanted to tear that other room apart, burn it all, but I couldn't. All I could manage was to make a mess. Your mother…" he turned, as if remembering there were others in the room. "Let's have a day out walking tomorrow."

Michael nodded and glanced at Ellie as Ross turned his attention to Bran.

"I hope you haven't been making a habit of going in there. You're here to look after the grounds not go snooping about my home. Don't ever go there again, Bran."

"No, My Lord."

"I won't hesitate to dismiss you if you do. Understood?"

Bran nodded.

"How did you find it anyway?"

The youngest Orman shifted uneasily. "One of the dogs was after something behind the bushes in the garden and I went to see what he was up to. When I got there he was halfway through the wire. There was already a hole in it. The wire was cut and pushed in."

"Are you sure?"

Ellie studied Bran, wondering whether he knew about his father's use of the tunnel. Maybe they'd been in there together.

"Yes. Anyway, I followed the dog and we found the stairs and priest's hole."

"And presumably the entrance to the library."

Bran looked down at the floor. "I came back later, at night. I found the entrance then. Took some doing."

"That's the last visit for you, Bran. Remember what I said. And fix the wire at the end of the tunnel."

"I'll do it first thing in the morning."

"Good. Now you get off to the courtyard and make sure any guests leaving aren't too drunk to drive home. I'll join the party in a minute when I've…"

The door, which had been partly open, suddenly swung wide on its hinges and hit the door-stop with a bang. As it swung back it almost hit Camden Orman who stormed in pointing at Ellie. Right behind him was Catherine, clearly distressed by the man's behaviour as she went quickly towards Michael.

"What the…?" began Ross, indignant and striding towards the intruder.

Camden took no notice of him, going right up to Ellie. It was as if he saw no one else in the room.

"You think you're *so* smart don't you, Ellie Madison. Nice and cosy with Glenn Thorley. Bet you never thought *anyone* would find out. Oh, we are *so* silly." He slunk around her, eyes glittering, and stopped in front, pushing his face close to hers. She stepped back, loathing rising. Spittle oozed out of the corners of his mouth. "Plotting behind our backs, waiting to take everything. You got Dad, got our money. You bitch!"

"Get out of here, Orman," Ross said, glaring at the intruder, his voice hard though not loud and carrying the authority of a man whose home had been invaded.

"And have I got news for you, Lord Strathvern," he continued, not moving away, but turning his head and grinning suddenly. "This Let's-Save-the-Highlands do-gooder and trashy painter is Glenn Thorley's cousin!"

The blood drained from Ellie's face and her mouth opened without anything coming out. There was just one name, one word – Byron.

The only sound in the room was Camden's heavy breathing. His eyes were full of rage one minute and sardonic glee the next. He was so close she could feel the heat of his skin touching her and stirring her to repugnance. The bile rose in her throat and so did her desire for revenge. She no longer saw him, only what he represented.

Her open hand hit the side of his face with such force it made him step backwards, the impact leaving red marks that she wanted to scratch until they were bloody and raw. Shock registered in his eyes, the muscles in his face tightened. Rage took over, but it too was supplanted and in its place came another thing, a hated thing – the gloating and arrogance of a victor.

Not this time. He was still standing there in that grubby, tatty green jacket, grinning, lips turned up in grotesque fashion. How she disliked him – so creepy and sick-minded. Before he could try anything else she raised her arm, hand curled and fingers ready to gouge out his eyes. No mercy this time. It was her turn for victory.

From behind, her arm was caught as she was about to strike. She tried to pull herself free, but the grip tightened.

"Let go!"

"No," said Michael quietly, "that's not the answer, Ellie. He's not the one."

"He's made of the same vile stuff." She glared at Camden who was giving her a peculiar look.

"Maybe, but beating him to pulp won't change…"

He stopped and Ellie looked at him, her anger unabated. Yet silently, she thanked him for not finishing the sentence.

"You're right. I can wait." She looked at Camden. "You're a sick man, Camden Orman, and a bully. One day you'll come unstuck."

"Not before you. I'll make sure of that."

She ignored the comment. "Who told you Glenn's my cousin?"

Camden grunted, looked her up and down, and turned his attention to Bran. "You can do some things right, then. Found Ellie

Madison. Pity you couldn't follow through with the rest of it. You'll regret it."

There was no answer from Bran. Everyone was staring at him, waiting, while Ross shut the door.

Impatient, and anger growing towards Byron, Ellie asked her question again – loudly.

"Who told you Glenn's my cousin, Camden?"

"Fen. She was at Thorley's swanky hotel in Inverness. Your lover boy was there too. Nearly beat Thorley to pulp." He laughed, a hard, discordant sound.

Ellie stiffened. Byron: treacherous, untrustworthy, teller of secrets. No lover of hers. In the next second she was ashamed of her thoughts.

She became aware of Camden studying her intently. "Thorley told them you and him were cousins. Oh, Bob Caraway was there. He's the chef, but you'll know that." His eyes widened and he grinned, gloating. "Oh, you didn't! Wonder what else you don't know?"

"Why would Bob Caraway work for Thorley?" Ross was glowering at the intruder. "He can't stand the man."

"Don't know, don't care." Camden jabbed a finger into Ellie's arm. She pushed him away. "That bitch's taken enough of mine. You'd better watch her, Lord Strathvern, or she'll be the next owner of your castle." He put his forefinger to his chin, tilting his head to one side. "Or maybe it'll be Fen. That'd be fun."

"Ridiculous! Get out of my sight."

"I'll be reporting the Madison woman for assault."

"Not unless you want charges laid against you for entering my house unlawfully and abusing my guests. Like father like son!"

Ellie watched Camden. Strangely, he did not immediately respond, but stood still and looked Ross up and down as if he was the interloper.

Over by a low curved settee with rounded dents in the leather cushions and worn patches on the arms, Catherine reached out and took Michael's hand. She looked up at him. Ellie envied the intimate glance between them. Sadness stirred in her heart.

"We are a bit alike, aren't we?" Camden said. "Except he cared too much about trees and mountains. Not good for family life really." Light-hearted banter switched in a second to anger. "And her! But you won't win, Ellie Madison. Your cousin's got plans for this small-minded village. It'll put us on the map."

"That's not true," Bran said, unexpectedly loud. "He's a blood sucker. There won't be any life left in the village if he gets his way. Dad... he tried, but he got side-tracked."

The quietness in the room seemed to go on for a long time, broken only when Camden walked over to his brother.

"Shut up! You know nothing. Never did, never will. That's why you're a lackey. Hopeless. You shouldn't have done what you did. Stupid! When Mum comes back you'll have a lot of explaining to do."

There was a muffled sound from Catherine and she looked at Bran with the softness of a doe not understanding why people had to be so cruel and she wanting only to comfort.

"She won't be coming back," Ellie found herself saying firmly.

"You shut up, Ellie Madison! You drove her away," Camden spat. The imprint of her hand was still red. "You were her worst nightmare."

"No, she wasn't," Bran said. "It was..."

"She'll never come back. She's dead. Her body's been found." Ellie didn't want him to say it, didn't want him to dishonour his father whether or not he deserved it. The whole world didn't have to know about Farley's failings.

"You lie!" Camden shouted.

"That's enough, Orman," Ross said. "You either listen to Ellie or you get out now. This is *my* house and I won't have you behaving like a lout in here. Do that somewhere else." He turned to his son. "Michael, would you go and let your mother know I'll be with her soon – and take Catherine with you. She doesn't need to be subject to any more of this."

Michael opened his mouth, then shut it and walked towards the door with his wife. "Fill me in, Father."

The older man nodded.

Bran sat down in the nearest chair, his face ashen. He was staring at the enormous dark green carpet, woven roses and leaves trailing all over it.

"Ellie, you'd better tell us what you know," Ross said, his expression grim.

***

Mary came out of the sitting room, her colour high, and let out a little, "Oh!" when she saw Byron bending down near Ruth.

483

He put a finger to his lips and shook his head as she came to help Ruth with the tray and broken mug and spilled milk.

"What're you doing here?" Ruth whispered, looking at him anxiously. "And how…?"

He shook his head again and she closed her mouth. She was, he thought, too calm.

"What's going on out there?" demanded Olga.

"Nothing you can help with," Mary said, raising her eyebrows as she picked up bits of china and dropped them noisily onto the tray.

Ruth went to find the dustpan and brush and a cloth to mop up the milk. Byron watched her until she disappeared into the kitchen. He sat quite still staring at the end of the dresser she had put the tray on.

It's almost finished, he thought, and she knows it.

"I need you in here," Olga said loudly. "Where's Ruth? There's something I want her to see."

"We're not at war now, Olga, and I don't take orders from spies. Ruth's getting a brush."

Mary was still picking up pieces when Ruth reappeared with a dustpan, brush and dishcloth. An indistinct sound from the sitting room brought Byron to his feet and he moved quickly and quietly towards the door, catching a glimpse of Ruth's eyes widening as if she'd read his mind.

He shook his head and mouthed, "No."

It was too late. She dropped the dustpan and brush and was running along the hallway, avoiding his outstretched arm. They reached the door together as the gun went off.

***

If they had been in the deepest part of the earth, entombed in silence and darkness, it could not have felt more remote from the world than the next few minutes in the Strathvern library. It was an odd feeling, reminding Ellie of times with Farley when he would withdraw and sit staring across the mountains, oblivious of her or anyone else present.

The Orman men were lost in their own thoughts; Bran was staring at his shoes, clenching his teeth, but Camden began tapping his knuckles on the edge of the desk, his lips pinched in a thin, tight line. From the settee, perched on its edge as if ready to pounce, Ross glanced from one to the other of the men and his frown deepened.

There was no more to add, thought Ellie, despite the questions in Camden's eyes; questions that she doubted anyone could answer yet. No one moved from their place; the voices and music from the entrance hall and ballroom were dulled, yet not less vibrant. The sense of remoteness lasted a few more seconds.

"Where's your lover boy now?" Camden demanded, a clanging symbol shattering relative peace.

"He's not. I've no idea where Byron is," she said, resenting his tone, "but you could ring your Uncle Jack. He'll know."

Reference to 'Uncle Jack' would, she knew, rile him. Having a policeman in the family frustrated and peeved him, due mostly to his constant misdemeanours. His answer surprised her.

"He's a fool of a plod, but he loved Mum. You know nothing, Ellie. What's family to you? You don't belong anywhere. How does that feel? It's what you deserve. You've ruined ours." He turned and walked towards the door. "Come on, Bran, let's get out of here and go to Mum."

The coldness of shock squeezed Ellie's heart as Camden's words sank deep into its chambers. Truth. How it hurt. Family – what was it to her? She'd left whatever there was years ago to escape the places and things associated with the pain and horror of her childhood. How long was it since she'd seen her mother? Three years? Five? And her dad – when did she ever think about him? Hardly ever. It still hurt that he wasn't around.

She saw Bran glance at his employer, who nodded; the young man followed his brother. The door opened as Camden reached for the brass door knob and he almost collided with the countess, but Ellie was staring at his jacket, ripped at the elbow. So, it was Camden who'd shot at them from the tree at the end of her garden.

"Tell *Uncle* Jack he's wasting the old bill's time," Camden said loudly without looking back and taking no notice Caroline. "He'll never find out how dad died. No one will."

He brushed past Caroline still ignoring her. Bran, sheepish, tilted his head and hurriedly followed his brother. Ellie said nothing.

Glancing from her husband to Ellie and back to him, Caroline asked, "Darling, what's the matter?"

"It seems Alice Orman's body's been found." He still looked shocked.

"Oh, how awful. Where?"

"Jimmy's Tarn."

Caroline stared at him, her mouth slightly open. "You can't be serious. What was she doing *there*? Alice hated it."

"I don't know. Any idea, Ellie?"

Ellie, who had sat down in a wingback chair, stirred herself, drawing away from the painful truth of her family. "I don't know either, but I think she's been there a while. I got a message from Byron just before the phone died. Bob identified her by her clothing and the bent finger. She had a ring in her pocket."

Caroline's eyes were troubled.

"What's the matter, my love?"

"I've just remembered something," she said quietly. "The day before Alice disappeared she and I had afternoon tea. We got on to family history and she said she'd been researching Farley's side for a while because he'd found out he was adopted. She said he was very angry and didn't want to know anything about his birth parents. She'd found one or two snippets of information – didn't say where – and felt she was close to finding out the name of Farley's mother." She glanced at Ellie.

"When you mentioned the ring it jogged my memory. I've seen it. Alice had it with her that day. It's a solid gold piece, quite big, with the initials DB engraved on it. She didn't say she knew whose initials they were. She also thought the woman had been a German spy. She said she was going to prove it, then surprise Farley."

"Not the sort of surprise many chaps would be happy about," Ross said in a matter-of-fact tone. "Did you know, Ellie?"

She shook her head. "Not the name, but in the bowels of your very big house is a pile of information. I think you know what I'm talking about, Lord Strathvern. Now," she said, standing up, "I have to find Byron and you have to talk to Michael. He'll show you. You wanted him to know, didn't you? That's why you didn't stop us."

The countess was studying them with intense curiosity.

"Yes, but *I* never wanted to know."

"It's time you did. Good can come from it if you let it."

He sighed and nodded, putting his arm around Caroline's shoulders. "I've asked Michael to come on a walk with me tomorrow, but first thing in the morning I've something to show you."

"Oh, Ross…"

There was a knock on the door and her husband went to answer it. It was his butler saying guests were waiting to leave.

"We'll be there in two minutes." Ross shut the door and returned to the women. "We have to go, Ellie."

"Yes, of course," she responded, only half listening. MM – *who* were you?

"Are you all right, Ellie?" Caroline's voice and eyes conveyed concern.

"Fine, thanks."

"Are you coming, Caroline?"

"Yes, darling. Don't do anything too adventurous, Ellie. I wish now I'd known how important Alice's words were. I might've been able to persuade her not to pursue that aspect of the family history."

"Don't blame yourself, Lady Strathvern. You couldn't have known how dangerous it was going to be for her."

She gave Ellie a hug. "It's Caroline. Take good care. Perhaps Jamie or Michael should go with you."

"I'll be fine... Caroline. Really. Byron's probably still at Jimmy's Tarn with Jack." She didn't feel as confident as she sounded, but had no intention of adding to their worries.

At the door they were joined by Michael and Catherine as many of the remaining guests were departing, some in high spirits, a few supported by another to prevent collapsing in an undignified heap on the steps of Strathvern Castle, and others sober and gracious in their thanks and good wishes.

"Who let you out?" Ellie whispered to Michael as they stood on the top step in the brisk air. Catherine was nearby laughing with friends.

"Father. He got anxious that we were gone so long. Hardly said a word all the way back to the ballroom. But tell me, how did you disappear out of that dreadful room? We both looked and pushed and prodded. Nothing budged. Father had no idea about it. He didn't believe me until you turned up in the library."

"There's a tiny flower in the centre panel. Have a look next time."

In the Land Rover, Ellie sat in the driver's seat for several minutes. Then she got back out and went into the castle where she asked Caroline if she could use the phone. Less than ten minutes later she was reversing out of the car park smiling to herself. It was a call she should have made a long time ago.

***

Byron would not let Ruth open the door. She was crying, her eyes silently beseeching him to let her in.

"Wait," he said, barely a whisper.

Getting down on his knees, he looked through the key hole. He was on his feet immediately, thrusting the door open. Ruth rushed by him, ignoring Olga who was lying back against the settee, her hand fallen onto the seat still clasping a gun. There wasn't a mark on her. Her eyes fluttered open and she gave him a strange look, almost victorious he thought, before she closed them again. Her pulse was weak.

Behind him he heard Ruth crying and trying to soothe Hugh. He glanced round. Blood was seeping into the fabric of Hugh's pyjama shirt and dressing gown.

"Mary! Call an ambulance. Tell them it's an emergency. Hugh's been shot. Olga's fainted."

"Oh my...!"

"Just do it."

She fled into the hallway and he heard her dialling.

"Olga," he said loudly. "Come on, old thing, wake up."

"Should've known... you'd... turn up," she murmured. "Too late."

"No, it isn't. The ambulance won't be long."

She attempted a smile and gave a slight shake of her head.

"My choice."

He studied her features closely. She was very pale. Out in the hallway he found Mary listening on the phone."

"I think Olga's taken something," he said quietly.

Her eyes widened and immediately gave the listener the updated information.

"Five minutes," she said, hanging up and entering the sitting room with him.

"Talk to Olga. Try and keep her awake," Byron said, walking over to see how badly Hugh was injured. Ruth had pulled an antimacassar from the back of a seat and was holding it against the wound.

"I'm all right," Hugh said, sounding uncertain. "Long time since I've seen any action. I'd forgotten how much being shot hurts."

.

"Shh, love. Don't exert yourself," Ruth said, touching his lips gently with her finger. "How's...?" She cocked her head in Olga's direction.

"Doesn't look too good," Byron said quietly. "I think she's taken something."

Ruth looked at her. Tears formed in the corner of her eyes, but she blinked and they were gone. No words came out of her mouth and her expression changed, hardening. She turned back to her husband.

"You knew about Hugh all these years, didn't you?" Byron said.

The Lawfords looked at one another in perfect understanding and silent communication. Such was the privilege, Byron thought, of those who'd known and loved each other for years. Familiar envy and yearning stirred. He shut them down. A little distance away, the high-pitched sound of an ambulance siren penetrated the room.

"Yes," Ruth answered quietly. "Within days of this man coming to England, looking like Hugh, but not quite him. At least, not to the wife. They'd done an excellent job of it and fooled everyone." She glanced at Hugh who gave a slight nod. "Well, except one person, but it didn't matter because no one took any notice."

Colin's contact, Byron surmised. "So I heard. Tonight," he added in response to their surprised expressions. "Why didn't you tell the authorities?"

The tears stayed in her eyes this time. "Because I knew *my* Hugh was dead and this man was so like him. We fell in love and we've never been out of it."

They held hands, Hugh regarding her with such tenderness that Byron glanced away for several long seconds.

"The other half of the story," Hugh said, "is that the hierarchy in the British army worked it out and decided they'd like to keep me, but on their side. So I obliged. Never told a soul. Never needed to. I served them longer than I did Hitler. You could say I got converted." He could barely raise a smile; pain was etched in his face. "And besides falling in love with Ruth, I also fell in love with England, then Scotland.

There was a strangled sound from across the room as Olga tried to sit up. Her eyes were wide open.

The ambulance siren was much louder.

"You… you traitor!" she wheezed and fell back into the cushion.

Mary gave her a sharp look. "You're a fine one to talk. At least he came to his senses."

The old woman grasped her arm, trying to speak, but could not. Byron left the Lawfords to sit on the other side of Olga. Death, it seemed to him, was waiting to claim her. Retrieving a lace runner from the coffee table, he removed the gun from her hand, wrapped it up and put it on the small table. She did not move. For a moment he studied her pale wrinkled features and wondered why she had clung so long to lost ideals and misplaced loyalty. What a tragic life, he thought, and gently took her limp hand in his. She had courage – there was no doubt of that. Pity she hadn't used it for Britain. He looked up to find Mary studying him as if she was seeing him for the first time. In a way she was, he supposed.

Ruth stood up, but Mary shook her head and disappeared into the hallway as the siren stopped and noises and voices sounded close by. Minutes later paramedics arrived in the room with stretchers and took control. Examining their patients, they asked questions, their voices calm, encouraging, and before long were wheeling Olga and Hugh outside and into the confines of the ambulance.

How strange, Byron thought, that after all these decades the two spies should end up in an ambulance together. Minutes later, he and Mary found themselves alone in the house. It was quiet, an odd quiet of the sort that happens after momentous events.

"Cuppa then?" she asked wearily. "Strong and sweet?"

Nodding, he watched her walk down the hallway, her shoulders hunched as if she was carrying a great weight.

He delved into his jacket pocket to retrieve his phone and found the ring Bob had given him. He'd forgotten it.

The phone rang a couple of times before Colin answered.

"It's all done here," Byron said to his sleepy friend.

"Meaning?"

"Olga and Hugh have been taken to hospital."

"What!" There was little doubt he was now wide awake.

"Hugh took a bullet in the shoulder. Olga's taken something. Not sure she'll make it."

"Oh." There was a second's silence. "Who shot Lawford?"

"Olga. It's more complicated than I thought, but your information about Hugh was right. Olga was here to tell Ruth all about her wayward husband."

From in the kitchen he heard Mary's voice, but she didn't seem to be calling him to tea.

"How did she take it?" Colin asked.

"She's known all along."

"Are you kidding?"

"No. I'll fill you in later."

"Be sure you do."

"Night, Colin – and thanks."

"Night, Byron. Glad you're still alive."

Mary came hurrying out of the kitchen, anxiety in her eyes and pinched features.

"He said I should go to the hospital," she said, looking at him as if she wanted him to say it was unnecessary.

Byron frowned. "Who did?"

"My husband, Mark. I used the phone in the kitchen. I didn't think they'd mind."

"You told him what happened here?"

"I'm not into blathering about national secrets, Byron. Only the bit about Olga saying she's my mother and… well, you know."

"I'll drive you."

"No. That's kind, but I need to be by myself for a bit."

"I'll follow to make sure you get there okay."

"Are you always this thoughtful? I saw you wi' Olga. She's betrayed our country all her life, but you said nothing to her, just held her hand."

Sometimes he wasn't sure himself why he felt compassion for enemies as well as friends.

They turned out the lights and shut the door behind them, walking out into chill, damp air. Byron held the car door open as Mary got inside and put the key in the ignition. As she settled herself he remembered the ring and took it out of his pocket.

"Thanks, Byron. It's only five minutes to the hospital from here and I'll be…" She stared at the ring in the palm of his hand. "Where did you get that?" The colour drained from her cheeks.

He went around and got in the passenger seat. "Bob," he said quietly.

"Bob Caraway?" Her voice was loud and surprised in the small interior. Her frown hinted at displeasure.

491

"Where'd he get it? I haven't seen it for years," she said, shaking her head. "Not since Alice wandered off. Never did understand that. She had her moments in the last few months, but she didn't seem to be losing her marbles to me." Suddenly her eyes grew big. "Have you... did she give it to Bob?"

Byron shook his head. "No. Mary... Alice is dead."

She stared at him, swallowing. "I always hoped she'd just turn up one day, smiling as she almost always did. I suppose it was nothing but a dream really, but she was one of my closest friends. They're hard to replace you know," she said, dabbing her eyes. "How d'you know she's... dead?'

Byron told her what he thought she needed to know.

"Oh, poor wee Alice! To die all alone in that place!" she cried, shuddering and then shaking her head. "And Jack – he doted on her. This'll be hard for him – and the Orman boys. She was their rock, especially when they were bairns."

"What about Fenella?"

Her eyebrows went up and down before she turned a stern expression upon him. "She was born independent and arrogant that one. Always preferred her dad. When she was about ten she started ignoring Alice, used to pretend she wasn't there. Even at home!" The eyebrows shot up again along with the pitch. "That hurt Alice. She told me once she felt like a stranger in her own home, especially when the boys weren't there."

"Camden doesn't seem the type to be close to his mother."

"Oh, aye, he was. I know it seems odd, being what he's turned out to be, but he's got a soft spot for frail elderly people, animals, and especially his mother."

They sat in silence, enfolded in darkness with the moon showing its face only when the clouds parted for a few seconds.

"So, who d'you think killed her then?" Mary said quietly, watching him with a candour he should by now expect.

However, he couldn't hide his surprise at the question and her lips twitched as if she wanted to laugh.

"Well, I don't know if she was." He sounded as uncertain of his answer as he felt it was pathetic.

"I'm not stupid, Byron Oakes. Alice hated Jimmy's Tarn. She wouldn't have driven herself there and then just died. Who'd have buried her? Besides, her car was never found. Where exactly did you find her?"

Byron hesitated and Mary glared at him until he told her. Tears ran down her cheeks and she fumbled in her pockets for a handkerchief.

"She didn't deserve that," she said thickly. "She didn't deserve any of it. Who'd want to kill Alice? She was no threat to anyone."

"That's obviously not true." He studied her while she wiped her eyes and blew her nose. Sighing, she put her handkerchief in her pocket and sat very still, staring out through the windscreen. Her lips were partly open. "What is it, Mary?"

She shook her head, biting her bottom lip. "How is it that at fifty-six I find out that my real parents were German spies! The two people I think of as Mum and Dad told me when I was quite young that they'd adopted me because my natural parents were killed in the Glasgow bombings along with my grandmother." She turned the ignition on. "I have to get to the hospital. I hope Olga Erskine, or whatever her name is, dies. She shouldn't have done this. She's made my whole life a lie. She's lived in the village seeing me, talking to me, knowing I was her daughter and never *once* saying anything! And Ruth – what's she done to that poor woman?" She turned to him, angry. "You want to know what it is, Byron Oakes? I'll tell you because I've just realised something that Olga said. Alice called me two days after she disappeared. Never said where she was, but that she had good reason to believe Farley was the previous Earl of Strathvern's son. His and a woman called Marian MacAdam. *That* treacherous woman who calls herself Olga Erskine! I didn't really believe Alice and put it out of my mind, but now I want to watch Olga die. She's a thief. She's stolen part of my life."

Tears trickled down her cheeks and dripped onto the collar of her jacket, her shoulders shaking. Byron reached over and turned the ignition off. He did not touch her, other than to give her hand a gentle squeeze. While her grief at such loss and deception absorbed her, Byron began to see the puzzle almost in its entirety. The war, now decades in the past, had grasped with its cruel fingers into the lives of another generation and tainted it. One woman who had struggled with her own troubled childhood already tainted by the adults who conceived her, had lived her life doing all she could to blot it out, wash it away, but without ever succeeding. Was it even possible? It hadn't been for him. Ena still lingered and the pain with it.

There were many strands linking Olga to the puzzle. Had she engineered the deaths of Farley and Alice to stop them talking?

Could a woman murder her own child? A cold shiver ran down his spine. Bile rose in his throat and his innards contorted into a tight mass as he remembered, and he got out of the car and took deep breaths of Inverness air. It was impossible to forget such things. Put them in a deep chamber somewhere in the mind, yes, but erase them? No. The memory of what he had witnessed one winter in a land he had never gone back to, reminded him that humans were capable of the most horrific violence when they believed that what they were doing was right. Could she have done it? Yes. Did she do it? That he had yet to find out.

"Byron, are you all right?" Mary's voice still had tears in it.

"Yes. You get going. I'll be right behind." He couldn't bring himself to engage in conversation with her; he had to put the memories back where they belonged.

Chapter 28

Dawn arrived cold, damp and misty, and Ellie was beginning to question her sanity in sitting huddled in her car watching the front of an old woman's house. Although she had parked a little up the road, partly obscured by a scrappy hedge, she couldn't help being concerned that neighbours had heard her vehicle arrive before the sun was up and thought it odd. There were few houses along the lane, and the residents probably knew every turn and odd rattle of every engine of their neighbours' vehicles. So far, however, she'd heard only cockerels advertising the new day, one or two dogs barking and a car, three doors down, heading off in the opposite direction. Exhaust gas puffed out the tail pipe.

The sun barely made an impression on the landscape, its light pale and ghostly. Leaves, windows and roofs, the bonnet of her vehicle, and a metal gate were damp with dew. A good morning to be snug in bed, she thought. The policeman at her house had been full of questions when she'd turned up in the middle of the night and furious when she went off again first thing in the morning. She'd had neither time nor patience with him and had driven off not bothering to look in the rear vision mirror. Jack would be furious.

She'd heard no more from Byron and hadn't gone to Jimmy's Tarn – she couldn't face it. When she'd phoned from home his mobile had been switched off. Staring across the lane at Olga's house, its bricks and tiled roof and the windows under the eaves were, somehow, unwelcoming. There was no sign of movement and the curtains were drawn.

Ellie closed her eyes and thought about Alice. What had made her to go out to Jimmy's Tarn? Byron's message had given few details. *'Under the floor'* meant maggots and decay, lifeless eyes. That wasn't Alice. A terrible thought surfaced, one she'd locked away before.

Alice had loved Farley so much. Too much some said. It had been suggested before, but Ellie had not believed it then and did not believe it now. Whatever his faults, whatever people knew or didn't know, Farley would never have done anything to harm his wife. She was, he'd said, his stabiliser, the one who kept him from getting caught in a rip tide and being swept away with the flotsam.

A gate clicked behind her and Ellie's eyes shot open. An elderly man with a walking stick opened an ancient gate and a young black Labrador scampered past him and began snuffling in the hedgerow. As they went past the man glanced at her, gave a curt nod and followed his dog along the lane. A couple of minutes later they disappeared into another lane. Ellie hoped he hadn't taken mental notes of what she looked like or memorised the number plate. Perhaps she was becoming paranoid.

Out of the corner of her eye she saw a curtain twitch in an upstairs room of Olga's house and she shrank into her seat. The lace curtain hid most of the face, making it difficult to identify who it might be. Yet, she was sure it was a woman. What was she was doing in the house? No one had ever mentioned Olga having relatives, but if she *was* Marian MacAdam…

The woman dropped the curtain and turned away from the window. Unable to sit cooped up for another minute, Ellie slipped out into the nippy air, shut the door quietly and walked up the lane until she was level with the far end of the hedge around Olga's house, which stood on a corner. She crossed the potholed lane in an unhurried fashion and went along the side hedge until she found a wooden gate opening onto a path planted on both sides by garden beds, one of them along the wall of the house. A window looked out on the hedge. Craning her neck over the gate she looked to her right. There was a washing line near a bird bath, and a large shed which looked as if it needed serious repairs. It occupied a generous space at the bottom of the garden. A seat underneath a tree faced flourishing herb beds and she'd have loved time amongst them, enjoying the scents, rubbing the leaves and flowers between her fingertips.

For a few seconds Ellie stared down at the gate. She had no idea whether it creaked, squeaked or grated when being opened or shut. However, before she could make up her mind about entering, the back door opened and footsteps pattered down the path. Ellie ducked behind the hedge.

Olga's visitor walked quickly towards the shed and a few moments later a car started up. As it backed out into the lane, Ellie went through the gate, which creaked, and was out of sight as the car turned into the lane. Peering round the end of the hedge, she caught sight of the driver in a dark red car and her heart missed a beat. It was Fenella Orman.

In less than two minutes the sound of the car faded. Ellie didn't move. Disturbed, she stared at a puddle in the lane. What was Fenella doing here and why had she hurried down the path? Ellie turned and looked at the house, then walked quickly to the corner of it where she listened for Olga's presence. There was no sound of a kettle on the boil, no water gushing into the kitchen sink, no clatter of cups and saucers. Maybe Olga was still in bed. Maybe Olga wasn't well.

Of all people – that self-centred Fenella Orman, she thought as she walked softly, but quickly towards the back door. She studied it for a few seconds. How was she going to get in? However, as it turned out, she didn't have to consider the matter for long. The back door was unlocked.

There was no sign of Olga in the kitchen or the front room. Curtains were still drawn except for a gap of two or three inches, and there was a mug on the coffee table with cocoa residue in the bottom of it. One of the drawers on the sideboard was open. Skirting round a plump seat, Ellie peered into the drawer; it contained silver cutlery set out in an orderly fashion, each implement in a separate section. Inexpert though she was, the weight of the various pieces was impressive. It was then she noticed the handle of a serving spoon engraved with the Strathvern crest.

Ellie left the room and went upstairs, several boards creaking underfoot. There was no sound of Olga stirring. It was gloomy on the landing and she stubbed her toe on the corner of a small cupboard, stifling a grunt of pain and annoyance. Still Olga did not call out. Coldness crept down her spine.

The first room she entered was small and spartan and set up as a study. The next door was partly open and she stopped and listened, peering through the gap between door and frame. It appeared to be the main bedroom. Puzzled, she stepped quietly into the room. The bed was made and unruffled. There was no sign of Olga.

Relieved, Ellie began looking around the gloomy room. The dressing table, wardrobe and bed ends were oak, Victorian, she thought, and similar to her grandmother's. Stepping across to the window, she peeked out. All that could be seen of the Land Rover was the bonnet and grill.

She turned on the bedside lamp and for some minutes gazed at the dark furniture and plain carpet. In contrast, the quilt was bright with pansies and pink roses. Directly across from the bed was a dressing table and over it hung a large painting of a big building with a small group of people in the bottom right corner. However, Ellie was more interested in finding evidence that Olga Erskine was Marian MacAdam than studying paintings on walls. The study, she decided, was the best place to start. A piece of silver in a cutlery drawer was not enough. It could have been a gift or she could have helped herself to it.

Passing the painting, she glanced at it, and stopped. A Nazi flag was hanging limp from the building. Her eyes rested on the group of people, five altogether. There was no mistaking the identity of two of them: Hitler, pulling on gloves, Goering, and three others, all looking relaxed, smiling. No doubt considering another of their warped and sinister plots, she thought bitterly. About to turn away, she peered at the two figures standing opposite Hitler. One of the men had his hand on another's shoulder. She stared at the features of the latter. It wasn't a man at all, but a woman, her winsome smile directed at Hitler.

"It's an awful painting. Brown, dull and ugly, but Olga loved it. As they say, there's no accounting for taste."

Ellie spun round, her heart thumping. Standing in the doorway was Fenella, her brown eyes regarding Ellie with haughty amusement.

"What're you doing here?" Ellie asked, shoving the fright aside. "You sped off."

"I had to make it look convincing. You didn't really think I hadn't noticed you hiding behind that tree, did you? A five-year-old could've done a better job than you did. I have a right to be here. You're trespassing."

She came into the room, elegant even in jeans, an olive-green angora jumper and walking jacket, and sat down on the edge of the bed. A twinge of envy ruffled Ellie which she promptly hid behind a cold study of the unexpected visitor and a blunt question.

"Where's Olga?" she asked, wondering at the same time whether she knew about the discovery of her mother's remains.

"I thought you'd know. You're the one who's been spying on her."

"Where is she, Fenella?"

The younger woman got up off the bed and went to the painting, her finger touching the figures.

"Haven't a clue. The old thing's not one to sit around and stagnate. I suppose you know she's my grandmother," she said in a matter-of-fact tone, without glancing around. "That's her there. I suppose you know that too."

"I do now. How long have you known about her?"

"Why is it you always know everything?" Fenella turned around, frowning and petulant. "Glenn says you're the only one we really have to worry about. You always work things out. He admires you in a funny sort of way. You look surprised. Not as surprised as me when he said you were his cousin. Did you know he told me and Bob? Byron Oakes already knew. You're quite good... chums... aren't you?" Fenella cocked an eyebrow before returning to the bed and sitting down. "Actually, I think Glenn'd rather have you in partnership than me. A bit odd, don't you think?"

"He'd be the *last* person I'd go into partnership with," Ellie snapped.

"I wonder why that is?"

"It's none of your business."

"He's got a soft spot for you and it'd keep it all in the family. Very tidy."

Ellie glared at her and then looked at the picture. What did Fenella know? Glenn wouldn't tell her, but he could have told her something that wasn't true. Right now she didn't care. Besides, in a few days he'd be out of Scotland. Her uncle had been very understanding, but then he'd always been very fond of her.

It was time to take control of the conversation.

"Your mother's been found."

"Don't be ridiculous."

"I'm not. They've found her body."

"That's impossible!"

The colour drained from Fenella's features and she sat unmoving, staring at the painting. Ellie didn't know whether she was in shock or denial, but it was clear the news was having a profound effect on her, and that neither Camden nor Bran had told her.

"I have to go," Fenella said abruptly and stood up, studying Ellie. "You *did* know Olga's my grandmother didn't you?"

499

Ellie was astounded. Her mother's body had been found and she was talking about Olga!

"Other than Glenn, you're the most arrogant, self-centred, uncaring person I've ever met." She didn't answer the question and she wasn't going to let Fenella know it had only been in the wee hours of the morning she'd realised Marian McAdam and Olga were probably one in the same. "How long have you known?"

A slow smile accompanied a sly, almost mischievous, expression in her eyes.

"Nearly all my adult life. Long before Dad stumbled on any of the stuff he found. He never knew I knew. It was our secret, mine and Gran's. So, as I said, I have a right to be in her house, but you're trespassing."

Ellie stared at her. "Why didn't you tell him?"

"And share my heritage with him and those idiot brothers of mine? Don't be stupid, Ellie." She peered at her, her expression hardening. "Have you told them?"

"No. What heritage are you expecting, Fenella?"

"You don't know?" She looked astonished. "I thought Dad told you everything."

"We didn't have that kind of relationship."

Her lips curled in a lascivious smile. "You can spare me the details. If he didn't tell you what he found out, then I'm not going to bother. Let's just say that Glenn came along at a very convenient time and I'll soon have what's mine."

"I doubt it. Glenn won't be around here much longer."

"He'll be here for as I long as I want him here."

"You have no say in it."

"And you do?"

Ellie didn't answer the question and kept her expression neutral. "By the way, your brothers do know about your mother's body being found."

"Stupid woman. She'd still be alive if she hadn't..." She stopped, biting her lip, and for a second her eyes glistened before she blinked and walked past Ellie towards the door. "I have to go. So do you. Can't leave you here poking around. Gran wouldn't like that. She's taught me a lot of things and one of them is not leaving people like you where you don't want them."

"Alice would be alive if she hadn't... what?" Ellie asked sharply, appalled by the implication.

Fenella didn't reply. She walked out of the room and Ellie followed her down the stairs. When they reached the kitchen, the young woman turned and looked at her.

"Don't meddle in what doesn't concern you, Ellie Madison. I'm sure you don't want to end up like her." She opened the back door. "After you. Don't come back here without Gran's permission."

As she walked down the lane, Ellie knew she was being watched to make certain she left. When she drove off Fenella followed her back into Kilcomb's main street before continuing on. She turned right at the crossroads and Ellie waited for a minute before taking the same turn. After all, her house was in that direction.

There were a number of turns Fenella might have taken, but as she hadn't asked where her mother's body was found, Ellie wondered if she already knew. There were two routes outside Kilcomb to Jimmy's Tarn. First, however, she had to make a phone call and stopped at her house. A police car was parked in the driveway and she remembered that she'd left without notifying them and then a second time without permission. Jack wouldn't be happy. She was about to back out of the gateway when she heard excited barking and Kipp came bounding around the corner of the house. Joy filled her and she stopped and got out of the vehicle. Seconds later he almost bowled her over in his exuberance and she wrapped her arms around his neck.

"Oh, Kipp! I've missed you!"

"Aye, and we've missed you, Ellie," said a familiar, though peeved, voice. "Where've you been?"

Jack was regarding her sternly, arms folded across his chest, while Tim Ashby stood almost level with him, his eyebrows raised and a look of annoyance on his young face. Behind them was another man.

"Hello, Ellie," he said quietly without smiling.

His brown eyes were studying her with an intensity that made her want to run to him and recoil at the same time.

"Hello, Byron." There was nothing else she felt to say, though her feelings for him were unexpectedly strong. Mistrust hovered over a desire for closeness and she returned her attention to the man nearest her.

"So," said Jack, "where've you been? You vanish wi'out the constable knowing until it was too late, turn up in the middle of the night, and then do another disappearing act this morning!"

"Sorry," she said, not sorry at all. "Something I had to do. Lord Strathvern will vouch for me. I was at the countess' party."

Jack stared at her, exasperated. "You should've told me, Ellie. That was irresponsible. You could've been dead for all we knew. If you try that again I'll lock you in the cells."

She attempted to look contrite, but doubted she fooled any of them. Fenella was getting farther away. If she didn't know where Olga was, where else would she go?

"...Ellie?"

"What?" She re-focussed on Jack. "Sorry. I missed what you said."

"You're beginning to irritate me and I'm not so sure how innocent you are," he said gruffly. "Where did you go this morning?"

Hesitating, she glanced at Byron who was still watching her, giving nothing away. Suddenly, she realised how they might perceive her behaviour. First, Farley was found dead at the Knobbles and she benefits from his will. Second, Alice's body turns up at Jimmy's Tarn, a woman some thought Ellie wanted out of the way so she could marry Farley. A shiver ran down her spine.

"I didn't kill either of them," she said, frowning, looking at each of them. "They were my friends. I'd never have stayed in Kilcomb if it hadn't been for them."

"I know that, lass," Jack answered, his expression softening, "but I still need to know where you went this morning."

"Olga's."

Even Byron looked surprised.

Jack stared at her, frowning. "What for?"

For a second she said nothing. There was suspicion in his voice and eyes, and she had the feeling that he was waiting for a specific answer.

"I think she knows who killed Farley. Besides, she's got an interesting history."

Jack's pencil hovered over a page in his notebook and he looked at Byron who walked towards Ellie and stood almost within arms' reach. Struggling with disappointment, she forced herself to look at him with as little emotion as possible.

He spoke first. "Her real name's Marian MacAdam. During World War Two she spied for Germany."

The sound of his voice was like music to Ellie, music once loved but lost and unexpectedly heard again.

502

"I wonder if Fenella knew what she really did." Ellie's words were almost to herself.

"Care to explain?" Jack asked testily. Ellie had the distinct impression he was annoyed that she seemed to know more than he did.

"She was at Olga's house. I don't know why. I told her Alice had been found. Seems no one's bothered to tell her."

"Not for want of trying. She didn't answer her phone," Jack grumbled.

"Well, she left in a hurry saying she had somewhere to go and told me to leave and not come back. Then she followed me to the village to make sure I didn't go back into the house. She also said she didn't know where Olga was."

"That woman's a law to herself. Could be anywhere," Jack said. "Camden and Bran turned up at Jimmy's Tarn last night. Said you'd told them about their mother. How d'you know?"

"I sent her a text message." Byron answered for her.

"Camden was at Strathvern as obnoxious as always – it's a long story," Ellie said in response to Jack's raised eyebrows, "and I just said about his mother being found. It kind of popped out."

"You should've let us tell the Ormans." Jack snapped his book shut and glanced from one to the other. "Camden made a nuisance of himself and almost destroyed the crime scene. Next time keep your mouths shut."

He looked exhausted and ten years older than the last time Ellie had seen him. Seeing Alice could not have been easy. They'd been close despite their different natures and feelings about Farley.

"I'm so sorry about Alice, Jack."

"Aye. She didn't deserve that. CID'd better find who did it before I do. I won't be as lenient as them." He looked from Byron to her and in his eyes she saw a message. "Right," he said curtly, "we'll be getting back to the station. Ellie, you still owe me a statement about your kidnapping. I've already had my backside roasted by Carter for not getting it. He thinks you're withholding information. So do I. I want to see you before the end of the day. Understand?"

Ellie nodded, but doubted it would happen.

The doors of the police vehicle banged shut and the two policemen disappeared down the road as the sun managed to send a few watery rays into Ellie's garden. Neither Ellie nor Byron

503

moved until Kipp began barking wanting attention. They both obliged.

"D'you know where Olga is?" Ellie resisted anything personal. There was too much to say.

He looked disappointed, but responded only to the question. "She's in Inverness Hospital. She tried to poison herself last night at the Lawfords."

The news appalled Ellie. "Why would she do that?"

"She wanted vengeance and in a way she got it."

"What sort of vengeance? She doesn't know the Lawfords. Olga's a loner."

Byron sighed and she could see he was annoyed. He had no right to be.

"Ruth Lawford's her sister," he said without hurry. "Olga's idea of inflicting pain was to gloat about the four children she'd had when Ruth, who desperately wanted them, had none. And to drive the point home she not only had one of her children with her, but told Hugh he was the father."

Ellie stared at him, blinked, and said nothing, her eyes darting away to the flowers outside the sitting room window. How on earth had he come upon such information? She wanted to ask, but it didn't feel right. Besides, her analytical processes were busy trying to make sense of what he'd divulged. She'd never heard of Ruth having a fourth sister. As to Hugh, she couldn't imagine him having an affair with Olga or any other woman. He was about as conservative as they came. Byron must've got it wrong. And the child?

"Farley's sister." She made the statement, but the unasked question was in her eyes. Her heart was thumping.

Byron didn't answer directly. "Are you telling me Farley is the Earl of Strathvern and Olga Erskine's son?"

"You didn't know?" She was surprised.

He shook his head. "It could explain a few things, but... Are you sure about this?"

"Reasonably. I've seen photos from the castle of a boy and girl. The boy *looks* a bit like him. It's hard to tell. And I showed Bran one of them and he thought it resembled him."

"Does he know where the photo came from?"

"No."

"I'm no detective, but I'm not convinced. As to Alice – buried at Jimmy's Tarn, Bromley ring in her pocket, Farley's wife. I'd guess she found out something she shouldn't have."

"What on earth's the Bromley's ring?"

"Handed down the generations from the Alisdair Bromley who was on the Klondike. Mary didn't think much about it when her mother gave it to her. She assumed it was from her mother's side."

A peculiar sensation buzzed in Ellie's head and ran down her spine.

"Mary?" she managed to get out.

"Mary Nevin. She's Olga's daughter. Olga and Hugh Lawford's."

Ellie stared at the hedge. Was it *possible* that a woman would live all her life in the same village as her two children and not tell either of them she was their mother?

"How long have you known this?" Her voice was hard.

"Since last night, just like her. Look, Ellie, don't stand there accusing me of something I haven't done. I had no idea where you were and only sent the last text message on the off chance you'd get it – and contact me. You didn't. The only conclusion I can come to is that you'd rather I disappeared into the Scottish mist and never reappeared. So, let's get on with it and then we can go our separate ways."

There was anger in his eyes, anger at her.

"Well, I couldn't get hold of you either, so don't go chucking all the blame on me!"

A long, tense silence ruled over them like a referee in a boxing match determined to keep the opponents separated. Today she had no desire for combat with him.

"What kind of a woman is she?" she said changing her tone and the subject, frowning, struggling to pull the strands together.

He didn't ask who she meant.

"A committed Nazi sympathiser who's never let go."

"But the war's been over for fifty years! She had two children right on her doorstep. That's not commitment, that's fanaticism. It's sick!"

"It's the only way she knows how to do life, Ellie. She was valued."

"Valued! The woman betrayed her country in cahoots with her brother and father! Don't excuse her, Byron. She doesn't deserve it."

"Maybe not, but you asked what kind of woman she is and that's the answer. She was an illegitimate child, like her older brother, and she needed to belong. The Nazi party filled that hole, at least in her mind, and she remained faithful."

"And poisoning herself was her warped way of joining with the great of the party?" she said sarcastically. Byron nodded. He was subdued and Ellie felt a surge of impatience. "You're being very defensive of her. Why?"

"I'm not. I feel sorry for her. She's an intelligent woman and she's wasted decades of her life waiting for the second coming of Hitler and it'll never happen. He was her hero and we all need one of those. Haven't you ever had one?"

The mist had been shifting while they stood in the driveway; the sunlight was strengthening. The front windows were bedecked with tiny droplets of water and the lawn was bright green in its wetness. In the cool dampness Ellie studied Byron's features while she thought about how to answer. Yearning stirred and she so wanted to touch his face and find in his eyes love and acceptance, eyes without condemnation or mockery. Yet the taunting question surfaced again. What if she was incapable of loving and trusting him even if it did turn out he wanted to be with her?

He turned his face towards her before she had a chance to hide her expression and for a second it seemed he wanted to say something to her. Then it was gone. Disappointment overruled the yearning and it sank back out of sight.

"No," she said quietly. "I've always been too busy being afraid someone would find out about my past and reject me."

***

No one moved or touched her. Against the law or not, Byron didn't care. He'd called in a forensic friend who'd done the testing and asked Ross a lot of questions. Now, as they stood in Byron's attic, a copy of the forensic report in Ross' hand, no one spoke for several minutes. Emotions travelled across the earl's face like shifting sand.

"I always knew somehow that she hadn't committed suicide. It was Nanny who told me she had seen sandbags in the coffin, but had been terrified to say anything and then convinced herself that the coffin bearers had used it to practise carrying the countess into the church. Why my... why that traitorous brute poisoned my mother and put her here we'll never know." He drew in a deep breath and said quietly, "I wish I'd been old enough to understand and prevent the awful thing that happened to you, Mother. You were snatched away from me. You deserved none of what he did to you. I've missed you so much!"

He clamped his lips shut, tears sitting on the ledge of his eyelids. Michael put his hand on his father's shoulder and the others quietly left the attic, gathering downstairs in the kitchen where Ellie put the kettle on and Caroline found mugs.

Byron said, "I think he'll need something stronger than that."

He disappeared along the hallway as Ross and Michael descended the stairs.

"Sorry, it's all there is," Byron said holding up a bottle of brandy.

"Don't be sorry, laddie. It's Scotland's best," Jack quipped. "Glasses?"

"In the cupboard behind you."

They watched as Jack poured and handed a glass to each one.

Ross said, "I've organised the funeral for the end of next week and the service will be held in the estate's church. She will be buried in the family cemetery." He looked at Byron, Ellie and Jack in turn. "Please come."

As if one, they responded with a nod.

Ross raised his glass. "To Margaret, Countess of Strathvern."

The five responded, their voices filling the cottage. "To Margaret, Countess of Strathvern."

Chapter 29

Byron stared at the middle-aged nurse. "What d'you mean she's not here?"

"I should've thought that was plain enough to understand – even for a southerner," she replied in clipped tones. "She's gone, taken away, flown the coop or, in this case, the ward. A young woman in a nurse's uniform, her granddaughter I believe, came and wheeled her outside for a breath of fresh air and that's the last we saw of them."

"And you just let her wheel her down the corridor? She tried to kill herself last night and was supposed to have been watched."

"And I don't follow every patient out into the gardens to make sure they don't scarper. I'm hardly going to mistrust a nurse." She regarded him intently, clearly annoyed.

Byron glanced at Ellie who raised her eyebrows.

"I doubt the young woman *was* a nurse."

The nurse pinched her lips together and gave him a withering look. "And *you* weren't here. She was a caring, knowledgeable young woman."

"Have you notified anyone?"

"Of course. I informed the doctor."

"What about the police?"

"That's the doctor's decision, not mine. If you wait around for an hour he'll be back and you can ask him yourself. I have a ward to run, so excuse me if I get on with it."

"How long has she been gone?" Byron ignored the hint that he should make himself scarce.

"About twenty minutes or so. Look," she said, glancing from Byron to Ellie, "the potion Mrs Erskine took wouldn't have killed her. It was a homemade remedy of some sort and I was told that within a couple of hours most of its effects had worn off. She would've had to take more than she did to end her life. The doctor was going to release her tomorrow morning."

Without waiting for any response, she turned and answered the phone, ignoring them.

He turned to Ellie. "Let's go and see Hugh Lawford."

She nodded, but did not look directly at him. He told himself it didn't matter, but it did.

They walked along the corridor without speaking. He wanted to take her hand. They were so close he could feel the warmth of her and yet, as he had done outside her house, he read her lack of communication as 'don't bother me'.

During the drive to Inverness he'd told her what had happened at the Lawfords' house, but not about Hugh's past or his real identity. It was not for him to reveal that information. When she'd asked about Alice he'd explained where they found her and had gone on to tell of his mad escape from the police, then the unexpected journey following Olga and Mary to Inverness. In return she'd given him details of the room under Strathvern Castle and what she'd found, and of Bran turning up in one of the tunnels that led through an old priest's hole and into the library. It made him think of the old war photos he'd had developed in Inverness. The one of the Nazi flag behind a desk had probably been taken in the room in the castle's tunnel Ellie described. Even so, he was sure it was not all, just as he had not told all. Miffed by her remoteness he'd briefly mentioned the hidden cupboard in Ross' study. The divide between them seemed to be widening and he didn't know how to close it. He glanced at her and his heart ached. There was no return glance from her.

They arrived outside the door of Hugh's room and stopped, listening to a conversation in full flow.

"Well, the nurse must know, Hugh. She's in charge of the ward. Said Marian had a visitor and neither of them came back."

"How can that fat old tart vanish? She's as slow as a Galapagos tortoise!"

"Shh, Hugh. You'll have the nurses running down here to find out what's wrong." Ruth's voice was low, strong.

"And you know as well as I do that Marian could turn up in somewhere like Edinburgh, totally transformed into another character, and tell anyone who wants to listen – and they will – who I am! And you, my darling, will not be spared."

Ellie looked at Byron and he saw the questions in her eyes, but said nothing.

"She won't get far. After all these years it'll blow over."

"You know better than that, Ruth," he said quietly, and then there was silence except for a faint snuffling sound.

Byron leaned towards Ellie and whispered, "Time to go in."

The Lawfords looked startled at their appearance, but it lasted only a moment. Ruth put her handkerchief away and smiled at them. Hugh, however, was studying them intensely.

"I'm guessing you heard some of that," he said bluntly.

Although Hugh was bandaged and sitting awkwardly, he still had the bearing of a soldier and his eyes sparked with life.

"Some," Byron said, "but Ruth's right, Olga's... Marian's disappeared."

"So, you heard all that then?"

Byron nodded. "Sorry, Hugh, Ruth. We didn't want to barge in."

"So you eavesdropped instead." Hugh's eyebrows arched upwards.

"Well, yes."

"Hmm. You should've joined the spy brigade."

"Not my cup of tea." He changed the subject. "The nurse we spoke to said Olga's been gone about twenty minutes."

"She's no fool. It won't be easy to find her. She's had a lifetime of hoodwinking people."

"Including her own family," Ruth added quietly. "How did she manage to get out on her own?"

"She had help," Ellie said. Byron glanced at her. "Actually," she went on in what Byron thought a defiant tone, "it was Fenella Orman parading as a nurse."

The Lawfords stared at her, then at Byron.

He nodded. "That's who the description fits."

They still didn't speak.

"Any idea where Olga would go?" Ellie asked.

Hugh seemed to gather his thoughts together. "I don't know." He reached for his wife's hand. "We'd had no contact with her since the war until last night."

"And she's focused on the war now from what I've heard."

"And her childhood." Ruth sounded regretful. "Last night she said that when she joined the Nazis she felt valued for the first time in her life. I was so shocked I didn't know what to say. How could anyone even *think* about them that way? But then I saw deep pain in her eyes, just for a second, but it was there. This morning I began to realise what a terrible childhood she must've had. Our father wasn't an easy man to live with, and I remember him telling Marian and Alisdair their mothers hadn't been good enough for him to marry. What a terrible thing to tell a child. I've often wondered what happened to those women."

"Mothers?"

"Yes, Ellie, mothers. My father wasn't a faithful man. He did marry my mother and had three daughters by her, but it wasn't a happy relationship. I wouldn't be surprised if there are other half-brothers and sisters dotted about the Highlands."

She looked out the window and no one spoke until Hugh said sharply, "She shouldn't have kept my daughter from me. She would've had a good life with us."

"D'you really believe that?" Ruth asked, touching his arm.

He sighed and shook his head slowly. "We'd have loved her, but I was consumed with army life and being the perfect loyal soldier. I was away too much, wasn't I?"

"Yes, but I never doubted you."

"I know, but I wish Marian had told me about Mary. I suppose she's sure I am the father. I mean she had…"

"She'd never have gone to all the trouble of coming last night if she hadn't been, darling. She wanted to humiliate me and show you she still had the upper hand. Or so she thought. Quite frankly, I think you outdid her last night. And Mary's certainly got your courage and pep," Ruth said, smiling, before turning her attention to their visitors. "You know, Marian went off to Germany just after the war started. For a holiday she said, but seeing her again now I don't think that was ever in her plans. No one thought the war would last more than a few months. I never saw her again. Never expected to. Even last night I doubt I'd have recognised her if I'd bumped into her. We rarely go to Kilcomb."

"What about you, Hugh?" Byron asked.

The man's brow wrinkled. "Actually, she did come up to me once a few years ago. I'd forgotten about it. I thought she was a batty old stick saying how much I reminded her of an old flame. There was nothing about her that remotely resembled Marian, but she always was the best when it came to disguise and deception."

"Jimmy's Tarn," Ruth said unexpectedly, looking at Ellie. "She might go there."

"The police are there," Byron said, taking control of the conversation.

"Whatever for?"

"Alice Orman's body was found last night."

Ruth went pale. "How awful! How did such a thing happen?"

"I don't know."

"My nephew Bob always spoke highly of her. He was very upset when she went missing. I think they'd been doing some kind of research together."

"D'you know what kind?" Ellie frowned, looking at Ruth intently. Byron wondered what she – and Bob – knew that he didn't.

"Can't remember if he even told me."

"Byron," Hugh said, trying to shift himself into a more upright position, "Marian was a first-class spy. So good in fact that Hitler twice invited her to dine with him and Eva. Don't underestimate what she's capable of and who she'll use."

Ruth plumped up his pillows. "She'll go to Jimmy's Tarn. Don't ask me why, I just feel it. Where was Alice found?"

"Under the floorboards in the house."

She closed her eyes, biting her lip. "There was too much badness in that place."

Byron watched as Ruth exchanged a long look with her husband, an unspoken conversation between them. Ellie was standing unmoving near the end of the bed.

Eventually, Hugh spoke, saying sharply, "She hated Jimmy's Tarn and her family. I'm sorry, Ruth, but you know she did. I doubt she'd go there."

"All right, Hugh. I know we weren't a perfect family. She made no secret of it before the war, telling us that the minute she could she'd be off and good riddance to the lot of us. I never did miss her and when she didn't return after the war I assumed she was dead. The only one who made any effort to find out what happened to her was my youngest sister Edith, and she didn't remember her all that well. Sounds awful, doesn't it?"

"What I don't understand," Ellie said, "is why she followed her father into Hitler's clutches."

It was Hugh who answered. "She didn't *follow* him, Ellie. She did it to show him she was a better spy than he'd ever be and would rise higher than him in the organisation. And she did. It gave her the greatest pleasure to give orders to her father, though he fought against her authority. Ruth never knew any of this until long after the war and by then we hadn't seen Marian for years."

"And how do you know all this, Colonel Lawford?"

Ellie sounded impatient, but Byron refrained from interfering. Watching had benefits.

"I can't tell you that. I'm bound by the Official Secrets Act."

"How convenient. And what about you, Ruth?"

"I was in the army, too." She avoided looking at the younger woman.

Byron watched Ellie's eyebrows twitch up and down quickly, her expression closed. He decided to steer the conversation back to Marian's whereabouts before it got stuck in World War Two.

"D'you have any idea where she'd go, Hugh?"

"Yes." His eyes were full of an ancient anger. "Strathvern Castle. She was besotted with it – and its owner."

"I'm not convinced about Strathvern Castle," Ellie said as they headed south in Byron's car, Kipp snoozing happily on the back seat. "Why would she go there?"

"To wreak havoc in the present earl's life. If Farley was the previous earl's son, and Olga's on a revenge binge, he'd be on the agenda."

"And Fenella's with her. I'm still not convinced. None of this is getting us any closer to finding out who killed Farley. And now Alice turns up!"

"Stop focussing on what you don't know. It's like a jigsaw. Try putting the pieces in place."

She almost pouted, but said nothing. That he was right, she couldn't dispute. She just wasn't in the mood to be told off. Staring out at the hills, some still wreathed in mist, Ellie allowed herself a few seconds to enjoy the scenery. Upon slopes and peaks, pale sunlight made the bronze bracken look richer in colour and the trees and grass greener. Black-faced sheep grazed in a field they whizzed past. It seemed to her the Ormans' deaths were part of the landscape, woven into the history of the region and perhaps to remain mysteries down the generations.

Another glance at Byron, but he was either ignoring her or was too intent on staying on the road.

Back to her own thoughts. There were too many possibilities of who knew what and who would benefit from Farley's death. The first possibility she considered was that Farley knew he was the Earl of Strathvern and Olga's son and had confronted Ross with the information. If he'd threatened to expose the facts or had taken it into his head that he was owed from the estate, Ross might have followed him on one of his hikes and killed him. His and his sons' futures would be secure. Was it that simple? What about Michael, earl-in-waiting? Any threat to his father's right to the Strathvern title was a direct threat to him. And then there was Jamie, creative, talented and unpredictable, but he'd never made any secret of the fact that he had no interest in being bound to Strathvern. Leith? She didn't know him very well. He was quiet and very much like his mother in temperament. As to the Orman offspring...

"Any ideas yet?" Byron's voice broke into the flow of thoughts and its sound made her thirsty heart do a little dance.

"Several." She looked straight ahead, afraid to look at him because she wanted to feel his arms around her.

"Care to share them?"

"No, I don't," she said more sharply than she intended. "You and your London friends probably have all the answers. Why is it I get the feeling you're playing a game with us locals. Just go and arrest the person who did it and let me get on with my life."

The car slowed and a few seconds later Byron pulled off the road near a bridge. Ellie could hear the rushing of water below them as he turned towards her. His eyes were intense.

"For a start I'm not a policeman and can't arrest anyone. Secondly, I don't know all the answers, and thirdly, I'm not in the habit of playing games with anyone. Whether you like it or not, this *is* part of your life and I'm in it. You've been out of contact, distant, stubborn, and so bloody independent you've almost got yourself killed! What was I supposed to do with that? You seem like you want to get to know me, but you keep withdrawing. I don't think you know what you want, Ellie. And if you don't, then we'll never amount to anything."

He drove back onto the road and picked up speed on a straight section around the next bend. For a few minutes Ellie wondered if he was going to end both their lives, but he didn't and they safely negotiated a corner before he continued on at a more reasonable speed. Conscious of how close they were in the car, there was a desperate struggle going on inside her to simply reach out and touch his arm. Another part of her was angry with him for being so blunt about his perception of her and she didn't know what to say. Though it galled to admit it even to herself, he was right and that fuelled resentment. She attacked.

"That's fine with me. I can't live with a man who keeps disappearing into a private world and won't let me in. I've told you the darkest secret of my life, trusted you with it, but you who accuse me of being distant, have never said *anything* about what makes you go into hiding. I've seen the pain in your eyes. Just drop me off at home and I'll not bother you again."

The silence lasted a long time. She bitterly regretted her words. It wasn't fine with her at all. She wanted to be in his life, but she'd said it now and she supposed he'd accept it.

The mist, blown by strengthening wind, shrouded only the high peaks by the time they were a mile from Kilcomb. Ellie allowed her mind to drift and she thought about Jamie at the Knobbles, angry and disturbed, then Bran in the tunnel. He, too, was disturbed, but burdened with knowledge about his father's death. And Camden? What was it he knew? Together they were withholding truth. She shoved her hands into her pockets and touched the metal object.

"Stop!" she said loudly.

Byron braked hard and the car skidded on the wet road before he pulled off to the edge.

"What's the matter with you? We could've had an accident!"

They had just passed the entrance to The Mill. She ignored his question and his tone. "We have to go in there."

"Why didn't you tell me you needed bread before we passed the bakery?"

"I don't need bread." Out of her pocket she took the silver card holder and handed it to Byron. "Open it."

Frowning, his mouth drawn in a thin line of annoyance, he opened it and read the card.

"Enlighten me," he said abruptly.

"I found it at the Knobbles yesterday in the cave. In all the time I've known Bob, he's been up in the hills only a few times – and not recently as far as I know. How could his card holder have got there?"

To her surprise his expression slowly relaxed and he smiled. Inside she felt a melting, but showed nothing of this to him. It meant another part of the picture had been painted, nothing more.

"One of the things I love about you is your ability to surprise." He touched her hand. "I don't want to make another life somewhere else, Ellie. I want it right here with you."

Several seconds passed before she found her voice, but all she could say was, "Oh, good."

A car passed by within inches, blasting its horn.

Byron smiled at her and nodded. It seemed to be enough for him for the moment.

He checked the rear-vision mirror and did a U-turn. Two minutes later they were sitting in The Mill's car park deciding what to do.

"Bob's car's here." Ellie turned in her seat to face him. "I don't want to do this, Byron. He's a very good friend."

"I'm not looking forward to it either. I like the man. Let's hope someone else left it there."

Long moments passed; he seemed as reluctant as she to step out of the car. Well, it was time to tell him what she knew about Jamie and Bran anyway. A good excuse to procrastinate. For the few minutes it took, he did not move or look at her, gazing out through the windscreen, impassive.

"What reasons would one of them – or Bob – have to kill Farley?" he said when she finished. "I think Jamie knows what happened. Bran I'm not sure. I've had little to do with him. What's the link?"

"Olga. But they won't know about her."

"Maybe they do. And what about Bob?"

"Bob? He's her baker." She frowned. "Oh, I see. She'd be his aunt."

"Yes, but she couldn't have got up to the Knobbles."

"What if Farley was taken there?"

"Maybe, but the police said it happened in the cave."

"Anything else I should know?" she asked, peeved he knew so much.

"I just happened to hear Jack on the phone one day." He squeezed her hand. "Come on, let's get this over with."

They found Bob at his kitchen table looking through a photograph album; several others were in a pile.

"Hi, Bob," Ellie said. "We knocked on the door and called out."

"I heard," he replied, looking up. His expression was troubled. "I've just put the kettle on. Have a seat."

"What's the matter?" she asked, when they were seated.

"Secrets. This village is riddled with them. Alice asked for my help a couple of times. She was trying to find out about Farley's family, but I was too busy. She wanted her children to know their grandparents on their dad's side, but Farley was too full of his own secrets."

"And which ones have you stumbled across? Your bakery was once a safe haven for smugglers haggling over their wares?" Her attempt to inject jocularity soaked into the heavy atmosphere as if it hadn't existed.

Bob stood up and made tea in the pot his grandmother had always used. Ellie had rarely seen him use another. He put biscuits, mugs, milk and sugar on the table. No one spoke. Ellie pulled the open album towards her and studied the black and white photographs. They were family pictures of Bob and his siblings, parents and others who she assumed were relatives. She turned the page as Bob returned to the table with the teapot and poured tea into each mug. They helped themselves to milk and sugar.

Still he said nothing. Ellie glanced up at him, puzzled by his silence. Studying him more closely, she noticed his skin was a peculiar sallow and there was no light in his eyes.

Alarmed, she said more loudly than she meant, "Bob, what's the matter?"

He looked from one to the other, shook his head, and became occupied with milk and sugar.

"I don't know how to tell you."

Ellie glanced at Byron across the table. He raised his eyebrows. Needing to occupy herself, she turned another page without having really looked at the previous one and cast her eyes over the photographs. Towards the bottom of the right-hand page was a picture that made her heart thump.

"Where did you get these albums, Bob?" she asked quietly.

Byron's expression was intense. Everything about how he was now sitting – upright, unmoving and focussed on her – showed her the strength of the man. It touched her need to belong.

Bob handed over the mugs of tea. "My parents wanted to sort their attic out a year or so ago and I said I'd help. I ended up bringing the albums home, but I've never had the time to go through them properly so I got them out this morning. There's a different reason now."

Ellie's pulse was racing. She didn't know whether to speak or wait for Bob, so she lowered her eyes and studied the photo. It was almost identical to the one she still had, but the others were taken with different people and at several locations. Byron hadn't moved. She knew enough of his life to understand that keeping watch for hours on end on high alert was built into him. A moment's distraction and he could miss a vital movement, or he and his men could be dead.

Bob was grasping his mug of tea, sipping from it. He doesn't know what to say either, she thought.

"I've seen a photo like this," she said, deciding to put things in motion.

"Where, then?" The words bolted out of Bob like a horse shooting out of the barricade and down the race track.

"Strathvern."

Byron got up and went around the end of the table, pulling a chair up beside her and looking at the photo she pointed to.

"So, you've known all this time and never said anything!" Bob thumped his mug on the table.

"All what time? I only saw it about a week ago."

She watched him gather himself together and take a deep breath.

"Sorry. You think you know who everyone in your life is until something comes along that knocks you sideways. Where did you see the photo?"

"Someone dumped me in Strathvern's cellars and I came across a room full of old stuff." She felt no compulsion to tell him the details.

"Strathvern," he mused. "Farley was right then."

Ellie looked at him, frowning, but he was lost in his own thoughts. She turned the page of the album. Now Bob knows, she thought. More photographs of children and adults posing for the camera. The elegant woman was not amongst them. Details of the boys and girls in some photos were fuzzy, a little out of focus. In others they were too far away. Who were they all?

"What is it you found out today, Bob?" Byron's voice, quiet and undemanding, changed the atmosphere in the kitchen.

The other man took a long drink of his tea before reaching for two envelopes partly hidden beneath another album. Faded in colour, they were, she surmised, quite old. Bob, hesitating a moment, slid both envelopes across the table to Byron. Ellie leaned towards him, watching as he carefully opened one envelope and unfolded two pieces of paper.

They were copies of birth certificates: Mary Emily MacAdam, parents' names Marian MacAdam and Helmut Bercht; and Robert Alec MacAdam, parents' names Marian MacAdam and James, Earl of Strathvern.

Ellie stared at the writing, her heart thumping. Bob? She looked across at him, but he was stirring his tea, intent on the contents in the mug. How could this be? And Helmut Bercht? Coldness squeezed her innards; she felt sick. It was Hugh. Mary was the daughter of a German and the woman known as Olga. Some of the stuff in the trunk in that awful room, the letters about the children, they were about Mary and Bob!

So Olga had lied to Fenella when she told her she was her grandmother. Why would she do that? Was she a convenient pawn, someone to continue the subterfuge of a warped life?

From across the table, Bob lifted his head and gave her a weak smile.

Without looking up, Byron opened the second envelope and unfolded two letters, also copies. One was addressed to John and Margaret Caraway and the other to Alexander and Rose Finley. He read them out. The content of both letters was the same except for the names, swearing each couple to secrecy regarding the adoption of the child. They were never to speak of the adoption or divulge to the child that it was adopted. The penalty would be cessation of the generous funds provided for the child's upbringing until the age of twenty-one, and of funds for the adoptive parents for agreeing to raise the child. The parents were never to enquire about where the child came from or seek the names of its natural parents. Neither natural parent would ever acknowledge their children either in private or public. It was a legal document, signed by the adopting parents and a lawyer from an Edinburgh legal firm.

Sounds outside were dulled by the thick walls of the house and for a long time there was little movement around the table. Stillness was broken when Bob's fluffy ginger cat, Marmalade, wandered in, purring, and went from one to the other rubbing his head against their legs.

"Where did you get these, Bob?" Byron reached down and patted the cat without taking his eyes off the other man.

"They were in this envelope. It was under my door when I came back from the bakery this morning. I didn't have time to open it until just before you arrived. That's when I got the albums out. D'you think it's somebody's idea of a joke?"

"No."

Ellie, irritated by the brevity of his answer, said to Byron, "Are you going to tell him about the girl?"

He raised his brows and sat back in the chair.

"It's Mary Nevin, Bob. She's your half-sister."

In all the years she'd known him, Ellie had never seen Bob cry, but tears now rolled down his cheeks as Byron told him what he'd learned the previous night. There were things she learned as well, things he hadn't mentioned in the car, and her heart ached for Bob when he found out he also had two half-brothers in Germany. His eyes revealed the depth of his pain and bewilderment, and she reached out and touched his clasped hands. The telling went on for some time, but she knew Byron was saying only what he knew could be told and for once her frustration at his secrecy barely registered. In hearing what she did, a measure of understanding settled her heart.

Sensing that Byron was coming to the end of what he had to say, she got up and put the kettle on. Then a peculiar thing happened. While she was waiting for it to boil and was collecting their mugs, she wondered whether Mary was at the shop. Catching Byron's eye as he was telling Bob that he didn't think Mary knew of their relationship, he gave a brief nod and Ellie excused herself.

She had not got halfway between the house and the bakery when Mary came walking up the driveway with Mark.

"Mary! I was just coming to see you. Are you... all right?"

Her words trailed off as they got closer and she saw Mary's puffy eyes. In her hand was an envelope, identical to the one Bob had received.

When they entered the kitchen, Bob was unscrewing the top of a bottle of scotch, his back to Ellie and the Nevins. Byron, halfway out of his chair, saw them first and Ellie smiled at his surprised expression. They had, she knew, been of one mind about fetching Mary.

"They were coming up the driveway," she said in a voice that sounded peculiar, not quite her own.

Bob turned around and the expression on his face was one Ellie knew she would remember for the rest of her life. As for Mary, she gave a half-strangled noise and hurried towards him, hugging him and hugged in return. Such was the power of restoration and knowing those to whom you belong that Ellie struggled to keep her emotions under control.

It was Mark who went off down the hallway and returned with glasses. Mary opted for a cup of strong tea, while Bob disappeared and came back with a large plate of cakes from the bakery. No one spoke much during the comings and goings, the making of tea, settling into chairs, and Bob and Mary comparing the contents of their envelopes. They were the same. Marmalade, apparently delighted by the company, made use of all the legs and rubbed against each pair.

"This all feels… unreal," Bob said, shaking his head, looking at Mary. "It's the stuff of novels not *my* life, *our* lives. And it raises a lot of questions."

"Aye, it does," she responded almost defiantly. "Why would she send them to us now?"

"You mean our… our… you mean Olga?"

"Or whatever else she wants to call herself."

A peculiar expression came over Bob's features. "I wonder who fathered the boys in Germany."

Mary answered. "A German officer. She was married to him, but he was killed a year after the second boy was born." She stopped and stared out the window.

Glancing at Byron, Ellie saw a closed and uninviting expression – he was watching Mary.

Bob didn't seem to notice. "What a sad life." He sighed and the subject changed. "When did your envelope come?"

Preoccupied, Mary took a few seconds to respond. "I found it slipped under the shop's door this morning."

"I wonder who it was."

Mary shrugged, but didn't respond, glancing at her husband who nodded.

"You'd better tell Bob who Helmut is, love."

Bob straightened in his chair. Mary was biting her lip.

"It's Hugh. Hugh Lawford."

Reaching across the table, she touched Bob's hand. "I'm sorry, Bob. This must be awful for you."

Without speaking, he pushed his chair back and went and stood at the window, staring out into the garden.

Chapter 30

From the end of the terrace, Ellie watched the Earl of Strathvern strolling along the edge of the loch, his two dogs splashing in and out of the water, carefree and full of life. Droplets of water flew into the air as they shook themselves, Ross laughing at their antics.

Kipp barked as they drew nearer and Ellie let him go, watching as he galloped across the grass and pebbles. Greeted warily by the gun dogs, they didn't take long to remember him and seconds later all three streaked off along the water's edge. She hadn't told Byron where she was going. He and Bob had begun talking about going up to Jimmy's Tarn and she'd left them to it. There was no doubt in her mind what she had to do.

"Hello, Ellie. What brings you to Strathvern?" Ross' tone was almost welcoming. In his eyes were reservation and a hint of suspicion.

Behind him, the dogs were coming out of the loch, drenched and about to shake themselves.

"It was you who sent the envelopes, wasn't it?" she asked without explaining further.

He frowned. "What envelopes? The post office delivers millions every day."

"Brown ones with papers inside. Copies of official papers to Bob Caraway and Mary Nevin."

The lines in his face deepened.

"Ellie, I've *no* idea what you're talking about."

"You know more than what you've let everyone believe. When you saw Michael and me at the door to the cellars you knew we weren't going to get wine, didn't you?"

"Yes. It was time he found out and you were the right person to show him. Oh, yes," he said, nodding. "I knew you'd been in that accursed room. I saw you in the tunnel the night you'd been abducted, although I didn't know that was how you got there until later. I left the door unlocked, hoping you'd do what I'd been unable to – rummage around and somehow begin putting an end to the past's effects."

"Well, I haven't put an end to that. *And*, it's not my place to do so." She was miffed by his presumption and, to be truthful, a little scathing of his lack of courage.

"But you have, Ellie. Already there's a difference in Michael. He's finally got the strength of his forebears pumping in his veins. We had our walk this morning, Michael, Caroline and I, and there was a lift in his head and determination in his eyes."

"And what about you?"

"It's not your place to question me, Ellie," he said sharply. "You judge from a distance by what you see, yet you know very little about my life."

"But you expect your son to right the wrongs of his fathers."

"Yes, I do. If he wants to keep this house together for future generations he'll need determination and fortitude *which,* until now, he hasn't had much of! Jamie's got more of the warrior in him than Michael, but he's not the heir. Anyway," he added less belligerently, "there's too much of the gypsy in him."

Ellie could see his point, but didn't determine how it was any different from the expectations of preceding Strathvern heirs, and she said so.

He sighed. "This is the supersonic, computer, hyper-marketing, we-want-more, we-expect-more age. If future heirs are to survive and keep their inheritances intact they have to be smarter about how they go about it and not just hope that their money, name and heritage will keep them afloat. It won't. Michael has to think outside the square."

Out of the corner of her eye, she caught sight of Michael standing up from a set of steps leading down into the garden. He'd been screened from view by shrubs growing along the stone balustrade and must have heard their entire conversation. Ross turned his head and saw his son.

"It was me," Michael said, walking towards them. "I sent the envelopes. Is that thinking enough outside the square, Father?"

"I don't know, Michael. It depends what they contained."

"Copies of birth certificates for Robert MacAdam and Mary MacAdam, and letters from an Edinburgh legal firm."

"Bob Caraway and Mary Nevin," Ross said quietly, his countenance now pale. "What was in the letters?"

"Come with me. You can read them for yourself."

They followed Michael to his father's study, a room Ellie had never been in. It was a masculine room, yet beautiful. In the bay window she'd be happy curled up with a book and occasional long looks across the loch where little waves were slapping about, touched here and there by sunlight. Shadows on the hills gave a hint of mystery and unpredictable weather.

The younger man unlocked a safe hidden behind books and retrieved the original documents. He handed them to his father.

Ross, reading glasses perched on his nose, sat for a long time in a wing-back chair absorbing the contents of the papers and letters without making comment. Ellie and Michael exchanged glances several times and he made a suggestion of fetching tea, but his father did not respond.

"Have you seen these papers, Ellie?" he asked in a wooden voice.

"Yes. Bob showed them to us."

"Us?"

"Byron was there too. Mark and Mary Nevin arrived a bit later."

"So, the net is drawing in – finally. And what about this woman, Marian MacAdam?"

Ellie swallowed. "It's a local woman called Olga Erskine."

"Olga Erskine? Isn't she that rather peculiar woman? Whatever makes you believe it's her?"

"Byron's been doing a bit of investigating. So have I actually. We're not all dimwits in the country."

Ross' lips twitched and Michael's eyebrows arched up over amused eyes.

"I have no reason to doubt you, Ellie," Ross said.

The brief interlude ended as she went on to tell them about Bob and Mary and the almost incomprehensible situation they found themselves in. They'd known each other almost all their lives without a clue they were closely related, Bob that he was adopted, and their mother a woman many in the village thought odd, to say the least. She said nothing of Hugh Lawford.

The moment she finished speaking, a strange, tangled emotion surfaced and she began crying, not for herself, but for Mary and Bob and the years lost, the shock of the revelation concerning their births.

And Farley – where did he fit? What was it he'd discovered – or thought he had? He had always hated everything the Nazi regime stood for and for that reason had banned his children from having anything to do with the Strathverns. When Bran had defied him and begun working on the estate, he'd almost disowned him.

As she thought about his frequent absences and times of sullen withdrawal during the last year or more, she was convinced he'd found out his father was the Nazi supporter in Strathvern Castle. To have hated the regime for so long... she could not imagine how he'd felt. Not once had he said anything of what he was doing or feeling.

"Ellie. Whatever's the matter?" It was Ross, who got up and put a hand on her shoulder.

She couldn't speak. Caroline, who had slipped in, sat next to her and Ellie drew comfort as a daughter would from a mother. She told them what she thought Farley had unearthed.

"Well," Ross said, returning to his chair, "that explains a lot. We had a blazing row a day or so before he died. He turned up when I was in the garden. I admit we never got on, but that day he was in a rage. He accused me of covering up my father's misdeeds and spawning another generation of Nazis. *And*, that he had evidence of children in the area who were my half-siblings and far more deserving of the Strathvern estate than I was! It did cross my mind he was referring to himself. He'd hinted at it often enough. I wasn't happy about it. Actually, I was furious and worried and told him to get off the property and not come back." He shook his head. "Poor man."

"The photo I saw, although I wasn't sure it was Farley, the letter I read about the birth of a son to Marian and your father, Farley's death... it all seems to fit," Ellie said.

Caroline was sitting quietly listening. Her husband gave her the documents and told her the names of the offspring. Her eyes filled with sorrow.

"What a terrible tragedy. And it affects *so* many people. What about this woman? Does anyone know who she is?"

Michael said, "I believe she's known as Olga Erskine and lives near the village."

"I've heard of her. Where is she?"

"She's disappeared," Ellie said, glancing from one to the other. "Byron and I went to Inverness Hospital – she was admitted last night. That's a long story I don't know much about. We were told a nurse, her granddaughter, had wheeled her out for some fresh air and never returned. The 'nurse' was Fenella Orman."

"What a very peculiar thing to do. And if she's this woman's granddaughter, does she know?"

"Yes. Olga told her years ago – another long story."

"If you stay for afternoon tea you can tell us. This is quite a saga."

"Thanks, but I have to get back. Anyway, there's enough information in the castle to keep you occupied for quite a while."

"And where did the documents come from?"

Ellie looked at Michael.

"In the Priest's Hole," he said, with a slight lift of his shoulders. "Sorry, Father. All those history books you made me read – well I couldn't resist it, I had to do some exploring of my own. I'm fairly sure Jamie and Leith don't know about it. Jamie would've said. I found the documents rolled up in cloth in a niche in the wall. I'd never have come across them except that the jar I was looking at wobbled and in steadying it, I knocked the side of the niche with my hand and found there was a hole. And there they were. Not intended for anyone to ever find them."

"Why didn't you bring them to me first?" His father looked annoyed.

"Because I thought you'd tell me to put them back and keep quiet about the Priest's Hole and the documents. Am I right?"

Ross pursed his lips and nodded. "This could have repercussions."

"They still have a right to know despite what that lawyer's letters say. Besides, Grandfather's dead and whatever monies he was paying out would have long since finished."

"Knowing my father he probably never paid a penny to anyone," he said bitterly.

***

By the time Ellie was five minutes from home the sun finally struggled free from mist and cloud and was shining brightly. A new bank of clouds was coming in from the north, without hurry. The sunshine's warmth on her arm through the Land Rover's window eased a lingering heaviness. Kipp was sitting in the front looking out, occasionally barking or swishing his tail.

Without really knowing why, she changed her mind about going home and turned sharply left onto a narrower road, causing Kipp to almost slide off the seat. She laughed as he scrabbled to stay upright. Ten minutes later she was outside the front of Olga Erskine's house.

There was no sign of life, but she hadn't expected there to be and got out without making any secret of her presence. She took Kipp with her, feeling less alone with him nearby, and walked down the side of the house and into the back garden. The side door of the garage was open and Ellie caught a glimpse of a red car. She took a deep breath. If Olga was inside the wisest thing was to get back in her vehicle, drive around the corner, call Byron and wait.

Kipp, however, had no such concerns and made his way towards the open back door and was inside while the frantic whisper was still in Ellie's throat. There was no shout for the dog to get out. Ellie had a peculiar sense that she was re-enacting a scene in a play and this time she entered the house with more caution. No one was downstairs, even Kipp had disappeared, but the front room looked nothing like it had that morning. Cushions, newspapers and magazines were scattered on the floor, pictures were off the wall and lying haphazardly on the settee and floor. A thief?

For the second time that day, Ellie, apprehensive about what to expect, climbed the creaking stairs. The landing was empty. Kipp was whimpering and a younger voice than Olga's was coming from the main bedroom. When Ellie reached the doorway and stood looking in, the same chaos as below met her eyes. Sitting on the end of the bed was a sobbing, dishevelled Fenella Orman. Mascara was running down her cheeks, her shirt was hanging out the back of her jeans and strands of hair had escaped their pins. She had an arm around Kipp who was looking up at her, then Ellie, with a soulful expression. It was the first time Ellie had ever seen Fenella in disarray and she stared at her, not knowing what to say, so she perched on a chair near the dressing table. Talcum powder had spilled out of its glass bowl and the lid lay sideways next to it, lace doilies were askew, bottles, brushes and combs were scattered across the wooden top.

"She lied to me. She even stole a locket from Jamie's grandmother. He saw me wearing it one day and told me I had to give it back because it belonged to his family. I didn't believe him until he took me to the castle and showed me his grandmother's portrait. All these years she's been lying to me. How dare she! How *could* she?" Fenella buried her face in Kipp's neck.

"Because she's lived a life of lies, Fenella. She's a master craftsman."

"But she shouldn't have done it!"

"No, she shouldn't," she said quietly.

The young woman looked up, mascara smudged and blotchy across her cheeks and on her eyelids. In any other circumstance, Ellie might have laughed and thought it was about time she looked less perfect, but not now. There was something pathetic about her, a daughter who needed her mother. As Ellie had at Strathvern.

"I suppose you think I'm a fool and deserve all this. You'll be glad to see me made the laughing stock of Kilcomb."

"No, I don't and no, I won't," Ellie said, holding out a box of tissues from Olga's dressing table. Fenella pulled several out and blew her nose, then took more and made an attempt at wiping her eyes and cheeks. She looked like a lost child. "Where's Olga gone?"

Fenella snuffled and blew her nose again, tossing the tissues into a waste paper basket near the dressing table. For a moment she gazed at the picture of the group outside the old building.

"She loved that picture. Said if I looked at it closely enough it would tell more than at first glance. I never liked it. It's too dull." She fondled Kipp's ears. "Two men were waiting here when we got back from Inverness. One stayed in the car and I didn't really see him." She looked up at Ellie with some of her old pride. "I fooled everyone in the nurse's uniform. I don't suppose you've heard about that."

"Actually, I have. I was at Inverness Hospital this morning. We went to see Olga, but she'd disappeared."

"It was a clever plan and it worked, but if I'd known…" She shook her head, clenching her teeth. "I hate her!"

"Who were the two men?"

"I don't know, but the one who got out of the car seemed to know her well. He gave her a hug and a peck on the cheek. He ignored me and Olga didn't say who they were. I didn't understand a word they said."

"German?"

She nodded. "When they were piling her suitcases in the car she said there was a letter for me on the coffee table in the front room. I wasn't to read it until after she'd gone. I was shocked. She'd always told me I'd be going with her, but she said I'd been a faithful friend and granddaughter, pecked me on the cheek and got in the car. She waved and that was it!"

528

"Any idea where they were going?"

"Germany, of course! Where else? I haven't a clue and I don't care. How could she have done this to me? What kind of woman is she? She was always so good to me, made me feel like I really belonged to someone. I made an enemy of my own mother because of her! And now I don't have her either. I don't have any parents."

Tears dripped onto her cheeks and she fell back on the bed, hands over her eyes. A few seconds later she sat up.

"I was so upset and angry I came back in here and messed up her front room. Then I saw the letter on the table and brought it up here to read. After that I made this mess. Go on, read the letter."

Ellie picked it up off the bed.

Our years together have come to an end. I wish it could be otherwise, but it can't. I don't want to stay here now and have been making arrangements for some time to leave. Your father was my son, but his father was not the Earl of Strathvern. I make no apology for leading you to believe you had Strathvern blood. It served my cause and you should be able to understand that after all this time. Back then, when your father was conceived, ours was a world of charade, lies, plots, deception and subterfuge for a cause we would have gladly died. I do not expect you to understand, but remember the good times we had not this sad end. So, farewell, my dear. Be proud of who you are – I am. Your loving grandmother, Olga.

Ellie stared at the letter. Farley *not* the earl's son? This was incomprehensible and made no sense, not one scrap. She put the letter down on her lap and studied Farley's daughter.

"I'm sorry, Fenella."

"Are you? You've always despised me, just like the rest of Kilcomb."

"That's an exaggeration and not entirely true, but then you don't make yourself very approachable."

"Well, I'm going to leave here. Glenn's in some kind of trouble and his father wants him back in London."

Ellie's cheeks burned and she bent down to Kipp, patting him. Without looking up, she asked Fenella what she was going to do now.

"I'll have to make a new life. Shame. We could've done wonders with that old castle."

"That *old castle* isn't for sale," Ellie said sharply.

"There are ways, but it doesn't matter now. By the way, I took some papers out of your filing cabinet. I got in through a window into your pokey laundry. Put the pot plants back just the way they were. Very clever I thought. Glenn wanted to know what you were up to with Maw's Hearth. Sorry you can't have the papers back."

Ellie stared at her. She was beginning to wonder whether Fenella had any sense that other people mattered and the whole world did not exist for her alone! She decided to change the subject. There was nothing she could do about the paperwork now.

"Did you and Olga go to Jimmy's Tarn on your way back to Kilcomb?"

The younger woman's eyes narrowed and she looked at her with an intensity that unsettled Ellie.

"We got to the gate and saw the police cars there. Well, I suppose they were all police. Olga wanted to collect some old photos she said someone had left there for her. She wanted me to get them a while ago, but I told her it was creepy and I wouldn't go alone."

Now she knew who'd written the note that'd sent her to the hated place with the photos. Ellie shuddered. Fenella didn't notice.

"You know the police will want to see you about Alice, Fenella."

"What for? I didn't kill her if that's what you think. I couldn't. She was my mother!"

"But you've got an idea. Just like Bran knows about your father's death."

"Don't talk rubbish. He wouldn't harm a fly."

"Perhaps not. So what happened to your mother?" Ellie asked quietly.

Fenella bowed her head and reached for Kipp again, stroking his head. Her voice was strained.

"I don't know, I really don't know. I came round to Olga's one evening. She wasn't expecting me. Usually I rang, but I just wanted to see her, ask her about a business idea I had. When I got here they were carrying something heavy wrapped in a sheet down the path to the shed. I stayed behind the hedge. When they returned to the house I went to have a look." She bit her lip, tears hovering in her eyes. "It was… it was Mum. I couldn't stop looking at her. She was so still. I couldn't move for ages, but they came back and I got behind the big trunk in there. They didn't say much. Olga said she shouldn't have been poking into affairs that didn't concern her and it had been an accident."

Ellie was aghast. "Why didn't you tell anyone?"

"I *couldn't*. They didn't, so I couldn't." She was gasping for air, sobbing. "I didn't know what to do. I was afraid, *so* afraid. It was my mum. My *mum!*"

Her cry filled the room and Ellie saw a young woman she'd never known existed, one who had hidden her pain, needing her mother without realising it, and who'd allowed ambition and the promise of greater things to steal part of her life. They had more in common that she realised – years spent in a wilderness, longing for love but never really finding it.

When the tears dried and Fenella finished dabbing her eyes, Ellie asked in a plain voice, "Who else was there, Fenella?"

Fenella did not move, wrapping herself in a cloak of secrecy, remaining silent.

The minutes ticked by and Ellie studied the painting on the wall, peering at the figures who'd been so bent on destruction. How could they have even conceived such horrific plans, thinking they were on this earth to create a pure race and eradicating anyone who didn't fit the mould? And Olga, who she'd begun to know and like, had been involved, somehow, in the death of a gentle and loving woman.

Ellie turned her attention to Farley's daughter, staring at her, watching as she wiped her eyes and pushed her hair back off her face.

This time Ellie was not so emotionless. "Who else was there? And don't think about lying. I'm very good at detecting it because I know Glenn Thorley better than you do and he's a liar of considerable skill."

The beautiful, tear-streaked face looked up sharply. "Now you're lying."

"No, I'm not. Tell me who else was here?"

Fenella swallowed. Her lips quivered and her hands trembled; she clenched them together.

"Dad," she whispered, swallowing again. "It was Dad. He was crying."

Ellie sat very still; she knew it was true. How clearly she could picture the scene Fenella witnessed. Olga, forcing her son to help and he, believing he knew who his parents were, had come and taken his wife to Jimmy's Tarn rather than expose his shame. Of this she was sure. It fitted.

Four years, Ellie thought. Four years of hoping Alice was still alive. Four years of watching Farley change, watching grief sap his

531

energy and for a while his passion, behaving like she and others who believed there was hope of Alice's return. She shook her head. Yes, he'd had grief, he'd loved his wife, but he had carried a lie and lived it out. He should *never* have taken up with an enemy.

"He didn't do it. He wouldn't. He loved Mum." Fenella's voice betrayed an uncertainty.

Without speaking to her, Ellie got up and went downstairs. She needed a few minutes of her own and reached for the kettle, filled it with water and switched it on. Whispered words on the stormy night about Fenella and secrets had, it seemed, been true, but she doubted Camden had any idea of their magnitude. Eventually, she found cups and tea bags in a cupboard. Normal things, comforting things. She felt far from either normal or comforted. Circumstances had altered that in less than half an hour. While the water heated up she phoned Byron.

The kettle boiled and she dangled tea bags in the cups of hot water. She hoped there was milk.

"I don't drink tea," said Fenella behind her. "There's a jar of coffee at the back."

Ellie spooned coffee into the cup, making no comment. There was half a bottle of milk in the fridge. Kipp was wagging his tail, looking at her hopefully, and she poured milk into a saucer. It was gone in seconds, spots of it landing on the lino.

"You should have gone to the police, Fenella."

"I told you I couldn't do that and I won't do it now."

"They'll find out eventually."

"Not if you don't tell them. Digging up the past won't bring my parents back. You have to live for the future."

"And what about the present?"

"It's a means to what's ahead. Now that Glenn's going away…" She frowned and put her cup down on the table. Fenella hadn't bothered with saucers. "What did you mean when you said you knew Glenn better than I did? I know he's your cousin."

Ellie wished she'd never said anything about him; she certainly had no desire to tell Fenella who would find a way of shaming her. She'd had enough of that.

"He was obnoxious, a bully." It would have to do.

A car drew up outside in the lane. Fenella pushed her chair back and stood up, eyes narrow slits and little dots of mascara on her eyelids.

"You've called the police, haven't you? You took our father, his money, and now you're going to have me arrested. Are you afraid I'll take Byron Oakes away from you, Ellie Madison? It wouldn't be hard. Look at you! But then, you'd probably sell your soul to get what you wanted! Can't think how else you'd keep Mr Oakes."

Ellie reached Fenella before the mockery in her eyes had time to fade, grabbed her hair and yanked her head to one side. The yelp of pain and indignation reverberated round the kitchen. A supersonic jet could hardly have made a better job of it, she thought looking down at her victim.

"I did *not* take your father or his money and you deserve to be arrested. You've covered up information about your mother's death, knowingly taken up with a Nazi woman, and…"

"Ow! Let go you lunatic! You're hurting me!"

"… you're as heavily involved in trying to turn Maw's Hearth and Strathvern Castle into havens for the rich destroyers such as Thorley. You're a pigeon pair. If anyone's sold their soul, it's you, Fenella Orman!"

"Let her go, Ellie."

Glenn's voice hit her as if a bolt from a crossbow, penetrating the thin armour of her defence system. Pain sought to reassert itself, dominate.

Beside her Fenella was struggling. Suddenly, there was a sharp pain as she shoved her elbow into Ellie's ribs. An abrupt grunt was Ellie's only acknowledgement of its impact. She would not allow Fenella any satisfaction over it. Instead, she faced her cousin. Their eyes met and a familiar quivering in her belly and legs almost tipped her back into the past, but she refused to allow the memories her body kept to dominate.

She could hear Fenella making her way round the table and turned to look at her. A discomfiting thought rushed to the forefront. In twenty-four hours she'd assaulted two of Farley's children. As she looked at Glenn she shuddered, repulsed by the memories, but there followed another terror. Did she too have violence in her blood? She turned the taunting voices off much as she would a dripping tap – with a sharp twist.

Before he could speak again, Ellie said, "What're you doing here?"

"I got an SOS."

Fenella, tucking her hair into place, stood beside Glenn. The arrogance returned to her expression, though with less vigour. Ellie ignored her.

"Were you one of the men who came and took Olga away?"

"What men? I didn't know the woman."

"You can't be as close as you obviously are to Fenella and not know Olga."

"I don't care whether you believe me or not, Ellie."

"He doesn't know anything about my... about Olga," Fenella said coldly. "I never told him. I never told anybody."

Glenn glanced at her, frowning, then stepped past her and around the end of the kitchen table. He was too close and Ellie, picking up the cups, walked over to the sink, keeping him in sight. The smirk she knew too well warned her.

"You rang my father," he said, the smirk gone. "Why?"

Ellie stared at his hands on the back of the chair. Hands of violence, hands that didn't know love or compassion. A trickle like ice ran down her spine. She shivered.

"Ask him. He's got other plans for you."

Suspicion showed in his half-closed eyes. "He doesn't discuss my business with anyone."

"Actually, Glenn, it's *his* business and you work for him." He stiffened, but made no move towards her. She wondered how far she could taunt him. Would he attack her while Fenella was in the room? "But don't worry, he didn't tell me. I don't care what it is as long as it's as far away from here as possible."

"You'll never be out of my reach, Ellie."

He began moving slowly towards her. At the other end of the kitchen Fenella stood still and Ellie knew she was watching every movement, every change of expression. When he was within three feet of her, he raised his arm. Kipp ran suddenly from Fenella's side and stood in front of Ellie, growling at Glenn.

"Get that dog out of here!" he shouted.

"The dog stays, Glenn. You always were afraid of them, weren't you? Something happened outside our house once and I didn't see you for a long time. Why was that?"

He stepped back, his countenance dark and troubled. Kipp followed, barking, the noise deafening in the small room.

"Shut him up, Ellie. He's a menace. You should have him put down."

"Don't be ridiculous, Glenn," Fenella said loudly. "He won't hurt you."

Glenn didn't answer; his eyes were fixed on Kipp who was slowly moving closer to him, growling. Ellie did not call him back. For the first time in her life she saw fear in Glenn's eyes and felt no pity for him. For years he'd tormented her. Now she watched him, doing and saying nothing. Fenella was telling Kipp to be quiet and telling her to take hold of her dog. Ellie didn't move. It was a moment in time she thought would never come, a moment in which she, the victim, had some kind of revenge. It didn't feel altogether right, but she continued watching like a mechanical toy that had no will of its own.

Kipp stopped, but didn't take his eyes off the man. In that moment Glenn raised his arm, the intention clear and Ellie cried out. Her dog took it as a threat and lunged at his arm. Fenella called Glenn's name and went towards him, but he was falling and knocked her, pushing her back against the table. For a second Ellie didn't react. She stared at her cousin, uncaring. She knew.

"It was you. You bashed Kipp. I think he wants revenge. Perhaps I'll let him have it."

"No!"

Fenella went towards him, but Ellie caught her arm.

Then she saw the terror in Glenn's face as Kipp's paws landed on his chest and his jaws opened. Ellie let go of the young woman's arm. The scene from all those years ago hurtled out of her memory and forced her to see what she'd long forgotten.

"Kipp!" she called sharply. "Come here, boy."

He dropped immediately, growling, and came back to her. She put him outside, but did not shut the back door when she returned indoors. They did not hear her come in and Ellie halted just inside the door, surveying the sight before her. Glenn was sitting on a chair and behind him was Fenella, one hand on his shoulder and the fingers of the other gently running through his hair. In Glenn's eyes the fear lingered, his hands were shaking.

Despite all her loathing and distrust of him, an unexpected rush of pity lodged in her heart. She didn't want it there or the empathy that followed directly behind it. How could her heart betray her so? And yet, she had seen true fear in his eyes and heard the echoes of his terrified cries for help while she'd stood at the window and watched, hoping he'd die.

"I've remembered," she said quietly.

Fenella spun round. "Get out of here you…!"

Glenn put his hand on hers and she closed her mouth.

"What is it you remember, Ellie?" he said, his voice sounding tired. He did not look at her.

"A lot of barking. It was evening and you were outside the gate. I was glad you were going." Her voice faded away and she hugged herself. He'd been there, but someone had come home. "Dogs. You were attacked by dogs. There's a scar on your leg and your upper arm. Your shirt had red on it."

He looked up at her in the stillness of the room and his voice seemed to come from a long way off, from down the years. "Your father saved my life."

She'd forgotten that. Quietly, she said, "Let me go, Glenn."

He didn't answer. Fenella, frowning, glanced from one to the other.

The sound of cars in the lane brought a sense of reality to the kitchen scene. Fenella moved away from Glenn, picked up her bag, and waited as he stood up. What energy he'd had before seemed drained away.

Out of the corner of her eye, Ellie saw Kipp walking towards the door and she went out to him, a cool breeze ruffling her hair. She breathed in deeply of its cleanness and scent of the mountains, seeking hope in its frivolous eddies. Would it bring a new season in her life, one free of Glenn and the past? Behind her she heard the other two coming out of the house. Without looking back, she walked Kipp to the Land Rover and put him inside.

When she turned around she saw Glenn and Fenella kissing. She swallowed, revolted. There was still too much pain and shame attached to the man. Ellie turned and opened the driver's door and got no further. Why would Olga leave behind a picture that meant so much to her?

She walked towards the house as Fenella was getting into her car.

"Shut the back door would you, Ellie," she called. "Oh, and if anyone's looking for me, I'll be in London."

Ellie watched her sink into the driver's seat of her bright red car, start it up, do a U-turn, and head up the lane. In seconds the car had disappeared round a bend. Over the roof of his car Glenn was watching her and she stopped. She did not want to get any closer to him. She knew only too well his unpredictable nature.

"That bloody dog of yours would've torn me to shreds."

536

"No. I wouldn't have let him, though it crossed my mind. I didn't think fear was part of your world, Glenn. I'm glad you're not totally dehumanised."

"There's a lot you don't know about me, Ellie."

"I know too much about you and you about me. It'll be better if we never meet again."

"I'm not sure that's what I want. You've got fire in you and you're strong. I like that."

"I don't care, Glenn. The past is over. Stick with Fenella. She'll have enough fire to keep you both going." It was too late for happy families. "Let me go."

He bent his head, staring at the ground and after a little while he nodded, slowly, as if reluctant to agree. When he looked up his expression shocked her for it was one of regret and sadness.

"Goodbye then, Ellie Madison," he said in a strangled sort of way and disappeared into his car before giving her a chance to respond.

He drove off quickly without looking at her. She was alone and didn't believe he would stay away from her. Eventually, he would turn up again. Still, there was a small knot in her stomach. He was still her cousin and she wished they could have had a healthy relationship. Tears stirred in her heart and stuck in her throat. Family – sometimes the yearning was too much.

"Come on, girl. You've got things to do," she told herself out loud. "Olga's not finished with us yet."

As soon as Glenn's car was out of sight down the lane and the engine noise could no longer be heard, Ellie went back and got Kipp. Going into Olga's house alone wasn't something she relished. This time she shut the back door and locked it before trudging upstairs.

Pale sunlight infiltrated the room through the lace curtains making patterns on the carpet and bedspread, dispersing the gloom. Heaviness, persistent since she'd entered the house and found Fenella, shifted.

She sat down on the bed and studied the picture. What was so special about it? Frowning, she got up to have a closer look. Why *had* Olga left it behind? Not for a moment did Ellie doubt the woman in the picture was her. It didn't have the look of Eva Braun, though she could go only by what she'd seen of the Fuhrer's mistress on television and in books. If Hitler and the warped Nazi ideals meant so much to Olga, waking up each morning and seeing her hero and herself in the same painting would feed the need of belonging and value. It did not explain why, if she was going back to Germany, she'd left it behind.

Maybe it wasn't only the front that was important. The stuff of novels, movies, and historical non-fiction, maybe, but Ellie grasped the frame and lifted the painting off the wall. Laying it face down on the bed, she began carefully peeling away the masking tape that kept frame and painting together. Beside her Kipp got up, staring at the open door. As the last piece came away there was a creak on the stairs. Her body tensed. Glenn. The pig! He's come back.

She picked up the painting and pushed it under the bed, Kipp between the wardrobe and the wall. She slid under the bed, hoping there were no spiders and Kipp kept quiet and still.

Her heart was thumping. For what seemed many minutes she lay still, breathing quietly, listening. There were no further sounds until Kipp suddenly barked and left his hiding place.

A silent groan filled her body. She was sweating and forced herself not to cry out in frustration and despair. If he touched her this time she would kill him. She couldn't stand being stalked and abused any longer. If he came near the bed she'd grab his ankles and push him over. With any luck he'd hit his head on something sharp or hard and that would be the end of him. This was too much!

Then she listened. Why wasn't Kipp snarling as he'd done in the kitchen? If it wasn't Glenn, was it Fenella? Ellie waited, turning slightly to the side.

She saw his shoes and his jeans-clad legs to mid-calf. A second later, Byron's face appeared, closely followed by the snout and shining eyes of Kipp.

The relief was so profound she closed her eyes. "Thank you, Lord," she whispered.

"Are you planning to spend the rest of the day under there?" Byron asked. She heard the smile in his voice.

"No, I'm not. You scared the living daylights out of me, Byron Oakes!" She bumped her head on the wooden bed frame as she pushed herself out. "Ouch!"

She put a hand to her head and looked up into Byron's face. He burst out laughing.

"It's not funny," she told him, her lips twitching. "That hurt."

"Have a look in the mirror."

Ellie scowled at him before turning to Kipp. "And you're no better, wagging your tail and laughing as well."

Then she spied herself in Olga's mirror. She was covered in dust and clumps of fluff, pieces of masking tape were stuck to her trousers at the knee, and in her hair was a piece of silver tinsel. Laughter burst out of her until she almost cried with relief at having him there. He peeled away the masking tape and removed tinsel from her hair as she dusted herself off as best she could.

"How did you get in?" she asked. "I locked the back door."

"The window over the sink. It wasn't shut properly."

"I didn't hear a thing."

"You weren't meant to. I'd no idea what'd happened to you or who might be in here," he said, sober now, his expression intense. "I saw Glenn driving out onto the main road just as I was about to turn in. I thought the worst."

Ellie swallowed. Still she couldn't cross the line she'd drawn for herself. "I'm fine. Kipp protected me. Anyway, Fenella was here and he wouldn't have done anything with a witness about."

She saw his disappointment yet again and felt a pang of guilt. To cover it she walked round the other side of the bed and pulled out the painting, holding it up for him to see.

"Olga told Fenella this was her favourite painting, that if she looked closely enough it would tell her more. I've looked at it and can't see anything special other than the woman in it."

Lifting it up, she let him study it for a minute or two.

"You think that's Olga?" he asked.

Ellie nodded. "But aside from that does it tell you anything else?"

He leaned closer, his eyes roaming over the entire canvas until they came back to the group outside the building. He studied each figure.

"It looks like she's carrying a bag, but I think it's a roll of papers," he said eventually.

Ellie put the painting face up on the bed and did as he'd done, looked very closely at what the woman was carrying. Nodding, she turned the painting over, flipped up the framer's clasps and lifted board and canvas out of the frame. Careful not to damage the canvas she peeled it back and lifted the board up. There, flat against the canvas were three envelopes.

Neither of them moved. The only sound was that of a tractor starting up and beginning its slow progress to an unknown destination. It was Ellie who carefully removed the envelopes and, one by one, opened them, removing the contents and laying them on the painting. They were all written in German. The sight of them unnerved her.

The loud jangle of the phone downstairs made Ellie jump.

"These look like certificates, but what? And is this a letter?" Byron's voice sounded tired and frustrated.

She looked at him, unblinking. Her throat had gone dry. "We have to see Bob."

Byron found a large bag behind a chair in the corner near the window as Ellie put the painting back together without the masking tape. They carefully put it in the bag and went downstairs. The papers, back inside their envelopes, were tucked into her bag.

In the kitchen, as Byron was opening the back door, he said, "What was Thorley doing here?"

"Fenella called him. Sent him an SOS – so he said. He's too old for her, but I think she loves him."

He glanced at her over his shoulder, an eyebrow quirked. "Not to mention his money."

Ellie didn't reply. She wanted to forget Glenn for a while – a long while. For Fenella's sake, she hoped Glenn treated her decently.

***

They found Bob in the bakery serving a customer. When he saw them, he turned and spoke to one of his staff, took off his apron and came out from behind the counter.

"I had a feeling you'd be back. Let's go to the house."

This time it was wine. He didn't ask, simply opened a bottle of red and poured generous measures into three large wine glasses. They toasted each other, swallowed mouthfuls of liquid and agreed it was a good drop. Delay. Did they really want to know?

Byron reached down and lifted the bag onto the kitchen table, removing the painting. Bob studied it at length, his lips drawn in a thin line.

"Doesn't look like Eva Braun. Olga Erskine?" He pointed to the woman.

"We think so," Ellie said. "Can you see what she's holding?"

Peering, as they had done, he eventually shook his head. "A bag I'd say, but it looks more like a roll of some sort."

"She's a clever woman, Bob," Byron said, glancing at Ellie. "You'd better tell him where you've been."

She did, leaving out little except for the scene in the kitchen with Glenn. Even Byron would never know about it. There was silence, the men lost in their own thoughts. Eventually, Ellie continued.

"Fenella told me Olga loved the painting and said to her that if she looked at it hard enough she'd see more than expected. I couldn't understand why she left it behind. Apparently, she got in a car with two men this morning, at least one of them German, and is on her way to the Continent. In the painting, Olga – or whoever it is – is holding a scroll of papers, painted to look like a handbag."

"And you being you probably took the back off and found something interesting," Bob said, a hint of amusement in his voice.

"It wouldn't be Ellie if she hadn't," Byron added dryly.

She ignored them, retrieved the envelopes from her bag and gave them to Bob. He withdrew the papers and unfolded them one by one, his eyes widening as he read the neat, fading script. He sighed and puffed out his cheeks.

"This is… *extraordinary!*" He lowered the yellowing papers, shaking his head. "One's a birth certificate and the other's a marriage certificate. The marriage certificate is between a Colonel Otto Heinrich and Frieda Wilbur, in Berlin on first of June, 1943. The birth certificate is for Franz Heinrich, parents Colonel Otto Heinrich and Frieda Wilbur, born…" He looked up at Ellie and held her eyes for several seconds, "born tenth of May, 1944 in Berlin."

Ellie closed her eyes and clamped her jaw tight. It couldn't be! She shook her head. This wasn't possible.

"Ellie?" Byron's voice came gently to her and she felt his hand cover hers.

"That's… that's Farley's birth date."

Byron's hand tightened and she opened her eyes. Bob, his expression grim, was reaching for the envelope. Her stomach was in tight little knots. He read the two pages silently, his expression growing more troubled as he progressed. Byron was frowning. She wondered what he was thinking. Two or three minutes later Bob put the letter down on the table, resting his arms either side of them, his palms downward.

"Now I understand," Bob said quietly, taking in a deep breath. "If only I'd known before, if only he'd said."

"I think you'd better tell us, Bob," Byron said.

Ellie wasn't certain she wanted to know. The baker reached for his glass and swallowed a mouthful of wine.

"It's from a Frieda Wilbur... Olga, I suppose."

"Yes," Ellie said. There were surprised looks from the two men. "I recognise the handwriting. Other letters. I'll tell you later," she finished lamely.

"This letter was written in July 1945" Bob began. "*Dear Siegfried, I'm writing to let you know that I've sent my son, Franz, to Scotland. I fear for his safety here in Germany and I was foolish to have kept him all these months. He cries a lot and now that he's beginning to walk always seems to be in the way of his father when he's home. I know Otto is your son and has worked hard to earn his high position in the Father's regime, but he's not a good father, Siegfried. He hates it when Franz cries or is toddling about and falls over or gets in his way. Often he will hit him leaving... leaving bruises and red marks. One night I caught him trying to suffocate him, but managed to stop him. Even I find this treatment of children unbearable, and this is his own child. I mean to have no more by him.*" Bob paused and Ellie saw his eyes slide quickly over the rest of the page.

"Best tell us all of it, Bob." Byron's expression was tight.

Bob nodded, swallowing. "*'Otto told me he would do whatever he liked with the boy; it was his son. He said he wouldn't last long anyway if the Fuhrer found out he had dark hair. I knew he was right. I came home the next day and found...'* Bob put the letter down, his jaw working away, tears filling his eyes. "Animal!" He picked up the letter. "*'I came home the next day and found Franz locked in a cupboard, tied up, bloody and bruised and a tape over his little mouth. Tears stained his face and his eyes were full of fear. This was too much! He is also my son. I think my heart will never mend. I know it will grieve you too, Siegfried. You have a great love for this boy and I'm grateful for it. So that is why I faked a kidnapping knowing Otto would do nothing about it. He managed a raised eyebrow.*

This letter will come to you by safe hands, but destroy it when you've read it. I do not know if you or I will ever see Franz again, but at least he's far away from the traumas of the war and the violence of his father. Scotland is a much safer place.

Our work for the Third Reich comes first, Siegfried, you know that. Franz will have better parents than either Otto or I could be to him. Be sure you never give any indication to Otto that you know anything about this because he will not spare you either. You will be classed as a traitor to the Reich.

His new parents have called him Farley. Do not ask how I know. Frieda.'"

He put the pages down on the table. No one spoke. Numbness. Ellie stared at the writing, Olga's writing. She wondered how she'd got the letter back, but didn't really care. The clock's ticking far too loudly, she thought.

Bob drained his glass and re-filled it, but before he'd got it halfway to his mouth, he suddenly began crying, loud cries that seemed to come from the depths of his heart.

"He was my brother. *My brother!* How didn't I know? I should've realised. I could've stopped…"

Ellie looked at a blurry image of him and yanked a handkerchief from her pocket, offering it to him, but he shook his head, got up and walked out the back door. She made to follow him, but Byron shook his head.

"I'll go."

She had no energy to argue and nodded, using the handkerchief to wipe her eyes. Marmalade rubbed against her legs and she picked him up, holding him close, needing the comfort of his soft fur and purring. She took him with her into the front room away from the sound of the clock and there they sat, Marmalade curled on her lap, little moving. She leaned her head against the back of the settee, closed her eyes and re-lived the years she'd known the passionate and often reclusive photographer. In the end she came to the conclusion that her understanding of him was greater now: a battered little boy who'd eventually buried himself in his work, trying to save a Scottish heritage that was only partly his and not knowing why he was so driven. He could not have remembered those first fourteen months of his life surely, but something inside his fragile soul and body would never have forgotten. A deep sorrow for him stirred in the deepest part of her and she knew it would linger for a long time.

When the two men returned she woke with a jerk; she hadn't realised she'd dozed off. Marmalade gave her a disdainful look such as only cats can convey and jumped down. Bob flicked on the light and she screwed up her eyes against the sudden brightness.

"What's the time?" she asked, sitting upright.

"About five thirty," Byron replied. He hesitated a second, glancing at the man beside him. "Ellie, show Bob what you found at the Knobbles."

Reluctant and uneasy, she withdrew the silver card holder, clasping it in her hand, slowly unfolding her fingers until it lay in the palm of her hand, exposed to its owner.

"Yes," Bob said hoarsely, "I was there."

Chapter 31

Bob would not begin until he'd rattled around in the kitchen, filled three plates with a pasta concoction and told them to start eating. Another bottle of wine arrived on the table.

Watching him from across the table, Byron pondered whether they would get the truth. The police were still deliberating and their investigation had stalled. It occurred to him more than once that Jack wasn't being his most helpful with them. Few in the village were being very helpful either. It was, as he'd often thought, a village of secrets held in trust and not to be divulged to outsiders or nosey policemen.

"It was no accident." Bob looked down at the letter and took in a long breath. "He hated everything the Nazis stood for and that's why he was so determined to keep his children from the Strathverns. You know this, Ellie."

She nodded, biting her lip. How much did she really know of Farley, of his absences?

Bob continued. "I got a call from Farley the day before his death saying he was going up to the Knobbles. All he said was that it was a special place. He'd arranged to meet Jamie there. It had something to do with a joint exhibition they were planning." He drew in a deep breath. "I don't know what it was, something in his voice, the way he said the words, but I knew I had to get up there. Bran came to the bakery as I was leaving. He said the Strathvern car had broken down and was in the garage to be fixed, could I give him a lift to the castle? I told him I was going up to the Knobbles because his father had phoned and I had to go. He wasn't happy, but called somebody at Strathvern and said he'd be late. He hardly spoke a word." He looked again at the letter. "Farley knew about this. I'm sure now."

Over the rim of his glass, Byron watched the baker's expression slide into fear. He'd seen it in his men's faces when they'd had to tell him dreadful news.

"It's okay, Bob."

"I wish it was." His face had lost its colour and there was great pain in his eyes. "I told Bran he could wait in the car, but he said he

544

was already late so what was another hour? We got up there. It was a beautiful afternoon, clear skies, bit of a wind blowing. There was no sign of Jamie, but we saw Farley leaning against a big rock near the edge, camera in his lap. I called him. He didn't answer, but he could be like that. It was Bran who noticed first. He rushed past me, shouting out to Farley."

Without saying anything, Ellie went around and sat beside him; she did not speak and she did not touch him. The clock chimed, but Byron didn't count. He didn't care.

"When I got there, Bran was pleading with him. Farley was swallowing liquid from a small flask. He had a gun in his hand." Bob opened his mouth; no sound came out, and he shut it, pinching his lips together. It was a full minute before he spoke. "He could barely talk. He said his whole life had been a lie and he couldn't live it any longer. He gave one of his quirky smiles and lifted up the gun, waving it around. He said it was in case the potion didn't work, which he hoped it did because it was a fitting end to one of his dubious pedigree. Bran tried to get the gun from him. It went off. Blood…" He shook his head. "It was terrible. That's when Jamie turned up."

Silence. It enveloped them like a blanket. No one moved. They did not look at one another. Only when the phone rang was there a shift, though small; a glass reached for, fleeting looks. Colour was draining from Ellie's face. She was so still Byron knew she was in shock.

When the jangling stopped, Byron roused himself. "Was it Jamie's idea to move Farley and leave him at the Knobbles?"

"Yes. I told them it was a bad idea, that we should tell Jack. Bran was a mess. He was crying and talking nonsense, hugging Farley and telling him to wake up." Bob drew in a long, ragged breath. He shook his head. "It was terrible, the whole thing. Believe it or not, Jamie was the only one who seemed to be able to think straight. In the end I shrugged my shoulders and said nothing. I'm ashamed of that, but of protecting Farley – no."

Ellie's voice sounded thin. "Bran said it was an accident, so who pulled the trigger?"

"I don't know, Ellie," Bob said gently. "Perhaps it was both of them."

***

Byron, with Jack in tow in civilians, found Bran and Camden in the pub. They were in the middle of demolishing big servings of fish and chips, pints of bitter near their hands.

It was noisy and crowded; an informal darts competition was in progress, tables were at their capacity and a number of people huddled around the bar. Better than a quiet night where everyone could hear everyone else's conversation, Byron thought. Ellie had wanted to come, but he'd told her she was better off staying with Bob. Jack had been brusque, saying she'd been too close to Farley and confronting Camden with her there would likely start off a fireworks display.

Jack invited himself to their table and sat down with no more than a, "Good evening, gents."

"What d'you want, Uncle Jack? And what's *he* doing here with you?" Camden said, scowling, stuffing food into his mouth.

Bran remained silent, moving quickly through the fat chips. Byron's stomach rumbled. It had been a long while since he'd eaten and he almost leaned across and helped himself.

"I need you to come down to the station, Bran," their relative said, his tone uncharacteristically even.

"Reason?" Camden stabbed a piece of fish.

"New evidence has come to light about your father's death."

"What new evidence? Someone killed him. You're slack, Uncle Jack. Wasting time, that's what you've been doing. Haven't got a clue, have you?" He stared at him, his lip curling, and then dipped a chip in tomato sauce.

Jack turned and looked at Byron, raising his eyebrows in an 'I told you so' fashion.

"Well, that's fine wi' me, but I'm sure Bran doesn't want to be a public spectacle."

The colour in Camden's cheeks was deepening, his blue eyes glittering. Any minute now, Byron thought.

"You tell me *why* I should believe you and I'll *say* whether he goes with you or not."

Byron wanted to shove fish, chips and tomato sauce into the man's face. A few hours clamped in a pillory would do him good. "You're a lot of noise, Camden. Pity none of it's done any good for your family."

"Shut up, Oakes! You know nothing. I turned your cottage upside down and you know *nothing*."

"Yes, he does," Jack said, still calm, before Byron could rebut. "In fact, he knows a lot more than you do. Now then, Bran, I just need a few words wi' you down at the station. Your brother can wallow in his dinner alone then. You know you have to, just to clear a few things up."

Then it came. Camden lunged across the table and grabbed Jack by the front of his jacket. The sergeant grunted loudly as his stomach hit the edge of the table. Beer flowed across the wooden top and Camden's plate scooted sideways, colliding with Bran's.

"You come in here making accusations about my brother and expect I'll be nice about it! If anyone's had reason to kill my father it's Ellie Madison. You bloody fool. You're worth nothing. D'you hear – *nothing!*" His voice bellowed across the room. The buzz died away and Byron could sense the tension behind him. "You'll pay for this, Kennart. You're a weakling, a misfit! D'you hear? Now get out of here and leave us alone."

Gone was any evidence that he wasn't quite right in the head. Who *was* the real man?

"Sit down, Camden," Byron said coldly, quietly.

"I don't take orders from you! You slimy Londoner. Who d'you think you are coming here and sticking your nose in where it's not wanted? And pairing up with that Madison woman who's…"

"That's enough, Camden!" Jack snapped, his cheeks bright red. "Now sit down!"

Patrons were stirring, conversation was beginning to buzz.

The man sat down, glaring at Byron, hating him. Byron had seen it all before, many times.

"Right," Jack said, straightening himself up and pulling his shirt down. "You've managed to make a show of this, Camden, and shame your brother. When will you ever get past your childish tantrums? Now, Bran, finish that mouthful. You're coming with me." He turned to Byron. "Remember, no more, no less, and be careful where you aim."

Nodding, Byron couldn't help thinking that Jack, though unorthodox and might not stand up to a microscopic inspection by higher authorities, had a way of getting things done that an outsider wouldn't. No more, no less.

They were still there close to closing time. Camden was thoroughly drunk and falling asleep. Byron wasn't far behind him in the sleep category and definitely not completely sober.

There was a quiet ripple of laughter behind him, then in the chair beside him.

"So, two of you to drive home tonight," said Ellie. "You really are a sight. How is it you haven't beaten each other to pulp?"

Byron turned heavily in his chair, but before he could speak, Camden lifted his head off the table and mumbled,

"He'sh not so bad after… all." His head was wobbling. "Got to do… got do to a job."

He slumped forward and his head hit the table with a thump. Ellie winced, though through Byron's tired eyes and to his sluggish mind it looked more like an expression of mockery.

"Not a laughing matter, Ellie," he said with difficulty. "He's a messed up boy."

"Messed up, yes, boy, no. Come on. Help me up with this lump."

"I'll do that, Ellie," said Andrew Stewart, appearing at the end of the table. "Your friend's not in any state to be lugging about the likes of Camden Orman."

Byron, with Ellie's hand firmly on his arm, followed Andrew down the path to the Land Rover. Camden could hardly stand. It was slow progress. Eventually, Andrew piled the drunken Orman into the vehicle and waved, grinning, as Ellie drove off.

At the Orman house there were lights on and three cars in the driveway. Byron managed to keep himself awake and between him and Ellie they half dragged, half carried Camden to the front door. Ellie, he noticed, was strangely detached and on edge. When Glenn Thorley opened the door he understood the reason. She must have recognised his car. He wondered what he was doing there.

"What the…?" he began, before Fenella arrived beside Glenn.

She stared at her brother and the two visitors, her mouth open. At that moment, in Byron's intoxicated state, she resembled a guppy. Not a very complimentary association, he thought, grinning.

"He's a bit drunk," he offered, looking at Fenella. "Had some news. I'm sure he'll tell you about it in the morning."

"What've you done to him?" she accused. "He's never been this drunk."

She looked from him to Ellie. "Get off this property and don't come back."

548

"As you're going to London with Glenn, Fenella, it won't matter whether we come back or not," Ellie snapped, and began turning away, grasping Byron by the arm. "Is Bran home?"

"No he isn't. Not that it's any of your business."

"He's still at the police station I expect," Byron said, and even in his lethargic state realised that might've been a rash thing to say.

"What! You're barking mad, the pair of you," she said. "Go home!"

"Why's he at the station?" Glenn said, ignoring her and focussing on Ellie.

"And *that*," Ellie said, "is none of your business, Glenn. Come on, Byron, it's time to go."

She almost dragged him away, leaving a snoring Camden on the doorstep in the care of his sister and Glenn.

By the time they were three minutes down the road Byron was asleep, but not before he'd stumbled through a sentence telling her Camden had found her gun in his dad's study and gone to Ellie's in the storm, got over her back fence planning to sneak it back. He wanted her fingerprints on it so the police would blame her for his dad's death. Except Fenella had followed him, found him under the leaves and taken it from him. Camden had no idea what had happened to it. Ellie did.

The funeral and burial of Farley and Alice was a distressing affair best forgotten. At least, that was Ellie's opinion. It was true it hadn't rained, the sun even poked its head out between the clouds once or twice, and Paul Shepley had spoken movingly and with considerable knowledge of the Ormans. Yet, the heavy atmosphere persisted, draining Ellie of energy. At her lowest point, Bob, not one for public speaking, suddenly stepped forward and gave a warm and lively epitaph, applauded by the large crowd gathered around. She just wanted to forget the whole thing. It was best that way. Remember Farley as he was, she'd told herself, walking away with Byron, Mary and Mark.

Chapter 32

Eating cheese and chutney sandwiches, they sat on the wall atop the ridge where she had told Byron of her childhood terror. The cold wind, she'd said, would clear his head. His eyes evidenced that his head was still hurting and he had a paler-than-usual complexion. He hadn't bothered to shave, afraid, he'd said, of taking off too much skin.

Two plastic mugs of tea from the thermos sat between them. He was on his second, having already had two cups of coffee at Ellie's. She'd shut the spare room door on him last night leaving him to his own undressing and getting into bed. What state Camden had awoken in she could only imagine. She was curious, however, about how the two of them had managed to stay at the same table in the same room for over three hours.

"So," she said, "what on earth happened to you and Camden last night?"

"You mean apart from getting drunk."

"Naturally. Andrew and Pauline said it was the best show they'd ever seen in the pub and the only reason they left the pair of you there was because they thought it was the safest place."

"They were probably right. Camden's one determined fighter. It took an hour just to get him to listen to me and that was after three beers and the assurance that there was a gun pointing at his legs."

"You had a gun? Byron!"

"Jack knew. It was his idea."

Ellie sighed. "What did you tell Camden?"

"No more, no less, as ordered by Jack. He already knew about Bran and Jamie up at the Knobbles and finding Farley. I said nothing about Bob. I told him about the birth and marriage certificates you found and the letter. He sobbed like a baby and one or two of his friends came across to see what was going on. They weren't too happy with me I can tell you. Nothing like having great big Scotsmen with fiery hair glaring at you to make you want to run and hide." He grinned at her over the rim of the mug. "It's freezing up here, Ellie. Let's get in the car."

"Not until you tell me the rest."

"You'd make a good interrogator," he muttered before going on. "I told him a bit about Olga, but not the stuff concerning Fenella. She can do that. He went into shock when he realised I was telling him Olga was his grandmother. Eventually, even after a couple of whiskies, he decided that his mother died because of what she'd found out. After that we rambled – I think. Can't remember too much."

"They'll have to sort a lot of it out themselves," she said, pitying them. What an unhappy state of affairs. "It won't be easy and there'll be loose ends if Olga isn't brought back here."

Thick clouds rolled in over the hills, picking up speed in the wind.

"Snow?" Byron asked, pulling his collar up.

"Maybe. Come on, you southern softie, let's get in the car. How will I ever toughen you up?"

Turning his head slowly, he looked at her with such intensity it went down deep into the core of her being.

"By asking me to stay," he said softly.

***

Six Months Later…

It was, she thought, a perfect way to honour Farley. His two great loves – Scottish history and the Highlands – forever displayed in his photographs. The Saxon artefacts were slowly being brought down from The Chimney under the careful eye of Jack and archaeological experts from Edinburgh University. The pieces would be shared, housed in Edinburgh and in a museum on the edge of Kilcomb. An old croft and large barn owned by the Earl of Strathvern, used occasionally for art and craft shows and jumble sales, were in the throes of conversion. Ross had agreed to pay for most of it, but the locals, keen to have a part in such an important event, raised considerable funds. A chunk of the money left to Ellie in Farley's will was also contributed. After a lot of arguing over who should open it, Fenella, who'd been demanding from London it ought to be her, suddenly changed her mind and said Camden and Bran should do it. She'd be there to sell copies of her father's books and framed photographs.

"I never thought I'd see the day," Jack said beside Ellie as they stood outside the barn surveying the comings and goings of workmen. "Farley would've loved this."

Ellie looked at him. He was glowing – if that was a word she could use to describe Jack.

"And you *are* loving it," she said, grinning. "Made any decisions yet about retiring from the police force? Curator of this must be tempting."

Nodding, he said, "Aye. The force has had thirty-four years of my life, so I've handed in my notice and finish in a month. Seems like a dream."

"I'm happy for you, Jack. And I heard you found some paintings and photographs of Alice's."

Again he nodded. "The best of them will go up in there. The rest the boys and I have shared between us. I'll make sure Fenella gets a few. Well, I'd better be going in a minute. Don't want Carter on my back about dereliction of duty. His spot visits are a damned nuisance." He gave a wry grin. "Canna say I'll miss *him*."

Ellie laughed. There was no doubt he was a happier man.

Out of the corner of her eye she saw two men coming out of the barn – Byron and Ross deep in conversation. It was strange how things worked out, she thought. As soon as the idea of a museum was mooted, Ross had not hesitated in asking Byron to oversee the project.

"You must be glad the investigation's over," Ellie said as Jack settled his hat on his head. Her eyes were still on the architect.

"Oh, aye. It was a bad business. I'm just glad Farley's death was found to be accidental and Bran cleared." Ellie nodded, returning her attention to him. "As to Olga Erskine, I think Interpol are having a hard time finding her."

He sighed, a weary, sad sound. It had been a difficult few months for him, for all of them. He'd aged, but some of the rancour between him and the Orman siblings had begun dissipating. To her utter amazement – disbelief, if she was honest – even Camden's ugly nature had mellowed. 'Just a wee bit', as Mary had put it.

"I think Olga will be somebody else by now, complete with new look."

"Well, whoever she is or pretending to be, she'll have Alice's death on her conscience forever."

"D'you think she's got one?"

He studied her for a moment. "Everyone has, Ellie. Some bury it deep, that's all. It's Fenella I feel sorry for. Thorley's lawyer did a good job getting her off withholding evidence. I don't bear her any ill will. She's just as much a victim of Olga's deception as the rest of us. I hope she'll be happy in London wi' that man."

"Time will tell, Jack."

"Aye, it will." He turned slightly. "Your Lordship, Byron. I'll be off now. Someone's been pilfering Charlie Adamson's piglets. You might chuckle, Mr Oakes, but you've seen his pigs and believe me they're worth a small fortune. Won championships up and down Scotland for decades."

They watched as he walked away and Ellie was sure there was a spring in his step she'd never seen before.

"I'm off, too," Ross said. "Thanks for going over those details with me, Byron. Another month or two and it should all be finished, thanks to you."

"Not to mention the small army of workmen and volunteers," Byron added, grinning. "We'd never have done it without them. Even Camden's turned up occasionally to see what was going on. A year or two from now he might be tamed enough to take on the marketing."

Ellie rolled her eyes. "Don't get too carried away. Reformation isn't always guaranteed."

"He's doing okay, Ellie. The loss of his parents is taking a huge toll on him. And he is good at marketing. Got some great ideas."

"I'm not convinced yet." She changed the subject. Like Glenn, Camden was still on her criminal files. "So, how's Jamie, Lord Strathvern?"

"He's been painting like a man possessed. He's up at Maw's Hearth today and taken Bran with him." He shook his head, his expression closing in. "He was hard hit by Fenella going off with Thorley, but she's not for him. They're too different. Jamie needs another creative mind in a wife."

With that he said goodbye and walked away to his car.

"So, Ellie," Byron said, "want to come and see what Bob's been up to?"

He held out his hand and she took it gladly, walking along beside him as if she'd done it for years. She glanced at him, warmth filling her heart, but still the old reservations and anxieties lurked in the background.

Inside the croft the wooden floorboards, which had long ago replaced the earth floor, were covered in footprints, bits of mud and plaster, and wood shavings. The old kitchen had been extended without detracting from the original building, although Bob insisted on more windows than were in most crofts. For once, she had no objections.

He was standing in the middle of the floor, overseeing the installation of cupboards.

"Ellie! Good to see you. What d'you think?"

"It's great, Bob. Ovens and refrigerators coming? Or are you thinking of keeping it simple – cooking in the old fireplace and sticking the milk and cheese outside in the snow. I'm sure it'll cut costs."

"I had thought about it, but didn't think our Lord of the Manor would be too impressed. Not to mention our resident architect here."

Byron laughed and clapped him on the back before wandering off to speak with the men installing the cupboards.

"Everything all right with you, Ellie? The hikers and painters will be back in droves soon, I suppose."

"Yes, but it's not the same without Farley, Bob. I love the Highlands, but I doubt I can match his energy in the preservation campaign. He had a passion that surpassed all of us put together. He never once caved in to pressure. Painting's my gift which I'll use to help people understand why they must be preserved. I'll still be part of the campaigns and do whatever I can."

He looked down at the ground then up at her, his expression tinged with what looked like guilt.

Frowning, she said, "There's something you haven't told me."

"Yes, a couple of things, but not here. Come for dinner tonight and bring Byron."

***

When he finished speaking, Ellie could only stare at him, shocked and disbelieving. That both of them, he and Farley, had betrayed the cause to stop development in the Highlands was beyond her understanding. He'd explained his part and reason, the fear of losing everything if he hadn't done Glenn's bidding. Yet, it was Farley's betrayal that gouged a deep hole in her soul.

She got up from the table and went outside into the dark garden, away from the light spilling out of the kitchen window. The writer of the article Jenny Browne had seen in the newspaper owed her, Ellie Madison, an apology.

What was it all for then this past fourteen years? Had Farley been playing games with everyone and everything, taking on the role of deceiver as his mother had done? How much damage would be done if it was ever found out! What was the point of going on with it?

"You know," Bob said quietly, unexpectedly, behind her, "he would never have gone through with it. In the end he'd have withdrawn his money and support because he loved the Scottish Highlands more than anything else. He was a troubled man, Ellie. Surely you must have known that."

"Yes! But to do this! At least you had the courage to tell me what you did and then refuse to take part in it. He hid it from everyone who trusted him for years! I don't think I can do this any more."

"But you will, Ellie. We should always fight for what is important and not give up. I almost threw away my whole career by sticking my neck out for Thorley. Don't you throw away what you have and the work you and the Ormans did. Others will step into the gaps – if you let them." He touched her arm and she turned to face him. "Ask Byron. He thinks you don't want him interfering because it's protected territory – yours and Farley's. He's dead, Ellie. It's time for new blood and new passion. Think about it. Byron loves you more than Farley ever did or could. More than I could."

He left her as quietly as he'd come.

Several minutes passed before she could bring herself to go inside and face Byron. What Bob told her about Byron made her feel ashamed. She'd had no idea he felt that way and little idea she was unconsciously locking him out of that part of her life. It had all been interwoven with grief over Farley's death and worrying about how the work would continue without him. Yet, if she dug a little deeper, there it was, a jealous guardian of the past.

There were visitors when she stepped into the kitchen – Mary and Mark, Michael and Catherine. She found the conversation, though full of spark and honesty, friendship and acceptance, unbearable, and she excused herself after half an hour. Byron went with her.

They walked along, huddled in coats, but not touching. The gap between them seemed to be widening again and it terrified her. This was her doing now. Strong, uncompromising Ellie Madison, strider of the Highlands in all weather and escapee from dangerous situations – are you now too afraid to speak to the man beside you? How brave are you really if you can't let him know who you are, can't trust him?

She stopped in the middle of the lane and turned towards him, but couldn't open her mouth. The words were stuck in her throat.

He was looking at her, waiting. Then he said softly, "I love you, Ellie and I'm not going away unless you send me."

He was giving her an opportunity to back away, to run, if that's what she wanted. As they stood in the cold night air he told her about the only other great love in his life, Ena, and about her death and the pit that drew him into deep despair from which he could see no escape. It had come only when he met her.

It was then she realised the strength of his love, a love that would free her rather than keep her captive, fighting inner battles in a lonely prison to which there were no visitors.

"No," she whispered, "I can't send you away. What would I do without you, Byron?"

He swallowed; there was fear in his eyes. She'd never seen it before and it hurt because she was the cause.

"But do you love me enough to let me into your life, Ellie Madison?"

She nodded. "Yes."

***

A week later they took a small group up to the Knobbles. It was overcast and the wind had a chill in it, but the hiking painters didn't seem to mind and found themselves crannies in which to shelter and haul out flasks and buns. Three of them discovered the cave where Farley had been found. Kipp was sitting near Ellie, eyes happy, tail lightly sweeping the stones.

Ellie stood with Byron gazing over the hills and glens.

"This is where it started, Ellie."

"You loved me then?" she teased.

"No, but I admired you. It was the day I started coming alive again."

556

He wrapped his arms around her and she looked up into his face, so close. There was no fear in his eyes now.

"And perhaps I did, too," she said softly.

It's time to let the past go, Farley. It's time to say goodbye.